To Julie

LEY RYDERS

Best Wishes

LEY RYDERS

HOLLY J. WILLIAMS

Matador
9 Priory Business Park,
Wistow Road, Kibworth Beauchamp,
Leicestershire. LE8 0RX
Tel: 0116 279 2299
Email: books@troubador.co.uk
Web: www.troubador.co.uk/matador
Twitter: @matadorbooks

ISBN 978 1785893 834

British Library Cataloguing in Publication Data.
A catalogue record for this book is available from the British Library.

Printed and bound in the UK by TJ International, Padstow, Cornwall
Typeset in 12pt Adobe Garamond Pro by Troubador Publishing Ltd, Leicester, UK

Matador is an imprint of Troubador Publishing Ltd

For my parents, Gill and Dave, and my Aunt Jack.

Chapter 1

THE DANCING STONE

The golden sunlight of the late autumn afternoon filtered through the trees of the copse, warming Hayden as he hurried along the ridge that led down to the stream. It would soon be dusk and if he did not start back to the village soon it would be dark and there would be no wood for the fire. His mother had sent Petronia out hours ago to collect logs while Hayden helped his father in the blacksmith's forge, but his older sister had not yet returned. Hayden was not surprised to hear that Petronia had not come home, for she often wandered off and lost track of time but he still worried.

He came to the grassy bank by the bubbling stream which was dotted with young saplings sheltering in the shade of their older siblings. Sure enough, he spotted Petronia's white cotton cap amid the rushes that grew on the far side of the river a few feet away, bobbing around like a pale bird as she busied herself at the water's edge. Hayden called out her name; at once the lass raised her head looking at him with her coal black eyes. Standing up, she slipped something into the pocket of her apron before gesturing with her hands.

'You'll have to come closer,' he called, cursing not for the first time his sister's muteness.

Shrugging her shoulders with frustration, Petronia hitched up her skirts and carefully picked her way across the large boulders that jutted out of the water. Hayden watched her. Short and stocky, like him and their father, Petronia was the picture of good health. In fact, there appeared to be nothing physically or mentally wrong with her apart

1

from the strange fact that Petronia could not or would not speak. As a babe, she never even cried. Not that it mattered much as their parents, consigned to the fact that their child might never utter a word, taught her to express herself through gestures and finger shapes, a method that Petronia was now well versed in.

She crossed the river and hurried over to her brother, an expression of frustration etched on her features. '*I was coming, you know!*' she signed, her fingers moving through the air nimbly. '*I don't need you watching over me all the time, little Brother!*'

Hayden sighed. 'I wasn't watching you. Mother just sent me to see if you were coming back with the firewood. Have you got it?'

His sister nodded and pointed to a large bundle of logs and twigs resting safely beneath a nearby oak. Hayden smiled and went to collect it, but Petronia held out her hands in protest. '*I can manage,*' she gestured indignantly. '*You've been working at the forge all day; I will carry the wood.*'

Stooping over, she gathered up the firewood under her arm and headed off up the ridge in the direction of the village. The hamlet of Ravensbrook had been home to Petronia, Hayden and their family for many generations. A small collection of huts and freeholds, it stood peacefully on the western edge of the deep wood, in the far south of Geoll. The Ley barely ran here and people barely spoke of it for the land was rich and life was peaceful. Travellers seldom came to Ravensbrook and did not stay long when they did for there was little in the village to interest people. When travellers did come with tales of far-off cities, their stories did nothing to stir Hayden's heart, as his feet were firmly and happily planted as apprentice blacksmith at his father's forge. Ravensbrook was home and if he lived there till the day he died, Hayden would be more than happy.

Glancing at the sun riding low in the sky, Hayden called to his sister. 'We'd better hurry, Petronia, it'll be dark soon and you know what they say. Strange creatures come out in the woods at night. Wood imps will steal your soul away if you're not in by dusk!'

Petronia stopped in her tracks and looked back at him with an expression of weary disbelief. She had large, striking eyes and full shapely lips that clearly stated with the slightest movement what her tongue could not utter. Right now, they declared that they were both way too old to believe the fairy stories told by the village elders.

To illustrate her point even clearer, she set down the firewood and twirled round on the spot, arms raised dramatically above her head, mimicking the way the wild folk were said to dance.

'Well, I believe them,' stated Hayden, as grinning Petronia picked up the wood again, 'and it wouldn't do you any harm to as well. You know what Mother says: it isn't your tongue that scares away prospective suitors, it's your stubbornness. You could have been married to a dozen fine men by now if you hadn't frightened them away! Only in August, Bartholomew the cooper's son came a-courting and Mother had to tell him that you were off wandering in the woods. It isn't maidenly!'

The humour drained from Petronia's pretty features as she crossly turned her back on her brother and marched off in the direction of the village. Hayden sighed reluctantly. He had not meant to hurt his sister, but the truth was there were aspects of her character that sometimes troubled him. Not only was she stubborn and fiercely independent, she also had a peculiar interest in collecting stones, juggling them skilfully in her fingers and sending them rolling in spirals across the ground. He had thought it a curious and fun game as a child, watching her send the small, round pebbles spinning across the dirt as they played, but they were no longer children and Hayden was sure that had he been born with his sibling's impairment he would want to make himself more accepted into the community, not drive people away.

He hurried after her across the leaf-carpeted ground, reaching her side just as the trees began to thin, revealing the small group of wooden longhouses that formed their village. Beside their own home, stood the small shed that housed the furnace, anvil and other items their father used in his craft. Through the open door, they could see the scarlet glow of the fire and the powerful silhouette of Godfrey as he put away his tools for the evening. The warming smell of fires and stew drifted on the autumn air, calling them home.

Hayden caught hold of his sister's shoulder just as she was about to hurry down the hill towards the village. She spun to face him, her pretty features still fixed in a cross frown. 'I'm sorry! I shouldn't have said what I did; I only try to look out for you. I would love you to find a good husband and be happy. After all, you are seventeen.'

Petronia's eyes grew wide with frustration as she angrily thrust the firewood into Hayden's arms. *'Maybe I don't want you, Mother or Father to find me a good husband!'* she gestured firmly. *'Maybe I don't want to marry at all! Maybe I want, I want...'* Her hands balled into frustrated fists as she tried to express the longing she felt in her heart. *'Something else, something different.'*

She sighed and an expression passed over her face that was so filled with sadness and longing it made Hayden's heart weep.

'A voice?' he queried as his sister turned to look at the rolling hills and farms that spread out to the west of their village. 'Is that what you want, Petronia?'

Petronia buried her hands in the pockets of her apron and shook her head as if to say she did not really know what it was she was looking for. *'Yes, no. I would like to be able to speak, Hayden, of course. But there's more.'* Inhaling deeply, she rubbed her eyes with the back of her hand as if to wipe away unseen tears before forcing a smile.

Standing on tip-toe, she affectionately planted a kiss on Hayden's forehead.

'I have the silliest notions,' she gestured. *'Ignore me, Brother, and do not worry.'*

Together they followed the dirt path into the village, returning homeward to their parents. Their mother Beatrice was waiting at the door to the small, two-room dwelling, her dark blonde curls tied beneath a scarlet barbette, while their father washed his arms and face in the village horse trough, scrubbing away the smuts and black soot of the forge. Hayden joined him while Petronia followed her mother inside with the wood for the fire and helped her to dish up the nourishing vegetable broth she had prepared. Proudly, Godfrey told his wife and daughter about the good work Hayden had done at the forge that day. The boy had learnt well from his father and displayed a great deal of skill in working with metal. Already, he knew how to fashion a number of

4

items from smouldering iron and could shoe a horse almost as quickly as Godfrey himself. Hayden smiled modestly beneath his father's praise but silently he felt jubilant. When the day came when his father grew too old to work, Hayden was sure he could manage the forge in a way that would supply his family with a comfortable income. They were rich of heart if not of pocket and Hayden was sure that a woman would see him as a suitable husband. He watched Petronia as she daintily ate her supper, her eyes wistful with unspoken longing, and wished that she too could find peace in her heart.

After eating, Beatrice and Godfrey sat beside the warmly glowing hearth and recalled stories of times passed. Feeling restless, Hayden stepped outside and paced leisurely around the house, looking up at the dark, velvety sky. It was a cold but clear night and the stars burned like bright fragments of glass against the peaceful blackness. The moon wore a misty glow of light blue like an ermine collar around its pale, round face, warning that winter was not too far away.

Leaning against the rear wall of the house, Hayden allowed his mind to wander happily over his life. He was sixteen, a man by all accounts and he pondered whether next spring he might find a sweetheart of his own. There were a number of attractive girls in the village, and although he knew his manner was awkward and coarse from time to time, he hoped that a man who was due to inherit a successful business would be seen as a suitable suitor.

The sound of light footsteps interrupted his musing and Hayden turned to see that his sister had joined him to partake of the cool evening air. Flashing him a polite smile, Petronia seated herself on the low fence where people tied their horses upon calling on their father's workshop. The cold moonlight shone brightly on her raven black hair which she had tied neatly back in a thick plait that reached down beyond her waist. The dull glow of evening made her skin look chalky white as she thoughtfully gazed out over the rolling hills and fields to the distant outlines of the neighbouring hamlets that dotted the misty horizon. Hayden saw, not for the first time, an enigmatic melancholy drift across his sister's beautiful features and wondered whether she had thoughts that she was unable, or unwilling, to express using her quick, clever hands.

After a few moments of silent contemplation, Petronia turned to her sibling and gestured. *'Do you ever think about what lies beyond the hills and wood? What exists out there?'*

Hayden shrugged his shoulders, having honestly not given this notion much thought other than what he had heard from the occasional traveller. 'On a night like this you can see Goodstone in the distance,' he stated blandly, pointing to the shadowy dwellings far off in the moonlight. 'Only the other month Father shoed the horse of that merchant who passed through on his way to market. Cocky fellow; I didn't much take to him.'

Stooping down, he plucked a long blade of grass and rested it between his lips. 'To the west, there's the Emerald Coast and all its ports, Mageswharf and the like. Rough places they are from the stories you hear, full of pirates and other sinful blighters, not suitable for good, decent folk like you and I. And, of course, north there lies Veridium, the capital, home to the Council and Prince Aarold as well as a thousand other people all jostling for room to breath. Noisy, smelly place. They say you can walk for a day in its streets and not see one green leaf or blade of grass.'

He watched Petronia as she listened to him speak and despite the negative opinions he expressed, Hayden could not but help notice excitement and wonder growing in his sister's eyes. He suddenly felt as if there was an unseen force tugging at Petronia, calling her away from the safe life in Ravensbrook.

'There is nothing so great in the world beyond that is worth us worrying about,' he told her gently, as Petronia looked wistfully towards the horizon. 'The outside world is filled with dangers and troubles we don't understand.'

Dismissively, Petronia wrinkled her nose and pulled an expression that said she thought her brother was exaggerating. Turning her back on him, she bent down and picked up a smooth, pale stone from the ground, running it skilfully through her fingertips.

'You only hear what you want to,' sighed Hayden, reclining against the wall, 'and one day it will land you in trouble.'

He watched Petronia with worried eyes as she sat on the fence, the moonlight reflected in her dark eyes like sparks of silver fire from a flint. Rhythmically, she rolled the tiny pebble between her palms, her silent lips moving in wordless contemplation. Skilfully, she flicked the stone in such a way that it wove in and out of the gaps in between her fingers like a shuttle pulling an invisible thread through a loom. Balancing it on the very tip of her thumbnail, so it sat like a baby bird preparing for flight, she flipped it up, catching it again in the palm of her hand. Hayden watched the tricks and flicks she performed, his frustration and puzzlement growing by the second. His sister was beautiful and bright so why did she insist on behaving in a manner that made her look like a child?

'Why do you do that, Petronia?' he murmured softly, not expecting her to answer him. 'Why are you the way you are? Why can't you speak?'

Warily he watched as his sister lightly rested the stone on the tip of her middle finger, bringing it up before her full lips and exhaling lightly so it rotated. Then, much to Hayden's astonished disbelief, she moved her hand a few inches away from the turning pebble, leaving it spinning slowly in midair, as if suspended in her breath.

A horrified cry caught in Hayden's throat when he saw the easy power his sibling held over the stone. Magic was a distant and fearful thing for country people such as he, the pursuit of which belonged to the scholars of the court and the mystical Ley Ryders.

Unable to contain his shock, Hayden rushed forward with a cry of, 'Petronia, no!' and fearfully seized his sister's hands. The moment he spoke, the stone fell lifelessly to the ground and Petronia stared at him with surprise.

Hayden hugged his sister fiercely, heart racing as he tried to make sense of what he had just seen. Desperately, he told himself that it was a trick of the moonlight and the stone had only appeared to be floating. But he knew in his soul that this was not true and he battled to understand what this meant.

'You mustn't do things like that, Petronia,' he informed her, 'it is wrong. There are things in this world too complex for us to understand, things that are better left alone.'

Petronia stared into her brother's face, her eyes like two pieces of polished jet, filled with longing and frustration. *'You're the one who doesn't understand, the one who's scared of the world,'* she signed crossly. *'I don't know why I'm the way I am but at least I'm not ashamed. I sometimes feel that there is something growing within me, setting me on a different path. I don't know what it is; all I know is I don't want to change it.'*

She stood up and turned her face towards the pale caress of the moonlight. The celestial orb held her in its silvery gleam, bathing her beautiful features, long, ebony hair and shapely form in its mystical light. She remained still for a moment and Hayden wondered whether the luminescence of dusk spoke just as clearly and silently to Petronia as she did to him.

'People would be fearful if they knew that you thought such things,' he warned her seriously. 'They would call you a witch or a changeling. They would cast you out.'

Glancing over her shoulder at him, Petronia laughed at his fears just as she had done when he talked of the wild folk. She drew a circle in the ground with her toe and a strange puzzled look passed over her face. *'Change is afoot, my dear Brother. I can feel it. Don't ask me what that change will be; all I know is that it will come and then, perhaps you will understand why I am, how I am.'*

Her gestures were deliberate and wistful but doubt gleamed in her eyes as if even she did not understand the forces that moved her. Compassionately, Hayden reached out and touched her arm. 'Whatever happens, I'll protect you, Petronia,' he reassured. 'You have nothing to fear.'

Glancing towards the small window of their modest dwelling, Petronia looked concerned. *'You won't tell Father and Mother, will you?'* she asked anxiously. *'About what happened with the stone?'*

Hayden thought for a moment. He wanted very much to speak to his parents about what he had seen, gain some reassurance regarding the unnatural skill Petronia had displayed. But he was sure that they would have no more understanding than he did of the strange phenomena. Moreover, it would cause them great distress to learn of their daughter's connection with such mystical powers.

'Only if you promise never to do it again,' he stated seriously. 'I mean it, Petronia. It could bring a lot of heartache and unhappiness.'

She did not respond to his request at first but gazed once more soulfully up at the moon as if searching for strength in its cool, silvery beams. '*I will try my best,*' she signed sadly. She smiled at her brother, but Hayden was sure that he saw disappointment in her eyes. Did Petronia hope that her brother would show more sympathy towards her actions? He wished that she could see that he only wanted to keep her safe.

With that thought he followed her back inside while the white moon continued to watch over the slumbering earth.

Chapter 2

DARKLIFE

The city of Veridium rested peacefully in the velvety blue night, slumbering beneath a moist coverlet of misty rain. Capital and jewel of the kingdom of Geoll, its sturdy dwellings of grey stone glimmered, the wetness of the rain making visible the specks and thin veins of magical colour that ran through every house and cobbled street, every statue and turret from the humblest hovel to the elegant palace that rested at the city's heart, home to the young Prince Aarold and the ruling Council that had supported him since the death of his father King Elkric three years ago. Elkric's clan had established Veridium in the distant mists of time – an ancient lineage of proud warrior lords who had created the city over the aeons, each building, lofty turret and resolute wall, as a monument to their kingly might. But even the wise and powerful rulers of history were aware that their will must bow to a greater force, the life-flow that blessed every living thing with the spark of existence, the mystical essence known as the Ley.

The whole of Veridium, noble and common born alike, were familiar with the mystical force of the Ley, running like an unseen river through the country, bringing life and nourishment to all living things. The Ley, it was said, had always been – the blood of the earth, flowing and ebbing with conscious intent a thousand years before the first human had uttered his first word. Only a select few, the Ley Ryders, were gifted with Its understanding. It was a secretive and all-knowing force, part of all living things, answerable only to Itself.

The Ley Ryders was a sacred order of women whose origins were almost as ancient and mysterious as those of the power they served. Theirs was a Calling few could comprehend, nomadically travelling throughout the land, bringing aid and protection to those in need. Part warrior, part holy woman, they answered only to the subtle command of the Ley and the Council of their fellow Ryders. A chapter of their Sisterhood always resided in Veridium. Relations between the royal household and the Ryders had been amicable during Elkric's reign. But as soon as the smoke from his funeral pyre had vanished from the cold winter sky, rumours of mistrust began to spread.

*

Along the dark, narrow streets that twisted like a gloomy serpent down to the city jail, a sleek, lone figure strode, her boots barely making a sound on the wet cobbles. A thick woollen cloak the colour of granite flowed from her shoulders, billowing with the swift pace of her gait, the hood drawn up to protect her from the elements. Her figure was strong, lean with a honed muscularity that was alien to both the fine ladies of court and the common women of the city. Her whole aura was that of a lifelong warrior and the myriad of crystals and coloured stones that studded her leather breastplate and leggings indicated to all her sacred Calling. The Ley Ryder felt the flow of the city's magic pulse around her, as she headed towards the city jail. The Ley had been unsettled by recent events and called to her to discover their cause. Not one week ago, at the prince's fifteenth birthday parade, a man had broken away from the crowd and launched himself at the royal coach, dagger in hand. The prince's personal bodyguards had dragged the assassin to the ground and disarmed him. He had been imprisoned and was due to be executed the following morning, but still the Ley whispered of danger circling the life of the young prince. With the Council's grudging agreement, the Ryders had on this night sent one of their number to meet with the condemned to uncover the true nature of his deeds.

She reached the great, wooden door of the jail, flanked on either side by armoured guards and gazed up at the narrow gatehouse that was home to the warden. The Ley that ran here was weighty with gloom and despair tainted by the many lives that had been ended within those towering walls. She noticed the soldiers grow tense at her presence, wary of the unknown power of her rank. It was common for people to fear her order.

Stepping into the golden glow of the lantern that hung above the gate, the Ryder lowered her hood and bowed her head respectfully to the men before her. The misty drizzle caught like newly born crystals in her long, ash-blonde hair and her eyes were sharp, keen discs of bright emerald. Had she lived another, less harrowing life, she might have been called beautiful, given that the structure of her features was clean and well formed, but countless years of travel, battle and endurance had hardened and marred them with a distant severity that cancelled out any feminine fragility that may have once dwelt in her face. The pale line of a scar healed long ago traced from the outer corner of her thin mouth to the centre of her right cheek and she stood with the confident alertness of a seasoned fighter.

'Sister Ammonite of the Ley Ryders,' she announced to the guards. Her voice was uncommonly soft in comparison to her tough appearance: a quiet level tone, calming but strong. 'I wish to see the individual condemned for the attempted assassination of the prince.'

The guard to the left of the gateway lifted the visor of his helm and regarded the newcomer warily. She appeared almost otherworldly in the dull gleam of the lamp, her russet leather breastplate and breeches glittering with tiny fragments of multicolour crystal like the shimmering feathers of some exotic bird. Shade and light seemed to cling to her as if the very fibre of her form somehow altered the air.

'On what authority do you come?' he enquired.

Ammonite gazed up at the imposing walls of the prison, her pale face chilled by the winter night. 'Only by the Ley Itself and my own compulsion,' she replied, her voice still, even and calm. 'May I speak to the sheriff?'

The young man eyed her warily. The Ryders never spoke to anyone without good reason, though their actions were beyond most folks' understanding. Turning his back to her, the guard unfastened the small portal to the side of the larger door of the prison and stepped inside, leaving Ammonite to wait with his comrade.

The Ryder drew her cloak around her shoulders to keep out the biting wind, but it did nothing to quell the terror in her heart. There was an unrest in the gloom of the Ley that ebbed from the prison that ran deeper than the mere atmosphere of sorrow that haunted the cells. As a seasoned Ryder of near on three decades, the disquiet spoke to Ammonite as clearly as a bird's song. It called to her, requesting that she and her sisters seek out the malady that disturbed it.

The guard shifted his feet slightly, unsettling Ammonite's thoughts. She gave him a compassionate smile, showing a glimmer of the beauty within her. 'It is a bitter night, my friend,' she said, reaching into one of the countless pouches that hung from her belt. 'Here, take this; it will help ward off the cold.'

She took out a small smooth beige crystal, run through with ripples of brown and cream, and offered it to him. 'Citrine. For warmth,' she explained.

The guard stared at the stone warily for a moment before taking it and tucking it away in a pocket of his surcoat. Ammonite saw a glimmer of mistrust in his eyes and her heart grew heavy. Had people's suspicion of them grown so great?

The door to the gatehouse swung open and the first solider returned along with an older, shorter man dressed in a slate-grey doublet and breeches. His head was bald but for a few strands of black hair and his face was egg-shaped with large, watery eyes and thick, wet lips. He was broadly set but the agility in his frame gave the impression of one who had been a fine warrior in his youth and was now enjoying the spoils of a rich, middle age. Ammonite regarded him with interest. The Council kept their pet sheriff well fed on the income from high taxation.

'Sheriff Knoxitch,' announced the guard as the older man bowed respectfully.

Ammonite returned the gesture.

'I apologise for disturbing you at this late hour, Sheriff.'

Sheriff Knoxitch's dark eyes cast their suspicious gaze over the female warrior, coming to rest on the glittering hilt of the sword she wore at her hip. 'No doubt you wouldn't have done so if it hadn't been a matter of great importance. Come in from this inclement weather and tell me what brings you here.' His words were polite and welcoming but Ammonite detected an air of mistrust in his tone. She recalled what her Sister Ley Ryder Onyx had said to her before she had set out that night.

Expect little help from those who work for the Crown. The favours granted to us during Elkric's reign are long forgotten.

The sheriff ushered her through the door into a small, dark room that served as his office. A simple, wooden table stood in the centre of the chamber, laden with legal decrees from the Royal Council and arrest warrants. A pair of plain chairs stood either side of the table for the sheriff and a guest, and a warm fire crackled in the grate. In the shadows of the far corner of the room, a strong, oak door barred with numerous heavy locks and bolts indicated the entrance to the cells. Ammonite stood silently for a moment, her chilled form slowly becoming accustomed to the heat thrown out from the fire as she once more felt the mood of the Ley wash over her senses. This was supposed to be a place of justice, of clear divisions of right and wrong but the wordless whispers of the stones told another story. There were laws now that went against the rhythm of the Ley.

Sheriff Knoxitch moved his well-set frame behind the table, shuffling the edicts and summons that were strewn there into neat piles. From a cabinet behind his chair, he took a dark glass bottle and a pair of goblets which he placed before him.

'Rum, good Sister?' he offered, uncorking the bottle and splashing some of the rich, dark liquid into one of the cups.

A polite smile traced Ammonite's thin lips as she shook her head. 'Thank you for the hospitality, Sheriff, but I must decline. Intoxicating liquor is forbidden to those of my Calling. It numbs the senses to the call of the Ley.'

She shrugged off her cloak and hung it on a nail beside the door. The many crystals and gemstones that encrusted her tough hide garments gleamed in the orange glow of the blaze, swirling in complex patterns and designs across her chest, shoulders, arms and legs. Gracefully, she crossed the chamber and sat down opposite the sheriff, her movements practiced and deliberate as if she suspected attack from an unseen adversary.

The sheriff took his goblet and raised the spirit to his moist lips. 'Darn poor role in this world if you can't enjoy the warmth of a fine toddy on a cold night,' he muttered, swigging a mouthful of rum. 'Though I must confess that I have little knowledge of the ways of your order. Tell me, what brings you to this sorry place on such a night?'

Ammonite removed her thick gauntlets and folded her hands on her lap as she regarded him. Every living creature, person and animal added their individual mood and mark to the Ley, their spirit colouring Its flow with what they were. A trained Ryder could gain some understanding of a person by reading how the Ley ran over and around them. From the way the power of the earth coursed around the sheriff, Ammonite could tell that he was a man who wanted to see justice done for his country and trusted his superiors to command him fairly.

'I wish to speak with you about the assassination attempt on the prince's life. The Ley compels me to see the condemned before he is put to death.'

A knowing smile pulled at the corners of the sheriff's mouth as he reclined in his chair. 'I thought that might be the case,' he said darkly, taking another sip of rum.

'Humour my curiosity, but why do the Ley Ryders show an interest in the prince's safety now, when at the time none of you acted to avert the attack even though a number of you were present?'

Ammonite clenched her hands together and battled to control her frustration. 'The Ley did not inform us that the attack was going to occur nor did It compel us to intervene. Prince Aarold's safety is, as you of all people know, the responsibility of the Royal Guard and while my fellow Ryders and I wish him the best of health, we cannot act unless instructed by the Ley to do so.' Her voice was impassioned but calm, demonstrating the strict self-discipline she had mastered during many years in the Sisterhood.

Sheriff Knoxitch fingered his goblet and gazed into the dark liquid it held. 'You must understand, Sister Ammonite,' he stated carefully, 'the allegiances of the Ley Ryders are difficult for laymen such as I to understand. You must be sympathetic to people's suspicions of you.'

Ammonite inhaled deeply and, closing her eyes, silently called upon the Ley to quell her disappointment in the negative way many of Veridium's citizens now viewed her Calling. She wondered, not for the first time, how this malicious mistrust had started when the Ryders' actions had always been for others' benefit. She reached for a smooth piece of dark, green moss agate that was set into the panelling of her tunic, drawing from it the strength she needed not to be offended by his words.

'The role of the Ryders is, and has always been, to listen to the guiding influence of the Ley and to offer help wherever it's needed. It is against our code to do harm.'

Something in her words must have touched the sheriff for he leant forward and gazed at her intently. 'There are rumours,' he confessed, in a voice hushed with both guilt and fearful mistrust, 'around the court, that since the king's death, the Ryders have been plotting to seize power of the kingdom. Many believe, though I am not among them, that a young prince with such ill health as Prince Aarold is a figure that could be easily usurped by a faction such as the Ley Ryders.'

Her thin, colourless lips tightened. Ammonite battled to recall the sacred ordinances she was taught when she first received her Calling, those guiding principles carved in granite by the first Ryders all those aeons ago. *Be not swayed by the judgements and accusations of others, only by the guiding of the Ley.*

'I can assure you and any others who fear or doubt our intentions,' she uttered, her voice as soft as the breeze through rushes, 'that the Ley Ryders have no ambition to rule or govern. We do not have the spirit to remain in one place and reign over our fellow men, not when the Ley may call us to move on at any time.'

Knoxitch's dark eyes narrowed shrewdly as he assessed her with the experience of one used to dealing with liars and ne'er-do-wells. 'Aye,' he said with a stiff nod. 'I believe you. You don't stay alive in my line of work without knowing who can be trusted.'

Ammonite's frustration lessened slightly on hearing this. Indeed, she had been correct: the sheriff was a good man at heart. 'The prisoner, then,' she reminded him. 'I am given permission to see him?'

Knoxitch drained the dregs of rum from his goblet and tilted it thoughtfully in his fingers. 'In my presence and that of the guards, I see no harm in granting your request.'

Setting down his goblet, he rose and moved over to the portal which led down to the jail. Ammonite joined him, her mind once more connecting with the spirit of the Ley as she focused on her task.

The sheriff took the bundle of heavy keys from his belt and methodically began to unlock the dozens of bolts and latches that barred the door. Finally, the sturdy, oak entrance swung open to reveal the long, dank corridor that led to the cells. A flaming torch rested in a holder on the thick granite wall and taking this in his hand the sheriff guided Ammonite down the gloomy passageway which stank of filth and despair. Trudging through the hopeless, icy shadows of the imposing prison, a great mood of Ley energy washed into Ammonite's awareness, condensed by the many forlorn longings of the prisoners to see the free world once more and the dark memories of the crimes they had committed. It flooded Ammonite's thoughts like a thousand unspoken, wordless whispers from the collective souls of the inmates. The Ley ran slowly and thickly through the cells of Veridium jail, like a broad river filled with the heartless ice of injustice. It was this great unfairness that drew the Ryder onward, compelling her to discover its source.

They passed a large, dank cell filled with many women and children. Some of the children were no more than babies and all were sickly and malnourished, eyes dark and haunting in the light of the torch. A rancid stench of sickness issued from the sorry mass, darkening the Ley with the awful promise of infant death; some of the babes would not see morning. Ammonite paused to gaze compassionately at the sorry waifs, torn between her oath to defend the needy and the call of the Ley to visit the condemned man.

'Women,' she puzzled sorrowfully, looking towards the sheriff, 'and children too? Tell me, Sheriff, what crime did these sorry individuals perpetrate?'

But the sheriff did not so much as glance at the sickly wretches, huddled behind the bars. 'The worst, in the eyes of the Royal Council,' he uttered in a noncommittal tone. 'They were unable to pay their taxes. The dues have been rising every month since the death of the king. The Council, under the advice of our wise White Duchess Maudabelle, feels that with a prince who is under-age and lame acting as sovereign, Geoll is in danger from avaricious enemies. The taxes go towards strengthening the army.' He gestured to the prisoners. 'Most of these are widows and orphans, with no income.'

Ammonite's eyes were drawn to one woman, a little younger than herself, trying to nurse her baby on her empty breast. 'What will happen to them?' she enquired.

'If they're lucky, they will be put into slavery and allowed to work off their debt.' Knoxitch's voice sounded grimly matter-of-fact.

The Ley Ryder attempted to glance at the sheriff's face in the dim shadows. It was difficult to tell, amid all the sorrow that washed through the Ley, whether he approved or not.

'And how long,' she enquired, 'will that take?'

The sheriff seemed reluctant to reply, but instead turned a corner leading Ammonite away from the sorrow within the main communal cells, down a dank and narrow staircase, away from the upper levels of the jail. 'The man accused of attempted assassination is being held this way,' he told her.

She felt her troubled thoughts once again being pulled by the Ley in the direction of the condemned man and cautiously followed him down the narrow stone steps. The sound of her heavy boots echoed off the thick, stone walls as they descended the deep shaft into the deepest section of the dungeon: the grimmest and darkest area resigned for those prisoners with no hope of salvation. The glow of the sheriff's torch flickered on the damp, shadowy walls, casting long, malformed shapes of darkness in the gloom. It was blackness mingled with the command of the Ley, drawing Ammonite onwards.

They stopped at a heavy iron door with a tiny, barred porthole. It was flanked on either side by heavily built, grim-faced guards, armed to the teeth with broadswords and spike-studded maces. They saluted Sheriff Knoxitch as he approached and he respectfully returned the gesture.

'Here we are,' he informed Ammonite, reaching to his belt to retrieve the keys to the cell. 'He says his name is Happenny but that's the only information we can get out of him. He denies all knowledge of the attack even though half the city saw what happened. My bet is, he thinks if he feigns insanity he might escape execution but there's no chance. His head will be severed from his shoulders in the morning, whether it's addled or not.'

Ammonite said nothing as the sheriff unlocked the thick, iron portal, her mind already thinking which crystals would aid her in uncovering the truth. Peering inside the dark cell, she regarded the sallow individual manacled to the far wall.

A sorry figure greeted her: a puny collection of bones wrapped in pallid skin which was battered and bruised from his time in the jail. Long scarlet wheals on his bare arms and legs displayed where he had been whipped and beaten, and his pale ginger hair and beard were matted with blood and filth. He barely had the strength to lift his head as Ammonite entered his cell.

She approached him cautiously, the Ley whirling noisily in her mind, telling her she was on the correct path. She motioned for the sheriff to stay near the doorway and hold his torch aloft.

Through the flickering half-light, Happenny gazed at her with frightened, confused eyes of pale greyish blue. His cracked and bloodied lips trembled. 'Why?' he bleated, pitifully. 'I do not understand.'

The Ley Ryder gazed at him compassionately, trying to read the moods of power that ebbed through his broken form. 'They tell me that your name is Happenny,' she said gently as the prisoner blinked in the orange glare of the torch. 'Is that correct?'

The man nodded weakly, tears springing to his eyes. He shifted nervously against the damp, icy wall, his chains clinking heavily.

'Tell me,' continued Ammonite, in her soothing, accepting tone, 'is it true that you tried to kill Prince Aarold?'

A terrified, guttural cry caught in the man's throat as his body shook with despair.

'I don't know,' he cried desperately. 'I don't remember anything. I keep telling them but they don't believe me!' He hung his head and wept.

Her eyes still trained on the sobbing prisoner, Ammonite unfastened one of the many leather pouches around her belt and retrieved from it a nugget of celestite, the truth crystal. Holding it before her, she focused her mental energy on the heart of the jagged, pale blue rock, feeling her will link with the properties and power held within the gem. As she had done countless times before, she allowed the intent of the Ley to pulse through her being, ebbing into the crystal where it became focused and clear.

'Tell me the truth, my friend,' she uttered to the frightened Happenny. 'You have nothing to fear from the Ley.'

The quaking prisoner sobbed even more bitterly as he gazed at the piece of celestite. 'I, I,' he began, then letting out a pained groan, slumped forward, his body convulsing uncontrollably.

Sheriff Knoxitch rushed forward when he saw the prisoner begin to twist and shake. 'Get a physician!' he shouted to the guards, but before he could finish speaking, Happenny's body fell still and his head jerked up to stare at the Ley Ryder. His features froze like stone. When Ammonite and the sheriff looked into his eyes their hearts were gripped with terror for the sockets now held nothing other than two dark globes of polished, black marble, darker than the finest jet.

A hissing voice echoed from the man's larynx, like steam escaping an underground geyser. His lips twitched as they tried to form utterances that were beyond the human tongue. The darkness that consumed Happenny's form called out tauntingly to Ammonite through the flow of the Ley, churning its rhythm like a squall churns the sea, colouring it with hues that Ammonite had not witnessed before. 'I am coming,' it spat wordlessly. 'Fear me, Ley Ryder!'

Ammonite battled to control her mastery of the Ley against this unknown threat. Steadying her will, she placed all her mental energy in the confessional power of the celestite, compelling the entity to reveal its name and nature.

The energy of the pale blue crystal vibrated through the dark force that had taken hold of the man's body. Happenny's flesh trembled as the malicious blackness cast it off like a serpent shedding its skin. The marble eyes melted into twin rivers of ebony shadow that oozed into the cell, ready to swallow Ammonite in a soulless death. Quick as a fox, she dropped the celestite and with one swift move, reached for the blade fastened at her side.

The sword arced through the putrid air swiftly. Skilfully aligned to the flow of the Ley, it rarely missed its mark, striking the wrath-like entity as surely as if it had been muscle and bone. Ammonite felt the forceful magic snag on the teeth of her weapon, tugging at it viciously, trying to get free. Reaching her belt with her free hand, she drew out a large piece of clear quartz, the mirror crystal that could both magnify and neutralise any magic that flowed into it. She threw it on the ground before her and with an agile flick of her wrist, brought the tip of her blade down on to its polished surface, dragging down the coils of dark magic. The violent power sent trembles of murderous intent through the stone and into the blade, causing Ammonite to feel its hatred course into her body through the golden hilt.

Muttering under her breath, she used all her mental will to connect with the Ley embedded within the sword, a power as familiar to her as her own hand. The rhythm of the Ley filled her mind from all around.

Like an empty vessel, her mind held the shades of the Ley, measuring and balancing them until each was equally at one with the other, before willing their flow down her blade to overwhelm the dark entity ensnared there. The twitching coils of inky shadow jerked and hissed like some mighty snake as Ammonite pinned them on to the clear quartz. Her blade twisted slightly, forming a small cleft in the pure, glass-like surface of the crystal. It opened its heart, greedily swallowing the unwilling, hateful cloud into itself, holding it securely imprisoned within the never-ending flow of the Ley that ran through it. Mentally exhausted, Ammonite withdrew her sword and replaced it into its scabbard. Sheriff Knoxitch hurried across to the unmoving form of the prisoner.

Anxiously, he pressed his fingertips to the man's neck. 'Dead,' he gasped, barely able to believe what he had witnessed. 'That *thing* sucked his life away before our eyes! What was that heinous blackness?'

Ammonite did not answer him at first; she simply did not have the words. Crouching down, she picked up the nugget of quartz and inspected it closely. A sable shadow tarnished the core of the crystal, a dark churning knot of vile intent. Her mind cast her troubled thoughts into the Ley like a line into a swiftly running river, but the guiding power gave her no answer. It only compelled her once again to follow It, seek out the truth where It led.

'I don't know,' she murmured thoughtfully, 'but it appears that the executioner will not receive payment for his services, not yet anyway.'

The sheriff huffed in bewilderment, looking from the lifeless body of the prisoner to the crystal in Ammonite's hand. 'His Majesty and the Council must be informed,' he stated. 'Having the prisoner die before his execution is most untoward!'

Ammonite rubbed her thumb over the angular face of the quartz and felt a dull heat stirring within its heart. 'Indeed,' she breathed, the Calling of the Ley tugging at her mind the way the wind tugs at a traveller's cloak. 'I myself wish an audience at the palace.'

She heard the sheriff giving orders to his men about what was to be done but his words did not register. Ammonite only heard the voice of the Ley, filling her senses, driving her to discover more about the unfortunate Happenny and the foul darkness that robbed him of his life.

Chapter 3

THE JOURNEYING TRIAD

Hayden awoke at dawn, the cold morning sunlight streaming through the window into the sleeping chamber he shared with his parents and sister. Petronia and their mother were already busying themselves in the living quarters, making up the fire to heat porridge so that Hayden and his father could have something warm and nourishing in their bellies before they started work. He dressed quickly, pulling on his breeches and linen shirt. The thin fabric did not keep out the autumn wind, but stoking the furnace in the forge would soon mean he would be warm. He ate the nourishing oats before kissing his mother and sister farewell and heading out with his father to start a day of honest toil.

Together the men stoked the great, black kiln until the fire that glowed within it burned with a powerful, orange heat. Working in iron and steel for countless decades, Godfrey knew how to encourage and master the flames, judging when they were hot enough to welcome the awaiting metal. Then he would plunge the cold dark iron into the heart of the coals, allowing the heat to embrace it, giving life and pliability to the rigid form. The metal pulsated, as if pumped full of life-giving blood before Godfrey moulded it with hammer and tongs, using powerful but skilful blows to sculpt it into form. With every strike the mighty anvil would sing a clear, ringing note, a rhythmic and hearty melody of honest life. Hayden worked the bellows – the great lungs of the glowing furnace – nursing the fire so it remained boiling and well fed, watching with pride as his father shaped tools, horseshoes and other implements.

He often thought how much energy there was pulsing through the small workshop: the heat of the fire, the sure strength of his father's hammer, the heavy ring of the anvil. It pleased him to know that all that force was being used to form useless lumps of metal into practical items. It was as if he and his father were masters of nature's power, commanding metal and flame for the good of their neighbours. Godfrey had taught his son to respect and understand the energies of fire and metal: treat them with honour so they might be useful allies. Hayden felt confident that his father had given him the knowledge he needed to one day be a great blacksmith.

Around midday, when the sun had melted the early frost from the earth and the furnace was crackling with a steady, constant heat, Godfrey instructed his son to walk down to the river and fetch fresh water for the barrel in which they cooled the burning irons. Hot from the blaze of the fire and aching from pumping the bellows, Hayden eagerly took two buckets and set off down the path towards the woods.

It was a pleasant autumn day, cold but bright and the birds twittered merrily as Hayden briskly walked to the stream. Nature seemed to be in her best garb: the lush green of the foliage tinged with hints of scarlet and gold as the distant pale sun rode high in the colourless, pure sky. He whistled merrily as he strolled along, relishing the beauty of his homeland. When the land was as lovely as this, how could his sister even think about wanting anything more?

Reaching the hillock that overlooked the stream, the blacksmith's son heard voices and looking down was surprised to see a group of three strangely clad individuals watering their horses at the riverbank. He watched with curiosity, unable to make out what manner of persons they were. They were dressed in well-fitted leather breeches, doublets and helms like soldiers, though they displayed no kind of standard to indicate who they served. Their armour was studded with countless shards of coloured crystal that gleamed and sparkled in the sun; even the tack of their steeds was dotted with precious gems. Their bizarre clothing gave them a regal, almost otherworldly air, although they moved and spoke as if they were used to living off the land.

As Hayden watched, one of the women, a broad-shouldered maid with long chestnut ringlets, stooped down to examine the hoof of her mount's right hind leg. Sighing, she shook her head and glanced over to one of her companions, a slightly rotund female with thick red hair fastened in twin braids, stretched out leisurely on the grass.

'It's no good, Sister Rosequartz,' Hayden heard her say, 'he's thrown a shoe. I shan't be able to ride him.'

The redhead sat up, stretching slightly as she did. 'Don't fret, Garnet,' she said with a smile. 'If needs be my faithful steed is strong enough to carry us both until we get to Goodstone.' Getting to her feet, she strolled across to her strong, piebald stallion and affectionately patted his muscular neck.

The third member of the group gave a snide chuckle. She was a tall, long-limbed maid with lank black hair that hung in soft curtains either side of her pallid, angular face.

'That old nag will keel over beneath the weight of the pair of you,' she said in clipped, elegant tones. 'He should have been put out to stud years ago.'

Rosequartz dismissively shook her head at this harsh remark and continued to stroke the horse's black and white coat. 'You pay no heed to Sister Jet,' she crooned lovingly to her mount. 'The Ley brought you to me and you're a handsome steed. Though I must confess, I have been giving you more weight to carry than I should be!' She patted her slightly rounded belly and laughed to herself.

Garnet finished examining her horse's hoof and turned to face her bickering companions. 'None of this is helping in the slightest,' she told them. 'The fact of the matter remains that I cannot follow the Ley on an unshod horse.'

'Excuse me,' Hayden called out. 'Forgive my impertinence but I couldn't help overhearing. Are you in need of a farrier?'

The trio turned to face him, surprised by the unexpected interruption. Hayden at once was made to feel slightly wary. The women had the quick reflexes of well-trained warriors and instinctively reached for their swords when they heard his voice. He froze, uncertainty filling his heart.

The air around these strange women seemed to be thick with a power and energy the like of which he had never felt before.

'Begging you pardon, mistresses,' he continued slowly, his hands instinctively raised in a submissive gesture. 'I mean no offence. It's just that my father is the finest blacksmith for near on twenty miles and he would be more than willing to shoe your steed.'

Rosequartz relaxed, a broad grin forming on her round, ruddy face. 'Well, what greets us here?' she chuckled. 'It seems the Ley has brought us assistance, and may I say it comes in a most dashing package!' She glanced over to her raven-haired companion who still had her hand on the hilt of her blade, eyeing Hayden suspiciously. 'Stand easy, Sister Jet, you'll scare the poor young fellow to death!'

Crossing her arms, Garnet regarded Hayden with knowledgeable, dark eyes. 'What is your name, young man?' she asked

'Hayden, son of Godfrey of the hamlet of Ravensbrook,' he said with a small bow.

Garnet grinned at her companions, amused by the youth's seriousness and formality.

'Well, Hayden son of Godfrey, may I introduce myself? I am known as Sister Garnet and this pair of bickering harridans are my companions, Sister Jet and Sister Rosequartz. You are indeed correct; my good steed needs shoeing but I am sorry to say that no common smith could perform the task, no matter how skilled they may be.' She took hold of her steed's reins, leading the fine animal gently forward, its glossy chestnut coat and gem-studded tack glistening in the sun.

'However, if your father would allow me to use of his forge so that I might complete the task, I would be happy to pay.'

Surprised by the woman's words, Hayden glanced down at her gauntleted hands. During his sheltered life in Ravensbrook, he had never met women such as these before; they seemed to address the world with the same confidence and power as any man, yet still possess a feminine, almost sublime, calmness of character. His father had always told him that women were delicate and needed to be protected. These females, however, did not appear to need protection.

26

'I'm sure Father would be more than happy to accommodate your needs. He's always taught me to offer help to damsels in distress.'

Hitching her foot back into her stirrup Rosequartz let out an amused chuckle. 'Damsels!' she declared, hoisting herself easily on to the steed's broad back. 'Did you hear that, Sisters? I haven't been addressed as a damsel since receiving my Calling nearly twenty years ago. The Ley has certainly led us to strange pastures this time!'

Garnet looked kindly upon Hayden, giving him a grateful smile. Her eyes were of the oddest and most beautiful shade: a golden brown colour like liquid honey or flawless amber droplets that glistened with untold knowledge in the sunlight. In fact, the warm glow of the late morning seemed to be naturally drawn to all of the three women like a moth to a flame.

'Take no offence from Rosequartz's jesting,' Garnet told Hayden kindly. 'Her temperament is governed by the need to find humour in all things.'

Filling his buckets from the stream, Hayden led the travellers along the pathway towards the village. As he walked, he could not help but admire the rich array of glistening gemstones that decorated the women's clothing and bridles. They glimmered with every conceivable hue and texture from flat shards of deep green and scarlet like polished glass to uneven crystals of milky white and lush purple, their natural forms as sharp as the finest blades. They swirled in complex, abstract patterns across the tanned hides of their breeches and breastplates, not set in mounts of gold and silver but firmly fixed into place with simple strands of thread. Hayden gazed at the glittering jewels and found his memory stirred by a semi-forgotten recollection of stories told to him in his infancy, of magic and noble warriors who roamed the land, righting wrongs and defeating the weak.

'Forgive the ignorance of a simple country lad,' he ventured politely, as they climbed the hill that overlooked Ravensbrook. 'But I can't help but wonder what role you good ladies serve? I have never seen folk dressed in your manner before, and wonder are you daughters of some foreign noble?'

The trio looked stunned by this remark. Solemnly, Jet shook her head. 'Has it been so long since we rode to this part of our land?' she asked her friends in her cool crisp tone. 'Do not people speak of us any longer?'

'Humility,' Rosequartz chided her; 'our deeds are not done for praise.'

Hayden's cheeks coloured with shame from his naivety. 'Forgive me, mistresses,' he whispered. 'I am uneducated and know little of the world beyond my village.'

Garnet placed a forgiving hand on the youth's shoulder. 'We are Ley Ryders, Master Hayden,' she explained. 'Humble servants of the power that flows through all living beings.' Sombrely she caressed a deep navy stone fastened to her shoulder.

'We devote our lives to following the flow of goodness that is harnessed in these crystals, focusing it where it is needed, to heal and protect.'

A memory stirred in the recesses of Hayden's mind. He had heard the elders of the village speak of the Ley Ryders, the noble deeds they had performed and battles they had fought. He had always believed them to belong to a time long passed.

'I have heard of your order,' he gasped awestruck. 'You fought alongside noble King Elkric in the war against Etheria, the country that lies beyond the Kelhalbon Mountains. Your reputation goes before you!' He bowed awkwardly, not quite sure how to show appropriate respect for such gallant warriors.

Garnet smiled modestly at Hayden's praise. 'You are most kind, Master Hayden, but neither my Sister Ryders nor myself can take credit for the bravery of our foremothers. We were barely children when King Elkric rode to war.'

'Hark at your vanity, Sister Garnet!' cried Rosequartz cheekily, raising her fine tapered eyebrows. 'She is older than she looks! Every morn she washes her face in water infused with albite and coral to keep her youthful.'

Garnet's cheeks flushed slightly at Rosequartz words. 'Perhaps it is true,' she confessed tactfully, 'that I recall the Great War in more detail than my sisters but I swear that I was too young to take up arms. I was merely an apprentice to the Ley, not yet given my Stone Name when it occurred.'

Hayden listened with interest as Garnet spoke of her Calling, although notions of the Great War and such were beyond his simple learning. 'But what brings you to our humble village, good mistresses? Nothing unfortunate, I hope.'

Rosequartz looked down upon the little hamlet nestled at the foot of the hill. 'Of course not!' she declared. 'The Ley simply brought us here so that we might bless the farmer's fields. We were heading back to our home citadel at Goodstone when Garnet's mount threw his shoe. The Ley always guides us where we are needed and supplies us with the tools to do Its work. Why look, It even guided you to us!'

Garnet nodded in agreement. 'Although,' she added thoughtfully, rubbing her chin, 'I have felt a disturbing darkness in Its energy of late. I feel It will soon call us to greater action.'

A distant look came into her amber-coloured eyes as if her thoughts were transferred to a far-off world.

'Don't speak of such things in front of our young friend.' Glancing behind him, the blacksmith's son saw Jet looking down at him from the saddle of her ebony charger. A polite smile touched her thin, colourless lips and her eyes were as dark as the gems that shared her name. Hayden did not think he had ever seen a woman look so beautiful and yet so cold.

'He has little knowledge of our ways and such talk will worry him. Believe me, Master Hayden, the Ley means you no ill will.' Her voice was polite and clipped but there was an aloofness in her words that made Hayden ill at ease.

Instantly, Garnet's eyes snapped back into focus as she gave Hayden a reassuring look. 'Of course,' she uttered, 'pay no attention to my concerns. We Ryders guard the Ley with the same sensitivity that a mother guards her offspring. Any slight change in Its mood causes us vexation.'

Hayden nodded politely although he did not completely follow

Sister Garnet's words. He understood, as all common folk did, that the Ley pulsed forever through the land, feeding the power of existence into every living thing. It had the power to give a farmer a lush harvest or bring famine and illness to a community. It worried him to consider the Ley not being an unchanging flow of goodness.

Jet dug her spurs into the glossy sides of her ebony mare. 'Time is short,' she declared, bringing her horse to a steady trot. 'I can see the blacksmith's forge from here.' Steadily, she rode ahead of the group, towards the village and Hayden's forge.

Rosequartz clicked her tongue disapprovingly and leant over to whisper in Hayden's ear. 'I apologise for my sister's impoliteness,' she said. 'Jet has been in an ill mood since we rode from Goodstone. She does not enjoy travelling in the company of others; she prefers to work the Ley alone. She has many skills. She is one of the best healers in our ranks, but lacks many social niceties.'

The Ryder's words about healing struck a chord with Hayden and instantly his thoughts flew back to his sister's unexplained muteness. If the Ryders truly did possess the power to alter the flow of sickness through someone's body, wasn't it possible that they could also remove the unseen ties that bound Petronia's tongue? He watched Sister Jet as she rode confidently into Ravensbrook and pondered whether the Ley had drawn her and her fellow Ryders there for that very purpose.

He escorted Rosequartz and Garnet into the village square where Jet had already dismounted. The arrival of such unusual strangers in the tiny hamlet had caused quite a flurry of excitement among the villagers and already many of them had come out of their huts to see the travellers. Housewives glanced at one another, intrigued at seeing fellow women dressed in armour and bearing swords, while the elders chattered with excited awe as they recalled the last time they had seen Ley Ryders in this part of the country. Some of the braver children ventured away from the safety of their mothers' skirts to curiously gawp at the brightly coloured stones that decorated the saddles and bridles of their mounts. Ever friendly and eager for company, Rosequartz climbed down from her steed to greet the inquisitive infants while Jet stayed reservedly by the horses. Glancing across at his own home Hayden saw that his mother and sister had left their chores and come to the doorway to investigate the activity in the square. He noticed that Petronia's eyes shone brightly and her face was flushed with excitement; he wondered whether she somehow knew that these women might have the power to bless her with speech at last.

Dutifully, Hayden took Garnet's mount's reins and led both the horse and its rider over to the forge where his father had paused from toiling at the anvil to witness the arrival of the travellers. 'By the powers,' he gasped, as Hayden secured the horse to the railing outside the smithy. 'I didn't think I would live to see your kind in the village again.'

Removing her gem-studded, leather cap, Garnet shook out her chestnut curls. 'Greetings to you, good blacksmith,' she said, bowing. 'Your son tells me that you are a fine craftsman and a generous one at that. I wish to ask for your assistance.'

Godfrey's dark eyes flitted over the Ryder's sturdy form taking in every aspect of her appearance, from her pale, golden eyes to the complex swirls of jewels fixed to her armour and the heavy sheathed sword at her hip. 'I was only a lad when the Ryders last rode through Ravensbrook,' he muttered, scratching his thick beard. 'Still I do remember how brightly the sun gleamed on their garments. I put it down to the wonder of a child's memory but one glance at you proves it is not the case. Tell me, is there still a woman by the name of Amethyst in your ranks? She cured my mother of a weak stomach.'

Garnet leaned against the fence and scratched Flintshank's neck. 'Sister Amethyst is the warden of our Keep at Goodstone,' she informed him. 'She is noble and wise. I myself was tutored by her.'

His mind still teeming with a possibility of curing his sister, Hayden approached his father. 'I met Mistress Garnet and her sisters at the river. Her mount has thrown a shoe and I told her she would receive assistance at our humble forge.' He was keen to show the Ryders as much hospitality as their lowly home could afford, both out of respect for their station and in the hope they would help Petronia in return.

31

Godfrey studied the fine tan-coated animal standing patiently beside its mistress. 'That should be no trouble at all, my lady.'

Gratefully Garnet smiled and removed her heavy, leather gauntlets. Hayden noticed how slim and smooth her hands were, so unlike the fingers of the village women that were red and sore with daily toil. These were the hands of a lady of breeding, at the very least someone who only used their fingers for the most skilled of arts.

'Forgive my rudeness,' Garnet continued, 'but as I explained to your son, it is against our way of life to allow anyone but a Ryder or a dwarf to shoe our horses. They carry us along the pull of the Ley and need suitable shoes for such a task.'

Godfrey regarded the woman suspiciously. Garnet was strongly built with a boyish physique but she certainly did not match the blacksmith in brawn. 'You've worked a forge before?' he queried doubtfully.

The Ryder arched her eyebrow in an expression that showed she was used to folk underestimating her due to her sex. 'I was trained to work with ore by the dwarves of Kelhalbon, finest smiths ever to raise a hammer. All Ryders receive an education from them in stone and metal; without such knowledge we couldn't do our work.'

The smithy shook his head in wonder. 'Such things are beyond reason,' he breathed. 'But your confidence is enough guarantee for me. You may use my forge and anvil.'

Garnet bowed in gratitude and climbed over the fence to enter the workshop. 'Your assistance is most gratefully received. I must inform you though, we Ryders are an impoverished order and carry no gold. However, I can repay you in favour with my use of the crystals. Perhaps I can give you a piece of aventurine or tiger's eye for above the door of your forge to bring you greater prosperity, or maybe you have a loved one who is in need of healing.'

Once again, Hayden thought of his sister and a miracle that could bless her with a voice at last. 'Father,' he began earnestly. Godfrey raised his hand to silence him, casting his son a reproachful look. 'Payment can be discussed once Mistress Garnet has received the help she needs,' he told him steadily before turning back to the Ryder. 'My forge is at your disposal as is the assistance of my son; he is my apprentice.'

Garnet nodded gratefully as she began to inspect the hammers and tongs laid out ready for use. Hayden made his way into the workshop, eager to address his notions about a cure for Petronia to his father. 'Father,' he enthused once more, as the Ryder removed her leather outer tunic so she was cooler and freer to work. 'Mistress Garnet says that she and her fellow Ryders are skilled healers,' he whispered to Godfrey, glancing over to where Petronia stood in the doorway of the house. 'Perhaps they could remove Petronia's muteness.'

A wistful glimmer of emotion flickered in Godfrey's dark eyes and his stalwart face softened for a brief moment that indicated to Hayden the same idea had crossed his mind. However, displaying any glimmer of feeling was not in the blacksmith's nature. Pushing past his son he gave the firm instruction, 'Give Mistress Garnet the same assistance you would me. I must speak with your mother.'

Filled with hope and anxiety, Hayden took his usual place at the side of the furnace and began to work the large bellows. 'There are bars of steel already cut to length,' he informed her, nodding toward a dozen or so black, metal bands laid out on a table nearby.

Without another word, Garnet rolled up the sleeves of her ebony tunic and set to work. Reaching into one of the numerous purses attached to her belt, she retrieved a small, smooth crystal of rich reddish orange and rolled it skilfully between her palms.

Hayden paused from his task of working the bellows to watch the woman twist and spin the gem between her agile hands and felt his spine prickle. He found himself once more standing in the moonlight of the previous evening, watching his sister juggle stones. The motion of the Ryder's hands was almost identical to that Petronia had used. His mind struggled to find an explanation of this coincidence, but could not.

Garnet noticed Hayden's transfixed stare and momentarily stopped the strange ritual.

'I'm harnessing the power of the fire agate,' she explained, 'easing the flow of the Ley through it so it may help the fire burn hotter.' Cupping the small, scarlet gem in her hands, Garnet stooped over at the mouth of the furnace, blowing gently over the gleaming jewel into the flames. At once, the fire crackled and blazed more fiercely, as if it had been suddenly fed by more fuel or oxygen.

The country boy watched, his mouth open in amazement. 'I would call such a thing witchcraft if I hadn't known the nature of your order,' he gasped in wonder.

Garnet simply smiled modestly and picking up one of the iron ingots with the tongs, thrust it into the golden flames. Within just a few moments, the dark iron began to glow with vibrant, liquid flame as Garnet skilfully began to form it into an even U-shape. Her use of the tongs and hammer was as competent as Hayden's father's but rather than using sheer brute strength to turn and mould the heated metal, she seemed to command a silent inner power that willed the iron to bend and turn with the slightest pressure from her tools. Hayden watched as she stared into the heat of the furnace, her golden pupils gleaming with the same blazing intensity as the fire, and thought how there seemed to be a silent, hypnotic dialogue between Ley Ryder, flame and metal. It was not just that Sister Garnet understood these elements: she was at one with them.

After a few minutes of toil the shoe had been fashioned from iron and flame and carefully Garnet dropped it into the water butt to cool. Dragging his eyes away from the Ley Ryder and her work, Hayden saw Petronia had come from the house, carrying a tray of water, bread and dried meat to offer their guests. She had placed the wooden platter on the ground beside her feet and was gazing wistfully at the leather surcoat Garnet had lain over the fence. Unaware that her brother was watching her, she reached out with curious fingers to caress a rough, light brown stone sewn into the hide marked with shallow lines that formed a cross. Shocked by his sister's boldness, Hayden hurried forward to stop her.

'Petronia!' he exclaimed, as the girl guiltily snatched her hand away from the stone, her cheeks flushed with the shame of being caught.

'What do you think you are doing? You know better than to touch that which is not yours!'

Hurriedly, she picked up the tray of food again and held it out in offering towards Garnet who had been quietly watching her with intelligent, amber eyes.

Bowing his head, Hayden apologised profusely to Garnet. 'Forgive my sister, I beg of you!' he stammered as she left the furnace to take the bread and water. 'Her mind sometimes wanders and she forgets her better manners. Ouch!'

Petronia had leant across the fence and dealt him a swift blow on his arm, her face crossly indicating that she did not appreciate being apologised for!

'What is the matter with you? This is no way to behave in front of noble guests!' He glared into her bright, black eyes, blazing with the strong gleam of wilfulness and defiance and pondered guiltily whether it was just Petronia's tongue that was touched by sickness. He thought of her behaviour the night before and how she had made the stone float in midair. Had some malicious spell taken hold of his sibling?

Garnet stepped forward, her face patient and understanding and gathered up the leather garment carefully in her arms. 'There is no need to chide her, Master Hayden,' she said gently; 'an inquisitive mind is a blessing not a sin.'

Carefully, she draped the surcoat over her arm so that Petronia might have a better view of its numerous stones. The girl's dark eyes danced in wonder as she watched the sunlight glisten on the many crystals, resting like water droplets on the tanned hide. 'This,' Garnet informed her, pointing to the dull, cross-marked stone that Petronia had reached out to touch, 'is chiastolite, a stone for courage and direction; it keeps us on the right path and links us to the Ley's will, and this one next to it, this deep green crystal, that's emerald; it draws all negative energies into it and protects us if we're under attack.'

Petronia's eyes marvelled at the intricate patterns and swirls of the crystals fastened into the thick material of the jacket and delicately rubbed a fingertip over a deep blue stone. As she caressed it, the shades within the jewel seemed to twist in the sunlight, revealing streams of dark indigo and violet. Garnet regarded the girl thoughtfully, her golden eyes cloudy with contemplation.

'What is your name, child?' she asked softly.

Petronia looked up, no longer transfixed by the numerous crystals. Her soft lips parted as if she had momentarily forgotton about her impairment and believed she had the ability to answer the question. However, no sound came from her throat and shame and frustration filled her eyes.

'Please, my lady,' interrupted Hayden delicately. 'She cannot answer you. Petronia is my sister and she is a mute. Hasn't uttered a single word since the day she was born.'

Colour rose in Petronia's tanned cheeks as she flexed her fingers agitatedly. '*Tell the good mistress I am not a fool!*' she implored her brother. '*It is only my tongue that is slow to learn, not my mind!*' She detested it when strangers judged her as imbecilic.

Hayden nodded and brushed his sister's hand.

'She asks that I might inform you that her mind is as quick as anyone's,' Hayden told Garnet respectfully. 'My sister has a pithy wit and bright mind for a maid of her limited learning. She is just unable to articulate it properly.'

A polite smile graced Garnet's mouth as if she had just remembered some private joke. 'I never doubted your intelligence for a second, Mistress Petronia,' she stated. 'Throughout my travels, I have encountered many a person who appears less than blessed with an able body and among them there are no more fools than among healthy folk. Why, even our Royal Prince Aarold is afflicted with a wasted leg!'

Petronia's bright, dark eyes grew wide with amazement at the prospect of hearing news from the glamorous, distant realms of the Royal Court and she gestured eagerly for Garnet to tell her more. Hayden watched his sister's flushed face and once more felt concern for the longing she had to learn of the dangerous world outside their simple existence.

'Do not beg Mistress Garnet for tall tales,' he reprimanded her gently. 'She is not a gypsy storyteller come for our entertainment. Now, hurry along and help Mother like a good lass.'

Petronia pulled a haughty expression that declared she did not much like to be talked down to like that and quickly gathered up the empty cups and plates. '*You're boring!*' she informed her brother before sauntering away with a swish of her glossy, dark hair.

Hayden sighed. 'Wilful girl!' he tutted to the Ley Ryder as Garnet fished the cooled horseshoe from the water barrel. 'A silent tongue does not hamper her headstrong nature. She certainly doesn't let it quash her character!'

Thoughtfully, Garnet wandered over to Flintshank and lovingly stroked the stallion. 'Your sister seems to have a strong, single-minded spirit,' she said, lifting the horse's rear leg to clean its hoof with a file. 'It will serve her well, whatever path the Ley leads her to.'

She glanced at Hayden and he saw the same, powerful, distant aura had returned to her golden eyes. 'Tell me more of your sibling. She has always been mute, you say?'

Sadly, Hayden nodded, burying his hands in the pockets of his breeches. 'As silent as a stone all her life, though it doesn't seem to damper her spirits. The village midwife has found no affliction in her mouth and throat, and by all other means she is as healthy as can be; you can see how comely and strong she is for yourself. My father, not that he is a learned man, has taught her to express her desires through gestures of the hands and face; this she does with the greatest of fluency. My parents and I as well as a few of our neighbours understand her perfectly.'

Garnet reached into a purse and pulled out a handful of iron tacks topped with tiny crystals of bluish green and began to nail the shoe on to Flintshank's hoof. 'A most clever maid indeed!' she commented.

Hayden looked doubtful as he leant against the fence. 'Aye, that she is,' he breathed. 'If only she would accept her place in the world. Her moods are fierce at times. Mother believes her temper is born out of frustration for the words that will not come from her lips. It would be a joyous day for all our family if she could speak.' He paused for a second and took a deep breath as he carefully considered his next words.

'Forgive my impertinence, Mistress Garnet,' he began carefully as the Ley Ryder completed the task of shoeing her mount, 'but did you not say that your order has among its skills, the gift of healing? I wondered whether you might have the kindness in your heart to turn your knowledge to my sister's plight and maybe find the force within the crystals to give her a voice.'

A good-natured grin tugged at Garnet's mouth. 'You would have your headstrong sister blessed with the gift of speech?' she teased. 'And dare that others hear the views of her spirited heart? My experience of men is limited but from what I know many would wish their sisters, daughters and wives to remain silent.'

Hayden gazed at her earnestly. 'I only wish to be a good and caring brother and provide my sister with all she deserves,' he replied sincerely, not understanding the humour in Garnet's words. 'It is my duty to take care of her until the time she takes a husband.'

The Ley Ryder chuckled at Hayden's seriousness. 'I jest, Master Hayden. Of course it would be most ungallant of us to accept your aid and hospitality without granting such a heartfelt request. The Ley has never granted me with much healing power but my Sister Jet is very skilled with using the crystals to ease illness. Speak with her and she will be able to tell whether Mistress Petronia can be given a voice.'

Hayden's heart leapt with excitement on hearing this and bowing low to express his deep gratitude he hurried away from the forge in search of Sister Jet. He did not want to speak to his sister or parents until he had truly secured a promise of aid. Such hope for an answer to a long-held problem was a fragile thing and he could barely allow himself to believe that the Ley Ryder Jet had the ability to rid Petronia of her affliction.

A small crowd of people had gathered in the village square, mainly children, and as he drew closer Hayden could hear the jolly melody of a jig being played on a flute. Curiosity distracted him momentarily from his quest and he wandered over to see who was playing the tune. Seated cross-legged on the ground before the enthralled audience was Sister Rosequartz, her lips pressed to the reed of a long, narrow pipe. Before her was a small puppet with long, jointed limbs of pale, carved wood connected to a hollow cage-like body, the belly of which contained a deep, ebony gemstone. As Rosequartz's fingers picked out the merry notes of the ditty, the tiny puppet hopped from the ground, its arms and legs flicking in skilful and comical movements like those of a tumbler or clown. It jumped and rolled, imbued with the appearance of life by the dark stone within and the jaunty song of the flute. The children giggled and squealed with joy and wonder as the doll stood on its head and performed somersaults, and even Hayden felt his heart grow light. As Rosequartz finished the song, the puppet collapsed to the ground; a lifeless piece of wood once more. The children clapped animatedly and cried for more.

Putting down her flute, her face wreathed in satisfied smiles, Rosequartz noticed Hayden and raised her hand in greeting. 'Master Hayden!' she cried merrily. 'So good of you to join us! Tell me, did you enjoy my little friend's performance?'

A strange, youthful happiness had filled the lad's heart at watching the puppet gaily cavort. 'Indeed!' he chuckled. 'He is a most talented acrobat! I didn't realise that Ryders such as you were also entertainers. Is there no end to your skills?'

Rosequartz picked up the lifeless doll and proudly brushed the coarse, woollen hair from its cheery painted face. 'Most of my sisters have little time or skill when it comes to jesting. But it is a gift I was blessed with and if I can use it in my work for the Ley, all the better. I say bringing laughter to a sad heart is as important as feeding the hungry and healing the sick. That's why I was given the Stone Name Rosequartz; it is known as the crystal of joy.'

At the mention of healing, Hayden at once recalled the purpose of his quest and asked the Ryder. 'I came in search of your fellow Ryder, Sister Jet. Mistress Garnet tells me that she is a skilled healer and may be able to help me. You see my sister, Petronia, lacks the ability of speech and I hoped that she would be able to grant her a voice.'

Rosequartz raised her pale eyebrows in understanding. 'Ah the mute girl,' she uttered; 'already I have made her acquaintance. She stopped by a few moments ago to enjoy my humble show. A very fair maiden indeed and one of determined character from what I could tell.'

Hayden nodded. 'That she is. Very spirited and knows her mind. You can understand how frustrating it is for her to not be able to talk. Do you think your noble sister might be able to cure her?'

Rosequartz glanced over to one of the huts. 'Sister Jet has healed many folk; her skill in using the Ley for such things knows no equal. If any of us can give your sister a voice it is her. Right now, she is with the old man going by the name of Otto, bringing him comfort for his strained back.'

Hayden turned to hurry over to his neighbour's dwelling, but Rosequartz called him back. 'A word of advice from someone who has ridden with Sister Jet,' she warned. 'She is a woman of blunt speech and doesn't suffer fools. Pick your words carefully when you speak with her.'

Nodding and thanking her profusely, Hayden made his way across to Otto's modest dwelling. As he grew closer to the old man's abode, he once more became aware of an intense power filling the air as if the warm force of a pulsing reverberation was being drawn towards the hut from all directions. Awestruck by this strong presence in the atmosphere, Hayden paused outside the house and took a couple of deep breaths before finding the courage to knock. There was silence for a few moments but just as he was about to knock again the door swung open and he found himself staring into the pale, beautiful but deeply austere face of Sister Jet.

The dark-haired woman studied him with intelligent black pupils. 'Oh, it's you, Master Hayden,' she stated blankly, leaning cross-armed against the door frame. 'Speak quickly; I am in the middle of a complex healing ritual and it doesn't help my patient if I am disturbed.'

Nervously, Hayden peered into the dim interior of the hut. He could see Otto, pale-skinned and body twisted with age laying on his front on the straw panel at the rear of the room that served as his bed. He was on his stomach, shirt removed and several large crystals of various colours rested on his lower back and shoulder blades. A long line of small shards of fiery orange amber traced the outline of the old man's bony spine. His head rested on one side and his eyes were closed as if he was peacefully asleep.

'Well, speak; boy, you have already disturbed my mental focus!'

Hayden's face flushed, both from Jet's beauty and the bluntness of her words. 'A thousand apologies, Mistress, for interrupting your complex work but I wondered if you would bestow some of your skill on a person dear to me who is in great need.'

Jet said nothing but tilted her head to one side to indicate she was listening. Apprehensively Hayden continued his explanation. 'My sister was born without the blessing of speech, a sorrow that weighs deeply on both her and the rest of our family. We would be forever in your debt if you were to lift her silence with a blessing from the crystals.'

Sister Jet's fine features remained unmoved as Hayden spoke of Petronia's plight, thoughtfully running her thumb across her bottom lip. There was no compassion or sympathy in her deep black pupils and as Hayden watched her he felt himself grow more nervous by the moment. The village midwife, his only reference to a person with any medical knowledge, had always displayed understanding and tenderness to the sick. But in the Ryder's eyes there seemed no compassion. He wondered how you could heal a person, change their life for the better and still remain totally detached.

Finally Jet spoke. 'Your sister,' she asked in clipped tones, 'is she slow of mind?'

Hayden fiercely shook his head. 'Not in the slightest, good mistress. She is as clear of thought as I. She can sew, tend house and cook and she understands everything that is told to her. She is merely unable to answer in words. Father has taught her to display her desires through gestures of the hand.'

The Ryder nodded but looked uninterested as if she had barely listened to what Hayden has said.

'Is she tongue-tied?' she queried. 'Does she have a tendon or piece of flesh binding her tongue to the bottom of her mouth?'

'Not that can be seen. The village midwife has checked her top to toe and truly in every other manner she is in rude health. I beseech you,

Mistress Jet; the power of the Ley may be the only thing that could grant my dear sibling a voice.'

The woman's inscrutable expression shifted slightly as she straightened up. 'The Ley only heals those who are meant to be healed,' she said curtly. 'It will only help those souls who allow It to. If your sister is truly meant to be whole and have a voice then the Ley will bless her with one, if not then there will be nothing that I can do for her. Do you understand?'

Sombrely, Hayden nodded although the truth was he struggled to comprehend what Sister Jet meant. He knew that Petronia had desired a voice all her life and wondered how the Ley went about deeming whether she was worthy or not of receiving one.

Sister Jet seemed satisfied with Hayden's understanding. 'Good,' she stated. 'I will complete the healing on this gentleman's back and then meet with your sister.' With that she shut the door.

His heart drumming wildly with excitement, Hayden hurried back to his own house. He could not wait to tell Petronia and their parents about the possible cure. Godfrey and Beatrice hugged each other, joyful at the notion that they might at last hear their daughter speak but Petronia herself seemed wary and uncertain. She kept asking Hayden if Sister Jet had told him what crystals she would use to free her voice. Hayden, wary of the Ryder's final words to him, told her no good was brought about by questioning miracles and she must show humble gratitude to whatever help Sister Jet and the Ley offered.

The sun was setting when Sister Jet finally exited Otto's dwelling accompanied by the old man himself. Otto was indeed standing straighter than he had done for some time and the new-found ease of his gait filled Hayden with hope in the Ryder's abilities. Jet strolled over to where Garnet and Rosequartz were unpacking their tents from their saddlebags and setting up camp for the night. Several villagers including Hayden's mother had offered them shelter, but they declined this saying that the ground was the Ley's cradle and it would serve them well. Jet looked slightly weary from her healing but after spending some time in conversation with her sisters and partaking of some food and water she approached Godfrey and told him she was ready to meet with his daughter.

Petronia nervously approached the small encampment, gripping tightly on to Hayden's hand. She had willingly agreed to allow the Ryder to examine her but now the moment had arrived her fear of the unknown threatened to overwhelm her. Garnet and Rosequartz had built a small fire to stave off the chill of the autumn evening and already Sister Jet was seated close to the orange blaze, her gems and crystals laid out on her cape like droplets of bright colour in the dusk. She looked up as they approached and without smiling motioned for them to sit down.

Petronia made a curtsey as her brother had instructed her to do and cautiously sat down beside the older woman. Jet examined the pretty girl's face with her shrewdly intelligent dark eyes, paying particular attention to her full-lipped mouth. 'So,' she said finally as Hayden sat down with them to give his sister comfort, 'your name is Petronia, is it?'

Shyly, the girl nodded, her bright eyes wandering apprehensively to the collection of gems strewn across the dark wool of Jet's cape. The Ley Ryder reached down and retrieved a glass-like wand of clear crystal. Petronia's breathing grew shallow and Hayden saw that his sister's expression had altered from trepidation to wonder and excitement. It was as if she had already seen the answer to her silent prayers within the depths of the crystal.

Composing herself, Jet motioned for Petronia to open her mouth and with eager willingness the girl parted her full, scarlet lips. Hayden felt the atmosphere around the campfire grow intense with an unseen power, just as it had done around Otto's dwelling. With well-practised skill, Jet was drawing in the flow of the almighty Ley, searching Its measureless depths for the power that would grant Petronia a voice. Hayden suddenly felt extremely fearful for his sister's safety. Unknown powers were swarming towards Petronia and he thought with alarm that they might swallow her up and whisk her away to a place beyond his understanding. But hope steadied him and stopped him interrupting the mystical ritual, the desperate faith that Sister Jet had the ability to master the Ley. Petronia's eyes were filled with joyous anticipation and

Hayden knew that if he said or did anything to stop the Ryder that Petronia would never forgive him.

Carefully, Jet caressed the inside of Petronia's mouth with the point of the crystal baton, tracing it lightly across the roof of her mouth, walls of her cheeks and length of her tongue. The clear gem seemed to glow with a pure, white light as it touched the girl's flesh, like a torch leading the way into a dark passage.

Hayden watched anxiously as Sister Jet peered into his sister's throat and heard her muse to herself in emotionless tones. 'Everything seems in perfect working order. No deformity or scarring, no signs of illness at all.'

She removed the wand from Petronia's mouth but continued to cup her chin firmly in her left hand so that the girl could not shut it. Putting down the clear crystal, the Ryder skilfully ran her dexterous fingers across the selection of jewels arranged before her. 'I think this should do the trick,' she decided at last, picking up a dusky, light blue stone.

Cupping the gem in her palm, Sister Jet brought it up before Petronia's open mouth and for a moment Hayden thought that she was going to force his sister to swallow it. But instead she held it inches away from the girl's lips and began drumming rhythmically on it with her nails. The night seemed to have become deadly silent; all sounds of village life and nature were muffled by the dense pressure of the Ley that cloaked in around them, the only audible noise the tapping of the Ryder's fingertips on the stone.

Tension gripped painfully at the centre of Hayden's forehead, making it hard for him to focus on what was happening. He felt overwhelmed, like the force of the Ley was washing everything away and wanted to stop it not just for his sister's sake but his own. The power was so intense, however, that he could not find the strength to do anything.

Quietly, Sister Jet began to murmur a low, hypnotic chant, her voice repetitive and soft as she skilfully caressed the smooth surface of the jewel. The angelite within her palm started to glow from within, its hues of sky blue and white twisting beneath its polished surface like cloud formations. They illuminated Petronia's lips with a soft, cerulean light and as Hayden watched, his sister's lips mimicked silently the words of Sister Jet's mantra. Trepidation and hope quickened his pulse as he anticipated Petronia's voice finally being awoken from her throat.

Suddenly, a fearful cry broke the intense atmosphere of the gushing Ley and at once Hayden felt the pressure of unseen power lift and a new force, cold and frightful, replace it. The entrancement of the healing ritual was gone and they were once more at the campfire. Garnet, whose voice had shattered the atmosphere, was on her feet, her long, jagged broadsword drawn and ready to strike, the minerals of its granite blade glittering in the firelight.

'There!' she cried, gesturing to the ground near Sister Jet's feet. Hayden followed the Ryder's alarmed gaze and saw that the dry soil had cracked apart as a plume of thick, black mist issued from it. It bubbled up like a putrid spring of oil and smoke, flowing over the ground in tendrils of shadow. Garnet lunged forward, bringing her blade down to smite the noxious entity. The dark mist billowed up into the cold, night air, avoiding the Ryder's blow with a graceful twist, tugging away from the rent in the ground, its menacing presence dimming the light from the fire. Swiftly, Sister Jet motioned for Hayden and Petronia to run as she and Rosequartz reached for their weapons. 'Get back!' she commanded as Hayden scrabbled to his feet.

The blacksmith's son seized hold of his sister's wrist and attempted to drag her back inside the safety of their home, but Petronia stood firmly where she was, her bright, dark eyes transfixed on the swarming cloud that swirled across the ground towards the Ryders.

'Petronia!' he yelled as Garnet lunged at the inky shadow once again, her blade tearing strands of wispy darkness from its indistinct edge. But Petronia remained exactly where she was, staring with fearless awe in to the colourless heart of the floating mass.

Skilfully, Garnet and Jet circled the hateful cloud, their weapons ready to strike. A low, gravelly hiss burbled from the core of the vapour as it thrashed out wraithlike tendrils towards them. As her sisters battled to guide the mysterious entity towards her, Rosequartz reached into a pouch on her belt and pulled out a chunk of copper which she ran along the edge of her broadsword. As the fiery metal of strength and energy came into contact with the razor sharp rim of stone, bright sparks of orange flame illuminated the night, drawing a golden curve along the perimeter of the blade.

'Sisters!' she cried to Garnet and Jet as the mist swarmed towards her, seemingly drawn magnetically to the power realised from the metal. 'Summon the Ley!'

Hayden saw the Ryders' muscles grow tense with effort as they wordlessly drew into themselves the flow of the Ley from deep within the earth. It rose up around them, like an invisible tide of crackling power, ancient and full of life, ever-changing with the life-forces of the Ryders. He heard Petronia's breathing become rapid and turned to see his sister reaching forwards toward the field of powerful energy. Her face was fearless, more alive than he had ever seen it, her glossy, black pupils filled with realisation.

Before he could stop her, Petronia had broken away from him and flung herself towards the collection of crystals still spread out on Sister Jet's discarded cloak. Her long, dexterous fingers danced over their colours and textures, sensing the energy locked within each one in a flicker of an eye. The stones hopped and trembled beneath her fingertips as she passed over each of them until at last she seized hold of an oval piece of clear quartz. The glass-like rock seemed to jump willingly into her hands of its own accord, ready to obey her command. Hayden cried out to her, fearful for her safety but the girl took no heed.

She rubbed the crystal's smooth, flawless surface intently and sparks of rainbow light flickered within its clear heart. Then, flinging her hands forward, she thrust the pure stone right into the heart of the ominous black cloud. Hayden bellowed in horror and rushed forward as the wraith of darkness swamped his sibling's form, the granite blades of the three Ryders slicing into it. The shadow let out an enraged hiss and curled in on itself like a wounded serpent. The swords gleamed within its twisting coils as they forced the sable vapour down into the heart of the stone clasped within Petronia's hands. With one final writhe of anger, the last tendril of smoke was dragged into the prison of the clear quartz.

Chapter 4

THE CALLING

Hayden fearfully hurried over to his sister who was crouched in shock on the ground, the quartz still gripped tightly in her hand. The pure crystal was now smoky black, the churning power of the mysterious entity trapped within its transparent walls, twisting like a snake within an egg. Worriedly, Hayden inspected his sister's face, but apart from the obvious shock of what had just happened, she seemed totally unharmed.

'Petronia!' he cried, wrapping a protective arm around her shoulder. 'Are you all right? Did it injure you?'

Petronia breathed deeply as she tried to regain her senses. Cautiously, she put down the crystal and looked at her brother. Much to Hayden's surprise, she looked elated.

'*No,*' she reassured him via her hands, '*I'm fine, dear Brother. I know now; at last I understand.*'

A joyful smile spread across her face and she had a look in her eyes as if she had suddenly discovered the meaning to her life, but disappointment filled Hayden as he realised the healing had had no effect.

The Ryders seemed unsettled by the strange occurrence for they had gathered together, speaking animatedly and glancing over at Petronia and the blackened crystal.

'It is as the message from Ammonite informed us,' Garnet said anxiously to her sisters. 'This is the second known appearance of this entity and it does not bode well. This must be why the Ley drew us here.'

Jet frowned, a dark look of misgiving masking her attractive features. 'You have no proof that this spirit of darkness is related in any way to the mystery our sister encountered in Veridium's jail,' she stated, gesturing towards the crystal that lay shadowy and blackened on the ground. 'There are many entities in this land, unexplained spirits, which are beyond even our knowledge.'

Inhaling deeply, Garnet ran her fingers over the fragments of crystal that covered her tunic. She turned her amber-coloured eyes to the stars and Hayden guessed that she was silently calling to the Ley for guidance. She stepped closer to Jet and Rosequartz and the three of them spoke spiritedly for several minutes in hushed whispers that he could not hear. Jet and Garnet were clearly disagreeing about something whilst Rosequartz battled to be peacemaker.

Finally, the group broke apart and Garnet proclaimed, 'We would be foolish to ignore what is right before our eyes; we must return to the citadel at sunrise.'

Jet's face grew pale and serious as it seemed she had lost the argument. Moodily, she marched over to the campfire and began to pack away the gems she had used in Petronia's healing.

As she turned towards her Sister Ryder, Rosequartz's freckled face filled with concern.

'What of the girl?' she enquired earnestly, gesturing to Petronia, who was still kneeling beside her brother.

Garnet looked troubled; clearly the disagreement with Jet had unsettled her. She regarded Hayden and Petronia with her intelligent, golden eyes and Hayden fearfully wondered if his sibling had committed some awful sin.

'It is a sign, Sister Garnet,' continued Rosequartz excitedly. 'A Calling. Don't tell me you've forgotten the indications from when the Ley first claimed you to serve It? It has brought us here so we might guide this child to her destiny.'

'Sister Garnet, Sister Rosequartz,' Hayden interjected politely, as he helped his sibling to her feet. 'I beg your forgiveness if Petronia has caused some offence to your order by her actions. I am sure she meant no harm.'

He looked at his sister who was staring intently at the darkened stone lying on the ground. Deep in thought, Garnet strolled over and picked up the crystal, running her thumb over its smooth surface as she examined it. Rosequartz crossed over to the anxious pair and placed a comforting hand on Petronia's shoulder.

'Have no concern,' she told them with a warm smile. 'Mistress Petronia has done nothing wrong. She has simply displayed that the Ley has spoken to her soul, commanding her to serve It as we do.'

Glancing up, Jet threw her fellow Ryder a disparaging look. 'There you go again,' she grumbled, 'always jumping to conclusions! You'll be choosing a Stone Name for her next!'

Garnet nodded in reluctant agreement with Jet's sentiments. 'The girl's actions prove nothing conclusive, you know that, Sister,' she informed Rosequartz. 'One lucky gesture does not declare her to have the spirit of a Ryder. Only years of study and training can determine whether the Ley wants her.' Turning to Petronia, she scrutinised her with gleaming amber eyes. 'Tell me, child, why did you seize that particular crystal and thrust it into the spirit?'

Petronia looked nervous under Garnet's questioning. Her mouth opened slightly as if she was going to make some verbal reply but no sound left her lips. She clasped her fingers tightly together for a moment or two before slowly beginning to move them, forming her answer carefully in the cold autumn air for Hayden to translate.

'She says she didn't think about it, it just felt like the right thing to do. She heard a voice from within the stones, compelling her actions.'

As he spoke on her behalf, Hayden could barely believe his sister's words. Petronia spoke of a magic and power far beyond his simple understanding of the world, yet had no trepidation towards it. There seemed to be a momentum, like a rushing river, within Petronia's soul as forceful and changing as the power that moved the Ryders and it scared him to see something so alien residing in someone he knew so well.

Garnet nodded knowingly, seeming to have come to a decision. 'I'm not knowledgeable in the summoning of apprentices to the Ley; teaching was never one of my blessings. Amethyst will be able to see the value of her heart. We must take her to Goodstone when we ride there tomorrow.'

Hayden's jaw dropped in horror at the prospect that the Ley Ryders might take his sister away from the safety of the village to follow their mystical and dangerous Calling. Protectively, he put his arm around Petronia's shoulder. 'You can't!' he cried. 'She has never ventured further than the woods and her lack of speech makes her vulnerable. My father would never allow it! Father, Mother, come quickly!'

Desperate for his parents' assurance that they would not allow Petronia to go with the Ley Ryders, Hayden called out to his parents to explain what the strangers were suggesting. The blacksmith and his wife rushed from the cottage, concerned by Hayden's anxious tone. They listened intently to their son's fearful words, and worried for her daughter's safety, Beatrice drew Petronia into her arms.

Sombrely, Godfrey shook his head when Hayden mentioned Rosequartz's suggestion that his child could possibly be intended to be a Ley Ryder. 'If I might say, good mistresses, I see such a notion as inconceivable. We are simple country folk with no knowledge of the ways of magic. That my daughter picked the correct gem was, no doubt, purely chance.'

Eyes growing wide with disbelief, Petronia stamped her foot, infuriated by her father's suggestion.

Garnet nodded understandingly as Hayden and his mother tried to placate the enraged Petronia. 'It may very well be but the Ley has mysterious ways of showing Itself. It doesn't often reveal one who is destined to serve and when it happens, it is foolhardy to ignore the signs.'

Godfrey looked across to his daughter, sitting silent and indignant beside the camp fire. The flames reflected fiercely in her black irises, echoing the strength of her spirit. 'But what could the mighty Ley see in a poor smith's mute daughter?' he asked helplessly. 'Surely there are nobler maids more worthy of joining your order?'

Clearing her throat, Rosequartz tactfully spoke up. 'The Ley pays little heed to rank and breeding,' she told him gently. 'Ryders can be born to Lord and peasant alike. It is the ability of our spirits and hearts which matters, not our parentage. I myself was born a simple baker's daughter.' She looked at Petronia and her warm, carefree spirit seemed to ease the girl's mood. 'It is a hard life but a rewarding one and she will receive many benefits. Apprentice Ryders are given a good education; she will learn to read and write, how to ride and care for a horse and live off the land, astronomy and fencing.'

'Fencing,' repeated Godfrey suspiciously. 'Why would she need to know how to use a sword? Weapons are carried by folk who need to protect themselves and I shall not place my daughter in the hands of those who would put her in danger.'

Taking a deep breath, Garnet chose her words carefully before addressing the blacksmith's worries. 'It is true,' she stated tactfully, 'that the life of a Ryder is at times perilous, but for the most part it is a peaceful and satisfying vocation.'

From her seat beside the camp fire, Jet regarded Petronia with inscrutable, dark eyes.

'Push the good fellow no longer, Sister Garnet,' she sighed coldly. 'It is his right to deem his daughter's future, not ours, not the Ley's.'

Rosequartz cast her fellow Ryder a puzzled glance but said nothing as Jet continued in her eloquent, refined tone. 'The writings of old clearly state that we are not to use the Ley to enforce our will over others, merely follow It and bring Its aid to those who allow us to. If Master Godfrey won't allow his daughter to come with us, so be it.'

'I think that would be for the best,' Godfrey uttered softly, placing his hand on his eldest child's shoulder. But Petronia let out an exasperated cry and turned to face her family, her black eyes burning with frustration and longing. Wistfully, she looked towards the three Ryders, mystical and resplendent in their gem-encrusted armour and all the desire of her heart was poured into her pleading expression. The answer to her unspoken dreams lay within the unknown depths of the mysterious Ley. Opening her mouth, she let out an angry sob before marching off towards the forest.

Worriedly, Beatrice called after her daughter, 'Petronia, we are only thinking of your safety!' But the girl did not even look back.

Anxiously, Hayden pushed past the others and hurried after his sister. He caught up with her a short distance from the stream where she had stopped to gaze broodingly at the reflection of the moon, flowing as a constant silver disc floating on the bubbling water. Catching hold of her arm, he pulled her to face him and was shocked to see the expression of rage and determination on her tear-streaked face.

'Petronia, listen to me,' he said, battling to keep his voice firm. 'What Father says is in your best interests. He wants to keep you safe; understand that.'

Gritting her teeth, the girl fiercely shook her head, gazing down at the riverbank as if searching for her lost voice amid the dark soil. With hands trembling with emotion, she formed her resolute answer. *'I can't stay here now and nothing will make me, not you, not Father or Mother. Please believe me when I say I am not being wilful. When I touched the crystal, it spoke to me, in a voice as clear and wordless as my own. It called me to the Ley and for the first time in my life I felt whole.'*

Hayden balled his fists in frustration and confusion. He wanted to seize his sister's wrists and stop her troubling words. 'You could try,' he bit angrily at his sibling's defiance. 'Show some self-control and not be swayed by your base emotions; be content with what we have!'

Tears brimmed in Petronia's large, dark eyes and at once Hayden regretted the harshness of his tone. Blinking away the dampness in her eyes, Petronia signed once more. *'I don't think I could fight this, dear Brother, even if I wanted to. It would be like altering the colour of my soul. The Ley has Called me and I have no choice but to answer. If you were to lock me away, break my legs and keep me in chains it would make no difference. I would find a way of answering It.'*

The expression on her lovely face was calm and resolute and Hayden saw a light in her eyes that he knew would be extinguished forever if she was not allowed to go with the Ley Ryders. It would kill Petronia's spirit to remain in Ravensbrook, the sad mute daughter of a simple blacksmith; slowly but surely she would die.

'You are a mere country lass, cursed by a silent tongue,' he uttered kindly, taking her hand. 'Even if you were to go with them, how could you make yourself understood?'

Petronia looked at him pleadingly and gently touched the palm of his outstretched hand. '*Then come with me, Hayden, and transform my simple sign language into spoken words, as you have done since we were children. You promised me that you would always take care of me, be my translator and protector until I married. If I am to be bride to the Ley, give me over to Its protection as you would to a good husband.*'

Doubt filled Hayden's heart as he looked towards the inky shadows of the forest. He had no desire to exist anywhere else than the safe hamlet of his birth, but equally he could not bear to see his sister perish from a shattered heart, never knowing fulfilment.

Gently, Petronia touched his cheek. '*Father trusts you with all his heart. If you were at my side as escort, he would allow me to go. Perhaps I am not destined to be a Ryder but not knowing would bring me misery for the rest of my days.*'

Hayden remained silent for a long while as he seriously pondered for the first time in his life about the world beyond Ravensbrook. Was it truly chance that the Ryders had come to the village that day or were there greater powers at work? He remembered what Garnet had said about her mentor, Amethyst. Surely a woman of such wisdom would at once see that his sister was not fit for the Calling of a Ley Ryder and send them on their way? Petronia's curiosity would have been sated and they could return home.

'It has never been my desire to travel, but for your own safety and sanity I will ride with you to Goodstone,' he told her earnestly.

A joyful squeal escaped Petronia's lips and she excitedly embraced her brother before twirling around in the moonlight, her arms spread wide in thanks. Hayden watched her worriedly as she stooped down to caress the stones on the riverbank.

'There are conditions, however,' he told her seriously. 'We shall not go without Father and Mother's blessing and we are to return here as swiftly as possible, no arguments.'

Eagerly, Petronia nodded her head before planting a grateful kiss on her brother's cheek. She hurried back towards where the Ley Ryders were still in deep discussion with her parents. Hayden followed her, his worry slightly lessened by the notion that no sane person would see his sister as a potential warrior.

They reached the fireside just in time to hear Garnet explain how many families had entrusted their daughters to the Ley to see them grow into satisfied and happy women. Godfrey still looked very doubtful and kept shaking his head wearily. 'We are simple folk,' he reiterated, placing an arm around Petronia's shoulder. 'I need to be sure my child would be well protected.'

Cautiously, Hayden spoke up. 'If it would ease your heart, Father, I could go along with Petronia and the Ryders, to ensure her safety.'

Godfrey still looked doubtful as Garnet glanced at her fellow Ryders apprehensively, 'It is not commonplace to allow menfolk to ride with us,' she uttered thoughtfully, 'but to leave your daughter behind when she has displayed such affinity for the Ley would be seen as an abandonment of our principles.'

The blacksmith looked from his son to the eager anticipation shining in his daughter's eyes. He wondered if his simple Petronia could be truly destined for greater things, but his parental instincts made him reluctant to let his children leave.

'Hayden accompanying her would make me more inclined to place his sister in your care,' he relented grudgingly, 'but I would still like some greater promise of her safe return.'

Rosequartz and Garnet exchanged a knowing look, heavy with the understanding of their Calling. 'A Blood Promise would ensure her return,' said Garnet. 'I am willing to make such a gesture; what say you, Sisters?'

Rosequartz shrugged. 'If it would prove to Master Godfrey that we would watch over his children, I am willing to bind my allegiance to this place.'

Seated beside the fire, Jet grunted disparagingly. 'Exclude me from any such promise,' she remarked. 'The Ley has deemed me to use all my energies for healing the sick. I shall not waste any of my life-force on a pledge made on chance. The girl has shown no firm proof she hears the Ley. Her choice of crystal could have been down to mere chance.'

Rosequartz frowned at her fellow Ryder's sceptical words. 'Your spirit is old before its time. You place no faith in looking to the future.'

Simmering rage gleamed in Jet's dark eyes. She glared hatefully at Rosequartz but said nothing and instead caressed one of the many crystals she wore around her neck.

Turning to Godfrey and his family, Rosequartz beamed a reassuring smile. 'We Ryders are nomadic by nature, but it is possible for us to bind ourselves to places and people, to pledge that we will return to protect them if needed. This is what is meant by a Blood Promise.'

Godfrey regarded the hope in his daughter's eyes and the fear in his wife's. 'And that would guarantee that Petronia and Hayden would return home unharmed?' he asked seriously.

Hayden thought he saw doubt momentarily gleam in Garnet's golden eyes but when the woman spoke her voice was firm and resolute. 'It would mean we would be bound to protect them with our lives.'

'It would mean instant death if they didn't,' Jet remarked darkly. 'In my opinion it is a foolish promise to make. There are unknown dangers afoot in the world, some of which even we are helpless against.'

Godfrey remained thoughtfully silent for a moment. Turning towards Beatrice, he asked, 'What is your feeling on the matter, wife?'

Beatrice looked from one of her children to the other, maternal compassion glowing in her eyes. 'It is the nature of a mother's heart to want the best for her children,' she said gently. 'It takes wisdom for a parent to know when the day has come to let go. Perhaps Petronia's future would be blessed by going. Hayden is a loving brother and a faithful son; he will protect her.'

Godfrey nodded, unable to deny the truth in his wife's words though he knew that worry would weigh upon them both.

'Your actions have proven to me that you are gallant women and can be trusted,' he answered. 'I will entrust my children to your care.'

Petronia let out a shriek of joy and gratefully threw her arms around her father's neck but Hayden felt a sinking feeling in the pit of his stomach. He was wary of the shadowy, unknown dangers that lay beyond the familiarity of the village and had no ambition to venture out into the wider world. His thoughts drifted back to the swirling mass of malicious darkness that had issued from the ground only moments before, altering their simple existence with its mysterious force. A tide of peril seemed to have swept into their lives, pulling him and his sister along unknown paths. He would ride with the mysterious servants of the Ley to Goodstone, for Petronia's sake, but it was a task that he accepted with a heavy heart.

Chapter 5

An Unwelcoming Audience

Ammonite stood with bated anticipation in the grand entrance hall of the Royal Palace, the crystal containing the strange, dark entity that had flown out of Happenny's body wrapped safely within three layers of cloth in one of her purses. She felt sick and unnerved having such an entity of unknown evil so close to her. But she realised that it was vital the court be made aware of its presence. She had presented herself at the palace gate as soon as it was light, but had been told that the Royal Household was still asleep. It would be several hours before the prince was able to meet with her, that was if he was well enough to hold an audience with anyone. It was not uncommon for visitors wishing to speak to Prince Aarold to be turned away or have to make do with lower courtiers. The prince's ill health and delicate physical state was well known and from an early age he had been wrapped in a cosseted cocoon of physicians, nursemaids and nannies orchestrated by the formidable influence of the Duchess Maudabelle, a cousin of the late queen.

The White Duchess, as she was commonly called because of her flawless white skin and her aloof disposition, was, like the late queen, born in the country of Etheria, north of Geoll, and for many centuries the two lands had been at war. Geoll had been victorious and the new-found peace, sealed with the marriage of King Elkric of Geoll to the Etherian Princess Neopi, had brought an amnesty to the warring nations. Neopi sadly died shortly after giving birth to Aarold, leaving the sickly child in the fanatical care of the White Duchess who had guarded the ailing infant with a svengali-like hold. Even now at the age of fifteen, she still deemed him too immature and unwell to take the throne.

As Ammonite waited to be addressed, she took in the lavish decoration and furnishings of the hall. The palace built by Elkric's ancestors utilised the greatest artisans of their time and was a structure of unmatched beauty. The vast ceiling of the entrance hall was of pale, grey stone and carved with skilful images to mimic the flora and fauna of the country. Coils of dog-toothed foliage twisted around bulbous flower heads, and rounded stone fruits and great birds of prey and majestic wild cats perched with elegant poise on the carved branches, their talons and eyes picked out in gold leaf. The lush cornucopia of the synthetic jungle was matched and echoed in reality by the collection of hunting trophies and weapons that decorated the walls, prizes of battle won by Elkric and the many kings who had gone before. Hides of bear, deer and wild cat littered the walls, flanked by skilfully forged swords, shields, axes and maces. The whole purpose of the hall was obvious. It had been built to display the great wealth and skill in warfare of the kings of Geoll. No wonder certain factions of the country felt a sickly prince unfit to inherit the crown.

The large gilded doors of the entrance hall swung open and a steward dressed in black velvet laced with silver thread stepped forward and bowed reverently. 'Her Grace The Duchess Maudabelle of Etheria,' he announced before stepping aside to let the duchess enter.

Ammonite had never met the White Duchess in person before but rumours of her beauty and coldness seemed to be well founded. Although well into her fourth decade, the duchess was a slim and strikingly handsome woman whose fine good looks would put many younger maids to shame. Her alabaster flesh was flawless and clear of blemishes, seeming almost luminescent in contrast to the thick, raven black curls piled high on her head. She had the classic bone structure and build of the Etherians: high cheek bones, sharp chin and long narrow nose. Her eyes were deep set, intelligent and a vivid shade of green and put Ammonite in mind of shards of emerald. Tall, but willowy in contrast to Ammonite's honed muscular physique, her narrow waist, slim arms and long neck shown off to full effect by her elegant tightly corseted gown of flowing dark blue silk, she looked as beautiful as she did imposing. Standing before the Ryder, she regarded her with an arrogant impatience.

Duchess Maudabelle extended a pale, long-fingered hand towards Ammonite in a gesture of polite but removed welcome. 'Greetings to you, Ryder. I trust you have been made welcome.' Her voice was clear and silken but still maintained the rounded vowels and clipped consonants of her homeland accent.

Gallantly, Ammonite bowed. 'Your Grace, I bring news of the utmost importance concerning His Highness Prince Aarold. Would it be possible to speak with him?'

A cold expression passed over the duchess's beautiful face but she skilfully masked it with a gracious smile. 'As I'm sure you are aware, the prince has a very delicate disposition and therefore we try not to burden him with too many troubling issues. It inflames his humours and makes him more prone to illness. I help him manage his affairs. Tell me your news and I will inform him.'

Unease knotted in Ammonite's stomach. The late king had placed his son's protection in the hands of the White Duchess, but the amount of control she had over the prince's life was disconcerting. No wonder there was mistrust in his abilities.

Maudabelle gestured to the steward to step forward. 'Have some mint tea brought up to the sun lounge for our guest,' she instructed. The steward bowed and departed through a smaller servants' door while the duchess motioned for Ammonite to follow her.

The Ryder found herself walking down a long passageway carpeted with rugs of rich scarlet wool. The high, white marble walls displayed broad canvases of the past kings of Geoll, broad-shouldered, powerful figures dressed in gleaming armour or rich purple robes; they gazed down upon the pair of women with brazen royal wisdom. At the far end of the hall hung the portrait of King Elkric and his young family, painted a few short weeks before the queen passed away. Elkric looked every inch the fairytale hero, his silver armour and flowing, golden curls gleaming in the sunlight. He surveyed the viewer with penetrating sapphire eyes, the very embodiment of goodness and kingly might. At his side, looking as lovely and delicate as a rare flower, was his young Queen Neopi. The artist had been careful to capture the Etherian princess's pallid beauty but the paint also hinted at fragility in her fine features, foreshadowing that she was not long for this world. She clutched her infant son lovingly on her lap and her dark eyes seemed to hold a secret, unspoken sorrow.

The duchess paused thoughtfully before the painting for a moment. 'Dear cousin Neopi,' she uttered softly. 'The Geollease climate didn't suit her. Fortunately, my own constitution has been able to adapt, but sadly the prince takes after his mother. The sun lounge is through here,' she added abruptly.

With an elegant sweep of her silken skirts, the duchess led Ammonite through another doorway into the sun lounge. Although considerably smaller than the vast entrance hall, this room was no less finely adorned. Its walls were decorated with abstract frescoes of leafy foliage in deep forest greens and it was furnished with stylish daybeds and chairs fashioned from light Tiki wood, their shapely arms and backs carved to resemble trees. One wall of the room was taken up by a full-length window looking out on to a neat courtyard garden. It had clearly been designed to let in the fullest amount of sunlight, so Ammonite found it strange that the glass was tinted black, which made the room shadowy and chilled.

Maudabelle noticed the Ryder looking at the darkened windows. 'I had them installed,' she explained with a slight flourish of her hand, 'for the prince's sake. Etheria's climate is much more overcast than Geoll's and exposure to too much harsh sunlight can irritate his skin and eyes. Shall we take tea?'

She lightly deposited herself on the pale, cambric cushions of one of the chairs and gestured for Ammonite to sit opposite. Ammonite took a chair and regarded the duchess's striking features shaded by the filtered sunlight coming through the tinted glass. Despite her many years of residence in the palace, the White Duchess was still an outsider from

Etheria. Ammonite could not help but wonder just how much power she held within the court.

Maudabelle took a small, steaming metal kettle from a stand on the table and poured the clear, green tea into two delicate pottery drinking bowls. 'Now,' she said, her voice as light and familiar as if Ammonite was an old friend. 'What was it you wished to tell me?'

The Ryder took a sip of the beverage. The refreshing taste of the brewed herbs coated her tongue, but as with everything she ate and drank Ammonite could also detect the constant tang of the Ley energy that had enabled the plant to grow. 'I came here on a most serious matter, ma'am, regarding the attempt on the young prince's life during his birthday celebrations.'

Spots of light pink colour came to the duchess's cheeks and the muscles of her elegant throat tightened. 'A most troubling matter indeed,' she murmured softly. 'The whole court was deeply concerned, myself especially. Prince Aarold is heir apparent of course but he is also my ward; he was placed under my protection by his father, King Elkric. I can only thank the stars that the Royal Guard intercepted the would-be assassin in time.'

Ammonite nodded soberly. 'The man named Happenny, the one who was sentenced to death. The Ley compelled me to visit him last night, before his fate was carried out.'

'Then you will have seen for yourself that the fellow is clearly insane,' interrupted the duchess, a slight laugh catching in her voice. 'A sick and deluded brain addled by violent fantasies on the prince's life. The sooner he is dead the better.'

The Ryder shifted uncomfortably in her plush seat as she felt the dark force trapped within the crystal in her purse wash over her like a wave of nausea. 'The man *is* dead. He died before my eyes. His body seemed to be possessed by some sort of evil entity. I have it imprisoned in this.'

With the utmost care, Ammonite drew the thickly wrapped cloth bundle from its leather pouch and laid it on the table. As the duchess looked on, she carefully peeled back the layers of rags to reveal the tarnished lump of quartz with its unnatural shadowy heart. The vaporous knot of darkness twisted and battled within its glassy bounds, issuing a low, barely audible hiss like a soul in torment.

Repulsed, Maudabelle raised her hand to her throat and swallowed hard. 'What is it?' she uttered in fear and disgust.

Ammonite studied the gloomy coils within the gem. 'It flowed from Happenny's body moments before he perished. As to what manner of magic it is, that I cannot say, not yet.' She gathered up the rags around the crystal once more, hiding its ghastliness from view.

The duchess's emerald eyes gleamed with deep intelligence and she inhaled deeply to cool her temper. 'As one schooled in the ways of magic,' she stated at last, 'I would say it was some form of malicious djinn or pukka. There are many learned scholars in the palace. Allow me to show it to them for further clarification.'

Ammonite felt the Calling of the Ley peak within her mind, clearly instructing her that it was her duty to solve the mystery of the dark spectre. Swiftly she re-wrapped the tainted jewel in its protective rags and tucked it carefully away in her purse.

'I would not see fit to impose such a heinous task on any of the Royal Household, ma'am,' she informed the duchess politely. 'The Ley has summoned me to complete this quest and I must obey. Besides, wouldn't you agree that it is better for this violent entity to be kept as far away from the young prince as possible? My only motive in bringing it here was to make His Majesty aware of the danger.'

The White Duchess's delicate features set in an expression of controlled irritation and her burgundy lips strained into a polite smile. 'I can assure you, Ley Ryder Ammonite, the young prince is in no danger within the palace walls. His every safety and comfort is overseen by myself personally. There is nothing to fear.'

'Fear from what, Aunt Belle?' Both women ceased their debate and turned towards the door at the far end of the room where Prince Aarold had entered unannounced. Recalling the painting of the late king she had seen earlier, Ammonite found it hard to believe this slight, pale-skinned youth could have come from such hardy stock. The prince had none of Elkric's masculine good looks; in fact he was rather dowdy. He was incredibly slim with a large, pasty face and weak jaw. His top teeth protruded slightly above his lower lip and beneath the delicate, golden coronet that rested on his brow, his fine locks were a shade of mousy blonde. The face was unremarkable apart from the eyes that in contrast to the rest of his appearance were bright and determined, deep navy blue like two spots of glossy ink resting on a sheet of colourless parchment. He was richly dressed in a doublet of deep forest green, decorated around the wrists and neck with gold thread and hoses of pale jade silk. Ammonite noticed that the right stocking hung loosely around the prince's calf as that leg was clearly wasted, bowing outward when he walked. He carried a finely turned cane of dark wood inlaid with a spiral of ivory which he leaned heavily on when he moved.

Ammonite and Maudabelle got to their feet as the prince entered, and bowed reverently. 'Your Majesty,' breathed the White Duchess, spreading her skirts wide in a flourishing curtsey. 'How pleasant to see you up and around. I thought you were too weak to leave your chambers.'

Aarold lowered himself carefully on to a chair. 'I get so bored resting all the time, Aunt Belle; sometimes I wonder if the physicians even know what's good for me. And besides, I wanted to continue my lessons with Master Grahmbere.' For someone of such a frail appearance, the prince had a remarkably strong voice, a clear and confident timbre that spoke of a youth who had shared his life with books and companions beyond his years.

The duchess smiled a placating smile. 'Now, Your Majesty,' she told him in a slightly saccharin tone, 'you know the doctors only have your best interests at heart, and you do get so tired when you exert yourself.'

The prince arched his fine eyebrows. 'Well, today I don't feel tired at all so I saw no point in wasting the day in bed. I was going to my lessons when I heard voices and wondered if we had visitors.' Before Maudabelle could reply, the prince had turned his attention towards Ammonite.

63

'Good morrow to you, mistress, Prince Aarold of Geoll, at your service,' he said with a polite bow of his head. 'My apologies for my late introduction. I trust my aunt has given you the best hospitality.'

Ammonite smiled. Despite his clear ill health, the young prince seemed to be determined to carry out his royal duties as fully as possible. 'It is an honour to make your acquaintance, Your Majesty. I am Ammonite, a Ley Ryder and your humble servant.'

The prince's deep indigo eyes grew bright with wonder on hearing this and his face became animated with childlike excitement and awe. 'A Ley Ryder,' he gushed, his eager gaze devouring Ammonite's heavy sword and jewel-encrusted armour. 'What an honour. How absolutely splendid! Aunt Belle, you're so naughty for not fetching me straight away!'

The duchess's pale cheeks flushed slightly as her elegant fingers gripped the arm of her chair. 'My Lord, as always, my only concern was for...' she uttered through gritted teeth.

'For my health, yes, Aunt Belle, I know.' Prince Aarold rummaged in the leather purse on his belt and pulled out a scrap of parchment and a small chunk of charcoal.

'But the opportunity to speak with an actual Ley Ryder, why it will further my knowledge no end. I try to be a student of all manner of folk in my kingdom you see, so that I might better govern them one day. Now tell me, good Mistress Ammonite, what *exactly* is the Ley? Animal? Vegetable? Mineral? I am learned in basic geology and alchemy, of course, but the books in the royal library only hint at the nature of the entity you serve. I'm keen to understand more.'

The change in the prince's face as he quizzed Ammonite was astounding. Blood flushed his pallid features and any sign of his delicate nature was overridden by youthful exuberance. The duchess watched him, her brilliant emerald eyes bright with concern. 'My Lord, I really must advise you not to agitate yourself so,' she stated in her rich Etherian accent, resting her hand lightly on his arm. 'It'll bring on one of your migraines.'

Prince Aarold stopped short as the duchess spoke, the colour draining from his cheeks. 'Yes, of course,' he murmured, resting a hand to his temple. 'Do forgive me, Mistress Ammonite, I was getting carried away.'

The Ryder nodded understandingly, sensing the shadow of sudden malaise that swum from the prince's form into the Ley. 'Perhaps I could speak to you about my Calling at another time, Your Majesty. But there was one issue I do think I should raise with you before I depart. It is regarding the man who attempted to attack you.'

The duchess's eyes, as sharp as an eagle's, swivelled back to Ammonite. 'I think it is best that we end this meeting,' she remarked crisply, 'before the prince becomes more perturbed.'

But Aarold shook his head and swallowed deeply. 'No,' he remarked, his voice as determined as ever as he mopped his damp brow with a silk handkerchief. 'I have been thinking a lot about the attack while I was convalescing and I think I know what might have motivated it.'

Ammonite listened carefully as Prince Aarold continued. 'Aunt Belle has always instilled in me the importance of maintaining the standards in our army, especially since my father died. She is fearful for the safety of both myself and our country, from outside invasion. But troops and weapons do not come cheap and taxes were raised to deal with the costs. It will do little good, however, if my people are resentful because they cannot feed their children.'

A tinkling laugh caught in the White Duchess's throat. 'Really, Prince Aarold!' she smiled nervously. 'Your young mind is so full of naïve imaginations! The populous is happy and contented and more than willing to pay for the protection of their beloved future king.'

The prince studied his guardian with intelligent blue eyes. 'Really?' he queried coolly. 'I doubt that description suits well the man who attacked me. If members of my kingdom wish me dead, is it not in my best interests to understand why? Have you discovered some new information?'

A flood of Ley energy barraged Ammonite's thoughts. She felt it was vital that she tell the prince of the spirit within the crystal, but the overbearing presence of the White Duchess made her uneasy. 'I have no firm facts, My Lord, only that the Ley has compelled me to investigate the history of your attacker more fully. I will inform you of all I find.'

The White Duchess's posture seemed to relax, but Aarold appeared deeply disappointed. 'I'm never told anything,' he muttered softly, losing for a moment his regal façade.

Unsteadily, he heaved himself to his feet, using the arm of the chair and his cane to assure his balance. 'I must leave you now, Mistress Ammonite,' he informed the Ley Ryder as she and the duchess respectfully stood. 'It is time for my history lesson and I do not like to keep Master Grahmbere waiting. It was a great pleasure to speak with you and I trust you will relay to me any further information you discover about this man Happenny. I bid you good day.'

With a respectful nod to his aunt, Prince Aarold walked unsteadily from the room. Ammonite watched the prince leave, feeling once more the complex pull of the Ley wash through her mind. It approved of the young prince, despite his clear limitations, and rushed strongly into his active mind.

'The prince shows great intellect for one so young,' she commented as the White Duchess took her seat once more. Maudabelle followed her gaze, her deep scarlet lips pursed thoughtfully. 'It takes more than an educated mind to rule a kingdom,' she uttered austerely. 'The court and royal physicians agree with me, his ill health wouldn't stand up to the rigours of kingship. It is best to wait until he is stronger before he takes the throne.'

Ammonite did not reply but felt the shadowy pulse of the concealed crystal run into the Ley as it urged her to continue her quest. She could swear the duchess sensed it too for the very next moment she said, 'I plead with you once more to place the burden of that malicious entity into my hands so it can be safely disposed of.'

Feeling the Ley pull at her thoughts, Ammonite solemnly shook her head. 'Thank you for your concern, Your Grace, but I am being told that this is a path I must follow alone. I came here only to share what little knowledge I have. I trust you will use it wisely.'

The White Duchess's emerald eyes sparkled brightly in the dim shadows of the shady sun room. 'I can assure you I will, Mistress Ammonite. Farewell and good luck on your quest.'

The Ryder bowed respectfully once more before departing. The force of the Ley added speed to her steps, turning her thoughts back towards Happenny and the darkness that seized his soul. She decided it was time she discovered more about the would-be assassin.

Alone in the silent shade of the plush lounge, Duchess Maudabelle's cunning mind whirled with many thoughts. The intrusion of the Ley Ryder was an unhelpful setback and had come dangerously close to putting her plans in jeopardy. But Maudabelle was not going to let over fifteen years' worth of work be ruined by some nomadic witch who could not mind her own business. Things would just have to be altered slightly, put on hold until the crystal was retrieved and she was sure that the Ley Ryder would learn no more.

Chapter 6

THE MAKINGS OF A SOVEREIGN

Leaving his aunt and the Ley Ryder in the sun room, Prince Aarold stepped out into the long, marble passageway hung with portraits of his ancestors, pausing for a moment as the wasted muscles of his malformed limb twitched in a gnawing spasm. He rested his arm against a pillar as the familiar pain eased itself, leaving him feeling the more annoying sensations of anger and frustration. Aarold loathed his body for its betrayal to the noble strength of his late father. He hated even more the excuse it gave his aunt, nurses and physicians for keeping him locked away in the safe world of his private quarters, denying him his rightful legacy of King of Geoll. The potions and daily medical massages prescribed to him helped fuel the seeds of doubt planted by his own mind that he was not worthy of taking the throne.

Aarold knew he was a lot of things he should not be, weak, unattractive, unskilled in the arts of combat, but one thing he was not was ignorant. He realised that the country needed a strong leader to depend on and despite his many shortcomings he was determined to live up to this role. He realised that what he lacked in physical strength he would have to make up for in intellect and therefore disciplined himself to hours of study, both with his royal tutor Master Grahmbere and in solitary research, poring over books in the palace library. Left alone within the catacombs of shelf upon shelf of heavy volumes, he could escape from his gilded cage, filling his active mind with knowledge of topics as diverse as geography, history, astronomy, art and magic. He was a keen and able student and hoped the day would soon arrive when the court would see that a studious king could be as good for the country as a great warrior.

Leaning carefully on his cane, Aarold cautiously put weight on his lame foot to check whether the spasm had indeed passed. As he did so, his eyes drifted up to the heroic portrait of his father hanging above the doorway and ruefully he recalled his parent. The king's death had not affected Aarold a great deal emotionally. How could you grieve for a parent you barely knew, a parent who only tolerated your company at state occasions and regarded you with incredulous disappointment that you were the product of such strong genes?

'I know, Father,' he remarked dryly to the handsome figure in the frame, 'your son and heir is a vast disappointment. But you followed your path and I'll follow mine.'

Confident that his leg was strong enough to continue the trek, Prince Aarold shuffled out of the corridor and through room after richly decorated room, following the familiar route to his tutor's chambers. The thick woollen rugs, finely carved statues and antique trophies of battle were the landscape to his entire life but as always the prince felt at odds with their opulence, as if he was an impostor in his own life. Aunt Belle and the doctors told him that this feeling of ill-ease was a symptom of his condition. But Aarold thought it had more to do with him feeling unworthy of his royal inheritance.

Finally he came to the narrow wooden door to the spiral staircase that led up to the tower where Master Grahmbere resided. The prince's doctors had requested that the scholar move to more accessible apartments to save Aarold the arduous climb but he had stubbornly refused, saying that moderate physical exertion increased blood to the brain and the prince would learn better if he preceded his lessons with a small amount of exercise. Secretly, Aarold was glad of this small rebellion by his tutor. Master Grahmbere was the only person in the palace who treated him like a person and not a china doll.

The climb was a challenge nevertheless and one made even more difficult by the fact that Aarold was late. He tried his best to make up time by taking the steps two at a time, but he quickly stopped this when a dull ache in his thigh threatened the arrival of another spasm. He paused to steady himself about a third of the way up and continued on at a more sensible pace, leading his stride with his healthy leg before bringing up his lame one to meet it. This was a great deal easier for him but he still felt quite out of breath by the time he reached the chamber.

The small circular room was, as usual, littered with an untidy array of books, scrolls and other paraphernalia belonging to the royal scholar-in-residence. Like his regal pupil, Master Grahmbere had an eclectic passion for knowledge and this was reflected by the collection of items that decorated his abode. Maps and charts of Geoll and beyond plastered the curved walls and there was a telescope and a large brass globe of the heavens near the window. At the far end of the room, next to the master's battered leather armchair, was a vast, glass-fronted cabinet containing various items that had sparked his interest including several large seashells, a fragment of bull's horn, the delicate bones of a small bird and an ancient piece of hide marked with some symbols of a long died out language. Near to the cabinet, propped up on a stand, was the scholar's beloved lute on which he would often pick out a melody as he considered a tricky idea or question. Aarold loved his tutor's room as there was always some new acquisition or wonder to uncover and explore.

Grahmbere himself stood beside the small eyelet window, studying the latest addition to his collection. He was a tall, spindly limbed figure with a slightly stooped back brought about from years spent hunched over books. His face had a slightly ratty appearance. Pinch-lipped and shrewd, though the grey eyes that rested either side of his sharp nose were kind and full of life. His pale skin was like in colour and texture that of old parchment and his long, thinning hair and drooping moustache were a light copper, white hairs mingling with the fiery red ones of his youth. The loose cap and houppelande he wore were of fine blue silk, but creased and stained with ink and various unknown blotches. He had in his hand a pair of pincers with which he clasped a dead beetle.

70

'Come on, my lovelies,' he chirped as he lowered the insect into the large glass tank before him. Aarold took a step forward to get a better look at what his tutor was doing. There was a high-pitched croak and a scaly, scarlet head with bright yellow eyes slithered over the rim. The lizard blinked twice before opening its jaws and emitting a small but fierce flame that lashed out and singed the cuff of the scholar's robe. Master Grahmbere let out a cry of shock, dropping the tongs and beating himself furiously to put out the blaze. Papers and quills scattered everywhere as he flapped his arms, finally managing to seize hold of a bottle of red ink and sloshing it over the burning material. The flame died with a splutter as the bright scarlet liquid soaked it, adding to the many stains that spotted the scholar's garment.

Master Grahmbere let out a relieved sigh before glancing at the label on the bottle. 'Dash it all and that cost me three gold sovereigns too!' he exclaimed, ringing out his cuff as the strange reptile sank back on to the dark sand at the bottom of the tank.

Prince Aarold carefully hoisted himself on to the tall stool at the desk in the centre of the room. 'Problems, Master Grahmbere?' he queried as his tutor checked his arm for burns.

The scholar glanced round and seeing Aarold for the first time, beamed an affectionate smile. 'Not at all, Your Majesty!' he grinned good-heartedly, searching along the many shelves that lined the room. 'Not. At. All. A mere mishap in animal husbandry, as you can see, no harm done, ah.' He found what he was looking for, a pair of thick, leather gauntlets, and pulled them on.

Aarold watched with a mixture of trepidation and excitement as his tutor crept back towards the tank. Master Grahmbere had always been bold in his exploration of the wonders of the world. Aarold could recall the time he had, totally accidentally, filled the tower with thick, pale green foam that smelt of roast pork when one of his alchemy experiments had gone awry. Not that the prince minded his tutor's foibles. Master Grahmbere brought some much-needed colour into the prince's dull, protected life.

With the utmost care, the scholar reached his gloved hands into the glass tank. There was a slight scuffling accompanied by a shower of sparks and black sand, but at last he managed to triumphantly scoop the creature up, holding it firming in his fingers for Aarold to see. The prince gazed in wonder at the reptile's slim, metallic body and tiny, golden claws, watching in fascination as tiny wisps of black smoke curled from its nostrils.

'Crimson Mountain Salamanders,' stated the scholar proudly, as the creature stared at Aarold with its corn-coloured eyes. 'These are only infants but amazing animals just the same.'

Aarold smiled as the tiny lizard opened its gullet and let out an agitated whine. Despite its fiery temperament, it was really quite adorable and fascinating; this made him ponder what other natural wonders lay beyond the protective walls of the palace.

'I bought two of them from a trader in the market,' explained Grahmbere as the salamander craned its serpentine neck. 'They have a gland in the roof of their mouth that secretes a highly flammable but very useful liquid. I hope to be able to extract some of it for my experiments before they grow too large and I have to release them.'

The salamander twisted its tail agitatedly as if it understood what the old man had said and did not approve of it in the slightest.

Carefully Grahmbere placed the creature back in its tank and shut the lid before it could cause any more damage. 'You're late for lessons again,' he observed dryly, as Aarold watched the scarlet lizard bury itself beneath the sand. 'No doubt that's due to that infernal gaggle of quacks and nursemaids your esteemed aunt insists on employing to hamper your educational development!'

The prince stifled a chuckle and tried to appear disapproving of the scholar's impertinence towards the Duchess Maudabelle. Grahmbere had made his views on the delicate treatment of the prince's condition very clear on a number of occasions and done so with such a passionate contempt that he was no longer welcome in the company of the White Duchess. His blatant disregard of the notion that Aarold needed to be handled with kid gloves was a refreshing contrast to what the prince normally heard.

'Master Grahmbere!' he cried in mock displeasure. 'How dare you speak of my aunt in such an inappropriate manner! Such talk could be seen as treason and lead to your neck meeting with the axe!' He chuckled as the scholar pursed his narrow lips at such a ridiculous notion.

'I'd like to see them try!' he declared, gesturing at Aarold with his quill. 'Treason, as you should know from our lessons in law, is a crime committed against the ruling monarch, which is you, and I will support and advise you till my dying breath. It's other members of the court I have issue with, members who are hampering you doing your royal duty!'

A tweak of doubt knotted in Aarold's stomach and he once more felt very aware of his physical limitations and how they impacted on his royal destiny. He wondered whether he should do more to claim the responsibility of kingship, but was fearful of what would happen if another bout of ill health rendered him incapable of rule.

'I am doing what I can,' he informed Grahmbere. 'That's why I was late for lessons. A Ley Ryder arrived at the palace and wished to speak with me about the assassin who made the attempt on my life. I want to learn from my people, what I can do to be a good ruler, but how can I devote myself to them when I am not even allowed out of the palace?'

The tutor regarded Aarold's mournful face as he gazed out of the small eyelet window that overlooked the city and land he was destined to rule. He remembered the late king, his quick temper and forthright character and marvelled at how different his son was to him and yet how the two shared the same determined spirit. 'You are a good student of men, Your Majesty. That will set you in good stead as this country's leader.'

Worriedly, Aarold shook his head. 'Will it, Master Grahmbere?' he said wearily. 'Will I truly be wise enough and strong enough to take the throne?' He was silent for a moment, lost in self pity, when an idea crept to the forefront of his mind.

'These Ley Ryders,' he queried, 'they travel among the people; maybe I could use their knowledge to guide me. Tell me are there any records of their deeds in the royal library?'

Grahmbere scratched his fine, orange beard and looked doubtful. 'I'm sorry to say that there isn't. The order is a very mystical one and those called to it share little of what they know with outsiders. Their duty lies outside your royal decree and they answer to nothing but the Ley Itself.'

Aarold nodded in understanding and tried to hide his disappointment. There had to be some way of escaping the sheltered world of the palace and prove to the court and his subjects that he was a worthy sovereign. He recalled what Grahmbere had told him of his family history, of how countless princes before him had proved their worth on the battlefield or in tournaments. Such options were not open to a cripple such as himself. He possessed a quick mind and a considerable skill for magic but those talents seemed to count little in the eyes of his aunt and the court.

'I am not very much like my father,' he pondered out loud. 'He was a great warrior who the people could trust to protect them in times of crisis.'

The scholar peered at the young prince knowingly through his eyeglasses. 'That is true,' he uttered seriously, moving to take down a thick tome from one of the shelves. 'It's also true that your father was quick-tempered, bombastic, with a habit of using his sword before his head. They too are traits that you thankfully lack. There is more than one way to be a good ruler, Your Majesty. The tongue of a diplomat can be at times more powerful than the blade of a soldier. Come now, we shall begin our lesson.'

He passed the dense book to Aarold and motioned for him to open it. As tutor and student studied the complex and noble lives of Aarold's ancestors, the prince found it hard to lose himself in his lesson as he normally did. His mind was distracted by other thoughts, tied to the notion of the man who tried to kill him and the mysterious Ley Ryder whom he had met earlier that day. If the Ryders were concerned about the assassin, he should be as well. He felt drawn to find out more about what was going on and the seed of a plan began to germinate in his active mind. It filled him with trepidation but for the first time in his life, Aarold decided to take control of his own destiny.

Chapter 7

THE PATH YET WALKED

Through the dark, still night, Hayden lay awake beside his sister and parents, his heart filled with trepidation and fear of the journey that lay ahead of him and Petronia. The Ley Ryders had brought an alien, unforeseen force into their simple, rural existence, full of danger and magic. It seemed to have ensnared Petronia's spirit, promising to fulfil a hunger within her that Hayden did not understand. *This is our home,* he thought, staring up at the thatched roof of their hut. *It is a good, safe place to live. What power could compel anyone to abandon this place in search of anything more?*

He looked over to where his sister lay on her simple straw mattress, the dim light of the moon shining like polished silver on her long ebony hair, and felt a stab of resentment pierce his heart. He cherished his sibling more than his life, but he could not help feeling bitter and wary regarding her actions. He loved her but disliked the oddness that drove her mind and spirit, robbing her of her voice and setting them both on a quest towards an uncertain goal. He swore that he would not leave her side while she journeyed with the Ryders, but secretly prayed that the endeavour to unite Petronia with her Calling would be fruitless.

Dawn leaked cold and pale into the sky as the birds that nested in the forest heralded its arrival with their usual melodies. Hayden wondered whether the birds in Goodstone sang as sweetly and whether the sky was the same shade of blue. He watched as Petronia and his parents arose and noticed how eagerly his sister dressed. *What are you hurrying for, Petronia?* he silently asked as he pulled on his jerkin. *What power do you feel that is driving you from our home?* He thought of how the Ryders spoke of the Ley moving them, a force that they could not resist. How could a power be so strong and yet remain undetectable to most folk?

They ate a good breakfast prepared by their mother, heartier than they would normally consume, to see them well for the journey ahead. Porridge made with goat's milk, home-made bread and a few green apples, the first fruits of the season. Afterwards, Beatrice braided her daughter's silken black tresses, a task that Petronia had done for herself since she was ten, and pinned them securely to her scalp to keep them tidy during the ride. Hayden saw sorrow in his mother's eyes as she fixed Petronia's hair. It was breaking her heart to send her children away with strangers, but she did so in the hope that Petronia would return with a clear voice and a more peaceful heart. Hayden wondered how an entity that was said to be wholly good could cause so much heartache.

As Hayden packed up his meagre belongings, Godfrey called to his son to walk with him to the forge. The morning cast its soft, golden light over the village as they left their hut, its brightness and warmth filtered by the mists of nightfall that still lingered. Hayden regarded the familiar scene surrounding him with troubled, keen eyes, trying to burn into his memory all that he had taken for granted: their hut and the forge, the similar, simple dwellings of their neighbours, the gently sloping green of the hill to the east and the ridge of trees beyond marking where the forest began. He saw the three figures slowly leading their mounts down the grassy bank, the early morning light glinting on their jewel-covered armour like multicoloured dew, and felt a stab of regret. Why had the Ley Ryders intruded on their happy existence?

'Come here, boy.' His father's voice called him out of his mournful thoughts.

Dutifully, Hayden followed him inside the workshop. Looking around, he took in the furnace, anvil and tools that were so familiar to him. This was where he belonged, toiling at the simple craft of ironwork, not riding off with mystical warriors. Godfrey stooped down to reach below his work bench and retrieved a long, thin item wrapped in cloth.

'Here,' he said as he removed the cover and handed his son the item. It was a sword, finely made, some of his father's best work: the blade narrow, light and strong, the hilt formed from a single length of curved metal that twisted serpentine over the hand to form an easy and protective grip. Hayden stared down at the weapon and marvelled at the artistry that had gone into making it. He and his father were born to craft such items not wield them.

'A wealthy merchant commissioned it from me a few years back,' Godfrey explained as Hayden cautiously drew the blade from its sheath.

'Unfortunately he met his death from a stomach complaint before he could claim it. I have met no-one else willing to pay the gold for the labour I put into it. Perhaps fate decided that I was to keep it, pass it to you so that you might use it to protect yourself and Petronia during your journey.'

Hayden slipped the polished metal back into its leather encasement and gripped the weighty weapon in his hands. It felt alien and awkward in his grasp and once more he became aware of the uncertainty of the path ahead. 'Father,' he enthused anxiously, 'do not tell me that you believe it is right to send your children on such a journey. You know that I am a craftsman, not a warrior and Petronia has no skill in her worthy of a Ley Ryder.'

Godfrey looked at his son and Hayden saw questioning fear in his dark eyes. He gazed at him as if he was a stranger, as unknown and mystical as the strange travellers who had disrupted their peaceful lives. Stoically, the blacksmith rested his hand on Hayden's shoulder. 'There are greater powers in this world than those that move our simple lives,' he said. 'If I have learnt anything in my time on this earth it is that change comes to all of us and sometimes if we learn to accept our heartaches it can bring us greater fortune. I trust you to take care of your sister, whatever challenges you may face.'

His gaze travelled from Hayden to the small crowd that had gathered outside their hut. The Ryders were ready to escort them to Goodstone, the hues of their crystal-encrusted armour gleaming dully in the morning light. Petronia and Beatrice had come out of the cottage to join them and Hayden could see his sister looking longingly at the polished stones that adorned their mounts' tack and saddles, as if each one held a fragment of her dreams.

He fastened the sword to his belt. 'I will bring her home again, Father,' he reassured, 'I promise.'

Together father and son left the forge and walked out into the cold autumn morning to join the others. Garnet and Rosequartz had dismounted but Sister Jet remained in the saddle of her ebony steed, her pale hands gripping tightly on the reins. She turned her dark eyes towards the colourless sky, the wind tugging at her silken hair like the unseen power, pulling at her spirit. 'We best make haste,' she told her fellow Ryders coolly as her horse Slatefoot pulled impatiently at the ground. 'We have a long ride ahead of us.'

Garnet held up her hand to indicate that Jet should be patient. Approaching Petronia, she regarded the girl with her wise, golden eyes.

'Are you ready, child?' she asked earnestly.

Hayden thought his sister looked slightly doubtful for a moment, but Petronia smiled broadly and nodded enthusiastically. She embraced both her parents and gestured that they should not worry as she was sure everything would be fine. Hayden wondered where his sister's certainty came from.

Godfrey watched as his daughter hurried across to Rosequartz, the knapsack containing her food and meagre belongings slung over one shoulder. 'Remember your oath,' he reminded the Ryder, 'to bring my children back safely?'

Garnet glanced across at Petronia who was running her fingertips across the bright stones on Flintshank's saddle in wonderment and Hayden thought he saw a look of doubt in the woman's eyes. Did she question her own ability to keep his sister safe? Hayden felt the sword at his side and knew that whatever pledge or promise the Ryders made, he would make Petronia's safety his responsibility

Garnet bowed her head respectfully. 'Of course, Master Godfrey, Rosequartz and I will perform the rite at once.' She glanced at her fellow Ryder seated astride her horse. 'Sister Jet, you remain firm in your decision not to join us in the Blood Promise?'

The dark-haired maiden rested her hand on her mount's neck to calm the disquiet beast. 'We have spoken on the matter, Sister Garnet, and my answer remains final. While I will aid Mistress Petronia all I can, the Ley does not move me to make such a commitment. I know you will respect Its choice to retain my skills for healing.' A polite smile alighted on her colourless lips as she placed her hand over her heart.

Garnet and Rosequartz echoed this gesture and in unison uttered, 'To each It speaks, may our hearts hear.'

Rosequartz stepped forward and looked at Hayden's parents reassuringly. 'Have no fear for your children's safety; both Sister Garnet and I will make the pledge.' Reaching into one of the many pouches that hung from her belt, Rosequartz took out a flat, light brown stone marked with a shadowy sign of a cross. It was not as beautiful as some of the gems that adorned the Ryders' armour and amulets, but still both Garnet and Rosequartz regarded it with reverence. Carefully, Garnet reached into her own belt and drew out a short, narrow dagger. Both Ryders closed their eyes, becoming very still and silent in the atmosphere of the newly-born day, breathing in the crisp, clear air, searching within it for the ever-present awareness of the Ley to fill them with strength. Silently, It spoke to them, hearing their intent and guiding their life-forces. Her eyes still closed, Garnet inhaled the cool morning air and spoke, her words soft and heavy with meaning. 'Ley be with us,' she uttered as Rosequartz cupped the chiastolite stone in her hands, 'in our blood and in our hearts. Hear us as we make this vow. With humble intent do we serve Your will, to bind our deeds to this individual so she might see her fate in Your rhythm.'

Rosequartz silently gestured to Petronia to draw close. The girl inhaled with nervous apprehension and cautiously stepped towards the Ley Ryders, her bright eyes fixed on the tan stone. Rosequartz gave her a reassuring smile and gently took hold of her wrist, moving her hand to cover the chiastolite crystal. A small gasp caught in Petronia's throat and her muscles grew tense as she touched the stone. Reverently, Garnet continued, her soft words echoed by Rosequartz. 'To this individual do we pledge our protection,' they said in unison. 'Know her life-force and our intent. We shall guard and guide her until she knows her Stone Name else return her safely to this place.'

For a moment all three women remained motionless, their hands resting lightly on the stone. Hayden watched his sister's eyes worriedly, searching for some indication of what she was thinking. Petronia's dark pupils shone brightly in the early morning light and she seemed to be filled with an inner strength and peace.

Rosequartz then indicated that Petronia should withdraw her hand and almost reluctantly she did. The auburn-haired Ryder nodded towards Garnet and with deliberate slowness Garnet drew the dagger from its scabbard. 'So do I bind myself to this promise,' she breathed almost nervously, pricking her index finger on the blade's sharpened tip. A dark scarlet orb of blood oozed from the cut in Garnet's skin, glossy and bulging like a rounded ruby. Carefully, she allowed a trio of droplets to fall from the wound on to the criss-crossed surface of the crystal. Wiping the dagger on the hem of her cloak, she passed it to Rosequartz, who mirrored her actions and words, allowing three spots of her own life fluid to pool with that of her sister's. The crimson liquid trickled across the curved face of the jewel, emulating the dark russet shadows in its depths and dripped sparingly on to the dusty soil at Garnet's feet. Stooping down, the Ryder dug a small hole in the ground before the blacksmith's dwelling and laid the crystal in it with the same gentleness as she would lay a body to rest.

'In Your name is this vow spoken,' she whispered, covering the blood-stained stone with soil. 'We are Your willing servants. To Your flow do we owe our existence; may You claim it from us if we break our oath.' She brushed her hand over the soil which now encased the crystal and stood up to address the smithy and his wife. 'It is done,' she told them, her voice returning to its usual clear tone. 'The vow has been made and Rosequartz and I are bound to your daughter and her birth place. The ground itself will bear witness to it.'

From her seat in the saddle, Jet turned her eyes towards the pale azure sky. 'The sun has begun its journey east,' she remarked coolly. 'We should follow it if we are to make good time.'

Hayden and Petronia embraced their parents one last time, saying farewell to the familiarity of the simple life they had grown up with, before setting out on their trek into the unknown. Rosequartz took Petronia behind her onto Graniteback, while Hayden mounted himself alongside Garnet on Flintshank and following Jet, the Ley Ryders and their passengers left the hamlet of Ravensbrook to follow the path that led into the wood.

*

Hayden remained looking behind him as Flintshank carried them away from the hamlet that was his home, his eyes focused on the tiny hut and workshop with his parents standing outside waving them farewell. The wind was at their backs as they rode and it blew in Hayden's face as he glanced over his shoulder, trying to keep sight of his mother and father for as long as possible. He felt as if he was a leaf caught in the wind, being carried helplessly away from all that was safe and familiar. He remembered his pledge to his father and steadied the trepidation in his heart. He had vowed he would stay strong for Petronia's sake and prayed they would be returning soon.

At last, the sight of Hayden's parents and homestead faded into the distant horizon, becoming no more than a memory as the autumnal foliage of the wood closed in around them, tinting the sunlight with shades of gold and scarlet. Jet led the way, picking out a stealthy and winding path through the trees on her ebony steed. She rode at a swift trot that the other horses could not match with their extra load and did not bother to look back to see if her fellow Ryders were following her. Garnet and Rosequartz seemed unworried by their companion's remoteness, being content to ride at a more sedate pace, chatting and singing songs as they went. But Hayden felt uneasy that the group was so spread out, especially when the landscape grew less familiar as they approached nearer to the forest's heart.

'Shouldn't Mistress Jet be riding closer to us?' he asked uncertainly. 'I would hate to get lost in these woods.'

Garnet tugged gently on Flintshank's reins to guide him around a large oak tree that was in their path. 'Fear not, Master Hayden,' she reassured him. 'The Ley is a master navigator. It will show us the path.'

At their side, Rosequartz drew Graniteback to a momentary halt just as a hare bolted out of the undergrowth across in front of them. 'It will do no good asking her to stay nearby,' she stated slightly disapprovingly. 'Sister Jet does not enjoy company other than her own. She prefers to follow the Ley in solitude.'

Hayden raised his eyebrows in surprise. 'If I might be so bold, Mistress Rosequartz, you do not seem sympathetic to your fellow Ryder's character,' he ventured delicately. 'I do hope there is not discord within your Sisterhood.' The notion of fractions between the Ryders filled him with mixed emotions. Part of him gained hope that it was an indication that they would be more open to debate on whether his sister was a suitable apprentice. But he was also concerned about the possibility of having to hand over Petronia's protection to a group of individuals who were not totally in agreement. They may not all have her best interests at heart.

Garnet smiled a knowing smile at Rosequartz's condemnation of Jet's solitary attitude. 'The path of the Ley runs differently for each Ryder depending on the nature and skills It sees in each of us. There are countless duties and tasks It may call on us to perform and no two Ryders are alike. Sister Rosequartz here, for example, is a great bringer of humour and comfort to those who are burdened by sorrow.'

The flame-haired Ryder sniffed sulkily and stroked the pipe she carried on her belt.

'You speak as though I am little more than a jester, Sister,' she remarked sounding slightly hurt. 'There is a great deal more to the skill of seeing the woe in men's hearts and alleviating it than jolly reels and dancing puppets.'

Garnet nodded her head in respectful agreement. 'And the Ley grants you such knowledge.' She gestured to the distant figure of Jet trotting stealthily through the trees ahead of them. 'For Sister Jet, on the other hand, the Ley has pulled her towards using Its power to draw out the sicknesses and ailments of the flesh. It is a great talent but one that causes her to see the faults and darkness in her fellow man, rather than the blessings. It tends to make her crave solitude when her skills are not needed, so she may purge herself of the blights she has witnessed.'

Hayden looked at the slim, brooding Ryder marking a path through the forest before them. She paused for a moment, astride her stallion, and looked back at her fellow travellers. With her dark-eyed beauty and detached regard, Hayden wondered how she could find the will to heal when she seemed to treat the rest of life with such coldness.

'And you, Mistress Garnet?' he enquired, as Flintshank carried them around a twist in the path, 'what Calling has the Ley placed on you?' He was keen to learn all of the duties required of a Ley Ryder so he could try and make sense of what talent the Ley could possibly see in Petronia. So far, he was still confused; his sister was not skilled as healer, councillor or clown.

He was seated behind Garnet as they rode so he did not see the troubled expression marring her handsome features. She was silent for a moment before stating with her usual confidence, 'I have done many tasks in my time, Master Hayden, some of which are not suitable topics of conversation. But, in short, one could call me a messenger of the Ley's will and champion of those unable to defend themselves.'

She then fell silent once more and it seemed to Hayden that there were certain tasks and rituals to do with her Calling that made Garnet uneasy. He looked across to his sister seated behind Rosequartz on Graniteback's broad croup. The mute girl's pretty features wore an expression of deep contemplation and her dark eyes remained transfixed by the myriad of rainbow crystals that hung glinting from Rosequartz's armour and the horse's tack. Now and again, she would shift her hands from their secure clasp around Rosequartz's waist to brush one of the gleaming stones very softly with her fingertips. Hayden saw the fascination in Petronia's eyes and wished that he could feel the power that seemed to speak to her through the crystals.

'Petronia,' he called in a slightly concerned tone, 'are you all right? Are you weary from the ride?'

Petronia dragged her gaze away from the glittering shades within the stones and gave her brother a reassuring smile. '*I am fine, Brother dear,*' she signed. '*I was just listening to what Mistress Garnet had to say about the undertakings of her order. It interests me to know what challenges my future may hold.*'

Seeing the excitement in his sister's eyes filled his heart with concern. He could not make out how a simple smith's daughter had such dangerous and ambitious plans for her future. Worry and slight resentment stabbed at his heart. 'Don't allow your dreams to run away with you,' he advised her soberly. 'The Ryders haven't consented for you to join their ranks yet. Remember, you still have a good life at home with Father and Mother.' Disappointment filled Petronia's features and without a further gesture of reply she went back to studying the jewels on Graniteback's saddle.

The company of five rode at a steady pace for the remainder of the day, twisting a knotted path through the large oaks that stretched up to the pale sky above them, turning its tepid light to dappled shadow with their tumbling foliage. The route they followed seemed to Hayden to have no direction to it, meandering in wide arches and hoops as Jet led the way across the soft forest floor, thick with lime-coloured moss and layers of fallen leaves. A number of times he felt as if they had doubled back on themselves, however Garnet kept reassuring him not to worry as the Ley would see them to their destination. At midday, they came to a part of the wood where the river cut in a still, deep expanse of water through the marshy ground. Here they stopped for a brief respite, allowing the horses to drink their fill from the slowly moving stream while Hayden and Petronia shared the provisions their mother had packed. Once both travellers and steeds had rested, the party set off again.

The autumn day wore on, the cold, dim sun beginning its slow descent into the west, drawing out the coldness and shadows of evening from every corner and tree hollow. Soon birdsong died away and other unknown sounds and movement stirred in the darkness, reminding Hayden of the macabre terrors of folk-tale. Sitting up straight, he reminded himself that he was a man and not a child, but the memory of the unnatural blackness that had oozed from the earth the night before ran through his thoughts. He was very aware that he had never been so far from home and certainly never this deep in the wood after sundown. He had always been told that when the sun set and the moon and stars were lords over the earth, that the forest became a realm of unseen spirits who did not take kindly to humans. He wondered whether Ley Ryders believed in such creatures and took precautions for their mortal souls. As the sky above the canopy of leaves turned velvety black and the moon cast its sharp, silvery gaze down upon the chilly world, Flintshank and Graniteback brought them to a small clearing where the trees withdrew their leafy protection and the ground was exposed to the watchful awareness of the countless beings that lurked in the shadows. Jet had already dismounted and was unpacking her sleeping blanket. She regarded her fellow Ryders and their anxious passengers from the centre of the gloomy glade, the bright light of the moon shining in her coal-like eyes.

'It is late,' she informed them, as she unfastened Slatefoot's saddle. 'We shall camp here for the night and then ride for Goodstone in the morning.'

The other Ryders nodded in agreement and dismounting, set about making up camp for the night. Petronia helped Rosequartz collect wood for a fire and with the aid of the same crystal Garnet had used the day before soon had a small blaze glowing in the centre of the clearing. Garnet searched through the packs strapped to Flintshank and retrieved a small slingshot. While the others cleared the campsite, she ventured back into the trees only to return some minutes later with the carcasses of three tree voles.

Sitting in the glowing orange light of the fire, the Ryder placed her hand on the creatures' russet bodies and uttered a prayer of thanksgiving for the sacrifice of their lives. Taking a small knife and skinning and gutting them, Rosequartz cooked the tiny cuts of meat on a flat stone in the embers and offered them to Petronia and Hayden, while she and her sisters ate the meagre innards of the creatures raw. This carnal display alarmed the young lad; surely only wild beasts devoured their kill bloody!

'You do not cook your meat?' he enquired, as Petronia watched with queasy unease whilst Garnet swallowed the offal in one gulp. The Ryder cleaned her bloodstained blade on the corner of her cloak and shook her head. 'We cook the flesh, but not the organs and never the heart,' she explained, gnawing on a chunk of bread that Hayden had offered her. 'To devour an animal's gizzards raw is to make sure that the Ley within them is not lost. It is a sign that we respect their sacrifice for our sustenance.'

Petronia pulled a grim expression and waved her hands in a repelled gesture. A smirk tweaked Hayden's lips; maybe his sister saw that the life of a Ryder was not so appealing. 'My sister says she doesn't think she could ever stomach such a meal,' he translated, hoping that this remark would show Petronia's unsuitability as an apprentice to the Ley.

Rosequartz nodded sympathetically. 'It does take a certain amount of training of the palatte,' she said understandingly, poking at the fire with a branch, 'and apprentices are not expected to take their offal raw straight away. But in time one finds the nutrition and taste of such a diet most pleasing and of great benefit to heightening one's awareness to the Ley. The heart and stomach of a rightfully caught rabbit, fresh on the day it was killed, served with some wild thyme and the flesh roasted on the side is a delicious meal.'

Both Hayden and Petronia smiled politely although neither could see the appeal of such a dish. The night grew colder, the biting autumn wind only kept away by the flames that danced in the campfire. The dark trees that edged the glade with their shadowy presence seemed to be filled with the movement and noise of countless beings who called the forest home. Wrapping his cloak around him, Hayden felt as if the night was creeping in to swallow them whole. His safe home seemed a thousand miles away and it was as if he was trapped within the core of another mystical world far beyond his understanding. Voices seemed to whisper in the wind and strange images kept crawling into the edge of his vision, like faceless eyes watching his every movement.

Once they had eaten, Garnet removed one of the numerous pouches that hung from her belt and loosened the drawstring. 'We'd better set up a circle of protection before we settle down for the night,' she said, taking out four large crystals, striped through with striking dashes of black and gold. 'Tiger's eye,' she explained to Petronia as she moved to place one of the four crystals at each compass point around the perimeter of the campsite, 'to act as watchmen as we sleep. There are spirits in the woods, both malicious and benign. We don't want to take risks, especially when we have people with us unfamiliar with the wildness of the world.'

Reverently, Garnet caressed each of the crystals as she set them securely in the earth. Petronia watched her nervously as she completed the ritual. Turning to her brother, she gestured, '*Surely fairies aren't real. I thought they only existed in folk-tales.*' Her face was anxious and it was clear her foolhardiness had been replaced by doubt.

'I told you they were real,' said Hayden, taking hold of her hand. 'You shouldn't be so quick to mock the old superstitions!'

He turned to the Ryders seated inside the protective ring. 'My sister has always been doubtful of the existence of nature spirits,' he explained to the Ryders.

Rosequartz and Jet looked grimly at one another. 'Oh, they are real,' enthused the red-haired Ryder, leaning her arms against her folded knees; 'seen them with my own eyes. Most are harmless, mischievous at best, but there are always dangers.'

Jet cast her gaze towards the murky shadows of the branches, her dark eyes gleaming with the orange flame of the fire. 'Strange powers ride at night,' she uttered, not looking at her companions, 'entities that the Ley has not yet given us knowledge of. It is wise to show caution.'

'*Like those that rose from the earth in the village last night?*' signed Petronia with an eager suddenness that almost made Hayden forget to speak for her. He stared at her, stunned for a few seconds before repeating her question to the Ryders. Jet regarded the mute girl intently for a few seconds, seeming to have almost forgotten the incident that had brought her to them. 'Yes,' she finally uttered, in a slow considered tone, 'you are most clever, Mistress Petronia.'

With a smooth, fluid movement she rose to her feet and drew her sword. 'I will do a patrol around the immediate area of the circle, just to be doubly sure.' With that she strode out of the ring of firelight and into the darker shade of the forest.

Hayden watched her silhouette dissolve into the gloomy shadows of the trees, his heart knotted with apprehension. 'She does not trust the safeguard of Mistress Garnet's ward?' he enquired anxiously.

Rosequartz eased off her boots and stretched herself out on the mossy green earth. 'She would not trust her own reflection if she saw it in a mirror. As I told you earlier, Master Hayden, Sister Jet is prone to see the darkness in the world. No harm will befall us while the tiger's eye looks on. Now settle yourself to sleep, both of you, we have a long ride to Goodstone tomorrow.'

Hayden and Petronia both reclined in the crackling glow of the fire, struggling to find comfort on the hard earth. It seemed to Hayden only a matter of moments before sleep claimed both Garnet and Rosequartz and he soon heard his sibling's breathing grow deeper as well, but slumber was not so swift to claim the smith's son. His mind was fearfully alert with thoughts about what unknown challenges lay ahead for Petronia in Goodstone and homesick longings for their simple cottage back in Ravensbrook. He watched his sister's still form curled in slumber a few feet away and thought how delicate and vulnerable she looked in the dying glow of the embers. The forest at night seemed to be alive with unexplained shrieks, sighs and calls, the world of night full of danger that they knew so little of. What good could come of travelling so far from all that was safe and known?

As these worries taunted Hayden's thoughts, he became aware of a lithe, stealthy shape step lightly from the primal darkness of the forest. His breath catching in his chest, his hand fearfully flew to the hilt of the sword his father had given him that morning. Like an ebony warrior goddess from some forgotten sect, Jet stepped into the orange light of the campfire, her striking features an inscrutable mask. Hayden relaxed a little when he saw her.

'Mistress Jet,' he whispered in relief, 'you startled me. I hope you found nothing of great danger on your patrol.'

The Ryder's coal-eyed gaze drifted over the slumbering bodies of the rest of the party, finally coming to rest on Petronia's sleeping form. 'There is much to trouble the mind within these woods,' she murmured, sheathing the narrow, stone blade of her weapon. 'But fear not, Master Hayden, those dark powers will not act tonight.'

With that she headed over towards the space her fellow Ryders had left for her at the fireside and laid down to rest, leaving Hayden once more alone in the disquiet night with his thoughts of unknown terrors.

Chapter 8

THE MARBLE SPECULUM

As dusk fell over the royal palace, the White Duchess Maudabelle stalked through its corridors and chambers in an agitated mood. For many years now, she had exacted almost total command within these walls, controlling the destiny of the court through subtle plans and delicate manipulation. Now, just as all her endeavours looked to be coming to fruition, Fate had dealt her the troubling card of the Ley Ryder Ammonite.

Maudabelle's mission had always been clear to her, right from the moment her uncle, King Hepton of Etheria, had given her it fifteen year before. Geoll may have overcome its armies and Elkric had claimed the Princess Neopi as his bride, but the Etherians were a proud people and Hepton wasn't prepared to give up defeat that easily. Neopi had been a fragile and innocent maid, easily won over by Elkric's charm and handsome features. She loved him despite the crimes the arrogant monarch had committed against her people. Hepton had been aware of his daughter's failings long before the wedding and so had charged Maudabelle, her stronger-minded cousin, with the task of being his eyes and ears within the Geollease court and keeping any offspring of the union firmly under control.

In the opulent banqueting hall of the palace, the White Duchess sat at one end of the long, dark wood table, delicately picking at her roast pheasant, her mind racing with what to do. Across from her, her royal nephew supped on the thin broth that the cook had prepared on her orders, his nose buried in a book. It had been so much easier, she brooded bitterly, when he was younger. A child, especially a sickly one, was easy to manipulate and keep under control. It had been relatively simple to keep the young prince away from affairs of state, surrounding him with medics and nurses. His weak body had been an easy tool to exploit but his mind was a different matter. As he reached adolescence, Aarold's independent spirit had grown stronger and now with his arrogant father dead, killed during some foolish hunting accident, the young heir was determined to take the throne. He was pulling away from her control and Maudabelle knew she had to resort to more desperate measures.

Like all Etherians of noble birth, she was well trained in the magical arts but the powers that she had been forced to utilise of late were unfamiliar and dark. Maudabelle feared that if she did not master them soon, they would reveal her true intent. She needed help from agents outside the court and fortunately knew exactly how to access them. After supper, the White Duchess bid her nephew a curt goodnight and retired to the east wing to consider things further. These were the apartments she had once shared with her cousin during their first weeks at the foreign court. In contrast to the rich, colourful sumptuousness of the rest of the palace, the duchess's chambers were decorated in the stark, gothic décor favoured in her homeland. No paintings or tapestries ornamented the granite walls and the few windows that peered out on the world were draped in plush curtains of black velvet that blocked out all daylight. With candlestick in hand, the White Duchess made her way through the morbid corridors of her quarters, heading purposefully towards the private parlour that only she was permitted to enter. Not even the late king had been allowed access to this part of the palace as it was where Maudabelle practised her sacred arts undisturbed. Not that Elkric had taken much interest in such intellectual endeavours, viewing study as a waste of time. Maudabelle recalled the late king with bitter contempt. To think that the regal blood of her cousin now was tainted with the brutish influence of that barbarian in the vessel of their offspring! It disgusted her. That was why the boy had to be dealt with and soon.

She opened the small, ebony door that led into her study and slipped inside, fastening the bolt behind her. The chamber was round with the narrowest of windows, lit only by the four torches fixed on the thick granite walls, the flames of which burned with a sickly, green glow that gave light but no heat. A small, iron cauldron stood on a spindle-legged tripod in the centre of the room. No fire burned beneath the pot and yet the insipid, grey liquid that filled it issued a constant plume of icy, pale vapour that filled the chamber with a cold, clammy atmosphere. Maudabelle inhaled, deeply, the musty air. Her magic had at least permitted her to create this haven from the scorching climate of Geoll, a refuge that imitated the gloom of her homeland. It had not been enough to keep Neopi in health but then again, the princess always did have a weaker spirit than her cousin. She had truly believed that her marriage would subdue the animosity between the two kingdoms. But Maudabelle knew there were larger plans at work, and now she was not going to let a Ley Ryder put them in jeopardy.

Swiftly, the White Duchess moved across the floor to a large, dark, wooden cabinet that hung off the far wall. Heavy and ornately carved with swirling, abstract shapes, the huge piece seemed to dominate the whole room, like a darkly cloaked assassin awaiting the duchess's command. Interlocked coils and spirals twisted in shadowy designs across its doors, disguising any hinges or locks from prying eyes. Broodingly, Maudabelle touched one of the thick curves of black wood and thought of what lay behind the doors. Her allies would not be happy for her to contact them, relaying information regarding her uncle's plan was always a risk, but she was tired of being expected to handle things alone. With alabaster fingers trembling, the Etherian duchess reached into a concealed pocket in the rich navy, silken folds of her gown and drew out a narrow silver key. It glinted brightly in the heatless glow of the pale torch flame, like a colourless finger bone inlaid with complex notches and grooves.

Her vibrant emerald eyes darted across the intricate motif of the cabinet's front until she found the tiny cavity among countless others that was the lock, and slipped the key smoothly inside. With a twist of her wrist, the concealed bolts and catches hidden within the cupboard's knotted design began to turn and loosen. Wheels and cogs of interlocked wood rubbed effortlessly against each other, shifting large sections of ebony. For a few seconds the whole cabinet appeared to come alive as its doors folded outwards to reveal the treasure held secretly in its heart.

The vast, polished stone sat motionless and imposing within its wooden frame, an immense dark tear-drop suspended in the damp, cool air of the duchess's hidden chamber. A thousand shades of blackness were captured within its still presence, more hues of darkness than could be thought possible trapped beneath the slick, glassy surface. There were nameless colours in the shadows, more subtle than pure black: the colour of midnight, of a thunderstorm, of the pelt of a vicious wildcat, the colour only seen by a blindman's eye, all shades of pitch frozen beneath its glossy façade.

Maudabelle saw her own strikingly beautiful features reflected within the sheen of the dark crystal, distorted in colour by the greenish light from the torches, and felt as if she was truly seeing herself for the first time. She always felt this way when gazing into the marble mined from her homeland, as if the true Etherian darkness in her soul was echoed within its depths, a homesick longing to strip away the genteel façade of servant to the Geollease crown and let the truth of her hatred for this land be known. She despised this country, the warm climate and carefree lives of the people. The White Duchess longed for revenge for the brothers, nephews and fathers taken during Elkric's bloody campaign along with other countless brave warriors. She had put all her efforts into creating the tool of her vindication, but as the moment of justice grew nearer, feelings of self doubt filled her mind. Mistakes had been made already and she dare not take any more risks.

Reaching into the sleeve of her gown, the duchess took out a delicate handkerchief of black silk and lace which she proceeded to wipe in broad circular movements across the already highly gleaming face of the stone. As she swirled the fine fabric across the glossy marble, Maudabelle pursed her scarlet lips and emitted a low, whistled note, barely audible to human hearing. The deep timbre was like a cord, an unseen, satin ribbon flowing from her tongue to the dark heart of the stone before her, piercing through its shadowy depths to a realm far beyond the watching eyes of the palace. Somewhere, many miles away from Maudabelle's secret chamber, another soul would hear her voice, a soul who possessed a fragment of crystal cut from the same boulder as the black stone and whose plans were in tune with those of the deceitful duchess. The low note fell to silence on Maudabelle's lips but remained as a trembling, purring echo caught within the smoky core of the crystal, making it quiver with an electric pulse. Gazing deep into the shades of blackness caught within the stone, Maudabelle saw them shift, subtly at first, like churning clouds of thought and consciousness, as another mind focused its awareness on their covert dialogue. The very texture of the dark marble began to alter, losing its solidity and bulging outwards as if sculpted by a will from the beyond. As she saw this transformation take place, the White Duchess summoned her own mental powers to transmit her own awareness into the fibre of the crystal. Training her mind, she could feel the fresh, icy air of a distant forest and hear the nocturnal rustle and calls of creatures of the woodlands. The glossy form of the stone bulged towards her like thick bubbles of boiling pitch. The hues of shade stretched and folded until Maudabelle's reflection vanished and another face appeared in three-dimensional relief within the inky marble. The features were nondescript, masked by magic to protect their owner's identity: circular eyes devoid of pupil, a long, sharp blade of rock for the nose, a narrow, smooth alcove of a mouth.

The likeness glared at Maudabelle and uttered in a voice muffled by distance and magic. 'This better be important; you know how dangerous it is for us to talk.'

The duchess gritted her teeth. She was familiar with her ally's impatience and mistrust of her abilities. 'Of course it's important! Would I contact you so we could gossip like common fishwives?' Crossly, she gripped the sides of the cabinet. 'Things aren't going as we hoped. There have been setbacks.'

The thin crack of a mouth stretched into a smug grin. 'Oh, we're all aware of that, friend,' it crowed sarcastically. 'How fortunate that our beloved prince was saved from the assassin's blade. What a show! What an absolute pantomime! Been enjoying the court minstrels too much have we, dear White Duchess, thought we'd have a go at play acting?'

A frustrated growl caught in Maudabelle's throat. Her colleague loved nothing better than to mock her comfortable court life, berating how her role in the fight against Geoll was so much harder. 'I am doing the best I can,' she snapped back. 'This entity we're dealing with is an unknown force. I used all my magic to bond it to that fool Happenny and it didn't work. It can't be held by living or dead flesh, it's too much of a risk.' She swallowed hard and bitterly confessed about her audience that morning. 'A Ley Ryder by the name of Ammonite called at the palace today, wanting to speak with the prince about the attempt on his life. She had some of the essence trapped in a crystal. This is your area. We have to get rid of her, permanently, before she figures out too much.'

The mask's eyes widened with shock and rage. 'You idiot, Maudabelle!' it shrieked in a hoarse echo. 'Do you know how much danger this puts us all in? Such magic can carry traces of those who use it. If the Ryders look into the power imprisoned within the crystal they will be able to trace it back to us.'

Cold panic spread through the duchess's chest. She did not need reminding of the jeopardy Ammonite could put them in. 'I know!' she hissed to the agitated phantom. 'That's why she has to be disposed of as soon as possible. You know more about the ways of the Ryders than I. It is an area you've studied long enough. Use what you know. Come to Veridium as soon as you can, seek her out and silence her tongue with your blade.'

The marble face became still within its ebony frame, like a statue immobilised by fear. 'I can't,' it uttered swiftly. 'Not now. There are other matters I must deal with here, unforeseen difficulties that I do not trust to leave unchecked.'

Maudabelle's vivid emerald eyes narrowed as she gazed at the stone face. The crystal features did not show the subtle emotions displayed by flesh and it had been many years since she had met with her collaborator personally. She was not convinced she trusted, even knew, the person behind the sable mask anymore. Her fellow Etherian now moved in mysterious and powerful circles and Maudabelle sometimes doubted her loyalty.

'What colour is your heart?' she purred suspiciously to the shadowy features. 'Are you still faithful to my uncle and the land of our birth or have your years of wandering led you to a new commander?'

Rage seemed to swirl within the coils of blackness as the face concealed by them contorted with fury. The crystal swelled and stretched once more as the characterless head leant forward towards the White Duchess as if the owner desired to leave its present location and travel directly through the mystical portal to confront her. 'How dare you!' it breathed angrily. 'How dare you question my loyalty after all I've been through in the name of my homeland. My memory is as clear as yours, my grief as strong. I lost everything in the war yet I had to continue with this charade. You can't begin to understand the forces that compel my life day and night, demanding my compliance but offering no consolation for my suffering. I request justice but it is denied me and yet I am still expected to express compassion to those I loath. I comply, only so I can ultimately avenge the deaths of those I loved. The fact that I speak to you now through this crystal window in space should be validation enough of my trustworthiness. How many more secrets of my path would you have me reveal before your faith is bought? I am not the weak link in this plan; it is you that has failed.'

As the voice raged, its anger unsettled the shadows of magic and darkness twisting within the stone causing them to ripple and undulate like the fierce waves of a stormy sea. The dull, vibrating tone that brought life to the crystal, rose to a buzzing pitch until its sound mingled with the irate words of the voice in the beyond, making them almost inaudible. The sable rock bubbled and seethed for a few moments until the speaker controlled its rage and focused its mind once more. 'I shall speak with you no more on this matter,' came the clipped toned at last, as the tempest within the crystal subsided. 'It serves no purpose in solving the Ammonite problem.'

A thoughtful expression passed across the shadowy crystal face as it regarded Maudabelle. 'Tell me,' it said coolly, 'is that dwarf you captured some months back still toiling at the project you set for him?'

Self-consciously, the White Duchess glanced behind her. 'Yes, even more feverishly now that our initial plan has failed. I constructed a cell of enchantments for him in the old palace dungeons and make sure he keeps to the design.' A sly grin passed across her face. 'The first prototypes are looking most promising but I wouldn't want to initiate our plan without testing them first.'

The face in the dark marble was still and thoughtful for a few moments, the coldness of the stone seeming to match a lack of feeling in its spirit. 'Then maybe it's time they were put to work,' the shadowy echo breathed. 'Summon the dark power as I instructed you to and harness it to the heart of the creation along with a fragment of our troublesome friend's name-stone. If your calculations are correct, White Duchess, the mechanism should do the rest.'

Excitement drummed quickly in Maudabelle's chest at the prospect of at last seeing months of work and careful design come to fruition. 'I will see that our mountain smith completes his work as swiftly as possible,' she cackled maliciously as she sensed her associate begin to withdraw from the mystic connection of the crystal.

In the chilly gloom of the chamber the pliable texture of the black looking-glass began to alter and harden once more. The characterless face formed from shadow and stone began to sink back into the blackness with the grim words, 'Remember, Maudabelle, if you fail in your duties a second time and I'm forced to assist you personally, your uncle will not take kindly to it. He is not an understanding man.' The reverberations of the final words echoed off the curved walls of the White Duchess's sombre halls before becoming lost within the final pulsating note of the crystal's dying tone. Their dialogue concluded, Maudabelle pulled the doors of the cabinet closed, locking its dark secret away within the heart of the ebony wood. She did not need reminding how merciless her uncle, King Hepton, could be to those who crossed or disappointed him. His blood ran with brutal determination and ruthlessness, but it was the same blood that ran within her veins. She had made a foolish mistake with Happenny but it would not be one she would repeat. As soon as the dwarf completed work on her designs, the Ley Ryder Ammonite would be no more. After that nothing would stand between them and their attack on the throne of Geoll.

Chapter 9

WITHIN GOODSTONE CITADEL

Hayden did not sleep well on his bed of moss and leaves, though it was not the coldness of the forest that kept him awake. It was the gnawing sense of fear and uncertainty in his heart, coupled with the constant wish to be back in the familiarity of his home. In the darkness of the forest, beneath the watching gaze of the sallow-faced moon and fiery tiger's eye stones that Garnet had set out to guard them, he laid barely breathing, hand on his sword, listening to the rustling and wordless murmuring voices of the wood, alive with unknown creatures of tooth, claw and magic. Fireside stories were all he had ever known of the powerful mysteries of the world, and if he had been in control of his own destiny they would be all he would ever need to know of beings that moved within the shadows. But uninvited, the enchantment of the Ley and Its faithful Ryders had swept into his life, stealing his sister's dreams of something more and pulling him along.

In the dying scarlet glow of the campfire, he had watched her sleep as peacefully as she had done when they laid beside their parents, and wondered how she could slumber so serenely in such a wild place. He considered her impairment, as familiar to him as her open face and long black tresses. For the first time he wondered whether it was not some misfortune of nature, but a sign of some deeper mystery that dwelt within her. It scared him to think that Petronia might be part of a greater power that he did not understand. It did not however lessen the bounds of protection and love he felt towards her as her brother. Hayden knew that whatever his sister was or was destined to be, he would always strive to protect her from harm. As night wore on, the tiredness caused by the long ride pressed in on him and when he did slip into slumber, his simple dreams were of Ravensbrook, his home and his parents.

When he awoke in the cool early light of the following morning, Hayden's brain was at first thrown into confusion as to where he was. Such concepts as the Ley and daring to sleep in the heart of the wild wood were so alien to him he thought he must have dreamt them. But upon opening his eyes and seeing the pale, grey sky stretching endlessly above, he realised that the uncertainty of his sister's future was indeed real and home seemed a thousand miles away. Sitting up, he stretched his aching limbs, cold and stiff from slumbering on the naked earth. Looking around, he saw that although Petronia had just awoken, Garnet and her fellow Ryders had already arisen and were packing up camp ready to depart. Jet stood with the horses, fastening their tack and preparing them for the ride to Goodstone while Garnet was carefully wrapping the tiger's eye markers, that had watched over them during the night, in soft, thick linen. At the fireside, Rosequartz sat nursing the crackling embers as a small, iron pot containing a pale brown tea simmered away. She smiled when she saw that Hayden and Petronia had woken.

'Good morning, my friends,' she cheered, her thick hair still a wild tangle from her night on the forest floor. 'I trust that you both slept well.'

Petronia rubbed the sleep from her eyes and gestured the affirmative. 'My sister says she had a restful night,' translated Hayden, 'but I was less fortunate. I cannot find the forest a peaceful place to sleep.'

Rosequartz gave the brew in the kettle a little stir with a wooden spoon. 'I found some dillberry root just outside the clearing,' she said. 'It makes a most invigorating tea. It should fuel our stomachs until we reach the citadel.'

Reaching into her pack, she drew out several, small wooden bowls which she ladled the brew into, handing one each to Hayden and

Petronia. Hayden warmed his icy hands around the steaming vessel and inhaled its hot, wet vapour. He cautiously took a mouthful and found that it had a strong, bitter, earthy taste similar to wood smoke and mushrooms.

Rosequartz supped her own dose and looked over to her fellow Ryders. 'Sisters,' she called, 'some tea before we set off on our journey?'

Garnet finished packing away the crystals and wandered over to join them, taking the bowl from Rosequartz. Jet, however, stayed where she was. 'I did not sleep well,' she declared in her usual austere tone. 'I do not have the stomach for any sustenance at this hour.'

Rosequartz scowled at her as Jet turned back to securing Slatefoot's girth. 'Miserable wench,' she muttered under her breath, taking a sip of tea. Hayden thought it must be unbearable for Garnet to accompany such a bickering pair for a long journey.

Garnet turned her face towards the pale autumn sky and watched as the tiny dark silhouette of a hawk circled high above them. 'It is a fine day for travel,' she declared to Petronia. 'The flow of the Ley is strong and will carry us swiftly to Goodstone; we shall reach the citadel by early afternoon.'

She motioned for Petronia to come and sit beside her. Taking the young girl's hand she gently pressed it against the cold, hard earth. 'Can you feel it, child?' she asked as Petronia cautiously flexed her fingertips against the soil. 'The pull and tide of the force that drives us? Does it move your spirit?' Petronia frowned with uncertainty as she moved her palm across the ground but gave no indication to what she sensed.

'Leave the girl be for now, Garnet,' said Rosequartz, draining the dregs from her cup. 'You know it takes time to tune the mind to the Call of the Ley and you are not experienced in tutoring apprentices. Leave her to Amethyst's guidance; we are merely her escorts.' She shook the last drops from her bowl on to the ground then emptied the remaining contents of the kettle over the smoldering embers.

The party gathered up the rest of their belongings and took to the saddle again to complete their journey. The day was bright and cold and as they rode north-eastward through the forest Hayden began to wonder what lay in store for them when they reached Goodstone. He had heard talk of the knights who protected the prince: they were set arduous trials before being deemed worthy of their title; and he wondered whether Ley Ryders had to complete some similar test. Although he secretly hoped that Petronia would fail any quest that would see her becoming a Ryder, he did not want her to be put in danger in doing so. He dared to wonder whether, if considerable risk was involved, the Ryders would allow him to act as champion in her place. As a man, it did seem the noble thing to do but from what he had seen of the Ryders, these independent she-warriors seemed to have little regard for traditional rules of chivalry.

'Forgive my impertinence, Mistress Garnet,' he asked as they reached the outskirts of the wood, 'but what can my sister expect to find at the citadel? We've never travelled this far from home and have little knowledge of the world. Is this Amethyst, of whom you speak, a good woman?'

Garnet smiled warmly as they left the dappled canopy of the trees. 'Very much so,' she informed him, 'the wisest, bravest, kindest individual you could hope to meet. You will be in good hands, Mistress Petronia; none knows the Ley better than she.'

Rosequartz nodded in agreement with her Sister Ryder. 'It is not in our nature as servants of the Ley to have a permanent home but if we do require a refuge from the trials of life, we can always find it in Goodstone. Sister Amethyst always offers advice and hospitality to those who are in need.'

They continued their journey through rolling fields and pastures, following the dirt track that led over the gentle hills of golden wheat and emerald grass. As they mounted one large hillock, Petronia let out an excited cry and pointed as they spied for the first time the sprawling town of Goodstone ahead of them, with its oak-beamed cottages, web of winding streets and, at the heart, the tall stone citadel of the Ley Ryders. This sight seemed to fill Garnet and her sisters with excitement for they quickened their steeds' pace to a steady trot and soon the group found themselves in the midst of the hustle and bustle of the town. For someone from a tiny hamlet such as Ravensbrook, Hayden found the colour, noise and smell of the throbbing village quite overwhelming. Everywhere people were hurrying about their business or chattering to their neighbours. Housewives hoisted their washing on clothes-lines strung high across the roads like patchwork bunting. From stores and street barrows, mongers displayed their wares, offering everything from freshly baked pies and fruit to brightly dyed cloth, calling in loud, sing-song voices to attract their customers' attention. Groups of young children played on the uneven cobbled streets, skipping across cracks in the kerb stones and chasing after wooden hoops. They cried out with joy and excitement when they spotted the Ley Ryders, calling out Rosequartz's name and running after her. The kindly Ryder slowed her steed when she saw the children. She beamed warmly at their excited, upturned faces, begging her for a song or tale of her most recent journey. Rosequartz knew each of their names and greeted them in turn as they crowded round her.

'Hello Ethan, hello Gwen,' she called. 'Have I been away that long? You're all getting so tall! No time for songs today, my dears, I'm afraid. We're wanted at the citadel.'

In fact, it appeared every resident of Goodstone seemed to want to welcome the Ryders for they were constantly stopping Garnet and her sisters to exchange greetings or news. They seemed filled with pride to live in a town surrounding the Ryders' refuge. Riding behind Rosequartz, Petronia took in all the busy newness of the town with bright, shining eyes. She beamed at her brother with such joy and wonder that Hayden almost felt guilty for his reluctance to be on the journey.

They followed the main market street uphill through the centre of the town towards the sturdy citadel of pale, bluish-grey stone. A high, curved curtain wall enclosed the cylindrical keep, topped by jagged battlements that twinkled in the sun with unseen crystals. A smooth dome of mottled glass could be seen peering just above the top of the battlements, like the moon had sunken down after its nocturnal vigil to rest within the safety of the fortification. Banners of gem-coloured silk fluttered high above, their shades reflecting the specks of brightness embedded within the strong granite and a clear, deep moat encircled the whole castle. Neither Hayden nor Petronia had ever imagined a building so powerful or beautiful.

Barring entrance to the keep stood a mighty drawbridge of thick oak in the centre of which was set a large clear crystal, like an unblinking eye gazing out at the travellers. Letting out a gasp of amazement, Petronia gestured towards the stunning castle. Rosequartz grinned.

'Yes, Mistress Petronia, the citadel is a wondrous sight indeed. Come, let's make our presence known.'

She reached for a medallion of blush pink crystal that hung around her neck and held it up before her to be reflected in the icy gleam of the clear gem before them. Garnet and Jet did the same thing, displaying gems of deep ebony and bloody scarlet, the stones whose names they had taken. The cold sunlight reflected on the jewel that guarded the way forward and within its transparent core shades of black, crimson and rose shimmered momentarily. Then with a creak of monstrous, hidden gears, the heavy drawbridge was lowered across the moat revealing a wide archway through which the party entered. As they rode through the gate, Hayden tried to spot the animals or people whose strength operated the drawbridge but saw no-one. Once within the courtyard, the mechanism shifted to life again, drawing the gate securely up behind them.

Unsure what he expected to see, Hayden gazed around the vast courtyard that stood in the shadow of the keep. Several smaller buildings sheltered within the thick curtain wall: a long, thatched stable in which stood, peacefully, a number of fine horses and in the far corner a small forge. There was an area of tilled earth set aside for a vegetable garden, overflowing with healthy shrubs and vines heavy with ripe fare. Half a dozen women of various ages went about the business of tending to the plants and horses or carrying fuel to the furnace. They did not wear the same padded leather armour that Garnet and her sisters wore, instead they were attired in simple, loose habits, each one a different shade. However, their thick girdles hung with numerous pouches and pendants showed that they too were followers of the Ley. Overlooking everything, stood the round, towering keep, like a solid granite pillar scarred with narrow windows and crowned by a high dome of metal and glass.

Garnet dismounted and strode across to an oval-faced woman dressed in deep emerald who was carrying hay to the stables. 'We wish to speak with Sister Amethyst,' she told her seriously. 'It is a matter of some importance.'

Before the woman could answer, a clear, calm voice rang out from the entrance to the keep. 'I know. Welcome, Sisters, I have been expecting you.'

All eyes turned towards the open doorway as Sister Amethyst stepped out into the sunlight. Slim and of average height, the mistress of the Goodstone citadel appeared much older than the other Ryders, seventy at least, but stood straight and moved with an easiness that Hayden had never seen in an elderly person. Her gait was quick and steady and although her hands were tanned and leathery, her fingers remained straight and free from any sign of arthritis. Her face seemed timeless, ancient yet filled with life, the lines of her jaw, nose and cheeks were square and straight. Her skin was dark, a rich mahogany shade, coloured by years of travel. It was a face of someone who had spent a lifetime surrounded by nature and so had grown to resemble Mother Nature herself. A glossy mane of straight, silken hair fell about her shoulders like a helm of polished steel, glinting in the sunlight against the deep purple of her robe. Her eyes, a pale shade of bluish grey, filled with steady intellect as she gazed at each of the visitors. When they came to rest on Hayden, he felt as if she was staring right through his flesh, studying without judgement the very core of his soul.

'I sensed your approach in the Ley when I woke this morn and spied you entering town from the observatory. It is not often that guests are brought to the citadel,' she continued, as Hayden and the others dismounted.

Garnet made a polite bow before addressing her elderly comrade. 'Sister Amethyst,' she said earnestly, 'we seek your counsel. We have encountered a strange entity near the village of Ravensbrook. This young woman helped us to defeat it. She shows ability in using crystals and may be a suitable apprentice to the Ley.' She gestured towards Petronia who stood nervously beside her brother.

With smooth, deliberate steps, the elegant Ryder moved towards the young country girl. Wetting her lips, Petronia curtseyed awkwardly as Sister Amethyst drank her in with a long considered stare. The creases in her tanned skin seemed like dark lines of text that Hayden was unable to read, but that held within all the secrets to life's mysteries.

'Ravensbrook, you say,' she breathed, toying with one of the many pendants that hung like ripe fruit from the chains around her neck. 'I remember that part of the world from when the Ley called me to follow It, before It set me down in this tower of sanctuary. What is your name, child, and in what manner did you feel the pull of the great power?'

Embarrassed by her inability to reply, Petronia focused her eyes on the cobbles at her feet although her graceful hands moved in the clear pattern she had formed for her name.

'She's a mute,' stated Jet in a dull, blank tone, 'and this lad is her brother. I tried to heal her tongue on the request of their parents, but before I could do so we were attacked by a pooka who the child aided us in vanquishing. Such a lucky incident makes Garnet and Rosequartz deem her as a possible apprentice, but I think they are overreacting.'

'It was not a pooka!' interrupted Rosequartz. 'You have no right to dismiss forces that we have little knowledge of as harmless sprites, just as you have no authority to judge the girl's powers!'

Jet threw her fellow Ryder a cold glance and tightened her grip around a pale grey howlite pendant that was suspended from her belt. 'Sister Amethyst,' she continued, struggling to keep her voice calm, 'I only wish to express my concerns for the girl's suitability for training. She is only able to communicate via her brother's translations and I for one am uncomfortable with allowing an outsider into the inner workings of our order. No man has ever understood the language of the Ley.'

Amethyst listened thoughtfully to Jet's objections. 'This is true,' she uttered solemnly. 'It doesn't seem to be in their natures to understand such things; they desire to follow their own goals rather than ones given to them.'

She took a step towards Hayden and elevating her strong chin, stared deep into his eyes. As their bright, grey depth bore into him, they seemed to act as sparks of fire, smouldering the dry kindling of his soul, stirring it with an alien sensation and pulling it into her so she could turn it over and examine within her mind a part of Hayden that he himself was not aware of.

'What is your name?' she queried.

Hayden felt his face flush beneath the elderly Ryder's scrutinising gaze, somehow feeling unworthy of her judgement, his life inconsequential and small. 'Hayden of Ravensbrook,' he replied. 'And believe me when I say I mean no offence to your noble Sisterhood by my presence or that of my sister's Petronia. I simply come as guardian and translator for my sibling but if you don't wish us to stay, we will leave at once and cause no further distress.'

Out of the corner of his eye, he saw Petronia shoot him a horrified look, appalled by the idea of having come so far only to return home none the wiser. Amethyst looked from one sibling to the other, her long fingers stroking the numerous jewels suspended around her neck.

'Give me your hand, Master Hayden,' she said at last, extending her narrow leathery palm towards him. Nervously, Hayden placed his rough-skinned hand in hers and silently Amethyst examined the lines and creases of his palm and the hard calluses caused by the scarlet heat of the furnace. 'You have a trade?' she asked, not looking up from his hand.

'Yes, mistress. I am a blacksmith, as my father is. It is a good trade to feed my family, but hardly one worthy of the noble company of yourself and your sisters.'

Amethyst looked up suddenly when Hayden mentioned that he was a smith. She turned her face towards the small forge that stood in the corner of the courtyard and she looked as if she was suddenly hearing a voice speak to her from far away. 'A worker in the ores of the earth, you say? And your sister might be drawn to the Ley? This is most interesting indeed.' She released his hand and took a step backwards, glancing between Hayden and Petronia. When she spoke again, her voice sounded firmer as if she had come to a decision and would not be shifted from it.

'The Ley doesn't pull people into Its flow by chance,' she stated clearly. 'We are all moved by Its tides whether we feel it or not. I will give the girl the education she needs if she is to become a Ryder. If she takes well to it then she is wanted by the Ley, if not her destiny lies elsewhere. Her brother will remain our guest while she receives training, aiding her to communicate.'

Jet stiffened. 'But, Sister Amethyst, I really don't think,' she began, but the elder Ryder silenced her with a gesture of her hand.

'I understand and appreciate your concern for our traditions,' she told the brooding Ryder levelly, 'but as you know the Ley is ever-changing. Perhaps It has a role for Master Hayden here, as well as his sister. By any means, I am sure he is an honourable fellow and means us no harm.' Jet gritted her teeth and once more fingered the gem that helped her control her emotions. Amethyst's eyes narrowed as she watched her, sensing the moods of the dark-haired Ryder as they flowed out through the Ley colouring It. 'You seem ill at ease, Sister,' she observed, moving forward to place a concerned hand on Jet's arm. 'Is the strain of your duties telling on your spirit? You are more than welcome to recover your strength here. It might serve you well to take a hot bath in an infusion of chrysocolla and amber and meditate with me a while before going on your way.'

She looked at Jet pleadingly but her fellow Ryder seemed unmoved by her concern. 'I thank you for your compassion, Sister Amethyst, but your worry for me is unnecessary. I know myself and the Ley well enough to heal any maladies that may trouble my spirit, body or mind and right now I feel It is calling me elsewhere. Once my steed is rested and watered I will depart.' She gave Amethyst one of her cold, courteous smiles before leading Slatefoot away to the stables. As she watched her go, Hayden thought he saw a knowing sadness in the older woman's eyes.

Rosequartz shook her head disapprovingly as Jet disappeared inside the stables. 'She would do well to mark your advice, Sister Amethyst,' she remarked tartly. 'Realign her passions with the flow of the Ley, or at the least carry some stone that would make her character more pleasing to the company of others.'

Amethyst's thin mouth pulled tight as she sighed sadly to herself. 'She will follow her own path, wherever that might lead her, as must we all,' she murmured before swallowing and continuing in a more cheerful tone. 'But I am being an abysmal hostess, allowing you to stand out in the elements for so long. Welcome to Goodstone, new friends and old. You must be tired and hungry from your journey. I shall fetch someone to make up appropriate accommodation for you.' She moved over to the open door and leant inside, calling out in a warm voice, 'Bracken, come here a moment and meet our guests.'

A few seconds passed followed by the sound of shuffling footsteps, then through the doorway hurried a tall, broad-bodied figure. Despite his manners, Hayden could not help but stare for the young woman was quite unlike any girl he had ever seen. Everything about her was overly large, as if she had been formed to illustrate in better detail the components of the human body. She stood a good head taller than Hayden, over six foot at least, with a square, bulky torso and long limbs, not so much muscular but chunky, like a doll a child might make of clay. Her face was round and uncommonly pale, like a white stone worn smooth by the wash of a river or sea. A network of light grey veins masked her cheeks and heavy brow and her eyes were small and a dark shade of liquid green, quite vivid against her pallid complexion. Her hair was long and wild, tumbling over her shoulders in unruly knots and tresses as if she had just awoken and had not had time to groom it. It was of the oddest shade, a pale non-colour, neither blonde, brunette nor mousy, that seemed to reflect more the colours of the world around her than possess a proper hue of its own. She had on the same, loose-flowing robes of the other women only hers were fashioned from a patchwork of long strands of different coloured fabric. She had a peculiar air about her, an awkwardness brought about by her size and strange complexion that made her at odds with her environment. Hurriedly, she scuttled over to Amethyst, stooping slightly to disguise her unusual height.

Warmly, the elderly Ryder placed her hand on the girl's arm. 'Sisters Garnet, Rosequartz and Jet have brought visitors to our humble citadel,' she informed her.

Bracken nodded earnestly, her dark emerald eyes shyly flitting to the strangers.

'Yes, Sister Amethyst, I saw them approach through the telescope in the observatory while I was polishing.' She had a hollow, deep, sweet tone to her voice, like air being blown across the neck of a large bottle. Her head bowed slightly as she turned towards the visitors and curtseyed awkwardly. Noticing Rosequartz grinning at her, a wide smile spread across Bracken's lips and she hurried forward to greet her. She flung her arms affectionately around both her and Garnet, greeting them as if they were much beloved but rarely seen relatives.

Fondly, the red-haired Ryder released the girl from her embrace. 'Greetings to you, young Bracken. I trust you have been keeping well since we last met and working hard on your studies.'

The tall maiden nodded, a hint of rose flushing her pale cheeks. 'I try my utmost, Sister Rosequartz, though it is a struggle for me at times. Sister Amethyst is most patient with me, though I am slow of study. My fencing, however, is much improved I think. I would like to show you if you have the time to coach me during your visit.'

Rosequartz patted her pale cheek as Amethyst looked on with maternal pride. 'I will look forward to our lesson and don't think I will go easy on you; you almost bested me the last time we crossed blades.'

Amethyst called Bracken back to her side. 'This is Mistress Petronia and her brother Master Hayden,' she told her, gesturing towards the two strangers. 'Our Sisters Garnet and Rosequartz believe that Mistress Petronia has potential to become an apprentice to the Ley, like yourself.'

Excitement flashed in Bracken's bright eyes. 'Really?' she breathed, regarding Petronia joyously. 'It has been so long since I've had a fellow student to share my classes! What fun!' She grinned broadly and curtseyed once again, holding out her multicoloured skirt like a large, ungainly parody of a peacock. 'Welcome, Miss Petronia, welcome indeed. I am Bracken, apprentice to the Ley. I hope that we will become friends soon; I'm eager to learn all about you.' Warmly she clasped Petronia's delicate hands, making them seem like those of a child against her own huge, fleshy palms. Petronia gave her a nervous but friendly smile.

'Mistress Petronia has not been blessed with the gift of speech,' Amethyst informed her gently. 'So her brother will be staying with her to translate her sign language. As the only other apprentice here, I'm making you responsible for their comfort in our citadel. Is that a task you feel capable of?' Bracken glanced from Petronia to her brother, blushing slightly when she looked at the dark-haired boy. 'I will do my best, Sister Amethyst.'

The old woman smiled affectionately up at the girl, and gently untangled a strand of her knotted hair that had snagged on the stitching of her gown. 'The guest chamber in the west tower, I think, would be a comfortable room for Master Hayden and his sister can share the apprentices' quarters with yourself. I'll leave it to you to show them the way. I must speak with Sisters Garnet, Jet and Rosequartz.' Amethyst seemed to have great maternal fondness for the awkward girl and this somewhat quelled Hayden's fears for how Petronia might be treated.

Shyly the tall, pale girl beckoned to Hayden and Petronia. 'Follow me, if you please,' she said softly, stepping through the small archway that led into the keep. The siblings nervously followed, leaving Amethyst in deep discussion with the other Ryders. They soon found themselves in a large, impressive hall, the curved, bluish grey walls of which were dotted like the night sky with gems of all colours and shapes. Rich tapestries of abstract geometric designs hung against the pale granite that seemed to emulate a dull silvery light in the empty atmosphere. A large hearth dominated one wall of the chamber, the heavy mantle supported by twin stone figurines of women in flowing robes whose eyes were brightly polished emeralds and sapphires. But the feature that dominated the entire space lay in the very centre of the room's black and white mosaic floor. A great pit, perfectly round and about five feet in diameter, gaped open like a dark, silent mouth leading into the bare rock of the castle's foundation. A grill of delicately scrolling ironwork rested over the hole, safely barring it from any misplaced foot, and an elegant canopy of fine, gleaming samite cloth hung with countless tiny crystals was suspended over it. It was clear the chasm was vastly important as every feature of the hall, even the gracefully spiralling tiles of the monochrome floor, led the eye subtly towards it.

Bracken shut the heavy oak door behind them as Petronia wandered curiously around the airy space, taking in every aspect of the strange but beautiful chamber. 'You must feel quite unsettled and anxious, being among such unusual company as us,' she said in her pleasing, deep tone as Hayden eyed their new surroundings. 'But I can assure you there is no need. As peculiar as our way of life seems to newcomers, the Ryders are a kind and wise order. Your sister will find life here most satisfying.'

'If she is to stay,' Hayden added sharply, casting Bracken a keen glance. 'Your mistress has agreed nothing yet.'

A shamed expression fell over Bracken's features and her cheeks coloured a dim shade of terracotta. 'Of course, *if* she has been chosen by the Ley, you are correct in being hesitant, Master Hayden. Few have within them the gift to sense the flow through the stones. I merely mean to say for those who do possess the blessing, it is an enriching path to a greater knowledge.' Sadness slightly echoed in her tone as her deep-eyed gaze drifted over to the dark-haired girl who had strayed over to the rim of the guarded abyss and was staring down into its gloomy shadows. Worried she might stumble, Hayden hurried forward. 'Petronia,' he warned, 'be careful now; best step clear else you fall.'

On hearing her brother's call, Petronia swiftly took a cautious half step backwards from the edge of the crevasse, her dark eyes remaining transfixed on the dim shadows beneath the elegantly coiling grill.

Bracken approached, her multicoloured gown sweeping softly across the tiles. 'Oh she is quite safe, Master Hayden,' she reassured as she reached the girl's side. 'The grating is locked securely in place so no-one can trip over the edge.'

Hearing this, Petronia once more leant forward, her hands resting on her knees as she studied the black tunnel that bore straight down into the foundations of the castle. Drawing close to her side, both Bracken and Hayden followed her gaze. It was indeed impossible to fall into the gap as the skilled metalwork of the iron gate left inlets no bigger than a man's fist between coiling bars twisted together in a massive interlocking knot. Through these openings, Hayden could see the smooth walls of the pit, pale grey like polished marble, stretching down into the silent darkness. A chilling air rose in intermediate wafts from the murky shadows, not clammy and smelling of damp as might be expected of the air from an underground space but dry, cooling and pleasant like a refreshing tender hand on a fevered brow. Hayden thought that the air had another delicate aspect to it that he was not able to define, a pleasant odour or comforting sound that his senses were not acute enough to detect. The breeze sighed in rhythmic puffs up from the grill, stirring their hair and the light curtains that hung above it.

'Our Ley Mouth,' said Bracken with a mixture of awe and pride. 'It is very rare and ancient which is why the citadel was built here.' She watched intrigued as Petronia reached out her hand to gently feel the soft, warm current of air rush over her fingertips, her face joyous, filled with wonder. 'Sometimes, the Ley is kind enough to brim out of the earth, forming an ever-renewed pool, the way a spring of water does. It's a constant stream of power and replenishment that brings strength and focus to all crystals and Ryders.' Her voice drifted into silence at the end of her sentence, tinged with a wistful sadness as she stooped down to press her long, chalky white fingers through one of the holes in the grate. 'It is very sacred.'

Hayden looked at the two maidens as they remained in reverent silence at the edge of the fissure. He could feel the warm current of air as it breathed out of the inkiness in the ground in regular, gentle gasps but found nothing in its heat or caress that was more remarkable than the air of a summer's day. So much of the Ryders' understanding was lost to him.

After a few moments, Petronia turned to her brother, her lovely face jubilant. '*Isn't it wonderful?*' she signed excitedly. '*The power and the goodness? I can feel it flowing right into my fingertips, filling me up like a vase placed in a stream. I can hear it talk! It's glorious!*'

Hayden frowned sadly, worried and disturbed by not feeling the same sense of euphoria as his sibling. Crouched close to the grating,

Bracken looked up at the girl with her vivid emerald eyes. 'Can you feel the mighty pulse of the Ley?' she asked.

Enthusiastically, Petronia nodded. Bracken reluctantly withdrew her large hand from the grill, gazing at her wide, soft fingertips with a mixture of controlled disappointment and jealousy. 'This is good,' she smiled, forcing herself to sound pleased. 'Sister Amethyst will be glad.'

She straightened up to her full height and adjusted the crystal-encrusted silk of the canopy. 'Come,' she said, stepping back from the Mouth. 'Sister Amethyst will explain more about the Ley Mouth tomorrow; her wisdom on it is much greater than mine. I will show you the rest of the citadel.'

She beckoned for Hayden and Petronia to follow her through a wooden door on the far side of the hall. Petronia was reluctant to leave the Ley Mouth but did so, and she and her brother walked with Bracken as she led them through the winding corridors of the citadel. The keep was quite unlike any building Hayden had ever seen. The walls were of strong, bluish granite and curved gracefully around each corner and doorway so that no passageway or chamber had a sharp angle or straight wall. Here and there, the heavy stone blocks were inset with large crystals of all colours and textures and the floors were paved with never-ending monochrome patterns. The citadel had a strange but pleasant atmosphere being at once grand and impregnable and yet filled with beauty and a feminine homeliness. Statues and paintings of past Ryders decorated many of the passageways and the walls were lit by countless torches and fires. On their tour, Bracken showed them many rooms for numerous purposes. There was a study with tall bookcases filled with ancient scrolls, a large kitchen where some of the Ryders were preparing a thick broth of vegetables for the evening meal and a vast armoury, equipped with weapons of all kinds as well as numerous suits of the Ryders' familiar jewelled leather armour. At one point, they stopped outside a long chamber with row upon row of beds. 'An infirmary,' Bracken explained, 'where people from the town of Goodstone and beyond can come and receive healing.' Finally, she showed them the apprentices' and guest quarters where they would be staying.

Hayden had been allocated a small round room that overlooked the courtyard. It was simply furnished with a dark wooden bedstead, chair and cupboard, although even such plain items seemed lavish compared to their humble hut back in Ravensbrook and Hayden was sure that he would never feel at home in such grand surroundings. Bracken then showed Petronia and her brother where she would be sleeping, in a long, almost empty dormitory, some distance from Hayden's chamber. Eight bunks lay in two neat rows along either wall, each one sided on the left by a washstand and on the right by a writing desk and stool. The room looked practically unused apart for the far right corner which Bracken had clearly made her own, sheets of parchment resting under a half burnt candlestick on the desk and a brightly crocheted shawl hung over the foot of the bed.

The tall, pale-skinned girl hurried into the dormitory, ushering the two siblings inside.

'And this,' she said proudly, sitting down on the bunk she had clearly made her own, 'is my own little corner of the citadel; well, yours too now, Miss Petronia, while you're staying here. Do pick out whatever bed you like; they're all free at the moment. When an apprentice becomes a fully fledged Ryder and takes her Stone Name, she is given a private chamber but we apprentices share our accommodation. It has been quite some time since I've had company for my lessons. I shall enjoy the companionship.' A note of wistful longing hung in Bracken's voice as she spoke of the notion of graduating from her training as if it was a distant goal. Glancing round the room, Hayden wondered just how long ago the last apprentice had left this dorm to follow the Ley.

Gathering up her small pack of belongings, Petronia hurried over to the middle bed on the left hand side and climbed on to it to look out of the narrow window above. '*Look, Brother,*' she beckoned. '*You can see right across the rooftops of the town to the fields!*'

Hayden strolled over to look through the wooden casement that was pulled halfway across the window. The view was indeed picturesque: the golden thatched roofs of the buildings set against the pale green of the countryside beyond. On the misty horizon was the darker, strangely ominous impression of the wood where they had camped the previous night. Seeing the land laid out so clearly like this made Hayden realise how far they had come from Ravensbrook and his heart lurched once more with the strangeness of his surroundings. Unable to suppress the question, he asked Bracken, 'How long before it is known for sure whether a maid is destined for the Ley?'

Petronia arched her brows crossly and pressed her hand to her chest to signal that she knew now where her destiny was charted.

'What I mean is,' Hayden clarified under his sister's silent objection, 'how long is an apprenticeship to this Calling? If my sister does have some mystical gift, in what manner can it be measured and trained?'

Bracken seemed slightly taken aback by his question. She nervously flicked through the pages piled on her bureau as if they held the answer, before saying, 'It is a delicate matter to answer, Master Hayden, as the Ley speaks to each of Its followers in a different way. Some see their Calling, know their Stone Name, in one great divine burst of energy that fills their emotions with such passion that their path of study is easy. For others,' she gazed down at her large, grey-veined hands, 'it is harder to hear above the everyday distractions of life a subtle tug or knowledge that drives you to seek out your place in the world. But Sister Amethyst always says that however the Ley moves your spirit, It does it in the mode that is right for you personally.' She once again forced an awkward smile as if she was trying to repress some deep regret or pain. 'I have bored you too much with my idle chatter. You have had a long journey and must be hungry and tired and I must return to my duties in the kitchen.'

With that she left the siblings in the long, bare dormitory.

Petronia excitedly enthused to Hayden about the beauty and wonder of their hosts' abode. She seemed already infatuated with the citadel and its residents and eager to begin any learning that Amethyst deemed suitable. Hayden saw his sister's enthusiasm but could not bring himself to share it. As grand and welcoming as the castle was, it was not his home and the thought that he might have to stay here while Petronia received tutelage for a vocation that he did not understand filled him with dread.

He sat at the long table in the warm kitchen where they were served a hearty broth of vegetables and regarded the collected Ryders, feeling lost and out of place. The women were friendly, welcoming and clearly as devoted to one another as any blood relatives. It was clear that if Petronia was taken into their order, she would have a fulfilling life and be well cared for. But Hayden could not see why Petronia would need the kindness and protection of strangers when she had a safe and loving home back in their village. He thought of the mighty rift at the centre of the great hall and the warm tide of air that rose up through its grating. How could something as indistinct as a summer wind compel a person to leave their home and family to follow it? It seemed to him to offer no financial protection or emotional support. He felt now as if he had to stay with Petronia not just as her brother, protector and interpreter but also as a reminder that she had something more tangible in her life than dreams of some mystical power.

*

He thought his mind would be too troubled to allow him much sleep but in the dim, silence of his room, tiny glimmers of coloured crystal blinked down at him from the granite walls – deep blue, silvery and purple – seeming to pour out a soothing power into his mind, making his body feel pleasantly heavy in the soft bed and filling his thoughts with the same familiar comfort of his home.

Chapter 10

PHEBUS

With his usual, careful gait, Prince Aarold made his way through the palace gardens towards the stables. It was mid afternoon and the sun was pale enough for him to go without the gauzy veil that his aunt insisted he wear to protect his eyes from harsh daylight. He had finished lessons early and although it would be, probably, more sensible for him to have a few hours' rest before supper, his mind felt too active with questions and worries for him to settle. The visit of Sister Ammonite, the Ley Ryder, had confirmed a suspicion that had long been rattling in his mind: all was not well within his kingdom and it was up to him as ruler to seek out the cause and put it right. His abilities were limited and he had few allies who would allow him the freedom he desired. There was, however, one individual who might be able to help him in the plan that had begun to form in his mind. But they might take some gentle persuasion, which was why he was heading down to the stables in the hope that his long-time friend was in an easy-going mood.

Aarold paused for a moment to check the peace offerings he had brought with him: a book of poetic philosophy by some long-forgotten scholar and a chunk of particularly smelly cheese from the royal kitchens; before he steadily descended the narrow steps that led down into the crescent-shaped courtyard surrounded by the numerous stalls that housed the royal steeds. His father had, among his many gifts, been a skilled horseman and owned many fine stallions. Aarold knew that before his birth, King Elkric enjoyed hunting in the forests to the north and galloping through the countryside of his kingdom with his beautiful wife at his side. He seemed to have held his fine stable of horses with more affectionate pride than his own son, who due to his weakened state was unable to engage in such athletic pursuits.

Aarold hobbled across the stable yard to where an elderly groom was sweeping the straw. The man looked up from his task and bowed respectfully when he saw him approach.

'Good evening, Your Majesty,' he stated, touching the wide brim of his straw hat. 'To what do we owe this visit? Does Your Majesty wish to enjoy a ride before supper?'

Aarold's gaze drifted warily to the number of strong, large beasts resting peacefully in their stalls and tried to disguise the unease that filled his stomach. The truth was that being around his late father's mighty steeds made him feel a little nervous. They seemed to be an echo of Elkric's power and ability, living reminders to his son of his mighty leadership.

'No thank you, Dermon,' he said briskly, leaning on his cane with both hands. 'I merely wish to speak to Phebus. I haven't seen him for some time. Is he free?' The groom pulled a sour face and sucked air in through his teeth. 'Aye,' he grumbled, 'the creature be free, though what kind of company he'll be is another matter. Foul animal tried to kick me in the head this morning.'

Aarold tried to repress a chuckle as the groom glanced bitterly over towards a small wooden shed set apart from the others. 'Oh I'm sure that it was an accident,' he stated, as Dermon broodingly poked at the debris by his feet with his broom. 'Equiles are, from what I read, normally gentle and even-tempered animals and he's always been most placid with me.'

The groom cast the prince a doubtful glance and chewed the inside of his cheek. 'You have more knowledge than I on these things, Your Majesty. But, if I might be so bold, it has been my experience that animals respond to a firm hand from their master. If you would allow me to use the whip on his scaly hide once or twice, not hard mind, when he gets a bit uppity, like I do with the other animals…'

Firmly, the young prince shook his head. 'Certainly not!' he declared, arching his fine eyebrows. 'Phebus is a noble beast and I will not allow him to be mistreated in any way. If he is getting ill-mannered I will speak firmly to him on your behalf but that is all. Good day.'

Dermon sniffed doubtfully and bowed his head in respect. 'As you wish, Your Majesty,' he grumbled, going back to sweeping the yard, before adding under his breath, 'Though I still think the animal would benefit from a few sharp lashes of the switch!'

Steadily, Aarold made his way across to the private stable situated on the shady side of the square. The once glossy, royal blue paint of the door was now peeling, but still the regal insignia of Etheria, a silver eagle with the tail of a serpent, could be seen on the upper half. Equiles were not indigenous to Geoll and Phebus had come to the royal household as part of Neopi's dowry. Aarold was very fond of the creature, partly because being with him made the young prince feel somehow connected to the mother he never knew. He was one of the few individuals who treated him as an equal, despite not being human.

Knocking thrice, Aarold waited for an indication that he might enter. The grooms might treat Phebus as simply another animal but the prince knew that his friend had a tender ego. When a throaty, somewhat effeminate voice called out from within, 'Enter, if you must!' he opened the door and stepped inside.

Phebus was standing in the far right corner of his stall, studying a slightly dog-eared manuscript that rested on a dais and looking, as usual, sorry for himself. For someone unfamiliar with the animal life of Etheria, the first sight of an Equile was at best shocking and at worst horrific. A few hands smaller than a full-grown horse, Phebus gave the first impression of some hellish, demon pony. His muscular body and neck were covered with a glossy hide of ebony scales and his spindly legs looked barely strong enough to support his own weight, let alone that of a rider. Instead of hooves, his slim calves ended in large, grey talons and in place of a mane sprouted a row of tiny, rounded horns that went from the base of his neck to in-between his small, sharp ears. The long face

120

ended in not a soft-lipped mouth like a horse, but in a tapered beak that added to the creature's dour expression. He looked up wearily at Aarold through heavy lidded, deep scarlet eyes.

'Oh,' he uttered dully, as the prince entered the stable, 'it's you, dear boy. I thought it was that dreadful man, Dermon, again.'

Leaving his reading material, Phebus stepped over to his master as Aarold carefully lowered himself on to a wooden stool. The young man smiled. Despite his worries, he always found Phebus's sardonic personality amusing. 'He's been telling me that you tried to kick him,' he informed the creature who was already sniffing the air hungrily at the odour of the concealed cheese.

Phebus lifted his head suddenly at this remark. 'Did he, indeed?' he snorted with an indignant twitch of his pointed ears. 'The bounder! How dare that common-minded bumpkin make such crude insinuations on my fine character! The audacity!' He eyed the leather satchel that Aarold wore with ravenous suspicion and ran a narrow pink tongue over his bony beak.

'So, there's no truth in it?' wheedled Aarold, good-heartedly.

The scaly, black beast pawed the straw on the floor of his stable guiltily with one of his massive claws. 'If I did deal any kind of physical action on his person,' he stated, at last, blinking his huge, scarlet eyes innocently, 'it was only in frustrated protest about the indecent way I have been treated under his care. Honestly, my good fellow, he and his ignorant minions are barbaric, simply barbaric. They treat me as if I were a common *horse*. The boorish fools know nothing about my noble genus, my need for mental stimulation, my dietary requirements. They expect me to eats oats, *raw oats!*'

With a melodramatic sigh, he bowed his long, flexible neck to allow Aarold to pet his crest of pale horns. His sharp bill resting lightly on Aarold's knee Phebus longingly inhaled the rank scent wafting from inside the satchel.

'Speaking of foodstuff,' he muttered slyly, nosing against the soft leather of the bag. 'I don't suppose you would have about you any morsel of decent quality to nourish a poor starving creature, such as myself.'

121

Grinning, Aarold opened the bag and unwrapped the hunk of cheese from its cloth. Eagerly, Phebus buried his narrow, hard muzzle into the prince's cupped palms, devouring the milky snack with fevered hunger. With a groan of delight, he raised his reptilian head, licking the stray crumbs from his beak and crowed, 'Sweet ambrosia!'

'And I brought you this too,' said Aarold, taking out the leather-bound volume of prose and holding it up for him to inspect.

Phebus grunted approvingly, reaching up with his front left claw to flip open the book's cover. 'A most satisfactory work of literature, no doubt,' he breathed wandering back over to the dais that supported the open manuscript. 'At least, it will keep my mind from rotting while I am condemned to be in the company of these idiotic laypersons. As for this laughable piece of writing,' he took the slightly gnawed volume from the stand in his mouth and carried it across to spit it out critically on Aarold's lap, 'you may tell the author, your so-called tutor, that his ideas on the effect of the moon's movements on the behaviour of animals are childish and lacking in proof!'

Taking a silken handkerchief from his sleeve, the prince wiped some of Phebus's thick saliva from the book. 'I'm sure Master Grahmbere will be very interested to hear that!'

The creature hung his narrow head self-pityingly and blinked his thick eyelids. 'I'm sure he won't!' he grumbled. 'That is the whole problem with this infernal country. The human populous shows no appreciation for the intelligence of species other than their own. I miss the camaraderie of my brethren Equiles, or at least the interaction with a true Etherian human who values my sparkling wit and lively debate. Apart from yourself, dear boy, and your good aunt I am starved of companionship, not that Maudabelle pays much notice of me nowadays.' With a mournful sigh, Phebus rested his head over Aarold's shoulder, allowing the young prince to affectionately scratch his scaly, ebony cheeks. Aarold shook his head as his thoughts once more turned towards his aunt. It was not only Phebus who felt frustrated by the duchess's treatment. 'I know,' he breathed, 'but Aunt Maudabelle holds a very important position; you can't expect her to have time for idle chatter. Why, until my health improves, she has to oversee all affairs of state; it's a very tiring and responsible task.' Frustration at his own physical weakness tightened Aarold's stomach once more, driving the fragile plan he had begun to formulate regarding the Ley Ryders to the forefront of his mind.

Tenderly, Phebus clicked his beak, clipping off a stray thread from the decoration on Aarold's tunic. 'Your late mother, may her sainted bones rest peaceful, she always made time to come and speak with me,' he recalled wistfully with a little shake of his head.

Aarold smiled sadly as he witnessed the fondness in the Equile's scarlet eyes for the late queen. 'You liked my mother a lot, didn't you, Phebus?'

The lanky creature straightened his long, elegant neck and gave his back legs a little stretch. 'She was an angel, dear boy, an absolute angel! Of course, I was little more than a foal, beak still wet with my mother's milk, when I accompanied her from her gloriously dusky royal home to be wedded to that social philistine of a father of yours, no offence intended. But she was always most considerate to me. Always took an hour or two in the evening to come down to the stables for a leisurely trot and a pleasant tête-à-tête. But, alas, for all her blessings, she was a delicate bloom, too fragile to exist in this blasted sun-drenched climate.' His throaty tones drifted off to silence as he gazed through the open door of the stable at the pinkish light of the setting sun. 'There is so little stimulation for me now in the company of these lower-orders and their beasts of burden. I do so miss her delightful recollections of our motherland.'

Awkwardly, Aarold hoisted himself up from the low stool, steadying his balance on his cane. 'Phebus,' he asked the Equile delicately, as the doleful beast gazed at the sunset, 'how would you like to accompany me on a little venture, away from the palace, just me and you.'

At these words, Phebus's sharp ears stood to attention as he turned to look at his friend, an appalled expression on his narrow, bony face. 'Leave the palace without a guard?' he whinnied. 'My good fellow, have you taken leave of your sanity? Such an idea! What with the world in the shocking state it is, assassins and all manner of ne'er-do-wells roaming the streets! Kindly no. I shall shut the door on my humble but safe abode and leave the outside world to its own devious business.' Huffing emphatically, he clipped around his stall, fussily kicking the straw of his bedding into a tidier pile.

'But a moment ago you said that you hated being stuck here with the horses and grooms!' Aarold protested, leaning against the wooden wall of the stable. He hoped that he hadn't misjudged Phebus's need for mental stimulation against the creature's reserved nature. Phebus snorted sharply, casting the prince a cool glance. 'It is simply a matter of assessing the risk to one's personage,' he remarked. 'True, I find the company within these walls for the most part tedious but at least I know that no peril will befall me. Or you, for that matter! You have a responsibility as heir to keep yourself out of harm so you might live to rule.'

Disheartened, Aarold stared down at his lame leg as a moderate pang of pain twitched his muscles. Phebus's words seemed to echo with the tones of his aunt and a hundred nurses and doctors. *Did his loyal friend think that he was unworthy of kingship too until a cure could be found for his condition? Would that day ever come?* 'But the histories of my family always show that the princes of Veridium took part in missions of bravery to prove their worthiness of their birthright. How am I ever to be seen as rightful king if I spend my life cloistered in this palace?'

Phebus's scarlet eyes flickered back in his head despairingly. 'That's the philistine blood in you talking,' he sighed, 'that hoodlum of a father of yours. Rule through might and bellowing. Cut your enemies' heads off so they can't contradict you. An effective manner of government, one could argue, but hardly a civilised one!'

'I'm not talking about some great crusade, Phebus,' explained Aarold as the Equile turned back towards his reading dais, delicately leafing with his beak through the book Aarold had given him. 'I'm not proposing we should set about slaying a monster or rescuing a damsel.'

'I kindly ask that you remove the suggestion of *we* at all from any plans you are having,' interjected Phebus.

'All I'm advocating is that as two scholars of the world, we should be more involved with the practical mechanics of life. Attempt to view the world as the common man does so we might better understand it. You can't truly claim to have knowledge of any subject if you only experience it through books.'

Aarold knew this was a daring remark to make to Phebus and hoped it would pay off. Equiles were notoriously proud animals and cherished nothing more than the idea that they were knowledgable about most subjects. To infer that Phebus's depth of learning was shallow because of his lack of experience with the outside world was bound to provoke a reaction. The scaly skinned beast stood still and unresponsive for a moment, his scarlet eyes fixed unmovingly on a line of script in the book, giving the impression that he was deep in study. But Aarold knew for sure that he was really milling over his comment and deciding on how to best answer without losing face. To persuade him even more, he added, 'There are many food stools and shops in the city. Bakers and delicatessens that sell fine cheeses and cured meats.' Phebus's pointed ears twitched automatically at the suggestion of access to fine food. He swallowed hungrily and gave his long neck a little shake.

'I am not saying,' he remarked coolly, as he turned to face Aarold, 'that I am wholly adverse to the notion of exploring the populous of the fair city of Veridium. In fact, a strong argument could be made that a short expedition into the bosom of the common man might be very enlightening. However, it does present many risks that one would be foolish to ignore.'

He paused for a moment and glanced at the untouched offering of oats that had been placed in his manger. 'Cured meats, you say,' he murmured wistfully. 'I don't suppose you would know what type, would you?'

Aarold grinned knowingly to himself. As he had hoped, the suggestion of learning coupled with that of food had worked wonders to motivate his Equile friend. 'I have no idea,' he shrugged lightly, 'but I think I once heard one of my nurses mention an outlet that sold nothing but different kinds of spiced sausage. The owner is somewhat of an artisan in the production of them.'

A heavy, lustful sigh escaped unchecked from Phebus's narrow nostrils as he ran his tongue over his beak. 'Sausages!' he groaned to himself, eyes growing misty with hunger. 'Oh that cylindrical masterwork of the chef's art! Freshly ground mince anointed with the most aromatic of seasoning. Thyme, parsley! What joy! What decadence!' His lanky legs trembled with the very thought of such a meal and flecks of white saliva formed around the edge of his beak. Regaining some composure over himself, he neatly licked the drool from his pointed snout and turned back towards the dais.

'I shall give the proposition due consideration, as it is not without merit,' he said, in a forced aloof manner, 'and inform you, at a later date, whether the mood takes me to accompany you on such a venture. Now if you don't mind, dear boy, I wish to indulge myself with some quiet study. Good-day.' With that, he raised his right fore-leg and delicately turned the page of his book.

Aarold studied the strange creature in silence for a moment, aware from Phebus's unsettled expression that he was turning over the idea of the trip in his head. Although Phebus gave off an air of cautiousness, Aarold knew that the Equile, like himself, felt bored and undervalued in the confines of the castle.

'You know I wouldn't allow anything to happen to you, don't you, Pheb?' the young prince said affectionately, reaching out to pat the animal's leathery hide. 'You're the only true friend I have.'

Phebus continued with his reading and made a doubtful, weary 'hmph' sound. Gathering up his cane, Aarold carefully began his journey back to the dining hall where supper no doubt would be waiting for him. As he left the stable, he heard Phebus muttering distractedly to himself about the 'uncivilised nature of Geollease stock' and 'heavenly prepared salami' as he tried to weigh up the risks and advantages of Aarold's suggestion. He really did hope Phebus would agree to help him in his quest. The young prince was beginning to feel more in need of taking control of his own destiny.

Chapter 11

THE IRON GOLEM

The hem of her fine, black velvet robe stained with dust draped the tall, elegant figure of the White Duchess as she made her way like a swift cutter on a calm sea, through the dingy and forgotten dungeons that lurked beneath the palace. These dank and filthy passageways had, fortunately for her, all but been disregarded; a grim echo of a more brutal time. There were few life-forms who knew the stench-filled, damp catacombs still existed, for their residents were now only rodents, insects and the lost ghosts of long-dead prisoners who had once been held in these hopeless chambers. Only one poor captive remained alone in the echoing blackness of the dungeons, an unfortunate soul incarcerated in the hellish depths by the malicious White Duchess to help her fulfil her wicked plan.

Maudabelle pressed a lace handkerchief to her delicate nose and mouth to dull the reek of rot and rat droppings and quickened her pace towards her destination. She was filled with a mixture of excitement and annoyance of being forced to activate her creation so soon, but the troublesome Ryder had to be stopped at all costs. If any whisper of her work escaped, years of planning and toil would come to nothing. It was easy for her colleague to tell her to put the mechanism to work, but the creature was a thing of elusive magic and clockwork; one misplaced cog or spell could destroy it. It had been difficult enough to find a craftsman skilful enough to complete her designs. Human metal-smiths and weapon-makers lacked the subtle talents needed for its construction.

Only a dwarf had the knowledge and expertise to fulfil the task and the mountain dwellers were not well known for taking such commissions. The White Duchess had to use force to press-gang such a being into her employment and that was not easy when said creature had flesh as hard as stone and could snap a grown man in two. Fortunately, Maudabelle had her own methods of persuasion.

The dimly lit corridor came to an abrupt end and the stone floor fell away into a narrow opening covered by a heavy metal lid held in place by six large nuts that glowed in the icy gloom with a dull, purple luminescence. Gathering up her skirts, Maudabelle crouched down on the damp floor and with the lightest of touches began to work her skilful fingers over the glowing washers. One by one, the light from the large bolts grew brighter, glimmering violent mauve in the blackness of the dungeon, twisting counter-clockwise until they finally released the thick cover from its setting in the cold stone. With the powerful spell of imprisonment lifted, Maudabelle slid the grating back to reveal the narrow entrance to a dark oubliette: the hidden cell of her captive.

There was a rope ladder coiled on the damp ground beside the opening and this the White Duchess lowered into the shadows beneath. Then with the careful, agile steps of a much younger woman, she descended into the mouth of the oubliette. As she climbed downwards, her way was lit by a dim golden light that glowed faintly from the far corner of the cell. A thin, beautiful thread of sparkling golden magic, like a long enchanted spider's silk, was coiled around a large pile of pale boulders hulked together in a miniature mountain against the wall. Gracefully, the White Duchess dropped to the ground from the last rung of the ladder and impatiently glanced around the grim catacombs. Tools of all shapes and description littered the floor along with shards of beaten iron, cogs, springs and other fragments of clockwork.

Stalking through the scattered debris, Maudabelle made her way across to the great mound of stone encircled by the delicate loops of gold twine. Stooping down, she hooked the thread up from the floor, wrapping it carefully around her fingers. Her face set in a heartless expression, she gave a short, sharp tug on the spool of bright light. A grating, weary moan issued from the piles of stones before her and with slow, heavy movements they began to shift and open outwards to reveal that they were not a lifeless collection of rocks at all but the crouched shape of a massive humanoid figure. The dwarf was seated on the floor but already his pallid globe of a head reached nearly to the duchess's shoulder. His body was vast, pale, naked and muscular, filled with solid potential strength and sheathed in a chalky, rough skin: the uneven texture of weathered granite. His arms and legs were short in proportion to his broad, heavy pectorals and immense rounded belly, palms thick and square ending in short fingers like broken stalactites. His stooped head was hairless and spherical, almost like that of an infant, yet his stony face was deeply set and rugged and looked to be as ancient as the earth. Tiny, beady black eyes nestled beneath a slanted brow and a misshapen nose hung like a long, craggy outcrop above a narrow crack of mouth. The fine thread of sparkling light looped tightly around his ankles, wrists and neck. The dwarf turned his brooding expression towards his beautiful captor but made no sound.

The White Duchess fixed the dwarf coolly with her glittering emerald eyes. 'Good evening, mountain dweller,' she uttered lightly. 'I trust you are not slacking from your work.'

The dwarf did not answer, but pulled back his heavy upper lip in loathing to reveal a set of stubby, pebble-like teeth. Crossly he picked at the shimmering cord knotted around his wrists.

Menacingly, the White Duchess took a half-step towards him, her fist curling around the gold chain. 'Don't ignore me,' she hissed threateningly. 'I know you can speak the common tongue as well as I. I asked you a question. How far have you progressed?'

The dwarf's black eyes glimmered with fury and his massive bulk grew tense as he hoisted himself on to his feet to tower a good three feet above Maudabelle. 'I am Krogg of Kelhalbon,' he declared in a deep, proud voice that grated and growled like jagged stones being shattered. 'I do not serve the puny whims of short-lived man. I demand that you release me from these enchanted shackles!' Fiercely, he yanked at his glowing bonds with all his immense strength but the thin loops of gold simply stretched and retraced, tangling him even more firmly in their grasp.

Cautious of the dwarf's rage, the White Duchess swiftly stepped backwards, careful not to show her prisoner one glimpse of fear or weakness. 'As I've told you before, *Krogg*,' she remarked crisply, her emerald pupils sparkling with determination, 'you will be free when, and only when, you have completed the task I have ordered of you. The skill of your kind with metals and stone is renowned. I do not understand what is taking you so long.'

Krogg's stony face contorted with rage, his features creasing and cracking like rocks in an avalanche. 'Vile witch!' he hissed. 'How dare you force me to use the ancient arts of my kinfolk for your contemptible ends. The crafts of dwarves were not meant to be enslaved like this!' With a bellow that shook the stale air, the dwarf lurched forward towards Maudabelle, his powerful hands outstretched to grab her throat. Like lightning, the White Duchess skilfully flexed her wrist, sending a large arch of energy and magic along the coiled length of the gleaming thread. Enchantment flared like shimmering fire along its looped span with a hiss of torn fabric and jagged bolts of light leapt from it to run like slim, fast vipers across Krogg's gritty skin. His roar of rage instantly transformed into a scream of excruciating pain and his heavy, muscular form fell to the ground like a vast granite tower that had suddenly been demolished. Contorted and weakened within his glittering bonds, he glared up at the duchess hatefully. Convinced once more of her power over the dwarf, Maudabelle swaggered deliberately over to Krogg's prostrate form and gracefully stooped down to regard his rough, loathing face. 'Try to understand,' she uttered in a light, creamy tone, as fading echoes of golden power rippled over his stony body, 'I don't want to hurt you, I don't enjoy it. I am merely a victim of circumstance, using what powers she has to right the wrongs done to her people. If you would agree to help willingly, things could be a lot more pleasant for both of us.' She sighed warily, placing a slim pale hand on Krogg's uneven cheek and her beautiful face looked, for the briefest of moments, compassionate.

The dwarf's grey jowls twitched with pain and loathing, and through gritted jagged fangs he muttered something hateful in his ancient, mountain language.

As suddenly as the tenderness in the White Duchess's face had appeared, it vanished, leaving her fine pallid features an aloof mask of indifference. With a sweep of delicate lace and velvet she got to her feet. 'Come,' she demanded unemotionally, 'show me what progress you have made.'

She nimbly twisted the glowing strand around her elegant fingers. A dart of agony and power shot down its length into Krogg's heavy body, making him twist and bawl out a growling profundity. The band's glow then dulled to a faint glimmer, loosening slightly to fall in slack loops. His limbs weighed down with shame and hatred, he dragged himself awkwardly to his feet and slowly led Maudabelle across the room.

Maudabelle's heart quickened again with trepidation as she followed the dwarf across his cell to a well-hidden item that rested swathed in dark material, lurking ominously in the far corner. The shape was flat, still and indistinct in the gloomy half-light of the prison but even cloaked in its cover, there seemed to be, within the stillness, a mass potential of awaiting energy, organic or mechanical, ready for some trigger to set it in motion.

Both human and dwarf's breath quickened as they gazed at the shrouded creation, one from fear, the other from excitement. Maudabelle's emerald eyes shot Krogg a dangerous, unspoken command and with movements stilted with dread and cautiousness, he slowly stepped forward, crouching down to retrieve a long, narrow screwdriver from the floor. Despite his immense size and obvious strength, the dwarf handled the tool with remarkable dexterity. Slowly, as if approaching the nest of some slumbering venomous snake, Krogg reached out with his free hand and with a single, deft motion pulled back the coarse cover that shielded his creation.

The device stood like an oversized iron beetle in the shadows: a dark, upturned dish of beaten and turned black metal, supported by six jointed legs. Complex curved grooves, markings and eye-holes swirled over its black surface. At the front of the shell was a small, hinged cube, like a sculpted parody of a tightly clenched maul, from which protruded a pair of rigid wires, like taut antennae, stiffly alert and aware. The whole contraption was a disturbing collection of paradoxes, a form not fit for existence, sickening and undefined. It was a creation of mechanics and magic made as a lesser echo of Nature's own invention, a deathly still and silent item holding within it an unspecified potential and energy: a soulless slave born of corruption.

Cautiously, Krogg stooped down and carefully picked up the iron automaton in his massive hands. Amazingly for a creature so large and strong, the dwarf's fingers had astounding dexterity. Cradling his creation against his stony forearm, he ran his hand lightly over its moulded shell, pressing a number of unseen switches and checking for any loose parts. With the same delicate skill of a surgeon performing a vital operation, he inserted the head of the screwdriver into various nooks and holes in the machine's armour, winding and adjusting its hidden workings. As he toiled, strange sounds issued from beneath its iron casement, the clicks and whirls of springs and coils as well as other more alien, almost beast-like sighs and murmurs. The dwarf's rough, haggard face was an intense mask of mixed emotions as he made precise modifications to the workings: a mixture of loathing for the thing he had been forced to create and a deep pride in the ancient art that his kind cherished as their own. The mixture of ironwork and arcane magic was precious to the dwarves and Krogg took pride in his craft even when it was being used in such a depraved manner.

At his side, the White Duchess tapped the toe of her velvet slipper like an impatient child. 'Well,' she hissed, 'stop stalling, dwarf! I need the mechanism primed before the spell can be performed. I have given you long enough to toy with it, haven't I?'

Krogg's mighty hands tightened around the disc-shaped body of the machine and for a brief moment it looked as if he was going to crush his creation and destroy it.

'It needed some fine-tuning,' he said in a gravelly, disheartened tone, setting it down on the floor once more. 'Your requirements were specific and unfamiliar to my craft.'

He took a step back from the crouching entity, glaring at it with venomous hatred.

'I have prepared the inner workings,' he spat, jabbing a stubby finger at the machine, 'but mark my words, what you have forced me to build is an abomination against the laws of magic and I shall carry my shame with me always. I beg of you, for the sake of every living creature, do not give that thing life.'

Maudabelle cast the dwarf an idle glance through her silken lashes. 'Your advice has been noted,' she snapped coolly as Krogg scuttled broodingly into the shadows.

The White Duchess intently examined the iron creature, a proud smirk creasing her mouth. Her elegant, pale fingers traced the markings on its metal body and she could already feel the dull quiver of slumbering consciousness curled within its gears and springs. With a dramatic step backwards, she spread her arms wide to form an unseen circle around her and the device. With a deep breath, she cleared her thoughts and focused on the power that dwelt in her mind. Within the silent gloom of the oubliette, she held her inner strength and blackness lightly within her mind, drawing it down through her body, so it passed through her heart and stomach and out through her soles where they touched the cold stone floor. Her body swayed slightly as her awareness leaked out from her flesh, but she kept her concentration and refused to give over to the urge to faint. Her thoughts sank deeper into the stone beneath her, into the eternal living vastness of the very earth itself until it connected with a wild and black power that throbbed and twisted like a thrashing worm waiting to burst up through the soil. Using all her mental might, she seized hold of the untamed energy and dragged a fragment up out of the recesses of the earth. The cold atmosphere of the dungeon trembled slightly, as if some sudden breeze from the outside world had leaked through its impenetrable walls, stirring them with whispering life. From the shadows, Krogg gripped his huge fists tightly and muttered to himself in fear.

Her thoughts still linked with the power of violence awakened from the earth. The White Duchess opened her eyes and focused her vision, blurred with effort, at the dark uneven cobbles of the prison's floor. Her lips moved noiselessly chanting words of command and enslavement as she drew from the earth beneath her a smoky strand of silken energy. Through the pores and cracks in the dark stone it seeped and oozed, a coiling, lashing tendril of viciousness that rose like a serpent between Maudabelle and the dwarf's mechanical creation, hissing and burbling with meaningless sounds of anger as it struggled to find some consciousness and purpose in its complete hatred and rage.

Intently, the White Duchess worked to gain and maintain power over the dark life-force that swirled like ebony fog about her feet. Wildly, she weaved her arms in broad circles and arches, her long fingers dancing through the air as she battled to bend the tainted entity to her will. Her deep, thick voice echoed bitterly in the stone chamber as she determinedly formed ancient words of magic, uttering enchantments of obedience and enslavement. The shadowy form bucked and thrashed angrily as it was pulled free from its root in the earth and rose in a heavy band of sable smoke that coiled and enfolded the duchess's slim body. She felt her mind become icy and dark like the flaky embers of a long extinguished fire as the sucking bleakness fought to overwhelm her. But she trained her mystic arts even more fiercely and thrust out her pale hands to seize the icy metal of the automaton. With a clawing slither, the hungry blackness slipped from Maudabelle's body to run in shivering waves across the polished iron. The inner springs and joints clicked and twanged as the malicious energy bled through the slits and screw holes in the mechanism's polished shell. Her body trembling with effort, Maudabelle willed the hateful entity to take hold of the mechanism and fulfil its violent desires. Her fingertips dragged over the symbols burnt into the iron, commanding them to activate the meaning held within their arcane imagery. '*Take*,' she enforced, as the curved lines began to glow with a dull, golden gleam. '*Obey. Destroy.*'

From the robotic heart of the metal Golem, sickening sounds started to come forth. Chugs and clanks of clogs grinding and wheels turning, all echoing with an unnatural undertone of something alive and bestial. It sighed and growled as dark enchantment and power imbued it with the gifts of awareness and movement. With awkward, jerky progress, the animated Golem flexed its spidery limbs as it struggled from the White Duchess's grasp and with a click of hinged joints landed agilely on the floor. Maudabelle let out a shrill cackle of triumph as she watched the Golem scuttle maliciously towards her. With a sudden snap, the middle section of the shell sprung upwards to reveal a vicious curved blade of jagged iron like a scorpion's tail, which it thrashed menacingly in the air.

'Look what you have forced me to build!' Krogg bellowed with spite and self-loathing, as the automaton stalked mindlessly about the floor, whipping its deadly tail. 'It is a thing of destruction and evil. An abuse of the crafts of metalwork and magic!'

'Silence!' barked Maudabelle, her emerald eyes gleaming excitedly as she watched her new weapon. 'Show some pride! It is a masterpiece. It will serve me well.'

Careful to keep her distance from the living machine, the White Duchess once more summoned her inner power and command of magic. Her hands drawing precise patterns in the still air, she addressed the lurking Golem as it prowled towards her.

'Hear me,' she stated in a clear, cold, steady voice, as the creature's mechanisms whirred and hissed, sensing its surroundings, 'understand me. I am your mistress. I have given you life. You will not harm me. You will obey me.'

The black creature stopped where it was, its body stiffly motionless, its narrow antennae twitching stiffly as if sensing the distinct vibrations of Maudabelle's voice. Sharply, the hinged box at the front of its torso snapped open to reveal an empty dark space, lit by subtle sparks of gold magic. The White Duchess smirked with triumph as the machine prostrated itself before her, awaiting her command.

'You are eager, my friend,' she crowed knowingly; 'you want to hunt, to kill, to feast on the energy of the living. Yes, I know. And I will give you your first victim.'

'You know not what you do, witch!' came the cry of warning from the dwarf crouched fearfully in the corner. 'You deal with an evil beyond your understanding. Once activated, it cannot be stopped.'

But Maudabelle took no heed of his words. Deftly, she reached her graceful fingers into a leather purse suspended from her waist and drew out a small, spiral of stone that resembled a snail's shell: an ammonite. Stooping down, she delicately placed the rock into the awaiting metal maul of the Golem. Bolts of golden fire rippled over the fossil's light brown surface as from within the iron beast, hateful whirs and snarls rose to a high pitch. Once more, the White Duchess's skilled fingertips danced across the carved symbols on the machine's hide as she instructed it to her desires. 'Seek out the Ryder who shares the name of this crystal,' she uttered darkly, as the sharp clasp snapped shut around the ammonite. 'She carries a quartz containing more of your dark essence. Slay her, feed on her life-force and bring the crystal back to me. Do this without being seen and I will have others for you to feast on.'

The whole of the iron Golem's body seemed to flex and shiver with delight at being given this task. With light, soundless claws, it scuttled across the cold stone floor and hooked itself up upon the rope ladder that rose to the world above, with the ease of a spider ascending its web. Filled with glee and morbid excitement that her plans were finally taking action, the black-hearted White Duchess watched the mindless assassin disappear into the shadows of the night.

Chapter 12

LEY ORIGINS

Hayden slept surprisingly well in his tower chamber within the Goodstone citadel. He believed that with the unfamiliarity of his surroundings and his worries for Petronia's imminent assessment by Sister Amethyst that slumber would elude his unsettled mind. But alone in the peaceful dark of his room, the pale winter moonlight shining through the narrow window twinkled soothingly on the fragments of amethyst, charoite and cerussite in the shades of night, making them glow with a comforting power that embraced him to the world of dreams.

It was not until the dawn broke and he awoke to find himself in a strange bed that the concerns about his sister returned, and he once more found himself somewhat lost as a welcome guest in the fort of the Ley Ryders. Easing himself off his bunk, Hayden wandered over to the tiny eyelet window of the tower that looked down over the courtyard. Far below, the community of women who had found their Calling to the mystical Ley were already going about their morning chores, their simple but brightly coloured robes like daubs of paint in the first light. Contented in their work, they went about tending to the few animals housed in the citadel's yard, clearing their stables and cording wood for the fire in the mighty kitchen. The family-like normality and contentment struck Hayden as puzzling considering that there were no men in the commune, no husbands or fathers to offer love or companionship, no promise of children to sooth the maternal longing he heard dwelt within most women. Only their unswerving devotion to the mysterious Ley that seemed to speak to them so clearly, but remained an enigma to Hayden's understanding. Was it possible his sister was destined for such an alien way of life?

A polite rap on the door interrupted his thoughts and Hayden went to answer it. In the hall beyond, he found Bracken, the tall, pale-complexioned apprentice to the Ley who had welcomed him and Petronia the previous day. She carried with her a shallow bowl of warm water and blushed slightly when Hayden opened the door to her shirtless.

'Oh, excuse me, Master Hayden!' she said, her fleshy cheeks blushing profusely as she modestly cast her eyes to the floor. 'Sister Amethyst requested that I bring you some water so that you might freshen yourself before breakfast.' Modestly, she kept her gaze lowered as she held out the basin towards him.

To spare her embarrassment, the young lad pushed the door half closed and retrieved his tunic, putting it on over his head before returning to take the wash bowl. 'Thank you, Mistress Bracken,' he said politely, 'your sisters are most gallant hostesses. I am much rested. I trust my sister, Petronia, had a good night?' He was keen to see his sister as it had been the first night in his life that he had not slept in the same room as her.

Bracken took a step inside the door but kept a modest distance from him, and Hayden was once more reminded of the strangeness of this wholly female environment. 'As far as I understand from her manner, your sister is in good spirits,' she informed him.

'I have provided her with suitable garb for an apprentice to the Ley and left her at her toilet in the dormitory. Sister Amethyst has spoken to me already and informed me that after breakfast she wishes to explain to both of you about the nature of the power we serve before assessing Mistress Petronia.'

Hayden grunted broodingly and studied the shards of jewels that peppered the chamber's walls. For all her pleasant manner, Bracken spoke as if it had been already decided that Petronia would join their order, however Hayden still had not given up hope of returning home to their old life together. As hospitable as this place was, he did not feel that he belonged here and could not understand how Petronia could feel differently.

Bracken folded her massive hands in front of the multicoloured patchwork of her dress. 'You are still concerned about your sister finding her place among us,' she noted gently, in her deep, hollow voice. 'This is understandable, especially with your sister's impairment. But, as far as my learning of the Ley goes, It would not have brought her to us without a reason. Sister Amethyst believes that perhaps It has a reason for bringing you to us as well.'

Shocked by this last statement, Hayden turned sharply to face her. Whatever the elderly Ryder might believe about Petronia's desire or abilities regarding the force they served, he was adamant that his sole reason for being in their company was as a guardian. 'I hope you will forgive my bluntness,' he firmly stated, 'but I seek no connection with the way of life you and your kin-folk follow. Rewarding and worthy it may be, perhaps even a suitable vocation for my sister, but I am a humble blacksmith and desire nothing deeper or greater. Sister Amethyst is wrong to think otherwise.'

A slight blush coloured Bracken's cheeks once more but she managed to maintain her composure. 'I understand your sentiments, Master Hayden, as I'm sure will my sister, but we do believe that the Ley moves all men and women along the path of life, even though they may not feel Its presence.' She nervously cleared her throat and made her way towards the door. 'I will escort your sister to the kitchens.'

Once she had left, Hayden stripped and washed in preparation for his and Petronia's audience with Sister Amethyst. He had been somewhat puzzled by the idea that his own fate might be somehow connected with the Ryders, but his good manners and strong nature meant it did little to anger or trouble him. He was adamant in his modest goals, to return to the simple life he had always known, free from the concerns of the Ley and Its power. If Petronia truly decided her future lay with the order, though it greatly saddened his heart to think such a thing could be, then he would ensure that the sisters had her best care at heart before leaving for home. He dared not think of the sorrow it would bring their parents to know their daughter had chosen such a strange and dangerous vocation, but he knew that it was not in him to find a permanent place among the Ryders. The time would come when he would return to Ravensbrook, be it with or without his sister.

Once dressed, Hayden made his way through the winding passageways and staircases of the keep to join Petronia and their hosts in the large kitchen for a breakfast of flat bread and fruits. As Bracken had informed him, Petronia greeted her brother in a loose robe of long ribbons of coloured fabric: the uniform dress of the apprentice Ryders. She was filled with glee and excitement for her new environment and enthusiastically signed to him about the wonderful night's sleep she had had and her eagerness to begin her education in the ways of the Ryders. Hayden watched her beautiful, keen expression, noticing how brightly her black eyes shone with happiness and was taken by how suited she was to the flowing garb. He knew it would break his heart to leave her in a world that she adored but he far from understood. Rosequartz and Garnet joined them for their meal, their bejewelled armour swapped for robes of respectively light pink and dark, earthy brown, a reflection of the stone colours whose names they bore. Jet was not present and with a distracted sigh, Amethyst informed her guests that the sullen Ryder had left in the late hours of the night, saying the Ley was calling her north.

After all had eaten their fill and the other Ryders of the citadel had gone about their daily tasks, Amethyst led Petronia and Hayden back up to the main hall and the Ley Mouth with its continuous current of shifting air. Eagerly, Bracken asked if she too might join them for the lesson to which Amethyst happily agreed but added that it would contain nothing that the apprentice had not already been taught. 'I'm aware of that,' informed Bracken as they took their seats on the floor around the rim of the gaping fissure, 'but it will do me no damage to refresh my mind of the old legends. And besides, my own understanding might help Mistress Petronia in hers; you did charge me with her comfort, after all.'

Amethyst nodded knowingly. 'That I did, child,' she smiled. Then leaning forward, the Ryder inhaled, deeply, the gentle cool tide of air that drifted up from beneath the iron grid they were seated around and a distant, thoughtful look came to her blue eyes. Without being instructed to do so, both Bracken and Petronia did the same, breathing in the subtle breeze that rose out of the fissure of the earth. Not wanting to appear impolite, Hayden followed suit, wondering if the air from the Ley Mouth would have some quality that would bring on a meditative trance, but his mind felt as clearly awake as ever.

Folding her tanned hands in the cradle of purple silk that her gown formed in her lap, Amethyst began to speak, her words echoing with the gravitas of aeons of time.

'To understand the nature of the Ley and why some are called to follow It, one must understand the origins of life itself. For it is the Ley that gives life to all things, as It always has and always will.'

'Ley is life, life is Ley. So says the First Dogma,' uttered Bracken in solemn answer as Petronia gazed keenly at the elderly Ryder.

Amethyst shifted slightly on the hard stone of the hall's tiled floor and brought her fingers together before her to form a circle with her hands. 'Before there was man or beast,' she told them softly, 'before there was time and memory, the world was as a great stone egg, its shell hard and clear of any life. But within this shell, there was a consciousness, the primary soul, the Ley. It knew Itself, alive and ever-changing and through this self-knowledge came into existence.'

'So It created Itself, with no mother or father, just by Its own awareness?' signed Petronia. Hayden translated, though his sister's words meant little to him.

Amethyst nodded. 'Indeed. As do we all, to some extent. For it is impossible to be alive without consciousness. Even the simplest bugs in the soil are aware of themselves. It is a memory from when we were all part of the Ley. For we all are, each entity that exists.'

Hayden turned his eyes unconvinced towards the peaceful shadows that rested in the deep recesses of the pit before him. He wanted to show respect to the Ryders' beliefs but found it very hard, almost laughable, to comprehend that something ancient and revered dwelt within him.

His life seemed so mundane, his existence too humble to hold within it a spark or fragment of immortality. To him, each life was fleeting: a tree, an animal, a man came into being by chance of nature, not orchestrated by some greater power.

The elderly woman continued her hallowed tale. 'As the Ley created Itself, It created life, breaking out of the still blackness of Its stone cradle and moving restlessly across the crust of the world. Everywhere It went, It left behind traces of Its spirit and they in turn formed themselves into the trees and the plants, the animals, birds and man. Each living thing It formed into its correct nature so it might exist in harmony.'

'You see,' interrupted Bracken, turning eagerly to Petronia, 'the Ley exists in all of us, even if we aren't always aware of It. It guides each being along their life path the way a seed fallen in a stream is carried to fertile ground.' She looked back to Amethyst for reassurance that her understanding was correct.

Amethyst smiled to inform her apprentice that what she said was right. 'Many are unaware of the Ley's influence in their lives,' she explained. 'They forget the source of their life-force just as they forget the months they spent in their mother's womb. But there have always been those, gifted women such as I and my sisters, who could sense the Ley's will and are able to manifest Its good in the world.' She spread her arms and gazed around her at the heavy stones and glittering crystals of the citadel's main hall.

'We are the Ryders,' she said proudly, 'dedicated brides and followers of the Ley, blessed with the knowledge and sense of Its power and sworn to serve and aid those It instructs us to. Our goal is to be empty vessels, brimming with Its goodness.'

An excited gasp escaped Petronia's lips and she reached her arms forwards to allow her fingers to be caressed by the soft stream of air from the Ley Mouth. Hayden regarded his sister anxiously. There was overwhelming joy and excitement in her eyes as well as a distant, hidden tranquillity that was beyond his understanding. Amethyst's words sounded very noble but she still did not clearly describe what the life of a member of their order actually entailed. 'You speak very eloquently, good Mistress Amethyst, about the birth of your Sisterhood,' he probed seriously, 'but say very little of its actions. What precisely are your duties to the Ley?'

Petronia pouted crossly at her brother and gave him a sharp blow on the arm for interrupting the Ryder. Amethyst grinned knowingly at the squabbling siblings. 'You have a mind that is both practical and caring,' she informed the young man, 'both worthy traits. You are concerned for your sister's well-being, perhaps think we are some kind of malicious cult that lures vulnerable maidens away from their families for devious practices. I can assure you this is not the case. Travel anywhere you please in this country of ours and you will find folk who will pay testament to the charitable deeds of we Ryders. Lame and sickly who have been healed, barren fields and women made fruitful again, vulnerable hamlets freed from the attack of scoundrels and wisdom given to those who have lost their way. All this and more have been brought about by this Sisterhood, with the Ley guiding our hearts and hands. As to what tasks It may require of you, Mistress Petronia, the Ley has planted in the earth markers of Its power over all things for us to read and use in our duties.'

She reached into one of the numerous purses suspended from the leather girdle around her waist and took out a number of brightly coloured polished stones which she held out for Petronia to examine in her cupped palm. 'Crystals,' she explained, as the young girl studied their glittering beauty intently, 'from deep within the ancient earth, pure fragments of the Ley's power. Each type in its uniqueness holds within its core a blessing of the force we follow, whether it be for healing, strength, wisdom, courage or a thousand other gifts brought about by the Ley. Through familiarity and study of these precious stones, we might better bring about the will of the Ley to others. Through learning their silent language so might each apprentice find her true Calling until one crystal commands her more than its fellows and compels her to take its name, thereby indicating her true destiny.'

Cautiously, Petronia stroked the smooth stones with her fingertips while Amethyst watched intently. Bracken too gazed at the collection of stones, a wistful frustration in her dark, green eyes. The grey-haired

Ryder seemed aware of the cause of this sadness for she said, 'But this clarity of the senses takes time and study to master. One must be completely familiar with all the qualities of many gems before the one whose name you will take will reveal itself. Very often, the longer the period of study, the stronger the final bond.' She flashed Bracken a reassuring smile before turning back to Petronia. 'But the time for words and legends has passed and you will not learn by my instruction alone. To understand the powers of the crystals, you must handle and work with them and this cannot start too soon. If you feel ready and strong enough, Miss Petronia, I would like to introduce you to some of the more basic crystals, just to see how you handle and relate to them.'

Eagerly Petronia nodded, her face set in a focused expression. Amethyst smiled gratefully before turning to Bracken and Hayden.

'Unfortunately, this teaching takes absolute focus of the mind and must take place unobserved. I would therefore kindly ask you to leave us for a short time, so there are fewer distractions. Do not worry for your sister's need of your aid, Master Hayden, as this exercise is one of silent understanding; she is merely asked to become aware of the aura of each crystal for her own knowledge, not to express to me how she feels. I will call for you if she indicates she needs your assistance.'

Unsure, Hayden looked at his sister, unwilling to leave her with a woman, however kind or wise, who had no knowledge of her language. But Petronia signed that she was fine in Sister Amethyst's company and when Hayden paused, gave him a good-hearted shove to indicate he should leave.

'I will go to my chores,' said Bracken, getting to her feet. She paused for a second and looked towards Amethyst expectantly. 'Will you help me with my studies later today? I have been meditating very hard on the crystals you gave me.'

Kindly, the elderly woman nodded. 'Of course. We shall continue our private lessons this evening. Do not worry, I shall not forget!' She glanced at Hayden. 'I believe you are on stable duty. Perhaps our guest would be gracious enough to assist you. Some light physical toil may make his time waiting for his sister pass quicker.'

A smile creased Bracken's mouth and she gave a respectful bow of the head. 'As you wish, Sister.' With an encouraging glance to Hayden she headed towards the door that led out to the courtyard. Nervously, Hayden followed, continuously glancing back to Petronia and Amethyst as they began their lesson. Gently, Bracken ushered him outside, locking the inner door to the keep behind them. 'Do not fret for your sibling,' she reassured him as they crossed over the cobbles to where the long wooden stables stood. 'The first introduction to working with crystals may exhaust Mistress Petronia's spirits but Sister Amethyst is an excellent teacher and will not push her beyond her abilities.'

Broodingly, Hayden stood beside the door to the stables as Bracken carefully led out the first of the animals from their stools. 'I cannot help it,' he confessed. 'Having Petronia learn ways of which I have so little knowledge unsettles me, even though I know your Sisterhood means her no harm. I'm sure your family felt the same, when you began your apprenticeship.'

The large, pale-complexioned girl paused for a moment in her duties, sadly stroking the nose of the fine chestnut stallion she was attending. 'Alas no,' she uttered sadly. 'I confess, Master Hayden, I am somewhat unique as an apprentice to the Ley for I had no kin to leave behind. I am a foundling, without parents and the citadel is the only home I've ever known.'

Hayden momentarily forgot his worries for Petronia, aghast at the faux pas he had just made. In the time he had spent in the citadel, Bracken had shown Hayden and his sister nothing but hospitality and friendship, and now his concern for Petronia had caused him to make a hurtful remark to the girl who had gone out of her way to make them so welcome. 'Forgive me!' he gasped, following Bracken into the stables. 'I truly meant no offence. I had no idea that the Sisterhood fostered orphans. I would never have mentioned your parentage had I known you were without family.' He felt very embarrassed for his misjudgement, but Bracken shrugged her broad shoulders and gave him a warm smile that reassured him that no slight had been taken.

'Oh, you mustn't feel pity or shame for me because of my lack of ancestors,' she said light-heartedly. Taking up a pitchfork she began to pile the horses' bedding into a nearby barrow. 'I bear none for myself. I lack nothing, physically or emotionally, from not knowing who sired me for the sisters have furnished me with as much love, care and nurturing as any woman could her own child. Especially Sister Amethyst who has been a mother to me in all but name and flesh. It was she who found me, you see. Would you like to hear the tale?'

'If it doesn't pain you to tell it,' said Hayden as he reached for a broom to help her in the chore. Bracken shook her head and loaded a large pile of straw easily into the barrow. Hayden was quietly astounded by her obvious strength and how easily she shifted the load. 'Not at all. Perhaps it might show you the caring nature of the Ley for it was that which brought me here. You see, sixteen summers ago Sister Amethyst still rode the Ley on horseback, as Sisters Garnet, Jet and Rosequartz do, bringing aid and protection to those who needed it. She was in the far north east of the country, where the Great Forest is; have you ever heard of it?'

Hayden shook his head. 'I am an ignorant blacksmith, Mistress Bracken. This castle is the furthest place I have travelled from my home.'

The lass cast him an almost affectionate glance. 'I only know it from the maps in the library myself and the tales the sisters tell. Anyway, she had been drawn there by the Ley to quieten a troublesome wood spirit that had been pestering villagers in those parts. It is not uncommon for a Ryder to settle such a dispute. Her task over, she was going to head south once more when her awareness of the Ley compelled her out of the woods to the Greyg Steppes at the very foot of the Kalhalbon mountains, realm of the dwarves and border between Geoll and Etheria. By all accounts I have heard it is a barren and desolate wasteland, not ruled over by any monarch nor truly belonging to any kingdom, merely a stretch of grassland between the forest and mountains. The stony ground and harsh northern winds mean few things thrive there, only coarse heather and the odd wild goat, so you can imagine Sister Amethyst's surprise when the Ley led her to such deserted climes. She was even more astounded when after a few hours riding she heard a babe's plaintive cry. Climbing down from her horse, she carefully followed the sound until it guided her to a large, low boulder rising out from the undergrowth and beside it, nestled among the woody gorse, she found me, only a few hours old and without a stitch of swaddling to protect me from the harsh elements.'

She paused and gave a sorry sigh, as if she herself was hearing the story for the first time. Hayden gazed at her in amazement and pity. 'What a brutal beginning, Mistress Bracken! It was indeed good fortune the kind sister discovered you. Was there no sign of your parents or indication of what caused them to leave?'

Bracken shook her head and continued to sweep the stables. 'Sister Amethyst tells me she searched the surrounding area for the tracks of a travelling caravan or wild beast attack that may have robbed me of my parents but could find none. She obviously couldn't leave me without a soul to nurture me so decided that the Ley must have sent her to carry me to a suitable nurse. So she gathered me up in her cloak and called to the Ley to guide her to a place where I could be raised in safety. It never crossed her mind at first that she would become my guardian; she had dismissed any notions of motherhood when she became a Ryder. But as she travelled south through the villages and towns, the Ley gave her no indication as to where I belonged. Oh, she met many good-hearted women who would have made excellent mothers for me, but each time she considered asking someone to take me on, the Ley would tell her my place was elsewhere and urge her onwards.

'We travelled south like that for weeks, me strapped to her chest for safety and weaned on what milk she could beg from people we met along the way, until the day dawned when we arrived at the citadel, where Sister Amethyst herself was tutored. Only within this house of the Ley did she receive the answer to her prayer that this was where I belonged, in her charge and that of the Ley. She said the compulsion was the strongest she had ever felt in all her years as a Ryder. It gave her to me and me to her and I am thankful every day for such a blessing.'

She smiled and took a large bundle of straw in her arms to lay down as fresh bedding for the horses. 'I was named after the common plants that formed my first cradle and have grown up under the most loving and wise eyes in the kingdom.'

Hayden leant on his broom and looked at her as he considered how eager he was to return to his own parents. 'But surely you must have some desire to know who your parents were?' he quizzed gently. 'As loving as Mistress Amethyst and the other Ryders are, they are not your kin. You must have some curiosity as to how you were left on that bleak rock.'

The tall girl looked thoughtful for a second and then shrugged. 'The Ley places all of us where we should be,' she told him simply. 'As I see it there are three options to what happened to my parents. Firstly, they may be dead and if so their energy is in the Ley and with me always. Secondly, they wanted me but couldn't, for some reason, care for me and therefore left me unwillingly; if this is so why trouble their lives with the burden of my return when the Ley placed my life into the hands of someone who could raise me? Or thirdly, they did not care for me at all and willingly left me to die by some force of nature; if this option is true, why should I give any concern to people who believed I was better dead?'

There was logic in her words but Hayden found it very hard to believe that Bracken could go through life without any questions about her origins. 'So you truly have no wish to know who you are?' he quizzed, as he helped lead the steeds back inside the stables.

Frowning slightly, Bracken paused and deeply considered Hayden's question. After a few moments of silence, she answered him with considered, honest words. 'I guess, when I was younger, I did fantasise about finding my birth parents, that they might be royalty or famed robbers or have some other thrilling life. But all children are prone to such playful daydreams, myself no more so than most, and as I have grown to womanhood I have put such thoughts away. No, the Ryders of our Sisterhood *are* my true family and I have no desire or need for any other kind. Although...' she stopped short, her thick lips tightly pursed as if to trap behind them some guilty secret.

'No,' she continued, turning her head away to hide the colour that had come to her cheeks, 'it is but a small insecurity of mine, barely worth the mentioning.' Hayden found himself becoming curious of this secret sadness within the girl's contented demeanour. She seemed to him such a strange creature, devoted to her life among the Ryders yet at odds with it, like an animal kept within too small an enclosure. 'What is it?' he asked gently.

The girl sat down on a hay bale, her oddly piebald face displaying uncertainty whether to trust him or not. 'You do seem an understanding gentleman,' she confessed shyly as Hayden sat down beside her. 'It's so pleasing to have someone my age to confide in and as you are not a member of our order it is doubtful that my confession would cause you offence or hurt. But you must swear not to divulge what I say to any of the Ryders; I would not worry them for the world.'

'Oh, on my sister's honour I swear I would not tell,' enthused Hayden; 'though I am merely a blacksmith my father has taught me to value a lady's dignity.'

Bracken blushed nervously and smiled in gratitude. 'Truly you are a gentleman,' she said. 'You see, my concern is this. As I say, I have been raised by the Ryders from an infant. At the age of five I was told the origins of our order and the noble deeds of our foremothers, at seven I began to learn the names and natures of all the crystals a Ryder might use in her duties and at ten I began to be tutored in the many skills a follower of the Ley needs: horsemanship, fencing, metalwork, not to mention the arts of meditation and self-discipline. But in all those years and for all my study, I have never,' she paused and clutched her hands together, '*felt* the Ley move me. That is, It has never spoken to me as It seems to, to your sister and the other Ryders. I can name the uses of each crystal as easily as you could name the trades of the folk of your village, but to use their gifts is beyond my mind.'

Ashamed by her confession, Bracken got to her feet and swiftly paced across the stable. 'Sister Amethyst knows that I struggle with my studies and is most patient with me. She says that the Ley will speak to me when It feels I'm ready. But my concern is, what if that day never dawns? What am I if I have been raised a Ryder with no aptitude for the Calling?'

Hayden watched the girl pitifully. It seemed to him unfair that Bracken, who seemed so fit and able, was denied the inner knowledge needed to become a fully fledged Ryder when Petronia, as handicapped as she was by her muteness, had seemed to be chosen to serve such a powerful force. If the Ley was truly benevolent, he thought, there did not seem much justice to the choices It made in the women It took for Its servants.

'It would seem,' he confessed, getting to his feet, 'that both our lives, not to mention that of my sister, would be a great deal fairer if the blessing Mistress Amethyst sees in Petronia could be, by some good fortune, transferred to yourself. Thereby, you could follow the vocation you have studied for all your life and we might return happily to our humbler existence.'

On hearing this remark, Bracken paused mid step and stared at Hayden, her dark emerald eyes filled with shock. 'Master Hayden!' she declared, resting her hands on her hips. 'I would never dream of contemplating such a notion! The thought of robbing another of their ability to hear the Ley; why, not only is it ludicrous, but offensive! Would you suggest that it would cure your sister's muteness to cut out another's tongue and sew it in place of her own?'

She shook her head and inhaled deeply to try and master her indignation. 'You are a stranger to us and our beliefs,' she uttered more calmly, 'so your ignorance must be excused. But you must understand that sensing the Ley is a great blessing and one that must be nurtured from within one's own heart. I am joyous for your sister's good fortune and natural aptitude and would not covet one ounce of it for myself. If and when the Ley reveals Itself to me, the event will be truly and uniquely my own.'

She began to collect together the shovels and brooms and tidied them neatly away.

Hayden was filled with shame for his lack of knowledge and that it may have hurt Bracken. 'Forgive me,' he said, 'for voicing such a careless observation. Your sisters have been nothing but the best hosts to me and Petronia and I would never deliberately say anything to offend your way of life.' He gave a thoughtful, sad sigh and gazed around, once more aware of how alien the existence of the Ryders was to him. 'I guess that as long as Petronia is deemed suitable for apprenticeship and needs me to act as her translator, I too am bound to learn your ways,' he remarked, 'although it does soften the task when it is done in such welcoming company, Mistress Bracken.'

Bracken smiled shyly, her cheeks once again flushing with girlish embarrassment.

'And what is this?' a teasing voice called out from the stable door; 'have I uncovered the seeds of romance in the stable? The Ley be thanked that I interrupted in time to save your liberty!' Both Hayden and Bracken turned to see Sister Rosequartz leaning easily on the lower door dressed in a loose pink blouse and leather breeches.

Hayden felt shamed and guilty, though he had no cause to, and took a modest step away from Bracken. 'Mistress Rosequartz,' he enthused, 'believe me, I was merely aiding Mistress Bracken with her chores. I am a gentleman and would never think to take advantage of my position as the only male guest in your citadel.'

Rosequartz chuckled and swung on the door. 'Who said it was young Bracken's liberty that was in danger!' she crowed, hopping lightly down. 'I remember what it was like to be an apprentice, locked away for hours with nothing but my studying and a bunch of old maids. What I would have given for the companionship of a strapping young fellow like Master Hayden in those days. In fact, I do recall one most handsome young farmer who visited us during the time of my apprenticeship.' Her sapphire eyes glittered with the recollection.

'Sister Rosequartz!' squealed Bracken, her broad face scarlet with embarrassment, 'enough of your coarse innuendo! You will shame Master Hayden!'

The portly Ryder clicked her tongue and tucked a strand of her long auburn hair behind her ear. 'Young folk,' she lamented light-heartedly, 'so easily offended these days!'

Reaching down, she retrieved a pair of finely formed scimitars that she had leant against the stable and fastened one on to her belt. 'Here!'

she called, tossing the other to the awaiting Bracken who caught it easily. 'Sister Amethyst has asked me to continue your fencing training if you are ready. I trust you recall all I taught you in our lessons: the appliance of not only physical strength in battle but that of mind and spirit, how you must control your actions but allow them to be guided by the Ley?'

Bracken nervously fastened her weapon to the thin girdle around her waist and nodded earnestly. 'I have meditated much on the crystals that aid us in battle while you have been away, Sister,' she told Rosequartz, pulling back the cuff of her gown to reveal a green bangle of jade and malachite fragments resting on her pale greyish skin.

Rosequartz grinned. 'Very well,' she observed, her merry sapphire eyes twinkling, 'let's see how you put it into practice with your blade. Master Hayden here can act as impartial judge.'

She looked merrily over at the earnest youth as Bracken hurried out to the courtyard, fiddling with the jewels of her bracelet as she prepared for her lesson. Hayden followed out into the sunlight, his mind once again drifting back to his concerns for Petronia and just what was being asked of her in her tutorial with Amethyst and the repercussions it would have on their lives.

'Mistress Rosequartz,' he interjected, as the Ryder prepared to begin Bracken's fencing practice, 'forgive my interruption but I wondered whether Mistress Amethyst will be finished with her evaluation of my sister's abilities soon?'

With a reassuring smile, Rosequartz placed her hand on Hayden's shoulder. 'Not quite yet, young master,' she said, guiding him over to a stool at the side of the square. 'But fear not, it won't be much longer. Sister Amethyst is a compassionate teacher and will not exhaust an inexperienced student in their first introduction to the Ley. Now you rest here while I test Bracken on her blade work. And do try not to look so handsome as it will distract her from my teaching!'

'Sister!' cried Bracken in embarrassment, her face flushing scarlet. Rosequartz chuckled, amused by her student's adolescent awkwardness. 'Coming, young Bracken,' she called merrily, jogging across to join her. 'Now let us begin with our warm-up motions. Wrist circles.'

Eager to distract his mind from what may be being asked of his sister within the great hall of the keep, Hayden sat in the tepid late morning sunlight and observed Bracken's own lesson in the ways of the Ryders. She and Rosequartz spent several minutes performing stretches and movements of flexibility to limber up their muscles. Then, drawing her long blade of metal-tipped granite, the Ryder went through a number of drills, attacks, parries and blocks of an imaginary opponent which Bracken mimicked with studied accuracy. Despite his distracted thoughts, Hayden found himself enthralled by the strong, fluid gestures of the weapons as they arced and thrust their swords with honed finesse. Both of them possessed sturdy, notably indelicate frames, heavy with strength yet each step they took, each flourish of the blades, was exacted with a deliberate grace and ability that Hayden never before thought a woman was capable of. Rosequartz was particularly talented in her swordsmanship, her blade slicing cleanly through the air as if guided by some outer force. Bracken, due to her inexperience Hayden guessed, possessed less poise but still showed herself to be a formidable opponent, using her height and brute strength to try and get the better of her teacher when the two ended their lesson with a lively sparring session. She lunged and swung at Rosequartz with a power that would put some men to shame and it would seem that she could easily better Rosequartz. But the Ryder, by summoning some inner guiding power, was always able to turn away her blows, forever encouraging her to try harder.

'Remember,' she instructed, as Bracken fell back in a defensive pose, 'do not rely on your physical strength; it can fail you. Allow the Ley to command your muscles; ask It for guidance. Feel It in you before you try and disarm me.'

Bracken pursed her lips and nodded. Her thick, pale fingers clasped tight around the handle of her weapon, she deeply inhaled and glanced down at her jade bangle before surging forward to attack. Her blow fell sharp and heavy on Rosequartz's blade, forcing the older woman's wrist to twist momentarily in a weak motion. But just when it looked as if the apprentice had won, Rosequartz thrust into her, her stone blade quivering with inhuman power. The vibration left the blade and shot through Bracken's own, causing her to tremble and step off balance. She tumbled awkwardly to the floor, her sword slipping from her fingers.

'Blast!' she exclaimed, as she landed heavily on her backside on the cobbles. 'I thought I had it that time. I was focusing inward, trying to find what the Ley wanted me to do.' She sighed, frustrated at her failure.

Smiling encouragingly, Rosequartz slipped her blade into its scabbard and offered Bracken a hand to help her to her feet. 'You did admirably, young Bracken,' she praised as the heavy set girl stood and brushed the dust and straw from her patchwork robes. 'Physically, I haven't seen an apprentice or Ryder with your brute power. Had we fought, using muscle and sword, as other warriors do, you would have beaten me for sure. It is only in summoning the strength of the Ley that you are inexperienced. It is on that you must concentrate.'

Bracken nodded as if she had heard this a thousand times and gazed thoughtfully at the handle of her sword as she passed it back to the Ryder. 'And the assistance of the Ley is important in combat?' she asked gingerly. 'I mean, if one trains well in fencing and becomes a master wouldn't that act as compensation, considering so few folk can summon the Ley in battle?'

Rosequartz looked thoughtful. 'True,' she replied levelly, 'but remember that there are other unknown sorceries and skills available to humans and magical creatures alike. It is best to arm yourself with as many weapons as possible in case of malicious attack.' Looking disheartened, Bracken sighed and Hayden remembered what she had confided in him before about her lack of sense for the Ley. Compassionately, Rosequartz rested a hand on her shoulder. 'It *will* come, dear child,' she said, lovingly; 'your talents grow each time I see you. Study as you have done and you will learn your Stone Name.' The girl gave a small, thankful smile and plucked at her bangle.

'Come,' said Rosequartz more cheerily, 'the lesson is finished. Refresh yourself from the well and then go and see if Sister Rhodonite needs any help with the crystal purification rituals. Caring for the crystals and preparing them for use is good practice for you.'

Just as she said this, the door to the keep swung open and Amethyst and Petronia came out into the sunlight. Hayden was on his feet in a second and hurried across to his sister. Petronia's pretty face wore a mixture of exhaustion, pride and euphoria and Amethyst too expressed a pleased smile. However, concern filled Hayden's heart once more when he saw the weariness in his sister's face. 'Petronia,' he asked earnestly, as she rubbed her eyes, 'are you all right? Were Mistress Amethyst's teachings too difficult for you?' Petronia enthusiastically shook her head. '*Not at all, dear Brother,*' she signed. '*I enjoyed it most thoroughly. It was a very fulfilling and enlightening experience. I am just overwhelmed with the intensity of it all.*'

Rosequartz was looking at Amethyst expectantly. 'The assessment went well?' she asked. The silver-haired Ryder smiled and placed a hand on Petronia's arm. 'Indeed,' she told them. 'I have witnessed Miss Petronia handling a selection of crystals and consulted with the Ley as to whether It desires her to serve It. Its answer was most clear.' She paused and took a deep breath, pacing a few steps away from the others, her keen, grey eyes flickering thoughtfully towards the heavens for a moment. The quartet waited tensely for her to continue and Hayden felt his chest tighten with trepidation. With just a few words, Amethyst had the power to decided his sister's destiny: whether she would be returning safely to the normality of Ravensbrook with him or start on a difficult and mystical path that ultimately he would be unable to follow. His thoughts were filled with an image of their simple home and loving parents and he silently tried to will it into Amethyst's mind.

At last she spoke, her tone plain and joy-filled. 'To my eye, Miss Petronia shows great initial aptitude in sensing the Ley and channelling It through crystals. I am more than happy to offer her a place as an apprentice under my teaching and aid her as she studies to become a Ryder.'

On hearing these words, Petronia laughed with excitement and happiness and clapping her hands, whirled round in a dance of delight before reverently kissing Amethyst's hands in gratitude. Both Bracken and Rosequartz cheered at the news that the girl would be joining their ranks and eagerly Bracken rushed forward to congratulate her.

'Another apprentice to share my lessons with at last!' she giggled, as Amethyst looked on proudly. 'Oh we shall be like sisters, I just know it!'

The courtyard seemed to echo with cries of happiness but in the centre of his sibling's celebration, Hayden stood, silent, still and lost. He saw the joy and contentment in Petronia's eyes and longed to feel happiness for her but could not. The world of the Ryders, as honourable and welcoming as it seemed, was still very alien to him and not the safe life he had wished for his sister. He could not leave her here, without his tongue to translate her expressions and gestures, but if he stayed he felt as if he was forfeiting his own life to become a permanent visitor in a realm he did not belong to. Joyfully, Petronia skipped across to him and flung her arms around his neck. Hayden embraced his sister protectively, wishing her happiness did not make it feel as if part of him was dying.

Releasing him, Petronia fixed her brother with her dark eyes, bright with fiery intellect. *'Say you're pleased for me in this, Brother,'* she signed, trapping him in her knowing stare. *'Give me your blessing.'*

Hayden's mouth felt parched as his sister searched his expression. He knew that it would do no good to placate her with lies. As skilled as she was in expressing herself without words, Petronia was equally as adapt at reading others' faces. 'I have always wanted you to find contentment and security,' he told her stiltedly. But Petronia's expression became straight, her fingers silent and Hayden knew she saw the regret in his heart.

Amethyst watched the siblings' exchange carefully and when the celebrations became quiet, she spoke again. 'Master Hayden,' she stated clearly as Petronia retreated to her side, casting her brother a disappointed glance, 'your concern is obvious and understandable, given your sister's unique situation. Be assured, you may remain a welcome guest here until your sister is tutored fully enough in the written word to express herself to others. I understand this whole situation must be quite unsettling and I will personally strive to make the transition as easy for both of you as I possibly can.'

Hayden felt his fists ball at his sides as he battled to repress the feeling of resentment he felt towards Sister Amethyst. He told himself that the wise old Ryder was not to blame for disturbing the peaceful future he had hoped for his family, that such interventions came from a higher, more knowing power that had laid before his sister a greater destiny. But his feelings of loss and concern made it very hard for him to believe that the Ley could be so benign when It was causing his family to be ripped asunder.

Chapter 13

THE BAZAAR ON THE QUAY

Engulfed by the busy atmosphere around her, Ammonite pushed her way through the hustling crowd of traders and barterers that thronged the portside of the river of Tuul as it sliced its way through the city, cutting Veridium in two with its wide, slick band of dirty water. It was nearing sunset, the hour of the day when the light grew low and bright to the eye, reflecting off the lazy broad waterway and deepening the colours of the fabric awnings that shaded the hundreds of tiny stools and barrows that were crammed in narrow, winding walkways along the dockside. All manner of fare was available from the vendors in this area of the city: grains, fruit and other crops from the farms in the south; tools and furnishings of metal and wood fashioned by craftsmen in the north; rich and exotic spices and vividly beaded materials and rugs brought into the western docks on the shoreline from far, nameless lands. Everything a heart could need or desire was brought into the hubbub of the city by the endless stream of barges and junks that travelled smoothly up and down the Tuul like long-bodied aquatic beasts on a never-ending migration. The quayside market was the filthy, breathing melting pot of Veridium where lord or layman was treated as equal as long as they had money to spare or goods to barter. Even now at the end of the day, when some traders were shutting up shop for the night, the air was heavy and suffocating: the cries of tradesmen offering last minute bargains; the clatter of cartwheels and low of oxen and the stifling concoction of odours: of the river, of spices and a dozen kinds of street food, of animals and people.

The ambience of the market made Ammonite's stomach churn and the inside of her skull felt dense and thick. A cloudy, dark illness had laden her spirits for some hours now and she was well aware that it was not simply caused by the claustrophobic business of the bazaar. In the pouch at her hip, the tainted crystal with its unnatural prisoner felt as heavy as a flagstone at her side and its quietly throbbing power sapped her strength every moment she carried it. Reaching into another pocket suspended from her girdle, Ammonite fingered a rough fragment of vibrant blue chrysocolla to draw on her strength reserves and fight off weariness from her thoughts. Within her tired mind, the Ley sense whispered urgently, compelling her to uncover the mystery of the malicious blackness that swirled within the crystal. The Ryder glanced around at the buyers and sellers on the portside. The Ley had drawn her here; the path to the answer must lay somewhere with these folk, but where?

Then, as if a blindfold had been suddenly removed from her eyes, Ammonite's vision was clearly drawn to one small stall of coarse black canvas and wood selling balls of brightly dyed wool. The memory of Happenny's dying face flashed into her mind and filled her with new determination; she hurried onward.

The individual behind the counter was a distinctly unattractive and dirty-looking hag. Stocky, fat and wizened with age and the hardships of life she stood a little under five feet in height, her leathery, sagging face set in a hard, unforgiving expression. A pendulous, black wart sprouting a coarse hair clung beneath her jowly chin and deep lines seemed to trace every inch of her harsh face. A singular, yellowed tooth protruded from her scowling lips and nestled beside it was a short black pipe from which she puffed foul-smelling smoke. Her brittle, wiry hair should have been greyish white but had been tinted a filthy brown by the fumes from her pipe and general dirt. Her stumpy, rough hands worked quickly at a spindle as she eyed Ammonite with suspicion.

'You be one of them Ryder wenches?' she asked in a gruff, thick voice, her eyes roving over Ammonite's leather tunic. Ammonite nodded, almost doubting that the Ley was correct in telling her that this individual would give her the answers she was in search of. 'Indeed, my name is Ammonite and I am a willing servant to the Ley.'

The woman sniffed unimpressed and sucked on the stem of her pipe. 'Thought as much,' she grunted, working the grey wool between her fingers. 'I's seen your type before, seen all types of folk I have. You do in this place. If you be looking for gems to buy or trade, you be out of luck. The traders from the mountains have all gone, packed up for the night.' She paused from her trade to scratch herself beneath one of her drooping breasts.

Ammonite felt the Ley surge urgently in her mind, driving her to pursue the issue of what she had witnessed in the dungeon days earlier. 'Actually, good mistress, it is information that I seek. Do you know anything about a man by the name of Happenny?'

Recognition glinted in the old hag's dark eyes but her features remained in a harsh scowl. Her face looked as if she would greet any news, whether good or bad, with the same bitter expression. 'The one they say tried to kill the prince?' she asked suspiciously. 'That I might. Old Moppet sees and knows a lot of things about this here waterfront. Trouble be, me old memory's not what is was, needs a little jogging along at times. Shiny things help it recall, coins and the like.' She paused knowingly for a moment, working her pipe back and forth with her tongue and eyed Ammonite hopefully.

The Ryder instantly understood. She carried gold and silver among her collection of gems. Both had qualities useful in working with the Ley and traditionally Ryders did not use them as currency. But the call of the Ley for her to uncover what the old woman knew was so strong, she was willing to make an exception. Reaching into one of her purses, she drew out a small nugget of gold.

'Would this heal your memory?' she asked, holding it between her gloved fingertips.

Moppet's eyes grew bright with avarice and she took a long draw on her pipe. 'Most definitely, good Miss Ryder,' she cawed as Ammonite placed the gold in her grubby, outstretched palm. 'It's all coming back to me now!'

Hurriedly, the old woman took the pipe from her mouth and spitting a disgusting globule of tobacco-stained saliva on the ground, proceeded to gnaw on the nugget with her one remaining tooth to authenticate its quality. Once satisfied she had not been duped, she tucked the nugget furtively into the pocket of her skirt. Holding back the filthy drapes of her stall, she then beckoned Ammonite behind the counter.

The tent was small, dark and reeked of dirty fabric. A worn rug, thick with filth, was spread over the cobbles and most of the cramped space was filled with tangled piles of greyish fleece ready for spinning. In one corner, snoring deeply, sprawled an unwashed and emaciated-looking wolfhound. Shuffling over, Moppet gave the animal a sharp poke in the stomach with the toe of her boot.

'Get up, you mangy creature!' she muttered as the dog dragged itself up on its long spindly legs, gazing at its mistress with the unwavering devotion that only a canine could display after being treated so abruptly. Flopping ungainly down on a pile of knotted wool, Moppet roughly invited Ammonite to take a seat in the spot recently vacated by her hound. Spreading her cape across the heap of dog hair and sheep's coat, the Ryder sat down.

Moppet shifted her broad backside awkwardly about on her grimy throne until she was finally comfortable. 'So, you want to know about that old sot Happenny, does you?' she declared gruffly, as her ancient wolfhound slumped its head adoringly into the tangled nest of her skirts.

Politely, Ammonite nodded and crossed her legs. 'The Ley indicates to me you might be able to tell me something about him,' she prompted, 'and why he did it.'

The hag's ugly face twisted into an even more hideous visage of scepticism. 'Bull droppings!' she declared coarsely. 'Old gezza never had the balls to do a thing like that. A slug has more of a spine than Happenny, believe me; I knew him for more years than you've been on this earth. He didna do it!'

Ammonite took in the old woman's words in surprise. Gazing at Moppet's coarse and filthy demeanour, it was hard to take anything she said as true, but when she inwardly cast the old woman's statement into the guiding flow of the Ley through her mind, It reassured her that this was fact. 'But half the city was at the parade,' she queried. 'A thousand witnesses saw him leap for the prince with a dagger.'

Moppet petted her dog's matted coat, absent-mindedly picking out fleas and crushing them. 'People don't see what they're looking at half the time,' she grumbled philosophically. 'All I says is what I knows and that is Happenny wouldn't kill the prince. He was a lot of things, were he, cocky, gobby, a skinflint but a prince killer? No. He was a royalist. 'Specially since he got that blasted commission from the palace.'

Ammonite's attention piqued at this revelation. Sheriff Knoxitch had mentioned nothing about the condemned man having any connection to the royal household before the incident. Surely such a major fact would have come up in the reports?

The old woman reclined lazily on her wares, rolls of loose fat rippling beneath her colourless dress. Despite her initial mistrust of the Ryder, she now felt quite flattered to have such a respected visitor hanging on her every word. 'Smug idiot wouldn't shut up about it,' she continued. ''Course, I tells him, I does, "you're still only a two-bit tinker, none the better than the rest of us", but on he kept going about how he got this letter requesting him to go to the palace by order of the White Duchess, to see about cleaning the royal silver or something.'

'The Duchess Maudabelle called him to the palace?' Ammonite asked. Her mind at once spun with the ebb of the Ley back to the memory of the duchess's beautiful yet cold face and she felt a chill in the pit of her stomach.

'So he said,' Moppet went on, unaware of Ammonite's sudden unease. 'Showed me the letter and all. Not that that was much good to me, never could make head nor tail of all that reading malarkey; as for the seals and heading, well you can get papers saying all kinds if you know who to ask round these parts. I could be an ambassador from Etheria if I went to the right people and gave them that bauble you donated to me earlier. But what I is saying is that no-one thought Happenny was telling the truth until he up sticks and went.'

162

She paused for a moment to catch her breath and rummaging in the waistband of her skirt pulled out a small leather flask from which she took a long swig. Smacking her toothless gums, she then offered it to Ammonite who politely declined. Moppet stared at the Ryder in disbelief for a moment before shrugging and gulping back another dram of the potent liquor. The alcohol brought a pinkish glow to her cheeks and she chuckled foolishly to herself before her face took on a more thoughtful expression.

'Gone about three days, he was,' she muttered, staring at the worn label of the bottle as if it held the answers to Ammonite's questions, 'and when he did come back, well, he wasn't, you know, himself.' She frowned and stifled a belch.

Growing steadily more uneasy, Ammonite shifted in her seat, the beginnings of a sickening idea stirring in her thoughts. 'What do you mean, not himself?' she urged, touching the old woman lightly on the wrist. 'Tell me, Mistress Moppet, and try to be as exact as you can.'

Moppet's glassy eyes wandered over the tattered drapes of her tent, cloudy with the beginnings of drunkenness. 'It was kinda like, something had got into that empty head of his,' she said tapping her temple, 'you know, behind the eyes. Something that weren't him, like his body was there but his mind weren't. A darkness. Gave me the willies it did.'

She gave an unnerved shudder and sucked on her bottle for comfort. Ammonite was suddenly very aware of the tainted quartz crystal she carried and the violent blackness captured twisting within it. In her mind, she once again saw it swarm out of the dying man's eyes, heard its inhuman voice thick with threat. There were many forms of magic in the world, both malign and evil, but as a follower of the Ley, her knowledge extended little beyond the power that flowed through the stones.

'Witchcraft,' she breathed thoughtfully; 'some kind of malicious sorcery.' Her hand instinctively went to the pouch on her belt that contained the shadowy crystal. The old woman nodded her head shrewdly and jabbed a short, dirty finger in Ammonite's direction. 'This be what I'm saying!' she slurred, the drink clearly taking quick effect.

'Happenny didn't attack Prince Aarold, some mystical hoodoo made him do it. Don't ask me what though, I know nought 'bout that kind of thing. In my opinion, it is best you stay away from all that hocus-pocus; it can land you in all nasty doings where you don't want to be. Look at how Happenny ended up, silly old goat.' She chuckled morbidly to herself and scratched her dog behind the ear.

Coldness filled Ammonite's centre as her mind began to piece together fragments of information into an appalling picture. The Ley pushed vivid images together in her mind: Happenny's dying form; the black vapour being sucked into the crystal; the shrewd and beautiful eyes of the White Duchess; and finally it all made horrendous sense. The threat to the young prince's life came from within the palace itself, from the one person who should have been protecting him.

'Thank you for your time, good Mistress Moppet,' she said as she hurriedly got to her feet, her heart beating wildly in her chest due to the new, terrible realisation of what was happening. 'Your words have been most enlightening. I fear I must leave now as I have much to attend to. Good evening.'

Moppet gazed up at her visitor bleary eyed and hiccupped. 'You not be messing with any of that hoodoo, my girl,' she slurred as Ammonite bid her farewell with a bow. 'I tells you, brings nothing but trouble.'

Tipsily, she watched the Ryder leave her tent and stride out across the near-deserted market. Rummaging in the pockets of her skirt, she once more pulled out the nugget of gold Ammonite had presented her with and merrily examined it. 'Not bad, not bad at all,' she muttered, giving her canine companion an affectionate pat on its hollow belly. 'More than decent payment for a bit of old gossip. We'll be having meat for our supper for a few nights with this.'

*

Dusk had been swallowed by night while Ammonite had been speaking with Moppet and as the troubled Ryder walked hurriedly along the riverbank, a damp, icy mist rose from the dark water, giving the silent evening an eerie atmosphere. Within her mind, answers flowed to Ammonite with alarming clarity as the Ley revealed to her the serious truth of the situation. The White Duchess's keenness to relieve her of the cursed stone was now too clearly understandable; it must be she who had hexed Happenny into attacking her nephew! The truth of this statement rang with the voice of the Ley but as to how and why the White Duchess would do such a thing was beyond Ammonite's understanding. All she knew was that she was the only other person to know the truth and she had to act before it was too late.

Her cape billowing in the autumn air, she turned swiftly into a narrow, shadowy alleyway that snaked between the warehouses on the quay. The night was peaceful but her thoughts bubbled and churned with numerous notions and influences. She was driven to act by the rushing flow of the Ley but a dulling, weakening sickness also washed through her body in waves, emanating from the poisoned crystal she carried. Bracing herself, she reached into the pouch containing the damned stone, and with careful movements drew it out into the palm of her hand and pulled back its linen wrapping.

Nausea and dread gripped her stomach as she laid eyes on the hateful swirling mass locked within the heart of the quartz. As she watched it, the smoky, gaseous entity twisted and pulsed within its prison, vibrating with a low, malicious murmur like the sound of distant thunder. Ammonite struggled to think how to act next. If the White Duchess was behind this terrible power, then she had to be stopped but Ammonite felt incapable of acting alone. She needed the support and wisdom of her fellow Ryders to defeat such a subtle, powerful foe.

A sudden sound from high above her head seized the Ryder's troubled awareness: an unnatural clicking, and whirring hiss of movement that shared no relation to any call or cry of beast. The crystal still gripped in her hand, Ammonite turned her gaze towards the sky. The insipid silver glow of the moon filtered between the vertical labyrinth of stairwells and wooden walkways that hung like a rigid web between the two buildings. Abstract shapes of light and darkness stretched high above her and in the maze she thought she caught a glimpse of a swift, black shape scuttling from one patch of shadow to the next, like a massive spider awaiting its prey. In the murky gloom high above, she believed that she had caught a glimpse of movement, just beyond the field of her vision: a small, half-imagined twitch of a slim, black limb or momentary glitter of a malicious pupil.

Her reactions were quicker than thought and without dropping her gaze, she placed the crystal back in its pouch and drew her narrow, granite sabre. Every sense alert to the unknown danger, she studied the darkness held like dusty fabric between the walls of the neighbouring buildings. The night was filling with lifeless shadows and the only sound that disturbed the silence was the distant rippling of the nearby river, a whisper of thoughtless tranquillity. Not a breath or heartbeat of life disrupted the stream of Ley that flowed through Ammonite's mind; all she felt within It was the trepidation and alertness of her own thoughts. Yet something beyond her senses, beyond even her feeling for the Ley, told her that she was not alone. She was being watched by a cold consciousness lurking within the shadows, stalking her movements, waiting to strike. Eager for the lurking presence to reveal itself, Ammonite reached into one of her crystal pouches and pulled from it a small, clear diamond which she swiftly passed in front of her eyes to enhance her vision. The power of the diamond flowed into her pupils a moment too late however, for as she made the gesture there was a sudden snap of metallic joints and a heavy black shape leapt from where it clung to the shadowy wall and landed powerfully right at Ammonite's side, missing her left shoulder by a hair.

The Ryder stepped backwards, caught off-balance by the ambush, her blade raised in defence as she saw her strange assailant for the first time. A dozen spindly legs lashed and twitched with silken quick movement from beneath its curved shell, striking out like deadly needles and shifting its bulky form as agilely as a cat. The pair of rigid, wiry antennae that protruded from its deeply engraved casing flexed and spun constantly, informing it of its surroundings and at its front end a duo of razor-like mandibles clicked with greedy intent. Its movements were a mockery of a living creature, displaying awareness without soul as it pounced at Ammonite with psychotic intent. The Ryder brandished her blade as the iron monster threw itself at her, sharp limbs and fangs slashing murderously as it searched for flesh to pierce. Frantically, Ammonite stabbed at its underside, trying to pry her blade into its workings and deactivate it but could find no point of vulnerability. As its weight bore down on her, she saw narrow ribbons of dull gold light and magic swirl around its iron form, giving it strength. With all her physical might, Ammonite thrust the abomination from her and sent it spinning on its rounded shell across the cobbles. The Golem emitted a piercing screech as it landed on its side and with a click of unseen gears, unhinged a vicious coiled stinger from its back, flipping itself upright again. Her heart trembling, Ammonite gripped the hilt of her sword and battled to immerse her mind in the power of the Ley. But as she did so, a fearful blackness swamped over her mind, blocking all sense of the power that had been her guide for so long. In the dank alley, faced with this unnatural monstrosity of metal and movement, she felt completely abandoned by the power that normally dwelt within her spirit, her only protection coming from her physical strength alone.

With light ease, the Golem's wiry limbs spun it across the cobbles towards Ammonite, lurching at her once more, its mandibles snapping viciously with the green and gold fire of enchantment. Her heart thundering wildly against her breastplate, she brandished her rapier in defence, thrusting its curved granite blade between the automaton's pincers to block their piercing bite. Bolts of jagged, metallic fire ran across the weapon's stonework, causing it to tremble within the Ryder's firm grip and sending shards of granite and dust tumbling to the ground.

The Golem's arched stinger flexed and thrashed like a jointed iron flail and with a strike like lightning it pierced through the heavily padded leather of Ammonite's breeches and embedded its tip deep into the flesh of her right thigh. She let out a cry of furious agony as the black metal of the razor filled the wound with burning pain, and struggled to master her self-discipline to ignore the injury and keep fighting; she had suffered worse flesh wounds in the past. However the searing heat of initial agony lasted only for the briefest of moments and was followed by a much worse sensation of icy, black cold that poured into her leg from the open tear in her skin, like liquid death deadening her muscles. The Golem withdrew its sting from her flesh with a swift, clear motion and slunk back from its attack with expectant triumphant.

Summoning all her strength, Ammonite attempted to seize this opportunity to finish off the creature, but already she felt an iciness within her begin to steal away her will. She had no feeling within her right leg and although it still bore her weight, the bones, muscles and tendons from her toes to her hip felt as lifeless as rock, solid, heavy and useless. In the dim light of the alleyway, she glanced down and saw the rip in her armour gaping open to display the fresh gash of ripped skin and muscle, the ragged edges of the wound marred by alien blackness. Fearlessly she lunged at the crouched Golem, her sword raised to strike but even as she moved, the paralysis that had gripped her leg coiled like chilling smoke upwards through her body, freezing every organ and fibre it touched. Her stride became a stumble as her whole form was gripped by unforgiving immobility and she tumbled to the ground like a lifeless statue pushed from its pedestal. Knowing that death must surely be upon her, the loyal Ryder prepared her spirit to become part of the ever-moving flow of energy that was the Ley, but the wicked darkness that had contaminated her physical being robbed her even of that final release and as she drew her last breath, its dark sorcery froze her final thoughts and awareness like a bug caught in amber within her lifeless skull.

In the unwatched shadows of that dank alleyway, the unthinking Golem twitched its antennae eagerly as it went about completing the task it had been given. Carefully, it circled round the Ryder's corpse, using its dexterous mandibles and feelers to search her clothing and purses until with a whir of excited triumph, it discovered the crystal containing the same dark power that gave it life. This it snapped up in a flash, storing it safely away in a concealed compartment in its underbelly. The malicious energy trapped in the heart of the quartz pulsed and vibrated powerfully as it felt itself surrounded by the flow of the matching life-force of the Golem. Its vitalised awareness heightened the magical activity that animated the iron automaton making it hunger for life the way a dog hungered for blood at the first taste of raw meat. With a violent clank of clogs, the metal beast leapt on to the dead woman's chest and plunged its iron fangs into her still warm throat. As the scarlet blood oozed over them, it carried with it the final echoes of her thoughts, feelings and consciousness, the last stirrings of her soul. It was this and not her blood that the Golem gorged itself on, the golden gleam of enchantment burning more intensely over its iron workings as it feasted. With its hunger satisfied, it then withdrew like a fleeting shadow into the night eager to return to its mistress.

Chapter 14

A Bottleful of Midnight

Aarold lay flat on his back beneath the silk sheets and satin comforter of his bed, trying very hard to be silent. The whole palace was commanded by the still, black peace of night, at rest and slumbering from the humble quarters of the maids and servants just above the kitchen to Master Grahmbere as he rested from a day of study and intellectual work in his chamber in the highest tower. Every mind and body was at peace in dreams except for one. The young heir to the throne's mind was acutely awake and buzzing with excited notions of what lay ahead. His heart pattered impatiently in his chest as he ran through the order of his scheme one last time to dispel any disheartening doubts that could hold him back. He must not let fear freeze his actions and keep him trapped within the cosseted gilded cage that had been his home for the past fifteen years. If he was ever going to rule as sovereign he had to prove himself more than a crippled weakling. He had to show that intellectual skills and mental ability could form as fit a monarch as the battle flair and brute strength of his late father. Thus he had concocted a plan to prove to all that knew him his worthiness of the crown. If a prince must take on a quest to receive his birthright, so be it, but Aarold would do so on his own terms.

When he was sure that the lateness of the hour had drawn a sleepy lid over every watchful eye, the young prince quietly pushed back the covers and carefully eased himself out of bed. Due to the damaging effect sunlight was said to have on his pallid complexion, night-time was the only time his nurses allowed the curtains to his chambers to be drawn and through the exposed window, a broad beam of silvery-white moonlight illuminated Aarold's familiar surroundings as clearly to his vision as the sun would have done. Perched on the edge of his mattress, the prince took a moment to survey the comforts that had been both his pleasure and prison: the countless books stacked neatly row upon row that had given only tantalising glimpses of a world he never knew, the map pinned on the wall charted the lands of his father's glorious conquests, numerous folios of his own sketches and writings, outpourings from his alert and frustrated mind. All this he was going to leave behind that night, as he ventured from the safe environment that had been his sanctuary into the dangerous real world.

Across the room, silhouetted by the moonlight where it rested on Aarold's desk, stood the broad square outline of his most treasured possession and the one that would give him the means to escape the palace: his chest of magical tools, potions and ingredients. Since being presented with it on his ninth birthday by his tutor, Aarold had spent innumerable hours studying the means to perform different spells and enchantments. In quiet investigation at his desk, untroubled by his physical limitations, he had discovered how to change the outward appearance of objects, make them appear to vanish in midair, conjure fire and water out of nothing, never guessing that such gifts would hold the key to his freedom. But once the bold notion had been ignited in his brain, the idea that he had the abilities to alter his fate had burnt with a fierce white light too potent to ignore and ferociously he began work on the necessary preparations. Now all was ready for him to put his plan into action.

Taking up his cane from where it rested against his bedstead, Aarold slowly eased himself to his feet. A sudden but expected tremble of weakness and pain darted through the wasted muscles of his right shin as they did every time he rose from his bed as if to make him remember the vulnerability of his state and what a risk he was taking. Swiftly he braced his bodyweight on his cane and bedpost, slowly stretching out the tight ligaments of his offending limb until the spasm and pain ceased.

No, he thought bitterly, as his leg once more came under his control, *I am a noble prince, damn it. I will not be dictated to by my own body!* Then with quiet, deliberate steps, he made his way across to the stool that was directly in front of the small cabinet and sat down ready to start work.

The richly polished mahogany box sat before him like a secret friend patiently waiting for him in the moonlight. The feelings of frustration and physical pain that had tortured Aarold moments before instantly ebbed away as he settled himself, and a warm sensation of pride and capability filled his chest. Sorcery took strength of mind and clarity of thought; it was something he had mastered despite his impairments and no fussing of doctors or worrying of his aunt could take that away from him. With confident hands, the young prince turned the key in the brass lock and opened the twin doors of the casket to reveal the dozens of miniature drawers and neatly stacked glass vials containing various powders, potions and fragments of dried plant and animal samples. A contented smile settled on Aarold's sallow face as he indulged himself by taking in his orderly catalogued and sorted collection before beginning the serious task in hand.

From a rack fitted to the inside of the left door, he carefully took a small bottle fashioned from pale, smoky blue glass and held it up to examine in the light of the moon. Inside, he could just make out the faint impression of the complex potion he had been carefully brewing in the past few days, clearer than water itself, glistening lightly in the glow of the moon. To his well-studied eye, the elixir appeared to be exactly as his books described and he prayed that years of learning had not been put to waste now that the time had come. Uncorking it, Aarold thoughtfully sniffed the contents to reassure his judgement. The odour of the brew was subtle, a barely detectable scent of night-time, indistinct and airy, just as it had been described in the tome he had found the spell in. Quietly pleased with his own skills, Aaorld placed the open phial atop the cabinet, in direct light of the moon. The pastel beams of the lunar orb sparkled metallic in the translucent liquid as the prince focused his gaze on the pale sphere in the sky above and uttered the incantation he had memorised by heart.

'Moon-glow of the midnight air, shield me from unwanted stare. Be my cloak, my shoe, my helm, as I travel through your realm.'

Apprehensively, the young prince dropped his eyes from the moon to the glass receptacle he had placed before the open window. The potion appeared still and unchanged by the final part of the ritual and for a brief second he feared he had got something wrong. Then he recalled that the spell had said that it took a few minutes of exposure to the moon for the magic to be fully effective, and aware that a watched kettle never boils moved on to the second part of his plan.

Opening a drawer in the desk, Aarold rifled through his collection of papers as quietly as he could before finding the two sketches he required. Putting one to one side, he smoothed out the second to inspect his handiwork and check he was entirely happy before he began; the drawing had to be perfect if the spell was to work. On the smooth parchment, rendered skilfully in ink by Aarold's own hand, was a depiction of a peddler dressed in modest garments and a simple, dark cape. His dark hair fell loosely around his shoulders and his features were strong and masculine but not overly handsome. Taking his quill in hand, Aarold regarded his work critically. The peddler, like him, possessed a wasted leg and stood with the aid of a simple wooden cane. These were unfortunately necessary details to include, for the simple glamour of magic could not strengthen lame muscles or misshapen bone, much as the prince longed that it could. He had toyed with the vanity of making the peddler rakishly handsome, but this was a passing fancy and would not aid him in his quest in the slightest. A compromise to his adolescent self-awareness had been to give the sketch a neatly trimmed beard and moustache, something Aarold had struggled to grow with any real success. He added the last finishing touches to the portrait with a few flourishes of his pen, before gently blowing the ink dry. His disguise was complete.

Aarold's heart caught unexpectedly in his chest as he realised what he was doing. Tonight, for the first time in his life, using the guise of this peddler, he would leave the safety of the palace and witness what lay beyond. He was briefly aware of the countless misfortunes that could befall him not to mention the rage and disappointment of his aunt when he did return. Realistically the whole scheme was madness but Aarold knew that if he did not do something to prove his own capability he would soon go insane.

Pushing all doubt to one side with the notion that he would not be entirely alone in the city and that he would take the utmost care, Aarold reached into a small compartment of his casket and took out a short thick brush and a box of polished dark wood. Careful not to spill the precious contents, he unscrewed the circular lid to reveal a finely ground powder of multicoloured granules, like flecks gathered from every corner of life. Aarold recalled using this reliable glamour several times before, to transform objects and animals under Master Grahmbere's careful instruction, but he had never before applied it to himself. He had to judge the quantity just right. Too little and the disguise would not cover him at all, too much and he would appear a comical parody that would fool no-one.

Diligently, he tapped out a measure of the powder on to a blank corner of his sketch and holding his breath with concentration, he began to sweep it across the line drawing with the soft bristles of the brush, his motions deliberate as he recalled the complex pattern of gestures. The coloured particles glittered and swirled over the image of the peddler as Aarold pushed them, first upwards and downwards and then in broad spirals, his determination set on reaching his goal. Shadows and shading within the drawing seemed to alter as the prince worked the bristles across it, before, slowly, hardly noticeably, the dark lines of black ink began to fade and grow less distinct as they were absorbed by the grains. Aarold's excitement grew as he worked and witnessed his drawing slowly vanish into the powder. The bristles of the brush twitched with static energy as they moved through the powder, telling him that the image had not been simply deleted but drawn into the granules themselves, the shape and design of it held like a memory ready to exist again. With one last serpentine movement, he removed the final pale imprint of his drawing before sweeping the glistening dust into a neat pile in the centre of the parchment. His new persona was ready. Shifting around in his seat, Aarold turned to gaze into the long gilt-framed mirror that hung on the wall. From within the glass stared back a pale and unremarkable-looking youth, with weak features and mousy locks. A faint, ironic smile tugged at the prince's lips as he saw himself. 'Farewell, Your Majesty,' he murmured. Then taking the brush in hand, he gathered a thick coating of powder from the parchment and began to sweep it across his face. Fragments of glittering colour fell into his eyes, blurring his vision, and particles of glamour tickled his sensitive nostrils, giving him the urge to sneeze, but Aarold continued to paste the enchantment over his features. The magic pulled and pressed at his skin in the most peculiar way, giving a not unpleasant sensation of thousands upon thousands of tiny fingers manipulating the tendons of his face into a new configuration. He wrinkled his nose as he felt it tweaked and pressed to be shorter and broader and scratched an irritation on his jaw-line only to find his chin was now covered by thick whiskers.

Blinking hard, he paused to examine his reflection and was greatly amused to see a ruddy faced and decidedly more masculine lad gazing back at him, his skin tanned from the sun, and hair and beard a healthy chestnut. Aarold stifled a triumphant chuckle to see his visage come to life as he thought of the shock on the faces of his aunt and nurses to see this rough and ready stranger in the prince's bedchamber.

Eager to complete the illusion, he reloaded his brush and began to coat the rest of his body, nightshirt and all with the powder. His pride and joy grew as he watched the spell darken his pallid arms and hands to a more healthy shade and transform the fine white silk of his nightshirt into the simple, dowdy robes of a common peddler. Finally, with the last flakes of powder, he coated his walking stick until the expensive ivory cane was turned to an unremarkable wooden staff. Then carefully drawing himself to his feet, Aarold took a few steps towards the mirror to examine his transformation.

The dark-skinned fellow looking back at him was a complete stranger and not someone you would give a second glance to as he moved through the streets and squares of the city. The only fragments of the sickly prince that remained were his startling blue eyes: bright with excitement and wonder at his own achievement. He touched his rough cheek, feeling the flesh of his face and the numerous hairs of his beard, as real as if they truly belonged to him. Spurred on by his success, Aarold hobbled back over to his desk and set about completing his work.

Meticulously, he tucked the other sketch and the pot of transformation powder into his leather satchel before doing a swift stocktake of the other potions in his cabinet to see if there was anything else that might prove useful. His lessons in magic had given him the ability to concoct a number of practical spells that could conjure fire out of thin air or bring about deep sleep, and aware that it was foolish to venture out on a quest unarmed he collected together a selection of these vials and pouches into his satchel.

During the planning of the journey, Aarold's mind had wandered to the mighty broadsword that had been his father's trusted weapon in many a skirmish. Should he, Aarold had pondered, steal into the royal armoury and take the blade for his own protection? However, he had quickly dismissed this idea as ridiculous. The sword was half his weight and he did not possess the strength to lift it from its stand, let alone wield it in battle. No, his weapons would be of his own creation: spells and decoys mastered by thought not muscle.

Tucking the last bottle carefully away, Aarold locked the cabinet and glanced nervously at the bottle he had left resting in the moonlight. Where moments before it appeared almost full, the clear glass now showed no tell-tale line of liquid and the young prince knew the spell was ready. Taking it down, he screwed an ionizer into the neck, and stomach churning with nerves stood up. In the dim gleam of the moonlight that illuminated his room, within the guise of a commoner he had skilfully crafted, the crippled prince squeezed the bulb of the ionizer, sending a light mist of silvery droplets of shadow and night into the air. Tilting his face upwards, Aarold watched as the microscopic fragments descended over his form like a soft, unseen cloak of ebony feathers. Darkness clung to him, swathing him in mute shadows and night until he became like a ghost venturing into the world of the living. As long as bright light did not break the spell, he was as transparent as the wind. Clothed in the veil of shadow, Aarold moved as swiftly as his lame leg would allow across his bedchamber and through the crack in the half-open door. The passageway beyond was black, still and peaceful, strangely unfamiliar through the cloudy filter of his invisibility. Cautiously, he made his way down the corridor, senses alert for anyone who might discover him. He felt like a bandit in his own home, an unwanted phantom boldly stepping through the hallowed halls of the palace, alive and daring for the first time in his life. His uneven footsteps and muffled tap of his cane against the plush carpet seemed unbelievably loud within the empty halls as he battled with all the physical control he had to place his feet and cane lightly.

Suddenly he froze beneath the camouflage of his shadow-cape, aware of another set of footsteps making their way towards him. His muscles grew taut with fear and with stiff, spasmodic steps, he tottered deeper into the shadows behind one of the oversized painted vases that lined the passageway. His weak leg jerked painfully, threatening to tip him off balance and he just grabbed the wall in time as the stooped and shuffling figure of the aged night porter came around the corner. The dour-faced servant trudged through the dark corridor, candlestick tightly clasped in his hand as he muttered moodily to himself about the numerous chores he was responsible for. Aarold held his breath and pushed himself tightly into the shadows as he watched the bobbing fiery glow of the taper carried by the old man. His invisibility enchantment was a delicate disguise only giving him cover under moon and starlight; the bright beam of a candle would destroy it and all his hard work would be for nothing. The elderly man crept closer, narrow green eyes sweeping every nook of the passage for signs of needed maintenance or unwanted vermin, lowering his torch to examine the skirting boards. 'Have to have a word with them maids, I will,' he grumbled to himself, pausing only a few feet away from where Aarold was hiding. 'Filthy here, it is; will be getting rats and 'er duchess will be blaming me.'

His body froze as if suddenly aware that he was not alone and he sniffed the air. The prince's mind whirred to conceive a plan to send the porter on his way and furtively he reached into his satchel and removed the cork from an empty vial. Careful not to shift into the revealing glow of the candle, he threw the stopper as hard as he could down the corridor. The projectile bounced and rolled across the carpet, ricocheting off the walls and once hitting an ornamental vase with a loud ding. At once, the porter spun in the direction of the noise, his candle held aloft, his eyes gleaming in triumphant. 'Rats!' he declared in a hateful whisper. 'I knew it! Little blighters! That does it, I'm getting the traps!' With that he turned on his heel and swiftly shuffled back in the direction he had come from in search of vermin.

Unseen beneath his shadow cowl, Aarold pressed his hand to his mouth to stifle a victorious chuckle. The decoy had worked. He barely dared believe it but it did seem that his wiles really equipped him to make his escape. At that glorious moment, the impairments of his body seemed no handicap at all and his blood sang with adrenaline. He remained perfectly still for a moment, waiting for the porter and his bothersome candle to completely vanish from sight before once more leaning on his cane and continuing his journey down the corridor.

He was even more alert now, barely daring to breathe in case he was overheard. Somewhere in the back of his mind, he was aware that his leg hurt, but his excitement and pride was at such a height it hardly troubled him. Recklessly, he partly wished that his aunt or one of the nurses would discover him so that he could look them straight in the eye and declare, *Yes, he was Prince Aarold of Geoll and he could achieve greatness.* But he knew that it would take more than an unseen stroll along the palace corridors to prove this.

At last he reached his destination: alongside the life-sized portrait of his father at the same age he was now, caught in the viral flush of his boyish youth, astride his favourite chestnut hunting mare. Pausing, Aarold took a moment to glance up at the brightly shining eyes of his deceased and distant father and for the first time in his life felt an affinity pass between them. Would Elkric be proud of his son's bold bid for freedom? Aarold truly did not know or really care; his father had certainly never displayed any sign of parental pride during his lifetime.

Without any further consideration for his father's opinion, Aarold placed his hand on the right of the gilt frame and gave a firm but gentle tug. With a whining creak, the painting swung away from the wall to reveal a narrow staircase leading into cold darkness. Aarold's heart trembled with apprehension as he peered downwards before swallowing hard and shuffling into the hidden exit, allowing the picture to swing back into place. Alone and blind in the blackness of the corridor, the prince steeled his nerve. This, he had known, was going to be the most tricky and dangerous stage of his plan and if he allowed his impairment or fear to overcome him it could mean deathly peril. If he put a foot wrong or his lame leg gave way he could tumble down the whole staircase without anyone to come to his aid. Cautiously, he reached out his free hand and gripped hold of the rough wall before tapping his cane forward to find the edge of the step. With slow and deliberate movements that made his muscles throb, he lowered himself on to the next step, making absolutely sure his balance was secure before repeating the torturous process. He edged downwards in this manner for what seemed like hours but was probably only a matter of a dozen paces or so before fear and vertigo froze him motionless on the dark staircase, his muscles too weak to go on. Aarold gripped the uneven stonework, his head disorientated by the blinding darkness and the ligaments in his wasted limbs twitching with the threat of collapse. This was too perilous; there had to be a better way. With slow, deliberate movements, Aarold lowered himself until he was seated securely on the step, his feet resting on the one below. At once his body felt more stable and his courage returned. With his cane resting across his lap, he felt for the edge of the step he was sitting on and taking his weight on his arms he cautiously lifted himself down on to the next ledge. This movement felt a great deal safer and easier than descending on foot, and despite his temporary blindness Aarold quickly got into a rhythm of shuffling from one stair to the next, using his legs only for secondary balance.

The journey down continued at a good pace in this manner with little threat of accident although after some time the lifting made the prince's arms begin to throb with effort. It was a good type of pain, however, not caused by his ailment but by his own labour and physical exertion, the type of ache that would leave his body stronger. The stone beneath him felt cold and damp and his soft palms soon were grated by the uneven texture of the steps against his skin. After what seemed like hours of toil, the gloom of the passage was enlightened by a narrow shaft of starlight seeping in through a crack beneath the door. Aarold's pulse quickened as he pressed forward, bumping eagerly down the last remaining steps until he could at last feel the wooden portal with the toe of his outstretched boot. Knowing that he was now at the foot of the staircase, he took his cane in hand again and stiffly hauled himself up. His muscles silently shrieked with discomfort as he stretched and shifted himself into a standing position but Aarold felt too proud to care; after conquering the challenge of the staircase he felt like there was no problem posed by his body that his mind could not overcome.

Pushing open the doorway that led out into the stable block, Aarold blinked as his eyes became accustomed to the silvery moonlight after the hopeless blackness of the stairway. The courtyard stood empty and still in the midnight hour and the night was silent but for the distant call of an owl and the peaceful snores of the slumbering animals. Unseen beneath his cowl of moonlit sorcery, the prince swiftly crossed the square to the far corner where Phebus's stall was housed. As deftly as he could and still unsure what his old friend's reaction would be to this midnight flit, Aarold slid back the bolt and slipped inside.

The Equile was snoozing peacefully on a bed of hay, a plush blanket covering his scaly hide as he muttered in his dreams. Reaching into a pocket of his tunic, Aarold pulled out a small silver tinder box and struck the flint. The tiny orange flame sprung to life, causing Aarold's aura of invisibility to disintegrate in a flurry of pale iridescent light, leaving him visible in his conjured guise.

The sudden flicker of flame disturbed Phebus's peaceful slumber and the creature snorted grumpily, flickering open his heavy leathery eyelids. Sight blurred by sleep, he glanced around his stable to see the unfamiliar figure of the bearded peddler looming towards him. With a snort and cry of alarm, Phebus scrambled to his feet, his ears pricked with shock and he lashed out with one of his front claws to strike his assailant.

'Intruder!' he cried in a throaty, fearful tone. 'Kidnapper! Summon the guards, we're under attack!' His polished beak frothed with specks of foam and his scarlet pupils flashed fearfully as he searched for assistance.

Aarold stumbled sideways, caught off guard by his friend's sudden outburst. Gripping the wall of the stable to gain his balance, he raised his hand peacefully and tried to calm the Equile before his cries brought unwanted attention. 'Phebus!' he hissed urgently as the beast glared at him. 'Calm yourself, it is I, your friend Aarold.' Ignoring the prince's pleas, Phebus stalked forward menacingly, stabbing the air with his sharp beak. 'Vile footpad,' he shrieked. 'You, sir, have tangled with the wrong Equile! I just happen to be the good acquaintance and loyal steed of His Royal Highness Prince Aarold and if anything were to happen to me, *well!*'

Careful to avoid Phebus's dangerous bill, Aarold reached forward to clasp the creature's head firmly but gently in his hands. 'Phebus, it *is* me Aarold,' he hushed, reaching under Phebus's chin to scratch him in the place he always did. 'Look into my eyes, hear my voice. I am merely masked by a glamour to hide my identity.' The spooked creature ceased his cries for aid and regarded the intruder more closely, realisation dawning on his features as he recognised Aarold's deep sapphire eyes.

'Aarold, dear boy?' he queried in disbelief.

The prince smiled proudly at the effectiveness of his disguise and stepped back so that Phebus could see it fully. 'It is an enchantment formulated by my own hand,' he explained as the shaken Equile curiously poked at his ragged cape with his beak.

'Convincing, is it not?' Taking a cautious step forward, Phebus quizzically sniffed Aarold's now-chestnut hair.

'Well, yes, old chap, it is,' he said eventually, when his suspicion was fully eased. 'But the purpose of such a ruse is, I confess, beyond me. If this is your idea of some prank I fail to see the humour in it. It is at best appalling taste and at worst foolish recklessness! Wandering around in the pitch of night dressed as some vagabond, what were you thinking in playing such a joke?'

Aarold felt his stomach tighten as he prepared to reveal his plan.

'No joke, Pheb,' he told him in a grave, serious tone. 'I have made this disguise so that I can travel unnoticed. I'm leaving the palace to explore the city, just as we spoke of. I have my spells and charms for protection and I'm leaving tonight.'

The Equile's jaw dropped open at his friend's bold confession as he tossed his long neck. 'Oh my dear boy,' he exclaimed with a mix of despair and pity. 'That was merely pie-in-the-sky, idle speculation between friends, a theory not to be turned into practice, surely? You'd be mad to consider it as anything more. You can't be fully *compos mentis* if you believe such a venture is feasible; you must be coming down with a fever. Let me feel your brow.' He attempted to press his beak gently against Aarold's forehead but the prince crossly batted him away.

'I am not sick, Phebus! Or if I am it is a sickness of boredom, a sickness of lethargy. An illness of being shut in this damn palace day after day with no means of proving that I am more than an invalid. Well, no more, my friend. I am going to prove to my aunt and doctors that I am master of my own fortune. I will leave this place tonight with or without your company.' The hushed rage in his voice surprised Aarold himself but he felt that it was legitimate. Too long had his frustration been silent and fruitless.

Phebus's red eyes brimmed with emotion and concern. It was astounding that such a brutal-looking beast could display such tenderness, but Phebus was a creature of deep loyalty and compassion. 'Aarold,' he pleaded, 'think for a moment I beg of you. The risk you're taking, your physical impairment. Surely you can see the danger. I could not live with myself if I left you in fate's careless hands. Your mother would never forgive me and your aunt would have my hide for riding boots if she knew.'

Touched by the animal's deep concern, Aarold affectionately scratched Phebus's neck. 'Then come with me,' he implored the shocked creature. 'Why else do you think I would tell you of my intentions if not to have you keep me company on such a journey? You are a fine steed and my most trusted friend. I would want no other comrade for protection and company.'

Disgusted by this bold suggestion, Phebus shuddered and gave his long neck a vigorous shake. 'The notion!' he snorted haughtily. 'I believe I have made my feelings on the risks of interaction with the lower classes quite clear!' Snootily, he pawed the ground. Wounded by his friend's cowardice, Aarold leaned heavily on his cane and began to move towards the door. 'Fine!' he hissed crossly, shooting Phebus an acidic glare. 'I will see you on my return.' His muscles tight with frustration and disappointment he began to turn away.

'Wait!' Phebus's urgent cry pierced the night dangerously clearly, sounding more like a wounded beast than an actual word. Aarold paused, more out of fear that the call had aroused unwanted attention than out of response to his friend's request.

Perturbed, Phebus glanced round his cosy stall, at his bed of fresh hay and velvet blanket and collection of half-read manuscripts and let out a weary sigh. 'I'll come,' he bleated unwillingly, trotting forward to Aarold's side, 'to warden you against any more spells of insane bravado. After all, *one* of us needs to be looking out for your personal safety.'

Grinning, the prince gave the morose Equile a grateful hug. 'Steadfast Pheb!' he whispered, giving the creature's horny neck ridge a firm rub. 'I knew you wouldn't let me down!'

The animal pursed his beak and gave Aarold a withering look as the prince rummaged in his satchel to retrieve the other sketch and the transformation powder. 'It begs the question who is more demented, the fool or the fool who follows him?' he remarked coolly, but Aarold did not hear. Already he had laid out his careful ink drawing of a sturdy chestnut pony and was sprinkling it with the magical compound that would turn it into a suitable disguise for his friend. Curious, Phebus leant his head over Aarold's shoulder and watched with great interest as he moved the fine multicoloured granules over the ink lines with the soft brush. 'And what, dare I ask, is this?' Unwilling to break concentration, Aarold paused, making sure to keep his brush carefully in place. 'A enchantment to make sure you're not spotted,' he explained.

'There are very few Equiles on the streets of Veridium. I have to disguise you as something more everyday.'

'As a horse!' cried Phebus, backing away in shock. 'One of those odorous, dim-brained animals! Oh, the shame! To trade my handsome scales and claws for common fur and clumsy hooves. You are fortunate I hold you in such kind regard to suffer this indignity!'

Straightening up, Aarold approached him with the heavily coated brush in hand. 'I know,' he hushed sympathetically, 'and I'm beyond grateful, dear, noble Phebus. When we return, I will buy you a bushel of gourmet sausages and a whole wheel of the best stilton as a reward for your friendship, I swear. Now hold still while I apply the charm.' Phebus shuddered slightly and looked distrustfully at the pile of bristles heavy with magic. 'Believe me, dear fellow, there isn't enough fine produce in the kingdom to compensate my humiliation. Now make haste with your foolhardy trickery before my sanity returns and I call for the guard.'

He braced himself forebodingly with rigid legs and eyes squeezed shut, as his friend gently began to dust the fine powder of transformation over his leathery hide. The enchanted granules shimmered slightly in the dull moonlight as Aarold meticulously applied them to Phebus's stocky form. In the dim shadows of the stable, the clever prince turned the creature's scaly, ebony hide into a dusty, chestnut pelt and his sharp beak into a soft-lipped muzzle. The bony ridge of horns that adorned his long neck loosened and fell into coils of coarse, black hair and in a few short moments Aarold found himself standing beside a rather ordinary looking pony. 'There!' he said proudly, tucking away the tools of his sorcery into his satchel, 'finished, and what a fine horse you make too!'

Phebus apprehensively opened his eyes, which although still remained deep red were now shielded by long, thick lashes. 'Mmm,' he pondered doubtfully, 'let's see the damage!' Slightly unwillingly, he turned away from Aarold and clopped over to his water trough to inspect his refection. Peering up from the black surface of liquid was the image of a sturdy beast of burden. 'Oh my stars,' he murmured in shock, touching the water gently with his newly pliable mouth. 'What do I look like? My own mother wouldn't know me.'

Smiling proudly at another spell successfully performed, Aarold limped over to his side to admire the picture of a common peddler and his faithful steed reflected in the trough. 'We'll be perfectly safe in the city looking like this and back home before you know it.'

Phebus sighed crossly, and self-consciously stomped his newly formed hooves on the ground. 'How is one supposed to perform the simplest of tasks with these blundering appendages?' he complained, kicking out his legs in the attempt to pick up a stray quill lying on the ground. 'No wonder horses are such foolish creatures. Any attempt at high art or skill is impossible.'

Carefully seizing hold of Phebus's mane, Aarold awkwardly hoisted himself up on to the creature's broad back, Phebus dipping slightly as he always did to allow his rider better ease swinging his weak leg into place. 'Horses don't write,' he huffed, slightly out of breath from climbing up, 'and they usually can't talk either so try and keep your voice down if we're in a crowd or people will get suspicious.'

'Oh nay nay whinny snort!' Phebus uttered tartly as Aarold secured his cane in the baldric across his back. 'My opinions fall mostly on deaf ears as it is. I knew it was only a matter of time before I was condemned to full muteness. And do you mind not yanking on my mane quite so hard. Hair is more sensitive to pain than horn.'

Willingly, Aarold loosened his grasp on the coarse dark hair. 'Sorry,' he said earnestly, reaching into his satchel to retrieve the ionizer of invisibility potion. 'Now, by my reckoning, the three o'clock guard will be taking their post any minute. That will mean the gate will be open and we can slip out behind them.' He felt his heart quicken with the excitement of their impending escape. 'Are you ready for an adventure, old friend?'

'No,' came the sardonic reply from beneath him, 'I am being press-ganged into one by a lunatic!'

Pointing the nozzle of the ionizer upwards, Aarold gave the small bulb a gentle squeeze and sent a fine cloud of misty silver and shadow into the air over them both. Phebus gave a little shudder as the delicate enchantment of midnight fell like a shower of ebony feathers over their bodies, merging them into nothingness with the moonlight. Cloaked once more with the fabric of night, Aarold's stomach knotted with apprehension and eagerly he gave Phebus a little kick in the sides to urge him out of the comfort of his stable. Phebus heaved a sigh as if to say the escapade had already exhausted him, and giving his safe and cosy abode one last longing glance, trotted unwillingly out into the moonlight.

Like ghosts from another time, the pair crossed the gravel yard and passed on to the wide pale path that meandered through the palace's immaculate gardens to the high stone wall and ornate iron gateway that separated the privileged royal household from the common city. Aarold gazed wide-eyed around him as he rode, feeling as if his shield of invisibility also bestowed him with fresh vision, seeing the familiar landscape of lawns, borders and statues for the first time. Seated comfortably astride Phebus's broad back, his leg did not hurt and he felt more at ease in his enchanted disguise than he had done in his normal robes of velvet and satin. An inner voice seemed to be calling him, from somewhere unknown beyond the palace walls, drawing him to follow his true destiny. Soon they were close enough to the gate to see the pair of guards, dressed in their surcoats of scarlet and gold, each with a halberd gripped rigidly at their side as they flanked the gate. Aarold regarded them jealously for a moment as he often did, envious of their muscular limbs and broad shoulders, but then reminded himself that strength came in many forms; surely the fact that he had managed to get this far unseen proved that he had cunning and talents of his own? He gave Phebus a light tug on the mane to indicate he should halt. Leaning forward, he whispered in his ear, 'We'll wait here until they open the gates to let the next shift through then pass through unseen.'

Phebus snorted briskly to show he understood and together they waited like unnoticed shadows in the moonlight for what seemed like an age. Then the still of the night was disturbed by heavy boots approaching from the same direction they had come and glancing over his shoulder, Aarold saw two more soldiers approaching. Blood seemed to sing in his ears and all his senses seemed to come alive as he readied himself to make their escape. The potion of moonlight made him as transparent as the wind, but Aarold had never felt so solid, so real, so alive! As the guards passed by, one of the men turned his eyes in their direction, gazing straight at them. Time seemed to freeze and Aarold felt so filled with adrenaline he thought his heart might stop. Too frightened to move, he knotted his fingers in Phebus's mane and stared boldly back at the guard until the man looked away again and carried on towards the gate.

Aarold felt as if this was not really happening, as if he was in a dream and would wake up any moment in his safe cosseted chambers, frustrated and impotent once more. As if in slow motion, he witnessed the huge, gilt gates swing open to allow the changing of the guard and seized the moment to dig his heels in and urge Phebus with an excited whisper. 'Now, Pheb, as quickly as you dare!'

The Equile trotted forward at a swift but cautious pace. The prince clung on tightly to his friend's mane, barely daring to breathe as Phebus passed unseen right under the watchful gaze of the palace sentinels. Terrified that the guards would at any moment realise what was happening, Aarold kept looking furtively at the men as they passed between them. A tiny doubting part of him desperately wanted his escape to be noticed, for the guards to suddenly become aware that their vulnerable master had fled from the safety of the palace and escort him back to his chambers where nothing could befall him. However for the most part this childish fear was overridden by an immense pride and thrill, a sense that as he left the royal grounds he was also leaving behind his restricted childhood and finally becoming a man.

He rode for what seemed like forever, exhilaration and the dread of his plan failing at the last moment causing the muscles of his torso to cramp and making him crouch forward as if they were galloping along like the wind, despite Phebus keeping a relatively sedate pace. Finally, he felt the Equile draw to a halt and took this to mean that they were safely through the gate. They had made it!

'Aarold! Aarold, my boy. Are you quite all right?' Phebus's whisper was filled with panic and deep concern.

Sitting upright, Aarold felt his spasms of fear and adrenaline ease at last and all the tension of their daring flight was released suddenly in a flood of emotion. He looked to the moon high above that had gifted them their cloak of invisibility and laughed with a youthful joy he could not remember feeling before.

'We did it, Phebs! We did it!' he hissed in an enthusiastic whisper. Twisting round, he stared back at the palace which now lay a few hundred feet down the road, looking as gilded and unreal as a drawing in a child's picture book.

Phebus followed his master's gaze, gracefully bending his long neck to look mournfully back at their luxurious home. 'Yes,' he mused glumly, 'you've certainly done something!'

Aarold was in no mood for his friend's foreboding sentiments. The night air was fresh and cool in his lungs and all around him streets and alleyways stretched out like the thread of a spider's web, filled with shops, houses, taverns and other wonders he had yet to know. The city, his city, was filled with mystery and adventure and the young prince was ready to face every last moment of it!

Chapter 15

SIEGE OF SHADOWS

A light, autumn mist hung in the air around the town of Goodstone, a dark moisture that filled the atmosphere, too light to be called drizzle but thicker than fog. In the library of the Ryders' citadel, Sister Amethyst moved her candle to the small eyelet window to inspect the troubled weather, before pulling the shutter firmly closed and returning to the piles of ancient manuscripts and scrolls she had been studying. Easing herself back on to her stool, she took one of the small honey cakes from the plate on her desk (a slight indulgence of comfort she allowed herself in her dotage) and took a small bite, chewing it slowly as she mulled over the rushing river of thoughts that challenged her wise and experienced mind.

Amethyst had been a Ryder longer than most of the women who dwelt within the citadel had drawn breath. She found it hard to recall a time when the benevolent Ley had not been her teacher and companion. Years of discipline and training had made it near impossible to distinguish Its quiet voice from that of her own consciousness and now they dwelt together as contented old friends. The Ley had brought her a long and fulfilling life but in the past few weeks Amethyst had felt within Its flow an urgent and chilling note that was unknown to her. There was a new mood in Its rhythm, a dark and desperate threat of change and danger that had troubled Amethyst. Now a new apprentice had joined their order. From the moment she had looked into the mute girl's eyes Amethyst knew that this young woman had been touched by fate in a way that went beyond even her great understanding. Amethyst realised it was imperative to know whether her suspicions were true; her vision of the young woman's path was cloudy and it would be foolish to jump to assumptions that had lain for so long as nothing more than myth and legend.

She sighed and briefly closed her eyes. A lifetime as mistress and servant to the Ley had blessed her with a certain amount of foresight into her own future and that of others. There were moments when she could see destiny with crystal clear insight while others left her unsure. But it seemed the Ley's will was only to reveal the sorrows that lay in the coming months, not give her the answers as to how they were to be resolved. The picture was only partly shown to her, but there had to be a reason for that.

'So be the Ley's will,' she muttered wearily to herself.

Suddenly she felt a great surge of melancholy sweep over her, weakening her resolute spirit and reminding her she was a woman in her winter days. An image of Bracken, her beloved ward, swept into her mind and she was overcome with feelings of affection and pride for the maid she had raised as her own. Reaching into a pocket of her purple robes, she fingered the small parcel she had prepared earlier that evening. The Ley did not reveal all things to her, but one fact Amethyst could sense was that soon their paths would part and Bracken, like the newcomer Petronia, would be forced to follow her own vocation.

A sharp rap on the chamber door interrupted her deep thoughts. Wiping a stray tear from her eye, Amethyst composed herself and pushed her personal sorrows to one side. 'Come in,' she stated clearly.

The door swung open and into the gloomy library stepped Garnet and Rosequartz, dressed respectively in their robes of earthy brown and pale pink. They both bowed respectfully to the older Ryder. 'You wished to speak with us, Sister Amethyst?' asked Garnet.

Giving a smiling welcome, Amethyst gestured to the bench across from her and bid them sit. 'Yes, good Sisters,' she said pleasantly. 'I am aware that in the past few days I have been somewhat busy and we have not had the opportunity to chat. I wish to remedy that. Tell me, has your stay here been restful?' Garnet and Rosequartz glanced at each other. Everyone who knew Amethyst knew that she was a Ryder of great wisdom and knowledge who rarely wasted words on idle banter. 'Yes,' Garnet replied at last, 'your hospitality has been most gracious, Sister; we thank you.'

Amethyst rested her fingertips lightly together to form an arch. 'And you both feel in good health, physically and mentally?' she continued. 'Received healing for any minor ailments that have been troubling you?'

Slowly Rosequartz nodded, unsure of the crux of Amethyst's questioning. 'Both Sister Garnet and myself are in rude health.'

The elder Ryder smiled with satisfaction at this answer. 'Excellent,' she said before looking down at the myriad of ancient parchments that littered the table. Her warm expression melted away for a moment and both Garnet and Rosequartz saw concern etch her weathered features. 'I wish to ask you,' she said, trying to keep her tone relaxed, 'what is your opinion on our two young apprentices? As their primary tutor I am somewhat biased; it would help me to get other views.' Both Ryders fell into an unnerved silence and restlessly Rosequartz wrapped one of her long auburn braids round her fingers. The Ley flowed clearly through their minds, as It had done the night that they had first seen Petronia's gifts but like Amethyst, prudence made it hard for them to speak out. Finally, Rosequartz tactfully began. 'Regarding our dear foundling babe, Bracken,' she started, hoping the slow approach would bring them to the matter of the other girl more easily. 'You must know how deeply fond I am of her. All the Sisterhood love her dearly. I know she has been struggling to find her Calling in the Ley, but truly she has a willing mind and pure heart. She is a credit to you.'

Rosequartz's kind words tugged at Amethyst's heart and she momentarily felt wistful. How, she pondered, had sixteen summers passed in a twinkling of an eye turning that sorry mewling infant she had found on the cold plains into a kind and hard-working young woman? 'Yes, I thank the Ley for allowing me to know and raise her,' she murmured softly to herself, before adding more firmly, 'but I was thinking more of the most recent individual to come to us, the mute child Petronia; tell me your impressions of her character. It was, after all, you who the Ley sent to bring her to my tutorage.' A tense atmosphere hung heavy in the air of the dimly lit study; the strong guiding flow of the power that the three women had devoted their lives to filled each of their minds with a fearful knowledge that seemed to reach beyond their understanding. All of them were aware of the potent issue that hovered over the silent girl and knew that it could no longer be ignored.

Amethyst leant forward and peered at her Sister Ryders with gentle and encouraging eyes. 'I know you both made a Blood Promise to protect her,' she stated softly, 'and you would have not done so lightly, or if you thought she had average potential. You both saw something more in her than a mere aptitude to sense the Ley.' Rosequartz and Garnet exchanged knowing looks, somewhat relieved they no longer had to bear the burden of their suspicions alone. It was a blessing on Ley followers that often Ryders' minds would become attune to each other without need for speech. All three of them now shared the same sentiment.

Rosequartz exhaled a relieved sigh. 'She is remarkable,' she confessed. 'Sister Amethyst, in all my years of devotion to the Ley I have never seen a woman with such innate talent for the qualities of crystals. They seem to fly to her fingers as if drawn there by some power she isn't aware of. She knows their uses without being told, seemingly without even thinking. It's astounding to witness.' The silver-haired Ryder nodded in agreement. 'I feel the same. As a teacher, one does not like to show too much shock at their pupils' gifts as it can cultivate both arrogance and fear of failure. But it is true I have never seen an apprentice so in tune with the Ley. It's almost inhuman.'

'A wild soul,' Garnet chimed in almost before she was aware she had spoken. Amethyst looked at her, her head tilted thoughtfully to one side. Outside, the wind howled in the distance. 'An interesting choice of phrase, Sister Garnet,' she said with a small amused smile, 'but an appropriate one. Indeed, Mistress Petronia does seem to be more akin to the spirits of nature than most.'

Pausing in contemplation, she carefully flicked through the selection of ancient documents lain out before her, grey eyes meticulously skimming the lettering inscribed by Ryders long since passed. 'I wonder,' she murmured thoughtfully, 'if either of you can recall from your own apprenticeships, learning about the first Ryder to bear the Stone Name Obsidian.' Rosequartz frowned for a moment then shook her head. 'I was never the most academic of students, Sister Amethyst,' she said with a rueful chuckle. 'You of all people should remember that!'

'I recall something,' Garnet said, her dark brows knitting together as she searched her memory for the lessons of her adolescence. 'They called her Obsidian the Oracle, said the Ley blessed her with the gift of divinity, a great scribe. But weren't her writings viewed as mainly fables, moral lessons to guide the conscience rather than hard predictions of future events?'

Uncurling a roll of paper, Amethyst gently ran her fingers along the lines of text. 'Many Ryders choose to believe that. But what if we did take her writings as literal, true predictions of what was to come? I would like you both to consider this passage.' She pointed out a section of text and both Garnet and Rosequartz leant forward to read it. The words and figures were faint, faded with time and dirt and in places blurred and smudged till they were illegible, but in the soft glow of the candlelight, most of the text could be read.

For It shall speak to all It calls to hear. And blessed be we who listen, like a bride dutiful to her husband, or daughter to her father's will, do as It bids for the greater peace and goodness of all Nature. For no human tongue can form the language of the Ley but one, and she will have within her Wisdom of the flows and ebbs greater than any Ryder. For there are more shades to the Ley than seen by human eye or tones heard by human ear. Only the One with tongue of stone shall utter the majestic power of the Ley.

'A warning, surely,' said Rosequartz, raising her eyes from the arcane text to seek the agreement of Garnet and Amethyst. Her tone was far from confident. 'A lesson to future Ryders to be humble in our gifts of understanding the Ley.' She looked at Garnet, for her to confirm her opinion, but the chestnut-haired Ryder remained silent and thoughtful.

Sister Amethyst swept her long silver mane over her shoulder with a graceful flick of her skilled, tanned hand. 'It is easy to take it so, Sister Rosequartz, I agree,' she stated in a level, wise tone, 'but suppose, for a moment, we took Obsidian's words literally. Say it was possible for a child to be born with the capability of speaking the language of the Ley, understanding It and working with It not passively as we do but as an equal, a physical embodiment of the power we follow. Think of the repercussions of such an occurrence.'

Both Garnet and Rosequartz silently considered the weighty meaning in Amethyst's suggestion. It seemed beyond their comprehension, beyond all that they had learnt and believed as Ryders to take in such a notion. But within each of them, the rushing energy of the Ley throbbed and burnt with hues more powerful and of different shades than any of them had felt before. Like heated water turning to steam, the fabric of the Ley seemed to be transforming into a new form and as always the Ryders knew it was their undoubting duty to serve It. Finally, Rosequartz swallowed and dared to speak. 'If such a child existed,' she said cautiously, 'I doubt she would instinctively know the importance of her existence. To bear such a blessing is one matter, to have the knowledge to use it is quite another. She would need guidance until such time she fully understood her place in the world, even if her fate wasn't fully understood by those guarding her.' She traced the scar on her hand where she had drawn blood for the oath they had made to Petronia's father to protect her. A slight smile ghosted over Amethyst's slender lips. 'A compassionate heart and a clear mind are useful gifts for a guardian to possess,' she uttered quietly, hoping silently she had used both in raising her own adopted child.

Garnet seemed pensive as she listened to the wind howl outside, an icy electricity prickling her spirit as if to ready it for action. 'She has not come to us by chance at this time,' she stated anxiously; 'one path of a river does not change without altering the flow of other streams. The child may have only just come to us, but the transformation of our way of life began long before we knew her name. We can deny our instincts no longer.'

In an instant, the air in the chamber changed, as if a mighty wave had suddenly risen in the night outside throwing its threatening shadow over the whole citadel. Like a cat woken from its slumber by a sudden noise, Garnet leapt to her feet, her eyes closed to block out any outside stimuli as she focused on the swelling urgency that bubbled within. With a cry of alarm, Rosequartz flew to the window, flinging open the shutters and peering out into the black night as all around the ramparts, lanterns sparked to life as Ryders took to their posts in unexpected panic. Amethyst rocked rigidly back in her chair, her long fingers knotted around the wooden arms as intense dread and adrenaline flooded her body and her mind burst into flame with a thousand images and thoughts of darkness and light.

Garnet's voice scratched at her throat as she battled to vocalise the horrific knowledge that cast a shadow across her mind's eye. 'The darkness,' she croaked, 'it's attacking the citadel!'

Breathless with her awareness of what was occurring, Amethyst gritted her teeth and gripped a nugget of chrysocolla in a pouch suspended from her belt. Summoning strength from the Ley she focused her mind and scrambled to her feet. 'I knew it would be tonight,' she breathed urgently. 'Sisters, to the observatory! I must see for myself!'

With hurried footsteps, the three women flew to the door of the library, flinging it open and rushing up the spiral staircase that led to the highest chamber in the keep, the great glass-domed observatory. As they ran, they heard more swift footsteps racing down corridors and urgent cries to arms as the other Ryder residents in the citadel experienced the same bleak and desperate terror informing them that they must take up arms against the evil threatening to infiltrate this most sacred of places. Bows and swords were seized as dozens of consciousnesses were attuned to the Ley to summon the strength needed to see off this unexpected and unknown foe.

At the top of the stairs, Amethyst flung open the portal to the observatory and she and her companions raced inside. The dome that formed the topmost room in the keep was wide, airy and circular, built totally of thick panes of mottled, curved glass set into polished metal frames like the gently bowing petals of a giant, drooping flower-head. Through the vast windows the sky, which was now pitch black and utterly moonless, could be seen and the chamber was bare, but for a massive telescope in the centre of the space, its gleaming brass barrel and stand set with numerous pieces of blue tourmaline and diamonds.

Pressing her eye to the lens, Amethyst frantically twirled the dials and wheels of the mighty spyglass. Her skilled fingers danced lightly over the crystals embedded in its casing as she drew upon instinct to focus the lens in the right direction. The power of the Ley flowed quickly through the diamonds and other stones into Amethyst's pupil, illuminating the black night beyond the citadel's walls and she gasped in horror and dread at what she saw. Around the base of the curtain wall that enclosed the citadel, a dark and churning cloud floated over the moat, totally covering the water with its putrid, undulating presence. The mass moved like a sentient being, its texture shifting between that of a thick fog and slippery globulous of mud. It moved shifting, nauseous, deliberate and menacing as it oozed closer to the castle. Thin, dripping tendrils of misty shadow flicked out from the main body of the entity to flail and caress the gleaming stones of the wall, sinewy with malevolent power as the formless matter attempted to worm its way through the defences. The fabric and force of the apparition, the constantly pulsing strength and malicious but mindless awareness stirred something terrifying within Amethyst, and she knew that the dark shadow was controlled by wickedness.

'We must stop it,' she told Garnet and Rosequartz grimly, stepping away from the spyglass in horror. 'Drive it back from the citadel at all costs. Join our sisters on the battlements and summon the powers of sardonyx and clear topaz to purify and disperse this evil.' Both Ryders nodded in understanding and headed towards the doorway. Her heart trembling with dread and sorrow, Amethyst breathed deeply, knowing the moment she feared was now at hand. 'I must find the apprentices,' she muttered, 'and Master Hayden.'

*

196

A sudden surge of adrenaline swept through Petronia's body, driving her concentration from the stones she was studying at her desk in the apprentices' dormitory, throwing her thoughts into urgent abandon. A hollow, breathy call swept through her mind, chilling and terrible like a wild animal springing upon her. The crystals beneath her fingers suddenly seemed ice cold and lacking in life as a greater power and instinct caught hold of her mind.

From outside the dormitory door, frantic shouts and calls to arms pierced the peaceful household, and in the distance, a rhythmic toll of a bell could be heard. Alarmed by the unexpected pandemonium, Bracken leapt from her bed, her eyes wide with childlike fear. 'The siege bell!' she stated in dread. 'We're under attack!'

Hurriedly, the two girls dashed to the window and threw back the shutters. Already, fluttering orange torches had been ignited along the parapets and against their fiery light, inky silhouettes of Ryders could be seen taking their posts on the battlements armed with narrow, strong bows and swords of metal and stone. The myriad of coloured crystals that peppered their leather armour and weapons danced like twinkling fairylights in the glow of the torches. From a distance, Petronia could sense long, thin, unseen bands of flexing power and energy flowing out of the gems, through the Ryders' limbs and fingers and into their weapons. Staring out onto the battlements in the half-light, the thick granite of the outer wall seemed to melt away before Petronia's eyes and she saw, or rather she felt, a great tide of deathly energy pushing its way across the moat with mindless intent. It was this that was the empty, sinister whisper that had echoed through her mind and Petronia felt as if she alone understood and could stop this evil.

'We must find Sister Amethyst.' Bracken's voice seemed tiny and far off even though the girl stood at her side. 'She'll know what's happening.'

Taller and stronger than Petronia, Bracken was practically dragging her fellow apprentice towards the door but the last thing that Petronia wanted was to flee. Her mind felt active and alive, searching for knowledge she felt she already knew but just could not quite recall: a thought or memory that haunted the edges of her awareness, tangible but unknown. She could sense what was happening but could not quite understand. She had to do something but what?

With a jerk, she snatched her hand out of Bracken's grasp and buried her face in her hands, trying to block out sight and sound and focus on the new sense awakening within her.

Bracken glanced at the door and then back at Petronia, feeling helpless and afraid. She knew that the citadel must be alive with the force of the Ley now, guiding the archers to hit their marks, protecting Its followers. But as always Its power left her spirit unmoved. 'Come, Mistress Petronia,' she encouraged desperately, 'don't be afraid. The sisters will protect us.'

Frustrated, Petronia lowered her hands from her face and glared at Bracken. More than anything at that moment she wished she could find her voice and declare loudly, 'I am not afraid!' The terror and threat of whatever was lurking outside the castle walls was very apparent to her, but she felt impervious to it. Instead, she was overcome with an electrifying wave of adrenaline that filled her body and mind with unconscious purpose. A sensation like a bolt of lightning ran through the nerves of her back and she suddenly found herself pushed gently but firmly forward as if by an invisible pair of hands urging her to run. Before she was even aware of what her body was doing, Petronia found herself sprinting full pelt out of the dormitory and through the dimly lit corridors of the castle, towards an ultimate goal that of which her mind was not yet aware. Bracken was close at her side, her long, powerful legs carrying her along easily as she frantically searched for someone to tell them what was happening. Petronia, however, needed no such reassurance. All her senses seemed to have been heightened suddenly, taking in at an alarming rate information that would normally go unnoticed. The jewel-scattered walls of the passages they were running through seemed to be streaked with smoky bands of light which illuminated their path. In her mind, she heard a soft but persistent voice willing her onwards in a wordless language that she instinctively understood. The unclear knowledge of what she had to do seemed to be glistening like a polished gem at the edge of her awareness and she ran desperately trying to grasp it in her mind. As they turned a bend in the corridor, the apprentices crossed the path of a staircase and almost collided with the two figures hurriedly descending. Bracken let out a cry of relief when she saw her beloved guardian.

'Sister Amethyst!' she cried, grasping the elderly Ryder's arm, 'thank the Ley! What is happening?' Amethyst gazed into her ward's fearful face and her grey eyes struggled to hide their sorrow. 'It's all right, child. You'll be safe, follow me.'

Hayden, who had been alerted to the attack by the tolling of the bell and had joined Amethyst as he had rushed to the apprentices' chamber in search of his sister, embraced Petronia. 'Petronia!' he gasped, out of breath from running and fear. 'You're okay. Stay with me, I'll protect you.'

Her brother's face and words floated into Petronia's mind like distracting fragments from the world of dreams. Somewhere in her heart, she felt thankful to see him and wanted to stay with him, but the growing sense of intent that seized her body and mind urged her onwards. The voice within her grew louder, uttering wordless instructions, the guiding beams of colourless radiance becoming bright as darting stars as they showed her the way. She could feel Hayden's hand firmly on her arm, trying to guide her to safety and knew she must push him away. Shrugging free of his grip, she quickly arched her fingers into an apologetic '*I must go!*' before bolting as fast as her legs would carry her down the dark passageway.

'Petronia!' Hayden's scream was frantic and fearful as he saw his sister dash away. He started after her, but Amethyst blocked his path, seizing his arms.

'Let her go,' she told him firmly, as Hayden tried to push her aside. 'That is her path, not yours.' The Ryder was elderly but fire seemed to fill the crystals of every colour that hung from her garments and her eyes were filled with determination. Hayden struggled to free himself. 'You don't understand!' he barked. 'She is my sister. I swore to our father I would protect her.'

The old woman's hands remained firmly on his arm. Despite her age, the Ryder seemed to have remarkable strength within her, a sturdy, constant force that allowed her not just to hold him back but to gently guide him back down the corridor. 'I know, Master Hayden, I know,' her tone was level and reassuring, 'but you must leave her. There are great powers guarding her and I swear on all I believe in that your sister will not be harmed. But the Ley has decided you must temporarily be parted and you and Bracken must come with me!'

Hayden glanced over his shoulder as Amethyst firmly shepherded him and Bracken along the candlelit passage, watching helplessly as his sister darted away into the shadows without so much as a backward glance.

He desperately wanted to shake the Ryder's hand from his shoulder but found that he did not have the strength to do so. Her fingers seemed to be glued there by some powerful magic that carried the three of them down the staircases of the castle at alarming speed.

'You must depart from Goodstone at once, both of you.' Amethyst's voice was firm, almost severe as she guided Hayden and Bracken through the corridor. Hayden glared at the old woman's grim expression. 'Mistress Amethyst, I am going nowhere without Petronia.'

Bracken seized her guardian's hand as she hurried alongside, her green eyes filled with horror. 'What?' she gasped. 'Sister, I beg of you no! The citadel is the only home I've known, don't make me flee. I will fight to defend it.' Amethyst slowed her pace for a moment to look at her ward's terrified face and lightly touched her arm. 'That isn't your destiny, my child, nor is it Hayden's. I hate this more than you can know but the Ley has spoken to me and must be obeyed.'

Pushing open the door before them, the Ryder marched the pair swiftly into the great hall at the heart of the keep. The atmosphere in the vast open chamber was icy and wild almost as if the roof had been torn away leaving the room open to the elements. A brisk breeze howled round the circular space and the delicate curtains that surrounded the wide Ley Mouth flapped wildly about.

Amethyst stepped forward, the churning air tugging at her silver mane and gown. Crouching down to the monochrome tiles, she began to pull numerous gems from the pockets of her robe. 'I will open a travelling portal for you,' she explained, as Hayden and Bracken nervously crept closer. 'I cannot say where it'll take you but it will be somewhere safe and on the path you are to follow.' Her long fingers moved skilfully as she set out four pieces of tiger iron on the black and white floor before her. One by one she flicked them so the fragments began to roll and spin in a circle about two feet in diameter. With subtle touches, she encouraged the momentum of the stones until they whirled and spiralled with energy of their own. The marble floor beneath them began to vibrate as the pieces of tiger iron danced over it, the solid pattern of the tiles melting away with the force of the movement, becoming a grey, loose texture like quick-sand.

Swiftly Amethyst stood up and extended her hand towards Bracken. 'Quickly, child,' she encouraged the frightened girl, 'the portal will not last long.' Bracken pursed her lips tightly as she battled the urge to cry. 'Sister,' she whimpered as Amethyst gently approached her. 'I'm scared; don't make me leave.'

Maternal sorrow etched Amethyst's wise features and tenderly she took Bracken in her arms. 'I know, dear Bracken, I know. But you must be strong. I know you can do this. Trust in the Ley.'

Reaching into a pocket of her purple robes, the Ryder took out a flat package of parchment sealed with wax, which she pressed into Bracken's hands. 'This will tell you all you need to know,' she informed her gently, before pressing her lips lovingly against Bracken's mottled cheek. The girl nodded mutely and allowed Amethyst to guide her to the edge of the muddy vortex that swirled in the marble floor. 'I will try not to let you down,' she gulped, taking one last fearful glance around the only place she had ever known as home.

Then with cautious, shuffling footsteps, she approached the area where the ground was melting and turning in a swift eddy of animated soil. Amethyst gave her hand one last reassuring squeeze before Bracken stepped into the vortex. The moment her toes touched the shifting ground, she slipped straight down into it, as if her body was being swallowed whole by some greedy subterranean creature. A second and she was gone without a sound, leaving the silky ground twisting smoothly once more.

Anxiety shone in Amethyst's pale eyes as she watched her ward vanish from sight but she battled to not let this show. Urgently she gestured to Hayden. 'You must follow.'

But Hayden stayed where he was, his face resolute. 'No,' he declared firmly. 'I told you, my place is with my sister. I will not leave her.' Amethyst bit back her frustration and gritted her teeth. 'You have no choice in this,' she told him frantically, 'any more than I do! Do you think it was my will to cast my adopted daughter into the unknown? But it is what must be; it is fate.'

The air around them was filled with noises, empty, hollow breath that demanded to be heard. Hayden glared at the old woman defiantly. 'A man makes his own fate,' he spat.

Turning his back on her, he began to head back towards the corridor to seek out his sister but as he stepped forward, the swirling air of the chamber hit him like a punch in the chest driving him back. Hayden battled against it, striving to push his way forward but every gesture he made seemed to double back on him, buffering his body in the opposite direction. His feet slipped on the smooth marble and he felt his heel catch on an obstacle, tipping him off balance. For a brief breath of time, he was held still in the air, balanced on an unseen axis before tumbling helplessly backwards to the ground. He felt his back collide with the floor but the moment he came into contact with it the solidity of the earth gave away, a million grains of loosely shifting sand scattered beneath his weight sucking him downwards into the dark, pliable safety of its womb. He attempted to let out a cry of shock but before the sound could leave his throat he found himself submerged in blackness beneath the crust of the earth, drawn onwards along an unseen path that led him away from the battle and his sister. The tiled floor of the chamber rippled with the final desperate throws of the boy as he sunk from view before once more becoming calm and flat. The portal opened by the tiger iron slid smoothly closed and the ground became solid, leaving no sign of the escape that had taken place. Amethyst stooped and swiftly collected together the fragments of tiger iron, taking a brief moment to pass her fingertips across the area of ground through which Bracken had slipped. 'Ley go with you, dear child,' she whispered.

*

Racing out of the corridor and into the icy storm of the night, Petronia paused for a brief moment and tried to gather her thoughts. Her senses were overflowing with information and rational thought seemed beyond her. She was aware of all that surrounded her: the chilled rain from above; the cries of the Ryders stationed on the battlements; the flaming arrows that flew from their bows, but all this seemed a faded shadow amid the greater power that flowed into her. Strands of vibrant colour and energy filled her vision, like brilliant tails of vanished comets that led her ever onwards to some unknown purpose her body cried out to fulfil. A thousand words uttered in some long unspoken tongue filled her head, instructing Petronia, a new and natural reaction as primitive as breathing. All she knew was she had to respond.

The colourless radiance that filled her vision dragged her onwards across the courtyard like a tether and eagerly she followed. It illuminated the stairs that led up to the catwalk where the Ryders desperately fought their strange and violent foe. As she climbed, Petronia became more and more aware of the entity that lurked outside the safety of the citadel for its mindless life-force seemed to shriek out to her, untamed and ravenous, unharmed by the arrows and crystals of the Ryders. It was a terrible, wild power but Petronia felt no terror, just a strange magnetism that drew her onwards.

Reaching the battlements at last, Petronia's energy suddenly seemed to be sapped as she became aware of dozens of Ryders summoning the strength of the Ley to ward off their attacker. A river of ever-renewing might banded the catwalk, like thick liquid gold feeding Its servants' muscles and minds. Petronia was overawed and her thoughts became frightened as she began to doubt her own instincts. She recalled her brother begging her to flee and felt a pang of fear for his safety. But the wordless language within her would not cease and frantically it urged her onwards through her doubts.

Through the glare of the Ley that hung about her like a cloak and the pelt of the rain, Petronia stumbled across the narrow wooden walkway to the thick granite battlement to peer through an embrasure at the attacker below. In the combination of moonlight and flame she saw the vast mass of creeping blackness that clung to the outer wall of the castle, greedily caressing it with tendrils of shade. A great sigh of despair and desperation issued from its core, filling her with horror and pity. The entity was featureless, but it seemed to stare up at Petronia with the eyes of a thousand souls, trying to communicate some message, begging her for something, *something*. But what?

A heavy, gauntleted hand fell on Petronia's shoulder, hauling her back from the precipice. Frustrated, she struggled to get away from the Ryder's grasp and return to understand what the darkness below wanted, but the power and Ley flowing from the Ryder was getting in the way. 'Get back to the dormitories!' the woman told her gently, as Petronia battled to free herself. 'You're not trained for battle.'

Aggravated, Petronia pushed the Ryder away, thrusting her palms angrily against the woman's chest. As her hands came into contact with the Ryder's form, she became aware of yet another energy flowing into her mind, the unique life-force of that particular individual. Through her armour and flesh, she could feel the steady beating of her heart racing with the adrenaline of battle. More than this, Petronia was conscious of the spirit that dwelt within the Ryder and for one brief second knew the quality of the stranger's character in intimate detail. The Ryder clearly felt Petronia's awareness penetrate her for her eyes grew wide with disbelief and she loosened her grip.

'Leave her be, Sister Sunstone. She knows what she must do.' A calm, fearless voice rang out clear from the courtyard below and both Petronia and the Ryder turned towards it. In the centre of the square, Amethyst stood motionless in the howling storm, her weathered face inscrutable and wise. Her grey-blue eyes bore into Petronia and she made a tiny movement of her head to indicate that the apprentice must follow her own instincts.

The Ryder Sunstone released her hold on Petronia and at once the awareness she felt of the Ryder's spirit slipped away from her mind to be replaced once more with the powerful call of the darkness that pressed in against the castle walls. Lines of light once more began to dance in Petronia's vision, filling her mind with whispered instinct. The haunted shadow was calling; it needed her. With liquid movement, Petronia snatched the sword of stone and steel that hung at Sunstone's hip and drew it smoothly from its scabbard. The illumination within her mind gleamed on the silver metal and minerals within the blade, drawing them in ribbons of energy. With a step and a leap, she had crossed the catwalk and mounted the battlements and was standing balanced in the embrasure looking down on the river of blackness that engulfed the castle. Once more she felt the pitiful, empty consciousness of the magic below turn its attention towards her, wordlessly calling her name, as silent and profound as her own voice. She became aware of her own tongue, lying muted and still behind her gritted teeth, a pointless appendage that served no purpose throughout her life, but now felt as if it was capable of uttering unknown words and phrases. What would it express; what wonderful or terrible language did it know? Petronia was too fearful to set it free so she tightened her jaw and pursed her lips.

Energy engulfed her body, balanced there high on the citadel wall. The night glowed as bright as midday as the power of the Ley swirled about her, in and out of her body and mind. She felt it push her, lift her, tilt her from her perch, into the cold night air. The shadows were reaching up to embrace her, calling out to her, and in thoughts Petronia replied, *Yes, yes, I am here. What do you want from me?*

Her own senses and actions overwhelmed as she dived through the light and shadow until all rational awareness slipped away and she was nothing more than a moment in time, a heartbeat, a breath of life. Only life and death existed to her now, only light and words, shadow and desperation, change and movement. Nothing solid, nothing inert, only the flow and pulse and rush of the Ley. But even in this state of pure energy and sound, Petronia fiercely bit her reckless tongue for fear of what remarkable things it might utter if it was set free.

Chapter 16

THE RAIN-SOAKED COPSE

The earth carried Hayden through its dark, pliable form at an alarming speed, snatching him deep into its life-filled bosom and whisking him away from the besieged citadel. As tightly wrapped as a caterpillar in a cocoon, he was pushed through the soil by the very throb and heartbeat of the earth itself. The cold, closeness of the undergrowth pushed in on him at all angles, but his breathing seemed completely unhampered for the earth itself had taken over all his physical responses. Its breath was his breath, its pulse, his pulse, as safe and as natural as a foetus in its mother's womb journeying through ignorant darkness to the cruel light of birth. The enchantment cast by Sister Amethyst and the tiger iron crystal formed a rushing canal of dark energy deep within the soil, through which Hayden found himself propelled at a most alarming rate as if within a boat sailing down a racing river. He wanted very much to do something about his situation, gain control once more of his body, thrust his head upwards into the still world above to get some sense of where he was, but the earth around him wound his limbs in a heavy, tight embrace that he could not fight. Throughout his gloomy journey, his eyes caught brief glimpses of rocks and roots, beetles and bugs that populated this subterranean realm and he wondered whether such common things of the earth understood this strange power, this Ley, that now pulled him away from his sister. His mind cursed the Ryders for the peril they had brought into their lives.

A sudden impact caused his body to shake as a blockage collided hard with the back of his neck and shoulders. He buckled at the waist as the power within the earth gave one final push, causing the darkness around him to crack and fall away in clods of wet mud, revealing him to the cold and rain-soaked night. Fresh, damp air with the scent of undergrowth rushed into his lungs and his heart pumped wildly with the adrenaline of the sudden release from his earthy prison. Instantly, he kicked away the soil surrounding the lower half of his body and stood up to see where he was. He found himself standing amid a dense group of trees that offered damp and gloomy shelter from the cold rain. The shadows were inky black and the icy air smelled of forest and rotten foliage. The branches and storm clouds above blocked out any moonlight and, filled with frustration, Hayden stalked about searching for a track or path that might indicate a way back to the citadel. He had to find Petronia and return home. The life of the cursed Ryders was clearly too dangerous for any sane woman and he would not allow his sister to be held captive by any league that had such violent enemies.

A twig cracked underfoot behind him, and filled with fear and rage Hayden spun to face the intruder, drawing his sword as he did so. Her mottled face as round and pale as the hidden moon, Bracken stepped from the shadows, her dark green eyes filled with trepidation. 'Master Hayden,' she uttered in a hushed whisper. 'Thank the Ley you survived the journey. I feared for a moment I was on my own.'

The mention of the Ley ignited Hayden's rage and cursing under his breath he crossly drove his blade into the soil. 'Thank the Ley,' he hissed. 'Thank It indeed, if It exists. Thank It for bringing those deluded wenches to my village and filling my sister's innocent head with foolish dreams! Thank It for dragging us away from our home to the fountain-head of an insane cult. Thank It for casting me out in the middle of nowhere and leaving my sister to face who knows what fate at the hands of an enemy that isn't even hers.'

Bracken's eyes widened at Hayden's raging tirade. 'You are fearful,' she said hoarsely, burying her hands in the folds of her skirt, 'and that is understandable. But Sister Amethyst is wise and would have not sent us away from the citadel without good cause.'

Anger grew hot in Hayden's chest despite the chill of the rain. 'Where are we then?' he barked back. 'If your beloved guardian is so wise then why didn't she think to mention where her spell would land us, and why would she allow my mute sister to face an enemy rather than follow us?'

The tall girl's colourless lips parted in protest but she was unable to find an explanation. Nervously, she fiddled with one of the bracelets of gems around her wrist. Hayden glared with loathing as he pulled his blade from the ground. 'Exactly,' he hissed. 'You don't know. You don't know and neither did she. She's just a stupid old hag worshipping a pointless idea that does nothing but bring trouble into people's lives.'

He turned to walk away; the sight of Bracken reminded him of all the trouble that had twisted his simple life. He had only taken a couple of steps through the undergrowth when a blow like a small boulder hit his right shoulder making him bellow with pain. Bracken had punched him. Not a small, feminine punch but a powerful thump that most men would envy landing. Pained, winded and filled with rage, Hayden spun back to face her. The stout girl loomed down at him, the strange markings on her face darkening as her features contorted with fury.

'How dare you!' she shrieked, in a voice that was oddly womanly in comparison to her heavy build. 'You take that remark back about Sister Amethyst, sir, before I forget I'm a lady! What she did she did to keep us safe and you should be grateful.' She was opening and closing her large, powerful hands as if she did not know whether to punch Hayden or slap him. Hayden massaged his shoulder to ease the pain. It had been a strong punch but he did not want to show that a woman had injured him. 'I do not strike women,' he muttered, 'and besides I am not going to waste time fighting when I could be looking for my sister. I don't expect an orphan to understand the loyalty of a brother.'

Bracken's emerald eyes glinted brightly. 'Sister Amethyst *is* my family, whether we share the same blood or not, and if you think that I am any less afraid for her as you are for your sister then you're very much mistaken. I would've given anything to stay and fight beside her, to defend my home. But what is done is done and it will do neither of us any good to return to Goodstone without reinforcements.'

Her tone trailed off at the end, losing its anger and displaying a note of fear. Hayden's fury quelled for a moment as he regarded Bracken in the dull, wet light of the wood. *What a strange creature she was,* he thought, *with her towering build, piebald complexion and manly strength. So solid and sure in her physicality and yet displaying within her such clearly feminine emotion; it was as if her spirit was too small for her form.* He watched as she broodingly rummaged in the pockets of her multi-coloured robe and pulled out the tiny package that Amethyst had passed to her just before their escape. She was trying very hard not to cry, however Hayden had become a master of reading expressions from his sister. If Petronia, wherever she was now, was as scared as Bracken, then he hoped that there would be someone with her to give comfort.

'What is that?' he asked quietly as Bracken carefully unfolded the parchment from around the object. Bracken gazed at him, her chunky fingers lovingly caressing the paper and what it contained, but said nothing. Hayden could see the dark markings of text and, ignoring his curious stare, Bracken sat down on the damp forest floor to read silently to herself. Studying her face, Hayden tried to guess what was written. Sorrow and puzzlement were etched on Bracken's features and when she had finished reading, she buried her face in her hands like she was weeping, but did not make a sound. Hayden wondered whether Ryders, even apprentices, took an oath not to cry, to remain as stoic as the crystals they carried. The gloomy copse was mournfully quiet apart from the constant tattoo of the rain. At last, Hayden spoke.

'My sister always had a strong spirit,' he uttered quietly. 'For whatever reason, she had already decided she would fight alongside your kin and Sister Amethyst wouldn't have been able to change her mind any more than I.' Bracken did not respond but kept her head bowed, one hand closed tightly around the item concealed in the parcel.

Hayden stooped down beside her and cautiously rested a hand on her broad back. Beneath her wet robes, Bracken's muscles felt as taut as iron and he could detect neither heartbeat nor breath. 'My words about your protector were cruel and untrue and I deeply regret them. Mistress Amethyst is, as you say, a wise woman and I realise that her actions were carried out to spare us harm. If Petronia remains with her I am sure she will be safe.'

Bracken sniffed and swallowed her unshed tears. 'I accept your apology, Master Hayden,' she muttered softly, relaxing the thick pale fingers of her tightly clasped hand slightly to reveal a glimpse of the stone shape she gripped between them. 'Whatever attacked the citadel has taken us cruelly from both our kin and arguing between ourselves will not return them. This is a path we must both follow ourselves.'

She did not look at him as she spoke, rather down at the item she clasped carefully in her hands. Hayden could see it now, illuminated by the dull light of the unseen moon: a short, dark pipe against her greyish skin. The cylinder was straight, about the length of a man's index finger and roughly an inch in diameter. Its surface was perfectly smooth and polished and formed of a strange dark material that looked to be part-way between metal and black stone. It had an odd hue to it, appearing at first to be jet black but on closer inspection showing interchanging dark shades of every thinkable colour. Tiny, metallic flecks dotted it, almost hidden in the darkness of the material.

'What is it?' Hayden asked, as she thoughtfully turned it over in her hands.

Woefully, Bracken shook her head. 'I don't know. It doesn't appear to be made of any crystal or mineral I'm familiar with.' She paused for a moment and pressed one end of the tube to her eyes, squinting through it up at the rain-soaked canopy above their heads. 'Nothing,' she sighed, after a few seconds. 'I thought it might be a spyglass of some kind but it shows nothing that cannot be seen by the naked eye.' She looked dejected and cast her eyes once more to the piece of parchment she still gripped like a child's comforter in her other hand. Hayden motioned towards the delicate dark ink marks. 'Didn't Mistress Amethyst explain why she gave it to you?' he queried. Bracken's dark green eyes once more wandered over the lettering and an expression of melancholy threatened her mottled features. 'No,' she said quietly, 'she simply said it belongs to me.'

Carefully resting the mysterious item in her lap, Bracken softly took the parchment in her hands and began to read it out loud. Her voice was soft, like an echo of the rain that dripped from the trees high above. Even though Hayden was standing right beside her he had to strain his ears to hear, for Bracken read not to inform him but to reaffirm what was written to herself.

'My dear Bracken, dearest child, as I write this I do so with a heavy heart for I feel that our time together is drawing to an end and I do not know whether our destinies will ever cross in this plain again. The path the Ley has carved for you will lead you, very soon, away from my loving gaze and although I know that it will take you to your true destiny it breaks my heart to think I may never look upon you again.

In the past sixteen years, not a day passed when I didn't thank the Ley for delivering you to my protection. My devotion to the Ley denied me the chance of bearing a child of my own and I would have never guessed that It would have bestowed on me the wonderful opportunity of being a mother and guardian to you. I couldn't hold in my heart more love and pride for a daughter of my own flesh.

I know of your doubts in your own abilities, that you feel you have no sense for the Ley but you must now believe in yourself as I believe in you. You have many skills and qualities within your loving heart and now the time has come for you to use them and discover the woman the Ley has created you to be.

I found this object with you when I discovered you on the heath. Not knowing what it was, I kept it from you, wrongly perhaps, so you might focus on the love of our Sisterhood rather that the sorrow of your origins. But whatever it is, it is rightfully yours. Maybe it will aid you in finding your future.

Dark times are upon us, child, and this land I feel will soon be filled with danger. But I trust you have learnt well the ways of the Ryders, the qualities of mercy, courage, love and compassion and these noble sentiments will see you well through any trials you may face.

I close by saying again that I love you dearly and give you my every blessing. Ley be with you always.

Your Guardian Amethyst

Bracken carefully folded the parchment and tucked it into the bodice of her robe next to her heart. Her face was an inscrutable pale mask as she sat silently in the wet grass, fingers resting lightly on the polished stone tube. Hayden watched her, and for a very long time said nothing. The nocturnal world around them seemed at once to be immeasurably large and cold and Hayden was aware that despite his rage moments before they were in the same position: helplessly lost and detached from those they cared for.

'What will you do?' he asked finally, his tone dull but soft.

Bracken sighed heavily and taking one of the many leather lanyards she wore around her neck, threaded it through the mysterious cylinder. 'I will do what I have been raised to do,' she uttered simply, tying the strap around her neck once more, 'and that, Master Hayden, is to follow the Ley. You may dismiss It as myth and superstition but It is the only way of life I know and I trust It to lead me from my sorrow.' Getting to her feet, she cast her eyes towards the dripping canopy above them, perhaps in prayer, perhaps to see if there was any lessening in the cold rain. 'It is late,' she stated calmly, stalking over to the base of a large, thick-branched fur tree. 'We have a few hours until dawn. I suggest we get what little sleep we can and then seek out help at first light. There is bound to be a village nearby.' She patted the ground with a questioning hand and deeming it dry enough settled down to make it her bed.

Alone in the clearing, Hayden repressed a shiver of cold. He hated the helplessness and ignorance he felt right now, unable to do anything to aid his sister in her plight. He recalled the last moments he had seen Petronia, her dark, expressive eyes so filled with clear emotion, not fear or panic as he felt now but a focused determination and understanding of knowledge that Hayden could not begin to fathom. *Did his sister really possess a sense for the forces that the Ryders claimed moved all their lives and if so what kind of peril would that bring?* Finding himself a sheltered spot in the crook of a split tree trunk, Hayden glanced across the glade to Bracken and felt an odd pang of jealousy. *It must be comforting,* he thought, *to have such belief that destiny had a purpose for keeping you alive.*

Chapter 17

AN APPRENTICE ABROAD

Energy flowed in an unending rush through Petronia's form as she flung herself from the battlements of the citadel. Her body was falling through the cold night air, this she knew, but the downward force of gravity seemed a minor influence on her state when compared to the tornado of other powers that surged into her consciousness. Her mind seemed detached from her physical self, an ever-changing but fixed point fed by her senses, taking in and processing the life and universal awareness that poured into her at every angle until her perception of the everyday world melted away and she became focused on something greater: mighty and intangible. She was blind but saw colours and forms too abstract to describe. Deaf, yet her ears rang with language. Her unconscious mind open and accepting like a celestial lotus flower, a chalice to be filled unendingly with the deathly black and blazing bright energies that surrounded her. She was in a snowstorm of time and movement, no two moments quite identical yet aware of one undeniable truth: everything that was happening – the pull of the Ley, the threat of the darkness that had called to her – was linked together, dual elements from the same mother origin. Through it all, a clear stream of ability channelled through her mind; an idiom and skill of almost godlike influence that had been awoken within her was waiting impatiently for her command. Such capability: an empowerment unworthy of human flesh or thought; it terrified Petronia to believe it was part of her, though she knew it had lain dormant in her mind for as long as she could remember, the immortal words that had a rightful claim to her mute tongue. She did not feel she had the strength or ability to master such power so she did nothing, simply allowing the rushing tides of abstract energy to flood in and move her mind and body, consciousness and spirit along the path of her destiny until it deposited her with gentle oblivion back into the physical world.

She awoke, as if from a deep and confusing dream, her mind and body struggling to connect and understand the real world. She could recall the assault on the citadel and her manic actions on the battlements but none of it made sense now and it all seemed so far removed. Where was she? Certainly not the Ryders' fort at Goodstone or her parents' humble cottage. She opened her eyes to see a patchwork of watery blue sky intersected by bare tree branches. Her body felt numb and painful at the same time, as if an immense weight had been crushing her flat. Thought came slow and sleepy and she found it a chore to take in where she was.

Cautiously, she pressed her hands against the soft, damp ground beneath her and forced herself to sit up. Her head spun with dizzy nausea as the world righted itself before her stinging eyes and the morning sunlight blurred her vision. Her mouth was dry with a vile metallic taste and she clicked her tongue to stimulate the flow of saliva. A strange noise dawned on her and she awkwardly flexed her tongue and throat, forcing stale breath from her lungs. A rasping bark emitted from her lips, like a feline coughing up a fur-ball. Speech was still beyond her. At least that sad fact was strangely comforting. Stretching her arms and back, she took in the panorama surrounding her, trying to make sense of her situation. She was on a grassy bank beneath a small tree at the side of a long, wide, sandy road, snaking through open country. On the near horizon, she could see the tall, pale sunlit walls of a vast city to which the road led. The path was dotted by numerous moving shapes of carts and travellers trekking to and from the city gate.

Petronia's mind slowly began to regain its awareness. This was not Goodstone and it certainly was not Ravensbrook! Where was she and what in the world had brought her here? In the battle, she had felt so certain of her actions, as if some outside force was guiding her to do the right thing. Had that force also transported her here and if so why? She recalled the dark power that had attacked the citadel and wondered for a second if the Ryders were still in danger. A deep insistence spoke calmly within her, reassuring her that whatever the threat had been it had passed and Amethyst, Rosequartz and the others were quite safe. At the same time, Petronia's thoughts were instantly drawn to her brother. Hayden had seemed so fearful, confused and desperate to protect her. He would have no idea what had happened and she could think of no way of finding him.

A desperate tremble of panic filled her chest. Hayden had been her only means of making herself understood; how would she be able to ask the way back to Goodstone without him? She glanced once more at the city in the distance. She was adept at making her views clear through gesture and expression, but would strangers in a busy city have the time or willingness to listen? Taking a deep breath she tried to steady her nerve. It would do no good to allow herself to descend into frantic terror. As frightened as she was, crying would bring her no aid. She gazed down at the rainbow patchwork robe in which she was dressed and at the stone blade laying in the grass at her side and felt a tingle of purpose. *What had Sister Amethyst said? Concern yourself with others' sorrows and the Ley will bring you comfort from your own.* She was, after all, an apprentice to the Ley, even if she was only at the beginning of her education. It certainly felt safer to think of herself as that rather than a lost blacksmith's daughter with no voice.

Petronia slipped the weighty stone sabre into her girdle and got to her feet, brushing the damp grass from her gown. She must trust her fears about her impairment and lost sibling to the force that had called her to Its service and take action to walk her own path. With a resolute attitude keeping her concerns in check, she took to the dusty road that led towards the city of Veridium.

*

'Isn't it amazing, Phebs?' Aarold leant forward over the horse's neck to whisper excitedly in his ear, 'Have you ever seen so many people?'

Beneath him, the disguised Equile gave a little shudder of discomfort and revulsion.

The pair had been travelling throughout the night, riding as swiftly as they could muster away from the watchful presence of Aarold's royal abode and as the sun arose they found themselves travelling down one of the narrow suburban thoroughfares of the city, lined on either side with high, thin houses that looked down on the street below with small slit windows. All around, the common people of Veridium hustled and bustled about their business, on foot and horseback, paying no heed to the tinker and his steed.

Aarold's senses were overloaded with all the new experiences surrounding him. For the first time in his life, he felt completely alone and free, at liberty to go and do whatever he pleased without overprotective eyes following his every movement. This new freedom was made even more thrilling by the knowledge that it came about via his own skill and ingenuity. With silent pride, he rested his hand on the leather satchel containing his magical potions. *Who said that having a physical deformity made you weak and incapable?* At this precise moment, Aarold felt like the most accomplished magician in the whole kingdom. After this daring escapade, he would be more than able to prove to his aunt that he was strong enough to take the throne. Why, in the fresh, busy air of the city, even the aching of his wasted leg felt less intense.

A woman mounted on an ebony mare passed by to the right of them, the animal's sweaty body brushing against Phebus's side in the crowded street. Disgusted, Phebus let out a horrified gasp and staggered sideways away from the beast. 'Foul!' he snorted sharply, struggling to make his speech go unheard by the throng surrounding them. 'That's what this place is! A rancid sewer of the great unwashed! I have never seen such squalor. Heaven knows what I'm walking through; I daren't look!'

Aarold patted his trusted friend's chestnut mane. 'Hush now, Phebs,' he reassured him, 'remember horses don't speak.'

'Well, I'm sure if they did, they would complain!' came the tart reply, 'This place is a travesty!'

Aarold sighed sadly as he gazed about him. It pained him to admit it but Phebus was right. Many of the people they passed by were filthy and malnourished and it shamed him to see his subjects in such poor condition. 'Was Veridium like this in my father's day?' he pondered.

'Your father was too pig-headed to notice if it was!' Phebus remarked icily, forgetting once more that he was meant to be a simple horse. 'As I've said a million times before, your father, ouch!' His monologue was cut short by Aarold sharply digging his heels in his flanks.

'Much as I enjoy listening to your strong opinions of my parentage and as keenly as I agree with you about my father, this is not the time or the place,' Aarold hissed. 'High-handed debate is not helping my people. And as you can see for yourself, they do need my help.'

His voice trailed off as his attention was drawn to a sorry scene at the side of the street. A girl of no more than seven years of age was begging for meagre pennies and food scraps from travellers, most of whom passed her by without a glance. She cradled on her hip a boy of about three or four and both children were clothed in filthy rags and clearly malnourished. Such a pitiful sight moved the prince's tender heart as he considered all the luxuries that had been bestowed on him since birth. He nudged Phebus to carry him closer to the sad pair. The girl stared up at him with large sorrowful eyes that made Aarold's heart weep.

'Spare a penny for two orphans,' she pleaded, holding out a filthy palm.

Empathy throbbed in Aarold's heart making him feel even more sorrowful for the poor mites. Reaching into his purse, he pulled out a silver coin which he pressed into the girl's hand. A grateful smile brightened her face.

'Thank you, sir,' she gushed, tucking her treasure into the pocket of her skirt. 'Now we can buy food for us and the others tonight.' 'Others?' queried Aarold with concern. 'There are more in your family than you and your brother?' Sadly the girl shook her head. 'Only my brother and I in our family, sir, but there are plenty more without parents running the streets.' She paused and scrutinised Aarold's face so intently that he thought she might have seen through his disguise. 'You not be from the city, are you, sir? Else you'd know about the taxes.'

Aarold stiffened, his hands tightening on Phebus's reigns. 'No,' he said quietly, 'I am a traveller from a distant land. Tell me, is it hard for the people of Veridium?'

The child nodded, her face creasing into a scowl. 'It be the prince who done it!' she stated crossly. 'He raised the taxes to pay for his father's war! Our father had to work himself to death to pay them. Then our mother got sick and died. It's the same all over.'

Aarold grew pale on hearing these words. He had suspected this was happening and why the assassin had tried to claim his life, but had no idea things had got so bad. He wondered if his aunt knew the dreadful suffering in the city. 'And you and the other orphans have nowhere to go?' he asked gently.

A small, woeful smile creased the girl's lips. 'The Ryders show us kindness when they can,' she said, gently stroking her brother's hair. 'They give us food and allow us to sleep in their lodge. But their duties call them far and wide and they do not have the resources to help all of us.'

Aarold listened with kind understanding and felt a deep stab of guilt. Too long he had been free from his responsibilities as monarch. His people clearly were in need of his leadership and he would not allow his ill health or influence of the court stop him from bringing succour where it was needed. Reaching into his purse, he retrieved another silver coin. 'For the Ryders,' he said, pressing it into the child's palm, 'to buy food for others such as you and your brother.'

The girl gave him a smile of gratitude and pressed her lips against his fingers in thanks. 'You are a most generous gentlemen, good sir. I shall ask the Ryders to lay their blessings on you.' She hurried away, her prize gripped tightly in her hand.

Aarold watched her disappear into the noise of the crowd and sadly shook his head. He had spent his whole life being told that he was poorly and incapable of taking on the role fate had cast for him. But his eyes saw clearly the need of his subjects and his heart was filled with compassion. He recalled what his tutor had told him, about a kind heart and a clear mind being as worthy tools in kingship as a strong sword-hand. There was much he could do, but he needed the support of those who understood the suffering of the people.

'Happy now?' Phebus's dull whisper broke into his contemplation. 'You have fulfilled a charitable quest and satisfied your princely hankering for chivalrous conduct. Can we now return to our more civilised existence?'

Aarold gave his mount a sharp, and somewhat cross, nudge to spur him onwards. 'Phebus, really!' he chided. 'Sometimes you are the most selfish and thoughtless beast. Was your heart not moved by that poor child's plight?' Phebus huffed dismissively as they continued down the road. 'I am not saying hers isn't a sorry tale,' he muttered. 'But you can't help every unfortunate soul you come across, dear boy.'

But Aarold knew that Phebus was wrong. As monarch of Geoll, it was his duty to care for the well-being of all his people. He felt his mind drift to the Ryders. Perhaps his meeting with Sister Ammonite had not been mere chance. Maybe the Ley, if such an entity existed, was driving him to join with the Ryders and bring the plight of his kingdom to the minds of those who had the power to change things. As leader of the nation, it was up to him to let their voice be heard.

*

Petronia stood still for a moment, her senses overwhelmed by the unfamiliar and busy surroundings she found herself in. She had walked with little rest for the most part of the day, following the broad dusty road towards the city, each step taken with the prayer that the strange metropolis would bring some aid to her confused situation. The trek had been long and hard, but the physical exertion of the journey had brought some relief to the fear and uncertainty that dwelt within. She felt that just by moving forward towards a destination, she was somehow at least mimicking the motion of the Ley, constantly pushing onwards towards Its self-known purpose. Even though she had no assurance the Ley wanted her to go to the city, it felt more useful than just sitting at the side of the road waiting for something better to arrive.

Now, here she was, within the sand-coloured walls of the city, immersed in more life and sound than she had ever experienced before. All around her, people moved about purposefully, making their way homewards through the narrow streets. The sound and smell of city life saturated her mind with unfamiliarity, making her question even more the certainty of what she should do next. Standing in a small piazza, a short distance from the city gates, she struggled to order her thoughts and compose a plan of action. She studied the unfamiliar face of each stranger who passed her by, trying to determine, by their eyes, whether they had the patience and kindness to understand her clearest gestures of communication. But even if they did, even if she could speak with a voice as audible as any other, what question or aid could she elicit? She had no real explanation why she had travelled here, just a faint, intangible yearning, a troubled restless drive that urged her to search for something. But what?

Petronia leant wearily against a sturdy, curved arch to one side of the square and cupped her face in her hands as her fatigue turned her mind towards the hopelessness of her situation. She thought of her brother, dear protective, dependable Hayden. *Where in the world was he now? All he had ever done was try to look after me and keep me from harm and how had I repaid him? Abandoned him without a thought, to pursue some reckless, primal urge, an infection of my spirit that compelled my actions with a power I did not understand. What did that say about my nature?* What *was* her nature, would be a more accurate question. For Petronia could not deny that there was something inexplicable within her spirit, that she did not have the power to repress.

Taking a deep breath, she chided herself for being so self-pitying. True, it was not within her to fight this unnatural sense that took control of her body and mind, but that did not mean she had to be under its control. She had, through ingenuity, overcome her muteness and found other ways of expressing her desires. How was this challenge any different? It was simply a matter of awareness, determination and self-discipline.

Her muscles ached from the long walk and her skin and mouth felt parched. Amid the hubbub of the crowd, she became aware of the cooling sound of rushing water and looked about her to see that on one wall of the piazza there was a large, stone font, filled with fresh, bubbling liquid that rushed from the open mouth of some mythical, carved beast. Thirstily, Petronia hurried across the square and fell to her knees beside the brimming trough. Cupping her hands, she scooped mouthful after clean, refreshing mouthful down her dry, parched throat before dipping her whole face and forearms into the cool, soothing reservoir to revive her aching muscles. The freshness of the water lifted her spirits and made her feel human again, awaking her tired mind. All at once, her senses seemed clearer and she was able to focus with more ease on her surroundings, her mind imbued with new positivity. The water sang noisily from the gargoyle's jaws, its burbles and splashes filling Petronia's ears with a half-uttered language. Once more, her thoughts were illuminated with a powerful, unseen light and motion, but this time she was not overwhelmed and felt determined to remain in control of her own consciousness. Mentally, she acknowledged the essence that infiltrated her senses, addressing it surely. She kept her mind focused on the rough texture of the font beneath her hands, the droplets of cold water on her face, her physical existence in the world as she silently spoke in her mind to the power that called. '*I will follow you, but my actions are my own. Lead me, do not control me.*'

At once the flood of brightness and wordless sound simmered down, becoming in Petronia's mind not a barrage of sensation but a clear and uncomplicated line, like a trail of thread for her to follow. Slowly and carefully, for she still feared that the strange power would once more flood her senses rendering her unconscious again, she stood up and took a moment to familiarise herself with the scene of the courtyard. She made a deliberate effort to take in the figures of the people surrounding her as well as the size and position of the buildings, holding all she saw firmly in her mind before mentally tuning into the call and light that spoke within her. Immediately, she saw a thin ribbon of gleaming luminescence stretching out across the piazza in a flowing band, like a glittering lock of hair from an unseen spectre which had swiftly departed down one of the thoroughfares of the city, with the insistent expectation that Petronia was to follow. Petronia felt a compelling urge in her aching muscles, a gentle tug in her mind, driving her onwards and without a moment's doubt started off to follow the mystical trail.

*

'You don't know where we're going.' Phebus's whisper held within it a fearful tone that struck doubts that had already begun to form in Aarold's heart.

The young prince pulled his cape tightly around his shoulders and surveyed the narrow, shadow-draped alleyway they found themselves in. It seemed like only moments before they had been travelling through the streets of Veridium in the brilliant light of the afternoon sun. But dusk had swept across the city within a blink of an eye, bringing with it a murky gloom that made every building, statue and lane look like the last, and chilling the air so it gnawed painfully at Aarold's wasted muscles. He pressed his palms against the heat of Phebus's sturdy back and fought off another threatening spasm of cold and dread. 'Don't be ridiculous!' he snapped, lips quivering slightly. 'The situation is perfectly under control. It's like I always say, the appliance of the mental can always override the emotional and physical if you just stay calm.'

Phebus let out a heavy snort, his warm breath floating away like smoke in the chilly night. 'A fine theory, good fellow,' he grunted, 'and perfectly adequate when one is amidst the comforts of one's home. But in an environment such as this...' Aarold felt Phebus tremble beneath him. It troubled him to admit that his friend's apprehension was not without cause. He had found it so easy in the light of day to deem their daring adventure a success, but the night and his unfamiliarity with the city brought the dangers and vulnerabilities they faced flooding with stark reality back into his mind. Turning his face towards the heavens,

Aarold studied the cloudy section of dim purple sky visible above the houses. 'If only I could make out the stars,' he mused anxiously, 'then I could work out what direction we were going in.' He squinted and peered at the dusky clouds more intently than ever.

Suddenly, a loud, brutal shout pierced the black shadows of the alley and Aarold felt his mount buck beneath him as an unseen hand struck Phebus's rump. Desperately, Aarold tried to cling on as Phebus instinctively bolted to freedom, but his lame leg was too weak to grip into the creature's side and he felt himself slide from the saddle. The world was plunged into black confusion as he tumbled, his hands frantically trying to grasp on to Phebus's mane. A muscular arm clamped around his torso, crushing his own arms to his side as his assailant seized hold. Aarold's breath was squeezed out of him by fear and the sheer strength of the larger man. His heart and mind raced helplessly as he tried to take stock of the terrifying situation he found himself plunged into. Instincts told him to struggle but a dull glimmer from the blade of a dirk warned him that any effort he made would end in bloodshed. Frozen and weak with terror, he prayed for his life as the thief roughly rifled through his pockets.

*

Petronia's heart pounded steadily in her chest as she hurried stealthily through the murky streets of the city. Her body buzzed with adrenaline but her senses were crystal clear to every stimulus that surrounded her. Her mind was focused and an unrelenting drive powered her tirelessly on her quest, though she had no idea where she was heading or why she was needed. Dusk had begun to fall over the city as she ran, casting shadows and turning the stones of the streets and buildings a ghostly pale violet. In the dim light of the approaching evening, Petronia was vividly aware of a persistent guiding radiance glimmering just beyond the field of her natural vision, hovering somewhere between her sight and mind, always with her yet always ahead, urging her to follow Its path. Her mind could detect voices, tones inaudible to her ears but which spoke to her from the moment she had requested their guidance beside the water fountain. Her mind strained as she hurried through streets and alleys, trying to understand what the wordless language was saying. There was danger, yes, danger and she was needed. But what danger and how she could help was unclear. All she knew was that she had to obey.

The force that drove her marked an unmistakable path through the streets, as apparent to Petronia as heavy footprints in newly fallen snow. She felt as if there was someone running in front of her, a guide laying a trail, preparing the way, trusted but unseen. A strange sensation had begun to surge through her, an electric tingle within her muscles. At first she thought it was cramp, her body reacting to her sudden burst of energy. But the feeling was not painful or hampering, in fact it felt like a new form of power awakening.

Suddenly, the drive that propelled her forwards ceased, dropping away abruptly like a curtain being pulled aside before her eyes, allowing her to take in her surroundings. She was just inside the entrance to a narrow and poorly lit alley, the atmosphere of the late evening, cold and murky with shadows. Her heart was drumming wildly and instantly she picked up the fearful sounds of a violent scuffle taking place within the brooding darkness. Urgency filled her body, like a possessing spirit, filling her with courage she never knew she possessed. She had to help whoever it was being attacked.

Her eyes searched the blackness of the alley and almost as if they had been outlined in golden ink, she caught sight of the silhouettes of two men, one stocky and brutish, the other slight and trembling with fear. The stronger figure had a blade pressed to his victim's throat as he roughly foraged through his pockets. Without thinking, Petronia's hand flew to the hilt of the stone sabre at her hip but almost before she could grab it, an urgent instinct hot within her brain told her that brute force was not what was needed. The burning sensation that had awoken within her ran like ripples of energising light and liquid over her skin, causing her to become aware of the numerous crystals within the pockets of her gown and purses on her girdle. Vibrant sensations of colour and texture flooded her mind, brilliant yellow and powdery crystals, filling her thoughts with the attributes of one particular gem until it felt as if her entire brain had changed its structure. Her fingers intuitively shot into a pouch suspended from her belt and drew out a small, rough nugget of mustard-coloured sulphur. The uneven, crystallised surface of the stone burned her fingertips as she touched it, not with heat but with a pulsating vibration as if the crystal itself had come alive as her skin caressed it, awakening and opening a path directly into Petronia's mind. In her hands it was a living thing, a detached component of her physical being, as much in her control as her eyes or hand. Petronia could feel herself within its form, imbued with the power to stop this unlawful attack and draw away the robber's violent intent.

'*Stop this*,' she commanded in a mental whisper, linking the crystal to her will; '*save him!*'

Stooping low, she sent the sulphur skimming across the cobbled ground of the alleyway in one liquid swift movement. Energy seemed to crack the air as the stone hurtled along its path, sending undulations of yellow-tinted power through the atmosphere. Shaken and disorientated in the thief's grasp, Aarold sensed the startling force wash over him, altering the ambience of the gloomy passage. Vast bands of power passed straight through his body, like the backdraught from a mighty charge of warriors, colliding with his assailant. The man let out a short groan of shock and pain, stumbling jerkily backwards, like a puppet whose strings had been seized by a heavy hand, before crashing in a lifeless heap to the floor. Aarold was caught off balance by the sudden rescue, tumbling forward as his lame leg gave way beneath him. He landed on his knees, his kneecaps colliding with the stony ground, and frantically gazed round to see who, or indeed what, had saved him. His attacker lay motionless on the ground and there was no-one else nearby, only a tall feminine figure hurrying towards him out of the shadows.

Petronia rushed towards the victim as fast as she could although her legs felt like water and she had the unnerving sensation that she was going to pass out. All her energy had left her the moment she let go of the crystal, leaving her feeling empty and powerless. She struggled to understand how she could exist constantly shifting between these two states, one minute filled with purpose and a power beyond her control, the next fully aware of reality and feeling helpless within it. She had a terrible, sickening feeling that in the last few moments she may have killed or seriously injured two men without any memory of how or why. She approached the younger man, the victim of the attack, crouched on his knees, and cautiously reached down to touch his shoulder. Startled, he looked up at her with large, bright eyes, the shade of sapphire, his tanned face pale with shock and confusion. Once more, Petronia was aware of how much her muteness handicapped her. She desperately wanted to say something reassuring, tell him he was safe and she meant him no harm. Instead, she forced a gentle smile and crouching down, offered him her hand in greeting. The boy, for now she was this close to him Petronia could tell that he was closer to her age than to full manhood, looked at her with a nervous but inquisitive glance. 'You saved me,' he stated, in baffled amazement, his eyes fixed on the stone sword at her side. 'Thank you.'

Petronia tilted her head to one side and spread her hands in a motion to indicate that she had had no choice. Looking at the youth, she noticed that one of his legs was twisted at an angle beneath the other. Concerned, she gestured. The youth winced bitterly. 'I'll be fine, thanks to you, good mistress, no harm done. I think I can stand, that is if I have my cane.' Looking round the gloomy alley, Petronia quickly spotted a wooden walking stick lying close by. Picking it up, she held it out towards the slim youth who took it in his right hand and with slow and cautious movement, managed to stand up again, leaning heavily against the wall for a moment, until he was certain of his balance.

Petronia watched to make sure he did not stumble and then when she was sure of his safety, turned her attention to his attacker who lay motionless on the ground nearby. The thief was stretched out, still and rigid on his back, like a fallen statue. His eyelids were closed as if he was asleep or unconscious, but his muscles were stiffly tense, elbows and knees slightly bent, fists tightly gripped. In one hand, he grasped a leather purse, the fruits of the robbery Petronia had averted. She took hold of the pouch and with a few firm tugs managed to prise it free from his clasped fingers before holding it out questioningly to the boy. Aarold took it from her with a hushed, 'Thank you,' and tucked it safely into his belt, all the time peering down at the lifeless villain with a mixture of fear and curiosity. 'Is he dead?' he asked finally, his voice heavy with trepidation.

Instinctively, Petronia shook her head. She did not know why but she was sure beyond doubt that the man was still alive. Lightly resting her hand on his chest, she at once became aware of his life-force still within his body, but temporarily held dormant by another power, the power that had moments before coursed through her.

'You're a Ley Ryder, aren't you?' The boy's astute observation cut through Petronia's thoughts, making her turn to face him once more. 'The crystals on your belt give you away. Tell me, what is your name?'

His tone was warm and friendly despite the awful ordeal he had just faced. Once again Petronia felt overcome with frustration for her situation. How ridiculous it was that she could render a man unconscious through uniting her will with a stone, but could not answer a simple question? Apologetically, she rubbed her fingers against her throat before pressing them to her lips and shaking her head.

The youth watched the gesture thoughtfully, his sapphire eyes filling with realisation. 'You aren't able to talk? Is that it?' he queried gently, to which Petronia gave a sad nod.

'Do you write then, express yourself with pen and ink? I have some parchment with me.' He paused as he saw Petronia shake her head. 'You cannot write either? No.'

He sighed and Petronia felt within her the familiar anger of appearing a fool before someone who did not understand her communication. Then, however, the boy chuckled ruefully and tapped his cane against the ground. 'So what of it? From what I've seen of life, most that is said or written is of little consequence and you are clearly kind and able enough to give aid to a person in distress. I thank you, Mistress Ryder, for saving me from my peril.' He bowed, somewhat awkwardly, due to his impairment, before adding with a hint of self-doubt, 'May I call you Mistress Ryder, in lieu of knowing your name?'

Petronia tilted her head thoughtfully to one side and considered whether it was wrong to be called a Ryder when in fact she was only an apprentice and decided that if the Ley was aware of her inability to speak her given name, It would take no slight in her going by a title given to her through her actions. Happily she nodded and the youth looked relieved.

'Good,' he breathed, 'and you can call me...' Aarold paused briefly, his princely name sticking in his throat. The attack had shaken him but was he so weak-willed to give up on his adventure so soon? He glanced at the Ryder and his adolescent eyes could not help but notice how young and pretty she was. Would it really do any more harm to his situation to spend some time with her before his journey was at an end?

'You can call me Aaron,' he stated with a smile. 'I'm a peddler of charms. I travelled here to sell my wares at the market.' He stopped suddenly, his hand clasped to his face in shock as his memory came back to him. 'Phebus!' he murmured worriedly to himself, 'my companion, I mean, my horse! He bolted when I was attacked.'

Petronia looked first up and then down the alleyway for any sign of the animal but could see none.

Leaning on his stick, Aarold began to hobble down the passageway. 'He won't have gone far,' he said stopping to glance back at Petronia. 'That villain who attacked us spooked him but he's very loyal, just a tad nervous. He's probably found some safe little nook and is hiding. Will you help me look?'

Willingly, Petronia indicated she would and together the unlikely pair set off back down the shadowy alleyway in search of the young man's runaway steed. Aarold felt very relieved to leave the unconscious footpad behind them, still comatose on the cobbled ground. The whole situation had left him more traumatised than he was willing to admit and part of him felt that once he had found Phebus it would perhaps be a good time to return to the castle. But there was something about being in the company of the young Ley Ryder, not simply her youthful beauty but also the fact that she, like him, suffered from an impairment but was actively following her destiny, that added courage to Aarold's spirits. With her at his side, his ambitions to venture out into the world seemed less foolhardy.

They walked together along several dark streets, Aarold calling for his horse while Petronia kept close watch for any sign of the animal. She watched the peddler with great interest as he shuffled along the cobblestone roads, dependent on his cane for balance. It was the first time in her life that she had come across another person blighted by an imperfection and she found it a curious experience. She admired Aaron's determined spirit to pick himself up after his attack. It was true that a great misfortune could have befallen him if she had not happened by, but he must have been aware of the vulnerability of travelling at night and that alone showed great courage. He had also taken on her impairment at face value, not phased by her inability to speak or write. For once she felt that someone saw her as something other than a vessel for her impairments; he saw her as a Ryder! Petronia felt the Ley resting quietly all around them, like a sleek furred cat slumbering contentedly by the hearth after a day of catching mice.

They searched for some time as the hour grew late, before discovering the spooked Phebus quaking with fear at the back of a house. Aarold calmed him by patting his chestnut neck and flanks and speaking to him in a soothing, almost human manner.

'See, Phebs? It's all over. I'm quite safe and so are you. We just need to be more careful in the future.' The beast whinnied in a tone that almost sounded to Petronia like scepticism. His shiny black eyes swivelled in Petronia's direction and he snorted sharply. Carefully, Petronia reached out a friendly hand to pat him affectionately on the nose, but the creature strained his neck and snapped his teeth at her fingers.

Forcefully, Aarold seized his head. 'Phebus,' he reprimanded as Petronia quickly backed away from the agitated horse. 'Phebus, no! Show some respect to the good lady. This is the Mistress Ryder who saved me from that vile footpad after you chose to abandon me.' The animal's head drooped heavily with shame as he gazed at his master piteously through silken lashes. Lips parting, he emitted a low, breathy sound that sounded uncannily like, 'Sorry.' Petronia gasped as the peddler affectionately scratched Phebus's ears. She had never seen someone talk to an animal so conversationally.

Lovingly, Aarold slapped his mount's side. 'I know, he caught you unawares. I won't hold it against you.' He flashed Petronia a knowing smile. 'Phebus is fine with me, he just doesn't get on too well with people who he doesn't know. He's a big scaredy cat really.' 'I say!' the beast seemed to whinny, clomping his hoof heavily and pressing against his master. Aaron looked unnerved and gave the animal a sharp slap. Tucking his cane into the baldric across his shoulders, the young man grabbed firmly hold of his steed's mane and awkwardly heaved himself on to his back. This, it was obvious, took a great deal of effort and Petronia thought about offering help but before she could do so, her new friend had succeeded in settling himself in the saddle.

'There now,' he sighed, trying hard to make the task appear easier than it had been for him. 'All back as it should be and we are a little more wary but nonetheless unharmed by our ordeal, much thanks to you, Mistress Ryder. Believe me, I can't express my gratitude for you stopping that awful villain. I don't know what would've happened to me if fate hadn't brought you to my rescue.'

Petronia grinned with modest pride and lowered her gaze in the hope that he would not notice her cheeks were reddened. She had completed her first mission of mercy as an apprentice Ryder and she could not help thinking that both her mentor Amethyst and her family would be proud of her.

Suddenly feeling very self-conscious, Aarold pulled his cape over his lame leg. The memory of his father drifted into his mind, mocking him for having to be rescued by a female. This was hardly appropriate behaviour for a disguised prince out to prove himself.

'I wish there was a favour that I could pay you in return,' he stated, trying to make his voice sound as deep and manly as he could. 'A kindness worthy of your noble role. Are you on a quest of some sort that I could aid you in?'

Uncertainty flooded Petronia's mind at these words, and she unconsciously fiddled with the leather pouch at her hip. She was once again very aware that she had no idea how she had reached the city or why the Ley had brought her here. Saving this kind young peddler was clearly the right thing to do, but now he was safe Petronia did not know what her next move should be. Silently, she tried to tap into the rhythm of the Ley for guidance, but was only aware of the very slightest pulse, compelling her to stay with Aaron.

Aarold examined her pensive expression. 'Excuse my boldness,' he ventured shyly as a notion dawned on him, 'but you do appear to be very young and I was wondering if it was possible that you had been sent to Veridium to be educated by your Sister Ryders at their lodge in the city?' He was rewarded with a broad smile and much nodding.

'Do you know how to find it?' Bafflement crossed her face as she looked one way and then the other before shaking her head.

Pride swelled within Aarold's chest as he thought of a way that he could repay his rescuer. 'I don't know the way myself but I'm sure if we find a tavern they would give us directions.' He shivered a little as the autumn wind caught his frail body. 'It's very late and the streets around here are clearly unsafe. Would it be an offence to your order if I offered to pay for meal and lodgings in an inn for us, in separate rooms of course! Then at first light, we could seek out your Sisterhood.'

Petronia considered this offer for a long moment. She had wisdom enough to be suspicious of the intentions of men; many in the village had thought her pretty and her mother had told her to be wary. However, the idea of a good meal and warm bed after the challenges of an extraordinary day was very tempting. Without any other place to turn for advice, Petronia silently uttered a request that the Ley give her a sign as to whether her new friend was virtuous and at once a rush of instincts flowed into her brain. Looking at his kindly face, she saw it gold-rimmed with the Ley's approval, his whole slim form momentarily imbued with strong, chivalrous energy that overwhelmed his physical weakness. The Ley displayed for her the goodness within his heart.

Aarold watched her study him intently for a moment, her dark eyes seeming to weigh up the nature of his spirit. Then, with sudden certainty, she smiled her agreement. 'Excellent!' he breathed happily and with that the pair set off together in search of lodgings, both quietly grateful for finding a companion with whom to face the unknown challenges that may lay ahead.

Chapter 18

A RELENTLESS PURSUIT

The portly, middle-aged nursemaid Gurta pressed a sodden handkerchief to her flushed and tear-stained face and let out a woeful sob of guilt and sorrow. Before her, seated poised and inscrutable on the couch in her nephew's sleeping quarters, the White Duchess regarded her with the cool, green-eyed stare of a hawk watching a chubby field mouse.

'I just don't understand it,' bleated the distraught nanny, plucking at the prince's tangled and abandoned bedding for the umpteenth time, as if the knotted sheets were somehow hiding her charge's form. 'I swear, Your Grace, I helped him to bed and gave him his nightly medication.'

With a distracted gesture, Maudabelle lifted her pale hand for silence and Gurta fell mute with a fearful sob. The discovery of Prince Aarold's disappearance had been made early that morning sending the palace into panic, yet the White Duchess had remained unnervingly silent and calm. This did nothing to quieten the servants' troubled hearts. Everyone knew the duchess took the safety of her nephew gravely. If she even suspected that one of her personally appointed staff was connected with the prince's disappearance, then the penalty would be most severe.

'Yes, Mistress Gurta, I understand fully.'

She swallowed hard as if to repress un-shed tears that were kept behind her mask of porcelain beauty and wet her scarlet lips. Her eyes swept from the empty bed to the tall, imposing figure of Captain Tristram Kreen who was examining the room for any signs of forced entry or foul play. The head of the Royal Guard paused for a moment and shot the duchess a momentary look of reassurance. With his thick mane of red hair and mismatched-coloured eyes, one deep brown, one pale blue, Kreen was a well-known figure in the palace. A boyhood friend of the late king, his loyalty to the royal family was almost as famed as his ruthlessness in battle. Rumours hung around his burly form like a cloak he was not concerned enough to shake off. It was said that he had killed over a hundred men on the field of war and that only the late king could equal him as a swordsman and rider. There were more lascivious stories too, regarding his closeness to the White Duchess. Some said that they were lovers, others that he was merely besotted with her icy beauty, but she thought herself too above him to respond to any of his advances. One thing was certain though, since the deaths of the king and queen, Kreen had turned his devotion solely on the duchess, taking orders from none but her.

Gurta tried not to notice the look that passed between the pair and continued her explanation. 'As I say, Your Grace, I settled the young prince myself last night. But when I came to raise him this morning, gone he was!' Her eyes became glassy with tears. 'Makes my heart weep to think of something happening to him, poor sickly lamb that he is. Cared for him like one of my own, I did.' She pressed her handkerchief to her face to wipe a droplet of moisture from her slightly hooked nose.

Kreen, who was standing next to the window, regarded the crying nanny, suspicion coldly glinting in his mismatched eyes. Resting his long neat clipped fingernails on the glass, he thoughtfully caressed the pane. 'You are absolutely sure this window was locked from the inside when you left the prince last night?' he quizzed her harshly.

Gurta's face flushed slightly under the captain's accusing gaze. 'Why, yes, sir,' she enthused. 'I always lock the window of the prince's chamber at night.'

She stopped crying as she became aware of Kreen's eyes boring into her intently. Their unusual colouring gave his stare an unnerving quality, as if while the brown one was taking in your physical state, the blue was dissecting your soul, seeking out anything you dared to hide.

'Well, at least I *thought* I'd locked it. No, no, I did, I did, I must

235

have. Mustn't I?' she lowered her head and rested her hand against her cheek as she tried to recall her actions of the previous evening.

The captain took a half step towards the unnerved matron, his posture mildly intimidating. 'Because if this casement *was* left open, say by someone who knew that there were folk who wanted the prince dead, it could be seen as treason. If His Majesty has come to harm because of your negligence it could be seen as a very serious matter.'

Gurta's mouth dropped open as she gulped and spluttered like a fish pulled from water. 'Why, sir, what is it that you are implying? I have toiled in the palace happily since I was a girl of thirteen. There is none in the kingdom more loyal to the prince, more loyal to the crown, as I.' Kreen's pallid, chiselled features remained inscrutable and suspicious. 'It is my duty to guard the prince's life,' he explained coldly. 'I must seek out treachery wherever it lies.' Before he could say any more though, the Duchess Maudabelle shot him a wary glance, a lightning quick look with her vivid emerald eyes which made him fall silent.

'Thank you, Captain Kreen,' she uttered in a hoarse whisper, 'but I believe there is no need to harass Mistress Gurta any more. I appointed her to the prince's chamber myself.' The very sound of the White Duchess's voice seemed to hold sway over the captain's will. His face remained grim and detached, but there was a subtle alteration in his demeanour, a twitch of an eyelid, a tightening at the corner of his mouth, that spoke of compliance, devotions and perhaps even lust. 'As you wish, Your Grace,' he breathed, bowing humbly.

Maudabelle rested her alabaster hands, like two white doves, on the dark material of her skirt. 'That will be all, Mistress Gurta,' she stated calmly. 'You may leave. I have much to discuss with Captain Kreen regarding the search for my royal nephew.'

The nanny curtseyed low and left the bedchamber. Once she had departed, Tristram Kreen allowed passion and guilt to flood his pale skin. Falling to his knees before his adored duchess, he pressed his lips reverently against the gold signet ring of her left hand as she gazed aloofly down through thick, black lashes.

'Oh, my most beautiful and wronged lady,' he uttered, 'I have failed both you and your royal nephew. The safety of our young prince is my duty and yet I have allowed him to be stolen from his own bed. I beg you, with all the passion I have, for the forgiveness I am unworthy of.'

Maudabelle prised her elegant fingers from the captain's fevered grasp and motioned for him to stand. 'Your self-reproach is most uncalled for, my noble Captain,' she said, a forgiving smile playing on her lips. 'I do not blame you for the loss of my nephew. As woeful as it is, there are grave powers in this world that control men's fates. I only beg of you, my most steadfast Captain, to seek out these villains and rescue my nephew before his fragile life is lost.'

Eagerness smouldered brightly in the captain's eyes as he once more got to his feet. 'My heart, mind and actions are always at the will of the crown, as they are to you, my lady,' he uttered earnestly, secretly hoping that finding the prince alive would at last win him favour in the duchess's heart. From the moment Tristram had witnessed Maudabelle's pale and foreign beauty when she first arrived at the palace, he had been bewitched, yet years had passed with no greater response to his fevered adoration than polite pleasantries and unfulfilled promises. Perhaps returning the prince to the safety of his throne would at last let the duchess consent to be his bride.

'I will order every one of my men to search the kingdom. We will not rest until he is found and these traitors are brought to justice.'

'No!' The duchess's sudden outburst shocked Tristram and he gazed at her concerned, as crimson flushed her cheeks. Taking a calming breath, Maudabelle regained her composure and made her way over to the window, sombrely looking out as if her nephew was just beyond her vision.

Cautiously, Tristram approached, torn between the desire to comfort the woman he worshipped and the conventions of their status. 'Your Grace,' he ventured, 'is there something wrong?'

She pressed her hand to the column of her throat, turning to him with the slight glint of tears in her eyes. 'I fear there may be, my good Captain. It pains me to admit it but I have suspicions as to who is responsible for the prince's disappearance, yet I have no proof.' Anxiously she paced the room. 'I am gifted, dear Captain Kreen, with a certain amount of second sight, an intuition linked to the safety of my dear nephew. It is through this that I am able to know what ails him and what dangers might strike at his well-being. And as heinous as it is to confess, recently my mind has been drawn to the suspicion that the Sisterhood of the Ley Ryders harbours dark notions on the prince's life.'

Captain Kreen regarded her with uneasy doubt. He had heard many rumours about the Ryders, both good and bad, but like so many, knew very few solid facts about the order. 'The Ley Ryders?' he queried quizzically. 'Forgive my bluntness, sweet lady, but the Ryders are an ancient and trusted order, as old as Geoll itself. They answer only to the mystic force whose name they bare and have no quarrel with any.'

Maudabelle stopped her pacing and looked at him, seeming for that moment totally without any stately grandeur, no more than a vulnerable and frightened woman turning to him in her hour of need. 'I know it sounds foolish,' she confessed, her voice throaty and heavy with her Etherian accent, a tone that seduced his senses, 'but if they believed this country was in danger because of my nephew's sickness, this so-called Ley might compel them to seize power, not for their own greed perhaps, but out of duty to the people and I fear what would become of Aarold if they do.'

Agitated, she pressed one of her white hands to the russet material of Tristram's doublet while holding the other against her brow. The love-struck captain's feelings were in turmoil; this was the most intimate gesture she had ever shown and he found himself lost in the maze of her emerald eyes. 'Captain Kreen, I trust you more deeply than anyone in Geoll. I must know if my nightmares are true and the Ryders are behind the prince's disappearance.'

Tristram would have given anything, given his own life, to kiss her scarlet lips at that moment but he knew his place and did not allow his lust to soil the one chance he had to win her favour. Instead, he took her pale hand from his chest and chastely kissed her knuckles. 'Have no fear, Your Grace,' he reassured, 'if the Ryders know anything of the prince, then so will I.'

A relieved smile graced the duchess's face as she lowered her eyes gratefully. 'You are most loyal and understanding, Captain Kreen,' she told him. 'By your actions, you will gain many rewards.' Tristram's heart skipped at these words but he did not dare to express his hopes. If the prince was found through his actions, surely the young man's gratitude would mean he would willingly grant Tristram his aunt's hand in marriage. 'I will seek out the Ryders' lodge at once,' he said bowing deeply.

The besotted captain departed swiftly on his mission leaving the White Duchess alone with her thoughts. Once she was sure that he or the servants would not return, Maudabelle allowed her true emotions to rise to the surface. Letting out a frustrated expletive, she pounded one of the velvet cushions on the couch to release her wrath. This had put everything into turmoil and although it would be of great benefit to have some random villain slit her nephew's throat for her, it would not look good back in Etheria to have a common cut-throat succeed where her hard studied magic had failed. There would be a new order after the invasion, a new government to rule over Geoll and Maudabelle was not going to sacrifice her place in it because she had been caught asleep on the job. Besides, there were opportunities and allies in the city for Aarold as well as dangers. Aarold might quickly grow to realise he was not as incapable as his aunt had led him to believe. No, there would be nothing else for it. The killing could not be delayed a moment longer.

Taking a breath to master her emotions, Maudabelle left the prince's chambers and swiftly made her way through the palace's winding corridors to her own apartments, like a black-sailed galleon travelling smoothly across an even sea. Any servants who crossed her path did not dare to address her, thinking that her bloodless countenance was the grim mask of a troubled aunt and never guessing the murderous hatred that boiled behind it.

She entered her private refuge and barred the door, the moist gloom of the room soothing her emotions and helping her to draw on the power within her blood. In one corner of the sparsely furnished chamber, motionless in its mechanical slumber, squatted the black shape of the iron Golem. A cruel smirk twisted the scarlet mouth of the duchess as she gazed upon it. It had returned successfully from its last lethal mission; now it was time for it to perform the true task it had been designed for. Crossing the floor, Maudabelle crouched down beside the automaton, laying her pallid fingertips lightly on its hammered sable shell. Straight away, she could feel a dark, mindless force coiled within its cogs and springs tremble with energy as her warm flesh caressed the engravings on its body. Words of sorcery formed clearly within Maudabelle's mind and in a low, hushed whisper she uttered them to the machine. '*Awaken. Kill.*'

Deep beneath the Golem's smooth shell, the swirling dark power that Maudabelle had bound to it stirred, flowing like blood through the veins of a beast. Cogs linked and turned, rods pumped and springs flexed as it once again juddered to life. Its movements jerked into action as it awoke, legs tottering anxiously on the stone floor of the chamber, its antennae twitching this way and that as its awareness was awoken once more. The hinged compartment that formed its jaws snapped open with a sharp whir, hungry for violence and ready for input.

Smiling triumphantly to herself, Maudabelle reached into a pocket of her robes and drew out a small glass vial filled with thick, crimson liquid. The White Duchess had taken regular samples of her nephew's blood from when he had been a baby, using it to better determine the weaknesses of his body and formulating potions to aggravate them. Now this sample would be used for the ultimate goal: to end his miserable life.

Carefully uncorking the vial, the White Duchess steadily poured every drop of scarlet fluid into the Golem's awaiting maul.

'Yes, my lovely,' she crooned, her hand resting lightly on the automaton's back, sensing the growing power within. 'Drink well and learn. You have a new victim awaiting, one that you were built to destroy. Taste his blood and hunger to spill it.'

As the thick red fluid flowed into the metal orifice of the Golem, the movements of its complex mechanisms purred and chugged more purposefully, the life-force of the prince coating them, mingling with its dark spirit like an opiate in its motorised brain. A mindless impulse seized its automated actions, filling it with the unquestioning desire to seek out and slaughter its new victim. Juddering agitatedly, it scampered from Maudabelle's controlling touch and scuttled across the stone floor in the direction of the shuttered window, its workings oiled with Aarold's blood buzzing and chugging with vicious eagerness. The violent eagerness of the Golem seemed to heighten the duchess's own dark desires and like a graceful black moth she flew to the barred window and flung open the shutters, letting a narrow insipid beam of sunlight pierce her shadowy cloister. Her emerald eyes gleamed as they surveyed the city which would soon fall to the might of her birth-land.

With an agile leap, the Golem sprung on to the window ledge, antennae twitching as it sampled the fresh morning air for microscopic signs of its victim. Glancing down at the marvellous and deadly machine, Maudabelle felt inspired by the genius of her own invention. The moment it had returned from its first successful quest, the cruel White Duchess had set her dwarf slave Krogg about creating an army of these wonderful brutal machines. When these Golems, driven by her dark power, joined with her uncle's legions of Etherian warriors, the kingdom of Geoll would not stand a chance.

Joyous, she watched as the automaton scurried from its perch, using its tiny hooked feet to cling to the stone of the palace wall, moving as fleetingly as the shadow of a swift over the ground. Let her dull-brained suitor continue his pointless quest for the prince; it would serve no purpose. The scent of victory was already in her nostrils.

Chapter 19

THE SIGHTLESS SEER

In the cold, wet cleat of a dead tree, in the heart of a forest that he did not know the name of, Hayden, the simple blacksmith's son, dreamed of home. As he fitfully slept in his cramped cradle, he pictured so easily the safe and mundane existence that he had once taken for granted that now seemed to be a million miles away. In his mind, he was in Ravensbrook where magic and danger had no business. He was assisting his father in the forge, partaking in hard but honest toil, the tools of his craft familiar in his hands. He saw his mother, her face pink from the heat of the hearth, welcoming them home with a hearty meal of vegetable stew and fresh bread and his sister Petronia, broom in hand, sweeping the floor, a million unuttered words held within her eyes.

Petronia. In his restless sleep, Hayden's heart called frantically to his wayward sibling in a mixture of urgency, fear and rage. She looked at him, her lovely face distanced and searching and then melted away along with their parents, their home and village in a burst of cruelly sparkling crystals, leaving nothing but a violent black gale and the sound of a thousand Ley Ryders being called to arms. He awoke several times during that dark and rainy night, and despite his masculine pride found himself compelled to shed a tear for all that had been suddenly taken away. His body was so exhausted and his mind so frantic that he found it difficult to know what was dream and what was reality. He had hoped that the terrible peril he had been thrown into was no more than a fearful nightmare and his heart broke once more when he awoke in the cold early light to find himself uncomfortably wedged in his wooden nest; all the terrors and losses of the previous night were a cruel reality.

He emerged into the chilled air of the woodland morning like the first man to be called man and looked about this new unfamiliar place with a heavy heart. It had stopped raining for the moment but a clammy, cold fog hung heavy in the air. A camp fire crackled softly in the centre of the clearing and the Ley apprentice Bracken, Hayden's only companion in this strange, new place, crouched on the ground beside it, her peculiar wiry locks reflecting dully the autumn hues of the foliage. The haunches of a freshly caught rabbit roasted on the fire but Bracken was slowly and unwillingly devouring the raw inners, as was the custom of Ryders, with her bare hands. She paused from her meal, like an animal interrupted after a kill, as Hayden emerged from the hollow and watched with large, mistrusting eyes.

Silently, Hayden sat on the ground across from her, his gaze resting warily on her pale round face. His heart still quickened at the memory of anger, the rage and blame he had felt the night before for her kinsfolk. If it had not been for the Ryders, he and Petronia would still be together and at home. But events of the past could not be altered by fury and Bracken could not be held to blame for the actions of her adoptive family.

Drawing a blade from his belt, Hayden skewered a chunk of rabbit meat from the fire and proceeded to eat. Bracken finished the offal with an unwilling swallow and then copied him. The two ate in silence for a long time, exchanging uneasy glances. Several times Bracken reached inside her bodice and retrieved the letter her guardian Amethyst had given her, reading it through for comfort. Putting it away for the third time, she touched one of the many crystals she wore before finally breaking the silence. 'The forest is deeper than I thought,' she uttered in her deep hollow tone. 'I walked for a good hour before you woke and could find no sign of human life. There are plants and trees I am unfamiliar with in the woods around Goodstone.' She lifted her head and sniffed the crisp mist. 'I think we are in the north.'

Hayden took all this in without a word, feeling the dull throb of resentment towards Amethyst and the Ley Ryders for landing him in such a place. 'Any sign of paths or tracks that might lead to civilisation?' he asked dully.

Bracken tried to ignore the accusation in his tone and cleaned her blade on a rag from her purse. 'Not that I've noticed. There are fox tracks and wildcat, perhaps even goblins. Sister Amethyst taught me how to stay safe in the wilderness as part of my training. It's important for a Ryder to know how to...' Her voice trailed off into silence as she noticed the scowl on her companion's face at the mention of the Ryders. 'Well, I know how to survive in the woods anyway, so we'll be quite safe.'

'You intend to stay with me?' Hayden's tone was disbelieving and sharp.

Bracken faced his coolness with friendly indifference. 'Why, yes,' she said, 'I must. It says in the 17th Dogma that a Ryder must bring aid to where her heart sees it is needed.'

Hayden let out a short, harsh chuckle and poked at the embers of the fire with a twig. 'Your character astounds me, Mistress Bracken,' he remarked coolly. 'You once told me that in all your years not once had you felt the guidance of this so-called Ley move your senses. And yet, in this moment of strife, when we are lost in a strange land, away from all that is familiar, it is in the Ley you put your hope. How can you continue to follow a deity that has left your spirit unmoved?'

Bracken's face grew tense as she listened to his austere words, her complexion draining of colour so that the bands of veins that masked her features became even more noticeable. She shifted her heavy form slightly and at once Hayden was reminded of the very unfeminine strength that dwelt in her thick limbs. When she spoke, however, her voice was gentle and without anger.

'Faith,' she simply replied. 'It is what compels each one of us. I don't ask you to understand the nature of my belief in the Ley, it is simply how I was raised and I know of no other manner of living. But I refuse to believe that you, or any other man, is without faith in something greater than himself.'

Hayden snorted dismissively and gazed at the leafy canopy high above their heads.

'Don't you want to travel from this place and find your sister again?' probed Bracken pointedly. 'Do you believe you will be reunited and see your parents again? What is that if not hope in a concept you can't guarantee?'

'I made an oath to our father that I would watch over Petronia, an oath that your guardian forced me to break by banishing us to this unknown forest without so much as an explanation. Even if I could find my way back to Ravensbrook, I could not face my parents without knowing what had happened to Petronia.'

Bracken nodding sympathetically. 'A promise to a parent, devotion to a deity, it is all built on faith, a compulsion to do what we believe to be right. My apprenticeship as a Ryder will not allow me to abandon you in your need just as your devotion as a son and brother compels you to seek out your sibling.'

Grunting, Hayden took the remaining rabbit meat from the fire and bundled it up in a kerchief. 'Do as you will, then,' he grumbled. 'Just do not hamper me in my search!' Getting to his feet, he collected up his meagre belongings and looked about to decide which way to head. Bracken heaved her large frame from the ground and carefully kicked soil over the embers of the fire. 'If it sits with you better,' she stated, 'look on my companionship as penance for the wrongs you see my kin doing to your family. I am your willing servant.' He cast a severe glance in Bracken's direction. 'A murderer would pay a less harsh price than to have one of your Sisterhood as a fellow,' he muttered as they set off.

Using the sun as a guide, the pair of uneasy travellers set out north for Bracken had said she had seen little sign of civilisation to the south. Although both of them were familiar with woodland, the landscape of the forest was vastly different to that which either of them knew. The trees that grew here were mainly evergreen, their upwardly curved, evenly spaced branches dense with dark, glossy needles. The ground was slightly spongy underfoot and every so often they came across large patches of alien squat, purple-capped fungi that neither of them could find a name for. The wood, even in daylight, was filled with wildlife, the swift scurrying sound of deer, fox and rabbit and the chatter of birds in the bowers, their song sounding so different to the thrushes, jays and cuckoos Hayden knew from his home. He thought that there were other beings lurking among the shade of the trees too, wily, humanoid creatures with mischievous glinting eyes and dark scrawny limbs that burbled and chuckled high above them in a language indistinguishable from the rustle of leaves. He remembered the cautionary tales he had been told about wood imps and kept his senses alert.

They struck out in search of flowing water, a stream, river or brook whose path they might follow out of the wilderness, but could find none. From time to time Bracken would stop and take out a crystal from one of the purses on her belt, holding it cupped in her broad hands as she desperately tried to focus her senses and request the Ley show them which direction to go. But these moments of meditation always ended fruitlessly, with her sighing and silently cursing her lack of skills. Hayden watched her attempts ruefully, holding no belief that the stones she consulted would give them any divine aid. It was not her that he doubted, it was the Ley as a whole.

They walked all day with little rest, neither of them tiring, driven on by the growing desire to find a path out of the never-ending forest. The winter sun arched swiftly across the sky and by late afternoon its light was beginning to fade. A thick, pale mist seemed to rise around them in an instant, chilling the air and making it harder to see. As it filled the forest, Hayden sensed they were not the only sentient beings in the wood and fearfully he kept his hand near his blade.

'This is the sort of place where fairies hunt for souls,' he murmured warily, as Bracken paused once more to consult her crystals. 'Tell me, Mistress Bracken, does your apprenticeship teach you about dealing with the troublesome sprites that vex travellers in the wilds?'

Bracken put away the gem she was studying and glanced about her, a perturbed and distracted expression on her face. 'Oh yes,' she muttered as they carefully picked their way across the forest floor. 'Of course, my knowledge of them is only theological, from books and lessons, but many a Ryder has dealt with fairy mischief during their duties and travels.' She smirked to herself. 'I recall one occasion when Sister Rosequartz arrived at the citadel early one morning in a most disorderly state with strange markings on her neck. She claimed that she had been set on by fairies while helping the farmers around Goodstone harvest their crops. But I don't think Sister Amethyst truly believed her.' She chuckled but Hayden shot her a disapproving look and they travelled on in silence.

The cool afternoon was quickly transforming to dusk and the twilight fog that rose with the beginnings of night seemed to grow thicker by the second as Hayden and Bracken made their way through the forest, growing more eager to find any sign of civilisation. Deep indigo shadows criss-crossed their path, vastly altering the appearance of the woods and making it hard to tell whether the trees they were passing were in fact the same ones they had seen hours before. Evening made concern and homesickness burn fiercely in their hearts again as they both recalled with longing the comforts of their respective homes. Hayden became troubled by the notion that they were walking in a massive circle and would never see human life again. He looked at Bracken and despite his earlier resentment felt a sorrowful pang of pity to see her sturdy form moving ahead of him, her heavy posture failing to disguise the fear and loneliness she felt.

The adrenaline that had kept them going throughout the day had burned itself to nothing during the long trek and both of them were suffering from aching muscles and growling bellies. Suddenly, the most mouth-watering aroma wafted across Hayden's nostrils. Hungrily he breathed it in, running his tongue over his lips. Someone was cooking vegetable stew. Eagerly he nudged Bracken. 'Sniff the air,' he told her excitedly; 'I smell food. We must be near a homestead!'

Bracken's eyes grew bright with enthusiasm as she smelled the delicious odour permeating the evening air. 'I knew the Ley would guide us!' she enthused as filled with new energy they hurried in the direction of the wholesome smell.

Soon, dim lights came into view through the shadows of the branches as the trees grew sparser to reveal the hazy outline of a small cottage.

Hayden and Bracken dashed almost deliriously towards it, laughing with joy at their luck to have found a sanctuary so deep in the forest.

They rushed out of the undergrowth into the open glade to approach the tiny shack but as they stepped into the open, the tempting aroma of food vanished and the shadowy shape of the dwelling became paler. To their horrific disappointment, the cottage's outline blurred, becoming nothing more than abstract shades in the mist. A sob of frustration caught in Bracken's throat and Hayden let out a bellow of disbelief.

'But I saw,' he stuttered, gawking at the empty glade. 'I smelled!'

Bracken gave a ragged sigh as if her own disappointment was struggling to get free.

'A mirage,' she stated sadly, her shoulders slumping, 'brought on by our tiredness and hunger.'

Hayden staggered around, touching the ground and trees as if there was some hidden switch that would bring the cottage back into reality. 'No,' he gasped shaking his head, 'it can't be, we both saw it. It – ow!'

He let out a cry of shock and pain as something tiny and sharp, like a shard of glass, hit his cheek. Bringing his hand to his face, he saw that his fingertips were smudged with blood.

Swiftly, Bracken turned to face him, her hand anxiously on the hilt of her blade. 'What is it?' she asked fearfully.

Hayden patted the tiny scratch on his face. It was not deep but the area tingled strangely with an icy pricking sensation. 'I don't know,' he mused uneasily.

Suddenly Bracken let out a startled cry and gripped her shoulder. Taking her hand away, she brought with it a small slither of purple material as if a blade moving too fast to be seen had lashed out and cut a hole in her gown. Her breath caught in her throat with fear and instinctively she cast her eyes upwards. 'Look!' she gasped in horror.

Hayden followed her gaze. Hung in the night air just feet above their head, was a vast glittering cloud of what at first glance appeared to be pale blue dragonflies. However, when Hayden looked closer he saw that they were surrounded by a host of thin-bodied fairies with translucent buzzing wings. It was a sight as terrifying as it was beautiful. Each fairy's body was no thicker than a blade of grass and their limbs shone like glass needles in the starlight. Their faces were so tiny it was impossible for the human eye to make out their features, but you could still, very clearly, get an impression of their expressions: a hungry amorality that gazed down at the pair from a thousand sets of microscopic, fly-like eyes. Amid the crowd were visible quick flashes of light and movement as the strange creatures whizzed back and forward through the air.

Bracken tightened her grip fearfully on her sword and prepared to draw it. 'Fairies,' she breathed anxiously, 'they lured us here with the glamour of refuge so they could ambush us. Get ready to flee.'

His throat dry, Hayden fumbled for his weapon and took a half step back. Time seemed to be captured in ice, freezing his actions, but above him the swirl of needle-like bodies still buzzed and clicked with eager anticipation. Then with one united thought, every single fairy dived on them, enveloping the pair in their frantic, stinging assault.

The first thing that overwhelmed Hayden was the noise, a piercing, metallic clamour, ear-splittingly high and deafening, that disorientated him and confused his instincts. Then came the pain, as the fairies set upon him with minuscule cuts and scratches, barely visible to the naked eye but acutely sharp, slicing through clothing and skin, tearing away tiny fragments to be devoured. He battled to fight back against the swarm, swinging his blade this way and that through the mist of hair-like forms that swirled around. He could hear a biting zing again and again as his blade collided with one small brittle body after another, but the sheer volume was staggering.

Likewise, Bracken struck out at the fog of clawing, scratching forms, trying with all her might to carve a pathway to their escape. She swung her thick stone scimitar in wide, powerful arcs, rending the bloodthirsty sprites from the air, but fiercely they kept coming at her, peppering her skin with thousands of tiny, agonising wounds. The stinging of the blows dissolved into her piebald skin, making it prickle and burn with an excruciating sensation of venom pouring into her, both icy and fiery in the same instant. Her mind raced with countless lessons from her apprenticeship and her free hand fumbled in the pouches at her belt to retrieve some crystal that might have the power to drive the fairies back. The pain that racked her body, however, made her fingertips clumsy and the stones slipped from her grasp.

At her side, Hayden reeled about inefficiently, the blows of his sword lazy and heavy. The venom from the fairies' bites had quickly worked its way into his bloodstream, numbing his nerves and hampering his coordination. He felt nauseous and tired and was not sure how much longer he could continue fighting when a manic cry filled the clearing and through his blurred vision, Hayden saw the oddest creature run out of the wood, brandishing a fiery torch.

'Aaaaeeeeooooooaaaaaah!' The figure leapt from the shadows whirling the burning branch in all directions as it ploughed headlong into the fairy hordes, a wild mass of tangled, grey hair, lean, muscular limbs and animal pelts. Exhausted and overwhelmed, Hayden fell to his knees, the agony of the fairy attack gripping his muscles. The wild figure jumped and danced around, thrashing his fiery weapon out at every angle, driving away the murderous forest spirits with its orange light. Her vision at last cleared by the sudden fleeing of the fairies, Bracken saw Hayden hunched in pain on the ground and worriedly hurried to his side. He shrieked with pain as each racing heartbeat pushed the icy poison deeper into his body and anxiously Bracken rummaged through her purses and amulets for a crystal that might bring him aid.

Meanwhile, the strange figure stalked around them at some distance, forming an uneven circle as he thrashed his torch from side to side. Now that the panic had ceased, Bracken could see that the peculiar beast was not a beast at all, but in fact a wiry framed, elderly man. His hair and beard were grey and straggly, knotted with twigs and dirt, and he was clothed only in a rough cape of crudely darned animal skins. He looked ancient and had an odd manner of moving: a crouched, ambling gait, spine bent, more like a bear than a human. Despite this, the muscles of his body were lean and ropey, his dark-skinned form not having an ounce of excess fat. The nails of his fingers and toes were thick and claw-like and his face an ugly mass of wrinkled, leathery skin and bristled hair. He swung his torch around like a club, screeching in a tone that barely clung to the rim of human understanding, somewhere between language and the snarls of beasts.

'Back!' he barked threateningly, stabbing his lighted branch towards the sky. 'Back fairies baaaack!' He snorted aggressively and tilted his head to one side, listening to the hushed sounds of the forest. Curled in spasms of agony on the ground, Hayden groaned and swore as the fairy poison twisted his insides with burning pain, making him want to claw his own skin off with its icy torture.

Hearing the cries of suffering, the wild man spun sharply to face them, his torch jabbed menacingly in their direction. The blazing glow of the flame clearly illuminated his hideous features: hooked nose, sharp uneven teeth and scarred, filthy complexion. Bracken gasped with shock. It was not these features that startled her, it was the eyes of the wild man. In the gleam of the fire, his irises were pale and milky, like two opaque marbles, displaying only the faintest shadow of pupils. He was completely blind!

The hermit took a lunging step towards them, his thick lips drawn back to show an uneven set of beastly teeth. 'Who there?' he growled, shuffling towards the frightened pair, his free hand stretched out, clasping violently at the air. 'You speak now! I know you there, can hear you, smell you!' He grunted and lurched towards them, his back stooped.

Fearfully, Bracken let out a little cry and instinctively reached for her sword to protect herself and Hayden from the stranger. But the moment she began to drawn the blade from its leather scabbard, the wild man let out a fierce cry and leaping in the air, skilfully kicked the blade from her hand. Bracken yelped with shock as the sword flew from her grip and landed a few feet away. Fearfully, she studied the man's cloudy eyes, finding it hard to believe someone with such damaged sight could land such an accurate kick.

Angrily, he jabbed a long-nailed finger in her direction. 'No weapons!' he barked sharply, stamping his foot. 'You speak! Who are you?'

Carefully, he pushed the handle of the torch into the ground and scuttled forward, hands outstretched to discover the intruders who had ventured into his woodland domain. Bracken's muscles grew taut as he approached. She suspected she was powerful enough to overcome the hermit, but doubted that she could do so and keep Hayden safe at the same time. Terror rippled her skin as the old man's filthy hands moved with rough swiftness across her face and shoulders.

'Girl,' he muttered decidedly to himself, roughly patting her broad cheeks, 'young, yes, strong too and...' He reached down and began to examine Hayden cradled in her arms in the same inquisitive manner. Bony fingertips pinched his nose and prodded his cheeks, plucking several hairs from his scalp and sniffing them. 'A boy also,' concluded the wild man, dropping the chunk of hair and shuffling back to where he had planted his torch. 'Both young, both stupid!' He scratched himself beneath his covering of furs, plucking an insect from them and putting it in his teeth.

Hayden let out another gasp of pain and seized hold of Bracken's hand. 'It burns,' he cried. 'Help me.'

Turning her attention back to her companion, Bracken frantically searched through her crystals, trying to recall her lessons in healing as she pressed various stones fruitlessly against his tender skin.

The ugly beast man crouched a short distance away, head tilted, listening to Hayden's cries of pain. After a few moments, he gestured at Hayden and then pointed to the sky. 'Fairy shot,' he grunted knowingly, as Bracken fought to bring him relief. 'Travel in woods at night with no fire. Stupid. Fire keep fairies away. He die now.'

Bracken looked at the old man horrified, her lips trembling with the dread that his words might be true.

'No,' she gasped, tears beginning to form in her eyes, 'he can't. The Ley wouldn't allow it.' Tenderly she laid him on the leafy ground and pulled open his shirt to get better access to his chest, pressing a small uncut diamond to his reddened skin. She prayed to the Ley that, if she had any ability to channel It, it would be awakened but still no flux of power flowed through her. The hermit's gruff words filtered into her brain. 'Only velvet cap mushroom draw out fairy shot. You not know? Stupid.' Wiping tears from her eyes, Bracken stared at the strange figure seated in front of her, rocking on his heels. 'Velvet cap mushroom?' she stammered. 'Is that the antidote? Tell me will it save him?'

Crossly, the hermit tossed back his head and yowled at the sky. 'No,' he snapped impatiently. 'Velvet capped mushroom draw out fairy shot. Whether he live or die, his choice!' He let out a frustrated bark like a kicked dog and leaping to his feet, shambled haphazardly into the trees.

Fearfully Bracken watched the lithe hermit vanish into the shadows of the forest and cradled the shivering Hayden, rubbing the fragments of diamond against his naked chest. Looking down at his handsome face, she felt a throb of tender concern and guilt that he might lose his life and she was unable to do anything. Yet again she feared all her education as a Ryder had been useless.

There was a rustle in the branches at the edge of the clearing and once more the terrifying figure of the ancient, blind wild man lumbered into the ring of firelight. In his claw-like hands were clasped a dozen or so, medium-sized, dusky blue mushrooms. He fell to his knees beside Hayden and roughly thrust one of the fungi into Bracken's face.

'See, see,' he barked fiercely, 'velvet cap draw out fairy shot!' He then began tearing the spongy flesh of the plants apart with his long, filthy nails, crushing it to a grey pulp in the palm of his hand with a bony knuckle. Bracken watched him work with a mix of awe and revulsion, doubting very much that a crazed individual such as this had the healing power to save Hayden. The hermit spat into the bowl of his hand to add moisture to the mushroom flesh and then roughly began to smear the mixture into Hayden's chest. Bracken reached out with her crystals to try and heal him once more, but the wild man bared his teeth and shoved her hands away.

'Get!' he ordered the frightened girl, continuing to brutally massage the fungus into Hayden's skin. The boy twitched spasmodically, his eyelids flickering and he let out a low grunt. The wild man took a clump of pulp and violently pushed it down Hayden's throat, forcing him to swallow. The lad gagged and spluttered and then sat bolt upright, blinked hard and looked around.

'The fairies,' he groaned placing his hand on his tender head and casting his eyes towards the now empty sky. 'What happened?'

Seeing her companion fully recovered, Bracken let out a cry of relief and, overcome with emotion, threw her arms around his neck and embraced him. 'Oh thank the Ley!' she exclaimed to the shocked boy. 'I thought you were going to die!'

Embarrassed by the sudden flood of affection she had displayed, Bracken quickly let go of him, her normally colourless cheeks glowing. 'The fairies attacked us,' she explained, too self-conscious to meet Hayden's eyes. 'And you bore the brunt of their assault. If it hadn't have been for this...' she paused, not knowing how quite to describe their saviour who had now staggered back to his feet. Plucking the torch from the ground, he was now stalking around the clearing muttering angrily to himself.

'This, um, good-hearted fellow, we would have both been overcome with their venom. He frightened the swarm away with fire and brought you healing herbs to revive you.'

Hayden turned to see his unlikely rescuer, equally as surprised as Bracken at his wild and hideous appearance. It was as if he had been born from the wood itself, more animal than man, all vestiges of human refinement stripped away, leaving only muscle, hair and instinct. Yet within those white and unseeing eyes, Hayden thought he saw a profound spiritual wisdom.

Cautiously, the boy extended his hand towards him. 'We are in your debt, good sir,' he said earnestly, as the wild man hobbled around the clearing, examining the grass for any further signs of danger. He turned his head slightly when Hayden spoke and grunted something that sounded like, 'Emouchet.'

Carefully Hayden stood up, watched by a concerned Bracken. 'Emouchet?' he queried as the hermit sniffed the night air; 'is that what you are called?'

The wild man twitched, shaking a straggly lock of hair from his face. Abruptly, he turned on them, his milky eyes glowing angry orange in the torch fire. 'Stupid!' he yowled, jabbing his torch in their direction like some hellish imp from a nightmare. 'Stupid, both stupid! You come to forest in night, no respect, no thought. Tis why fairies attack. Folk no understand forest, only Emouchet know forest, know fairies and spirits, know beasts and birds, know tings that grow. Is Emouchet's home. Stupid folk, get away!'

He spread his long, muscular arms wide and tilted his head back to let out a blood-curdling cry of dominance, spinning round like a sorcerer in a trance. The trees surrounding the clearing rustled with the sounds of birds and animals awakened by his terrible howl. Fearfully, Hayden and Bracken huddled together, hearts in their throats.

Hayden swallowed hard as Emouchet lowered his arms, the flame of his torch flickering. 'We meant no harm,' he panted. 'I am Hayden of Ravensbrook and this is Bracken, ward of the Ryder Amethyst and apprentice to the Ley. We did not come to your woods by choice but were sent here by a spell cast by Bracken's guardian so we might escape an attack on her citadel.'

The hermit took a lurching step back towards the pair, pressing his hideous face close to them, and inhaled deeply through his hooked nose as if their very scent would supply him with information about their characters much greater than vision ever would. He remained perfectly still, his gnarled features barely inches away from Hayden's own.

'All folk be the same,' he muttered menacingly to himself before adding in a croaking whisper, 'Though perhaps...' Then his features contorted into an unsightly scowl and grunting dismissively, he turned back towards the shadowy woods.

'No,' he sniffed crossly to himself, 'if them not know about fairies, then what they know about themselves? People, yeugh!'

He began to traipse back towards the trees, leaving Hayden and Bracken to look at each other baffled. Neither could quite make out Emouchet for although he had saved them from the fairy attack and healed Hayden over their poisonous influence, the hermit seemed to regard them with utter contempt. Why show such clemency for people you dislike?

At the edge of the clearing, the strange old man stopped, head tilted as he took in the sounds and atmosphere of the forest. 'You come with?' he barked abruptly.

Unsure, Hayden glanced at Bracken. 'He wants us to follow him,' he mouthed, as the hermit broke away some twigs to clear a path for them in the undergrowth, 'and he does seem to know the perils of this landscape more than you or I.'

Doubt marked Bracken's face and she fingered her amulets nervously. 'It is at times like this when I most regret my lack of Ley sense,' she confessed, 'for It would surely know whether this strange fellow came as blessing or curse. I myself have no idea.' She sneaked a glance in the hermit's direction, but then quickly looked away when she saw that he had lifted his cape of animal pelt and was urinating copiously against a tree. After leaving his mark in this manner, Emouchet wrapped his furs about him once more and stated, 'You stay here, you die. Emouchet care not either way.'

Then with the fiery torch gripped firmly in his claw-like hand, he scuttled into the woods.

In the new gloom of the eerie clearing, Hayden was once more aware of the unnatural noises of the forest and breathed a reluctant sigh. 'I admit, he is not the most genteel of guides,' he said, retrieving Bracken's sword from where Emouchet had kicked it, 'but surely if he had meant us harm, he would have shown it by now and I fear there are worse beasts in this place than a blind hermit.'

Unwillingly, Bracken was forced to agree. 'By actions of virtue and mercy, so may the Ley be seen, so says the 37th edict,' she quoted, securing her weapon. 'A Ryder never judges by appearances.'

Together, Bracken and Hayden set off once more into the shadows of the forest, this time following the flickering orange flame of the torch carried by the blind hermit Emouchet, a creature that seemed as animal as he was human and as wise as he was insane. To their surprise, they had to move swiftly to keep up with him for despite Emouchet's obvious lack of sight, he moved deftly through the forest, like a grey haired spectre or ancient primate. His remaining senses and memory of the landscape were remarkable as he powered himself forward, skilfully traversing hidden roots and vines that tripped and snagged Hayden and Bracken. A combination of his blindness and age and his familiarity with the woods seemed to have robbed him of all fear as he leapt from the forest floor to tree trunk, to low-hanging branches and back to the ground with no thought that he might fall. It made Hayden's heart catch in his throat to watch him.

'How can he find the safe path when he cannot see?' he puzzled to Bracken as Emouchet disappeared once more into the lower canopy of the trees. Hayden let out a shriek of horror as with a sudden angry cry, Emouchet's ugly face appeared before him upside down. 'Emouchet is blind!' he snarled, dropping to the ground before him and giving the boy an aggressive shove. 'Does not mean Emouchet can't see. Is two different things. Many, many folk have two working eyes still they see nought!'

The gleam of the torch danced over his twisted features, reflecting into his opaque pupils so they looked like two amber discs. 'This place,' he uttered, in a low, hallowed tone that pricked at Hayden's skin, 'this wood, it taught me to see. See clear, see far, to distant lands and folk, see who folk really are. Now you must learn. Both!' Roughly, he thrust the handle of the torch into Hayden's hand before swiftly turning on his heel and darting ahead of them into the inky darkness.

Cautiously, Hayden and Bracken crept forward, picking their way carefully through the trees, ears pricked for the shambling footsteps and strange calls and yelps of Emouchet as he beckoned them onwards. Soon they caught sight of another orange, crackling light, casting long, dancing shapes of brightness and gloom between the trees. Their senses alert and fearful that this may be another fairy trap, the pair pressed on until they came upon the small campfire burning beneath a massive, ancient tree whose thick, gnarled trunk stretched sturdy and high above its siblings. The atmosphere surrounding it was mystical and awe inspiring and the night air was alive with the sound of caws and cries and the flutter of countless wings. Hayden held the torch high and peering up into the shadowy canopy gasped with shock. The broad branches of the tree were tangled and knotted like uncombed hair, with countless untidy nests and eyries built in every notch and fork. Thousands of bright, keen eyes stared down at them from every bough, scrutinising their visitors.

Hayden had never seen so many birds gathered together in one place and felt quite unnerved to be under their unblinking stare. The tree was a kingdom of carrions: birds of prey of every species and size from the smallest blue-winged merlin to great and imposing eagles with chests of copper feathers, each one peacefully roosting, watching the dark night like silent spectres, their beaks and talons gleaming like polished blades in the light of the campfire. Way beneath their perches and nests, on the bare and pellet-littered ground, a single arresting figure stood erect in the orange glow of the fire. Emouchet seemed too to be a bird trapped in the flesh of a man, doomed to walk on the earth instead of soar heavenward. The untrimmed nails of his bony fingers and toes were like curved talons, his large prominent nose echoing the shape of an eagle's beak. His arms were spread wide to either side and his cloak of fur hung from them in a curved semicircle like the wings of a falcon riding the air. Even his beard and hair fluttered feather-like in the night air and the light from the fire coloured his opaque pupils gold. He heard the pair approach his camp and slowly lowered his arms, gracefully crouching to sit on the forest floor like a bird coming to roost.

'So, you come, you live,' he uttered in a surprisingly soft tone. 'This is good. Interesting. We will see, I think.' He made a gesture that they should come closer and sit with him at the fireside, which Hayden and Bracken did with some reluctance as the ground was filthy with droppings and smelt like an unclean aviary. Reaching out, the hermit firmly grasped Hayden's hand between his own, bringing it roughly to his face to sniff his skin. Meticulously, he studied the boy's palm and fingers, tracing his own emaciated digits over the shape of his hand as if reading some invisible words etched there. He followed the lines of his palms, pressed the soft, rough pad at the tip of each finger, sniffed his nails and pinched his knuckles. Finally, he released Hayden's hand and looked into his face with unfocused eyes.

'You wish to live,' he observed, the inky shadows of the fire flickering over his lined and whiskered features. 'Why? For what purpose is your life?'

Hayden was surprised by such a searching question, but quickly found his answer in the goal he had set himself. 'To protect my sister.

Fate has taken her from me at a time of peril and it is my duty to find her.'

Emouchet's face puckered as if he had tasted sour fruit and he crossly shook his head.

'No, no, no,' he chided, jabbing him painfully in the arm with a long fingernail. 'That is no purpose, no purpose at all. Are you man or are you shadow, hm? You empty, here,' he tapped Hayden's chest. 'So you look for others to fill you up. Not know who you are. Your sister, she find her own path and where does that leave you?'

'That's all very well and good,' retorted Hayden, heatedly, his emotions raw from the recollection of his missing sibling, 'but you do not understand. My sister is a mute and none but I, our parents and neighbours have knowledge of her manner of communication. Alone in the world, she is vulnerable.'

Emouchet threw up his hands and pointed to his throat. 'Is not a thing!' he exclaimed to an agitated Hayden. 'What is a voice? What is sight? Or limbs? Lizard loses tail, it still lizard, then what is tail? Each has what it needs. She find a way or else die. How things is. You not change that.'

The hermit's harsh words filled Hayden with rage and his hand flew to his sword. 'You filthy, evil old man!' he cried. 'What do you know? I have a good mind to...'

High above, in the tangled branches, the hordes of eagles, owls and other birds of prey, screeched and beat their wings as if they understood Hayden's threat, but Emouchet simply pointed at the boy fearlessly.

'Kill Emouchet, then what? Does that magic your sister to you or you to her? No! Does that take you from this wood? No! You brave, good heart but know not your purpose. So you shout, you run, you wave sword and make threat but why? Because you frightened and not know who you are. What if your sister die? What if she survive without your tongue? What then?'

Hayden's hand tightened on his sword but he did not move for the hermit's words had struck deep within him. In the past few days, he had seen power and magic the like of which he had never guessed had existed. Indeed, he had cast himself as Petronia's defender but not once in their time with the Ryders, not even during the attack on the citadel, had his sister looked to him for protection. Hayden had put this down to stubbornness and naivety but what if he was wrong and Petronia really did have a knowledge or skill beyond his understanding. He thought back to the night before the Ryders came to Ravensbrook, of how Petronia had made the pebbles dance in the moonlight and once again felt within him that frantic fear of something he had not the power to define let alone fight. If Petronia was part of this greater entity, if, for better or worse, it did engulf her with Its power, what did that leave for him? Emptiness sat uncomfortably in his belly, making him feel as vulnerable as he thought his sister to be, but masculine pride and the duty he felt towards his kin would not allow him to admit to it.

Sightless, Emouchet seemed to read the boy's pensive expression as if it was carried to him as a scent or sound on the warm air of the fire. 'You must look within not without,' he told him solemnly. 'Find in your heart what you are.'

Bracken nodded in reverent agreement. 'The Ley has a path for us all,' she reminded him in a sincere whisper.

The hermit let out an incredulous grunt and twisted his shaggy head towards the sound of Bracken's voice. 'You think?' he cawed harshly, 'you think you see your way? Ley, pah! Didn't stop fairies, did it? What are you? Let Emouchet see.' Abruptly, he seized Bracken's hand and began examining it even more intently than he had Hayden's, pinching and poking her pale, fleshy palm roughly and feeling the shape of her stubby, thick fingers. Bracken let out a cry of protest as the wild man unceremoniously brought his face down and sucked the tip of her thumb ponderously before spitting over his shoulder, muttering, 'Curious, yes, yes; no common sort this one!'

Bracken tugged her hand away from the old man's grasp. 'Indeed I am not!' she said huffily, wiping her hand on the skirt of her robe. 'I am a loyal apprentice to the Ley and will become a noble Ryder when It deems it the right time to reveal to me my Stone Name.'

At this remark, Emouchet rocked back and forward, letting out a manic cackle of mirth so loud that it disturbed the birds roosting high above. Greatly offended, Bracken gripped the pendants that hung around her neck.

The hermit slapped his naked thighs with merriment. 'Say who?' he mocked, waggling his finger at the wounded girl. 'You be Ryder? How you know?' Bracken's thin lips tightened as they had done when Hayden had spoken ill of her guardian, but Hayden saw uncertainty glimmer in her dark green eyes.

'I am the ward of Sister Amethyst,' she stated clearly, sounding more as if she was trying to reaffirm her own knowledge than convince the wily old man. 'The Ley guided her to me when I was a helpless baby and instructed her to raise me to follow the path of the Sisterhood. My awakening will come, it will!'

Emouchet grunted knowingly and shifted on to his bony knees. 'You worse than he!' he chided, gesturing towards Hayden. 'Him not know what he is, goes looking in all wrong places. You think you know who you is but is wrong, is not that at all! Like snake that tried to be squirrel or bat that think it be fish. Is the wrong shape!' As if to emphasise his point, Emouchet seized Bracken's hand again, poking his bony finger against her chubby palm. He then proceeded to go further, patting up her broad arm and gripping her muscular shoulder. Seeing his companion being manhandled in such a rude and unseemly way, Hayden reached out and pushed the hermit off her. Not expecting to be grabbed like this, the blind man fell gracelessly backwards, slapping Hayden away with sharp blows.

'You mad old fool!' he declared, as Emouchet scrambled to sit up again, screeching and flapping his cape about like a bird knocked unexpectedly from its perch. 'What's wrong with you?' Crouched on all fours, Emouchet looked towards the sound of Hayden's angry voice, his cloudy eyes seeming to glow with the light of the fire. 'Nought wrong with Emouchet,' he burbled shrewdly. 'Emouchet know who he is; learnt it from the forest. You two be the ones with no clue. But it is not hopeless, if you learn to see, oh no, no, no!'

He motioned for Hayden to calm himself and sit down again and then gestured towards Bracken. 'She,' he uttered cautiously, 'is made from great power, great, great power from within. Not of the common magic. Not of that she been taught, that she is trying to fit to. But from uncommon fate. She is special, is rare.'

Hayden looked across the fire to Bracken's unnerved, pallid face framed with hair that at this moment seemed to glow with the russet gleam of flame and saw that her hands had moved subconsciously from her crystal pendants to the strange cylinder Amethyst had given to her.

'What kind of power?' he queried softly.

At this, the hermit's unsightly face twisted and puckered into an expression of inscrutability, as he dug into the soft soil with his long fingernails. 'Is not Emouchet's place to say,' he barked abruptly, slapping at the ground. 'Only you can know who you be. Same for both. Look with heart, look with true self, then you see.'

Hayden's eyes returned to Bracken's abnormally tall and pale figure seated pensively gazing into the fire and his mind puzzled on the mystery of her true parentage. She gripped the strange cylinder tightly in her large hand and remained silent for a few moments while Emouchet fidgeted and fussed, flapping his pelt cloak about and picking at the leaves dropped from the flock above them.

Finally she spoke in her calm, low tone. 'What did you mean, Emouchet, when you said the forest told you who you were?'

Emouchet stopped still as a statue when he heard these words. Slowly, he drew himself to his feet, arching his head back and inhaling with solemn reverence. 'My story,' he whispered as the birds roosting high above shifted and squawked knowingly, 'Emouchet's story, yes. I will show, you will learn.'

He pointed his right index finger in the direction behind Bracken. 'To the south,' he uttered, 'many, many summers gone. My family, my mother and father. They were poor, poorer than soil but with many, many children. My brothers and sisters had to work, work hard to feed themselves, was no succour, no charity for those who could not. Emouchet was born sightless, was unable to toil in the fields, pay his dues, make his worth for others.'

'That is a very sad tale,' exclaimed Hayden compassionately. The old man scowled and waved his hand dismissively. 'Is not sad,' he muttered, 'is not sad, is not happy, is just what was, cannot be altered. Emouchet was blind, therefore served no purpose to family. Weighed them down, took and never gave. Whole family would starve. So in Emouchet's seventh summer, my father took me deep into this forest and Emouchet was left for good of family.'

Bracken's eyes grew glassy as she listened, contrasting the hermit's childhood abandonment with her own. 'What a heinous thing for a father to do,' she said, clutching at her pendants. 'It was ill fortune that a member of the Ryder Sisterhood couldn't give your family aid in their hour of want.'

Emouchet pouted angrily and stomped his foot on the ground. 'Does you not listen?' he barked as the birds of prey in the trees screeched crossly. 'No Ley come to us, so what of it? My father was a good man, did what he had to for his children, gave up one for sake of many. Twas his choice. No duty to Ley, to gods or spirit, only to himself and his own. His decision was right. Bear him no blame; human life small part of my story.'

The hermit lowered himself to the ground, sitting cross-legged before the fire. His face was calm and unemotional and his opaque eyes seemed to rest without any command from him at a point within the flickering flames. 'So was my father's choice,' he repeated softly. 'He leave his son to the forest. Now is coming Emouchet's choice, at the age of seven, alone in the wild, blind, scared. Is the choice all folk make at least once, the choice you make when fairies attack just now. Do I want to live or do I want to die?'

Entranced, both Hayden and Bracken leant forward in anticipation as Emouchet fell silent, lost in memory. 'What happened then?' asked Hayden with trepidation. Abruptly, the old man reached across and without even looking away from the fire, landed him a swift blow across the back of his head.

'You idiot, are you?' he exclaimed as Hayden nursed his bruised scalp. 'Am I not here? I choose to live! To survive! With my family, twasn't no life for me. But here, here. I learn. Listen to the beasts and live as they do, eat as they eat. Very tough, hard life, much strife and pain. But is how Emouchet is made. Was not my time to die when father left me, tis not my time yet. Emouchet may not see, but I is always finding a way. In here.' He pressed a clawed hand to his bare, wood-like chest and then repeated the gesture on Hayden. 'Here!' he enthused, pressing his nails against the boy's flesh. 'That's where you find who you are to be, both of you! This wood.' He slowly turned his back on the pair and crept across to the trunk of the giant oak under which they were sheltering to caress its knotted bark reverently. 'These trees, this air and plants, the beasts, they speak to Emouchet.'

Throwing back his head, the wild man opened his throat and let out a shrieking squawk that echoed through the inky shadows, making the branches of the mighty oak tremor and disturbing the flocks that nested just out of sight. From the blackness above, countless cries and calls rang out in reply as powerful wings took to the icy air. Emouchet chuckled merrily and swirled his cape in a sweeping circle as his adopted family of hawks and eagles responded to his cry. Lifting his arms high, he danced in a manic ring, feet barely still for a moment as several birds swooped down like clawed shadows. Hayden and Bracken jumped back in shock as a pair of large white-tailed eagles dived out of the darkness, landing just a few feet away from Emouchet. They were joined only seconds later by a smaller blue sparrowhawk that came to perch happily on the old man's arm.

Lovingly, Emouchet petted the smaller bird's orange breast before stooping down to extend his fingers to the eagles in familiar greeting. 'The birds,' he continued earnestly, 'they be Emouchet's family now. They teach me and I am one of them. Have no need for eyes, for the hawk, the osprey, the eagles, the owls they show Emouchet how to see with the heart and mind. On their wings, my spirit soars, see many folk and distant lands.'

One of the massive eagles folded its wings and with deliberate, shuffling footsteps crept towards Hayden, its head bowed, eyeing him intently with its huge, unblinking gold eyes. He found himself caught in the creature's gaze and was overcome by the strangest sensation that someone else was watching him through those hunting irises of fire. That this bird, all birds within this strange haunted glade were in tune with Emouchet's mind and through their faultless vision he was given access to the world.

'You not need eyes to see,' came the hermit's solemn words, 'and you no need tongue to speak. You will learn, you will understand.'

Hayden felt unnerved, every hair on his body alive with energy. He managed to tear his gaze away from the eagle's piercing stare to look upon Emouchet's hideous face. 'The birds really allow you to see anywhere you wish?' he asked nervously.

Emouchet lifted his chin slightly and sucked on the filthy, grey whiskers that drooped over his top lip. 'Emouchet learn,' he stated firmly; 'took many, many years to know what is to be bird. Now birds and Emouchet be one mind, one heart. Is who I am.' He bowed his head and cawed affectionately to the small hawk perched on his hand. The bird twisted its head and blinked its bright beady eyes, making a soft chirp as if it had understood perfectly what he had said.

Filled with fragile hope, Hayden scrambled to his feet. 'Then you could seek out my sister, see if she is okay! She is a maid of my age, dusky complexion and very pretty. Her hair is long and black and her eyes the same shade as mine. She is a mute, as I say, and when I last saw her she wore a gown matching that of my companion. I would owe you my life if you could tell me where she is.'

'Hayden,' Bracken said, her round face pale with doubt and trepidation, 'do you truly believe such a thing is possible?'

Hayden cast her an impatient glance and saw that she was still fingering her bangles of multicoloured stones for comfort. He felt almost spiteful towards her; this strange wild man had offered them more practical aid that day than her beloved Ley. Silently, the hermit raised his arm and the sparrowhawk took to flight. 'Emouchet may see your sister,' he told an overjoyed Hayden, before adding sharply, 'but will not lead you to her! If she lives, I will say, if she dead, I will say. But her path is her own, not yours! She must find her own way! Like you.'

'But,' stammered Hayden dismayed. Before he could continue, however, Emouchet let out an enraged bark and jabbed a pointed fingernail against the boy's chest. 'I tell you tomorrow then show you way from forest. That is all,' he snarled angrily.

'You two not belong in forest, have no respect for it. Sooner you go is better! That is Emouchet's offer. Take it if you wish or leave alone, get lost, die. Your choice.'

Turning his back on the pair, he hobbled back towards the tree, flanked by the two eagles who stared expectantly up at him.

Hayden remained silent for a moment, his hand resting on the spot above his heart that Emouchet had gestured to. He looked at Bracken, seated stoically at his side, the orange light of the fire dancing over her pallid features. She met his gaze, but her dark green eyes were filled with indecision. She shrugged her shoulders to gesture that it was Hayden's choice.

'We accept your offer of help,' he said finally as Emouchet stooped to run his fingers ceremoniously through the eagles' feathers. His cloudy pupils shone like orbs of flame in the burning firelight and he made a strange sound, halfway between a growl and a chuckle. 'Is good decision,' he uttered knowingly; 'perhaps, perhaps there be hope for you yet.'

He straightened his crooked back and turned his head towards the sky. 'Late,' he remarked as the eagles at his feet unfurled their wings and took off, 'sleep now.' Without looking back at Hayden and Bracken, he launched himself at the broad trunk and climbed up it as quickly and skilfully as a polecat, disappearing into the tangle of branches and shadow above.

Bracken and Hayden watched him vanish, leaving them alone beneath the mighty oak and the watchful gaze of dozens of birds of prey eyes. Filled with uncertainty, they made their beds side by side near to the protective light of the fire and waited with lonely apprehension for the arrival of dawn, both of them wondering what new and odd mysteries tomorrow would bring.

Chapter 20

THE PATH OF BLOOD

Goodstone citadel stood in trance-like silence in the cool light of the early evening. Two days had passed since the halls of the Ryders had been attacked by the insidious darkness that rose from the soil surrounding the castle. The brave followers of the Ley had fought courageously, but it had been only when the mute apprentice had thrown herself from the battlements, vanishing into the chilling storm, taking with her the shapeless threat, that the danger had subsided. Many had witnessed what had occurred and despite their unwavering belief in the Ley, all were baffled as to what had happened. All, that was, except Sister Amethyst. No doubt was left in her mind now that a great change in the energy of the Ley was coming about and Petronia was indeed the stone-tongued maiden written about in the ancient text. Amethyst's senses were acute and honed and she was aware of things that many of her fellow Ryders were not. Sometimes the hidden character of folk struck her like a veil of silk hung behind their eyes, unnoticeable even to themselves. She knew that had been the reason the Ley had given her the Stone Name Amethyst, the teacher crystal, so many decades ago. Her duty had always been to draw out what was in others' hearts, helping them to develop what was good and turn away from the more negative tendencies in their nature. But each person ultimately had to make their own decisions and the Ley did not give Amethyst the power to shape the paths of others, merely guide them on their way.

A still cool had fallen over Amethyst's heart recently. She could see that the world was altering shape, ready for a great trial and knew that the assault on Goodstone was only the beginning. The Ley filled her up like an empty chalice and turned her thoughts to the truth of her own future. She was a woman of many decades and although her body and mind still felt strong, her age was something she could not deny. The power she had devoted her life to spoke in her spirit and told her she would soon be part of It. Amethyst would not be witness to the great battles that were to come and although she had absolute faith that her Sister Ryders would stand firm against evil and aid Petronia in fulfilling her destiny, the stubbornness of old age still formed part of her character. She had confessed this flaw to the Ley, admitted her desire to be part of the great crusade that formed Petronia's fate and the fate of her cherished ward Bracken, and the Ley had been merciful to her wishes. Not for Amethyst the peaceful sickbed death of the elderly; she would die a warrior's death and in doing so, she hoped, offer one last lesson of salvation to her murderer.

When the siege on the citadel had ended and the apprentice Petronia, her brother and Bracken had all taken to their respective paths, Amethyst began readying herself to fulfil her final duties. Her fellow Ryders also sensed the call of the Ley, drawing them away from the citadel, some to be warriors, some to bring strength to the weak and frightened, others to try to heal the sickness in the land left by the dark power that had sullied the earth. Rosequartz and Garnet set out to attempt to track the mute apprentice who held in her unknowing grasp the power to alter the fate of their world. In ones and twos they left the citadel and Amethyst blessed each of them as they departed with wise words, a tender hand or kiss on the brow, not letting them know that it would be the last they would see of her.

Finally she found herself completely alone in the castle that had been her home and would soon become her mausoleum. Calmly, she walked through the familiar chambers, recalling with fondness her life spent there and her acts of devotion. She went into the courtyard and offering a prayer of thanksgiving, mercifully slaughtered one of the hens which she gutted expertly in the kitchen, separating the inners from the carcass, making them into a paste which she ate quietly with some bread. She went to the well and stripping naked, washed herself head to toe of any earthly impurities, plaiting her long, silver mane into a single braid which she fastened tightly to her scalp. Then as nude as the first human, she entered the armoury and took from the straw dummy on which it was hung, the suit of brown leather armour studded with crystals that she had not worn since the Ley had made her guardian to Bracken. The padded jacket and breeches felt heavy and stiff to her after years of wearing her gown of purple silk, but the feel of them on her form was familiar and almost comforting, making her recall the challenges the Ley had lain before her in her youth. She touched the gems embedded in the chest-plate and shoulders and felt the Ley burning powerfully within them. Amethyst knew that if she was destined to die that day, no jewel or crystal would protect her but she prayed they would imbue her soul with courage so she could face her end without fear. From its rest, she lifted her weighty sabre of metal and rock, taking time to familiarise herself once more with the heaviness and balance of the blade. This too would not protect her from her assassin, but it may ward them off for long enough so they would have time to take in what she had to say and maybe alter their course. She practised a few sparring moves in the silent armoury; her elderly muscles twinged slightly with effort, but still retained in them the action memory of thrusts, parries and blocks. Then she smoothly slipped the blade into its scabbard and descended, with slow, deliberate footsteps, the stairway to the great hall.

The soft, lifting pulse that rose from the Ley Mouth shifted the pale canopy surrounding it as Amethyst entered the chamber. Her heart tranquil and prepared, she stepped forward, carefully mounting the latticework of iron that rested over the gaping abyss. A powerful stream of air and energy drifted up, encircling her in an unseen embrace. It seeped into her mind and spirit, filling her with stillness, strength and peace. Amethyst felt a great love for the Ley as it enveloped her and was joyful that soon her soul would become part of Its flow. Sitting cross-legged on the grill, she rested her sword across her knees and closed her eyes, falling into a deep meditation as she allowed the Ley to ebb through her. That great power of life and love spread like a vast silver cobweb across Amethyst's mind, thousands of unseen strands reaching out to touch and link the lives of countless beings, overlapping and interlinking. Each action and thought was a tremor that vibrated along an iridescent filament of Ley light to touch another soul whose thoughts and actions would cause another tremor, over and over without end. Past, present and future were one entity, all and the same, for the Ley existed in them all like a string through the centre of a line of beads. Ley was love and love was everlasting. Amethyst could sense her beloved Bracken's soul and sent her a prayer of strength and love.

She felt the approach of the bringer of her death as they rode up to the drawbridge and summoned it to open. She was aware of them as they strode across the courtyard and sent out a plea through the Ley, not for her own salvation but for that of this approaching, fallen spirit. She remained perfectly still as she heard the door to the keep swing open and sensed the brooding gaze of her killer rest upon her back, as they stood waiting in the shadows of the doorway. Darkness, rage and grief were in their soul and Amethyst could sense them tarnishing the brilliance of the Ley. Taking a deep breath, she addressed the visitor in a calm, level tone.

'Welcome, Aerona, you are expected.'

From the shadows of the doorway, Sister Jet stepped forward, her sword ready. Her beautiful face was a pallid emotionless mask but pain and anger blazed bright in her eyes. 'It has been over fifteen years since I went by that name,' she uttered coldly, circling the Ley Mouth with cautious, deliberate steps. 'It surprises me that you of all people should call me it.'

Amethyst turned her head slightly to see Jet, but her body remained in the same, tranquil cross-legged position. 'I thought it was unfitting for me to use your Stone Name, now that you have decided to leave the Ley's path.' Her grey eyes softened with disappointment as she gazed at Jet's taut expression. 'Oh, my Sister, I hoped so much you would overcome the sorrow within you. You have so many gifts.'

Fury flashed across Jet's face as she took a menacing step forward, her sword brandished before her. 'Do not try and counsel me!' she growled, the tip of her blade aimed at Amethyst's throat. 'You know why I'm here. Where is the girl? Tell me where you've hidden her and I won't harm you.'

A rueful chuckle caught in the old Ryder's throat as she gently caressed the stone and metal of her own weapon. 'The Stone-Tongue is not here,' she said lightly but firmly. 'She had to continue her journey. Besides, there was nothing I could teach her; you know that or you wouldn't fear her so. And you are afraid, Sister, I can sense that. But you needn't be.'

A muscle twitched slightly in Jet's top lip and her eyes glinted like silver. 'I am not afraid,' she hissed, her fingers shifting on the hilt of her sword, 'not afraid of some foolish girl with no voice. I know a greater power, old woman; I have witnessed it and soon so will this land and all its stinking inhabitants.' On hearing these words, Amethyst felt her stomach tighten with unease but called to the Ley to help her maintain her calm and understanding composure. 'I see,' she said gently as Jet glared down at her, her whole body cloaked in an unseen mantle of fury and violence. 'And would this power be greater than the Ley?'

The younger woman flinched at the mention of the power she claimed to serve. Her body contorted with fury and letting out a cry of livid anger she reeled her blade in a glistening semicircle, striking at the canopy that hung over the Ley Mouth. The sharp stone and metal cleaved through the delicate gossamer and fearfully Amethyst watched as one of the fragile drapes fluttered to the ground. 'The Ley,' Jet spat, her tongue dripping with contempt, 'what power does It have? What mercy? None for me, though I served It faithfully all the days of my womanhood.' She turned her eyes towards the carved walls of the chamber glistening with countless jewels. 'To think I once believed,' she croaked hoarsely, 'that the Ley would heal the grief in my heart. Mend the sorrow of two brothers and a father slain in war by the Geollease army. A betrothed who came back, not a man but a shell.'

She looked at her trembling right hand gripping her blade as if it did not belong to her and seemed to be fighting the urge to cast her weapon away. 'I thought my Calling was a blessing,' she uttered to the compassionate Amethyst. 'That under the name of Jet, Healer of Woes, the Ley would ease my own suffering. But although I brought health to countless others in the Ley's name, It has brought me no peace.'

Tenderness filled Amethyst's heart as she heard Jet's bitter words, making it swell with the pulse of the Ley. 'Sister,' she breathed gently, extending a weathered hand towards Jet, 'hear me. You are not alone. The Sisterhood cares for each other as they care for all folk. Ask and you shall be supported. The Ley moves with love.'

Jet's form shook. Her beautiful face was damp with tears but her features were cruel and fixed and her green eyes grew cold with hate. 'Too late, Sister,' she hissed coolly, her hand once more tightening on her sword. 'I serve a darker incentive now. Grief is greater than love. Revenge soothes what sympathy cannot.'

Deliberately, she lowered her sword and ran its tip firmly across the marble floor. The blade rasped as it scraped against the stone, its razor edge giving off a faint shadow of curling, dark vapour. Amethyst's heart caught fearfully in her chest as she witnessed the fine mist of darkness float from the blade to circle Jet's form in loosely coiling trails of wickedness.

'Sister,' she breathed, 'take my counsel, for your own sake if nothing more. You are following a path of blood and death, and no good will come from it.'

Swiftly, Jet raised her weapon so the tip of the blade rested mere inches away from between Amethyst's eyes. 'I outgrew your teaching a long time ago, old woman,' she uttered menacingly. 'I will find the Stone-Tongue.'

Jet's eyes gleamed with fury and as Amethyst looked into their dark depths, she knew there was nothing she could do to heal the young woman's tormented soul. The breath of the Ley Mouth engulfed her elderly form and her weathered fingers tightened on the hilt of her sword where it rested across her knees. This was what she had been preparing for.

'Perhaps you do speak some truth,' she told the hateful Ryder as a vaporous cowl of smoky anger and bitterness swirled around Jet's form. 'I am, indeed, a very old woman.'

Her breathing grew short with adrenaline as she felt a sudden build-up of Ley energy boil from the depths of the abyss beneath her, filling her muscles with strength and courage to fight her final battle. 'But then old women tend to be uncommonly stubborn.'

A wave of power like a mighty breaker crashing on the shore rose up within Amethyst as the Ley took command of her actions, dismissing any signs of age or infirmity from her body. Like a bolt of granite lightning, Amethyst raised her blade and with a swift blow, struck Jet's sabre, catching the younger woman by surprise. Letting out an enraged shriek, Jet took a step backwards to guard herself as a great thrust of Ley power, like a sudden wind, lifted Amethyst from her seat on the grate and deposited her lightly on her feet before her startled adversary. Amethyst's knees buckled slightly as she landed, somewhat overcome by the intensity of the Ley. Glaring at her, Jet sharply drew breath and the shadowy essence that swam around her drew close to her body like an armour of ebony feathers. 'Foolish old woman!' she spat as Amethyst fearfully brandished her sword. 'Call the Ley if you must but your body is still elderly and as you of all people should know, It cannot intervene when the moment comes when you're destined to die!'

Jet charged like a creature possessed, the dark force that she commanded streaking out from her form like a cape of sable as she ran, her blade tip aimed at Amethyst's belly. But the old woman quickly and skilfully deflected her attack, the Ley guiding the angle of her sword. The atmosphere of the great hall was alive as if the roof had been torn away, all elements of storm, wind and rain poured down in a maelstrom of chaos. The wide Ley Mouth roared with angst like the gaping maul of a wounded beast, sending out a great bellow of unseen power and energy that ripped the silk awning asunder and shook the walls as it cried with grief for Jet's wayward soul. The fallen Ryder paid no heed to Its lament. Jet's mind and spirit had been tainted by grief, bitterness and fury, and the immense mass of her sorrow fed into the darkness that was bound to her soul. It loomed behind her in a shapeless cloud of murky vengeance as she stalked towards Amethyst, her blade raised high. In this swirl of movement and violence, Amethyst felt her spirit grow peaceful with the nearness of the Ley and her own death. She was beyond mortal terror and knowledge as the world seemed to slow down and the only sorrow within her heart was the sadness of Jet's misguided faith. Mentally, she uttered one final entreaty to the Ley that It might fill Jet's heart once more and save her. The great, unending flow of love and life washed over Amethyst's spirit, seizing it and merging Its energy with her own life-force as Jet swung her blade in a deathly blow; all that Amethyst was altered and rushed into a new state. The biting blade sliced easily through her throat and her body sagged to the ground in a fountain of crimson as her head was severed mercilessly by Jet. But this corrupted form was no longer the Ryder Amethyst, Keeper of the Goodstone citadel and adoptive mother of Bracken, for Amethyst was now something else. She was part of the Ley, energy transferred and not ended, life everlasting with a never-ending flow that would travel through the world.

The atmosphere of the great hall was still as Jet stood alone, cloaked in silence, watching the ever growing pool of scarlet pour from the severed body of the woman who had once been her teacher. Blood. There was so much blood, turning the monochrome floor glossy red. It dyed the fallen canopy and spattered the grey stones. It painted her hands and blade, hot and sticky, but she felt nothing. Just burning fury. Above her, hanging in the air like a misty embodiment of her hatred and rage, the pulsating shadow of malicious energy hung, besmirching the holy ambience of the chamber just as Amethyst's spilt blood defiled the floor and walls. Twisting tendrils, like emaciating strands of greasy hair, ran from its shapeless form into Jet's mind, simultaneously feeding off her dark and poisonous feelings. Her thoughts were tortured and without compassion. Remorse was beyond her heart and she knew only perverted bitterness. Her actions were driven solely by revenge, like an addict hoping the next fix would sate the pain of hunger.

Collectively, intent stirred within the hateful mass and Jet's thoughts and with heavy, deliberate steps she approached the growing pool of scarlet that flowed from the corpse's open neck. She gazed down into its glossy depths, seeing her own pitiless figure reflected back at her in a crimson looking glass. The teachings of the Ley had been correct about one thing. Everything was connected and those bonds could never be severed. Not even knowledge could be hidden by death.

The vengeful entity that shadowed her drew close once more, linking and encouraging the intent of her deeds. Feeling its sinister support, Jet crouched down at the edge of the bloody pool and dipped her fingertips into its shallow, gory depths. It was still warm with the energy and experience of the slain Ryder's life and Jet knew she had to act fast or lose her trail. Silently she opened her mind to resentment and loathing, allowing the murky force to slip into her mind, becoming a channel for it as she had once been for the goodness of the Ley. Her skin tingled as the blackness seeped easily into her, making the memories of sorrows and losses burn bright. Her pale lips twitched and uttered a silent phrase of command, '*Feel her memories. Show me the path taken by Stone-Tongue.*'

Her slim form trembled slightly as the darkness rushed through, a subtle spasm between pain and euphoria. The warm, red liquid at her fingertips shook slightly as her hands quivered, forming tiny ripples of motion. Her eyelids fluttered over her vision and a small, elated cry escaped her throat as the spiteful shadows ebbed from her body into the mire of death. A black swirl of cloud billowed gratefully into Amethyst's spilt blood to form twisted spirals and eddies in its shining scarlet. A low, inaudible note vibrated the air, ancient and godless, like a memory of a long-ago unforgivable horror.

The shape of the pool altered slightly as a thin trickle of blood stretched out from it, like a ruby finger of accusation. It rolled steadily across the chequerboard floor, leaving behind it a narrow clear path. Jet opened her eyes and grinned triumphantly as she saw the rivulet of gore seep beneath the keep's heavy doorway.

Swiftly, she removed her hands from the pool of blood and stood up. Thanks to the power of vengeance, Amethyst had revealed the secret of Stone-Tongue's location and soon she would fall. Wiping the fresh gore from her fingers and blade on a scrap of gossamer from the destroyed canopy, Jet cast it mockingly into the gaping darkness of the Ley Mouth before glancing at the headless corpse of Amethyst, a cruel smile twisting her lips.

'Ley go with you, Sister,' she sneered before following the betraying crimson stream out of the citadel, towards her unsuspecting prey.

Chapter 21

THE SABLE SPIRIT

In his narrow bed, in the room of the inn he and Petronia had come upon the previous night, Aarold lay awake, waiting for day to dawn. After the dangerous and exhausting events of the previous day and night, his weak body begged for sleep but the young prince's mind was too active and excited to allow it. Scenes from the last twenty-four hours kept running through his head and he relived them again and again in disbelief that he was the protagonist. His daring escape from the palace, his travels undetected through the city, the terrifying attack by the footpad and his ensuing rescue by the silent but pretty young Ley Ryder all seemed like chapters from one of the adventure novels he had read in the palace library. For as long as he could remember, people, in particular his aunt and father, had told him he was feeble and incapable of any kind of challenge, but here he was in the midst of his own adventure. Aarold's sensible mind knew that the whole situation was ridiculously perilous. The violent attack on his person alone illustrated that the city was a dangerous place and an individual of his political importance and physical vulnerability was safest behind the thick walls of the palace. But these facts did not counter the truth that Aarold was a boy of fifteen and like most youths was filled with an anarchic longing for exciting activity, especially if it was connected with attractive young women like the Ley Ryder who had rescued him.

The prince thought of the mysterious mute girl and sighed wistfully. She was undoubtedly a beauty but it was more than this that intrigued

Aarold. He had never before met someone who, like himself, suffered from such an acute physical ailment and it piqued his curiosity to know how she had overcome such a handicap to fulfil her duty as a Ryder. He thought that the Sisterhood must be a very accepting and fulfilling vocation to allow her to overcome her struggles and wanted to find out more, in the hope that he could maybe apply some of their teaching to take a more active role as leader of Geoll. It would be a tricky task to converse with her due to her inability to speak or write, but it was a challenge Aarold felt he had the patience and knowledge to overcome. He was, after all, a gentleman of learning and good breeding and as such felt he owed her a debt. She had rescued him from peril and the least Aarold felt he could do was to be civil company and escort her to the house of her Sisterhood.

Such thoughts filled his mind as he succumbed to a fitful night's slumber, and awoke the following morning, very early, feeling surprisingly good. He sat himself on the edge of his bed and, as he did every day, silently assessed his physical well-being. He was aware of the usual, dull ache in the hip of his lame leg as well as some new and interesting bruises beneath his nightshirt brought about by his fall from Phebus's back. But his breathing felt clear and easy and despite his somewhat restless night his spirits felt at peace and positive. In fact the overall attitude of his mood was a great deal happier than he had felt in a long time. Hobbling over to the dressing table, Aarold peered into the mottled glass and almost let out a horrified cry. The glamour that he had carefully applied the night before had begun to wear away, leaving his face an unsightly mish-mash of the features of peddler disguise and his own. His skin was a piebald patchwork of tawny and pasty complexion and great chunks of mousy blonde hair were protruding from his chestnut curls. 'Oh my,' he gasped, grabbing his knapsack and rummaging through it to find the remains of the concealing powder. 'That won't do at all!' He quickly applied the spell to his features and gradually his own pale face and hair withdrew behind the dark-skinned mask of the peddler. He then quickly dressed and hurried downstairs to the inn's stables to find Phebus before anyone else awoke and found a half-horse half-Equile monstrosity sheltering morosely among the other animals. Great patches of shiny black scales had begun to reappear through his russet fur and clumps of his mane had started to harden back into horny plates along his neck. He broodingly lifted his head when he heard Aarold enter and stared at him ashamedly with one brown and one scarlet eye.

'Don't look at me,' he lamented as Aarold closed the stable door, 'I am an utter disgrace!'

Aarold hobbled over and gave the creature an affectionate pat. 'You vain old thing, Phebs, it's only the magical glamour wearing away; I will put that right in no time.' He found the necessary items and began to carefully apply the sparkling camouflage to the patches of Phebus that betrayed his true form.

The Equile shuddered as his black scales were once more transformed to fur. 'I am not talking about my current shoddy appearance for that is entirely your fault. I am referring to the display of unforgivable cowardice in my character last night. Fleeing from that footpad like a shameful poltroon. I am thoroughly disgusted with myself. No way for a noble Equile to behave when a friend was in peril. I would not blame you for shunning me.'

Aarold breathed a sigh and worked the powder into a spike of horn protruding from Phebus's mane until it softened into an ebony lock. Phebus's abandonment had rankled him slightly, but Aarold knew enough of his friend's character to realise that Phebus's tender devotion to him far outstripped his faint-hearted nature. Male Equiles were well documented as nervous creatures, leaving any military duties to their female counterparts and Phebus could not be expected to override his genes. 'I forgive you, Phebs,' he sighed, moving forward to look into the animal's shamed face. 'If I had the physical ability, I would have run for my life too. Besides,' a small smile teased his lips as he recalled his rescuer, 'no true harm befell either of us, did it?' He cupped a pinch of the bewitching powder in his palm and softly blew it in Phebus's singular scarlet eye. Phebus snorted and blinked hard as his pupil darkened to chocolate brown. 'I will say, in my defence, that my intention was to raise the alarm and summon help from the first person I met, heedless of my own base façade,' he said, pressing his snout lovingly into Aarold's hand. 'My only consolation is you are safe and fully aware of what a dangerous environment the city is. It goes without saying that we are now returning to the safety of the palace post haste and shall chalk up this reckless escapade as one of the follies of youth.'

Aarold did not reply but pursed his lips guiltily and avoided his friend's gaze. Phebus immediately began feeling wary. 'I reiterate, dear boy, it goes without saying we're going home now.'

Aarold's cheeks coloured as he fiddled with a strand of hay. 'Yes, Phebus, we will go home, eventually. But I am indebted to the young Ley Ryder who saved me and I think it would be terribly improper if we were to leave without at least escorting her to the lodge where her Sisterhood dwells.' An austere gleam flecked Phebus's eyes and he sulkily clopped over to the water trough to get a drink. 'I see,' he muttered coolly to himself as he lowered his head; 'the hypnotic effect of adolescent lust!'

'I beg your pardon!' exclaimed Aarold, his face turning a deep shade of crimson.

Lazily, Phebus lifted his head from the water and observed his friend. 'Tell me, dear boy,' he stated in clipped tones, 'would this young Ley Ryder be considered attractive in your species?'

Aarold felt the skin on the back of his neck prickle. 'I suppose she is fairly pretty but I fail to see what that has to do with showing her the gratitude she deserves, Phebus,' he stuttered.

The chestnut horse gave his ears and tail a knowing flick. 'Oh, the ensnaring wiles of womanhood!' he lamented. 'How often do they cloud the vision of even the keenest scholar. Hormones, Aarold my friend, primeval urges brought to a heated frenzy by your tender age, a rising of the humours that can overwhelm rational thought. Beware for there lies the path to disaster!'

'I have no idea what you're talking about!' blustered Aarold, staring down at the toes of his boots.

Lowering his silken lashes, Phebus gave his friend a sardonic stare. 'No, of course you don't,' he remarked dryly. 'Needless to say, I could not call myself a friend of your dear departed mother, nor of yourself, if I was to allow you to become entangled in the satiny tendrils of your adolescent libido and throw all logical consideration to the wind, especially as you have displayed such lax judgement of late.' He sniffed and lowered his head to rub an irritating spot on his right foreleg.

Annoyance rankled Aarold slightly. 'Are you saying that we shouldn't escort Mistress Ryder to the lodge?' he quizzed pointedly. Phebus shuddered at this insinuation and pricked his ears. 'I am insulted!' he remarked. 'We Equiles are renowned for the importance we place on good manners and proper behaviour. Yes, dear Aarold, yes you must escort this female back to her fellows; a gentleman can do nothing else. I am merely warning you not to allow yourself to fall into greater peril due to any attraction you might have formed.'

Aarold stifled a sigh as he caught his reflection in the still surface of the water trough. His peddler disguise was complete but the twisted nature of his leg was still clear to see. He felt his early morning positivity dip as the shadows of his father and aunt flitted through his thoughts. How foolish to think the young Ley Ryder would show him anything more than dutiful kindness. 'Don't worry, Phebs,' he breathed, 'I won't.'

The Equile nodded seriously. 'Well be assured that I am going to act as guardian to your royal modesty,' he chided. 'You may look like a pleb but that is no excuse not to act princely.'

Aarold reluctantly nodded in agreement before leaving the stables to return to the inn for breakfast. As he stepped out into the courtyard that linked the two buildings he came face to face with his Ley Ryder as she exited the inn in search of him. Despite Phebus's staunch warnings, Aarold could not help but notice that she appeared even prettier in daylight than she had done in the gloom of the alleyway. Her face had a pinkish blush to it that spoke of a less cloistered life than the ladies in the palace and the multicoloured robe and leather baldric she wore gave her a slightly exotic air. She smiled shyly when she saw Aarold and raised her hand in greeting.

Self-consciously, Aarold brushed the dust from the stables from his tunic. 'Good morning, Mistress Ryder,' he said, trying to sound polite and confident, 'I trust you slept well?'

Petronia nodded in answer, feeling very aware and irritated by her muteness. Since rescuing the young peddler the previous night, she had been troubled by a great urge to speak to him, even if it was only to reassure she meant him no harm. He had shown her politeness and gratitude and from the very start seemed unphased by her inability to speak. He spoke to her in a clear but non-patronising way that she could answer by nodding or shaking her head. The Ley had aided and compelled her to save his life and now Petronia felt a responsibility towards him. Despite her better manners, curiosity kept drawing her eye towards his wasted limb and she was full of questions to find out whether he experienced the same challenges and frustrations with his impairment that she did with her own. With cautious concern she gestured to his leg and rubbed her own in a nursing motion.

Aarold understood her question immediately. 'No, Mistress Ryder, I wasn't injured too severely by last night's misadventures, thanks to you. I am greatly in your debt. Unfortunately, this accursed limb has always been the blight of my life but that ruffian hasn't crippled me any more than I already was,' he chuckled, trying to make light of his situation, but at the same time moved his cape to hide the offending limb.

Petronia nodded and smiled with empathy, pointing first at Aarold then at her own throat to indicate that she too had been born with her handicap.

'Oh I see! You were born mute, just as I was born lame. I understand. I thought at first you may have taken a vow of silence to help your work with the Ley. I have heard that some scholars pledge such oaths so that they might better focus on the mechanics of learning.' Petronia shrugged and gave a sad half smile to indicate that her lack of speech had no such noble cause.

'Still I am grateful for your aid last night,' continued Aarold. 'If our paths had not crossed at that moment I would surely have come to a sticky demise. I owe you more than I could give.'

Lowering her gaze in modesty, Petronia spread her arms to show there was no need for thanks. She truly did not feel worthy of any credit for the actions she had taken the night before; for even as she had enacted them she had felt that the will that compelled them was not her own. She had been driven by instinct beyond her conscious mind, that undeniable energy that welled with unexpected intensity in her body and thoughts only to disappear, like now, to leave her as she had always felt. She curiously reached out within her awareness to see whether this strange power was still within and sensed it stir, but only very slightly, like a shallow breath or barely remembered dream. She certainly did not feel like she was, or ever had been, capable of fending off such a villain. She had to find her way back to the Ryders and turn to their wisdom to discover what was happening to her.

Unaware that this notion had entered her mind, Aarold continued. 'Nevertheless, as I said last night, it is the least I can do to escort you back to your Sisterhood's residence in the city.'

The pretty young Ryder greeted this statement with a level of enthusiastic nodding and gesturing that made Aarold feel as if she was desperate to escape his company. Seeing the relief and gratitude on her face, he reconsidered Phebus's words of warning. It was understandable that the young Ryder was devoted to her Calling and would rather share the company of her sisters than him. He chided himself for even considering otherwise. 'Of course,' he said with a forced smile, 'we will leave at once.'

The two of them then went inside where Aarold paid the innkeeper for their food and lodgings. The helpful man was also able to provide them with directions to the Ley Ryders' lodge on the other side of the city and a local stable where they could hire a mount for Aarold's companion. Then with Aarold riding Phebus and Petronia seated in the saddle of the rented pale grey mare, they set off on the route they had been given. It was a cold, dull day but the innkeeper had assured them they would reach the lodge before dark, and quite soon the pair found themselves enjoying each other's company. Aarold deduced that it must also be his new friend's first time in the city as every few minutes she would gesture to a building or monument with an expression of wonder. Although this was his first venture outside the palace, Aarold had a great deal of knowledge about Veridium from writings in the royal library and was able to amuse his female companion with stories and trivia about landmarks they passed. Petronia listened to him, hungry for knowledge after her mundane, village childhood and it gave Aarold a sense of growing pride to display his knowledge to an interested audience. Despite the challenge of Petronia's muteness, they quickly fell into an easy form of conversation and Aarold was astounded by the clarity with which his new friend expressed herself through gestures and facial expressions.

'I still feel it's terribly impolite of me not to know your proper name, Mistress Ryder,' he confessed as they made their way along the cobbled streets. 'May I guess at it?'

Petronia tilted her head to one side and gave him a lopsided grin. During their morning ride, she had grown to like the shy young peddler. He spoke to her in such a genuine manner and she found his politeness rather endearing.

Aarold studied her playful expression and considered what gem or stone best matched her character. 'Is it Ruby?'

A firm shake of the head.

'Emerald?'

The same reply.

'Diamond then, to match the sparkle in your eyes?' He blushed at the boldness of this compliment. Beneath him, unable to express his disapproval verbally, Phebus snorted.

Petronia lowered her eyes coyly at his awkward attempt at flirtation. She guessed that the young lad liked her but was inexperienced at wooing. She chuckled and indicated that his remark flattered her, but he was still wrong.

Aarold thought hard. He always felt that his mental ability was his greatest asset and unable to impress the young Ryder with either his physical strength or looks was determined to do it by guessing her name. 'Citrine, Galena, Peridot.' He fired off the names of every stone and crystal he could remember from geology.

Her reply was a shake of the head, then a quizzical frown. Curiously Petronia turned over each crystal the peddler named in her mind, wondering if by some happy accident one would sparkle as her Stone Name and reveal itself not only to him but to her for the first time. However all felt flat and wrong despite the fact she was rather enjoying the game.

Aarold sighed in despair, having named every jewel and crystal he could recall. 'This puzzle is beyond me, for now,' he chuckled wearily. 'My kind and noble Mistress Ryder you will have to remain, at least until your sisters at the lodge reveal your proper title.'

Petronia once again felt sad frustration at not being able to speak and reveal who she was; suddenly the guessing did not seem so much fun. She reached across and softly patted his hand to show that it did not matter. Phebus bristled at this gesture and took a step to one side, carrying Aarold away from her. 'Hussy!' he snorted under his breath.

Aarold cleared his throat to disguise this remark and quickly changed the subject. 'Your family must be awfully proud of you joining the Sisterhood,' he stated.

A melancholy expression crossed Petronia's face as she recalled her family. She had been so wrapped up in the excitement of her adventure that she had not thought about her parents and Hayden for some time. Now she did, her heart was filled with concern. Her father and mother would be fretting over her safety and the last time she had see her brother was during the siege on Goodstone. She prayed that the Ley Ryders had kept him from peril.

Aarold saw her sad expression and was concerned, 'I haven't said something to upset you?' he asked worriedly. 'You *do* have a family?'

Petronia dismissed his anxiety with a reassuring smile and indicated that her parents were both alive and healthy.

Aarold looked relieved. 'I am glad,' he breathed. 'The influence of one's upbringing is so important to how the character is formed.' He sighed sadly to himself as he recalled how his own father's coldness towards him had deeply affected his confidence. 'And siblings then, do you have any of those?' Petronia held up a single finger and then stroked her chin with her index finger and thumb to mime a beard. Aarold understood the message. 'One brother, I see. A good man, I warrant, if his character is the male equivalent of yours.' She wrinkled her nose and gave a doubtful look. She hoped greatly that Hayden was safe and loved him but she could not deny the fact that he struggled to understand her carefree nature and gave her cause for frustration.

'You didn't get on, then?' asked her companion, noticing her unsure expression. 'What is the problem?' Petronia thought for a moment how best to express her brother's nature. Fixing an exaggerated severe expression on her face she wagged her finger in chastisement then plucked at the material of her gown and shook her head. Aarold carefully watched her and slotted together the clues. 'He told you off? And didn't approve of you becoming a Ryder? Is that right?' Sadly Petronia nodded as she recalled Hayden's aversion to her wanting anything other than marriage and a safe, homely life. Tenderly, she stroked her chin again before pressing her hand hard against her chest. 'But there was great love between you, I understand. Sometimes we are hardest on the people we care for the most.'

She sighed. The peddler was right, of course. Hayden loved her a great deal and had devoted himself to her safety and care. Now they had been parted Petronia realised how ungrateful she had been to force him on such a dangerous journey so that she could follow her dream. The Ley, or was it her own stubbornness, had driven her onwards with little care for Hayden's own views or desires. She had no idea what had happened to him and she prayed that if the Ley was a truly benevolent entity It would not allow Hayden to be sacrificed for the benefit of her education. Pressing these thoughts to the back of her mind, she pointed to her companion to encourage him to speak of his own family.

'Me?' Aarold asked, seeing her expectant gaze. 'Do I have a family?' He paused and focused on Phebus's dark mane as he carefully formed a truthful answer. He knew it was foolish to tell this stranger his true identity but her silent and patient nature gave him courage to speak about his deceased parents. 'I have no-one,' he said honestly. 'My mother was of ill health and died soon after my birth and my father passed away a short time ago.'

Her heart filled with compassion, Petronia reached out and rested her hand softly on his arm. Aarold forced a smile. 'Oh you must not pity my loss, Mistress Ryder. I was too young to grieve for my mother and as for my father...' He paused as the image of the painted eyes in the late king's portrait filled his mind, more real and familiar to him than his father's actual face.

'We were not close. By all accounts of those who knew him, my late father was a virtuous man, brave, strong, respected by those whom he had business with. But as for how he was to me.' He stopped, almost expecting the ghost of the late king to appear and chastise him as he had done a thousand times in life. The palace, Aarold's home, had been a mausoleum to Elkric's memory: trophies of his hunting prowess hung on the walls; his deeds in battle recorded in tomes in the library; his imposing masculine presence etched in the minds of all who served him. But Aarold was no longer in the palace and for the first time he felt free to utter how he saw his father. 'My father believed a man should have and display physical strength to master all that was rightfully his, that fitness of body mirrored fitness of spirit and lacking in such was a sign of failure.'

He glanced at his companion and saw that her gaze was resting knowingly on his wasted leg. 'Quite,' he uttered grimly. 'I was, to him, unworthy of his genes, not a man. When I was a child, he believed that my, defect, could be overcome by force, as he had overcome so many obstacles, bullied out of me through physical exercise and medical treatment. When this turned out not to be the case, he rejected me and concentrated on other areas of his life. Our relationship was a tense and unfamiliar one.'

Petronia shook her head sympathetically and tutted. She drew her fingertip in a line downwards across her cheek to mimic the track of a tear, before forming a fist and rubbing it in a tender circular movement against her chest after which she pointed at Aarold once more.

'No, don't be sad, Mistress Ryder. No, me? Am *I* sad? Because of my father?' Aarold pondered the question hard before answering. 'I guess I don't grieve for him as much as people might think I should. I am sorry for the fact that he didn't live to see my achievements. If you'll excuse my pride, I do consider myself well-read and quite the scholar. I have studied numerous subjects as best a peddler can. Art and the sciences, the workings of the natural world, the history of my, I mean, the royal family. A little magic also. But even if my father had survived to a greater age I doubt he would have put credit in such work. As I said, he never did.'

Gasping with disapproval, Petronia shook her head. The peddler seemed to have knowledge of so many different things and she greatly envied his obvious literacy. She could not believe a father could put so little confidence in his only child. She pointed to Aarold and then tapped her temple and gave him an admiring smile.

Aarold tried not to blush when he saw that she had been impressed. 'Me, clever? No, not really. I am too young and have not lived long enough in the world to be deemed wise. I just enjoy reading and improving my mind. It is the most capable part of me.'

They continued their journey a short time more, winding through the narrow streets as the afternoon wore onwards. In time they passed into the alleyway on which stood the modest but sturdy lodge that was the residence of the Ley Ryders. Not as grand or imposing as the citadel at Goodstone, the lodge was a simple, long, stone chalet with a small porch running along the whole of the front supported by a dozen thick granite columns. In the gaps between the stonework, fragments of gems and crystals had been set in geometric patterns. The door was a smaller twin of the drawbridge of the citadel, deep oak wood with a clear, angular crystal set in the centre. Petronia gazed at the lodge, hoping to feel a sense of relief or excitement as she had done when she had first arrived at Goodstone, but instead was overwhelmed with a strong unease. It was not the building itself that unnerved her, it was more of an awareness of a sickening and twisted shadow of malevolence that lurked, hidden from her view, like a viper at the bottom of a well of refreshing water. She felt the Ley stir within her, awakening to crouch like a nervous creature in the pit of her stomach.

Aarold noticed her anxious expression. 'You look troubled, Mistress Ryder,' he observed. 'Are you perhaps unnerved by the prospect of returning to your studies? I have heard that the work of a Ryder is arduous at times.' Petronia forced a smile to reassure herself and her companion that she was fine. She told herself that it was tiredness that had unsettled her nerves. They dismounted and secured their horses to the columns of the porch before stepping on to the veranda to approach the sturdy doorway.

Due to his naturally inquisitive mindset, Aarold could not help feeling a little excited at the prospect of spending even a few short minutes in the residence of the Ryders. Despite the danger he had faced, he was grateful that he had taken the risk of this journey. Not only had he got to spend a most pleasant time riding and chatting with a very pretty Ley Ryder, he was now set to see the inside of the dwelling place of her Sisterhood, a fellowship that intrigued him greatly. Petronia, however, could not shake the unnerving notion that something was amiss.

Politely Aarold rapped on the door and waited for a reply. 'You see, Mistress Ryder,' he observed happily, 'did I not say I would escort you home? I expect your Sister Ryders will be awaiting you with open arms.'

Petronia nodded unsure. She hoped that the young peddler was right and wished with all her heart that the door would be opened by Garnet, Rosequartz or even Amethyst: a familiar and reassuring face that could dismiss her unease and bring hopeful news of her brother. Dark thoughts of death and unrest kept rising like black bubbles in her brain and she could not understand why. An urgent whisper echoed, but she was too filled with fear to hear what it was asking of her.

After a few minutes they heard the latch being lifted and the door swung open to reveal the figure of a short and wizened Ley Ryder. The woman looked ancient, like a dead tree or preserved prune, shrivelled and dehydrated. Her features were sharp and puckered and she had the passing resemblance to a small tortoise that had been deprived of its shell. Her nose was small and pointed and her mouth a barely visible furrow as if she had just eaten something very bitter. Her colouring was astoundingly pallid, her wrinkled, sagging flesh bone white and her brittle, blonde hair pulled tightly away from her face. She wore an earth-brown gown marked with a criss-cross pattern of dark thread that hung loosely from her almost skeletal form. Her sleeves were rolled up to her elbows as if she had been interrupted from some task of housework and she wore a small, round black cap on the crown of her head. She regarded the pair standing before her with large, watery black eyes.

'Yes, may I help you in some way?' Her voice was a shocking contrast to her emaciated and ancient appearance. It was soft and full with a compassionate tenderness that spoke more than any words.

Aarold made a small, polite bow. 'Good morrow, Mistress Ryder,' he stated. 'I am Aaron, a peddler and stranger to this city.' He then went on to explain his story, how he had been attacked the previous evening by a thief, how the young Ley Ryder with him, despite her muteness, had saved him and how it was his gentlemanly duty to accompany her back to her fellow Ryders.

The old woman listened in silence, a look of mild surprise on her leathery face. When Aarold had finished his tale, she asked if she might see his hands. Somewhat puzzled, Aarold obliged and allowed her to examine his palms with the light, professional touch he recognised from the royal physicians.

'Mmm,' she pondered softly, 'you have had much death in your life, am I not right?'

'Yes,' he murmured quietly, as she shuffled across to take Petronia's hand. She held it for a moment and then slowly let it slip from her grasp with a puzzled sigh. 'As for you, well. I don't know quite what to make of you but you are, clearly, very interesting, my dear.'

She stared at Petronia and then shook her head as if she was unable to decide. 'I am Sister Chiastolite,' she said, looking from her to Aarold, 'or you may call me Cross-Stone, if it suits you better; the meaning's the same. I must confess you come at a bad time, but I will act as hostess best I can. Enter if you will.'

Beckoning them to follow, she shuffled back into the gloom of the doorway. Aarold and Petronia stepped over the threshold and found themselves in a dark and somewhat austerely decorated stone chamber. The room was a great deal more modest than the intricately decorated halls of the citadel at Goodstone but did echo in a lesser extent its style.

The granite floor and walls were embedded at regular intervals with geometric motifs of crystals like angular eyes blinking in the shadows. The furniture was sparse, a dozen or so simple wooden chairs around a table on which lay a pitcher of water, tumbler, loaf of bread and small dish containing what looked like minced raw offal. Thick black velvet drapes blocked out the sunlight through the windows and a small candelabrum was the only source of light. Chiastolite hobbled slowly across to the table and taking a seat, motioned for her visitors to do the same. She cut herself a thick slice of bread, on which she piled a large helping of the prepared gizzards.

'Eat if you're hungry,' she told the pair, her slack jowls wobbling as she chewed the unappetising snack.

Both Aarold and Petronia grimaced at the sight of the glossy, scarlet flesh but they were hungry after their day of travel and so Petronia cut them a chunk of bread each. Chiastolite took a sip of water from the tumbler and wiped a stringy, scarlet strand of food from her creased lower lip. 'This is not a good time for you to visit this chapter of the Sisterhood,' she sighed apologetically, 'not a good time at all.'

Petronia once more felt the growing, unsettling feeling that had come over her spread through her body. Her muscles felt twitchy, as if she knew that at any moment she was going to have to flee; her eyes kept being drawn to a doorway in the back of the room.

Aarold took a small mouthful of bread and chewed, swallowing hard before he spoke. 'Forgive my impoliteness, Mistress Chiastolite, but why is that?'

The old woman gave a dry, ironic chuckle and gestured to herself. 'I am Chiastolite,' she said simply. 'It is never a good time when I am in a place. Ask my sister here.'

She pointed to Petronia. Aarold looked at his companion for some kind of explanation but Petronia shook her head and indicated that she had no idea what the old woman was talking about. She was ill at ease in this place, feeling that she should be doing something but was not sure what. Her head was filled with a wordless whisper and it seemed to be speaking to her from whatever was behind that door.

291

Chiastolite sighed and clicked her tongue. 'You are so young,' she said to Petronia, regarding her apprentice's robes. 'Perhaps you are not yet familiar with the crystal whose name I share. Chiastolite means stone of the dead and grieving, handmaiden of the grave, steward that helps prepare souls to join the Ley.'

Aarold glanced around the chamber and at last recognised the thick, velvet drapes for what they were: curtains of mourning like those that had hung in the palace when his father had passed. 'This is a house in mourning,' he exclaimed sombrely. 'Oh forgive us, Mistress Chiastolite. We did not mean to intrude on your grief.'

The old woman showed him a compassionate, toothless grin and reached across to pat his hand. 'Do not apologise, young sir. I am no more in mourning this day than I have been every other day since I became a Ryder. It is my life duty to attend the dead, ready their bodies for cremation, give succour to those they leave behind.'

Petronia felt her skin prickle as she took in Chiastolite's words. She felt in her heart that death was in this place, but there was something very wrong. Like a steady line coming to an abrupt conclusion or a thread that was cut too short, the dead of this house were not at rest. She could feel a heavy pressure in the centre of her chest, like a barrier or a lock holding back a path of energy.

Eagerly she nudged Aarold and gestured her distress. He carefully watched her frantic signals until he managed to decipher the message. 'My friend asks,' he stated slowly, 'who has died?'

Chiastolite looked troubled and glanced towards the doorway. 'Alas, it is one of our sisters, young miss. A Ryder by the name of Ammonite. Her end shocked even me.' She shuddered slightly and pressed her pale hand against a crystal she wore around her neck. 'Ley forgive me,' she breathed. 'I have seen countless deaths; the last moments and most defiled bodies leave me in no horror for I know their life-force is in a better state. However the remains of my young Sister Ammonite leave me troubled.' She moistened her creased lips thoughtfully. 'I have performed every ritual and rite for the dead and dying that I know, but something is not right. My sisters have left me alone in the lodge so I may clearly attune myself to the Ley and prepare her for her final journey, but Ammonite's spirit is blocked somehow and her remains cannot be disposed of respectfully until she is at peace.'

Aarold looked into the old woman's troubled face and felt a pang of empathy. He racked his brain for some suggestion that might help but his tutors had taught him very little on the rites of death. 'Are your fellow Ryders not able to assist you?' he asked as Petronia stared intently at the door at the back of the room.

Sighing thoughtfully, Chiastolite leant back in her chair. 'I am the Ryder who serves the dead and dying,' she answered simply, 'the only one who bares the Stone Name at this time, so I must follow as the Ley wishes. But I do not deny that I am old; perhaps my senses and mind aren't as sharp as they once were.'

While Aarold spoke with the elderly Ryder, Petronia tried very hard to concentrate but began to find their words growing muffled beneath the urgent whispering that filled her brain. A force tugged at every fibre of her being, trying to drag her out of her chair and over to the far doorway. She wondered if the Ley had brought her here at this moment to somehow help the deceased Ryder. Shocked by the boldness of her own actions she pointed sharply at the closed portal.

Chiastolite followed her gesture, puzzlement clouding her eyes. 'My Sister Ammonite lays in rest in that chamber,' she murmured.

A bitter taste filled Petronia's mouth as she became aware that the rush of the Ley was welling up within her once more. Her thoughts were still very much her own and in her conscious mind she felt there was nothing she wanted less than to see a dead body. The Ley was calling to her with all Its strength and she knew if she did not obey, the dark disquiet that filled this dwelling would never leave. She slowly once more motioned to the doorway and then back to herself.

The dark eyes of the old woman danced intently over Petronia and carefully hoisting herself to her feet she padded round the table towards her. As she approached the young girl, Chiastolite could sense the air was charged so powerfully with Ley energy it almost overwhelmed her. Fearfully, she rested her pale hand on Petronia's shoulder. 'Does the

Ley compel you to view my Sister Ammonite's remains?' she queried gently. *What am I doing?* Petronia thought to herself in disbelief. *I, a simple smith's daughter, knows nothing of the paths to the spirit world.* Her thoughts screamed that what she was doing was folly and she could do nothing to aid the woman whose body lay within that room. Once again it was not her thoughts that compelled her actions, but a subconscious instinct that existed solely in that moment.

Slowly she nodded. Chiastolite caressed one of the pendants that hung about her neck. 'As the Ley wishes,' she murmured. 'Perhaps you may bring her peace where I have failed. Follow me.' She shuffled off towards the foreboding doorway and, leaving her companion seated bewildered at the table, Petronia followed her into the Ryder's final resting place.

An electric chill prickled Petronia's skin as she entered the small room with Chiastolite at her side. The chamber was as stark and dim as the previous one, long and narrow, more a passageway than a room. The high granite walls were marked by line upon line of neatly carved inscriptions, names of fallen Ryders engraved in memorial, each one preceded by a small, round medallion of the crystal or gem that shared that Ryder's name. In the centre of the room, atop an oblong tablet of stone, the still body of a young, ash-blonde woman lay, her rigid form draped with pale white cotton. A table stood at the bedside laid with a bowl of fresh water, numerous large crystals, phials and other tools of the coroner's grim craft. Around the bier, there was fastened a strange framework of pliable brass struts that curved over the body and from which were suspended various gems on thin strands of thread, twinkling slightly as they twisted in the candlelight. More stones had been meticulously laid on the bare flesh of the body, in neat lines along her naked shoulders and throat and on her forehead. Petronia's gaze locked on the still body of the young woman but her vision seemed to be blind to her unmoving form. She saw something else: a shapeless mass of putrescence that hung like a shadow. Death brought stillness, but to Petronia, the atmosphere in the chamber was ever-shifting. Chiastolite gave a sad sigh and took a pair of spectacles from the pocket of her apron.

'It is always a burden to my heart to perform my duties on the young,' she said, shaking her head. 'The Ley takes them too soon and in this sorry case I am unable to detect by what means.' She rested a withered hand on the crystal around her neck and uttered a silent prayer to the Ley before tottering across to the bier.

Petronia also silently approached the corpse, feeling as if a dark string in the core of her stomach was drawing her in to it. Expected feelings of dread and revulsion fluttered faintly in her mind but they were overshadowed by the consuming compulsion that seemed to be calling out to her from the dead woman. The same wordless language that spoke to her before burbled and cried distractedly in her skull and images glimmered unclear through her thoughts, teasing her with indecipherable flashes of the Ryder's last moments: a glint of iron, the coldness of the night air, a splash of blood.

Together Petronia and Chiastolite stood gazing down at the pale form beneath the sheet. The face of the deceased Ryder was youthful, pretty even, but even in death there was unrest in her features. Her eyelids were only half closed, frozen as if the last sight she had witnessed still dwelt horrifically before her gaze. Her jaw gaped open slightly, her lips fixed back as if pinned in place to form a terrified cry. This was not the face of someone slumbering in the never-ending sleep of the hereafter, this was a person caught forever at the agonising moment of death. Petronia felt an urge to lean closer to that terrified face and press her ear to the colourless lips in the hope that the woman might utter what had left her in such a piteous state.

Chiastolite moved her hands expertly over the corpse's features to try and shift them into a more peaceful expression but to no avail. 'Be at peace, Sister Ammonite, go to the Ley,' she begged. Hopelessly she shook her head. 'A porter from the bazaar found her body in an alleyway off the quay a few days ago,' she told Petronia. 'I was summoned and began the rituals of death as soon as I could, but there is something unnatural about Ammonite. I know the feeling of peace in the flesh when the soul has returned to the Ley, but this poor soul has no such respite. It is sinful to cremate her before her spirit has joined the flow of the Ley. She is not alive, but I still sense a force within her that will not relent.'

Petronia stared down at the outline of the body beneath the white sheet. A pool of throbbing energy had formed within her and her nerves felt uncommonly sensitive to sensations beyond the mortal realm. The sound of the rushing darkness filled her head, surging up from the woman's pale form from an intangible hunger. Sensation began to tingle in her thigh, quickly growing from a niggling throb to a searing agony of ice and flame. Once more, scenes darted across her mind as if the dead Ryder was desperately trying to reach out. Like a far-off echo, she heard Chiastolite speak. 'I believe she perished from some kind of toxin but I do not recognise it.'

Sombrely, Chiastolite moved and carefully folded back the linen of Ammonite's shroud to reveal her naked right leg. A sickening gasp caught in Petronia's throat as she saw the fatal wound and felt the energy in the pit of her belly surge upwards. Along the length of the dead woman's pale thigh was a deep gash that sliced open her skin and flesh, leaving the texture of her muscles exposed. Petronia shuddered inwardly for even her inexperienced eyes could see there was an unnatural influence on the flesh. The muscles and tendons were still moist and remarkably red, with no sign of clotting or darkening of the blood. In fact the exposed cut did not resemble human tissue at all, being closer in colour and appearance to a deposit of rubies in a fissure of the earth. The pallid, bathed skin around the lesion was marked by a lace-work of thin, black lines, too regimented to be mistaken for veins, that rested beneath the skin like a veiled fretwork of cold iron. Petronia saw these marks and an instinct cried from within her brain; these were no mere symptoms of decay, but a consciousness within themselves, a consciousness that had ended the Ryder's life and was now aware that Petronia stood before them.

Chiastolite spoke but Petronia was barely aware of her words. 'I know of no creature, weapon or curse that would leave such a mark.'

She tried to listen to the old woman's words but already her awareness had begun to lift away from the physical world to a higher plain of alertness. The energy within her began to swirl throughout her body, like gusts of smoke rushing through her veins, carrying unspoken messages of action to her limbs. She saw her hand reach out before her, stretching towards the glistening scarlet and sinful black of the putrid wound and felt a heave of repulsion at what she was about to do. Yet she knew she had no choice. Her touch would be a catalyst: a powerful command of release that would purify the remains of the Ryder.

Chiastolite watched the young apprentice with horrified eyes. 'No, young Sister,' she begged. 'You do not know what manner of toxin is in her body.' She reached out a withered hand to stop Petronia but was overwhelmed by a surge of Ley energy that ordered her to allow the girl to continue.

Her nerves on edge with trepidation and fear, Petronia's fingertips hovered inches away from the crimson wound. Already, she could feel something powerful and malevolent stirring violently within the dead woman, calling out to her in hushed wordless whispers that only she could fathom. But Petronia was not afraid for she knew that this dark entity was the only thing in the world that truly understood her soul.

Her skin came into soft contact with the crystallised, ruby flesh as she felt the chilling solidity of its unnatural nature. The darkness that tainted the Ryder's mortal body gasped and shuddered. In Petronia's mind, powerful words began to form and within her mouth, a strange texture and flavour coated her tongue, compelling it to move in long unspoken phrases. She reached out with her thoughts into the deepest part of the defiled corpse, commanding the hateful force to relinquish its covetous grasp. *'I am here!'* she told it, *'show yourself!'*

A sudden, low creak like a key being turned in an ancient, corroded lock issued from Ammonite's dead body and the corpse's petrified muscles trembled and relaxed as the force that held her rigid spirit at the brink of death was drawn out by Petronia's command. Uncertain what she had done, Petronia withdrew her hand and stepped backwards, fumbling to grasp the blade fastened to her belt in protection from the horror that was about to be released.

In the shortest of moments, the scarlet wound in the dead flesh had turned jet black, the deep gash becoming filled with a thick, dark matter like oily smoke, undulating and heaving just as it had done when it had surrounded the citadel. With a lazy heave, it oozed as one shapeless mass from the Ryder's remains, slipping like liquid shadow over the edge of the bier, trickling towards Petronia with coiling tendrils and wordless utterances. Horrified by this unholy abomination, the elderly Ryder Chiastolite staggered back, reaching instinctively for the crystal pendants that hung from her belt. 'This is a place for the restful dead,' she shrieked, holding out a fragment of milky white selenite; 'you shall not taint it with evil, whatever you are!' However neither Ryder nor crystal seemed to have any effect on the shadowy mass.

The pulsating darkness loomed up like a monolith of ebony fog before Petronia, its black depths swirling with perpetual movements of violent energy. She stared into its colourless, formless fibre and felt her heart and mind flame with power. Her breaths were deep and steady, her heartbeat a fearless rhythm of certainty, her thoughts totally locked with the intent of this powerful entity. Words filled her mind, as clearly as ink on parchment, and with a process that seemed so natural to her, she felt them drift from her mind to her mouth. Her tongue curled against her teeth and palate, her lips flexed and her throat expanded and constricted as she attempted to give sound to the phrases that filled her awareness. Yet she still remained silent and her communication with the living smog that loomed before her hung like a taboo manuscript locked in a casket of iron, a secret dialogue between her and the amorphous evil.

'What are you? What do you want?'

Her reply came soundless and clear from the churning power that rippled before her, uttered in blood written behind her eyes. 'Death,' it hissed. 'Murder. Blood. Destruction. Carnage.' Petronia could feel the violent hunger of the shadow rising within her as she shared its own hellish desires. Slowly she backed away, eyes aflame with challenge, every moment taunting it to pursue and consume her. A wild instinct grew within, making her feel like a vicious beast encased within human flesh. The dark, tacit language whispered and scrawled its message of action through every vein of her being. In a fluid motion she drew her blade from its scabbard and brandished it before, raising her chin in arrogant challenge.

'*Come then. Take it if you dare!*'

'Mistress Ryder! Oh mercy, what is that abomination?' The young peddler's shocked and fearful voice struck into Petronia's mind as she backed into the outer chamber to see him standing anxiously against the table. Her mind was a maelstrom of death and destruction, but through the blackness that swarmed her vision there came a sudden strand of light. Aaron's life-force was brilliant. As if in tune with her own awareness, Petronia sensed the consciousness of the dark malevolence settle hungrily on the young man as it surged into the room like a flood of black water. A hateful desire pierced its awareness as it encountered him, and it coursed towards his frail form with murderous intent.

Overwhelmed with fury, Petronia flung every bit of her conscious thought into the swirling core of the shadow, latching on like a horseman digging his spurs into the flanks of an unbroken stallion. '*Not him!*' she ordered as the venomous tendrils of death began to coil around Aaron's body. '*It is I who you truly desire!*'

The influence of the entity had already begun to set itself upon the young lad and Petronia heard him let out a shrill gasp of desperation. With movements as natural as breathing, Petronia's hand dived into the pouch on her belt, her fingertips commanding the power of the stones. A fragment of fire opal, sparking and flecked orange like an ember plucked from the grate, adhered itself obediently to her hand and with one skilful flick of her wrist, Petronia flung it in the air, catching it on the upper edge of her sabre before batting it lightly in the direction of the helpless peddler. The crystal glimmered with beams of glowing orange light as it rolled down the blade, jumping like a summoned animal to land against Aaron's chest, wrapping him in a pale cowl of burning light.

The young lad let out a cry of surprise as he found himself being dragged backwards across the room away from the rippling ebony shadow towards the door of the lodge. Petronia spun to once more face the amorphous threat looming before her, her mind linking with its unnatural, unspoken nature. Though she could not see any evidence for it, she felt as if tiny threads of the blackness had already wormed their way beneath her flesh. Far from weakening her, she felt the power within her mind becoming stronger, more concentrated. All those unuttered words and desires locked within her were becoming solid, real, tools for her to command, not through echoing gestures on hand and facial expression, but something greater. Her tongue burned like magma in the base of her mouth as she felt the unexplained urge to spit, free her gullet of the thick, bubbling sensation of power that swelled within. Her movements felt heavy and deliberate, every gesture or flicker of motion expertly placed by instinct.

With precise footsteps, she moved directly between the peddler and the flowing mass that loomed up before them, tresses of silken deadly mist outstretched to penetrate the air. His body shaking with terror, the lame youth struggled to get his balance. Flecks of orange still clung to his waist and hips and using this influence together with what meagre strength he possessed, he staggered fearfully and as quickly as he could back out into the street. The shadow instinctively responded to his unsteady escape and with a low, empty howl, surged forward in a tide of murderous energy. Petronia felt every atom in her body shake as the oily darkness buffered against her, pushing into her body like water seeping between cracks in a dam. She took a deep breath of shock as wisps of the shapeless evil entered into the pores of her skin and clenched her muscles in preparation for death; instead of a sapping poison robbing her of life, Petronia found herself being filled by a supernatural strength and knowledge that overrode her mortal awareness. A raging hunger to envelop the shadow within her flesh had awoken and the new unspoken language that drove her thoughts cried out.

'*Take me! Fill me!*'

Petronia found herself being driven out of the Ryders' lodge by the sheer power of the shadow's movement. She staggered into the blistering light of the street, each inch that she travelled taunting her opponent to follow and join her. The panic of the crowded street was a shallow echo as the blackness billowed from the door like ebony smoke. Cries of horror from women and children barely registered in her thoughts;

suddenly her dark connection with the spectre was merged with an awareness of an individual nearby, desperately trying to climb on to his mount.

His heart in his throat from what he had witnessed, Aarold frantically tried to pull himself on to Phebus's back and ride to safety. The terrified animal reared up with a scream of terror as both shadow and Ryder came tumbling out of the building. A flood of murderous energy welled up in the pitch black depth of the shadow as it became aware of the fleeing boy and it ploughed towards him, engulfing Petronia as it went. A rush of power ignited in her heart as the blackness flowed over her, just as it had done on the battlements at Goodstone. Her body seemed to disintegrate into nothing and all that was left was the rushing force of her soul. At the same time, she was acutely aware of being sandwiched between two forces – the frightened and vulnerable soul of the young man and the addictive, consuming hatred of the shadow – and realised she was the only thing that separated them. Words ripped through the air, deafening and powerful, torn painfully from her non-existent throat.

'*Away! Away from this!*'

Movement poured around her in a typhoon of power, blurring all that was solid – herself, the peddler, and his horse – into nothing as once more her consciousness left her and she succumbed to the power within.

Gasps of horror and confusion rippled through the crowd as the unsuspecting passers-by saw the mass of evil vanish as swiftly as it had appeared. Fearful words were exchanged and many looked towards the elderly Ryder who had come to the door for an explanation. However, one individual who had seen what had happened placed no faith in the followers of the Ley. Captain of the Royal Guard Tristram Kreen's heart felt unnervingly cold as he realised that there had indeed been truth in his beloved duchess's words. Something was very amiss in the Sisterhood of the Ley.

Chapter 22

BRACKEN'S BIRTH-LAND

The first traces of the cold dawn sun broke across the colourless sky, filtering down through the tangle of branches to bring icy daylight to the forest world. The misty woodland air was alive with sound as the nocturnal spirits and creatures handed over the ownership of the land to their day dwelling brethren. The chilled morning atmosphere was alive with birdsong and from his bough high in the ancient oak, the strange, blind being called Emouchet was at one with every note and trill. Many heard the dawn chorus but few experienced and understood it the way the hermit did. One leg hooked around a sturdy branch for balance, he raised his lithe arms to the cold moist atmosphere like a cleric in holy rapture; the voices and tones of his feathered kin filled his consciousness. Emouchet was a man only in form; his heart and soul were that of a soaring bird, free and unrestrained by any human law and though his milky eyes had never witnessed the sun rise, in his sacred communion with the eagles, doves, wrens and countless others, his soul was carried on their wings high and far to watch over the business of the people he had been cast out by as a child. It was from this unseen celestial vantage point that the aged hermit saw the world, captured through a million sets of bright eyes and transferred through twittering song and spiritual connection to his mind; a far removed, Godlike view that witnessed all manner of nature, war and love, trade and family, birth and death, but passed no judgement or interest in the matters of men. He understood the character of the race who had given him life but had little desire to re-engage with creatures so constricted, selfish and arrogant. This morning, however, one individual did pique his interest, like a glinting fragment of metal catching the attention of a magpie. At one with the mind of a soaring hawk hovering high above the city of Veridium, he witnessed through its keen eyes a female of great potential with a power she was fearful to control. The trills and warbles of his adoptive species told him that this was the sibling of the boy who had intruded in his forest home, and he wondered in disbelief why the lad felt the need to protect her when she clearly had power beyond measure. The human heart, he thought, was an odd and foolish thing and he felt grateful that his own bore wings and feathers even if his body did not.

The dawning light heated the surface of his leathery, tanned skin and with a small shudder Emouchet shook the dew of the early hour from his tangled grey hair. Night was over and it was time to awaken. Uncurling his leg from around the branch, he dropped lightly through the canopy, slowing his fall by grabbing and hopping on the lower branches. His blindness bore him little hindrance as he knew the limbs of the tree as well as his own fingers and toes, and within a matter of moments had jumped down to land safely on the soft forest floor, directly in between the slumbering figures of the lad and his female companion.

Scuttling over to the sleeping boy, Emouchet leant over and roughly poked him in the stomach with a long, curved fingernail. Hayden awoke with a snort and blinking his eyes, let out a shout of horror to see the hermit's hideous face looming over him. Scrabbling on to his knees, he had already drawn his blade to ward off the terrifying visage, before he remembered who the creature was and that he had saved his life the night before.

Emouchet shuffled agilely out of the way of Hayden's sword and grunted disapprovingly. 'Still think it do you good to harm Emouchet?' he quizzed sharply, reaching out to pinch the narrow blade of the weapon between his finger and thumb.

Slowly, Hayden lowered his weapon and sheathed it back in its scabbard. 'No,' he said softly, 'I don't. I apologise. I woke suddenly.'

Emouchet ran a fingernail through his filthy beard and sucked the tip thoughtfully, making a low growling sound as he did so. 'You have much to learn,' he grunted to Hayden; 'tis better you start soon else you not know where you end up!'

Roused by the ruckus, Bracken stirred from her bed among the fallen leaves and yawned wearily. 'Is it morning?' she asked, sleepily stretching and gazing around her with the realisation that the strange events of the previous night had been more than a dream.

Hayden nodded and getting to his feet brushed the dry leaves from his body. 'It would appear so,' he muttered as Emouchet shuffled around in the undergrowth grunting and gabbling to himself.

With a small sigh, Bracken sadly nodded and reached into the pocket of her robes where she had stowed Amethyst's letter. Taking it out, she held it delicately in her hands but did not unfold the paper. After a few moments, she put it away carefully and lightly touched the strange stone cylinder that had accompanied it which was now threaded on a lanyard around her neck. Finally, she took hold of one of her crystal pendants and pressed it to her lips, uttering some silent words of prayer.

The haggard hermit emerged from the undergrowth, a pile of large, light blue berries clutched in his cupped hands. 'Here!' he croaked, thrusting a dozen into Hayden's hands, 'you eat, then Emouchet show you way out of forest. You be too long here messing with tings. Emouchet be glad when you've gone!' He practically threw some of the fruit at Bracken before crouching down on his haunches to gobble up the rest himself.

Seated cross-legged on the ground, Hayden began to pick at the sour berries as he attempted to put his thoughts in order. Each day that passed while he was away from Ravensbrook, the world around him grew more and more strange; he could not begin to wonder what marvels or perils lay ahead. All he wanted was to find his sister Petronia safe and well, but a gloomy concern weighted his heart that he may never see her again. A thousand and one dangers could have befallen her and he did not have the faintest idea how he could aid her. He looked across at the old blind man, chewing noisily on the fruit he had gathered. A number of small birds, sparrows and wrens mainly, had flown down to land on the ground near to him, quite unafraid of his company, even perching on his wiry limbs and shoulders to peck and groom bugs from his wild and filthy hair. Emouchet remained perfectly still as they hopped over him, twittering and croaking softly to them. Hayden could honestly say that he had never come across anyone like Emouchet. How had the blind man survived in the wilds of the forest for so long? Was he completely insane or had all those years away from human company blessed him with a knowledge and awareness that was even beyond the capabilities of the Ley Ryders?

'Emouchet,' he called softly, as the hermit sucked the remaining dark juice from his fingers. 'Last night, you told us that the birds gave you the power to see without your eyes, see far from the forest. You said that you would be able to see whether my sister was safe.' The hermit did not seem to hear or at least showed no sign of response. With hands as gentle as a mother's, he scooped up one of the sparrows in his palms and held it close to his face so that its feathers caressed his leathery skin as he whispered to it. Hayden glanced at Bracken, unsure why he was receiving no answer.

'Emouchet,' he repeated, slightly lower as the old man raised his feathered friend up so it might take off, 'do you remember what I asked you? About my sister?'

Emouchet gave an impatient growl and leapt to his feet. 'Emouchet knows,' he grunted, pacing around the clearing. 'Emouchet saw her. She is on her path, on her Ley,' he added patronisingly as he gave Bracken a shove to indicate she should get to her feet. 'She is alive. That is all.'

Relief flooded Hayden's heart at this small glimmer of hope. 'Good,' he breathed. 'Tell me, is she still at the citadel in Goodstone? Is she safe?'

His anxious questions were answered by Emouchet letting out an angry squawk and flapping his tattered fur cape like a bird caught in a trap. 'Did I say I would tell you these tings?' he demanded, his opaque eyes rolling in their sockets as if they were trying to find where Hayden was. 'No I did not! Emouchet say that I tell you if she be alive or dead. And I say she be alive and on her path. That be enough. E-nough!'

He landed a hand heavily on Hayden's arm, pushing him to face away from the mighty oak before reaching out to roughly grab Bracken's robes, dragging her in the same direction.

'You both go now,' he shrieked, the pitch of his voice painfully shrill. 'Get! I show you the way and you get gone. We leave now and you be at forest edge by time sun cools. Emouchet not take care of you another night. I is not your mothers!' Crossly he pushed past them and gambled ahead into the trees, muttering and squawking angrily to himself.

Hayden looked at Bracken who was checking she had not lost any of her precious crystals and securing her baldric around her waist. 'I guess that's his way of telling us to follow him.'

They set off away from Emouchet's nest, aware that if they dawdled the short-tempered hermit would not wait for them. He had soon disappeared from clear view, diving into bushes or scuttling up trees to leap from branch to branch, almost totally unhampered by his disability. He was easy to track, however, from his continuous birdlike chattering and seemed to have memorised every tree, plant and rock in the wood by touch or smell. Sometimes he would stop for a brief moment to caress the bark of a tree trunk, sniff the air or taste a leaf to get his bearings and these pauses gave Hayden and Bracken a chance to keep pace. They were both very aware that their guide through the perilous landscape was blind and also very likely mad, but knew that he was more aware of the dangers of this place than either of them and saw no other option but to follow.

'Do you think he knows what he's talking about?' Bracken asked softly after they had been walking for a while. She had remained uncommonly quiet that morning and this was the first time she had engaged Hayden in conversation since they had left the oak.

Hayden watched Emouchet as he roughly batted a low hanging branch out of the path.

'I must admit I thought it was unlikely at first,' he confessed as the old man stooped down to sniff at the droppings of some animal before grunting approvingly and lurching onwards. 'But he is clearly of a good age and has made his home here for a long time. He must know the woods well to thrive in them as he does despite his blindness.'

Bracken nodded in agreement but her eyes looked thoughtful, almost sad. 'One grows accustomed to the environment one finds oneself in,' she said quietly. 'I wasn't doubting that he would lead us down the wrong path. I was thinking more about what he said about me last night.' Hayden stopped for a moment, careful to keep one eye on Emouchet so that they would not lose him. 'About you being special? Having great power? I don't know. What do you think, Mistress Bracken?' Part of him prayed that the hermit was right, not for Bracken's sake but his own. It reassured him to think Emouchet did have some kind of divine sight, that he had truly seen Petronia alive and was not just saying so to make them leave his sanctuary.

Bracken cupped an amethyst crystal she wore about her neck in her palms and gazed into it as a woman might gaze into a looking glass to check her appearance. 'It scares me that he could be right,' she confessed, 'but it also scares me to think he is wrong.'

Hayden frowned. 'I don't understand.'

She gave a sad laugh and touched Hayden's arm as they continued to walk side by side. 'Of course you don't, Master Hayden,' she said kindly, 'you are sure of who you are. You desire nothing more than your family and their safety. I envy your certainty. If our friend speaks the truth, if I am destined for a life different to my sisters, it would explain why the Ley has never spoken to me. Yet I have no other desire than to be a Ryder and use the teaching bestowed on me. If my power is so great wouldn't it have shown itself by now?'

She focused on the winding track Emouchet was cutting for them as she kept talking and Hayden began to suspect that she spoke not to him, but simply to voice her own uncertainty. 'But if he is wrong then,' she paused, before confessing honestly, 'I am nothing, I have nothing. No sense for the Ley, no purpose in life, no reason for Sister Amethyst to have raised me.'

Her words sounded so empty and lonely that Hayden once again questioned the virtue of the Ryders' belief system. 'I was always taught that a man has the right to choose his own path,' he told her. 'If you have no duty to the Ley, doesn't it give the freedom to settle on a role you choose for yourself? It does't say any less of the ethics taught to you by your Sister Ryders, kindness, charity, courage, they are all admiral values, but you do not need a Stone Name to possess them. No-one can take them from you without your consent.'

He was afraid that he might have once again said something to offend Bracken's adoptive kin, but the tall girl simply nodded thoughtfully and replied, 'Choice is only free if you can choose what you wish. As Emouchet said a lizard cannot be a bat or a bird be a fish. I have no other desire than to be a Ryder. If it must be, I must learn to dismiss that dream from my heart. I pray to the Ley that It will allow me to do that even if I cannot feel It act on me.'

She lapsed back into silence as they continued on their trek, following the impatient calls and gestures of Emouchet as he led them through the wood. As they walked, Hayden pondered on Bracken's strength, not simply the robustness of her heavy physique but her stoic character. It took great discipline to devote yourself to any cause so fully; what he had once seen as clinging faith he now began to understand as an act of enormous willpower. Bracken believed in the Ley and what right had he or anyone else to dismiss something that had such a powerful effect on her character.

They followed the trail Emouchet led them on for several hours into the early afternoon, not pausing for rest or nourishment as midday passed. The blind old man seemed to pay very little attention to the conversation of his unwanted companions, focusing his efforts solely on finding his pathway through the forest using what senses he still possessed and his almost animalistic familiarity with the terrain. He switched between lurching across the forest floor and bolting up tree trunks to leaping from branch to branch, grunting and squawking all the time, either to himself or to the birds that fluttered in the canopy. Hayden could not understand what he was chattering about most of the time but had the feeling that Emouchet was complaining about the two ignorant strangers who had blundered into the tranquillity of his solitude. Part of him did wonder whether the old man did really have any idea where they were heading but in time he began to notice a definite but subtle change in the landscape. The undergrowth became less lush with not so much variety in the plant life. The ground was rockier and the trees younger and not so well established. They were definitely coming to the edge of the forest. With a loud grunt, Emouchet dropped from the lower branch of a tree, nearly landing on top of Hayden and Bracken.

'Is here,' he announced, gesturing northwards through the sparse pines and aspens.

Bracken peered curiously through the outskirts of woodland. In the far distance, she could just make out a vast plain of long grass. 'What is here?' she asked.

The blind man burbled angrily and threw up his arms as he stalked around. 'Is here! Is here!' he screeched in his birdlike tone. 'Edge of forest, like I say. Emouchet take you no further. Is sick of you both! I help you enough; now find your own way. Now you head north, is okay way. Emouchet has no business there.'

With a powerful leap, he launched himself back into the lower branches of the tree, his milky eyes rolling back in his head. Hayden glanced up at him, a wild creature of fur, hair and leathery muscle and called out a word of thanks. 'We are grateful, Emouchet,' he called. 'We could not have survived the night without you.' The old man did not seem to hear or show interest in a farewell. Paying them no further notice, he scuttled higher into the green canopy, disappearing into his woodland kingdom until his calls and screeching were indistinguishable from his adopted family of birds.

Hayden searched the network of branches till he could see him no more, feeling as if Emouchet had been no more alive than a dream or nightmare. 'Such a strange person,' he murmured before he and Bracken carried on their way.

Despite his clear dislike of Hayden and Bracken, Emouchet had stayed loyal to his promise to lead them from the woods and the pair only had to walk a short distance before the forest completely disappeared and they found themselves in a strange, barren new country.

*

The panorama that greeted them was austere, almost monochrome in its blandness. The ground was level but rocky and the wind chillingly cold. The only plant life to be seen was a blanket of coarse, brown grass that grew to above their knees and rippled in waves of liquid movement. It stretched out in acres before them up to the dark solidity of an imposing range of mountains that squatted like a dark crouching giant on the horizon, its caps dusted white with snow. The air was silent apart from the biting howl of the wind.

Hayden looked in awe at the severe landscape, searching hopelessly for signs of civilisation. 'What an unwelcoming land,' he breathed. 'I wonder where we are.'

He looked round at Bracken for a response and saw that the girl's features had set themselves in an expression of brooding wistfulness. The wind blew her colourless hair like a veil across her mottled face and her dark eyes were cloudy with thought.

Hayden spoke her name. 'Mistress Bracken, are you all right?'

Slowly she nodded but did not look at him. 'I know where we are,' she whispered hoarsely. 'This is the Greyg Steppes. I was born here.'

She stepped past Hayden and wandered through the long, billowing grass, taking in every bare detail of the barren landscape. Hayden watched her intently, realising she felt a sudden bond to this empty land. 'Are you sure?' he asked gently.

Bracken licked her lips as if to taste the essence of the place in the air and nodded. 'I'm sure,' she told him. 'I mean, I don't remember, of course. But I've seen maps and sketches. Those are the mountains of Kelhalbon that mark the border between Geoll and Etheria. This is the pampas that belongs to no kingdom. This, this is where Sister Amethyst found me.'

She stood perfectly still amid the drab shrubland and lowered her hand to run her palm against the tips of the rustling grass as if in the hope that its caress would awaken something within her. Hayden wondered what was stirring in her thoughts, whether returning to this lonely place brought to her mind familiarity through memories she could not recall. He surveyed the empty, whispering pampas, searching for the smallest signal of homeliness that might betray to Bracken the truth about her origins but could see none.

'I never thought my life would lead me back here.' Bracken's voice was a low, soft whisper and she crouched down to sit amid the dull prairie grass. 'It is not how I pictured it in my mind. That is if I pictured it at all. I can't say I gave it much thought when I was with Sister Amethyst and the Ryders.'

Hayden approached and took a seat on the grass at her side. The ground beneath him was stony and cold and Hayden found his thoughts drifting back to his own more pleasant homeland of Ravensbrook. He recalled with familiar fondness his parents and their simple home, the neighbours and uncomplicated life that he still hoped to return to. Even this far away Hayden still felt its tug of belonging. Looking around, he wondered whether Bracken could feel the same sense of ownership to this desolate plain.

'How do you feel?' he asked gently.

Bracken plucked a blade of long, rough grass and ran it between her plump fingers. 'Sad,' she answered softly, studying the blade as it twisted in the wind. 'Being here makes me realise that my parents, whoever they were, were real people, that I existed, even if it was just for a short time, outside the care of the Ryders.' She raised her arm and gestured to the bland landscape. 'Look at this place,' she commented. 'I mean, they couldn't have come from here, this couldn't have been their home. No dwellings, no farmland. Why would they come to a wasteland like this to bring a child into the world? Why did they leave me behind?'

Her deep voice grew throaty and hoarse but her expression was enigmatic and Hayden knew by now that whatever lay behind her mottled mask she would not cry. Bracken had once told him that she had no desire to know who her birth family were, but now that they found themselves back where Amethyst had found her, he wondered if that was true.

Sighing deeply, Bracken reached for the purple crystal that hung around her neck and tenderly pressed it to her lips. 'Oh Master Hayden,' she breathed, 'I do miss Sister Amethyst, so very much. She is so wise. I know if she were here she would be able to reassure me.'

The loneliness in her voice plucked at Hayden's heart and his thoughts were painfully drawn back to his own sorrow for the loss of his sister Petronia. Emouchet had declared that she was still alive but what proof could a half-crazed hermit give? Even if he were right, it did not help Hayden find his way back to her. Whether bonded by blood or adoption, both he and Bracken were far away from those they cared for.

'Do you think they would be proud of me?' Bracken uttered the question quietly as she gazed at the mountaintops encircled with cloud and mist that overshadowed them. 'My parents, Sister Amethyst too – do you think I've acted in a way that they would have approved of?'

Hayden felt a sick sensation settle in the centre of his chest. Touching the hilt of his sword, he recalled the last moments he had spent in his father's forge and the promise he had made to protect his sister. That promise now lay broken and Hayden wished with all his heart he could find the power and means to find her and bring her home.

'I think,' he said slowly, 'parents, guardians too, are always proud of their children if they try and live a good life and help others.'

Bracken looked weary and stretched out her long, thick legs. 'I don't know if I can lay claim to that,' she said wistfully, rubbing her palm against her right eye. 'I try but all my efforts seem to end in failure.'

'What do you mean?' asked Hayden as Bracken fiddled with her pendant. 'If you hadn't stood firm when the fairies attacked us in the woods, they would have overwhelmed me. If you hadn't fought them off, I would have perished long before Emouchet had the chance to revive me. You swore to protect me and you kept that oath. A parent could not ask for a nobler deed from their daughter.'

Bracken looked up, a small smile tugging at her thin mouth. Hayden looked at her and for the first time noticed that there was a strange beauty in her unusual features. Not the same conventional prettiness that Petronia was blessed with but a striking attractiveness about her shadowy skin, deep-green eyes and ever-altering hair colour that was pleasing. 'Really?' she said, sounding truly heartened by what he had said.

Hayden tried to shake off his observations of Bracken's looks and think of other matters. 'Of course, the sisters have taught you well. Despite what I may have said, I am grateful of your company.'

Bracken's pale cheeks coloured with pride. 'The 17th Dogma,' she said softly, getting to her feet: 'a Ryder must bring aid to where her heart sees it is needed. Thank you, Master Hayden, you have lifted my spirits.'

She glanced around, a small frown creasing her brow. 'But I still would like a few moments of meditation on my crystals. This is such a desolate place and holds so many mixed emotions for me. I know that I might not feel the Ley but it would quieten my heart and mind a little if I were to cast some of my worries to It, even if It gives me no answers.'

Silently she paced away from him, casting back a thoughtful glance as she went, until she reached a spot amid the rustling grass that she felt was private enough to perform her meditative rituals. Hayden stayed where he was, half watching her and half lost in his own thoughts. He leaned back on his elbows and observed as Bracken fastidiously removed each of the crystal pendants and bangles, holding them one at a time towards the sky before laying them out in a semicircle in front of where she was kneeling.

After observing this routine for a few moments, Hayden allowed his concentration to wander as he gazed at the desolate landscape. His thoughts were, as ever, on his sister, and in the lost emptiness of the Greyg Steppes he could not help but feel lonely and hopeless. Bracken had given him her vow to aid him all she could but he very much doubted that she, like him, had any idea how they could find their way back to the citadel. He looked at the greyness of the world before him and the barrenness of the place seemed to echo with his own powerlessness. At least Bracken could take comfort and solace in her faith in the Ley. He thought about this and about how Bracken still committed her worries and prayers to It even when she sensed nothing in return, and as he did so the notion seemed to become less foolish than he first thought. The

313

tepid sun that glowed overhead was the same sun that lit his sister's way, the chilled wind that caressed his cheek was blowing south, perhaps by chance to blow on Petronia too. These tiny sensations brought Hayden some comfort and not daring to think too deeply about what he was doing, he closed his eyes and held a quiet thought in his mind. A thought that he loved his sister and that she would keep herself safe and well until he could find a way back to her. He tried to imagine the icy wind taking this thought from his mind and carrying it like a light feather high over the vast forest and countryside to wherever Petronia was, so that she might know that he had not abandoned her. He tried very hard to picture this but Hayden, by nature, was a more practical man and had little faith in thoughts and wishes.

A sudden cry of alarm shook him from his contemplation and in a fraction of a second his eyes were open and he was on his feet running towards Bracken and the direction of the sound. The girl was standing amid the long grass with her right arm stretched out in front of her. In her hand, she tightly grasped a leather lanyard from which was suspended the strange, polished stone cylinder that her guardian had given her. The small tube was spinning on the axle of the thin strap at an alarming rate, like the bobbin on a spinning wheel. The energy created within it was so powerful that it lifted the lanyard taut so it was pointing in an almost horizontal line toward the mountains. The cylinder whirled and tugged like a hunting dog on its leash, eager to pursue its quarry, drawn unquestioningly in the direction of the mountains. It emitted a strange, low noise as it turned, a dull, grinding sound like millstones at work.

Hayden's eyes grew wide with amazement when he saw it. 'What's happening?' he asked fearfully, his hand resting on his sword in case he needed it.

Bracken wound her fingers tightly around the leather band, fearful that the tube would pull it from her grasp. 'I don't know,' she gasped. 'I was removing my pendants and amulets to lie them on the ground to connect them with the Ley but when I took this off, it started spinning like crazy and swinging in the direction of the mountains.' As if in agreement with this statement, the cylinder gave a strong tug at her hand.

Hayden's jaw dropped at what he was seeing; it was almost as if the pipe had come alive. 'Maybe, maybe it's the Ley,' he pondered as the dull groan of the tube drowned out the wind. 'Maybe this is your Calling, Bracken.'

Excitement flashed momentarily in Bracken's eyes but she frowned and looked doubtful. 'I'm not sure,' she said. 'I mean, I know every crystal used by the Ryders and this doesn't appear to be made from any of them. And besides, wouldn't I *know* if it was my Calling? I don't feel any different.' She looked pensive, the whole of her stocky frame taut as she struggled to hold on to the persistent tube and what its movement might mean. Her breathing was shallow and excited and her free hand twitched with eagerness to do something, even if she had not yet decided what that was. After a moment's thought she spoke, more to clarify her actions to herself than to inform Hayden. 'I think I should touch it,' she stated.

Hayden looked apprehensive. 'Are you sure that's wise?' he asked, staring suspiciously at the whirling artefact struggling to break free. 'It could be an evil talisman of some sort.'

Bracken looked worried for a brief second but quickly shook her head. 'No,' she said surely, 'Sister Amethyst is well learned in such matters. She wouldn't have given me any item that was tainted or harmful. Besides, a Ryder must always show courage in following her destiny.'

Cautiously, she stretched out her left arm towards the rotating cylinder, firmly pulling back with her right so it came within her grasp. Her thick fingers trembled slightly with a mixture of fear, excitement and apprehension as she reached out, but mastering her nerve she boldly pressed the tips of her index and middle digit to the polished, rotating surface of the tube. There was an instant and frantic buzz of sound as Bracken's flesh came into brief contact with the smooth stone, a high-pitched cross between the shift of gears and a cry of recognition in a foreign, guttural tongue. A fork of brightness like miniaturised lightning

315

broke across the tube's curved face, sending threads of gleaming brilliance like veins through the solidity of the stone before vanishing seconds later. The cylinder jerked, lurched forward with a desperate energy that nearly tugged its leather bonds out of Bracken's grip. She took a stumbling step forward to catch her balance, overwhelmed and amazed by the strength and will within the cylinder. What she had first assessed as animalistic power now seemed more abstract, more cerebral, a wish and persistent intent to draw them onwards.

Hayden witnessed his companion stumble and quickly reached out to catch her arm and help her regain balance. 'Are you all right?' he gasped as Bracken staggered to her feet.

The girl nodded, her dark, forest green eyes darting back and forth between the whirling cylinder and the mountains towards which it was pointing. 'Kelhalbon,' she gasped in realisation. 'The Kingdom of the dwarves. Of course!'

Hayden frowned in confusion as Bracken knotted the leather thong restraining the cylinder more securely around her wrist. To his disbelief the solid stone seemed to be buckling and bowing in desperation to move forward. Enthusiastically, Bracken explained. 'This, whatever it is, must be made by dwarves. They are skilled craftsmen, masters of metalwork and magic. This artefact must be imbued with an enchantment to guide the carrier back to Kelhalbon. It must be my quest to return it!'

Full of doubt and mistrust, Hayden scratched his head. 'But why would you have it?' he asked as Bracken began to gather up her crystals and pendants from the ground.

She paused for a moment, a look of uncertainty masking her piebald face. 'I don't know,' she murmured before adding a surer tone. 'But the dwarves and Ryders have a long and profound affinity with each other. They believe in the Ley also, and the caves of their kingdom are where all our crystals and stones come from. They will be bound to help us if I tell them I'm an apprentice to the Ley.'

Turning towards the austere mountains, Hayden felt apprehension grow cold and empty in the pit of his stomach. The stony peaks of the imposing crags looked jagged, dangerous and unwelcoming, wrapped in their cowls of ice and snow. He had been wary of magical creatures before and after the attack of the woodland fairies, he dreaded to think what horrors dwarves could exact.

Noticing the fear in his eyes, Bracken placed a hand on his arm. 'Take heart, Master Hayden,' she reassured. 'From what I've read in the citadel's library, dwarves are mostly benign and show little interest in attacking humans. They follow the acts of my sisters with interest and will surely have news that will guide us to your sister.'

Hayden swallowed hard at the mention of Petronia but uttered not a word. To him it seemed like life and Bracken were pulling him further and further away from her side. Each moment that passed the world seemed to open up with more and more miracles and dangers and he wished that he could see one certain sign that he was doing the right thing. He looked at the dark, stone tube, tied to Bracken's wrist, buckling with power and urging them toward the mountains. Bracken had sworn on her faith in the Ley that she would be loyal and help him find his sister, but the mysterious cylinder was the only link Bracken had to her lost family and Hayden knew painfully how strong the urge to find your kin could be. Bracken seemed to have a noble and true character but could you really know what desires drove a person's heart? That fact could be as enigmatic as the workings of the Ley or the unknown dangers that awaited them amid the craggy slopes of the Kelhalbon Mountains.

Chapter 23

THE MASKED HUNTRESS

His heart heavy with concern and disquiet, Tristram Kreen pulled his cloak more tightly around his shoulders and peered into the gloomy night. It was gone midnight and the city gates had long been bolted against malicious intruders. The noble captain now knew that the risks to Veridium's safety and that of its young prince lay within the walls of the city not from the outer shadows where he now waited for his nameless contact. Once again he ran through the events of the last days trying to dispel the incredulous disbelief he had felt for what he had witnessed. His love and devotion for the White Duchess knew no bounds but even he had been filled with doubt when Maudabelle had spoken of her suspicion that the Ley Ryders were behind Prince Aarold's disappearance. Like so many people, Tristram had always viewed the followers of the Ley as benign and merciful, only bringing aid and comfort to those who needed it. That was before he had stood before the lodge and witnessed with wordless horror the billowing spectre of evil oozing from within, in murderous pursuit of the royal heir. If that had not been enough to shake his beliefs then the sight of a young woman in the garb of a Ley apprentice commanding the smoky foulness to strike the prince had displayed for him the heinous truth: the Ryders were set to overrule the kingdom by means of this indescribable wickedness. Tristram's instincts had been to strike out against this terror in defence of his master but the incredulity of what he was confronted with rooted him to the spot and he could only watch in helpless horror as the mighty shadow descended and both prince and attacker disappeared into its rushing billows.

Trembling like a child awoken from a nightmare, Tristram had staggered back to the castle and on bended knee before his adored duchess spoke in hushed fearful words of what he had seen. He had expected her to crumble with grief and terror at the confirmation of her fears but although passion and distress burnt bright in her emerald eyes, the White Duchess had more resolve and mettle than lesser females. Her quiet strength made Tristram desire and admire her even more and once again he pledged his devotion. For a long time she remained silent, contemplating what to do before addressing her trusted captain in cool calm tones. She told him there was only one other person she trusted as much as him in this time of great peril, a warrior/tracker of great skill both magical and physical who had long ago swore allegiance and would serve her at a time of her greatest need. She was wise in many things and if the prince still lived, she would be able to find him. The duchess would send for her at once and Tristram would accompany her on this vital mission, that was if the tracker deemed him worthy. Tristram had greatly professed his devotion to this quest (and his beloved duchess) and declared he would not fail.

*

Somewhere in the black night an owl hooted. The torches that burned in holders on the city wall had begun to splutter and dim with the lateness of the hour, and a clinging icy fog had begun to rise. The eeriness of the night magnified Tristram's concerns and fears of dark magic. He had been waiting patiently for several hours and had begun to wonder whether the White Duchess's champion would show when a low, feminine voice, soft but authoritative, uttered his name.

'Captain Kreen. Captain Tristram Kreen.'

Tristram quickly turned toward the sound of the voice to see a figure step silently out of the night. One moment he was alone and the next she stood before him, as if drawn suddenly into existence out of the shadows, like a wildcat pouncing from its lair. She was a woman, this was the only true fact Tristram could state about her with any conviction and this was only from the timbre of her voice. Her shape was entirely obscured by a thick woollen cloak that seemed to merge with the night as she moved. The hood was drawn up and the manner of her features, that could have perhaps been distinguished in the pale light of the moon, were completely covered by a black leather mask that sported only the narrowest slits for sight and air.

A vague sense of unease crept over Tristram as he viewed the figure. 'I am he,' he said cagily, his muscles tensing instinctively in preparation for a sudden attack. Beneath the cowl, he could feel the stranger's eyes sweep over him. The figure in black tilted her head slightly. 'I believe you were expecting me.'

Tristram's eyes narrowed as he searched the stranger's loose garments for the glimmer of a sword or other weapon. 'That would depend,' he uttered suspiciously. 'Who are you?'

A soft, muffled snigger echoed from beneath the woman's mask and with a swift silky movement she reached into the folds of her cape and drew out a small, sapphire medallion that she threw to Tristram. Catching it, he examined it in the palm of his hand. A serpent of expertly carved silver coiled across a mottled field of rich blue enamel, an expensive rendering of the White Duchess's private insignia.

'And you, Captain Kreen,' came the woman's cool, low voice. 'A similar gesture would seem appropriate, if you are who you claim to be.'

Still slightly suspicious, Tristram passed the medallion back to its owner before removing his right gauntlet. He held out his hand so she could inspect the much treasured signet ring Maudabelle had presented him with as a mark of trust. He saw a dark pupil glitter through the eyelet of the black mask as the woman studied the metal snake coiled around his little finger before nodding with satisfaction.

'You still have me at an advantage,' he told her, withdrawing his hand and pulling his glove back on. 'You know my name but the duchess didn't inform me of yours.'

He seemed to sense the lips beneath the leather form into a smile.

'How impolite of me,' she breathed, her tone heavy with irony, 'you may call me Coal-Fox.' She spread her cape slightly and bowed. Tristram's trained eye instinctively fell on the hilt of a finely made blade fastened to her hip. He was devoted to the White Duchess without question but couldn't help thinking that this faceless footpad was way below her approved social circle.

'You will forgive me if I seem mistrusting, you understand,' he uttered knowingly, 'but I am a captain of the Royal Guard and in my experience individuals who call themselves by names other than their own, who use masks and cowls to hide their faces, nearly always do so because they do not want themselves attached to the deeds they do. I wonder if that is the case with you.'

Coal-Fox stood before him as motionless as an ebony statue. 'You are most observant, Captain Kreen. It is true that there are many people in this land who would want me dead if they knew my true agenda. I am understandably fearful for my own safety. Even the most virtuous sometimes need to act in secret, if they suspect evil-doers will put pay to their plans. But know that I speak plain and with no deceit when I say my allegiance lies with no other but the Duchess Maudabelle.'

Tristram rolled his saliva thoughtfully around the inside of his mouth as he considered Coal-Fox. His military training left him with the nature that he would be happier to see the woman in black behind bars than at his side. If she was to suddenly turn, he wondered whether he would be able to overpower and subdue her. If she was indeed a mere woman, he had no doubt of this, but who knew what dark skills lay beneath that emotionless mask. 'I have only your word for that,' he pointed out.

'And the duchess's mark does not buy me your trust?' came the brazen question.

Tristram fixed her with his penetrating, mixed-coloured eyes, a stare that could turn a thief's heart to ice. 'Such things can be stolen or forged.'

This remark seemed to amuse her greatly. Slowly clapping her hands, Coal-Fox took a step back, turning her featureless face toward the half-hidden moon so that its light shone on the patterned texture of her mask. 'As you will, Captain Kreen,' she said almost amiably. 'I do not wish you to override your better judgement. I am far too busy to waste my time attempting to win your approval. Return to the palace if you wish and inform your beloved White Duchess that you deem her most trusted Coal-Fox a charlatan and rogue. I'm sure it will make for a most entertaining conversation when she and I next converse. Or perhaps you intend to set out to find the prince on your own. A man of your clear intellect must surely have at least some idea where he is.' She paused and tilted her head, awaiting his reply.

Tristram felt an unpleasant chill as he recalled the smoky horror that he witnessed bursting forth from the Ryders' lodge to sweep Prince Aarold away to who knew what terrifying fate. He was an intelligent man but there were some things, dark and heinous atrocities, that were beyond his imagination. He did not have a clue where to start searching for the prince nor what malicious dark power had swept him away. Looking at the stranger in her sable robes, he wondered if she indeed had subtle skills, magical or otherwise, to track the path he needed to follow. Was that why the White Duchess had employed her as her servant?

'Are you saying you could find the prince's whereabouts?' he quizzed sternly.

Coal-Fox softly rubbed the tips of her leather-clad fingers against one another as if she was feeling the very texture of the cold night air. 'I do possess certain talents and knowledge,' she breathed softly. 'The fox always finds its prey when it has the scent.'

She peered at him intently, her dark eyes glinting like black diamonds through the slits of her mask. Tristram felt a stab of mistrust but realised that if he was going to find the young prince, and win Maudabelle's heart, he would have to take whatever help Coal-Fox offered.

The masked tracker extended a gloved hand toward him and beckoned Tristram to dismount. Cautiously he obeyed and came to her side. He could almost sense the grin of triumph beneath her mask. 'Step only where I do,' she told him; 'the path that leads to the prince runs nearby.' Turning away from him slightly, she proceeded to stalk with light, careful footsteps across the stony earth. His senses alert for any sudden trick or betrayal, Tristram followed, studying her movements intently as he tried to detect what she was looking for.

After a few moments of intense searching, Coal-Fox let out a triumphant gasp and swooped down like a black-feathered falcon. In a split second, Tristram was at her side to see what she had discovered.

Beneath the dim gleam of the moon, the dusty earth at their feet looked chalky white and across its colourless face trickled a thin line of inky dark fluid as if some unseen quill had marked the land. It was impossible to detect the colour of the liquid in the dimness of the night, but it was glossy and slowed steadily like a tiny bubbling stream. Apprehensively, Tristram reached out with a gloved hand and lightly dipped his fingertips into its narrow flow. The liquid was thick and sticky with a recognisable tart, metallic odour. His heart froze.

'Blood?' he queried. Slowly she nodded but said nothing.

Fearful, Tristram lowered his voice to a hushed whisper. 'The prince's?' he asked, his stomach tightening with the notion that his quest might already be at an end.

Flexing her fingers slowly to form a fist, Coal-Fox stared at the bloody trail with eyes as dark as the flowing liquid. 'No,' she said with grim certainty, 'not the prince's. I can guarantee it.' There was an icy coolness in her tone, a dark and brutal knowledge that told Tristram more than her words. Once more, his suspicion grew keen in his chest. He sat back on his heels and looked at the outline of her form partly hidden beneath the folds of her cape but clear enough to tell him that she was young, lithe and strong.

Sensing his gaze, Coal-Fox turned her grim featureless face towards him, her eye sockets shadowed by the brim of her cowl. 'I told you before,' she said dully, without a hint of emotion, 'there are people who would stand in the way of me serving the White Duchess. I have certain skills that she makes use of. Not all of them are pleasant.' She gestured offhandedly to the trickle of gore that ran ever northward. 'Surely a man of your military background isn't squeamish?'

Standing up she stepped away from the stream of blood and let out a low whistle. There was the sound of hooves as her black steed appeared from the shadows. 'I suggest we ride as soon as possible,' she said, taking hold of the horse's reins; 'every second we dally the prince is in danger.'

Tristram remained looking at the flowing rivulet of dark liquid as Coal-Fox spoke. As she prepared to pull herself into the saddle, he reached out and roughly grabbed her arm. Her posture stiffened and beneath her mask her dark eyes burned.

'Understand,' he hissed as she pulled away from him, 'I do not trust you, Coal-Fox. I will follow your lead because I serve Prince Aarold and the White Duchess but if you betray them, if you betray me, I will take it as an act of treason. Do not forget that.'

The masked woman sharply jerked her arm from Tristram's grasp. 'Your feelings are clear,' she hissed, as they mounted their steeds. 'I will not dismiss them.'

Without another word she set off following the bloody path, the watchful captain close on her tail.

Chapter 24

UNVEILED AND IN PERIL

The cruel mountain wind howled outside the mouth of the cave, carrying with it icy flakes of bitter snow. The cold air made Aarold's lame leg muscles ache painfully but this was the least of his problems. One moment, he had been patiently waiting in the outer hall of the Ryders' lodge in the city for the return of the pretty apprentice and the Ley Ryder Chiastolite, the next a vast inky cloud of shapeless darkness surged into the chamber like a murderous wolf, intent on ending his life. The young maiden who had befriended him soon followed, battling to control and rein in its brutal will. She had sent a sparkling crystal tumbling towards Aarold, alive with a burst of power that had momentarily blessed him with the strength to escape the heinous apparition and flee into the street, but as he struggled to mount Phebus and ride away from the nightmare, the shadow flooded out of the lodge, like a river of tar bursting through a dam, engulfing Aarold, body and soul. He felt himself buckle and pivot on the brink of death. However, there had been a presence at his side, a mystical touch of ancient magic, fixed and unyielding, dragging him firmly back from his demise, breathing a powerful, forgotten sorcery that harnessed the black cloud like a snorting, bucking beast. The world spun, a sickeningly fast rush of colour and movement, as they were whisked away quicker than thought. His senses were overwhelmed by the force that bombarded them as he plummeted into unconsciousness. He awoke once more free from the wild, shadowy peril, in the chilling rocky surroundings of a lone mountainside. The simple enchantments he had placed on himself and Phebus were smashed like a wooden sword against steel. The motionless form of the young mute girl lay next to him, her shapely lips painted scarlet with blood.

He and his loyal Equile swiftly searched out a sheltered inlet in the rock and with Phebus's strength they managed to drag the girl inside. There, Aarold used a phial of liquid flame from his trusty satchel to start a fire and did his best to make the slumbering apprentice comfortable as he tried to think what to do next. His father's voice echoed inside his head, saying a prince must be courageous and take charge in times of danger, and for once in his life Aarold did not disagree. He had to do something. Wearily he crouched down beside the fire and tried to think of a plan but fear and confusion mixed together with the fatigue and pain in his body made logical thought very hard.

At the mouth of the cave, Phebus cast his crimson eyes skyward and let out yet another melancholic wail. 'You've murdered me!' he bleated, as Aarold warmed his stiff fingers before the fire. 'I don't understand what I've done to make you despise me to such an extent but you really must want to kill us both. Haven't I always been a devoted friend, a loyal steed? Haven't you always had the best education, every comfort that your royal status afforded? Yet despite this, you have condemned us to perish here, to become an icy monument to your youthful pigheadedness.'

Aarold sighed wearily and slowly shifted his leg back and forth to stop it completely seizing up with spasm. 'Phebus, please,' he begged, as his friend pecked angrily at the stony ground with his beak, 'please just, be quiet while I try to think.'

The Equile squawked in disbelief and banged his front talons against the hard floor of the cave. '*Think?*' he spat, his spiny tail thrashing with irritation. '*Now* you decide to *think!* How about *thinking* back at the palace when you had the idiotic notion of us pantomiming about the city as a peddler and horse? How about *thinking* about going home after we escaped by the skin of our teeth from that robber instead of aligning ourselves with that ill-omened harpy? Why didn't you *think* then?'

'All right, it's my fault!' Aarold's voice rang out crossly above the wind. 'This entire situation is a complete disaster and it's all my fault!

But you are not helping the slightest by laying there, whining and complaining.'

Wistfully, he looked down to where the comatose Ryder lay, his bundled up cape tucked under her head to form a makeshift pillow. Despite his despondency, he could not help but see how beautiful she looked lying there, like a maiden in a folktale placed under a spell of eternal sleep; however, such romantic fantasies were foolish in this situation. It struck Aarold that she was, or at least had been, a great deal more powerful than any storybook heroine. She had saved him twice in the past day and during the terrifying attack by the shadowy entity at the lodge seemed to have mastered at least some command over the heinous power that had threatened to rob him of his life. He prided himself on his intellect, but the truth was he did not have a clue what the nightmarish spectre had been or how it linked to the mystical abilities of the young apprentice. More worryingly though, he did not have any idea of how to find a way out of this hostile environment. One thing was apparent, with the young woman in a deep coma and Phebus on the verge of a nervous breakdown, it was up to him to get them to safety.

A sudden, jagged gasp caught in the sleeping girl's throat and Aarold jumped. Her body twitched and shook violently and her lips parted as she made a series of gagging, guttural noises. Swiftly, Aarold reached for his satchel and scrabbled inside as he tried to recall the medical knowledge from his own convalescence.

'She's having a seizure!' he declared anxiously, as he searched for smelling salts to revive her. Phebus turned his head and momentarily glanced at the fitting girl before making an uncaring grunt and returning to his gloomy self-pity.

Before Aarold could find the jar containing the salts, she stopped her violent shaking, blinked her eyes and became lucid. Cold and fear clung to Petronia's body as she awoke and became aware of the world again. Just like she had done after the attack on the citadel, she could recall everything, only this time she was aware of a small but profound change. The feeling of command and control over the energy that she had drawn from the dead Ryder's body had not vanished. Instead she could still feel it churning and bubbling inside, as if she had swallowed whatever had attempted to murder her new companion, locking it safe within her heart and mind like a second soul shadowing her own. Within her mind she could hear it speak, no longer wild and murderous but tame within her own form, unpicking the strange, ancient language that filled her brain. She thought if she just lay quietly and listened, the meaning and sound of the mystical dialect would become so clear that her muted voice would speak. But her body was too cold and uncomfortable and her consciousness would not allow her to concentrate.

She was aware that she was in some kind of cave and more worryingly, that she was not alone. Agitated voices surrounded her and moving shadows flickered in the firelight. She turned her head and let out a gasp of fear when she saw an unfamiliar, pale-faced boy with mousy hair and a hideous, black-scaled, red-eyed beast staring at her. Her terror grew even more when the creature opened its sharp beak and uttered sarcastically, 'Oh joy upon joys, the blessed damsel awakens!'

Scrambling to her feet, Petronia drew her blade and brandished it fearfully in front of her as she glanced warily from the creature to the boy, and back again. The lad grinned with relief to see her awake while the leathery-skinned creature just glared at her with loathing.

Raising his hands in a calm gesture the boy spoke. 'It's all right, Mistress Ryder, be at peace, it is I, your peddler friend.'

Confused, Petronia frowned and sharply gestured to his face shaking her head to indicate she did not recognise him. She then pointed her sword in the direction of the strange, speaking animal and glared at them both, demanding an explanation. Aarold gently patted his own cheek as he tried to understand her frightened gestures. 'Oh, you don't recognise me without my disguise, of course. But it really is me. See? My leg is twisted and lame just as it was before.' He stretched out his twisted limb for her to see. Suspiciously, Petronia glanced at his wasted and bowed shin before studying his unfamiliar face. The features were indeed much altered, but when she looked into his deep sapphire eyes she recognised the same warmth and integrity she had seen when she first saved him.

Despite the vast change in his appearance, this was indeed the same kind gentleman she had met in the city. However, the unusual crimson-eyed animal still filled her with wariness and she motioned towards it with her sword.

Phebus blinked and snorted impatiently. 'What is it now, stupid girl?' he demanded tartly. 'What do you want? Haven't you brought us enough woe for one day?' Petronia gasped in amazement and offence at having such a peculiar animal speak to her in such a sharp and condescending manner. Cautiously, she took a few steps towards him brandishing her blade. Seeing her approach, Phebus hauled himself to his feet and gave his serpentine tail a threatening thrash. 'You can put that sword away for a start, missy,' he sneered, lowering his hooded eyes. 'Because, believe me, if you're going to start any more trouble, I won't be responsible for my actions. My patience has been worn paper-thin by what I've been through.'

'Phebus!' declared Aarold, from his seat on the ground. 'We all know you're upset, just let me explain.' He looked at the young girl with the sword in her hand and once more felt the hopeless weight of the situation he had got himself into. Unwillingly, he realised that he had no other option but to tell the truth. 'Phebus is an Equile. He's completely harmless, if a little distressed at the moment.'

'A little distressed?' Phebus interjected. 'Well, that's the understatement of the century! I think I've got every right to be *very* distressed, don't you?'

Sighing deeply, Aarold pressed his hands to his forehead. 'Look,' he breathed, 'I think the best I can do is tell you the truth. It must be quite clear to you by now that we are not who I led you to believe us to be. I am in fact Prince Aarold, son of Elkric and heir to the throne of Geoll.'

Petronia slowly sheathed her weapon and stared at the lad in disbelief. At first glance, he could not appear any less royal with his weak frame and tatty clothes but as she looked at him she could feel the Ley draw close by, like specks of golden light attracted by the honesty in his words. It flowed over his sorry frame like a golden mantle reflecting the blue blood in his veins. She was in no doubt that he now spoke the truth, but the situation of finding herself in the cold and desolate cavern with a disguised prince was bewildering to her and she struggled to comprehend how it could have happened. She somehow felt deep in her gut that it all should make perfect sense, that the Ley was setting a challenge for her to prove herself and Aarold was somehow involved. But in the dire situation she now found herself in, Petronia found it very hard to summon the mental strength to work out what the Ley wanted from her.

Curious, she sat down next to Aarold at the fireside and with circumspect fingers, reached out to touch his altered face to see if the Ley would allow her to detect any residue of sorcery. Aarold blushed considerably as Petronia gently brushed his pallid cheek and examined the change in his hair colour. When she was truly convinced of the realness of his appearance, Petronia gestured to his tatty garments and shrugged quizzically.

'You're wondering why a prince disguised himself as a commoner and got himself attacked by a footpad, aren't you?' asked Aarold sadly. Petronia nodded earnestly.

'That,' Phebus remarked dryly, 'is a very good question and if you were to ask me, I would put it down to juvenile insanity.'

Sighing, Aarold gazed into the flickering flames of the conjured fire, too weary and disheartened to argue with this statement. 'I wish I could tell you that it's all part of some great military plan but right now I'm not sure if I even remember why I thought it was a good idea.' He then proceeded to tell Petronia the whole of his story, how it was indeed true that his father, the late king, had disapproved of him because of his physical weakness and how all his life he had been shackled by the demoralising bonds of his aunt and her army of nurses and physicians. Petronia listened sympathetically as Aarold told her how by using his magical and intellectual skills, he had hoped to discover more about his kingdom and prove himself worthy of the throne.

She found it a painfully familiar situation: to hope that you had discovered within yourself the key that would overcome your shortcomings, only to find out that the world was bigger and filled with more danger than you ever dreamt. Hearing Aarold's remorseful story made her realise how cocksure she had been when the Ryders had offered her the chance to become an apprentice. She could still feel the restless movement of the Ley churning within, but she was no longer sure that she would find the teaching she needed to understand it. Perhaps her brother had been right and it would be her downfall.

'Well, now you know the truth of who I am,' finished Hayden, massaging his aching shin to keep the circulation going so his spasms would not return. 'But as to where we are and how we got to this hostile place, I really have no clue. I don't suppose the Ley gives you any knowledge as to our present whereabouts, Mistress Ryder.' He gazed at Petronia hopefully with his deep, sapphire eyes.

Petronia thought if she could talk there would not have been any words that could express how she felt. Somehow she felt responsible for the shadowy darkness that she had drawn from the dead Ryder's body, like it was a dark extension of her being, awakened by the Ley, something wild and powerful that it was her duty to tame. Even now she could feel it in her mind uttering its ancient and mystical language, commanding her spirit and tongue to become its mistress and vessel and unleash the ability within. All Petronia wanted to do was act for good, and help and tame the murderous blackness that seemed to well up wherever she went. Every time she attempted to face it, seize control and unleash the phrases of command that were imprisoned within her head, the energy in her grew intense and her grip on reality was whirled away like the snowflakes tossed on the bitter wind outside the cave. However, she knew if she gave up, turned her back on whatever power she had, they would just be two sorry souls lost in the snow, waiting for ice and death to claim them. Perhaps if she had been on her own she would have been happy to consign herself to that sorry fate but Aarold, apart from being the heir to her homeland, was a good and kind person who deserved a better chance.

Silently, she got to her feet and walked to the cave mouth as if drawn there by a magnet. Phebus lifted his head and watched her suspiciously as she passed him. 'Aarold, Aarold dear boy,' he alerted his friend nervously, 'she's going to do something. Be on your guard, I don't trust her!'

Petronia blocked out the creature's concern and concentrated on the energy that swirled within the hostile climate. High above, the sky was clear and dark like unpolished jet and the stars glinted with the acute bright sharpness of diamonds. The dim light of night-time etched the mountain landscape in blocks of jagged monochrome, brutal granite ledges and outcrops dusted with an icy coverlet of powdery snow. The wind howled with bitter fury, tossing countless microscopic icy flakes through the air like unheard syllables of a mystical language fluttering together in the hope that their meaning would be revealed in profound words. Petronia breathed in the chilly but pure air, tasting its essence and letting its energy mingle with the rippling awareness that churned within. She could feel the rush of powerful movement surge up and was seized by the fearful notion that once more this power would overwhelm her and she would become lost. Anxiously, she looked back at Aarold, in need of the validation of his friendship and connection to the real world.

Her hearing was acute to the eerie silence of the mountaintop and suddenly above the roar of the wind, she heard a strange clicking and whirring sound echoing from the shadows beyond the cave, like a key being turned in a lock. It clearly was not a trick of her senses for Phebus's ears twitched and Aarold peered nervously out into the darkness. 'Something is watching us,' he uttered fearfully, shuffling closer to his Equile friend and taking a small dirk from his satchel.

Swallowing hard, Petronia drew her sword and with a final glance back in Aarold's direction, stepped out into the snowy night to investigate. She could feel the Ley rising within her heart and mind but struggled with all her might to push Its influence to her subconscious thoughts, wary that if she allowed it to overwhelm her, she might pass out. Instead, she focused on her senses of sight and hearing to detect the danger. She listened for the tell-tale noises of nearby creatures: a paw, foot or claw crushing the snow; a snort, low growl or heavy breath, but could hear no such thing, only a rhythmic, soft tapping like a chisel against the rock of the mountain. Her vision swept the dimly lit landscape, taking in nothing more than abstract shapes of grey and black. Then in the orange glow of the campfire she caught sight of something more, not so much an animal or even a shadow, but a shape, smooth and dark like polished wrought iron, scuttling just out of the corner of her eye, shuffling up the incline towards the cave. In a flash, she turned her head but could see nothing in the darkness, only sense that something was there, almost like a spirit, beyond sight of mortal eyes. Petronia was aware of a most peculiar sensation. A sense of being watched but by something that had no vision, an entity out there, meant to do them harm but its actions had no thought or intent, a thing of motion but not life.

The will of the Ley broke through her mental barrier, staring through her eyes at the lurking entity and filling her mind with Its powerful language, giving her courage. Petronia could sense the golden path light of the Ley reaching out before her on the virgin snow like a thin chain passing through her body ready to link her to that cold oddity in the shadows. In a split second, the icy night was filled with the metallic noise of gears, pistons and wheels as the deadly, beetle-like automaton powered itself from its hiding spot towards her. Petronia was struck motionless for a moment, overcome with terror and amazement at the sight. Jagged mandibles clashed viciously together as it galloped over the stony ground on three pairs of spindly legs. Its domed shell was coal black and carved into its surface were countless symbols of magic. A sheen of mystical energy ran across its shell, dripping like oil into the lines and curves of the symbols, giving the Golem life and intent.

Brandishing her blade, Petronia rushed at the metal abomination ready to attack but with a skilful leap, it swerved in between her legs, carrying on its relentless path towards the cave, causing her to skid on the icy ground. She tumbled, landing on her hip, only to recover just in time to see it disappearing into the cave and realised that its target was Aarold.

An awkward, grunting scream left her throat as she tried to cry out in warning, but already she could feel her vocal cords and tongue twisting and knotting as the Ley began to pull them into shape. Struggling to her feet, she dashed back towards the cave to defend him, her throat brimming with bitter bile, her tongue sharp and heavy.

She crossed over the threshold into the bright firelight to witness a scene of absolute chaos. Aarold was cowered against the wall of the cave, his dagger clutched feebly in his hand. In front of him crouched his loyal steed, shrieking with terror and horror, lashing out with his talons as he battled to fend off the whirring Golem. The vile automaton twitched and lashed out with its pincers, snapping mechanically at the air as it scurried about, trying to force its way past Phebus. A compartment down the centre of its black casing had snapped open and from it uncoiled a vicious, curved stinger like a barbed, metal scorpion's tail which it slashed and stabbed violently. Petronia stared in horror at the brutal weapon and saw that its sharp edge appeared to be dripping with deadly, dark energy, like an icy poison that could end a life with one single scratch. She felt this evil energy, just as she had felt it surge from the Ryder's body, awakening something powerful within her, flooding her muscles with action. Instinct made her lunge at the beast, sword drawn to pierce its shell and rip out its workings. Stone, iron and magic collided as the tip of her blade stabbed at its side, but its metallic hide remained unbroken and the force of the blow simply pushed the Golem squealing and clunking to one side.

Phebus's claws scrabbled awkwardly on the ground as he moved backwards away from the attacker, practically crushing Aarold with his weight. 'Fear not, dear boy,' he declared in a terrified voice, his scarlet eyes agog. 'I will protect you. Stay at my side and prepare to mount. We will flee!'

Gasping for breath, the young prince battled for the strength to stand but fear and cold had left his weak limbs paralysed. In his head, he could hear the echo of his father's spirit, declaring that a prince would stand his ground and fight, not run like a coward. Aarold might not have the ability to defend himself or the young Ryder but he definitely was not going to flee. If the Golem overcame them, it would overcome them all.

Her veins rushed with adrenaline, Petronia stepped in front of

Phebus, blocking the Golem. The automaton's movements were swift and jarring, like a spider knocked from its web, as it scampered across the icy floor, trying to regain its bearings. It turned swiftly to face its prey, hungrily sensing the heat of their life-forces. The two rigid antennae atop its smooth brow twitched and whirred with precise movements, taking in information about its surroundings, and beneath its shell, countless wheels and cogs clicked and whirled at an alarming speed. As she gazed at it, her sword gripped tightly, Petronia was acutely aware of a vast flowing mass of silky black energy rippling like a shadow from the Golem across the ground, as if drawn by something that dwelt within her. Her lungs felt like two immense bladders filled with a bewitching gas, the muscles in her throat flexed and contracted with the feeling of flame and rock that scorched her oesophagus and she was forced to clamp her tongue between her teeth to control its unnatural undulations. She felt sick and wild and out of control and was fearful that if this change within her was released she would slip away from reality.

Thoughtlessly, the metallic beast lurched, its razor-like maul gaping open, the squealing and chugging of its workings piercing the air. Using all her might, Petronia swung her sword, jabbing the uneven blade lengthways between the Golem's jaws. The black metal fangs crushed down on the stone blade, neither breaking it nor yielding to its might. Petronia's whole body trembled as the two of them locked in combat, her muscles straining against the weight of the iron beast. The dark flood of their twin powers crashed and thrashed hopelessly against each other, each one as mighty and wild as its opponent.

She felt her sight grow weak, not out of fatigue but merely from the growing acuteness of her other senses. The granite-hard, molten heat of her insides roared and the strange, arcane language that filled her brain grew louder and louder, pushing its way out of her thoughts and into her larynx. For the first time in her life Petronia could feel language: words like fresh seeds ready to be flung from their mother pod, full of life. These were no ordinary words, these were powerful phrases formed by no flesh tongue or mortal alphabet, magical utterances of rock, power and life that tore from Petronia's tongue like a knife being drawn from the scabbard of her gullet, over her palate and scorched lips in a trail of thin, scarlet blood. Their sound was borne to the cold world as if it had issued from the very centre of the earth, grating, forceful and divine, so unfamiliar to mortal ears that Aarold wrapped his head in his arms to shield himself, and Phebus pressed his head to the stone floor with a whinny of dismay. Neither prince nor Equile could understand the language uttered by their companion, but Petronia knew the meaning as soon as it flowed from her mouth. It was an uncompromising command. *'Yield to me!'*

The sound and the magic of the words trembled the bitter air, running in sharp zigzags of darkness over the Golem's black shell. The gears and springs, energised by sorcery, meshed and jarred as its lifeless awareness was transformed from the command it had initially been impregnated with to a new mistress. Petronia felt a grateful shift within her body and mind as the metal creature relented in its attack and responded to her will and words. The traces of the Ley ran from her thoughts like reverberating echoes of the powerful order she had uttered, knotting the wild beast to her service. With a singular click, the vicious mandibles snapped open, releasing her sword from its grasp. Then it grew still, held in patient immobility as it awaited her next command.

For a second, Petronia did not dare move or even think. Within her head she could hear two rhythmic tattoos throbbing with life, her own heartbeat twinned with the ticking consciousness of the halted automaton. Beneath this, murmured and rushed the potent words of her newly awoken language, filling her mind and throat with awkward but persistent energy. With acute concentration, she inhaled, filling her lungs with the breath she needed to push the magic from her body, before allowing the newly mobile tendons of her vocal cords, tongue and lips to shape the command that was held in her mind.

'Sheath your weapons.'

The strange arcane dialect filled the cave again with its heavy, forceful power, echoing like the sound of the earth's spirit. It filled the air for just a moment like a crashing wave upon a stony shore, withdrawing as suddenly as it had come. The Golem quivered at the touch of the sound, its iron workings ringing with the force of the note. Springs and hinges tightened and snapped as the energy flowed through, causing it to stiffly close its jagged jaws and fold the deadly sting back into its shell. Its inner workings seemed to emit a sigh of release as it fell motionless and as it did so, Petronia felt her energy flag as exhausted she sank to her knees.

The icy cave fell silent for a long moment. The only movement stirring was the flickering flame of the fire. Aarold crouched shocked and fearful, curled into a ball behind the protective weight of Phebus's trembling body. He could scarcely believe how close the violent machine had come to ending his life. Once again it had been his Mistress Ryder, his strange and lovely guardian angel, who had saved his life. His body ached with spasms of terror and pain but most of all his head echoed with the unnatural sound that had issued from her mouth and ceased the Golem. In all his years of study, Aarold had never heard or read of such powerful magic. The force of the words uttered by the Ryder had nearly pushed him into unconsciousness and he struggled to believe that any mortal could survive speaking them. They had filled the mountain crag momentarily with their might and strength, only to die away, leaving complete silence.

Struggling to gather his wits, Aarold stiffly manoeuvred himself on to his knees and gave Phebus a gentle shove. The dazed animal shook into awareness, his leathery eyelids fluttering over his scarlet pupils and muttered nonsensically.

'You may tell the chef from me, he has put too many red peppers in the soup,' he burbled as Aarold squeezed himself from between the cave wall and his friend.

Cradling the Equile's head in his lap, the young prince tenderly stroked his beak. 'Phebs,' he whispered gently, 'are you all right?'

Phebus's red eyes looked glazed for a moment as he slowly tried to figure out where he was. 'Oh Aarold,' he breathed, 'Aarold, my boy. What a frightful nightmare I was having. We were in this horrid ice cave, under attack by this awful metal scarab and it was all because you had fallen in with this mute Ley Ryder who,' he twisted his long neck, blinking hard as he saw the immobile Golem and the young woman kneeling motionlessly beside it, 'is not five feet away from me. Oh my claws and scales, it wasn't a dream after all!' Exhausted and disheartened, he rolled heavily on to his side with a whimper of regret.

Giving his friend a commiserating pat on his flank, Aarold crawled by him and cautiously began to approach the motionless Ryder. She was facing away from him and sitting very still, shoulders slumped, hands trembling ever so slightly where they rested on her lap, staring at the squatting, metal beast that stood static before her. Aarold felt terror rise in his throat as his eyes wandered to the immobilised Golem.

Right now, it appeared completely inert, no more threatening than an iron carving or unwound clockwork toy, but Aarold was understandably ill at ease. Instead he remained some distance from both the girl and the metal beast and cleared his throat to attract her attention.

On hearing the sound, the young Ryder swiftly turned to look. Her face was sallow with exhaustion and she looked terrified. Anxiously, Petronia wiped her mouth on her hand. Her lips and tongue felt like they were caked in congealed blood and tasted foul. She was still aware of the whispering, mighty power within her, but even contemplating it or what she had achieved moments before left her feeling dizzy and overawed. She felt different somehow despite her tiredness, more real and alive but unsure as well.

Aarold extended a friendly hand. 'How are you?' he asked.

Petronia paused for a minute, acutely aware that moments before her long-silent voice had uttered words so powerful they had restrained a nightmare of metal and sorcery. Did this mean her muteness had somehow been cured? Cautiously, she strained her vocal cords to voice a simple answer, but could only form the same husky, dry retches she always had. Pursing her lips, she settled for a small nod to indicate she was unharmed.

Reaching into his satchel, Aarold retrieved a flask of water that he passed to Petronia so she might wash the blood from her mouth. Gratefully, she took it, rinsing and spitting a small mouthful to rid her tongue of the taste of metal before taking several more greater gulps to quench her thirst. Handing the flask back to Aarold, she sank wearily on to her knees.

Pensively, the prince twisted the flask in his grasp as his sharp mind began to work through the odd events he'd just witnessed. His fear was slowly dying but his bafflement at what had happened was acute. 'You spoke,' he stated softly, as Petronia stared thoughtfully at the motionless Golem. 'Pardon my rudeness, but I didn't think you were able to speak.'

Sighing wearily, Petronia shrugged and shook her head to show that she did not think she had the ability to talk either.

Aarold took a sip from the flask and thought for a moment. 'I thought that your Sister Ryders might have taught you some kind of sorcery. I am quite an adept student of various types of magic and spell-work, but never in all my studies have I come across words with such power as the ones you uttered to stop that beast.'

Anxiously, Petronia raised her hand to her mouth and bleated nervously. Her mind was still full of the strange and mysterious language that had halted the Golem, and she could feel the will and power of the Ley flooding back and forth between her consciousness and the dormant metal beast, keeping it in check. She had always known that she was different, partly because of her muteness and partly due to the restless nature of her character. Now it seemed that these suspicions had good grounding but what it meant, who she was and why she was able to utter only phrases with such power and magic, was beyond her. Suddenly Petronia felt very small and scared, as if she had discovered and unleashed something she had no idea how to control.

The young prince saw the worry in her brown eyes and guessed that despite what she had achieved she still felt as frightened as he did. 'I don't think you know *how* you spoke those words any more than I do,' he said. Sadly, Petronia shook her head. Aarold reached out and compassionately placed his hands over the young girl's own. Her fingers were chilled and he thought he felt them tremble slightly with nerves. 'Well, however you managed to do it, you did stop that dreadful metal beast and for that we must both be grateful. It would seem some power has sent you as my own guardian angel to keep me from harm and for that I am thankful.'

'Or to put you in greater harm!' grumbled Phebus, still slouched exhausted to one side of the cave. Neither of them paid any attention to this remark and he groaned in despair. 'I don't know why I bother to open my beak anymore.'

Petronia forced a small smile. It comforted her slightly to know that Aarold looked on her as some kind of protector sent to him by fate. It meant that perhaps despite all the unpredictable changes happening within her that the Ley did have a clear course for her destiny.

Equally heartened and embarrassed by her smile, Aarold grinned slightly, his cheeks scarlet, as he shyly moved his hand away from hers. 'Facts,' he said brightly, tucking the flask back into his satchel. Petronia looked baffled at this perplexing statement but Aarold continued.

'Grahmbere, my tutor, he told me that whenever you're in doubt as to how to solve a problem you should concentrate on what is known, what is solid and work from there.' Awkwardly, he heaved himself to his feet and leaning heavily on his cane looked around. 'It is very cold,' he stated, 'and from the terrain I would say we were in a mountainous climate.'

His eyes then fell uneasily on the static metal bug resting near to where Petronia sat. 'And then there is our friend here,' he said nervously, gesturing towards it with his cane. 'Do you think it's completely immobilised?'

Petronia glanced in the direction of the ominous dark Golem. In her mind she could still feel taut strands of control pressing down on the automaton, repressing its movement. The murderous energy which moments ago had ignited its workings now flowed docilely into her thoughts, a mindless link awaiting her command. It would not stir unless she asked it to. Slowly she nodded to confirm that the beast was now harmless.

With utmost caution, Aarold limped towards the Golem, stopping far enough away to feel safe from its silent fangs. He peered at it intently, examining its ruthless blades and dark metalwork with a mixture of apprehension and fascination. When it was clear that it was not going to spring back to life, he daringly reached out and gently tapped its iron shell with the tip of his cane. After a few moments' inspection a broad smile of understanding broke across his face. 'I think I know where we are!'

Both Petronia and Phebus regarded him expectantly as the young prince explained.

'It's obvious really. The cold, mountainous environment, the mechanised guard to ward off intruders. We must be in the Kelhalbon Mountains, between Geoll and the kingdom of my mother's birth. We're in the land of the dwarves.'

Petronia looked completely baffled by this having never heard of such a race and Phebus simply grunted moodily and uttered, 'Oh wonderful, uncultured troglodytes, what a thrill!'

Aarold cast him a chastising glance. 'Don't be such a snob, Phebus,' he said, lowering himself to sit beside Petronia. 'Dwarves are in fact a very ancient, noble and wise race. They fought alongside my father in the Great War and are very skilled craftsmen and metal workers. Granted, as a rule they do not welcome visitors to their lands, which explains our iron friend, but they are for the most part benign and I am sure they would willingly aid a lost young Ryder.'

Phebus looked unconvinced by his friend's words. 'You're certain on that point?' he queried dryly. 'If your father approved of their company, I would take it as evidence that they were barbarians.'

'Ignore him,' Aarold told Petronia. 'Phebus disapproves of most people.'

Petronia had barely heard the Equile's tart comment. Her thoughts were still racing with the momentary achievement of speech and how it had occurred. As her mind throbbed with bands of power, binding the Golem to her will she began to wonder whether the creators of such a beast would be able to explain why she had been able to do so. The Ley seemed to be guiding her along a path and altering her mind and abilities from within, granting her the speech she so longed for, but along with it came a power much greater than she could comprehend. Petronia now felt like she could talk but if she did the words would have such force and magic, the repercussions could be immense. She needed someone to explain what was happening and without Amethyst and the Ryders around maybe she could turn to the dwarves.

Aarold shivered, his fragile body suddenly very aware of the bitterness in the air. Pulling his cloak around him, he shuffled near to the fire. 'The night is so cold,' he muttered. 'As much as I think it would be helpful to seek out the dwarves, I fear that I am not strong enough to do it until morning. Would you agree to camp here until dawn, Mistress Ryder?'

Looking broodingly at the motionless Golem, Petronia slowly nodded in agreement. Although she felt like the black automaton was completely under her mental control, the effort of the battle had left her both psychologically and physically exhausted. The power that had flowed through her had taken a toll that only sleep could heal and her many questions would have to wait till morning.

Wearily, Aarold crawled over to Phebus's side and snuggled down against the creature's warm smooth body for comfort. Within a matter of moments he was fast asleep. Lovingly, the Equile pulled at Aarold's cape with his beak so that it was securely tucked around him. 'Foolish boy,' he chided affectionately as Aarold's breathing grew heavy, 'what would you do without me? And as for you,' his scarlet eyes swivelled in Petronia's direction, 'I am going to keep a very close eye on you, don't you worry! Goodnight.' Lowering his head on to his folded claws, he closed his heavy eyelids and focused his mind on the pleasant memory of his warm stable, velvet blanket and other luxuries of the palace that were now very far away.

Turning her back on the two friends, Petronia curled up on her side facing the iron beetle. Her body felt heavy with weariness but her mind was a whirl of thought and activity. The strong, weighty bond that tied her to the Golem coiled like an unseen lazily flowing river across the cold stone floor, burbling quietly with the strange language of the Ley that Petronia was slowly beginning to understand. Curiously, she caught hold of one of these strange phrases within her mind, silently trying to breathe the form of its sound with her lips. No words left her tongue this time, but across from her the curved mandibles of the metallic beast twitched stiffly open and closed, responding to her will. A force of both darkness and light had been awoken within Petronia that night but right now, as the icy mountain storm howled outside the cave, she felt too tired and baffled to understand it. Wrapping her cape around her, she closed her eyes and lost herself in dreams of a time when her existence was simpler.

Chapter 25

A DISTRESSING DISCOVERY

Rosequartz shifted nervously in her saddle and glanced over her shoulder at the elderly, pale-skinned Ryder on the dusky coated donkey behind her and Garnet. Chiastolite looked like a bundle of bones and sticks wrapped in brown cloth as she slowly drove her mount along the path towards Goodstone. It went without saying that all Ryders felt a sisterhood towards each other and although Rosequartz held no personal dislike towards the old woman, her presence, and her unlucky Ley Calling as handmaiden to the dead and dying made the younger Ryder feel uneasy.

'It doesn't bode well,' the normally cheerful Ryder whispered to Garnet as Chiastolite reached round to adjust her belongings strapped to the mule. 'I am not comfortable having her with us. Never have I seen her do the Ley's work without it ending in grief.'

Looking towards the overcast sky, Garnet appeared stoic. 'Patience, Rosequartz. We've already learned good tidings from her, that the maiden Petronia is alive and well. The Ley may have simply sent her to us as a messenger.'

Like the other Ryders stationed at Goodstone at the time of the strange attack, Rosequartz and Garnet had left the citadel in the early morning on the orders of Amethyst. No-one, not even Amethyst, seemed to be able to explain the dark entity that had laid siege to the castle so suddenly nor the sudden disappearance of the mute girl. Those who had fought on the battlements had spoken of seeing the newest apprentice for the last time. Her actions had surged with the energy of the Ley as she grabbed a sword and hurled herself like a bird from the wall into the throbbing blackness below. There had been a burst of power, of dark, hungry magic and restless Ley force, causing the air and ground to tremble with the aftershock of their unity. Then, stillness. As suddenly as the hateful entity had appeared at the base of the castle walls, it vanished, sucking itself into non-existence as if being drawn back into another realm and gone with it was any trace of Petronia. Mortal dread had struck at the hearts of Garnet and Rosequartz when they heard this. Had the spectre been sated with a sacrifice of the young girl's life like an arcane, pagan deity? If that was so then the covenant they had made to her father had been broken and the Ley surely would make them pay with their lives. Indeed, as they allowed the Ley to lead them out into the peaceful countryside, Garnet and Rosequartz were sorrowfully preparing themselves for a justly deserved death. On the following morning when they encountered Chiastolite, bearing her mortician's robes, they suspected that she had come to attend them in their final hours. However, it appeared that the Ley had drawn the elderly Chiastolite to them for a far more extraordinary reason. After greeting each other the three of them exchanged their remarkable stories of the silent young lass who appeared to be the Stone-Tongue of ancient legend.

Chiastolite urged her donkey between her two companions' mounts and glanced up at them with her watery dark eyes. 'I see you fear my company, Sisters,' she observed knowingly. 'I am used to this. My presence does tend to be the harbourer of mortality.'

Rosequartz blushed slightly. 'Forgive my coldness, it was impolite of me. May the Ley bring blessings and good health upon you.'

The elderly Ryder licked her puckered lips and shifted the folds of her ill-fitting brown garment around her bony frame. 'You've no need to fear me, my Sisters,' she told them both with a wag of her crooked, pale finger. 'I can sense both your life-forces and they are equally long and strong. Not untouched by death, that is true, but I will join the Ley long before you will need the sad skills It has blessed me with.'

Garnet gave a small smile, unable to deny the relief she felt on hearing this. 'It is not only our lives we fear for, good Sister,' she informed the old woman. Chiastolite nodded knowingly. 'The mute apprentice,' she said, her crinkled face growing serious. 'I agree, hers is a stranger spirit than any I've ever aided. But I swear by the Ley that every word I have told you about her releasing Ammonite's trapped soul from her corpse and the strange darkness stealing her and the peddler away is true. With the knowledge of life and death I have acquired, I am sure she is still among the living.'

Wincing she shifted her scrawny hide awkwardly in the donkey's saddle and shifted a chunk of tiger iron onto her right hip. Ryders, of course, were used to the nomadic life but Chiastolite was getting on in years and tended to ache on long journeys.

Seated on her horse's broad back, Garnet silently ran through the remarkable events of the last few days along with what Chiastolite had told them, calling upon the Ley to grant her insight and guidance.

'Do you believe what Sister Amethyst said about the legend of Stone-Tongue, that this girl Petronia could speak the language of the Ley?'

The old Ryder sniffed thoughtfully and scratched her mule's short mane as she considered her answer. 'I have seen many strange deaths and great sorrows in my lifetime, but none compared to what I saw that young girl achieve in our city lodge.' Tilting her head to one side, she half-closed her eyes, listening to the clear, quiet inner voice of the Ley as it drifted through her thoughts, murmuring half-disclosed messages. 'I know a great change is imminent in the fabric of life and that as handmaiden to the dead I will have more work to do than ever as the balance shifts. But as to legends and destinies, Amethyst had a clearer sense of the Ley in such matters than I.'

They had entered the outskirts of Goodstone by now and could clearly see the citadel on the misty horizon. There was a chill in the air and both Garnet and Rosequartz noticed that there were very few villagers about. All three Ryders felt strangely tense as they slowly made their way through the town. In each of their minds, they felt the Ley grow thick and dark, tainted with a perverse foreboding that lingered there like a deadly virus. Shadowy colours twisted with jagged sorrow as if someone had reached a hand into the Ley and knotted Its natural flow with some heinous deed. It left a dreadful sickening in the pit of their stomachs like the haunting memory of the terrible darkness that had surrounded the citadel.

As the three Ryders began their wary approach to the citadel, a child's, both joyous and fearful, voice rang out, stopping them in their tracks. 'See? See? They are back. I said they wouldn't abandon us!'

A waif-like girl of about six with long, dark-blonde hair ran out of one of the side streets, hurrying towards them, her eyes shining brightly. Bringing her horse to a stop, Rosequartz dismounted and dropped to one knee to greet the child.

Overwhelmed with relief on seeing the friendly Ryder, the girl threw her arms around her neck and hugged her as if she was never going to let go. Instantly, Rosequartz felt the dread in the child's spirit and tenderly stroked her hair, allowing her natural gift from the Ley to bring joy and comfort. 'Hey now, Buttercup,' she soothed as more of the villagers emerged from doorways, alerted by the child's call, 'what is all this about?'

Calmed by the Ryder's warm presence, Buttercup relaxed slightly but still kept her fingers knotted securely in Rosequartz's red hair for comfort. 'We thought that you had all gone away for good,' she bleated timidly, peering up at the other two Ryders, 'and you were never coming back!'

Rosequartz chuckled good-heartedly and tilted her head to one side. 'Now why would you think such a thing?' she asked. 'Don't we always return after the Ley has called us to do Its bidding?'

Buttercup sucked her finger and looked very uncertain. 'Yes, Rosequartz, but that was before,' she whispered shyly, shuffling her feet in the dust of the road, 'before the monster.'

A tremble of dread ran through Garnet's heart when she heard the child's words and her mind was transported back to the night of the siege. Had the strange, black entity returned to wreak havoc on the townsfolk while they had been away?

347

'What monster?' she asked gently.

The young girl looked up, her hands still gripping on to Rosequartz for comfort. 'I didn't believe it, Sister Garnet, not what they said. But my big brother Jarrid, he said that a monster attacked the castle and drove all the Ryders away. He said it would come in the night and eat all my fingers and toes! Will it?'

Rosequartz gave the girl a reassuring hug. 'Not on your life!' she told her. 'I have met a number of monsters and have it on good authority that they think little girls taste horrid and never eat them!'

This remark made Buttercup giggle, and reassured she climbed off Rosequartz's lap and marched indignantly over to her brother and parents who were part of the crowd that had slowly surrounded the Ryders. Rosequartz cast the young Jarrid a knowing glance and pursed her lips as his sister poked him roughly in the arm and declared, 'Told you so!'

The boy scowled as his sister climbed into her mother's arms. 'But I swear it is true. Well perhaps not the bit about fingers and toes, but I did hear father and the other men talking about a black serpent that surrounded the castle walls.'

A murmur of affirmation ran nervously through the crowd at the mention of the heinous, dark oddity that had arrived so recently and unexpectedly in their midst. Rosequartz raised her hand and called for order and calm among the villagers, although her own mind remained troubled. Her compassionate heart was filled with the force of the Ley, compelling her to take up her given role as joy bringer and ease their worries.

'People of Goodstone,' she stated in a commanding but soothing voice, 'take heart. Indeed there are many dangers in the world but they are no more perilous or impending today than they have ever been. You are fortunate to live under the gaze of we Ryders and our citadel and if any peril did attack this town, I swear that I and my sisters would defend you from it, for this has always been our duty.'

These words seemed to calm many in the crowd but there were still a number who wore anxious expressions. In her mind, Rosequartz heard the Ley whisper words of instruction, urging her to bring succour to the wary. Under the watchful gaze of Garnet and Chiastolite, she went from person to person, offering each individual words of comfort, a reassuring gesture or crystal for protection. Her Sister Ryders did not aid her in this task, knowing that Rosequartz was more skilled than they in soothing troubled spirits. Rosequartz's heart was more hopeful and resilient than most, and she well suited her Stone Name.

When the villagers had finally returned to their homes, the red-haired Ryder mounted her steed and she and her companions continued their journey towards the citadel.

Glancing at her fellow Ryder, Garnet scrutinised Rosequartz's round, pleasant face. 'Do you believe your own words, Sister?' she asked. 'Do you truly believe there is no need for fear?'

A troubled expression flashed across Rosequartz's face that seemed at odds with her usual carefree nature. 'I am the bringer of joy,' she softly uttered. 'The Ley compels me to say and do what will bring comfort to those in need. What I feel, what we all sense at this moment, will not bring reassurance. It is a trouble that we must face, not they.'

Knowingly, Garnet nodded at her companion's words. Rosequartz gave the impression of being merrily trivial but that did not mean she was any less wise than her fellow Ryders. The three of them continued on towards their destination with little conversation. All of their minds were focused on the strange, unsettling mood of the Ley that drifted out to greet them from the castle. A sickening chill tainted Its flow, gabbling Its normally clear language with misty impurity. It tore at the definite lines of certainty, flexing them out of order so that the pain of the memory of what had been mingled with the dread or anticipated horrors to create a present that was unnervingly disorientating.

Finally they halted at the barred drawbridge of the citadel, gazing silently up at it, each one of them praying for the Ley to give them strength to face the unknown horror that seemed to echo in their minds. The moat and ground surrounding the citadel appeared pure and totally unharmed by the immense entity of violent magic that had swelled over it. The grass was green and healthy, the water looking as clear as ever. To the eye, all seemed to be as it had been, but as the Ryders examined their surroundings, they could clearly sense echoes of terrible horror and evil.

Climbing down from her horse, Garnet inhaled the cold autumn air, hoping the taste of it would reveal to her some hidden secret. 'Something's not right,' she muttered to Rosequartz, her hand resting nervously on the hilt of her sword. 'The Ley brought us here to show us something.'

From her seat astride her mule, Chiastolite straightened her crooked spine and blinked her watery, black eyes as the familiar sensations of Ley and mortality rushed through her mind. 'Death was here recently,' she stated surely, thin strands of her white hair dancing in the breeze.

Garnet and Rosequartz looked at her in horror, awaiting her next words. The old woman sighed and blinked her eyes shut for a brief moment as the Ley revealed to her hazy images of what the citadel had witnessed. Death was like the perfume of flowers: each life, each bloom, leaving a lingering scent that betrayed its unique nature, and Chiastolite knew them all. Slowly she spoke, using the knowledge of a witness to a thousand departed souls.

'It was a good death, one of honour. The soul was ready to meet the Ley and departed swiftly. But it was unjust also, violent, at another's hand. The peace in it was brought by the victim's readiness to die not by the attacker. It was a murder.'

Garnet swallowed hard, her chest tightening with trepidation. 'Does the Ley tell you the identity of the victim and who killed them, Sister Chiastolite?' she asked fearfully.

Chiastolite looked grim and solemnly shook her head. 'We will discover who has met their end here soon enough,' she said ominously. 'I can tell that the body lies not far from here.'

Dismounting, Rosequartz strode over to join Garnet, her eyes roving over the high citadel walls and surrounding landscape. 'We must inspect the area,' she murmured. Soberly her fellow Ryders agreed and together the cautious trio began to circle the castle, inspecting every inch of the walls and grounds for signs of misdeeds and murder. Anxiously, they pressed their thoughts to the Ley, feeling Its mood and flow as

It lingered close to the home of the Ley Mouth and finding It to be troubled, cold and restless. Darkness shadowed the Ley's power but it was not till the Ryders returned to where they had started their search, before the mighty drawbridge, that they discovered any physical sign that the sanctity of the keep had been violated.

'Look!' Garnet fell to her knees in the muddy road that stretched out before the citadel. Swiftly Rosequartz and Chiastolite came to her side and looked to where she pointed in the damp earth.

Across the moist ground, almost unnoticeable at first glance, trickled a narrow, straight rivulet of scarlet, a crimson line that ran out of the clear water of the moat. The red liquid hung in misty curls as it leaked from beneath the barred drawbridge, swimming eel-like to emerge on to the ground near their feet before carrying on its secret pathway over the fields, like a red-scaled adder stalking its prey.

Garnet held her gloved fingers inches above the gory stream, too fearful and disgusted to even touch it. 'Blood,' she stated dully, her mind already conjuring grim notions of what could have caused this tiny, gory trail.

With a creek of aged bones, Chiastolite leant forward to inspect it. 'Not just blood,' she breathed in a steady voice, 'magic too.'

Anxiously Rosequartz had followed the blood's path to the edge of the moat, staring ponderously at how it crossed unhindered through the water. 'It's coming from the citadel,' she murmured, puzzled. 'Whatever is bleeding must be inside. But how can that be? Only we Ryders can lower the defences.' There was a note of fear in her tone, as if her upbeat nature would not quite allow her to believe there might be something so powerful it could break through the Ley's protection.

Garnet rested her hand reassuringly on her fellow Ryder's shoulder. 'You and I were both there when the blackness attacked,' she reminded Rosequartz. 'Only Petronia was able to stop it. Sister Amethyst warned us that the nature of the Ley is changing. Who knows what is possible?'

Placing her hand on a medallion of the stone from which she took her name, Rosequartz sighed. 'I guess there is only one way of finding out,' she said as Chiastolite hobbled over to join them. Together the three of them displayed crystals of rose quartz, garnet and chiastolite to the large, unblinking stone eye set in the centre of the drawbridge. For a brief moment it seemed that the Ley power that guarded the keep had forgotton its duty, the vast door remaining secure, unwilling to reveal the horror that was hidden within. Then the hues in the colourless rock altered, shimmering momentarily with shades of ebony, pink and brown and the heavy workings began their metallic grind as the drawbridge was lowered before them.

For a moment the three Ryders stood, unmoving at the entrance to the keep, sensing the unnerving, weighty stillness that hung in the familiar courtyard. The place, which had not long ago throbbed with the life of the Ley and Its loyal servants now stood open before them like a ransacked tomb, lifeless and filled with an air of sickening desecration. The stables, forge and gardens stood abandoned, as if their fellow sisters had been spirited away by the call of the Ley at a singular moment. The power of the Ley still lingered within the walls, but it felt troubled and wounded and as they made their way inside, the Ryders could sense It screaming to them in a noiseless, pained howl, swirling over the swept cobbles like a distracted dog left too long without its master's attention.

Across the smooth, swept cobblestones of the courtyard, the thin scarlet line marked its ominously straight path, disappearing beneath the heavy door of the keep. With dreading hearts, the three Ryders followed the glinting strip of blood. Already their minds were icy with fear and knowledge as the agitated Ley plucked at their thoughts, revealing tiny snatches of the heinous event that had defiled Its flow. Sensing the familiar presence of death, Chiastolite drew a fragment of carnelian from a pouch on her belt, working it skilfully between her fingertips as she prayed to the Ley to give her strength in the work It brought her here to perform.

Garnet swallowed the rising bile in her throat and steadied her hand as she took hold of the iron ring and hauled open the door to the hall of the Ley Mouth. Both she and Rosequartz believed they had steadied their hearts for any horror that lay inside, but the scene of violence and debasement that met them made them gasp and gag with repulsion. The immense hall was chillingly cold as the gaping hole of the Ley Mouth belched forth wave after wave of powerful energy in an attempt to purify itself of the bloody horror that now scarred this sacred place. At its side, upon the monochrome field of black and white tiles, a vast, bright pool of blood spilt out like a ruby mirror and it was from this that the constant rivulet of crimson was magically being drawn, as if by an unseen quill. The source of this glossy gore was painfully obvious for beside it, dressed in her jewel-studded armour, was the decapitated body of Sister Amethyst.

A choked sob caught in Rosequartz's throat as she saw her fellow Ryder's murdered corpse. 'Sister Amethyst?' she gasped in horror, fearfully approaching the body. 'Oh by the Ley Itself! It cannot be!' Her heart beating wildly with grief, shock and unjust rage, Garnet surveyed every inch of the vile scene, her golden eyes gleaming with unshed tears. 'But how?' she gasped. 'By what foul means did this crime occur? The drawbridge was locked, the door bolted. What heinous monster could have killed her in this, our most hallowed and safe refuge?'

Her round cheeks sallow with grief, Rosequartz fumbled for a nugget of lodestone, the crystal for conquering mourning and reconnecting with the world and pressed it systematically to her forehead, lips, heart and stomach. 'Blessed be the Ley, for It is life everlasting,' she whimpered mournfully, as she repeated the ritual over and over to console herself. 'Joyous be the spirits of the dead, for their energy is part of the Ley. Give me strength in my sorrow for the sake of the name given to me. I am Rosequartz, bringer of joy, bringer of comfort.' Her words died away into a hoarse sob as she clasped the crystal tightly in her hand.

Shuffling forward, Chiastolite tenderly placed her arms around the weeping girl. 'Courage, Sister,' she whispered to her, her gentle voice filled with compassion and the soothing love of the Ley. 'Show mercy to yourself. The Ley will support you. Take heart in the knowledge that energy and spirit is ever changing. Amethyst exists now in another form. It was the right time for her to transcend.'

Garnet drew close to Rosequartz's side and offered her hand in comfort as Chiastolite mournfully shuffled towards Amethyst's corpse, drawn by her duty to the Ley and the dead. The powerful rhythm issuing from the Ley Mouth drifted over the murdered Ryder's body, forming ghosting images of her last moments in Chiastolite's experienced mind. With a sigh of effort and sorrow, the old woman knelt down beside the body and rolling up the sleeves of her robe, placed her pale, wrinkled hands on Amethyst's lifeless back. Closing her eyes, Chiastolite cleared her thoughts and allowed the Ley to dance across the blank canvas of her mind forming shadowy shapes and moods of Amethyst's death. The mighty force allowed her to acknowledge past truth and emotions, telling her of the manner of the Ryder's last moments. Feelings and information came to her in snatches as if glanced through a keyhole. At the side of the hall, Garnet and Rosequartz stood in silent and shocked reverie, uttering heartfelt prayers to the Ley for Amethyst's soul.

When she felt that the Ley would reveal no more to her about what had taken place, Chiastolite sat back on her heels with a satisfied sigh. 'Hers was an honourable death,' she stated, resting her hand compassionately on Amethyst's form.

'An honourable death?' declared Rosequartz in anguished disbelief. 'Murdered in the keep that was her home for the past fifteen years, slayed before the sacred Ley Mouth? How can you say such a thing?'

The elderly Ryder turned her compassionate eyes on her companion and calmly raised her hand. 'I mean no offence or disrespect by my words, Sister Rosequartz. I simply state that my senses tell me Sister Amethyst knew her death was coming and was prepared to meet it with dignity and peace. Her soul joined the Ley with the swift easiness of someone who knew Its flow, leaving behind no trace of sorrow or unrest.' A disturbed frown crossed over her wrinkled features. 'I do not deny, however, that it was a bloody and brutal death brought about by a hateful hand.'

Garnet looked earnestly at Chiastolite as the old woman wiped some of the blood from the back of Amethyst's severed neck and leather tunic. 'Does the Ley show you who did this foul act?' she asked.

Blinking at the feelings and sights of Amethyst's death, Chiastolite sadly shook her head. 'Alas, It chooses not to grant me such knowledge at this time,' she uttered woefully. 'I can tell that the murderer acted with powerful and dark magic that sickened the flow of the Ley even more than our sister's death, but that darkness also masks their name and face.'

A sob of grief choked Rosequartz. 'Then try harder, Sister Chiastolite!' she begged tearfully. 'Summon your strength and probe the Ley deeper for knowledge for you are the Handmaiden of Death. Use crystals if you must, for there cannot be anything right in letting this sin go unpunished!'

The old woman breathed a heavy sigh and a weary expression passed across her face. 'I shall not lecture you while your heart is sore with loss,' she told Rosequartz evenly, 'merely remind you of what you surely must know. The Ley only divulges what It sees fit to and will not reveal more if badgered or begged. It has brought us here to the site of Amethyst's killing, therefore It decrees that we must put it straight.'

Garnet placed a comforting hand on the distraught Ryder's shoulder. 'You wear your passions and moods too tenderly on your heart, Sister Rosequartz,' she told her softly. 'It is a blessing from the Ley to have such empathy but hot tears and wails of grief will not bring justice to our fallen sister. We must view her death scene with the mind not the heart if we are to discover the truth.'

Rosequartz gulped back her tears and gratefully patted Garnet's hand. 'True words, Sister Garnet,' she breathed; 'your mental faculties were always stronger under stress than mine. I will try to put aside my grief for the moment else it will cloud my thoughts.'

Calling upon the Ley strength, Rosequartz forced herself to look at the desecrated scene, as did her fellow Ryders, desperately searching for sense amid the violent chaos. It did not take long for their attention to be drawn to the glossy scarlet pool of blood that gushed from Amethyst's severed throat. There was something highly unnatural about it for it showed no sign of dehydration and as they studied it closer they noticed tiny tidal ripples pulsing over its surface, pushing the thick redness out to form the long, narrow line that they had followed into the keep. Silently, it stretched out from the dead Ryder's life-fluid like an accusing finger. Carefully, Chiastolite rested her hands on the tiled floor and stooped down to examine it more closely as Rosequartz and Garnet stepped forward to do the same.

The elderly Ryder delicately sniffed the blood as the empty atmosphere of the hall howled with the disquiet churn of tainted Ley energy. 'There is something abnormal in her blood,' she murmured thoughtfully as her gaze followed the narrow stream as it trickled out of the door. 'Something is compelling it to make this trail.'

'The Ley perhaps?' queried Rosequartz, stretching out her hand above the gleaming surface of the pool. 'Amethyst is, well sadly was, very attune to the Ley. Maybe she used her last moment to imbue her blood with her will, so that it would lead whoever found her to her killer.'

Chiastolite sat up again with a groan and the creak of arthritic joints. 'Perhaps,' she mused. 'There are always traces of the soul's energy in the blood, as you know. It is why we eat our meat raw; it is the purest way of absorbing the remaining energies after the soul has joined the Ley. But think on, what else do you sense?'

Cautiously, both Garnet and Rosequartz reached out to hold their fingertips just above the surface of the bloody pool. As they did so, both were gripped by a steely cold, dark force, quite different from the warm strength of the Ley, which pulsed deep within the crimson fluid, driving it on in its search.

'It's the same force that attacked the keep,' observed Rosequartz, 'but what is it and why did it murder Sister Amethyst?'

Grimly, Garnet stared out of the open door of the keep as the autumn sky was darkening with approaching dusk. 'She wasn't its intended victim,' she uttered soberly, 'but it needed her to show it where she hid her.'

Realisation dawned across Rosequartz's pale face. 'Of course!' she exclaimed. 'Petronia, Stone-Tongue. It's trying to destroy her. That's why the castle was attacked. Amethyst must have sent the girl to safety. Now, whatever this darkness is will use Amethyst's blood and knowledge to seek her out.'

Garnet looked melancholy and gazed at Amethyst's remains. 'That must be why she sent us and our fellow Ryders away so swiftly after the attack. She sensed that evil would soon penetrate the citadel and decided that no more than she should bear its wrath. She sacrificed herself so that we and our sisters might fight another day.'

Rosequartz nodded in sad agreement. 'A noble death,' she uttered softly before gasping in horror. 'A terrible thought has just occurred to me,' she gasped. 'Dear Bracken. She would be broken to learn of her guardian's death. Ley be merciful and not allow her to witness this evil with her own eyes. I pray for her.'

Seriousness froze in Garnet's gold eyes. 'I pray for both of them,' she said forbiddingly, 'but more I pray for Petronia for it is she who this foulness seeks to destroy. And it is she we pledged to guard. I suggest that we use Amethyst's final message and follow this bloody trail as swiftly as the Ley will allow us to. With good fortune we will catch its maker before any further destruction is wrought.'

Unsteadily, the elderly Chiastolite stood up, gripping Rosequartz's hand as she straightened her stiff legs. 'I agree,' she croaked, 'but not quite yet. The correct rites must be observed for our fallen sister. I could not bear my Stone Name if I didn't dispose of her remains with respect.'

Garnet nodded solemnly. 'Of course. Amethyst was a woman of great honour and devotion to the Ley. She deserves no less than her earthly remains being returned to the Ley womb of the earth. Rosequartz and I will bear witness as you perform the ritual. Then will you ride with us or does the Ley call you on another path?'

Chiastolite looked thoughtful and sad for a moment as she silently listened to the whisper of the Ley as It revealed to her what road she must take, a road, which by her very presence, would be surely marked by more death. 'I will ride at your side, my Sisters,' she informed them reluctantly, 'for I fear that I will be called to my work again by the actions of this supernatural murderer. But worry of that not now, for it is the hour of mourning Amethyst. I shall get the tools of my craft.'

With that, she hobbled back towards the open doorway. Garnet and Rosequartz watched her go, the Ley seemed cool and silent in the air, allowing the grief they felt for the loss of their wise comrade to fall over them like a widow's dark veil and they clung to each other, weeping.

*

In the hours that passed before dusk, Chiastolite worked her funereal arts with reverent tenderness. She washed Amethyst's body and head, perfuming them with heavy oils and placed crystals against her lifeless skin. She put her in a shroud of white linen and carefully Garnet and Rosequartz carried her remains into the courtyard where they built a pyre. The fire was lit and kindled to intense heat with pieces of fire agate until the brilliant flames engulfed Amethyst's mortal form like robes of orange silk. They stood sombrely around the sacred pyre as the Ley transformed her muscle and bone into new matter of flame, smoke and ash, crying bitter tears of loss and pain and calling to the Ley to touch them with Amethyst's essence as smoke and embers twisted in the icy air. For they knew, as all Ryders did, that life and energy cannot be destroyed, only transformed and transferred from one state to another. So they watched with hearts of faith as human matter became fire, fire became ash and ash cooled, knowing that Amethyst's life had become one with the Ley. With gentle hands and words of final prayer, they gathered up the pale, dusty embers into a dish of vivid green dioptase, casting them out, some to the soil of the land where they might feed new growth, some into the holy murmuring Ley Mouth to re-enter the core of the earth's ancient womb, where they danced like fragments of thought in the Ley's breath. What little remained was collected by the wandering wind, the shadow and likeness of the Ley force which Amethyst's spirit was now part of. When this final rite was observed, Garnet, Rosequartz and Chiastolite rubbed their fingertips stained with the blackened embers of Amethyst's memory in solemn gestures against their foreheads, lips and hearts, massaging the dark marks of grief left on their skin with the purple stone that bore their sister's name. Part of her essence would be absorbed into their bodies and live within them forever. But these rituals for her cast of husk were simply tradition and comfort for the grieving, as the true life-force of Amethyst was not in flesh, fire, blood or ash but swirled peacefully, as all souls of past Ryders, within the flowing love of the Ley, watching, felt, but unseen as her sisters mounted and set off on the blood-stained trail that her killer had laid.

Chapter 26

THE SNOW LISTENS

Hayden anxiously drew his cloak around him and turned his eyes toward the late afternoon sky that seemed to be pressing down on the rocky earth with ominous threats of bad weather. He searched for any heavenly body: milky, cold sun, pale, fingernail of moon or silver dot of starlight, but could see nothing but the threatening grey shapes of churning cloud-cover that promised to unleash their burden over the slopes and ravines of the mountains. Ahead of him, Bracken climbed ever onward, her sturdy limbs picking out a narrow and uneven path. Her journey was made even more difficult by the fact that her left hand was occupied with keeping firm grasp on the leather lanyard to which the spinning stone cylinder was fastened. The strange artefact was swinging and rotating at alarming speed, bucking and jolting out in front of her like a hunting hound on an irresistible scent. Frantically, it drew them higher and deeper into the mountains, growing more frenzied and powerful with each step they took. Hayden looked at the stone tube with mistrust. Bracken was convinced that it was connected with the dwarves that dwelt beneath these rocky peaks and would lead them to safety, but Hayden was not so trusting. It was not so much the cylinder he was wary of but the environment it was drawing them into: steep narrow valleys and perilous cliffs where one wrong footstep could lead to death. If the storm broke, rain could make the rocks treacherous and snow could be even more deadly.

'Bracken,' he called, his voice mingled with the bitter wind, 'are you sure this is wise? The weather looks like it could turn at any moment.'

The tall girl paused and glanced back, her face filled with doubt and worry. 'I am a little uncertain,' she confessed, a tremor of fear filling her voice, 'but the power in this amulet is so strong, I am sure it wants to show me where my destiny lies.' The arm with which she was holding on to the tube remained straight, pointing towards a narrow, gloomy canyon between two immense cliffs of unforgiving stone. All signs of life and vegetation were now far below them on the windy steppes. All about him Hayden could see nothing more than uneven crags and plains of iron-coloured rock coated here and there with layers of ice.

'I know,' he begged, unnerved by the loneliness of the place, 'but maybe we should turn back now and try again in the morning. We could make camp on lower ground and wait for the storm to pass.'

Fear shone in Bracken's dark green eyes as she regarded warily the darkening clouds and flecks of sleet that peppered the air. 'Perhaps you have a good point, Master Hayden. We will turn back.'

As the words left her mouth, her whole body jolted and she let out a scream of surprise as the strange cylinder pulled her onward, bowing almost into a horseshoe shape with the eagerness to carry her forward. She stumbled, running as quickly as she dared over the slippery ground. Hayden sped after her as she disappeared into the threatening, chilly blue shadows of the stone gorge, his boots sliding over the treacherous terrain as he ran. The bitterness of the air burnt his cheeks, and his muscles ached with cold and fear. Before he knew it, he had entered into a slim valley and found himself hemmed in on either side by vast walls of granite, dusted with snow and ice.

'Don't run off like that!' he hissed through teeth gritted against the biting chill of the chasm. 'We could lose each other out here.'

She spun to face him and for a moment Hayden's heart was stopped by the eerie beauty and terror that seemed to have come over her appearance. Her long, coarse hair looked like it had turned to strands of silver wire and stood out around her circular face like a halo of crackling energy. Her face was smooth, colourless as snow, the strange shadowy, grey veins that masked it lining her cheeks and nose like an intricate lace veil. Her emerald eyes glistened wet, not with tears but with the cool clarity of polished glass. Her expression was calm, almost bewitched, as though her thoughts had been lifted by the icy wind to an ethereal plane. She held her arm steadily out in front of her, her stubby fingers knotted tightly around the lanyard as the shiny, dark tube suspended from it twirled and spun like a compass unable to find north, specks of brilliant silver shooting like comets over its polished surface.

'Hayden,' she called out in a euphoric voice as he staggered towards her. 'Listen! Can't you hear? It's singing! It's singing to the mountains, to the Ley, to me!'

Fear bit Hayden with a harsher chill than the snarling wind. He listened but could hear nothing more than the deadly howl of the storm and the frightened throb of blood pulsing against his eardrums. He looked at Bracken in her beautiful, entranced state and felt a stab of terror. He was sure that the strange cylinder had ensnared her in some kind of spell.

'Bracken,' he growled, 'for both our sakes, drop that talisman this second. It has some malicious enchantment on it!'

Uncertainty cracked the elated expression on Bracken's face and she looked between Hayden and the whirling tube. 'No,' she stuttered, her voice hushed with overwhelming emotion. 'I can hear it! I almost understand.'

In the few moments that had passed, large fragments of snow had started to tumble from the heavens, waltzing and swirling around in the powerful wind. Looking up, Hayden saw the sudden violent beginnings of a snow storm as it broke from the heavy clouds. The cliffs and sky looked almost the same colour now, a hopeless, brutal black that loomed in above them with the threat of falling snow and rocks. Frustration and terror raging in his chest, he lunged at Bracken, desperately trying to snatch the lanyard from her grasp.

'Let it go!' he screamed, his voice reverberating off the lifeless, stone curtains like the snarl of a wounded beast. The two of them grappled awkwardly, feet sliding on the frozen ground, equally matched in strength and passion. Chilled hands grasped for the twisting cylinder that swung and whirled before breaking free of its restraint as it tumbled down to land on the solid, icy floor.

The instant stone collided with stone, an earth-shattering boom echoed all around them as if the very cliffs and cavern floor were crying out to the wintry world. The foreboding rocks, the heavy sky, the whole world around them seemed to rattle and shake with sound. It issued up from below their feet, like a great, unseen monster disturbed from slumber, bellowing out in some ancient guttural language grating words of triumph. The bitter air quaked with the sound, turning from gloomy shadows to blinding whiteness as the snow rained down, summoned by its call. The immense crags shook, releasing a deadly curtain of ice, snow and rock. Hayden tried to run but his legs felt like jelly.

'Avalanche!' he screamed, his voice little more than a dim note through the rumble of falling ice and snow. Turning on his heel, he struggled to flee, the burning fear within him fuelling him onwards out of the chilled, doom-filled valley, but against the might of nature it did little good. The elements of the mountains coiled around him like a frosty serpent, snow, ice, stone and wind, robbing him of his bearings and strength. He was blinded by the unending whiteness of the world, his breath feeling like frozen liquid in his lungs. Cold seeped up through his body from the hard, lifeless ground, seizing his muscles with every step, making them cramp with spasm. He battled onward, fighting to stay alive, recalling thoughts of his sister and family but with every second that passed he knew the fight was a futile one. Beneath the monstrous echo that swamped the bitter air, Hayden could hear the deadly call of sleep and surrender. His toes were painfully numb as he blundered blindly on, and his weakened body sagged with weariness. In the heartless climate, even thought was an arduous chore as darkness swam into his mind. With a final gasp, Hayden slumped to his knees in exhaustion, the powdery, flawless bed of the newly fallen snow enveloping him in a tender, icy embrace as he tumbled unconsciously into it.

The mighty blankness filled the valley. Lost in the cold and the sound, Bracken could see nothing. The only sense she could make of the world was the low, grating howl that echoed from every direction, the essence of the mountains calling out to her. It was more than a deep sound that rung out through the bitter air, it was a language, muffled words of a foreign tongue that spoke to the most basic and primitive part of her mind. She was sure that if she tried a bit harder, if she could reach into her most ancient of memories, she could understand what the mountains were telling her. Her body felt deathly cold, her bulky form heavy as granite as she stumbled this way and that, trying to find some definite path through the whiteness. Was this her Calling from the Ley at last? She had long prayed for this moment, thought it would be a brilliant awakening of her spirit when all realisation and purpose would finally dawn and the Ley would reveal the colour of her soul. But she felt confused and afraid. She battled with all her might, all the knowledge her guardian had bestowed, to summon up the Ley inside her, for warmth and strength. But even now Its loving flow remained absent.

Thoughts filled her skull, of her dear guardian Amethyst and the other Ryders she loved so much, of Hayden, the first boy to stir her youthful feelings, who for all she knew could be lying just feet away, his life seeping into the deep snow. Tears of grief and frustration froze on her broad cheeks. She was nothing and she had brought death on to herself. The solid ground beneath her feet trembled with the grinding note of the storm. Exhausted and racked with angst, Bracken fell to her knees and sobbed. 'I don't understand!' she bleated to the stony echo of the valley. 'I don't know what you want from me!'

Tears blurred her vision as her limbs cried out for rest. Cold wrapped itself around her like a sapping cloak, sending bitter tendrils into her muscles. The snow had laid claim to her every sense so she did not know whether it was a dream, death or reality when a vast, grey silhouette loomed silently out of the ground as if born from the landscape, to tower over her barely conscious body.

Chapter 27

THE HALLS OF KELHALBON

Wherever Hayden was, it did not feel real. He felt as if he had been in a heavy dreamless sleep for years and even now was not fully awake. Strange sensations slowly filtered into his mind as he struggled to place where he was. The air on his face and hands was mercifully warm, muggy even, like when his mother had been boiling a pot over the fire. A faint odour filled the air, earthy and unpleasant, sulphur, and there was the distant rumbling sound of voices speaking in a language he did not understand and the churning clack of machinery. To make sure he was not still asleep, or even dead, he carefully shifted his limbs. His body was stiff and ached but seemed uninjured. He was lying on something soft but uneven, a pile of furs perhaps, warm and slightly musty. Blinking, the world gradually came in to view: blurry at first through the fog of uncertainty and weariness but then slipping into focus as reality dawned.

His first thought was that by some magical fortune, he had been transported back to the Ryders' citadel at Goodstone, for the chamber he found himself in did resemble the sturdy, stone rooms of the keep. The walls were formed of bluish-grey rock but bore no lines of interlocking bricks or blocks, rather a singular uneven surface like that of a cave. Here and there recesses had been expertly carved out from the stone into which large crystals had been placed. The golden flicker of fire illuminated the space, sparkling off the crystals and minerals in the stone, cast out from four ornate black iron torches resting in claw-like brackets fixed at each corner of the room. There were no windows, only a heavy door of expertly crafted metal, held together with studs as big as apples and locked by some complex mechanism of cogs and bolts.

Weariness quickly slipped away from Hayden as he realised he appeared to be in some kind of prison. Sitting up he saw that he was not alone. Across the cell on a bench made of twisted iron sat Bracken. She was engaged in animated discussion with an odd, grey-skinned creature the like of which Hayden had never seen. He stood about eight feet tall with a broad muscular back and shoulders. His limbs were stocky and thick and his hairless, pallid skin the coarse texture of granite. His head was like a boulder into which had been carved deep eye sockets, a prominent bulbous nose and thick-lipped maul. He gestured excitedly at Bracken with stubby fingers that looked like broken shards of flint and spoke in a low guttural tone, a monosyllabic language that Hayden could not understand.

Frowning, Bracken shook her head. 'I'm very sorry but I don't understand what you're saying.'

The creature let out an enormous sigh of frustration and reached out to reverently pick up a small item from beside Bracken. It was the strange tube that had led them into the valley. Pointing at it, the being spoke a short phrase before earnestly sinking to his knees and seizing hold of Bracken's hand.

Afraid for her safety, Hayden leapt from the iron cot he was laying on with an outraged cry. 'Unhand her, you brute,' he shouted, reaching for his sword, which he was surprised to find was still in its scabbard.

The creature let go of Bracken's hand and turned his face toward Hayden with a grunt of surprise. He glanced at Hayden's blade and livid expression and uttered something in a tone that almost sounded amused, his short, pointed teeth bared in an awkward grin.

Fearfully Hayden edged forward, brandishing his sword. 'I demand you tell us why we have been taken prisoner. Release us at once!' he declared as the being drew himself up to his full height.

Hayden felt quite unnerved as he loomed over him. His bright, black eyes blinked in understanding as he tried to find the words to express himself. 'Pre-san-or no,' he grunted, stooping his head slightly to bring his uneven face closer to Hayden and somehow managing to look more threatening. He then gestured toward Bracken and uttered the same phrase he had done when holding the stone tube.

'I don't think he means to harm us,' ventured Bracken quietly. 'I have been awake for some time and he hasn't threatened me at all. He keeps trying to tell me something, about myself and this tube, but I don't understand what.'

The creature watched Bracken as she spoke, a look of wonder, even awe, in his eyes. Carefully, Bracken stood up and wandered around the small cell, inspecting the thick walls and crystal-lined niches. 'I think we may be in Kelhalbon, Kingdom of the Dwarves.'

It was at that moment that the chamber was filled with the whirring and clicking of oiled machinery as the cogs and bars that locked the iron door slid into action. The heavy portal swung open and the dwarf hurried over to greet the new figure that entered, its head bowed in respect. The stranger shared some of the features of the dwarf and while it was clear that they were of the same race it was obvious from the appearance and manner of the newcomer that she was female and of a higher rank. There was a clear beauty about her but a beauty that belonged to a work of art more than a real woman, something not of this world. She was a little shorter than their captor, but still towered above both Hayden and Bracken. Her figure was womanly but she had powerful, broad shoulders and full, smooth hips, her waist was slightly tapered and her bosom well proportioned. But these comely curves were strangely lacking in feminine softness, her complexion a cool, pale grey like dull marble. In fact she more resembled a living statue than a human female. Her face made it all the more clear that she did not belong to the human race. It was tranquil, bordering on aloof, with sharp, perfectly symmetrical bone structure, long, narrow nose, sallow cheeks and angled jaw. Her mouth was full, the lips almost rectangular in shape, and the corners turned downwards slightly which gave her a melancholy look. She had wide, deep eyes like polished discs of shiny jet, with no white surrounding them or rim of coloured iris, kind, wise eyes that noticed every detail of what was before her but was patient in judging what they saw. Her scalp was completely hairless but even and smooth like a river-tumbled pebble and this strange lack of hair only added to the power and authority of her remarkable features. She was robed in simple but finely made garments that indicated she held some kind of office. She wore a plain jerkin fashioned from a remarkable fabric that shone like woven iron in the dim torchlight. The collar was cut in a low circular style and a thick, heavy choker of intricate gold and silver ingots, fragments of stone and crystals rested over her pallid neck and chest.

She listened patiently as the other dwarf gabbled excitedly, making wild gestures in the direction of Bracken and the stone cylinder. As she listened, Hayden thought he saw her eyes widen with excited surprise, but her expression remained calm and level. When the dwarf had finished his story, he presented her with the stone cylinder, which she examined closely before uttering some kind of instruction in a low, firm tone. The dwarf nodded earnestly before bowing and hurrying out of the chamber.

Stepping forward, the She-dwarf studied the confused humans, in particular Bracken, for a long moment before addressing them perfectly in their common language. 'I hope you are not alarmed or injured by your ordeal,' she said politely in a husky tone. 'Rett found you in the snow storm and brought you here for safety. Unfortunately, he is a crafts-man and does not understand the human tongue but I can assure, he, like all dwarves, means you no ill. If you would permit me to introduce myself, I am Bahl, vizier and steward of Kalhalbon and servant to the dwarf Queen Penn and her Prince Consort Ion.' She elegantly bowed her head.

Hayden's spirits were at once put at ease by her calm, level tone. 'We are grateful of your hospitality, Mistress Bahl. If it hadn't been for your kinsman, we would have surely perished in the snow.'

The dwarf smiled in gratitude, revealing a set of small, sharp, flint-like teeth. 'Normally we dwarves shy away from intervening in the day-to-day endeavours of humans. They pass through the mountains and we pay them little heed. But yours was clearly a significant case.'

'Because of me?' Bracken chimed. Bahl regarded her in surprise, her dark eyes shimmering with intelligence. Bracken swallowed hard and her cheeks coloured slightly with embarrassment at making such an assumption. 'Pardon my frankness,' she stuttered, plucking nervously at one of the crystal bangles around her wrist, 'but I am an apprentice to the Ley, and from my teachings I was led to believe that the Ryders and dwarves share a unity, both believing in the Ley, am I not correct?'

Bahl tilted her head to one side and remained silent for a moment as she scrutinised Bracken with intense curiosity, drinking in every inch of her nervous, pale face.

'What you say is true,' she finally uttered, her guttural tone picking out each word carefully, 'and it is indeed you that caused us to intervene. But your apprenticeship has little to do with the matter, although I do find it curious that the Ley has called you into Its service. May I ask, what names you go by and where you hail from?'

Bracken and Hayden glanced at each other, neither of them sure why the dwarves showed so much interest in their lives.

Finally Hayden spoke. 'If it pleases you, Mistress Bahl, I am Hayden, son of Godfrey of Ravensbrook and my companion here is Mistress Bracken, ward of the Ryder Amethyst.'

The dwarf nodded thoughtfully but barely seemed to register what he had said. Taking a seat on the bench next to Bracken, she asked, 'And who raised you, Mistress Bracken?'

Bracken looked upset and slightly ashamed to be asked so bluntly about her heritage. 'I am proud to say I have no family but Sister Amethyst and the Ryders,' she uttered softly. 'I was a foundling babe, abandoned on the Greyg Steppes. The Ley guided Amethyst to me and she nurtured me as her own.'

Slate eyelids slipped over Bahl's glossy pupils as she uttered something that sounded like a prayer in throaty Dwarfish. Opening her hands, she held out the strange tube that had led Bracken and Hayden to them. The material from which it had been made had transformed. No longer shiny, dark and solid, its hues were now ever-changing, altering from deep emerald to violet to bloody scarlet and brilliant sapphire, blooming within a soft, pliable, tactile cylinder like the tubular flower of a rare lily. Bracken gasped when she saw its beauty.

'And Sister Amethyst gave you this?' Bahl's voice had an almost fearful tone.

Slowly Bracken nodded. 'She presented it to me when I left the citadel at Goodstone; she said it was the only thing I had with me as an infant. I thought the Ley might be using me as a messenger. Am I right?'

An excited cry caught in Bahl's throat and losing her reserved demeanour she leapt to her feet and began pacing the room muttering breathlessly to herself. Bracken watched concerned, afraid that she had inadvertently committed some awful sin. Glancing at Hayden, she mouthed, 'What have I done?'

Bahl sharply stopped pacing and sighed. 'I am wasting time! Bracken, you must come with me to meet with the Prince Consort Ion, at once.' She held out her wide, grey hand and motioned for Bracken to stand up.

Bracken remained seated. 'Am I in trouble?' she asked anxiously.

Bahl's thick lips cracked into a broad grin and a low chuckle rumbled in her throat. 'By the Ley, no! This is a wondrous event. I shall explain more as we walk. Come now, it's very important.'

Indignantly, Bracken crossed her arms and remained seated. 'If I'm not being summoned because of some crime, I refuse to leave Master Hayden's company. I swore by the Ley I would aid him until he was reunited with his sister, a fellow apprentice, and I will not abandon him!'

Bahl sighed in frustration and regarded Hayden with slight annoyance. 'It is not the done thing but if you insist then he can come with us,' she said, moving over to turn the cogs securing the door. The heavy portal slid to one side and with a hurried gesture, Bahl bid them follow.

Getting to their feet, Hayden and Bracken entered the dark corridor after the dwarf. The passageway was gloomily lit with only a dull glow picking out the mineral fragments embedded in the stone walls. The passage was mercifully short and after a few minutes walking, opened out into an immense subterranean grotto full of light and sound, the magnificence of which dazzled their senses.

It was as if the entire mountain had been hollowed out from within, leaving a vast cathedral of stone that could fit the town of Goodstone in twice over. The floor was formed from vast, smooth plateaus of rock, separated from each other by deep gorges and linked with countless ornate iron bridges, stairways and ladders, that twisted, stretched and coiled like the curved, black bones of some prehistoric bird, delicate but incredibly strong. No two pathways looked alike, all of them decorated with spirals, abstract shapes, arches and minarets that reached up in tall spires to the domed roof high above. Some were broad, heavy thoroughfares at least thirty-feet wide, while others looked as if they had been spun by huge metal spiders, their steps almost appearing to hover in thin air. On every plateau there were two or three forges, where skilled dwarf craftsmen toiled. Hayden watched them hard at work, bending and forming thick, metallic ingots with their coarse grey hands like potters with clay and he marvelled at their incredible talent. He thought about his own father and how amazed he would be to see these artisans at work.

The thick walls of the cave glittered and gleamed with vast patches of natural crystal in every shade, reflecting the glowing light of the forge fires so that the space remained as bright as a sunlit day. Interlocking trellises clung to the walls, delicately hugging every contort of the rock, their complex mesh-work embellished with huge metal flowers, rigid petals glinting with swirls of innumerable colours like oil separating on water. Large cradles travelled across the frames in every direction, pulled by a network of pulleys, chains and wheels, carrying dwarves high into the gleaming, crystal atmosphere of the cavern as they toiled on the winding grid, reinforcing its struts and joints and polishing the decorative blooms. In the apex of the rounded roof, a giant system of coils, hooks, arms and bowls joined seamlessly to form an immense chandelier of pale, gleaming silver. Countless claws clasped cauldron-like braziers of brilliant orange flame that lit the subterranean kingdom as brightly as sunlight. The whole atmosphere of the cave was noisy and filled with life, an echoing, clattering song of metal against metal, the buzz of well-oiled clockwork and guttural dwarf voices.

Bracken's head was constantly twisting this way and that as she and Hayden followed Bahl along the walkways and over the bridges, her greedy eyes not knowing what amazing sight to take in next. 'Look, Master Hayden, look!' she gasped as the unnatural light of the grotto gleamed off her long, wiry hair, changing its hue moment to moment from gold, to fiery scarlet to coal black. 'Have you ever dreamt of such a place of wonders? I have read descriptions of Kelhalbon in the citadel's library, heard stories of it from the Ryders, but nothing does it justice!'

Hayden, a blacksmith by trade and familiar with the art of the forge, was overwhelmed by what he saw. Such marvels in iron, brass, tin and rarer materials left him lost for words. He paused for a second to admire a miraculous likeness of an exotic bird, three-feet high, perched delicately on an ornate pedestal. Its feathers were individually rendered in paper-thin pieces of silver and bronze and it moved and preened itself, brought to life by some wondrous hidden workings of clockwork and magic. Blinking its cut jewel eyes at Hayden, its sharply hooked beak snapped open and a tinkling melody of high-pitched notes issued forth, leaving him slack-jawed in amazement.

Bahl smiled proudly when she witnessed their amazement at her home. 'Beautiful, is it not?' she said, guiding Bracken onwards. 'Our menfolk are the finest artisans in metal and jewel-work in any realm or kingdom touched by the Ley. We are long-lived by your standards; death doesn't visit us often. Many workers you see here will have spent hundreds of years perfecting their craft.'

She paused for a moment and gestured, watching one particular dwarf bent over a vast pot of bubbling, molten metal. Hayden and Bracken grew wide-eyed with surprise as the dwarf very gently reached into the searing, orange liquid and drew out a long, flexible portion, moulding and turning it in his bare hands. His fingers were stubby but unbelievably dexterous as he formed the cooling metal into a delicate bow, like a mother plaiting her daughter's hair. When he was happy with the shape, he breathed delicately on it in the palm of his hand until the glowing iron cooled and hardened before holding it out to Bahl for her approval. She uttered a few short words of praise in Dwarfish before leaving him to continue his work.

Hayden gasped in astonishment at what he had just witnessed. 'The hot iron,' he exclaimed, 'it did not burn him!'

Bahl tilted her head slightly to indicate that they should carry on their journey. 'No more than it would hurt you to touch cool water or woven cloth. We have a stronger physical state than humans; some of your kind believe us to be immortal but this is not true. All beings return to the Ley eventually.'

They had arrived at another astounding bridge, an extraordinary structure of swaying, circular discs joined together by rigid iron cords that spiralled upwards to a higher stone plateau, seeming to defy gravity in its levelness and balance. Bahl proceeded to climb, and reassured that it would bear their weight, Bracken and Hayden clambered after her.

Not looking round to confirm the safety of her guests, Bahl continued her monologue. 'The roles of gender in dwarf society are very clear,' she explained as Hayden and Bracken battled to match her long, steady paces, while all the time trying very hard not to look down at the dizzying abyss below. 'The males concern themselves with manual labour: miners, smiths, artists. It is they who build and maintain our kingdom. Females, such as myself, are in charge of more intellectual matters: record-keeping, government, diplomatic relations, anything that is not to do with metal or stone. We have warriors of both sexes, but on the whole we are a peaceful race. Our queen is our ruler and her mate, the prince consort, is chosen for his skill and craftwork from among all the adult males but he has no power in his own right. It is our queen who governs, or it was until...' she sighed deeply and shook her head as if suddenly remembering she had company and was not simply vocalising her own thoughts. Resting her hand lightly on the chain railing, she paused for a second, glancing over her shoulder at Hayden and Bracken, who were several steps behind, struggling to keep apace with her steady progress on the hovering stairway.

'Are you able to keep up?' she asked, unclear as to whether she was referring to the climb or her explanation of dwarf culture.

Slightly short of breath, Hayden and Bracken drew level with her and stopped for a moment to rest, daring to glance down at the amazing landscape of Kelhalbon spread out below them like overlapping fragments of a complex metal and stone jigsaw. From their raised position, the whole realm of the dwarves appeared to be a massive, living machine, sturdy stages of rock supporting churning forges, laced delicately together with threads of black iron, while all the time strange carts, pulleys and levers moved with almost animal grace as they fulfilled countless tasks.

Turning away from the vision of industry below, Bracken ventured a question. 'If the queen is your ruler, why are you taking us to her consort? You just said male dwarves have little to do with government.'

A look of embarrassment crossed Bahl's thick features as she turned away to continue her climb. 'It is complicated,' she stated stiltedly, seeming for the first time to struggle expressing herself in their language. 'Things are... how do you humans put it? Not how they should be. But hopefully change is coming and it will be for the better. If all goes as I hope it shall, you will meet Queen Penn.'

She flashed them a nervous smile and continued up the final few steps to a rounded outcrop jutting from the wall of the cave. Baffled by her vague sentiments, Hayden and Bracken followed, feeling somewhat glad to be on firmer footing again. The projection formed a natural balcony overlooking the work below. A wide angular archway was cut into the stone wall set with a thick, heavy portal of blackened iron. A large, complex mechanism rested in the centre from which protruded a dozen or so bolts jutting rigidly against the frame of the doorway to keep it firmly shut. A small window, about three-feet square, was set high in the door at dwarf eye-level. The door was flanked on either side by a female dwarf attired in a long, hooded robe of finely woven chain-mail. *There is something peculiar*, Hayden thought, *about the style of their garments that make them look to be both guards and nurses.* They bowed in unison as Bahl stepped off the staircase.

'Is our royal spouse fit to receive guests?' she asked.

The dwarf to the left of the doorway nodded soberly. 'He has been breakfasted and completed seven devotions in prayer to the Ley, Chief Vizier Bahl,' she uttered in a guttural whisper. 'As you know, yesterday he did several hours of work at his forge; activity is always good for his spirits. I would say this is a good time for him. He has been informed of the arrival of our guests.'

While the dwarves talked, the remaining guard, who seemed to be somewhat younger, stared at Bracken with fascinated intensity. Edging closer to her fellow guard, she folded her hands excitedly in front of her and muttered in a gravelly tone, 'Is it she, Vizier Bahl? Only I have heard rumours and while it is true that it is foolish to believe in miracles, one cannot dismiss the dearest hope for our people.'

She was sharply silenced by her fellow guard authoritatively raising her hand, her dark eyes boring into her crossly at her impertinence. 'You speak out of turn, young Qam,' she reprimanded dryly. 'It is not our place to ponder such things. Maybe if you concentrated more on your duties and less on the talk of others!'

Qam lowered her glossy black eyes and adjusted her cowl. 'Yes, Captain Chy,' she whispered shuffling back to her post beside the door.

Glancing at the secured door to check that neither of the guards had been slacking in their duties of keeping the prince consort secure in his private refuge, Bahl spoke, her voice somewhat distracted. 'Nothing is confirmed as fact,' she told them, 'nor will be until we meet with Prince Consort Ion. You may make him known of our arrival, Qam.'

The junior guard nodded silently and took hold of a long, delicate gold chain that hung down beside the door and tugged it sharply three times. From within the stony recesses beyond the portal, a hollow clang of inharmonious chimes echoed out, soon followed by a deep, growling utterance somewhere between belch and yawn. Suddenly fearful, Bracken edged closer to Hayden, her fingers knotting with the crystal pendants around her neck.

A voice creaked, low and weary from the tiny window in the door, sounding more like heavy slabs of granite being dragged along the ground than actual words. 'What is it?' it burbled lazily.

Stepping close to the slot in the door, Bahl called politely inside. 'It is

I, the Vizier Bahl, Prince Ion. I wish to speak to you if it is convenient.'

A great noise issued from behind the door, a combination of mighty boulders being heaved about and the snarl of an awoken bear. 'Is it important?' came the slurred reply. 'If it is then you should deal with it. You're the vizier, not me.'

Qam and Chy exchanged knowing looks and Qam whispered. 'He will go the way of the Queen and become Ac-Nu if his temperament does not change.'

'No-one asked you,' snapped her superior, 'so keep quiet!'

Ignoring the guards' bickering, Bahl continued her conversation through the closed door. 'I would not bother you if it weren't of the deepest concern to you and our queen. I believe you have been informed about the issue.'

There was a momentary silent pause as if the prince was mulling over what Bahl had told him, followed by a woeful, almost pained groan and a heavy, sorrowful whisper of, 'Bring her before me.'

Chy stepped up to the door, and delicately moved her short, grey fingers over the mechanism in its centre. With smooth, liquid movement, the bolts and bars that snaked across the iron portal retracted into the metal knot at its centre and with a weighty groan the door swung open. Bahl moved forward and beckoned for Bracken and Hayden to follow – Bracken remained motionless.

The dwarf vizier regarded her with almost tenderness. 'It's all right,' she said gently, 'the prince is ill-mannered and moody at times but quite harmless.'

Unwilling, the anxious guests allowed themselves to be guided into the gloomy chamber of the dwarf queen's consort, the iron door slamming shut behind them. Neither the smith's son nor the Ryder's ward had ever had the honour of being in the presence of royalty before, but naturally they imagined that the husband of a queen would live in more regal surroundings than those they now found themselves in. The room was relatively small, a little over ten-feet square, and bore a striking resemblance to the cell they had first found themselves in when they awoke. Twin torches were fixed in brackets, casting their fiery light in long bands of orange and shadow across the room. The place was unbelievably cluttered, filled with piles of twisted, knotted iron, buckled wheels and half-completed fragments of machinery, looking to be more of a scrapyard than a throne room. It was virtually impossible to see what anything truly was and the only definite item of clear shape was a massive ornate throne of carved iron decorated with coils of gold and silver. Slumped on this beautiful crafted seat, looking like he had not moved in centuries, was the heavy, hunched figure of the Prince Consort Ion.

At first glance, he made an impressive, if decidedly ignoble, figure. This was due to his massive frame; even seated he towered somewhere between seven and eight feet tall, with broad, bullish shoulders and an immense stomach that lolled over his thighs like a globule of melted grey wax. It was clear that, at some time, he had been a creature of great physical power, but all that had once been toned muscle now drooped in great swathes of inert fat, like curtains of dark granite hanging from his underarms, turning his bare pectorals into sagging breasts. He had no jaw or chin to speak of, rather a veil of loose jowly flesh like wet clay connecting his bulbous head and body. His lips were thick and baggy, hanging down in a forlorn scowl, and his cheeks were flabby and sallow. Pupils like lumps of unpolished coal were set deep amid a mass of creases and bags, so dark and lifeless they appeared to belong more to a soulless corpse than a living being. In fact nothing about his appearance or manner struck of life at all; it was as if his whole form was being weighted down by life itself, physically dragged into despair by his colossal bulk. His sorrowful façade was made all the more pitiful by the fact he was so richly dressed. A massive sable cape, fashioned from the pelts of, at least, three black bears was draped haphazardly around his shoulders, embellished with countless jewels and crystals of all shades and a jagged coronet of battered gold encircled his hairless pate.

He stared vaguely into the dark shadows of his chamber barely moving to acknowledge the trio which had entered. Stepping forward, Bahl sank to her knee in a bow of respect. 'My Prince,' she said in a reverent whisper, 'First Smith of Kelhalbon, Regal Husband to our Queen.'

The flabby dwarf shuffled his huge weight uncomfortably on his metal throne and parted his lips to emit a deep, sighing belch. 'Have you brought my dinner?' he grunted. His tone was like distant thunder far out at sea and his words were slurred and half-formed.

Bahl raised her head and blinked. 'No, sire,' she uttered patiently. 'Pok is your cook; he feeds you. I am your vizier.'

An irritated scowl creased Ion's wrinkled face and he made a strange, almost childlike whimper. 'I'm hungry,' he whined, 'and when I'm hungry I can't think.' He rocked forward on his throne, clasping his boulder-like head in his powerful hands and groaned as if he was in pain. 'Where is my wife?' he moaned feebly. 'Where is Penn?'

Sighing, Bahl got to her feet. 'Sire, if I can just have your full attention for one moment, then I can deal with this matter. The sooner it's dealt with the sooner you can eat.'

Ion uttered something coarse in Dwarfish and reluctantly nodded his head. Broodingly he gestured vaguely in Bracken and Hayden's direction. 'Which one is it?' he grunted.

Turning towards the nervous guests, Bahl motioned for Bracken to step forward. Swallowing hard, Bracken stared at Bahl's sallow, coarse-skinned hand reaching out toward her. 'Come closer so that the prince might see your face better.'

A sudden anxiety gripped Hayden as his companion stepped away from him and he pondered whether despite the beauty and sophistication of their realm, the dwarves were as civilised as they seemed. Old tales from his youth of monsters who feasted on human flesh ran through his mind and he wondered whether they had been in fact brought to the queen's spouse as a rare delicacy.

As Bracken fearfully drew nearer to him, Prince Ion gripped the sturdy arms of his throne and leant forward, his breath ragged and sharp. She battled to keep the fear from her face, telling herself that a Ryder must show calm courage at all times. The chamber was gloomy but even so she was struck by this horrid visage. It was not so much the ugliness of his slack grey skin or the countless wrinkles that etched his eyes and brow like a spidery mask of age that struck her, it was more the emptiness of his expression, quite unlike anything she had witnessed before: a hollow, soulless abyss filled his eyes, gnawing hungry loss draining him to the core of his soul. The prince twisted his heavy head slightly as he inspected her resolute expression as if searching her features for the answer to some unknown mystery.

'Fire,' he grunted, beckoning to Bahl awkwardly, 'I cannot see.'

Straight away, Bahl moved to one of the iron wall brackets and removed the heavy metal torch, carrying it over to the immense throne. The orange light danced across Bracken's tense face, turning her wild locks auburn and gold. Clumsily, Prince Ion raised his brutish hand and roughly ran his stumpy fingers over her features, clasping her jaw in his palm and twisting her face so he might view her profile.

'There is,' he wheezed, '*something* about her. Perhaps. But I don't remember. I am not sure.'

With a defeated grunt, he slumped back in his seat. Pensively, Bahl stared at him as if unsure whether she dared continue. Summoning her nerve, she reached into the pocket of her tunic. 'She came bearing this.'

Extending her hand towards him, Bahl unfurled her fingers to reveal the strange, shimmering cylinder resting in her palm. Soft, almost flesh-like, it formed a perfect O like a slumbering animal curled and dormant, its bright hues ever changing beneath the light of the torch.

A gasp of shock caught in the dwarf prince's throat and for a brief second Bracken thought she saw vitality glimmer in his lifeless eyes. He clasped his hand to his bare chest as if struck through the heart by an arrow of pain, his breath heavy. Once more his gaze danced over Bracken's face, his anguished features suddenly animated.

'Your hand,' he uttered in an urgent whisper.

Puzzled and fearful, she did nothing but stare back at him in bewilderment.

Frantically he gestured towards her, rocking agitatedly in his seat. 'Your hand!' he shouted, his voice echoing like iron tools off the stone walls. 'Hold forth your left hand!'

Trembling with terror, Bracken raised her left arm, extending it so that the dwarf prince might examine her hand. The golden firelight flickered across her pallid skin, revealing the dark veins and arteries on the back of her hand like shadowy pathways across her flesh. Prince Ion stared at her hand, his breath held in trepidation. 'Bahl,' he whispered anxiously, his eyes swivelling to the vizier, 'you do it. I do not have the courage.'

Sombrely, Bahl took the glistening tube carefully in her hand and delicately slipped it over Bracken's extended index finger. The frightened girl tensed as the cool, polished stone came into contact with her skin, half expecting some torturous magic to flow from the cylinder and wrack her body with agony. Instead, her terror was filled with wonder as the tube gently tightened and shrunk around her digit like a fine satin sheath. Its texture changed from solid, smooth marble, becoming pliable and soft as if becoming part of her own flesh, flexing easily to encase her knuckle. Threads of metallic light glittered, running like wispy snakes of ruby, sapphire and emerald over her hand. A joyous cry escaped Bahl's mouth as she clapped her hands to her face. 'It is she,' she gasped as the dwarf prince trembled with disbelief. 'My lord, it is she!'

The weathered visage of the woeful consort crumbled with emotion. His soulless eyes grew dark and wet with tears and he gripped his sable mantle for comfort. Overwrought, he tossed back his globe-like head and let out a mighty wail of agony, grief and joy, a bellow so loud and long that it seemed to fill every cave and cavern of the dwarves' realm.

Terrified, Bracken staggered back towards Hayden, seizing his arm for comfort. Like an awakened mountain, Prince Ion heaved his colossal mass on to his stumpy bowed legs, tottering forward like a drunk as he reached out pleadingly towards Bracken, his eyes wide with amazement. 'She lives,' he cried, 'my granddaughter lives!'

Chapter 28

THE PRINCESS'S STORY

Hayden suddenly felt the great weight of Bracken's sturdy form slump against him and quickly wrapped his arm around her thick waist to support her as she swooned. She was by no means waif-like and it was a struggle for him to stop her collapsing completely. Quick as a flash, Bahl replaced the burning torch in its bracket and hurried over to stop Bracken's semi-conscious form from crushing him. The dwarf was clearly stronger than Hayden and easily took Bracken in her arms, helping her to her feet again. Bracken's eyelids fluttered as her brain swam back to consciousness.

'Easy, Your Majesty,' Bahl said in a soothing, almost maternal tone. Glancing at Hayden, she nodded to the immense pile of twisted metal at the side of the room. 'Fetch her something to sit on.'

Quickly, Hayden hurried across the chamber and searching through the mound of knotted, black bars managed to uncover a small, heavy, low stool.

The shocked girl slumped down upon it, breathing heavily and staring at her left hand with large, bewildered eyes. Awkwardly, Prince Ion ambled over, mewing and huffing like a wounded bear. Muttering something in Dwarfish, he reached out and touched Bracken's head, partly to comfort her and partly to reassure himself she was real. 'She lives!' he burbled. 'She lives!'

Ever attentive, Bahl took gently hold of the prince's arm and guided him, muttering giddily, back to his throne. Hayden remained just behind Bracken, staring down at her in concern as she trembled and panted nervously, running her hand over the strange ring that encased her finger. The hue of the cylinder had paled, becoming almost the same shade and texture as her skin, only distinct from the flesh by countless metallic threads of light that sparkled over its surface.

'Are you all right?' Hayden asked softly, crouching down at her side.

Agitatedly, Bracken shook her head, her wiry locks shining brilliant copper in the glow of the torches. 'No,' she panted, her eyes lowered to the floor, 'no I am not. This is wrong. There has been a terrible mistake made. I am not your granddaughter. I can't be, I just, I just can't.'

She held up her left hand before her eyes, staring at the strange ring bound there like it was some hideous blight or scar on her flesh. 'There must be some other explanation,' she muttered frantically, gripping her index finger roughly in her right hand and tugging at it, trying to remove the item that clung there like her own skin. 'My parents must have been vile thieves who stole this from your people. If so, take it back with my deepest apologies for any harm they caused.'

She attempted to press her fingernails beneath the object to prise it off her digit but it stayed there, sealed to her flesh. 'Some soap,' she begged frantically, 'or oil to lubricate its path. I will not take what isn't mine.'

Bahl left Prince Ion's side and silently walked over to Bracken to kneel soberly before her. Gently taking the girl's hands between her own darker, stronger ones, she rested them in her lap. 'The ring,' she said, in a simple, clear tone, almost as if she was talking to a child, 'is the Royal Band of the Dwarf Queens. It has been passed from mother to daughter down the line of our regal leaders for millennia. Its magic and craftwork binds with royal blood and once placed on an heir's hand it cannot be removed until she herself has given birth to a daughter. There is no mistake, you are of royal blood.'

In the shadows, slumped upon his mighty throne, Prince Ion made an odd, whining noise somewhere between overwhelming joy and heart-rending sorrow. 'Duun,' he whimpered, his eyes rolling back in his head. 'Duun, my daughter, forgive me, I did only what your mother would allow. Your actions made her sick with rage.' He whined and cried, a deep, sickening sound like lava bubbling through underground trenches. His stubby hand clawed anxiously at the rich pelt of his mantle as he arched back, banging his head repeatedly against the iron of his throne. 'I loved you, Duun. But she is my Penn, my wife, my queen.'

Sighing, Bahl glanced back at the bereft consort. 'No-one blames you, my lord,' she uttered, sounding as if this was the thousandth time she had reassured him. 'Queen Penn ruled over us all.'

Shivering with disbelief, Bracken tucked her hands into the pockets of her gown, unable to gaze at the mystic band that marked her true lineage. 'But this can't be,' she implored. 'Look at me, my hair, my eyes. Admittedly, I am tall for my years and my build is brawnier than I would wish. But I do not resemble your kin.'

She twisted on her stool to look at Hayden. 'Master Hayden,' she begged, 'answer me honestly and do not flatter. Do I look like a dwarf?'

Hayden gazed at her thoughtfully for a moment. It was true that from first sight of her in the citadel in Goodstone he had thought Bracken looked quite unlike any other woman he had ever seen. Her form was large and heavy and her hair possessed no definite hue of its own, changing with the light she was in. But her features did indeed more resemble that of a human than the craggy faces of either Prince Ion or Bahl, and, he thought secretly, not altogether unattractive.

'No,' he told her gently, 'you don't, not to me anyway.'

Prince Ion grunted and pressed his hand to the bridge of his nose. 'You're only half dwarf,' he groaned wearily, 'and therein lies the sorrow.'

Bahl glanced at him anxiously. 'My lord,' she ventured, 'do you have the strength to tell the tale or may I?'

The prince's jowly mouth fell open as if he was about to begin some great saga, his dull eyes filled with woe, but instead, he simply whimpered woefully and hung his head. 'The pain,' he wheezed, clasping his furs to his chest. 'Oh the tragedy of it! My Penn, my Penn. The memory still tortures my soul. I am weary with loss and a hunger that can't be filled. I do not have the strength. You speak of it, Bahl, you explain.'

The vizier sighed mournfully and shook her head, seemingly

embarrassed by the prince's melodramatics. Clasping her hands in her lap, she gazed earnestly at Bracken and began.

'You say you were raised by the Ley Ryders,' she began gently, 'so I take it you have a reasonable education in history and are familiar with the Great War between Geoll and Etheria.'

Silently Bracken nodded, her eyes wide and expectant.

Bahl, seated on the stone floor at her side, straightened her back, her smooth, grey head held high and proud. When she spoke, it was obvious from her clear tone what she meant by female dwarves being the record-keepers of their race, as her words seemed to be recalled from some book stored deep within her mind. 'The hostilities were primarily between the people of Geoll and Etheria, humans, you understand. Kelhalbon sits between these two realms separate from either. At a point when it seemed Etheria had the advantage through sorcery, King Elkric sent a plea to Queen Penn to send dwarf warriors and weapon-smiths to his aid. He spoke of the purity of the Ley and how black sorcery would soil Its flow.'

She paused for a second and glanced sympathetically at Bracken. 'You must understand,' she added, 'back then, Queen Penn was a reasonable and wise ruler, with a great respect for the Ley.'

Prince Ion snivelled woefully at his wife's name and stuffed the hem of his fur cape into his mouth. 'My Penn, my Penn,' he whined like a sickly child.

Bahl ignored his laments and continued. 'Queen Penn agreed that it would be prudent to intercede in the humans' affairs and join forces with Geoll for the sake of the Ley. The Princess Duun, her daughter and only heir and your mother, would act as envoy, leading a band of fine warriors and weapon-smiths to join the Geollease ranks.' She stopped for a moment, breathing a melancholy sigh as her own memories intermingled with the narrative. 'I knew your mother,' she recalled softly. 'I wouldn't be so bold as to call myself her friend, but I acted as her prefect, assisted her in her duties. She was a fine dwarf, learned in the ways of politics and cerebral arts and a fine warrior if the need called her to be. She would have made a noble queen if the Ley had chosen that path for her.'

Bracken lowered her eyes, gazing at her powerful forearms and wrists. Sister Rosequartz always told her she had good sword skills and she now pondered whether she had inherited these from her mother.

Bahl shook herself out of her personal thoughts on the princess and continued her tale in the same, emotionless tone as before. 'I do not need to tell you of the outcome of the war. With our help, Geoll was victorious and the peace was settled with the marriage of King Elkric to the Etherian Princess Neopi. We lost few dwarves in battle, as I say we are a hardy breed, and the princess returned to Kelhalbon triumphant.'

She fell silent and it appeared that her tale was complete or at the very least she was unwilling to speak of what happened next. There was a look in her eyes of secret shame. Lowering his cape from his face, Prince Ion leant forward in his throne, his hands tightly gripping the arms. 'But we were betrayed,' he breathed in a hushed whisper, the torchlight forming ugly patterns on his etched and twisted face. 'That's what my wife said: betrayed by the human king and our own offspring. Sullied and shamed. Although, I don't think, I don't know, I...' Fear flashed in his dark soulless eyes as he glanced around the chamber, his hand pressed to his lips as if the room was suddenly filled with unseen spies. 'We were betrayed,' he repeated a little lower, as if to hide his own thoughts behind the words. 'Our queen was betrayed.'

Bahl raised her hand to hush his muttering. 'Do not vex yourself, my lord,' she comforted. 'The story is known to me and I will continue. You see, during the campaign of war, it would appear that the Princess Duun and King Elkric began a liaison. They laid together and when she returned to us, you, Bracken, were already forming in her belly.'

A shiver of electric disbelief ran over Bracken's skin as her mind battled to process the incredible origins of her life. It was barely within her capability to accept that she was the daughter of a dwarf princess but to also learn that her father was the legendary King Elkric seemed more like a fairytale than real life. She suddenly became aware of her own existence, every memory she possessed, every facet of her personality. She searched inwardly for any slight indicator to her royal heritage, but could see herself as nothing more than the humble lass who grew up in the citadel at Goodstone beneath the gaze of the kind Ryders. Hearing the names of her true parents left her with no connection to them or rush of affection. It only made her lonely for the advice and guidance of Sister Amethyst, the woman she had looked upon as both her mother and father.

Bahl paused from her tale and taking a deep breath rested her smooth firm hand compassionately on Bracken's arm. 'The rest of the story is, I'm afraid to say, painful and dishonourable to our people,' she confessed, 'and I must ask if you truly wish me to continue.'

Bracken blinked and for the briefest of seconds looked uncertain but then said, 'Yes, you must. If I am truly who you claim I am I must know why I was left abandoned.'

Withdrawing her arm, Bahl nodded sombrely. 'The Princess Duun kept her pregnancy hidden for some months before the truth made itself clear. When it did and Queen Penn found out, she was incandescent with fury. Rage and hatred twisted her heart and turned her emotions black.'

A horrible sound, somewhere between a fearful cry of pain and a wordless call for aid, escaped Prince Ion's cracked lips. Throwing his sable mantle over his head, he pressed his hands to his ears, rocking frantically back and forth and burbling to himself in a mixture of Dwarfish and the common language. 'Memories, the hurt, the terror, her anger! Oh Penn, oh Penn! My Duun, my Duun! I've lost so much!'

Hayden watched this manic behaviour in absolute horror and amazement. He had always thought that the members of the ruling classes possessed an aloof intellect that put them above the common man and made them fit to rule. He had never seen anyone, high or low born, human or not, act like Prince Ion. He seemed quite insane.

'Is your lord quite well?' he asked timidly.

Bahl gazed at the immense hulk of the prince quaking fearfully beneath his cape and, muttering something in Dwarfish under her breath, sadly shook her head. 'No, Master Hayden, no he is not. What happened to his family causes him great anguish and tortures his spirits. But the past is unchangeable and cannot be denied; however, we wish it could. People act as they will and not even the Ley can alter a person's choices.'

She turned back to face Bracken to continue her story but when she spoke the low timbre of her voice was woefully soft and her words seemed shrunken with shame.

'When Queen Penn found out her daughter and heir had been impregnated by the human king, her soul turned wicked with fury. Traditionally, the best dwarf craftsman is selected as mate for the queen, as this is a quality that we value most highly. It is also true that human blood is believed to weaken our stony nature, making us more susceptible to death. She saw you as a tainted and unfit heir to her royal blood line and demanded, as her mother and queen, that she abort you.'

Sickening bile rose in Bracken's throat as she heard this and her stomach churned. It was her secret dark fear, as it is with all orphaned children, that she was an unwanted addition to the world. She tried to think about the Ley and how It had carried Sister Amethyst into her life so that she might know love, but as always she could not sense Its movements and the dear memory and support of her beloved guardian felt very far from her. She prayed the Ley would bring them together very soon. Weary she leant against Hayden for support.

'But she didn't,' she uttered in a small voice. 'I survived.'

'Indeed,' whispered Bahl gently. 'Although she risked her birthright and life in doing so, your mother defied our queen and fled Kelhalbon. Queen Penn declared her a treasonous rebel and ordered her own warriors to hunt her down and kill both of you. They searched, fearful to go against the queen's wishes, but returned empty-handed. Everyone believed that your father's human blood had weakened both you and your mother and you had perished, returning to the stone of the land as all our people do. But even the thought of this death could not quell the queen's wrath. Anger and betrayal had infected the core of her soul like a tumour and she could not forget. She became what we dwarves call Ac-Nu, a state between life and death, when your hate and grief and sorrow grows so great that very little can distract you from it and it eats at all that you once were. She has been that way ever since, unable to let go of the loathing in her heart and rule us as she once did. I, as vizier, have overseen the well-being of our people these past fourteen years. It has been my privilege and duty to do so but I have never given up hope that the queen would return to her rightful place.'

Pale-faced, Bracken lowered her eyes as she carefully mulled over the amazing events of her conception and birth. 'Princess Duun, my mother,' she began, the words seeming awkwardly alien to her. 'She must have died giving birth on the Greyg Steppes; that's where Sister Amethyst found me. This ring was the only indicator of who I was and she had no clue what it signified.'

By now, Prince Ion had ceased his woeful lamentations. Lowering his cape from over his head, he studied Bracken's face with intense and hopeful desperation. 'Our bodies turn to stone and soil the moment our life-force returns to the Ley; she would have found no trace of my daughter's body. Oh Duun, my Duun. I loved you but you were foolish to think your mother could be ignored. But that's all in the past now!' he enthused leaning towards his apprehensive granddaughter. 'Kelhalbon will have a queen once more!'

Bracken's eyes widened, her face flushing hot with panic. Surely Prince Ion could not expect her to rule? The words of the blind hermit Emouchet filtered into her thoughts, of her possessing a rare kind of power. His acute senses must have felt the mix of human and royal dwarf blood in her veins. She was descended from two proud regal lines but felt she was unworthy and unprepared for the responsibility this would bring.

She was about to attempt to raise her anxiety when the sound of a bell ringing within the shadows of the chamber interrupted her thoughts. Gracefully, Bahl got to her feet and moved across to the doorway. As she swung the portal open, the two guards, Chy and Qam, pushed their way impatiently inside.

Unable to contain her excitement, the younger of the pair, Qam, edged nearer to peer at Bracken curiously. 'Well,' she asked Bahl nervously, 'are the rumours true? Is it she? Is it?'

Disapproving of this impertinence, Chy poked her comrade sharply in the shoulder with her stubby forefinger. 'Speaking out of turn again, Qam,' she chided briskly. 'I will transfer you to record-keeping if this keeps up. That is not why we are here!' She turned to speak to Bahl, deliberately blocking Qam's view of Bracken with her bulky form as she did so. 'Vizier Bahl, visitors have been found near one of the Eastern Gateways. We believe they are associates of the Ryders.'

Bahl sighed, clearly not happy about having such an important conversation interrupted by guests. She mumbled something to herself in Dwarfish before adding, 'Ley be blamed, you don't see a human in Kelhalbon for decades and then two parties arrive within hours.' She cast Hayden an apologetic smile. 'No offence meant, of course. We dwarves aren't used to hosting company.'

Chy's interest had wandered surreptitiously to where Bracken was patiently sitting as Bahl prepared to go and greet the newcomers. 'Vizier Bahl,' she queried lightly, 'is there any definite information regarding this girl's identity?'

Behind her, Qam gasped indignantly and stamped her foot. 'That is exactly what I asked!' she declared.

The senior guard grunted and swivelled round to glare at the younger dwarf. 'I have greater authority than you!' she snapped. 'I don't go round listening to idle gossip from every other smith and miner. If the vizier and the Prince Consort are concerned with the matter then there must be some validation behind it.'

Groaning, Bahl pressed her fingertips to the bridge of her nose. 'I swear, you two will send me Ac-Nu one of these days!' she said shaking her head.

Taking a deep breath, she tried to regain her composure and considered whether it was time to reveal the truth. Finally, her dark lips formed a smile and she kindly gestured towards Bracken. 'Yes, the truth can be known. This is indeed the lost child of Princess Duun. She has returned to us.'

At this remark, all animosity between Chy and Qam vanished as they were overcome with joy and excitement at confirmation of their people's long held hope. Happily, they clasped each other's hands, gabbling animatedly in Dwarfish before throwing themselves on their knees before the alarmed Bracken in joyous genuflections of gladness. 'Princess!' cried Chy, merry tears running down her marbled cheeks. 'We are your humble servants. Oh this is a wonderful day!'

Quite embarrassed by this display, Bracken blushed crimson and looked towards Bahl for some kind of prompt as to how to handle the situation. 'Oh please,' she begged as the pair grovelled before her, 'I don't want, I mean, I don't expect...' The sudden elevation of her position was alien to her and she did not quite know how to deal with it. Sensing her discomfort, Bahl kindly stepped in and motioned for them to stand.

'Yes,' she agreed as Chy and Qam got to their feet, 'it is a joyous day for the dwarves of Kelhalbon and our people must be informed. Remember though that this news also comes as a surprise to the Lady Bracken herself. She knew nothing of our ways until today, let alone her parentage. So I ask that we be patient and not pressure or crowd her.' Earnestly, the pair nodded and grinned at each other as Prince Ion burbled emotionally on his throne. Qam then timidly raised her hand. 'If Captain Chy will allow me to suggest it, might some kind of celebration be in order to mark the princess's return?' She looked at Chy, expecting to get disciplined for the suggestion, but the other guard seemed happy to allow it to slide.

Suddenly alerted by the idea of food, Prince Ion shifted heavily on his throne, his snub nostrils flaring hungrily. 'Yes, indeed,' he grunted, slapping his pendulous chops, his hands folded across his huge belly. 'I think that would be just the thing. Bahl, if you would make the arrangements.' Merrily, the vizier smiled and bowed her head. 'It would be an honour, my lord. Qam, if you would speak to the cooks and the novelty makers to provide us with suitable refreshment and entertainment. Chy, make sure the joyous news is known by every dwarf. Tonight Princess Duun's daughter has returned!'

Filled with excitement, Chy and Qam bustled towards the door. As they were about to exit, Chy looked back at Bahl and gently prompted, 'And what about the humans who have arrived at the Eastern Gateway?'

Clasping her hand to her smooth, hairless scalp, Bahl let out an exclamation. 'So much at one time! I quite forgot. Yes, I must attend to them. No doubt the Ley has brought Ryders to celebrate and bless your return to us, Bracken. We must show them gratitude for watching over you all this time. Come, follow me!'

With a final bow to the prince, Bahl headed for the door, beckoning Bracken and Hayden to follow. Shaking with emotion, Bracken got to her feet. Her broad face was alive with emotions of happiness, sorrow and disbelief but as always her eyes remained dry. As she went to leave, Hayden caught her arm. 'Mistress Bracken,' he asked with concern, 'are you sure you're able to cope with all that has happened here?'

She shook her head, too filled with emotion to meet his eyes. 'I don't know,' she answered in an unsure tone. 'So much to take in. My heart can't conceive all of it. I am numb with shock.' She thought for a moment. 'But if it is true, then it is what the Ley has destined for me and I will meet it. It's why I did not perish.'

Awkwardly she cast an uncertain glance in the direction of Prince Ion. The dishevelled dwarf partially acknowledged his granddaughter and burbled something nonsensical about dinner, his wife and great pain. It struck Bracken sadly that, despite his obvious joy at her return, Prince Ion seemed incapable of engaging in logical conversation for any great length of time. She wondered, if given the chance to present herself before the queen of the dwarves, she might be able to heal the pain brought about by her birth. Despite the truth of who she was being finally known to her, what filled her heart with the most joy was the news that Ryders had arrived in Kelhalbon and that she might have her adopted family at hand to help her through this difficult and emotional time.

Together she and Hayden followed the loyal vizier out of Prince Ion's chambers back on to the suspended, metal staircase that led to the vast grotto below. As they exited, they could hear the warm air of the cave already filled with the excited grunts and chattering of dwarf voices as the news spread about their princess's return. Toil and craftworks ceased as eager black eyes swivelled towards Bracken, rough, stubby fingers pointing her out. As Bracken shied from this sudden attention, Hayden's eyes were drawn towards the unusual group of newcomers standing in the centre of one of the great stone plateaus. An odd creature, like a giant black iron scarab, crouched on the ground near to them, being intently prodded and examined by several curious dwarves. Another peculiar creature, resembling a sturdy, scaly-skinned pony, paced anxiously about, muttering outraged complaints in a husky, effeminate tone. But neither of these strange sights held Hayden's attention when his eyes fell upon the human visitors to the dwarves' kingdom.

Chapter 29

Ac-Nu

Following the violent attack by the threatening, beetle-like Golem, the world seemed to be a strange and powerful place for Petronia. Obviously, she was very aware of the intensely vulnerable situation she found herself in, sheltering halfway up a snowy mountain in the company of a physically weak prince and his semi-hysterical Equile steed. The onslaught of the mysterious metal beast should have left her even more afraid but overpowering it in such a remarkable way, by speaking no less, left her feeling curiously strengthened, if somewhat shaken and confused. The words to stop the murderous beast had slipped so easily from her tongue and had such power in them, Petronia could hardly believe that they came from her broken and mute throat. Even after their forceful echo had quelled to silence, she could still feel the source of their magic residing deep inside her heart and mind, like a still, dark pool of black water in some hidden chamber of her body, waiting to rise mystically with the tide of her will. It was a sinister force, but strangely one she did not fear as it felt as much part of her as her own hands or thoughts.

In the damp chill of their cave shelter, Petronia made a bed for herself on the icy ground and lay, half curled on her side, facing the now dormant Golem and trying to make sense of the new abilities that were awaking within her. As she studied the strange marks engraved on its glossy, metal shell through half-closed eyes, she could feel a gentle tug of connection between the creature's mechanical inner workings and her own silent thoughts, as if the beast had somehow been brought to life by some detached part of her soul. Weariness weighed down her body and in that docile, almost hypnotised state between wakefulness and slumber, she idly tried reaching out dull, silent commands of movement to the automaton. In the half light of the cave, Petronia swore she could see a thin, coiling band of dark shadow worming out from her form to that of the Golem and witnessed its spidery legs and antennae quiver with movement. It was all too strange though, too frightening and unfathomable and soon she ceased this exercise, allowing herself to drift into an exhausted sleep.

She awoke the next morning, her body bitterly cold and stiff but with a sense of relief just to have survived the night, and a hunger both mental and physical to move on and find some security in this strange place. Her first thoughts were of her sickly companion who she now knew, much to her disbelief, was a royal prince. Her heart lurched with fear upon rolling over and seeing his still form, curled in a tight unmoving ball beneath his cape, with only his mousy hair visible to the bright, cold sunlight. Terrified he might have perished in the low temperatures of the night, she pulled back the mantle from his colourless face and shook him abruptly, grunting as loudly as her broken voice could muster to arouse him. His face was as white and chilled as the snow that drifted around the cave entrance and his delicate, almost girlish features were tinted a worrying shade of blue. He did not stir at first and all Petronia's frantic motions did were to wake Phebus who was slumbering next to him.

Startled at being awoken so suddenly and alarmed by his master's deathly appearance, the nervy beast started to noisily lament and yell accusations of murder at poor Petronia and it was these cries that finally awoke the catatonic prince. Unable to move through numbing cold and agonising spasms, he remained huddled and quaking for a long time while Phebus pressed his heavy, warm flanks against his slight body and Petronia rifled through the crystals on her belt to find one that might ease his suffering. In one of her leather pouches she found a red-green fragment of bloodstone that seemed to pulse and emulate heat and thrust it into Aarold's numb hands. He fingered it shakily, his skin quickly absorbing the soothing Ley-sent warmth as it flowed up his arms and into the rest of his body like a bath of steaming water. Soon his muscles began to relax, allowing him to sit up and shuffle close to the fire Petronia had rekindled, although his wasted leg remained bent and knotted beneath him for some time.

As Phebus fussed over him like a mother hen and Petronia looked on in concern, Aarold emptied bottles, pouches and phials from his satchel and began mixing together a number of powders and potent-smelling potions to form a slimy, dark blue brew which he gulped down with a grimace. A few moments later, the colour began to return to his cheeks, his breathing grew deeper and within the hour his withered leg had relaxed enough for him to straighten it. Petronia's relief grew as she witnessed Aarold's health slowly return and by mid-morning he declared he felt well enough to travel although Phebus would have to carry him as the cold made it difficult for him to bear his own weight. Petronia had the feeling that Aarold was trying very hard to play down the damaging effect the night in the icy cave had had on him and felt both admiration and concern. She knew too well the prideful tricks you played on yourself and others when you bore an impairment, making out it barely affected you, even when it caused you pain and anguish. It would have been easy for her to show great compassion for his health, she was, after all, growing very fond of him, but guessed it would wound him even more to have her make a fuss. It was best to let him wait until he felt strong enough to continue their journey and then keep a watchful eye on him as they did so.

When Aarold felt strong enough to journey onwards, they collected their meagre possessions together and prepared to go on their way. Aarold mounted Phebus's broad back, wrapping his cloak tightly around his form to muffle out the clawing chill, while Petronia walked close at his side, the weighty iron Golem cradled awkwardly in her arms. Both Aarold and Phebus were baffled as to why she insisted on bringing the hateful automaton that had attacked them and Petronia did not blame them for feeling wary. It did seem, on the surface, a foolhardy thing to do when there was the real possibility that it might spring to life and continue its murderous campaign. As strange as it was Petronia felt a strong connection to the dark machine, as if something hidden within its workings was twinned with part of her soul. She felt that it belonged to her somehow and was unwilling to abandon it before she fully knew what it was.

*

Before they set out, while Aarold rested and recovered his strength, Petronia took the time to examine the Golem closely, studying the delicate joints of its legs and weapons and the strange carved scrolling over its shell. These things were completely unfamiliar to her and she felt that it was something deeper, hidden in among the cogs and wheels, that her newly awakened senses were battling to understand. Mustering all her will, she timidly leant close and forced a dull, whispered sound from her twisted vocal cords. The legs and pincers of the Golem seemed to tremble slightly with the reverberation of this sound, like an animal stirring quietly in its sleep, but it made no further action. Nevertheless, this minute response confirmed Petronia's notion that she did have some command over it even if she was unsure how this came to be.

*

They did not venture back out into the snowy tundra of the mountains, but instead set off deeper into the cave mouth following Aarold's theory that they might be near Kelhalbon, Kingdom of the Dwarves. Petronia could not help feeling a certain amount of doubt about this notion; being a naïve village girl she did not truly know if dwarves existed or where they could be found if they did. Even if they were real, by Phebus's grumbling account they were brutal and violent, and she did not feel keen on meeting one. Still, the cave was relatively warm and dry and Petronia supposed it was safer for Aarold's fragile physical state to stay out of the biting wind for as long as possible.

To begin with, she saw nothing strange or unnatural about the tunnel but after some time wandering through the gloom, a faint orange glow in the distance indicated that there was fire and possibly life within the heart of the caverns. With both apprehension and eagerness they moved towards it to discover the light came from a fiery torch mounted on a large ornate bracket high on the wall. This sign of civilisation spurred them onwards, now reassured that Aarold's assumption about dwarves had been correct. Away from the bitter chill of the outside world, the tunnels gradually became more maintained, reminding Aarold of the passageways of his palace home more than any structure of nature. Brightly gleaming crystals of vibrant emerald and purple protruded in angular spikes from the smooth, dark wall, making the musty air full of the active buzz of the Ley to Petronia's newly opened mind. It filled her with hope and excitement and no longer afraid she eagerly hurried on.

Suddenly, their path was barred by a massive barrier of thick metal, fixed firmly across the passage. The door was at least twelve-feet high, fashioned of grim, cool iron with no visible bolts, handles or hinges, just a vast sheet of unforgiving metal. Ever the curious scholar, Aarold dismounted and after examining the solid portal, decided they had no other choice but to knock and hope for a response. Phebus's scales practically turned green with fear at the notion, but Petronia and Aarold braced themselves and drummed firmly on the polished surface of the metal, their blows ringing out surprisingly loudly in the empty, silent space of the caves. There was a heavy clunking of grinding metal and the vast barrier slipped with silken ease into a hidden slot within the cave wall, revealing the immense and imposing figure of a towering dwarf clutching a thick mace the size of a small tree. This awesome sight was simply too much for Phebus and the overawed Equile passed out on the spot, leaving Aarold and Petronia to strengthen their nerves and face the guard alone.

It was times like this when Aarold wished he was more like his father but, swallowing his quaking terror, he drew himself up to his full height and explained in his most chivalrous and polite manner who they were. To their surprise, the dwarf guard was most congenial. She examined Aarold's royal signet ring and the multicoloured robes that marked Petronia as an apprentice to the Ley, and once assured of their identities bid them welcome. Once Aarold managed to bring his trusty Equile friend out of his nervous swoon and reassured him they were in no danger, the party was led to the great hall at the heart of Kelhalbon.

Petronia marvelled at the beauty and size of the mighty chamber. Her wonder, however, had been suddenly transformed to joy as amid the intricate bridges and metal pathways of the land of the dwarves she caught sight of Hayden, her dear brother. All that she had felt over the past few days, her fear for this strange, new environment, her awakening emotions for the young prince, even the powerful and dark ability growing within her, seemed to vanish in a mighty flood of relief as she heard him call her name.

Moments later, they were hugging each other tightly, neither quite believing that they had found their sibling alive and well in such a strange and alien world.

Hayden held her face between his hands and kissed her tear-stained cheeks.

'Petronia!' he wept with happiness. 'Dear Pet. You're alive!'

Unable to contain her excitement at seeing him, Petronia let out a squeal of joy, peppering his face with kisses until he begged her to calm down.

Beaming, he took in her joyous visage. Her multicoloured gown was stained and torn, her hair matted and her face pale and weary but none of this mattered. All that counted was that the sister who he had begun to fear had perished in the battle at Goodstone had been delivered back to him. 'My sister,' he breathed, 'I never thought I'd see you again. Tell me, you're unharmed?'

Eagerly Petronia nodded, her fingers trembling as they tried to form her silent language, relief swelling that now she was at last back with someone who she could converse with clearly. Her phrases were stilted as she did not know how to explain so many of the strange and wondrous things that had occurred since they had parted.

'I am fine, Hayden, I am well. I have come so far; the Ley has taken me so far and showed me so much. But It kept me safe, Brother, through it

all and showed me what I had to do. I want to tell more but I can't. I don't know how.'

She clasped her hands tightly together, unable to form any more words, but Hayden could see the joy and relief in her eyes. 'It's all right, Petronia, it's all right. You don't have to say anything. We're back together and that's all that matters.'

'Petronia?' the timid voice broke into the joyous reunion. She glanced round to see Aarold hobbling shyly towards her. 'Is that your name? At last!' He grinned triumphantly and blushed as she rushed from her brother's side to gently take hold of his arm and usher him forward.

Both of the men watched as Petronia excitedly gestured at Aarold as she tried to explain who he was. Slowly, Hayden translated her proud messages. 'She is saying, you are her dear friend, that you met her on her journey, that you have been kind and helped her while we've been apart. She also says that you are... no I don't believe you.' Hayden frowned in disbelief. 'She says you are a prince!'

Aarold flushed scarlet and lowered his eyes. 'It is true,' he said with a modest nod, 'I am Prince Aarold, heir to the throne of Geoll.'

Overawed to be suddenly in the presence of his sovereign, Hayden bowed in reverent respect. 'Your Majesty,' he gushed, 'I am honoured to be in your company.'

Aarold shifted uncomfortably and leant on his stick. It felt odd to be treated as royalty again and made him recall the cosseted protection he had endured back in the palace. 'Please,' he begged, 'do not stand on ceremony. It is I who should pay homage to your sister. She is a most remarkable woman and noble Ryder. She has saved my life no less than three times since we met and I cannot go far enough to express my fondness and thanks.' He gave Petronia a shy smile which made her cheeks grow red with pride and embarrassment.

Hayden also felt his chest swell at the prince's words. He had been acutely fearful of his sister's ability to take care of herself without him but now he saw that she had been more than capable of protecting not only herself but the young prince.

'*Excuse* me!' A nasal cry attracted their attention and Aarold looked round to see Phebus eyeing the assembled dwarves with wary disdain. 'Yes, my friend here is indeed royalty and as such we would like to see a person of appropriate authority, do you understand?'

A concerned dwarf shuffled towards the agitated Equile, his hand extended in greeting, and muttered something calming in Dwarfish. Outraged, Phebus snorted loudly and backed away from him. 'Keep your filthy hands to yourself, you great grubby plebeian!' he declared, glaring at the dwarf's soot-stained fingers. 'Are you in some office of note? I don't think so!'

Hurriedly Bahl managed to cut a path towards the assembled group, Bracken trotting closely behind her. Petronia let out a cry of recognition when she saw her fellow apprentice Ryder and ran to greet her as Bahl swept towards Aarold and Phebus with a respectful bow.

The Equile extended his long neck and gave the dwarf vizier's garment a suspicious sniff. 'Are you the leader of these motley troglodytes?' he asked tartly. Aarold gave him a sharp shove to remind him of his manners. 'I apologise for my friend,' he smiled politely; 'our journey has been a long and arduous one and he is extremely tired and emotional.'

Bahl gave both Aarold and Phebus an understanding smile. 'Of course, the mountains are a cruel environment for those not familiar with them. All of you are our most honoured guests and shall be treated as such. I am Bahl, Steward of Kelhalbon. This is a night of celebration, for our long absent Princess Bracken has returned to us at last. It would bless the feast if the heir of Elkric, a noble Ley Ryder and a member of the learned race of Equiles would sup with us.'

Phebus's mood at once changed from indignation to contentment and he gave his horny plume a vain shake. 'Well,' he breathed lightly to Aarold, 'this is more like it. Did you hear her, dear boy, the learned race of Equiles! Finally, someone who appreciates my species' intellect!'

Petronia looked at Bracken in amazement, astounded at what Bahl had said. '*Is this true?*' she signed, open-mouthed. Gazing at the signet ring bonded to her finger, Bracken grinned, barely able to believe the truth herself. 'She's right, I guess,' she shrugged happily, 'although

I've barely had time to come to terms with it myself. My mother was apparently the daughter of the queen of the dwarves!'

Stepping forward, Petronia clasped Bracken's hands and planted a congratulatory kiss on her cheek.

Meanwhile, a short distance away, an interested group of dwarves had begun to form around the strange, metal Golem Petronia had brought with her. The skilled craftsmen and mechanics were babbling animatedly in Dwarfish until at last one of them motioned for Bahl to join them and examine the strange item. The wise vizier approached the motionless automaton and crouching down cast her eyes intently over the markings on its shell. Noticing the commotion, Aarold awkwardly made his way between the tightly crowded dwarves to where the Golem lay.

'It attacked us,' he informed Bahl, gazing nervously at the tightly closed pincers, 'ambushed us as we made camp in a cave on the mountainside. Mistress Petronia bravely managed to fight it off and disarm it. I guessed it might be some kind of Dwarfish mechanical guard.'

Bahl grunted thoughtfully and lowered her head to peer beneath the strange creature. 'You are knowledgeable for one of such few years, Your Highness,' she told him sullenly. 'It indeed shows the signs of dwarf metalwork but I haven't personally witnessed any of our smiths designing or working on such a peculiar item.' She looked up from the Golem and, raising her arm in the air, called out in a single short utterance. The crowd parted and the imposing, muscular form of a towering dwarf stepped forward. He was clothed in a kilt of heavy, closely woven metallic fabric with a thick girdle from which was suspended various tools and blades. Two more baldrics crossed over his broad, powerful chest, holding even more hammers and chisels. He nodded respectfully at Bahl who then proceeded to issue some instructions in Dwarfish, gesturing at the Golem.

When she had finished speaking, he stooped over and with surprisingly delicate fingers, picked up the dark-shelled automaton and carried it off with him back into the crowd. Bahl nodded satisfied and turned back to the humans. 'Tunk is one of our most skilled mechanics,' she informed them, 'and has an acute talent for understanding the origins and workings of all machines. If any dwarf can say what this strange creature is it will be Tunk.'

She smiled graciously and uttered some words in Dwarfish to the assembled throng who straight away began to disperse to prepare for the feast. 'But this is a time for celebration and such things can wait a few hours while we welcome our princess. Our guests must be allowed to bathe before we dine. Rett will escort the men to the spa pools while I will attend to Mistress Bracken and our esteemed apprentice Ryder Petronia.'

The dwarf who Bracken and Hayden had first encountered on awakening in Kelhalbon shuffled towards them excitedly and with a reverent bow in the direction of Bahl and Bracken, beckoned to Hayden, Aarold and Phebus to follow him. Hayden was reluctant to be parted from his sister so soon after their reunion, but soon found himself being ushered along one of the many long stone corridors that led off the main chamber. Soon he, the prince and the Equile found themselves in a low-ceilinged cave filled with clouds of warm, pungent steam. As his vision became accustomed to the foggy atmosphere, Hayden discovered that Rett had led them into some kind of subterranean bathhouse. Several large pools, each one big enough to comfortably accommodate around five dwarves, bubbled and steamed with naturally heated water from some underground spring. A broad, iron bench curled around the edge of the chamber so that visitors who had bathed could sit peacefully and enjoy the relaxing effects of the hot air. A number of dwarves were already enjoying the spa, some submerged neck deep in the simmering water like great, grey walruses while others reclined leisurely on the benches, chatting and joking in their gravelly, monosyllabic language and slapping their shoulders and limbs with long, thin-bristled wire brooms.

Rett motioned that Hayden and Aarold should disrobe and wash. Tentatively, Hayden removed his clothes and plunged into the foaming pool. The water was scalding hot at first, making him cry out with shock, but soon his body grew accustomed to the temperature and he found that the aches and tiredness of his long journey soon ebbed away in the heat and were gently massaged by the bubbles. The pool was incredibly deep, having been made for lofty dwarf physiques and Hayden had to tread water to keep afloat while Aarold remained clinging warily to the edge as Rett gently supported him beneath the shoulders with one broad hand, like a mother bathing an infant. The water was cloudy like diluted milk, with a sulphuric odour that betrayed the presence of earthly minerals and Aarold found the intense heat and movement of the waters relaxed the painful twinges in his wasted leg. Grateful of this release, he kicked out gently, reclining against the pool's rocky side and wiggled his toes. Phebus, after some suspicious dithering and muttering about being boiled alive like a prize ham, finally braved a separate pool from the humans, finding it to be quite pleasurable. Submerged with only his long, black face showing, he wallowed languidly, droplets of water trickling down his shiny hide, his eyes glowing scarlet through the mist.

When the moist temperature got too much for them, they climbed out into the seemingly chilly air, drying themselves on vast woollen towels the size of ship sails. Rett then took up one of the long, coarse-looking wire brushes and pantomimed how they should beat themselves with its bristles. After much frantic signalling, Hayden and Aarold finally made the dwarf understand that the spiked wire would not benefit their human flesh the same way it did hardier dwarf skin. Phebus though, with his leather, tough scales, announced that he was happy to, 'indulge in the local custom, for etiquette's sake' and allowed Rett to briskly pat and scrub his sides and flanks. Much to Aarold's surprise, his normally sensitive companion declared the experience, 'highly stimulating' and said it had managed to dislodge a number of dead scales that had been irritating him.

When he had completed Phebus's massage, Rett vanished from the spa only to return a few moments later with fresh garments for Hayden and Aarold to wear. He presented them with two lengths of strange, pale, metallic cloth that appeared to be woven out of spun silver. Carefully he demonstrated how they were to be worn. The robes were meant to be wrapped around the waist before being hoisted over one shoulder but due to the fact that the men, Aarold in particular, were considerably smaller in stature than most dwarves there was a great deal of excess fabric which had to be folded, knotted and gathered to make the robes suitable. Rett was most helpful, providing them with a number of delicately decorated brooches and pins to fasten the unwanted pleats until both Aarold and Hayden found themselves suitably garbed. They then left the spa, along with Rett and Phebus, to return to the Great Hall where the feast was already underway.

Immense tables of black and silver metal had been placed on the stone plateaus, around which dwarves sat talking, eating and drinking. Great sides of roasted meat, goat, wild boar and bear, were served on mighty platters along with their carefully prepared entrails which, like the Ryders, the dwarves ate raw. Numerous varieties of lichen and mushrooms filled bowls as big as bathtubs as well as loaves of strange, coal-black bread, the size and firmness of anvils.

Rett guided them along bridges and pathways until they reached the plateau where Bahl, Prince Ion, Petronia and Bracken were seated. Hayden moved towards the table to take a seat next to his sister but stopped dumbstruck when his eyes fell upon Bracken. No longer did she resemble the wild-haired, ungainly apprentice of the Ley that had accompanied him through the woods. Her multicoloured robe of rainbow patches had been replaced with a finely tailored gown fashioned from a gleaming fabric of gold and bronze thread. A thick, silver girdle of swirling knots circled her waist, accentuating her womanly figure and forcing her to extend her back rather than slouch. The dress was cut away at the elbows and neck to reveal her smooth, strong forearms and softly curved cleavage and the grey shadows of veins that hung across her flesh like lacy cobwebs seem to merge with the pallid, almost translucent quality of her skin giving it a nameless delicate hue: somewhere lingering between ice blue, snowy white and polished silver. The locks that normally hung in a coarse, crinkled mass over her shoulders had been teased and plaited into countless, chainlike braids and looped in perfect overlapping coils around her head like one of the intricate metal decorations that adorned the bridges and stairways. Her mother's ring still encircled the strong fleshy finger of her left hand, casting odd reflections of jewelled colour across her pale flesh. Dressed in such a manner, in metals and crystals formed by the genius craftsmen of Kelhalbon, Hayden could truly see the Dwarfish splendour of the girl's nature. She possessed a unique beauty, powerful and glittering.

Seeing her brother, Petronia beckoned him to sit between her and Bracken. Hayden did so, as Aarold and Phebus took their places alongside the Prince Consort and his vizier. 'Bracken,' he breathed, 'you look, you look beautiful.'

Bracken's silvery skin flushed dark crimson as she lowered her eyes. 'Thank you, Master Hayden,' she murmured. 'The gown was my mother's, I am told. She wore it when she was a child. I am a lot smaller in stature than she apparently.'

Ignoring his granddaughter's words, Prince Ion stretched a shovel-like hand across the table and tore half the ribcage from the blackened goat carcass that rested before them, shoving it unceremoniously into his jowly maul with a slurping crunch of shattered bones. Bahl gestured to the dishes laid before them.

'Please,' she said, above Ion's grunts and belches, 'eat, all of you. The meat and bread are nourishing for all stomachs, although I would advise our human guests to avoid the fungi as it is poisonous to your constitutions. However, we consider it quite a delicacy and I hope that our Equile guest will sample some. It is one of the foods common to the herds in his homeland.'

She offered a large bowl of ominous-looking, black capped mushrooms to Phebus who sniffed them carefully before taking a small portion in his beak. 'Oh yes, indeed!' he remarked, greedily knocking several of the larger vegetables into his bowl. 'Reminds me of my foalhood; haven't had these in decades. You're really missing out, Aarold dear boy. Who would have thought dwarves were such amicable hosts? I pride myself in admitting when I'm wrong and I was wrong about dwarves. This place is a veritable oasis after the horrors we've had to face.'

Concerned, Hayden looked towards his sister and took her hand. 'Is that true, Petronia?' he asked gently. 'Oh, dear Sister, I regret any harm that might have befallen you during our time apart.'

Between hungrily devouring the coarse bread and roasted meat, Petronia carefully described her journey through the city of Veridium, how she encountered and saved Aarold and what they had seen at the lodge of the Ley Ryders. As she signed, Aarold filled in verbally for her, praising her courage and describing more fully all that had occurred. There was a great deal, however, of their sudden flight to the mountain and how Petronia had managed to overcome the thief and the Golem, that Petronia could not explain to her brother. The best that her simple finger language allowed her to do was to say that the Ley helped her but she did not feel that these words conveyed fully enough what she had achieved. If she had tried harder, Petronia could have probably found a way to say that she could feel a change beginning within her, altering her thoughts and spirits, that it was dark and powerful, but she knew how her brother feared for her and was reluctant to burden him before she herself could figure out what it all meant.

In turn, Hayden and Bracken spoke of their journey through the great forest, their encounter with the half-mad-half-wise blind hermit Emouchet and the astounding story revealed to them by Bahl and Prince Ion regarding Bracken's true parentage. As ever, the astute Prince Aarold took in every scrap of new information and when Bahl helped Bracken recall the affair of her mother, accompanied by much howling and lamenting from the woeful Prince Consort, his deep sapphire eyes grew bright with excitement.

'Forgive my interruption,' he interjected, replacing a bone on the plate before him, 'but are you truly saying that your father was King Elkric?'

Modestly Bracken shrugged and glanced at Bahl for confirmation. 'All the signs declare it so,' she said simply. 'From the accounts told by Princess Duun they did lay together.'

Ion squirmed his heavy rump agitatedly on his throne, making a mewling, babyish whine. 'Penn,' he lamented, blinking his squint, soulless eyes, 'it was a great betrayal!'

Predicting the start of a tantrum of grief, Bahl broke a chunk of coal-black bread the size of a small boulder from the loaf set before them and thrust it gently into the Prince Consort's hands.

'Here, Your Majesty,' she soothed as Ion began to gnaw at it between blubs. 'Console yourself.'

Revolted, Phebus sniffed, lowering his leathery eyelids. 'Philandering!' he snorted. 'Hardly civil subject matter for the dining table. Still, I am not in the slightest bit shocked, not where your brute of a father was concerned. How dear Neopi tolerated it I will never know. All the bellowing, fighting and whoring.' He paused to pull Aarold's plate away from him with his beak. 'I think you've had enough meat. Remember what your aunt says. It will inflame your bowel.'

Aarold tutted, embarrassed by Phebus's bluntness but not at all hurt by the character assassination of his father. He held no illusions about the nature of his reputation. 'I only raise the subject,' he continued delicately to Bracken, 'because if it is true, if Elkric was indeed your father, it would make us half-siblings.'

'Oh,' said Bracken, in a soft, slightly stunned voice. She had, of course, figured this fact out the moment Aarold announced who he was but like so much of the new information she was discovering about her family, it was taking her a while to process.

The waif-like prince beamed excitedly as he considered this new revelation. 'I always secretly wanted a sister,' he confessed, reaching out to gently touch Bracken's hand, 'a confidante and companion to converse with, and now fate has brought one to me, I feel blessed. Trust me, I swear, you will be honoured as the truest sister of the monarch of Geoll and have a high place in the court.'

A strange, almost unnerved expression passed over Bracken's face as if all that had happened since arriving at Kelhalbon was suddenly flooding over her, leaving her spirits dazed. Taking her goblet from the table, she gulped down several sips of water and took a moment to breathe deeply to compose herself before speaking. 'Please,' she said at last, 'truly, I want to say, to all of you, that I expect nothing. I am overwhelmingly grateful of the joyous news I have received in the last few hours, happy beyond words to learn I have grandparents and a brother to call family but as for accolades and titles, I expect none.'

She gently clasped her hands together as if in prayer, caressing the iridescent ring in her left hand. 'I was raised by Sister Amethyst and schooled in the ways and beliefs of the Ley Ryders. The 41st Dogma decrees a Ryder must not bear any mortal honours or earthly rewards for her work. I am aware, of course, that I am only an apprentice to the Ley but Its teachings are precious to me. The Ley has chosen to guide me back to my roots and I will gladly serve any and all duties you expect of me but I beg of you do not treat me with favour.'

An appreciative smile graced Bahl's face as Bracken spoke. 'Of course,' she uttered understandingly, 'we must not forget the intensity of the revelations disclosed to you this day. Your adopted culture is a most noble one and we dwarves hold the Sisterhood in the utmost respect. It would be unthinkable for us to ask anything that contradicts the lessons of the Ley.'

Bracken nodded thankfully but a thoughtful, almost melancholy expression passed over her face. Fingering the stem of her goblet, she uttered softly, 'I wish very much that Sister Amethyst could have accompanied me on my journey. I'm sure she would have been most proud and pleased to see me return to my natural family.' Instinctively, she reached to her breast to touch the purple pendant bearing her adoptive mother's Stone Name as she always did when feeling in need of comfort, forgetting that she had left it along with her other clothes and crystals in the chamber where Bahl had helped her dress before dinner.

The wise dwarf vizier's shiny, ebony eyes skimmed over the crystal-dotted walls and ceiling of the immense cavern as if she had suddenly caught sight of the delicately coloured trails of the Ley dancing over the stone. 'I am sure,' she said kindly, 'that the Ley will bring news of your return here to the Ryders and compel your guardian to come to Kelhalbon to celebrate with us.'

A strange chill ran over Bracken's skin, causing her to momentarily forget the happiness and excitement of being returned to her family and filling her with an inexplicable sensation of dread. She recalled

Amethyst's note and suddenly was overwhelmed by fear that she would never see her beloved guardian again. Straight away she chided herself for letting such a selfish gloomy thought intrude on such a momentous occasion. Bahl was right, the Ley would reunite them when the moment was right, just as it had Hayden and Petronia.

The feast continued for some hours, with much revelry and celebration. When everyone had eaten their fill and the remainders had been cleared away, a number of male dwarves retreated to their workshops to retrieve various automated musical clockwork organs and percussion machines with intricate pipes, hammers and finely tuned strings. These were carefully wound and set to work so that they emitted tune after rhythmic tune of complex percussive music for the assembly to enjoy. Alongside these ingenious instruments, there appeared delicately crafted automatons in the form of birds and stylised human figurines, fashioned from brass and silver, their eyes and joints adorned with glittering gems. As the music played, the guests watched in wonder as vibrations of Ley power rippled over the polished bodies, imbuing them with energy and movement so they danced and whirled rhythmically to the melodies of the organs. The orange fire of the torch flames high above glinted their blazing light on the smooth, metal panels of the dwarves' creations as they cavorted. Not even Prince Aarold who had had many entertainments brought before him in his own palace to distract him from his ill health, had ever witnessed a show quite as wondrous and enchanting.

While her companions remained enthralled by the dwarves' entertainment, Bracken sat quietly, half listening to the music whilst going over in her head the story she had been told of how her mother had fallen pregnant with her. The Ryders had taught her that no momentous event or discovery happened by chance, each was a gift from the Ley to drive you onward towards merciful deeds, and Bracken was sure that her return to Kelhalbon at this time was not by mere chance. She must be here for a reason.

Reaching across, she lightly touched Bahl's elbow to gain her attention. 'Mistress Bahl,' she asked softly, 'may I speak with you?'

The striking dwarf vizier turned in her seat. 'Yes, Your Majesty,' she replied with a slight tilt of her head. 'How might I be of service?'

Bracken flushed at being addressed so formally. 'Please, Bracken is just fine. It's just that I've been thinking about what you and my grandfather told me about the circumstances of my birth and well, I think that I would very much like to speak with my grandmother, if it could be arranged.'

A troubled look graced Bahl's face and her smooth, domed forehead crinkled into a deep frown. Worriedly, she clasped the stem of her goblet and blinked as if trying very hard to comprehend what Bracken had asked.

Anxiety bubbled in Bracken's chest and she wondered for a moment whether she had done the right thing. Swallowing hard, she concentrated on forming her thoughts as reasonably as she could. 'I understand this may not be possible,' she continued; 'you have explained that she is sick, Ac-Nu I believe you said, and that she felt greatly betrayed by what happened with my mother, but if I could I would like to show her that I wish only goodwill to her and her people.'

She felt a sudden tight grasp on her wrist and turned to face Prince Ion who had frantically seized hold of her with a mewling, terrified cry. Looking into her face with his soulless, harrowing black eyes he whimpered fearfully, 'Understand, child, our queen, my Penn, she is Ac-Nu, the darkness, the hate, both within and without. There is so little. All is anger, all is stone.' He clawed at his face with his free hand, tears leaking on to his sallow skin.

Bahl reached across and with her strong but gentle hand managed to prize Bracken's arm from her grandfather's terrified grip, tucking his hand safely back into the folds of his cloak. 'You were raised by humans,' she explained as she tended to Ion, 'therefore you cannot fully understand what Ac-Nu means. It is not a sickness, as your physicians might describe a sickness. The closest term I can use to explain in the common tongue is a mood, a state of not living but existing. A choice some dwarves make when they reject life but do not succumb to death.' She gave a heavy sigh as if even discussing Ac-Nu was exhausting.

Bracken looked thoughtful and Petronia thought that she could see in her face the same determined intellect that she had witnessed in her half-brother, Aarold. 'But, as I understand, you dwarves share the same belief and faith in the Ley as Ryders,' she continued thoughtfully. 'I was taught that the right crystal, the right influence of the Ley, can sooth any grief or ill. I cannot claim to have much skill in crystal work but I do believe I was brought back here by the Ley for a reason. Perhaps the right words from her kin might have some effect.'

Bahl's thick lips twitched slightly and she looked almost amused by the idea. 'Such an altruistic notion could only come from a soul raised by Ryders not dwarves,' she said diplomatically. A desperate whimper issued from Prince Ion on hearing Bracken's words and he shifted animatedly in his seat. 'Bahl,' he cried excitedly, 'might it be true, my Penn, might she be returned to us?' Sighing wearily, Bahl shook her head as if she had suddenly created a lot of troublesome work for herself. 'My lord,' she uttered patiently, 'you know as well as I the nature of Ac-Nu. I wouldn't want to cause the queen or anyone else any heartache or pain. Things are, sadly, as they are.'

Prince Ion's whole demeanour had altered drastically in the last few moments and he looked, for the first time since they had met him, alive and engaged. Leaning his full bulk on the arm of his throne, he urgently motioned to Bahl with his thick hands. 'But they aren't as they were, are they, Bahl? Duun's child has returned and she has been raised by Ryders. They have skills. Who knows how my Penn will respond? If the Ley grants us the smallest chance.'

Bahl looked at the desperate Prince Consort with doubtful, almost pitying eyes. 'But my lord,' she said warily before continuing her remark in level, emotionless Dwarfish. Vizier and Royal Consort continued with their heated discussion in their short-phrased, guttural language for several minutes while the baffled humans struggled to follow what was happening. Prince Ion was adamant on some matter while Bahl seemed warily cautious. Finally, the vizier seemed to relent in her argument and with a placating nod to the prince turned to Bracken.

'Lady Bracken, guests, would you excuse the prince and myself? We have matters to attend to regarding Queen Penn.' Her voice sounded flat, almost angst-ridden. Standing up, she eased her hand beneath Prince Ion's broad arm and with much grunting and heaving hoisted him out of his chair. The prince belched unapologetically and still clinging to Bahl for support trudged away in the direction of a nearby table to converse eagerly with several other dwarves.

Once they had left, Hayden, Petronia and Aarold turned quizzically to Bracken. 'What made you ask about your grandmother?' Hayden questioned curiously. 'Surely if you were to be brought before her, Mistress Bahl would have arranged an audience the moment it was proven who you were. From the story she told, it doesn't appear that Queen Penn has any longing to be reunited.'

A look of uncertainty crossed Bracken's face as she nervously brushed the glossy material of her skirt. 'Perhaps,' she murmured softly before adding, 'but she still remains my relative and I can't believe the Ley would have placed me here and not have me attempt to heal old wounds. Time and the Ley are always moving on and hurt eases given time. It is a gift of the Ley that It moves us past such things.'

Aarold nodded wisely in agreement at this sentiment. 'Well said, dear Sister,' he uttered affectionately, reaching out to brush her hand in reassurance. 'While it is true that I know little of the teachings of those who raised you, in my own education I have come to the conclusion that tactful words and kind motives can put aside much ill-will, especially where family is concerned.'

Bracken regarded him intently. 'Did you learn that from our father?' she asked earnestly, curious to hear any anecdote that might inform her of the character of her parents.

Snorting in scoffing disbelief, Phebus opened his beak to give his considered opinion on the late king's manner of diplomacy but was silenced by a knowing glance from his master. Aarold took a sip from his goblet before answering Bracken as tactfully as he dared. 'I was fortunate in that father supplied me with many scholars learned in the arts of rhetoric and peacekeeping,' he said, being careful not to add that this was only a secondary consideration for Elkric who would have much preferred his son to have the ability to learn the arts of war rather than peace.

Seated beside her brother, Petronia considered her fellow apprentice Ryder's situation and as her thoughts lingered on the dwarf queen, she experienced an unnerving surge of energy as the Ley ran through her body, chilling, black and foreboding. Even holding the name Penn in her thoughts sent a shiver up her spine. Seeing her shudder, Hayden looked at his sister. 'What do you feel about Bracken's predicament, Petronia?' he asked.

She remained pensive for a moment, unwilling to inhibit any reunion Bracken might have with her lost family but unable to deny the ominous feelings in her heart. Finally, she made a simple, clear gesture, indicating that it was Bracken's choice alone and she had no view either way.

It was at that moment when the sound of swift, weighty footsteps announced that their host had returned. The group turned to see the lofty form of Bahl standing at the end of the table trying very hard not to look anxious or perturbed. An insincere smile of congenial politeness graced her thick, grey lips and her glossy, black pupils seemed to swim with a hundred troublesome issues and problems that were none of the present company's concern. Her posture was that of someone who had just lost a bitter argument but was still maintaining they were in the right. Prince Ion was nowhere in sight.

'Your Maj-, sorry, I mean Lady Bracken,' she said, attempting to display a smooth and untroubled tone which was difficult as her voice was gravelly at the best of times and she was clearly bothered about something. 'I can inform you that arrangements have been made and you may now have an audience with our queen.'

Bracken blinked, her confidence in meeting her royal grandmother wavering slightly. 'Right now?' she asked uncertainly.

Bahl replied with a curt nod before adding in an almost hopeful tone, 'That is, of course, unless you have changed your mind.' Swallowing her fear, Bracken got to her feet, brushing the creases from her shimmering skirt. 'No, no of course not, I would be delighted to deliver my best wishes in person.'

A sneer of disappointment, almost embarrassed disgust crossed Bahl's features before they returned to their usual stoic expression as she beckoned Bracken to follow her. 'Very well,' she sighed, 'I will take you to her. You must come alone. I'm sure your friends will understand the delicacy of the situation.'

Bracken suddenly felt a little overwhelmed by the idea of presenting herself to the wrathful queen alone. Glancing at Hayden and the others, she asked timidly, 'Will not Prince Ion, my grandfather, be attending his wife?'

A strange, cold chuckle of irony issued from Bahl's mouth, humourless and knowing. Swiftly she raised her hand to her face to disguise this disrespectful gesture and recover composure. 'Prince Ion is at rest, Lady Bracken. The day has been quite emotional for him. I will be more than happy to address any questions you may have. Now if you will come with me.'

*

Turning on her heel, Bahl strode away with merely a quick glance over her shoulder to make sure Bracken was following. Leaving the others at the table, Bracken took a deep breath and uttering a prayer to the Ley to give her courage, gathered up the weighty skirts of her gleaming dress and walked swiftly after the vizier. She expected, perhaps, for Bahl to lead her back up some spidery staircase to a hidden chamber similar to the one in which they had met her grandfather, but instead the dwarf walked across to one of the many ornate bridges that spanned the wide cracks between the plateaus. Stopping, Bahl turned her attention to a small door in the side column that secured it to the stone floor. Opening it, she skilfully turned a wheel hidden inside. There was an almighty sound of machinery creaking and clanging to life and with a heavy shudder, the far end of the overpass lowered into the shadowy abyss before them to form a set of steps. Bahl peered into the inky blackness below almost fearfully and lifted a large torch down from a tree-like lamppost nearby to light their path. She seemed full of apprehension and

Bracken wondered whether it was Queen Penn she dreaded or whether there were other unnamed horrors lurking in the darkness. Bahl was tall and clearly stronger than most human warriors and Bracken puzzled at what could cause her hand to tremble as she held the flaming beacon.

The wary vizier turned towards her, a serious expression on her striking face. 'This is the way to Ac-Nu,' she informed Bracken bluntly. 'Stay close in sight of the torch and watch your step. The staircase is narrow and one false step could be perilous. You may use the chain rail as a guide but touch nothing else; there are many things in the ravine that can be deadly. Do you understand?' Earnestly, Bracken nodded and cautiously shuffled a little closer to the edge of the stairway.

With a sigh of resignation, Bahl held her torch out before her to illuminate the path ahead and began descending the narrow iron steps into the pit. Carefully, Bracken followed, not daring to dawdle more than a couple of paces behind, and gripped hold of the icy cold links of the rail as if something would snatch her away if she let go. The stairs beneath their feet were incredibly smooth, as difficult to walk on as a frozen lake or highly polished metal, and it took all Bracken's concentration and balance not to stumble. The orange fire flickered coldly off the wall nearby, revealing that it was studded with countless razor-sharp fragments of metal until it was barely possible to see the stone in between. The whole journey possessed a feeling of difficulty and foreboding as if the dwarves had designed the shaft to keep people from entering or, Bracken thought with a shudder, keeping whatever was down here from escaping. She puzzled that such a place, such a prison, could be the throne of a ruler. It seemed more like the realm of the damned.

'My grandmother chose to come here after my mother died?' she murmured in disbelief, gazing at the cruel edges of the spikes that littered the walls.

From behind, she thought she saw Bahl stifle a shiver. 'This is Ac-Nu,' she breathed mournfully, pausing to peer into the unforgiving darkness below. 'I tried to explain to you the best I could, Lady Bracken. But those who do not know Ac-Nu can never understand it and those who understand it have known little else. If a dwarf allows hurt and rage and sadness to consume them, it is what they become. Without hope, without Ley, they choose to dwell within a place where they can bathe in and nurse their poisonous emotions undisturbed.'

'That's horrible,' gasped Bracken feeling a pang of pity for her grandmother's plight. 'Don't you try to help them? Give them any succour?'

Wearily, Bahl hung her head and issued a bitter chuckle. 'It would do them no good,' she said darkly. 'Pity, reason, any emotion is only fuel to the blackness within them. They twist it so it supports their own fury and hate. You are too human, Lady Bracken. You sense the world as your father's race does, with a heart of flesh. A dwarf's heart is made of stone. It is why we live longer but can never sense the Ley.'

There was darkness in Bahl's words, as bitter and gloomy as the cavern through which they travelled, and it brought a disturbing chill to Bracken's heart. Gently she rested her hand on her own bosom and felt through the cold metallic fabric the dull, regular beat of her own pulse. She had heard the phrase *heart of stone* before, but only as a metaphor for people who were cruel and uncaring. What harsh gravitas there was in the knowing of having a core formed literally of rock that wavered little with emotion? The Ryders had always taught Bracken to cherish love, tenderness and compassion and it troubled her greatly to think that a great part of her lineage came from a people who possessed such a brutal mindset. Deep inside, did she too have such dark tendencies?

They journeyed deeper together, descending into the gloomy bowels of the earth, each step taking them further away from the light and sound of Kelhalbon, further from any sign of life or hope, as if they were entering some bleak and forgotten mausoleum. Bahl's blazing torch did little to illuminate the blackness that surrounded them, its dancing scarlet fire only lighting the area a few feet ahead. Bracken was suddenly aware that the metal stairs down which they had been travelling had long ago vanished, transforming somewhere along the way into crude stone steps hacked into the side of the cliff. It was as if all the proud craftwork that had been used to build the dwarves' kingdom had stopped here, fear and despondency forcing out any attempt to maintain or claim anything from the natural grottos. Peering at the towering walls, Bracken searched for any opening or sign that something was alive down here and in doing so noticed that the rock had taken on a very strange appearance. It looked almost soft: bulbous, fleshy ripples drooping and hanging over each other, like swollen, boneless corpses preserved in granite. Countless limbs, stomachs, chests, faces seemed to bulge semi-formed from the dark stone, grasping and twisting over each other in a trapped orgy of loathing and despair. Now and again, narrow, round holes pierced deep into the frozen waves of rock: dark, empty sockets that could be thought of as hating, black eyes had it not been for their hollowness. The chilling, motionless atmosphere pressed in like a smoky fog, threatening, almost violent, and Bracken knew that even the most skilled Ryder would not sense the faintest glimmer of Ley in this hateful place. A faint sound filled her ears, like white noise in the grave silence, heard and unheard, a hissing, muttering, burbling wordless whisper of rage and grief. Bracken now understood Bahl's unwillingness to lead her here: there was nothing of life in this pit, even death seemed too afraid to enter.

Raising her torch high above her head, Bahl turned in a semicircle, looking behind her to check that Bracken had not been left behind. A brief expression of relief crossed her face when she saw the nervous maiden standing just behind her.

'If I recall correctly, Queen Penn resides very nearby,' she told Bracken, her black eyes skimming over the wall. 'I will try and seek her out for you.'

Turning away, Bahl continued to search the bulging contours of the shadowy grey cliff face for the purpose of their journey. As she did so, she called out a hushed, throaty salute in Dwarfish which hung dull and un-echoing in the claustrophobic air, the heavy atmosphere seeming to greedily snatch the words the moment they left her lips. As her guide struggled to raise the attention of the hidden sovereign, Bracken gripped the cold chain rail and gazed fearfully up at the fleshy, heavy forms that towered above her, oozing like dusty wax over the stone. The more she looked upon them, the clearer she could make out individual bodies, lounging listlessly, seemingly unaware of their neighbours, pressed so close that their inert limbs and torsos had begun to grow together like a clod of soil pressed back into the boggy earth. As it became clear that the mass that formed the bedrock of the cliff was not stone but what remained of semi-living dwarf flesh, a lazy, heaving motion could be seen within it: a heavy, arduous undulation of despair and unrest, like a restless sleeper tossing in a fitful half-slumber, rippling over the wall of bodies in a wave of grief, emitting as it did so a terrible, low sound: rumbling, moaning, slurred words of morose nonsense.

Bracken gasped in horror and dismay as a segment of the mournful mass near by her opened up into a fist-sized gawping mouth that belched out a whining, heart-rending groan that chilled her soul. Fear and grief filled her heart to hear such a sound, and as these emotions welled within her Bracken believed she saw two narrow, greedy eyes peer from the folds of flesh and sorrow, hungry to create and devour more ill-feeling.

'Come.' Bahl's sharply official tone captured her attention from the wailing mass of sorrow and Bracken found her hand being taken from the guide rail as she was led forward a few steps. 'I have found your grandmother but we cannot stay long. This way.'

Carefully Bahl manoeuvred Bracken into position before a segment of wall and gestured towards it. Bracken gazed blankly at the bulbous shapes before her for a moment, unsure what she was meant to see when another undulation of raw discord trembled the wall and the shadows and forms shifted just enough so that her eyes could focus on an immense body pressed sideways, half absorbed into the bulk of the rock. The silhouetted head was dominated by a huge, hairless scalp, the smooth outline of which cracked into a singular, deep eye-socket, narrowing to a slit by a heavy brow above, which was forced down into a resolved scowl. A piggish snout with an indignantly flared nostril snorted angrily above a thick, sneering upper lip. The lower jaw jutted out slightly, revealing a collection of sharp but unevenly spaced fangs that protruded at unnatural angles. The skull dissolved into shapeless billows and cracked jowls that merged to become one with the enormous flabby shoulder and bicep that stuck out proud from the wall. The area that should have been her forearm and hand was clutched back into the deep creases of her coiled body, pressed tightly somewhere between the amorphous bulges that formed her breasts and belly. There were no legs, none that could be clearly defined of as legs anyway; the lower quarters of her body merged seamlessly into the stone that cocooned her foetus-like shape, like an immense maggot half encased in its chrysalis. Despite the appearance of being fossilised, twitches of heavy, furious movement contorted the queen's form irregularly the coiling flex of her muscular, trapped arm, as if she had been restrained from lashing out violently. Snarling groans and sighs trembled the curves of her torso as she breathed noisily and the almost constant recoil of her lips and grinding of fangs as she muttered and fumed in an inaudible tirade of cursing wrath, uttered intermittently in Dwarfish, aimed at no other audience but her own loathing. As she raged and complained, a thick river of steaming, oily black fluid poured like coiling smoke from her trembling maul and soulless eye-socket, staining the pale rock of her flesh like seeping tar before dripping and evaporating into the bitter darkness of the cave. Bracken watched this stagnant stream of vaporous loathing issue out from the craggy orifices in her grandmother's semi-visible face, at the inert body crushed with hate and anger into the rock and wondered how this being, barely a being in fact, this *thing* could be related to her. She wanted to feel reverence, respect, a connection, perhaps even love for her newly found family, but all she felt was fear.

Bracing herself, Bahl shifted as close as she dared to the seething figure enveloped by stone and dark emotion and addressed it in a clear, loud tone, as if her voice had to carry right into the core of the cliff to be heard. 'Queen Penn, with humble respect, will you speak with us?'

Another great shudder of crushing emotion shook through the weight of the wall, this time focusing mainly on the area that enclosed the queen's body. A fearful, grating growl, like rocks tumbling combined with the snarl of some beast, trembled the air as the body trapped within the wall moved into consciousness, tautly flexing her confined girth. The slit, pupilless eye glared open, burning its hateful glower at the intruders of her eternal hibernation and the maul gaped open with a snarling splutter of foul saliva.

'I am Queen Penn,' the fanged mouth bellowed in a hoarse and raspy growl of fury. 'I am wronged! Vengeance! I am the wounded mother of the foulest whore soiled by a worthless human maggot whose name is too vile to utter. Bring me vengeance!'

Every word, every utterance was filled with bubbling poison, vomited out from the gnashing, spitting rent in the harsh stone with a splutter of dark, hissing liquid and clawing gas. Bahl bristled slightly, caught by the onslaught of the wrathful tirade, but managed somehow to maintain her composure. 'Your Majesty,' she continued, her voice remaining remarkably steady, 'I wish to bring someone before you, someone who might move you to alter your nature. The Ley has brought the offspring of your noble bloodline back to Kelhalbon.'

The petulent queen muttered and spat something sinister and vicious-sounding in Dwarfish, her boorish features twisting into an even more hideous configuration of wrathful recollection. 'I had a daughter once,' she muttered slyly, seeming to not take any notice of what Bahl had said; 'little slut of filth she turned out to be, little human breeding whore! Not now though, gone, little piece of excrement expelled from my body, good! She's dead; is she dead? I hope she's dead.'

Bile and shock rose in Bracken's throat as she listened to her grandmother's profane utterances. She had been somewhat sheltered growing up in the citadel and, aside from the infrequent cursing of Rosequartz when she burned herself working in the forge, had never heard such coarse and offensive speech. What made it even worse was such foul and hateful language was used by Queen Penn about her own kin. It made Bracken question her eagerness to be presented before her.

Just as this severe doubt took firm hold of Bracken's mind, Bahl turned and beckoned her to step closer to the seething figure cocooned in the rock. 'She is aware of our presence,' she informed the wary girl. 'Now would be a good moment for you to say your piece, before she gets lost in melancholy again.'

Bracken was too terrified to move at first, paralysed by the inability to know how to address the raging queen; she stood, clinging to the cold metal of the banister. With a deep breath she summoned her dwindling nerves and shuffled timidly forward, past Bahl, into the arena of Queen Penn's awareness. She could feel icy, odorous puffs of the queen's black-tinted emissions coil around her as she got closer and shakily knelt down before the twisted, flexing mass of solid muscle and flesh, her genuflection brought more out of terror than respect.

Queen Penn contorted awkwardly in her snug cleft within the wall, her bullish neck straining as her head lolled to one side to regard the individual before her with irritable contempt. Her thick, bulbous lips moved slowly, glossy black with the strange and vile substances that issued from every orifice that indented the wall. With what seemed like immense effort she grunted three short words, oozing with disdain. 'Who. Are. You?'

Bracken clasped her hands together on the shimmering fabric of her skirt in an attempt to stop them trembling and swallowed hard to lubricate her numb vocal cords. She wondered for a moment whether this was how Petronia felt all the time, unspoken words bottled up tightly, crushed inside, imprisoned by a force, in Bracken's case fear, that robbed them of all sound. Somehow, through sheer will, she managed to speak, reciting her name and identity in a small, nervous whisper. 'Your Majesty, my name is Bracken of Goodstone and I am the ward of the Ley Ryder Amethyst.'

A moist, loud retch issued from Queen Penn's fang-like maul as if the very mention of the Ryders disgusted her. A thick globule of dark, oily ooze drooled lazily over her lower jaw, glittering malevolently for a brief second in the glow of Bahl's torch before slipping into a long, thick strand of liquid blackness that dissolved soundlessly into the gloom around them. 'Ley,' hissed Queen Penn with sluggish loathing, 'Ryders. They did nothing for me. Did not sooth my wounds or bring justice where I was wronged.' Her face creased with weighty rage and her globular, scowling countenance seemed to crush into her heaving bosom as another quake of woe echoed from her and the other despondent, half existing dwarves of Ac-Nu. Bracken's skin felt icy, more than ice cold in fact, it felt as if the darkness and the ill-will in the atmosphere was turning her to stone. It was a fearful thought and she dared not dwell on it for more than a few seconds.

The quake of despair subsided and once it had Queen Penn lifted her protruding brow to gawk down at Bracken with loathing. 'Who. Are. You?' she demanded again, in the same, effort-filled tone. It was as if her mind had been sent senile by rage, only choosing to seize on to and comprehend what fed its own anger and self-pity and dismissing anything not connected to her sorrow as irrelevant.

A strange feeling fell over Bracken's heart, as she knelt before her grandmother, that seemed to quell the terror within her. The memory that, even if Bracken could not feel it, the Ley existed, coupled with the acute realisation that nothing she said could possibly worsen the queen's condition any more than it already was, gave her courage. Raising her head, Bracken stared straight into the grimacing face of the dwarf queen and said in a steady tone, or as steady as she could muster, 'Your Majesty Queen Penn, my name is Bracken of Goodstone and I am your granddaughter. I am the child your daughter Princess Duun gave birth to after you expelled her from Kelhalbon.'

The end of her statement was lost, however, beneath the terrible sound that filled the cave. It started as a distant rumble, but quickly escalated into a deafening, chilling roar of incandescent fury that shook the thick atmosphere like the sudden crashing rush of a tsunami. Bracken crouched low and clung on to the outcrop that she was kneeling on in fear that the very force and fury of the bellow would snatch her up and throw her against the walls of the cavern. She felt Bahl's broad hand against her back and was sure that somewhere beneath the avalanche of sound, the vizier was urging her to leave this hate-filled place. But she could not bring herself to depart without completing her mission to explain herself to Queen Penn. Before her, the semi-shaped form of Queen Penn twisted and bucked with wrathful fury in her stony cradle. Her misshapen maul gaped open, spitting great droplets of odorous venom into the icy air. Her hideous features contorted with infuriated disbelief and somewhere, deep, deep within her pupilless pit of an eye, the malformed and damaged fragment of what remained of her soul burned coal red. Her massive bulk struggled, flexing and bulging with tautly restrained strength as if at any moment she would burst free from her rocky prison, but the sturdy wall of her own creation held her firm.

After what seemed like an age, the ghastly roar ebbed and died away, transforming into a string of slurred and wrathful curses. Once again, Bracken felt her heartbeat grow steadier and with trepidation she turned back towards Queen Penn who glared at her, the foulest depth of her lone, black eye socket glowing dull scarlet.

'You,' she spat, her fat lips and gritted teeth daubed a thick coating of hateful black residue, 'you smear, you little discharge. Do you know what my whore of a daughter did to me?'

Bracken felt a solid coldness armour her heart as she stared into the queen's loathing face. The cruel words stung like venom-tipped spears and it took all Bracken's mental resolve not to let them cause her harm. She recalled her childhood training in meditation and willpower and breathed in a slow steady rhythm, trying hard to imagine the goodness of the Ley flowing in and out of her, but in the kingdom of hatred and self-pity even the air she inhaled seemed intoxicated with fury. 'Yes, Your Majesty, I was told,' she began calmly.

Queen Penn's jaws snapped sharply open and a terrible roar of indignation, rasping with a dry heat so dense that it seemed to clog her throat, nearly drowned her with her own wrath. 'Listen!' she shrieked as Bracken cradled her head in her arms to protect herself from the heat and the noise. 'LISTEN TO ME! My daughter, ungrateful scourge, trollop, pervert. She wronged me, ME, who granted her life and existence. Her mother, her mistress, her queen. A pox on her rotting flesh for challenging my will. I am the fountain-head of royal dwarf blood, blood she sullied with her vile rutting with a creature not of her species. I hunger for justice!'

As she raged, each word oozing with loathing, the queen grew more and more agitated, her stony flesh juddering and trembling with constrained emotions. She seemed almost to enjoy recalling her betrayal, the hot rage within her building up to an orgasm of hate. Her unrelenting prison held her convulsing form firm as she babbled and cursed. Finally, her energy lulled once more and she sneered silently at Bracken's crouched form.

'Bastard,' she slurred in a low, despising whisper, 'little mongrel, filthy, dirty half-breed. What are you? Why haven't you dropped down dead? Why are you here?'

Bracken felt her breath catch like thick smoke in her chest as her reserve faltered and the loathing in her grandmother's voice stabbed deep into the loveless origins of her life. There were hot tears within, not in her eyes but in her mind and heart, black, burning and filled with a sinister darkness, tears that her body would not allow her to cry. She swallowed hard, pushing them down, down, down, as deep as she could, trying to find a hidden spot somewhere inside where they could be trapped.

'The Ley,' she breathed jaggedly, somehow hoping to gain strength by uttering the name of the force she deeply believed in but never felt. 'I believe the Ley brought me to Kelhalbon to mend the pain brought by my birth. I offer only good feelings of respect and compassion to you as your kin.'

A strange, smug grin contorted Queen Penn's craggy face like a toothy fissure opening up in the cliff face. 'So,' she breathed, gaseous bubbles of dark hatred seeping from between her fangs, 'you admit I was wronged, that I deserve vengeance for the foul sin of that dirty, deceitful harlot. Vengeance! Reprisal! Her foulness created you with that human swine.' She seemed to have reached some sort of peace for the briefest of moments but that instant passed as suddenly as it had come, shattered by another howling shudder of dark emotion quaking from the choir of warped stony bodies of Ac-Nu that surrounded them. Trails of odorous vapour billowed out from her throat, encircling her head like an unholy halo as another snarl of rage ripped through her form.

'Unworthy half-breed!' she shrieked, her bulging shoulder straining as she tried to loom over Bracken. Bracken scrambled back on to her heels to escape the queen's wrath but still the foul, intangible wickedness that coloured her breath and poured in a dripping torrent from her eye seeped over her. 'How dare you lie to me! I see you for the stinking traitor you are! You want my throne, my power. You have wormed your way back to usurp me. Never! I will rip your flesh from your bones! I shall crush your meaty inners to diamonds with my bare hands!'

She bellowed and snorted like a rabid boar caught in a snare. All around Bracken was noise, darkness and loathing in the cavern of Ac-Nu. More terrifyingly it bloomed within her own heart and thoughts, bubbling to the surface of her mind with notions of worthlessness, pain and loss. Through her grandmother's manic tirade, she heard her own voice scream 'No, I swear, I have no desire for your throne!'

Before her, the twisted visage of Queen Penn warped repulsively with blistering fury. Her shoulder and elbow jerked violently and it looked very possible that she could at any moment shatter her rocky bonds and rampage manically free. 'So you don't think you're worthy of my noble bloodline, do you? Ungrateful little bitch, fleshy human offspring! You are scum; you are nothing!'

Bracken felt such pain and grief well up in her chest that she thought she would burst. All she could see, feel and comprehend was rage and hurt that swallowed her up like a relentless sea. Then out of nowhere, she felt a pair of powerful, muscular arms seize her round her waist and drag her roughly to her feet, like a frightened parent hauling their child away from a fire.

'Enough!' Bahl's cry was commanding, angry even, although it sounded like a mouse's squeal when compared to Queen Penn's manic tirade. Seizing hold of Bracken, she began bundling her along the narrow stone pathway away from where Queen Penn ranted and contorted within her cramped fissure. Bracken barely felt aware of Bahl manhandling her away from her grandmother's wrath. Darkness seemed to be gripping hold of her consciousness, dragging her back, forcing her to struggle against Bahl and continue to stare back at Queen Penn's fierce fury. She continued to look back at her hateful visage, snout snorting with indignance, the dull, soulless scarlet glow burning in the shadows of her eye socket, her fanged maul snapping violently as she shrieked, snarled and cursed, slathering globules of venomous black drool from her lips into the cowl of darkness that surrounded not only her but all in Ac-Nu. A cold, hurtful splinter in her heart told her that all this hatred, pain and sorrow was justified. The grim depths of the cave seemed to echo with the voice of her own insecurity, calling her an unwanted bastard, the product of sin and betrayal, unworthy and useless.

Behind her, Bahl held her torch aloft and pressed her palm firmly against Bracken's shoulder blades, driving her forward up the staircase. 'I said enough!' she barked angrily above the howling laments of the cave. 'Come on! Walk, climb! As fast as you can! Now!' There was no patience or compassion in Bahl's tone.

Bracken wanted to get away from this terrible, horrible place but her body and mind did not seem to want her to leave. Her limbs were like they were encased in molten lead, wearyingly heavy and cumbersome to move. Dark, woeful emotion filled her up inside, saturating every space in her thoughts till it threatened to overflow and wash her away. She wanted to cry, to vomit, to scream, to push out all the darkness that brimmed within. Behind her, Bahl relentlessly drove her on with sharp commands and urgent shoves. When Bracken felt unable to shift another inch, she would feel Bahl's stony fingers clasp the back of her thigh, forcing her to lift her knee and climb another step.

The climb seemed to take forever, every stair feeling like a mountain before them, all the time the wailing lament and shrieking anger of Ac-Nu sapping their strength. Finally a crack of light and clamour of lively noise sliced through the gloom from above, like ebony clouds slitting open to reveal a bronze sky. Bracken felt a shift in the darkness that welled within her, an alteration from grief and hatred to absolute fear as her mind comprehended that Ac-Nu was hungrily trying to claim her for itself. Inertia ceased in a sudden burst of terrified adrenaline that released her body from its driving paralysis. Like a fleeing animal, she bounded up the stairs, not daring to glance back to check that Bahl was still with her for fear that if she did just for a moment, the sapping misery of the caverns would completely overwhelm her. Breath escaped her lungs in long, hard gasps, each one accompanied with a choked cry of distress. With every step she climbed away from the awful misery she had witnessed, more and more of the shadowy effects it had on her came gushing out, like her body expelling some noxious poison. Hot tears flooded from her eyes as if brought on by some allergic reaction. Her stomach spasmed again and again, contorting her gullet with foul dry heaves. At last she reached the top of the stairs, flinging herself desperately back into the fiery light and mechanical sound of Kelhalbon. Exhausted, she collapsed on to the cold, hard ground, hugging herself tightly for comfort as she quaked and wept, eager to remove all trace of what she had experienced. A few seconds later, Bahl ascended from the cave, looking troubled and drained, her large, black pupils looking strangely dim. Fatigued, she sunk to her knees beside Bracken, muttering something softly in Dwarfish and turned the ratchet that withdrew the stairway from the cavern.

Anxiously the other dwarves drew in around the tired pair, accompanied by Hayden, Aarold and Petronia. Seeing his half-sister lying shaking on the ground, Aarold shuffled forward and reached out to comfort her. 'Sister,' he implored tenderly, brushing her trembling shoulder with his delicate hand, 'what has happened to you?'

Bracken did not, could not, reply. All the rage and heart-rending woe she had witnessed played like a hateful tableau in her mind, making her recall again and again her fears and feelings of rejection. Her fingertips clawed at the fabric of her sleeves as she cradled herself and tried to remember the comforting, encouraging teaching of Amethyst, but still Queen Penn's vengeful words tortured her thoughts. Quietly Hayden approached and stooped to help her sit up. 'It's okay, Mistress Bracken,' he murmured gently, 'it's over now. You're safe.'

His words seemed to break a bond of silence within Bracken and she managed to speak. 'It was terrible, *she* was terrible. My grandmother, the things she said, hateful, cruel, wicked things, with no Ley or love in them. Yet they seemed to be so true. I cannot believe I'm related to such a, such a monster.' She gagged with disgust as the queen's loathing filled her thoughts with blackness, her tongue tasting bitter with bile.

Taking a long, strained breath, Bahl drew herself carefully to her feet. 'Such is the nature of Ac-Nu, as I did warn you, m'lady,' she uttered grimly. Gracefully, she waved her hand and uttered a swift order in Dwarfish. At once, a female dwarf stepped forward from the crowd, carrying an unpolished, metal tray with two large, squat, stone beakers on it. Bahl took both and thirstily drained one before passing the second to Bracken.

Wrapping both hands around the vessel, Bracken peered inside to find it filled with fresh, cool spring water with a number of pieces of deep green dioptase crystal resting at the bottom. She recognised the brew at once as a crystal elixir, like Amethyst would make for her whenever she felt ill or fatigued, and greedily gulped it back, allowing the crystals to rest lightly on her lips as she drank. The water was pleasantly cool and the slightly bitter, metallic taste familiar to Bracken's palate but once the cup was dry she still felt the dark grief of the caves linger in her spirit.

Petronia had been watching all this intently from a distance, the now familiar feeling of pulsing Ley energy swelling up through her body once more. She watched Bracken trembling bitterly on the floor and as she did so became aware of traces of smoky, black vapour coiling like transparent serpents around Bracken's body, an unseen, whispering veil. Petronia's fingertips started to itch and burn with urgent power and inside her mind she could hear the murmurings of the same dark, wordless language that had filled her before. The entire back of her body, from her heels to her crown, tingled and pricked with the shimmering power of the Ley as It gently urged her on. Carefully she stepped towards Bracken, keeping her mind very focused in fear that the power within might unexpectedly surge up and overwhelm her.

Kneeling down beside the distraught girl, Petronia gazed into Bracken's eyes and as she did so became aware of a distant echo inside her own thoughts, like a barely recalled memory filled with words of hate. Looking into Bracken's eyes, Petronia felt as if she was seeing a freshly cut wound, painful and bloody but clean and shallow enough to heal. She turned her attention away from Bracken and on to the angrily churning and swarming billows of black energy that rippled around her. Carefully she reached out her hand so that it was not touching

Bracken but hovering within the space occupied by the tendrils of grim, woeful darkness. At the very presence of her touch, the strange, dark aura began to greedily caress Petronia's skin. Her body grew tense as she felt its cold, hateful energy speak to her of its despair and hunger for Bracken's life. She was filled with anxiety for a brief moment, afraid that the darkness might want to devour her also, but that worry was soon overwhelmed by a feeling of familiarity, confidence and utter control as once again the strange, unspoken language within her awoke. Soundless words and phrases drifted like a secret treasury of powerful tools and Petronia carefully examined each one, selecting what was needed for purpose. She breathed deeply and steadily as she mustered her mental strength and focused her mind on a singular command to send into the blackness that clung to Bracken's aura. *'Leave her,'* she demanded. A vengeful ripple of greed swirled defiantly in the dark mass. A sob caught pitifully in Bracken's throat as she trembled recalling what she had seen. But Petronia was not interested in conversing or comforting the girl at that moment, her voice had no words to address human ears, the only language at her command belonged to unseen and unheard darkness and evil. The muscles in her throat began to tighten as Petronia flexed and strained her vocal cords, trying to find the sounds that matched what she needed to express. Her tongue and palate felt rough and heavy like stone but lacked the pain or taste of blood that had scarred them before, as if her mouth and gullet were becoming harder, more resilient. *'Leave her,'* she commanded again, this time the words blooming into solidity within her throat, rising up like dull molten lead to fill her mouth before spilling out from her lips.

The sound Petronia made was not the same deafening roar that had halted the Golem in the mountain caves, in fact Petronia was not even sure that anyone else could hear it. The order to the darkness to depart from Bracken's spirit slid like a cunning and swift adder out from her, riding on an exhalation of breath, seizing the shadow of Ac-Nu that hung over her and drawing back inside Petronia in a smooth, easy movement. Rage, woe and icy bitterness gripped Petronia's heart as the dark hate departed Bracken's form and entered hers instead. All life and

Ley dimmed before her as she felt a great urge to break away from all that was good and wholesome and wander forever in the realms of despair. Once again, the Ley burst into her mind in a cloud of shimmering language and frantically she snatched at It, this time calling upon the phrases to drive the feelings of rage and terror down deeper into her, away from her conscious mind and emotions. A dark space opened up somewhere within, a spinning, evil vortex that was at the core of her growing abilities, something intense and alluring yet deeply terrifying and dangerous. With every ounce of will she had, Petronia thrust the draining shadow and bitterness into that place that boiled and muttered with words of might and control before sealing it and grabbing her way back to reality. Around her, she could feel the soothing blessing of the Ley drift over her spirit, renewing her strength. Even in her almost trance-like state, she had been aware of her brother's anxiety and the horror he would feel at witnessing such strange power issue from his sibling's silent tongue.

Bracken was sitting beside her. Her tears and sobbing had stopped and although her expression was still troubled she seemed more at peace. Sighing deeply, she gratefully took Petronia's hand. 'Thank you,' she breathed. 'The Ley worked through you and brought me comfort after my ordeal. I feel better now.'

Petronia smiled modestly and nodded her head. She found it easier to think it was the Ley that banished the grief in Bracken's spirit than it being transferred to somewhere within her. As remarkable as her new abilities were, each time she was compelled to use them she was left feeling drained and uncertain.

Hayden looked from his sister to Bracken. He had noticed a strange far-off expression come over Petronia's face as she had approached the sobbing girl, a powerful wildness in her eyes that made him think of all the times back home in Ravensbrook when she had handled pebbles and made them dance. He found it harder to doubt now that what the Ryders said about his sister was true and that she did have mystical powers. However, this did little to ease his worries about her. Tenderly he placed his hand on her long ebony hair in a gesture of both pride and concern. Turning her head, Petronia gave him a reassuring smile and gestured that she was fine.

Bahl moved across to where Bracken sat and extended her wide, grey hand to help her to her feet. 'Has Sister Petronia eased the effects of Ac-Nu, Lady Bracken?' she asked earnestly. Standing up, Bracken brushed out the folds of her shimmering gown, 'A little,' she confessed, resting her hand on her temple. 'I do not feel so woeful although my emotions still feel very raw. I have learnt so much this day of who I am, I still don't know how to process it all. I pray the Ley gives me the strength to deal with it.'

The dwarf vizier nodded wisely in agreement. 'It has indeed been a day of great revelation for all involved, but no more so than you, m'lady. I regret your audience with our queen was so harrowing, I trust now you understand my reluctance to introduce you. Rest assured that the hospitality of Kelhalbon is extended to both you and your companions and I am always at hand to offer my advice. This is, after all, your homeland.'

Bracken took a moment to look round the grand cavern with its bridges and automatons, at the tall, noble figures of the dwarves, thinking over all that she had been told and witnessed. For the first time the reality of her situation truly dawned, that this strange land of terrible woe, ingenious craft and glimmering wonder was where she had come from. It was indeed her homeland but not, Bracken thought, her home. Nor did the blood kin now known to her, the wrathful Penn, the grieving and confused Ion and the wise but delicate Aarold, feel like family.

'I think I, we all, would benefit from a night's rest,' she said softly. 'All of us have travelled far and while I am keen to talk with you about the role the Ley seems to have guided me to, I do not feel strong enough at this time to do so.'

Bahl bowed graciously. 'Of course, m'lady. The visit to Ac-Nu has left me drained of energy. Sleep will bring comfort and clearer heads to us all. Bed chambers have been prepared. I will guide you to them.'

With a graceful gesture she beckoned to Bracken and the others to follow her into one of the smaller antechambers that led off the cavern. Down a long, stone corridor that sparkled with crystal-indented walls, they soon discovered a number of small alcoves furnished with metal bunks and silvery silken bedding, one of which had already been occupied by Phebus who was snoring peacefully to himself. Hayden, and in particular Aarold, had not realised how tired they both were until they saw their beds and gratefully climbed into them to fall asleep almost immediately. Petronia's mind still felt active as she stripped off her apprentice's gown and climbed into bed in her chemise and drawers. Her mind kept drifting to the strange darkness she had witnessed and with each thought she felt it grow and churn, forming strange patterns and phrases. At last she felt weary and fell into a fitfully exhausted slumber leaving Bracken the last awake, trying to forget the harsh words spoken by Queen Penn and missing very much the simple, orphaned existence that had so recently been her life.

Chapter 30

ATTACKERS OF THE LEY

The chilled wind of an autumn dusk filled the branches of the great forest with rustling movement. Night was on its way and already the nocturnal creatures and malicious woodland spirits were stirring, transforming the woods from Nature's peaceful abode to a dangerous and foreboding realm. Garnet pulled on the reins of her steed to slow him from his canter and peered upwards through the network of bowers and leaves to see the darkening sky. It pained her to stop her trail even for a second and allow their wicked but unseen quarry to gain a moment's advance, but she was worldly enough to know what perils lurked in the forest after sundown. It had been a night and day since she, Rosequartz and Chiastolite had left the nightmarish scene of Amethyst's bloody murder at the citadel. Driven by the Ley, they followed doggedly the unrelenting scarlet trail that had been drawn out for them by the aged Ryder's life fluid. They had ridden with little rest, their senses peeled for any clue to the perpetrators of the heinous crime or the mute apprentice who might be the Stone Tongue foretold of in legend, but had so far found neither. Now another evening was upon them and the dim atmosphere of the forest coupled with their painful grief for Amethyst filled their spirits with unease and agitation.

Looking over her shoulder, Garnet called to her Sister Ryders as they drew near. 'I do not trust this place to travel through it by night,' she declared. 'We will make camp and ride on as soon as dawn breaks.'

Rosequartz lowered her flute from her lips and regarded Garnet with troubled green eyes. She had been playing continuously as they travelled, a series of achingly sweet, tender laments that soothed the souls but also spoke of great loss. Her sensitive, spirited heart had been pained by Amethyst's demise more than her sisters', her Calling being to revel in the joys of life rather than the reverence of death, and she played to summon the Ley to her own heart as much as to comfort her sisters.

'Surely we cannot stop to rest for a moment, not when such vile evil runs free,' she enthused. 'Every second that passes Petronia is in danger.'

Garnet sadly shook her head and clasped her crystal medallions for strength and comfort against the growing sinister atmosphere of the wood. Shadows were beginning to darken and in them she thought she could sense the malicious gaze of watchful eyes. 'Believe me, Sister, I do not want to cease our hunt any more than you do but these woods are filled with strange magic that clouds the awareness and I fear that once the moon rises we will not be able to trace the path. Besides, Sister Cross-Stone isn't as strong as us and I feel she is in need of respite.'

She glanced with concern at the elderly Ryder, bundled crook-backed in the saddle of her horse. She did indeed look tired but at the mention of her name, raised her pale head and straightened her hunched shoulders. 'Don't you concern yourself with my well-being, Sister Garnet,' she said, wagging her bony finger. 'The Ley gives me strength to carry on my duties when there is a killer to be brought to justice. I can journey all night if that's what's required. Nevertheless, I can see Sister Garnet's point, perhaps we should...'

She stopped short, her body suddenly tense and alert, and age seemed to drop away from her ancient form as something caught her senses. The others felt it too: a shrill heightening in the rush of the Ley that betrayed danger was nearby. The shadowy trees around them remained inscrutable and mysterious, dark shapes moving between tree trunks, figments of imagined vision or flesh and blood enemies.

In a second, Rosequartz had sheathed her flute and gripped the hilt of her weapon fearfully, her watchful gaze searching the blackness of the woods. 'We are not alone, Sisters,' she whispered, straining all her senses to detect the dangers that lurked out of sight. The forest was alive, its moist air filled with an orchestra of creaks, moans, shrieks and calls that muffled many a soft footstep on its leafy carpet.

With a prayer of summoning to the Ley, Garnet dismounted and drew a piece of unpolished diamond from a pouch on her belt and held it out before her, silently drawing on its power to sharpen her eyes in the gloom. But even before the Ley had a chance to improve her vision, there was a movement in the undergrowth and two figures, leather-masked and cloaked in black, stepped ominously before them, their swords glinting in the half-light of the wood.

The taller one spoke, his voice firm and threatening. 'Drop the gem,' he ordered, his blade pointing at the diamond clasped in Garnet's fingers.

Dutifully, the Ryder severed the crystal's link to the Ley and tossed it lightly towards the pair. It landed softly amid the leaves beside the shorter bandit's feet. 'Take it,' said Garnet, her hands spread to show she was no threat. 'If robbing us means you allow another traveller to pass through this forest unthreatened, it is our service to the Ley.'

The taller bandit eyed the jewel suspiciously but his companion kept her steely gaze firmly on the Ryders. She edged menacingly forward, her face a featureless oval of darkness beneath her cowl.

'We do not want your jewels and crystals,' she hissed sinisterly, her voice muffled by her disguise.

Quickly, Rosequartz slid down from her saddle, motioning for Chiastolite to stay safely where she was. 'Then what can we offer that will allow us to continue our journey?' she asked, trying to be amicable. 'We are Ley Ryders and mean you no harm.'

The male bandit circled round till he stood beside Garnet, his eyes carefully watching her sword hand which remained free at her side. 'You will come with us,' he said sharply, his hot breath drifting from between the slits in his mask like smoke, 'without question and without challenge.'

Bristling fiercely, his companion hissed, eyes burning maliciously in her shadowy sockets. 'No,' she barked, sweeping forward to bring her blade fearfully close to Rosequartz's cheek. 'That won't do. They must be dealt with more thoroughly. They will not leave this place.'

Shocked by his partner's ruthlessness, the male bandit faltered. With her captor's attention lost, Garnet seized the moment and with one great surge of Ley energy and adrenaline she gripped hold of her blade, drawing it swiftly out of its scabbard, dealing an upward blow to the robber's chin with the hilt as she did so. Caught off guard by the sudden strike, he stumbled back with a shout of pain. His cry alerted his partner and she broke her attention from Rosequartz who took the opportunity to land a sturdy punch in her stomach. Rosequartz staggered back towards her fellow Ryders, drawing her rapier for protection as the woman reeled, cursing like a banshee from her blow. Chiastolite clung desperately to the reins of her mount as it reared up, spooking the other horses to flee off into the trees. It did not take a second for the female bandit to recover from her winding. Wheeling her sword manically, she screamed to her cohort sprawled on the ground. 'Get up! Get up, you fool, and finish the job!'

With a grunt of effort, he powered himself to his feet and lunged expertly at Garnet with his blade. He was wiry, but strong, quick and well-trained as the two of them fought, blade against blade, blow against blow, equally matched in skill. Garnet's mind desperately assessed the fight; she could usually match any man in combat, but she was tired from the day's travel and her grief at losing Amethyst dulled her senses. She called to the Ley for strength and in an instant saw it gleam long, narrow bands of silver in the moonless night, marking the movements her blade should make to guard herself and deflect his attack.

Nearby, the enraged she-thief let out a bellow of fury, like a possessed animal. '*I'll* finish it,' she spat. 'I'll finish all three!'

In one fluid movement, she reached into her boot and drew a small but deadly sharp dagger which she tossed directly at Rosequartz's throat. The Ryder ducked, skilfully twisting her head so the blade did little more than nick her right cheek, leaving a thin dash of scarlet. 'Missed!' she laughed triumphantly.

Lowering her sword, the bandit tilted her faceless head at an odd angle. 'It's enough,' she sneered darkly, spreading her gloved hands wide.

She inhaled and with the sigh of her inward breath the atmosphere of the woods grew still and more chilled. Movement rippled amid the shadowy trees surrounding them. Not the movement of an unseen creature or person, but of a formless energy of darkness awoken from the deathly violence of nature. As the bandit gestured with her arm, tendrils of oily blackness slithered from the shadows like smoky serpents drifting over the grass. A cruel discord of power filled the clearing as the murderous darkness drew close, responding to its mistress's commands.

Locked in her duel with the male robber, Garnet sensed the sudden change in the air. Just as it had encircled the citadel, the violent, hateful energy flooded into the clearing like a river bursting its banks, its bubbling strength of anarchic force overwhelming the guiding clarity of the Ley, making Its silvery bands dim and flicker in and out of vision. Frantically, she fought on without Its aid, using only her physical strength and skill of blade to ward off her attacker.

Coils of silken blackness twisted around the female bandit, twisting around her legs, waist and right arm as if drawn there by some magnetic power. Beneath her leather mask, her eyes glinted maliciously and with a sudden, graceful swipe of her arm she extended her hand towards Rosequartz. Powerful waves of cold, black energy flowed out over her body, lashing across space towards the Ryder. Brandishing her sword, Rosequartz reached into a pouch on her belt to retrieve a crystal but before she had time to summon the Ley, ribbons of deathly, mindless power swirled silently about her, filling her aura with their hungry, numbing rage. Greedily, they homed in on the shallow gash on her cheek, seeping swiftly into the thin trail of scarlet blood with an iron-strong grip. A guttural scream curdled in Rosequartz's throat as brittle, icy fingers of blackness and death crept swiftly into her flesh, making her nerves freeze with agony and fear. Dropping her weapon, she fell to her knees, clawing manically at her face in a vain attempt to draw the poisonous vapour out. Life and Ley fled from her body as the blackness wormed itself deeper into her mind and muscles. The injured Ryder battled valiantly, summoning every ounce of might she had to battle the infection. As the masked attacker chuckled maliciously, Rosequartz clawed at the earth, shrieking for mercy.

A sense of untimely death filled Chiastolite's mind as she clung to the reins of her terrified mount. Her acute awareness could feel Rosequartz's life-force twisting in a dance of mortality with the black power that threatened to overwhelm it. Lost and unprepared for her final journey Rosequartz's spirit detached from the merciful flow of the Ley. This would not be a just death and Chiastolite could not allow it. Slipping down from her saddle, she silently prayed for the Ley to flood through her with an intense power of release. '*Away!*' she called within her thoughts, as flashes of brilliant Ley force glinted like brutal blades in her mind. '*Into death or elsewhere into life!*' Her arthritic fingers seized a large nugget of tiger iron crystal from her belt and squeezing it as tightly as she could in the palm of her hand, she commanded the Ley to pass through her body into the stone. Her ancient form sagged with shock and exhaustion as a mighty surge of energy crashed through, burning into the core of the mottled brown and golden stone, filling it with a pulling, surging desire to escape. With all her might, Chiastolite tossed the stone to the ground. The earth beneath their feet shook as if cracked by a mini earthquake, throwing up a shower of dirt, leaves and grass as a swirling, muddy vortex opened like a grave beside Rosequartz's trembling form.

Their attackers stared dumbstruck at this phenomenon as the elderly Ryder flung herself on top of Rosequartz's screaming form, rolling them both over into the gaping mouth of soil and Ley energy. Seeing her chance, Garnet rushed forward, shoving the male bandit forcefully out of her path before diving into the dark, moist safety of the earth, letting the powerful flow of Ley whisk her roughly away. Swiftly, the man ploughed after her, falling to his knees and driving his blade powerfully into the earth as he battled to land one last fatal blow. The portal, however, had shut just as swiftly as it had opened and his sword embedded itself in nothing more than cold mud.

*

With a growl of frustration, Tristram Kreen snatched off his leather mask and hurled it angrily to the ground. 'They're gone!' he spat, beads of sweat chilling against his flushed face, 'escaped into the earth via some kind of Ley power.'

He looked towards Coal-Fox who was broodingly stalking the perimeter of the clearing. The oily, shadowy mist still hung, coiling viciously in the air, weaving around her form like a headless serpent, awaiting the command to strike. The masked woman waved her hand in a swift gesture and the vapour dispersed, merging into the shadows of the forest and her own dark garments. 'You should have killed them when you had the chance,' she stated in a tone that chillingly lacked emotion.

Tristram sharply got to his feet and tugged his sword from where it stood embedded in the earth. Every moment he spent in the company of this mysterious servant of the White Duchess made him trust her less. 'You said nothing about killing them,' he bit broodingly. 'I was under the understanding that we were to capture any Ley Ryders that hampered our search for the prince.'

Coal-Fox glanced around, searching the shadows of the forest for any further threats or spying eyes. 'Then you were very much mistaken,' she murmured, her voice muffled beneath the taut material of her mask. 'I presumed the White Duchess sent you to accompany me on this quest because you were a great warrior who understood the grave peril her nephew was in. There are powers at work greater and more dangerous than your unschooled mind could imagine.'

Bitter bile tainted Tristram's tongue as the blow of Coal-Fox's words hit him. 'I have battled many foes,' he informed her menacingly, 'many of whom possessed magic, and through courage and skill I have overcome them. But I have never, in all my years of soldiering, been called to attack a follower of the Ley. It is an unchivalrous deed, not that I would expect one such as you to comprehend the rules governing noble battle.'

His rage did not seem to frighten or unease Coal-Fox, in fact she appeared highly amused. An uncharacteristic girlish giggle caught in her throat as she gestured to the gloomy forest surrounding them. 'Did you not take part in the battle here?' she quizzed. 'Did you not witness the immense and violent power the Ryders summoned from thin air? That black and murderous mist they drew from the shadows?'

Tristram glared deeply into the slits of his fellow traveller's mask. He could not deny the presence of the deadly fog that had filled the clearing moments before, had felt its icy power caress his spirit and weaken his senses. It had indeed been the same shadowy vapour that he had witnessed pouring from the doorway of the Ryder's lodge in Veridium in pursuit of Prince Aarold. But Captain Kreen was not blind or a fool and he had noticed that the tendrils of mist responded more to Coal-Fox's gestures and commands than any of the Ryders' actions.

'It appeared to me,' he hissed through gritted teeth, 'that that black energy, whatever it was, was most firmly in your command. Tell me, Coal-Fox, just what powers do you possess?' His mismatched eyes glinted suspiciously as he intently regarded the confident woman.

Coal-Fox squared up to him brazenly, her hands resting lightly on her hips, any trace of emotion totally hidden beneath her inscrutable mask. 'I do not deny that I am schooled in certain arts of sorcery,' she stated firmly, 'nor can I say I held no power over that murderous entity that we witnessed. It was necessary for me to mentally wrestle control of it from the Ryders so that I could use its strength against them. If I had not, we both would have perished.'

Tristram made no response to this statement but continued to stare mistrustfully at the strange and merciless huntress, trying to catch one glimmer of personality or motivation beneath that featureless mask. 'I don't trust magic,' he stated, aware and annoyed at how much his voice sounded like a sulking child's.

Coal-Fox crossed her arms and shrugged glibly. 'As I've always told you, you have no bonds to compel you to follow me in my quest nor have I to you. If you wish to depart and search for the prince's whereabouts on your own, I will bear you no spite and neither I suppose would Her Grace the Duchess. Personally I would find it an interesting test to see how a warrior of your *obvious* calibre copes in an environment such as this. These woods are rife with all manner of wicked magic and not just that which is commanded by the Ryders.'

Captain Kreen tensed as he stalked over to where she stood. He was more than a head taller than Coal-Fox and determined to let her know that she did not intimidate him, no matter what powers or magic she possessed. 'If you think I would leave a vicious rogue like you responsible for Prince Aarold's safe return, you very much underestimate my duty to the crown,' he growled.

Coal-Fox lifted her chin, revealing a small patch of pale throat between the edge of her mask and her high collar. 'You still do not think your beloved was right in placing her faith in me?' she taunted. 'How little you know of the depths of our confidence.'

There was something sickening about the way she spoke the word "beloved" that made his skin prickle and passion swirl violently in his belly. He was a proud and strong man, not the romantic sort that wore his love blatantly on his sleeve for the world to view. His passion for Maudabelle was something that he had locked deeply in the most private part of his heart, waiting for the time that he would grow worthy enough before attempting to woo her. To know that the sly Coal-Fox saw it within him made him feel sullied and uneasy.

As if reading his thoughts, Coal-Fox spoke. 'You think you could hide such a passion, Captain Kreen?' she said, sounding almost compassionate. 'Your love for the White Duchess hangs about you like a rose's scent.'

Tristram felt his passionate devotion to Maudabelle mingle with his disdain for Coal-Fox, overwhelming his self-control. Fiercely he seized her by the shoulders and shook her. 'Another word of disrespect and I will drag you back to the jail in Veridium, whether it means abandoning my search for the prince or not!'

Coal-Fox tensed in his strong grip, seeming genuinely shocked by this sudden outburst. She struggled to free herself and Captain Kreen was at once aware that despite her bravado and fighting skills she was still female and no matter how much he loathed her, it was unseemly of him to manhandle her. Letting go, he backed away as she straightened her dark robes and regained her composure.

'Forgive me, Captain Kreen,' she said earnestly, 'I did speak out of turn. I meant no scorn or disregard towards your feelings for the duchess. I simply wondered whether there was a way she could validate my loyalty to her, prove that I can be trusted.'

Tristram had taken a seat on the ground and was gazing with shame at his gloved hands. He felt conflicted; his feeling of mistrust and dislike for Coal-Fox grew with every passing moment and for a brief second he had wanted very much to strike her for mocking him. However, that would have been against his vows of chivalry. He felt as if even being near her was corrupting.

'There is no way to contact her,' he said grimly. 'If we return to Veridium now we will put the prince's life at risk.'

Coal-Fox remained silent for a moment, staring at him as if trying to decide whether a risk was worth taking. At last, she spoke. 'I could call her to us,' she said; 'it is within my power to do so. But it requires me to use magic. Do you trust me enough?' Tristram was thoughtful for a moment. Would calling on the duchess when they had not found her nephew be a sign of failure? Would it be better to rely alone on the guidance of her strange and powerful servant? There were so many issues and powers he was unsure about; would guiding words from the woman he loved aid him on his quest? 'Do it,' he said firmly.

Silently, Coal-Fox nodded and removing her leather gauntlets reached into a concealed pocket in her clothing and took out a small package wrapped in delicate black silk. Tristram watched as she carefully unfolded the fabric to reveal a long, narrow fragment of polished marble, darker in hue than blackness itself, which she cupped delicately like a globule of molten oil in her pale palms. Then with infinitely soft and deliberate movements, she began to caress its glossy, smooth surface, her fingertips not leaving the slightest smear or mark to disturb the faultless black. As she stroked and fondled the stone, Coal-Fox began to hum, a low and guttural sound muffled beneath the tight fit of her mask. Tristram could barely detect the note that she uttered but the stone she clasped seemed aware of it for the darkness that dwelt within trembled and churned at the noise like stormclouds, until curves and shapes started to reveal themselves from the toneless shade of the stone. A face began to take shape, or rather aspects of a face, drifting in and out of view from the shadows, a singular eye, a lower lip and chin, the outline of a nose, as if someone was peering out of a chink in space, spying from another realm.

A voice murmured, cold and echoing, sounding like the owner was standing in a vast cavern, a disembodied tone that startled Tristram until he realised that it sounded very much like his beloved White Duchess. 'What news?' the stone asked sharply as Coal-Fox gripped it in her palm. 'Has the prince been found? Is all as we planned?'

Coal-Fox's pale fingers tightened anxiously around the slither of rock. 'Alas no, Your Grace,' she muttered, sounding as if she was battling to conceal her true feelings in front of Tristram, 'there has been a minor setback. We have just encountered a group of Ryders in the Great Forest. We tried to capture them but they got away. I fear they are tracking Prince Aarold as well.'

A frustrated moan issued from the stone, sounding so full of rage that it might crack the very rock that transmitted it. 'I thought I made my instructions perfectly clear,' the voice of Maudabelle bit fiercely. 'Anyone or anything that hampered your pursuit of Prince Aarold is to be dealt with swiftly and brutally; we cannot afford distractions.'

Coal-Fox took a sharp breath, her eyes flitting from the stone in her hand to where Tristram sat watching her suspiciously. 'I am quite aware of the situation, Your Grace,' she replied, each word heavy with unspoken meaning. 'But your loyal servant, Captain Kreen, has his doubts. He is wary about using force against followers of the Ley.'

Agitation prickled Tristram's spine when he heard the sarcasm in Coal-Fox's tone. 'Let me speak to Duchess Maudabelle myself,' he demanded, reaching out to snatch the crystal. Sharply, Coal-Fox balled her fist around it. 'You do not possess the sorcery to maintain the connection,' she told him briskly. Tristram felt the urge to reach for his blade and had to fight not to do so. Coal-Fox's mystical power was one of the many reasons he disliked and distrusted her.

Through the gaps in Coal-Fox's fingers, the tones and shadows within the stone twisted impatiently and the duchess's cold but angry voice filled the air. 'I cannot help feeling disappointed in both of you,' she stated firmly. 'The welfare of my royal nephew is of utmost importance to me as it is to the whole kingdom. I would think that a captain in the Royal Guard would be willing to take any measures to find him, especially when I myself have tasked him personally to do so. And as for you, *Coal-Fox*, I believed dealing with Ley Ryders was somewhat of a speciality of yours. But I guess I was wrong. No, it would seem that I will have to deal with things personally. Where exactly are you?' Coal-Fox sighed heavily, angry that her plans were being interfered with. If she had not been burdened with Captain Kreen she would have dealt with the Ryders herself; in fact it would have been a pleasure. 'North,' she said, giving the stone a brisk tap, 'in the Great Forest. We will continue to follow the trail throughout the night.'

Fragments of the Duchess's face glimmered within the chunk of crystal, a sneering curve of a full upper lip and flash of eye. 'Head for the mountains of Kelhalbon. I shall take my swiftest steed and meet you in the foothills. It is obvious to me that you are both incapable of carrying out simple instructions without direct guidance.'

Coal-Fox's demeanour bristled with irritation as her fingers flexed around the enchanted stone. 'As you wish, Your Grace,' she uttered coldly as all trace of Maudabelle's features vanished from the dark shadows of the stone.

Swiftly, she returned it to the hidden pocket of her tunic and marched across to mount her horse. 'You heard the duchess,' she told Tristram sharply. 'It would seem that our rendezvous with the Ryders fell below her expectations. We'll head north and regroup there and then we will see what she makes of her champion.'

Tristram smiled grimly as he climbed into the saddle of his own stallion, soothed at the notion of seeing his beloved White Duchess at dawn and telling her about the disrespectful behaviour of her masked servant. 'I am confident my actions will not disappoint,' he sneered. 'I'm sure the Duchess Maudabelle has more respect for the chivalrous ways of the Royal Guard than she does for some deceitful and ruthless assassin.'

An ironic snigger caught in Coal-Fox's throat as she took up her reins. 'Really?' she said lightly, turning her featureless, black face towards Tristram. 'I wonder how well you know your beloved duchess.'

Before Tristram could reply, Coal-Fox had dug her heels into her horse's flanks and headed into the shadows of the forest.

*

The intense pressure of earth, flesh and speed pressed in on Chiastolite's elderly body as the urgent flow of the Ley transported her beneath the ground, carrying her steadily onwards away from danger. It had been some years since she had travelled by portal and her somewhat frail form battled to withstand the strength of the surging rush of movement through stone and soil. However, she was still a Ryder, mentally and physically trained to work with and respond to the Ley. She knew that despite her aged body's instinct to fight against the claustrophobic cocoon of damp dark mud clogging her mouth and nostrils, it would make an easier journey if she submitted wholly to Its pull, trusting It to do with her as It saw fit and hopefully deliver her safely from danger.

To distract herself from the pain and discomfort of the journey, Chiastolite focused her attention on her semi-conscious companion who she gripped tightly. Even in the subterranean chaos they found themselves in, the elderly Ryder remained acutely aware of Rosequartz's sickened state and the churning, icy darkness that burrowed deep into her body and spirit. Chiastolite sensed Rosequartz's strong and quick mind battling, fighting to remain in control beneath the onslaught of the greedy attack that gobbled up each thought and mental barrier she threw up. Worriedly, she searched the Ley for the inevitable shade that was familiar to her, the colour of death that she had witnessed in a hundred different hues, to see if it would now claim Rosequartz, but could not feel Its forgiving release reach out to claim her. Instead, there was only pain, fear and grief tugging greedily at the cursed Ryder's form.

With one powerful thrust, the clogging, wet earth that surrounded their bodies gave way, cracking open and belching them back out into the cold, airy atmosphere of the forest in a tumbling heap of mud and limbs. The agony of old age tore through Chiastolite's bones as she sprawled ungainly on the grass, Rosequartz's spasming and shrieking form crushing down on top of her. With a heave, the old woman rolled her friend's twitching body off and scrabbled to her knees.

The glade in which they found themselves was sparsely dotted with trees, the ground rocky and uneven. Muttering prayers for strength and assistance from the Ley, Chiastolite awkwardly crawled over to where Rosequartz, twitching and convulsing, cried out in half-intelligible utterances of agony and rage. Her spine bowed and flexed, her legs lashed out and her hands clasped desperately at her pallid face as if it was doused in acid. In the dim starlight, Chiastolite could clearly make out a sickening black stain, blighting her pale cheek where the bandit's blade had sliced it open, allowing the sapping magic to seep in. Already, dark, vein-like threads were weaving out from the wound like a spider's web of infection, seeping beneath her skin in twisting paths across her face and towards her throat. Another gut-wrenching scream tore from her lips as her voice echoed with a strange, animal tone.

Wiping the soil from her hands, Chiastolite reached out to examine Rosequartz's injury. She gently touched the exposed, scarlet flesh, finding it unnervingly solid and stony beneath her skilled fingers, colder than any corpse she had prepared for burial. Fear and uncertainty trembled in the elderly Ryder's mind but she battled against them and sent out a strong, silent call to the Ley to fill Rosequartz's body and save Its faithful servant.

At that moment, the ground not far from where they were bulged and cracked with a juddering groan, throwing damp soil upward in a shower as the Ley delivered Garnet from her journey. Picking clumps of mud from her hair and garments, the Ryder scrambled to her feet and anxiously hurried over to her companions. 'Is she going to be all right?' she asked earnestly, seeing Rosequartz's convulsing and shrieking form. 'She's not going to die, is she?'

Chiastolite looked pensive and rested her fingers against Rosequartz's icy flesh, sensing the battling turmoil of her life-force. 'No,' she said certainly, 'but believe me, Sister, there are worse fates than death. I've seen this violent power before, only recently though and I do not know what manner of magic brings it into being. We must call upon the Ley and pray that It allows us to free her of this darkness. Set up a ring of tiger's eye to guard us while we work.'

As her fellow Ryder requested, Garnet marked out a broad circle on the ground around Rosequartz and Chiastolite, setting down pieces of russet and black tiger's eye crystal at all four compass points. She then returned to Chiastolite's side, kneeling down to assist the elderly Ryder as she began working to save Rosequartz. The cursed woman twitched and gasped bitterly as Garnet and Chiastolite joined hands, focusing their wills intently on sending out a forceful plea to the Ley to strengthen their comrade. As their breath steadied and their heart rates quickened, the Ryders felt a sudden, powerful shift in the Ley, sensed a sweeping wave rush across the ground before them like an incoming tide flooding forth with compassionate, silvery energy to engulf Rosequartz's being. Within her chilled flesh and muscles, the angry blackness roared and raged as the gleaming strength of the Ley battled to fill the ensnared Ryder's soul. The insipid magic lashed and boiled violently, making her body tremble and convulse as if it was possessed by demons. Swiftly Chiastolite reached into the pouches on her belt and pulled out two medium-sized crystals, reddish pink thulite for strength and dark lodestone for grounding, uttering breathy words of prayer to summon their powers.

Rosequartz's hands were clasped tightly in angry fists as she struggled inwardly not to let darkness overwhelm her, but Garnet somehow managed to pry her knotted fingers open, allowing Chiastolite to thrust the thulite into her right palm and the lodestone into the left before her hands snapped shut around them. Rosequartz bared her teeth in a grimace of agony and determination as her eyelids blinked open, revealing a glint of spirit and life in her green pupils.

Heartened, Chiastolite cried out, 'That's it, Sister Rosequartz, fight it! Hang on to life!'

Urgently she moved towards the thrashing Ryder's head, her elderly body trembling. Turning her attention once more on Rosequartz's scarred and tormented face, she saw that the power of the infection had increased, drawing all colour from her flesh and distorting her features with round bubbles that bulged like trapped pockets of poison beneath the skin. The wound that split her cheek was open and shiny but displayed an unnatural lack of blood or raw tissue, appearing instead to be a stony fissure of deep, grey, lifeless granite.

Taking a deep breath, she tapped her spirit into the eternal strength of the Ley, letting Its energy fortify her elderly bones. 'We must draw the darkness from her,' she told Garnet, taking out a large chunk of glassy clear quartz; 'try to capture it.' Bracing herself, she gripped the colourless crystal in her fingertips and with a powerful cry to the Ley, pushed it firmly into the gaping cut in Rosequartz's flesh. At her side, Garnet reached out and rested her hand on Chiastolite's, feeling the sudden, lifeless chill of Rosequartz's skin.

Together the two Ryders focused their consciousness and felt the warm instant power flood in, churning, ebbing, ready for action. Like thick, silver mercury It pooled within their minds, hearts and stomachs and melded within them. An unseen aura as light as air and strong as steel emanated from their fingertips, making the crystal tremble as it sent out a summoning note from its faultless, empty core, searching to latch on to the poisonous power that simmered hungrily within Rosequartz's tortured body. Chiastolite moved the crystal lightly from side to side beneath her fingers, forming pulses and waves of Ley energy vibrating out into the stricken Ryder. Rosequartz shrieked and gargled, her hands gripped vice-like around the fragments of lodestone and thulite until her nails scratched across their surfaces in narrow, white lines. She arched her neck in agony, banging the crown of her skull against the rocky ground, her lips drawn back as flecks of black-tinted saliva foamed from her mouth. Suddenly, a violent force shook her body as tendrils of insipid dark vapour began to emit from the dark flesh of her wound. A terrible coolness started to encroach into Garnet and Chiastolite's thoughts as the smoky, oily coils of sorcery were dragged from Rosequartz's being, viciously twisting around their fingers and the crystal they clung to. Acutely, they could sense the ravenous, mindless consciousness of the curse, searching in every direction for life to consume and destroy. Using every atom of mental power they possessed both Ryders allowed the Ley to thrust powerfully through them, filling the clear crystal and transforming it into a strong, empty vortex to gulp up the blackness as it was flushed from Rosequartz's body. She let out a terrible cry of pain and effort as the vileness was sucked from her, the Ley forming a brilliant barrier around it within the heart of the crystal. Her fellow Ryders allowed the tainted stone to tumble from their grasp like a red hot coal and stared in concern at Rosequartz as she clutched her cheek and wailed in shock and pain.

'Sister!' cried Garnet as Rosequartz struggled to sit up. She saw that the wound on her cheek had started bleeding again, healthy, scarlet and untainted. All signs of the curse's infection had left her.

Rosequartz gritted her teeth with agony, her breathing heavy. 'By the Ley,' she exclaimed, 'I have never known such pain and wicked hatred! It desired all joy and life within me, wanting to devour and turn it to blackness. A thousand blessings of the Ley upon you, Sisters, for saving me from such evil.' Earnestly she clasped Chiastolite and Garnet's hands in gratitude.

'But you are well now?' asked the elderly Ryder. Inwardly, she was monitoring the way the Ley interacted and mingled with Rosequartz's aura, searching for the signs of encroaching death that she knew so well from her work.

Grimacing with weakness and exhaustion, Rosequartz dabbed the gash on her cheek and winced. 'I will not lie, I have felt better. I thought myself a better swordswoman than to be defeated by some common thief and their halfpenny market sorcery. The Ley taught me a lesson in humility.'

Rummaging in her satchel, Garnet retrieved a vial of smoky quartz elixir which she passed to Rosequartz who gratefully swallowed a mouthful. 'You belittle yourself, Sister,' she said grimly. Taking a cotton pouch from her satchel, she stooped down to pick up the infected crystal. 'I do not think that this was merely a trick of common witchcraft.'

Garnet and Chiastolite studied the stone intently for a moment. It was easy to see fragments of churning, dark power filter about within the core of the stone, wrathful and trapped in its prison of Ley energy.

Chiastolite sucked her puckered, brown lips thoughtfully. 'I do not think we are dealing with some simple spell attack, Sisters,' she mused soberly. 'I have witnessed this entity before, though I fear I cannot put a name to it. Blackness such as this rose from the corpse of our fallen Sister Ammonite and I would warrant it is also what laid siege to Goodstone.'

Rosequartz finished supping her elixir and dabbed the last dregs on to the wound on her face. 'I spoke merely in jest. I do not doubt that there are serious and violent powers at work.' She gazed warily at the crystal. 'What shall we do with it? I shall not sleep easy knowing it is nearby.'

Chiastolite nodded in agreement. 'Sister Garnet,' she said, 'see if you can find a spot in this wood where the Ley runs strong and bury this damned stone there; allow the power we serve to heal its poison. I trust you know the appropriate ritual. I shall remain here and make camp. Rosequartz needs rest and I am too old and weary to travel further this night.'

She passed the crystal to Garnet who knotted the pouch's string and set out from her companions to find an appropriate spot to dispose of it. In the quiet, cool air of the forest she allowed the Ley to draw her to a place near a small spring where a young willow sapling was beginning to grow into maturity. The Ley swirled here almost giddily and there was no hint of darkness or foreboding. Garnet dug a small, deep hole in the soft soil next to the spring and deposited the hateful bundle, casting along with it any unpleasant memories of the ritual she and Chiastolite had performed to save Rosequartz. She packed the earth firmly around it, uttering a prayer to the Ley that It would disperse and destroy the darkness and hate within. When all traces of the stone and its wrapping were buried from sight, Garnet placed a small fragment of turquoise on the freshly dug ground and waited a few moments for the Ley energy to unite and purify the area. Once this had been done, and Garnet felt that no vicious energy could escape the crystal, she washed the turquoise in the spring water, filled a few flasks from the pool for future use and returned to where Chiastolite was setting up camp.

450

The elderly Ryder had built a small fire and had captured a night lark whose meat she was roasting on a spit above the flames. She had already crushed its gizzards in a stone mortar and pestle and was searching through the undergrowth for wild herbs to flavour them when Garnet returned. Rosequartz had already fallen asleep wrapped in the cocoon of her cloak with only her gleaming auburn hair to be seen. Her breathing was steady and deep but every now and again she would murmur softly to herself. Careful not to wake her, Garnet sat down near to the fire.

'It is done,' she breathed wearily, warming her hands in the orange light of the flame. 'With the Ley's blessing, that darkness shall harm no-one else.' Looking at Rosequartz's slumbering form, she asked, 'Has our sister eaten?'

Chiastolite gave up on her quest for garnish for the meagre offal and flopped down at Garnet's side like a bag of bones. 'Slumber will nourish her better than food in her state,' she croaked. 'But you and I must keep up our strength.' She offered her companion the bloody paste she had made but Garnet declined and instead tore the carcass from the spit. 'You need the innards more than I,' she sighed, tearing into the flesh. It was warm but still good and bloody and as she devoured it Garnet could feel her stomach churn with the need for sustenance. She had been running on adrenaline for the last few hours and now that was beginning to subside she was feeling wrought, exhausted and raw. The Ley and her conscience told her she must carry on but Garnet could not dismiss the horrors she had witnessed. Amethyst had been murdered and they had been attacked for seemingly little more reason than they were Ryders and she could not fathom where this hatred was coming from.

Sombrely, she watched as Chiastolite sucked the bloody remains of the bird guts from her bent fingers and wondered whether she too was feeling uncertain. 'Times are black,' she mused as Chiastolite gathered together the bones in a pot and placed them on the fire to boil down for morning. 'Sister Amethyst warned us that she saw a great change in the Ley but I never thought that it would bring about such violence on those who serve It. I cannot comprehend this hatred towards us that now lurks in folks' hearts.'

The elderly Ryder paused from her meal, her wrinkled face softening in the glow of the camp fire. 'You seem to lack knowledge of the brutality that runs in the Ley,' she said. 'I take it that your service to It has been a peaceful one.'

Grimly, Garnet shook her head. 'I do not claim that my duties to the Ley have been without bloodshed and battle,' she muttered quietly; 'in my life I have witnessed sights and committed acts that no gentlewoman should. But always I have called on the Ley to bless the lives of those who have hindered my work as much as those who I have aided. You of all Ryders should know each soul returns to the flow of the Ley when its life has been spent.' She heard her own voice grow soft and sorrowful as the last words left her tongue, her mind once more gripped by the memory of Amethyst. No doubt, given time, the Ley would bring succour to Garnet's grief and she would be at peace with the knowledge that Amethyst's life-force flowed onwards as part of the never-ending tide of Ley power, but that comfort struggled to come tonight.

Chiastolite turned her gentle dark eyes towards her fellow Ryder and rested her bony arms on her bent knees. 'Do you know how I came by my Stone Name, Chiastolite, Sister Garnet?' she asked quietly.

Amid her weariness and sorrow, the younger Ryder felt a narrow coil of merciful Ley energy twist into her mind. Chiastolite was the Handmaiden of Death and Dying. Perhaps the Ley had sent her with Garnet and Rosequartz to counsel them in their grief.

The old women shuffled closer to the red flames of the fire, gazing deeply into the patterns of smoke and ember as if they were the record-keepers to her past. 'I was beautiful once,' she murmured wistfully, almost seeming to forget Garnet was there. 'Not that you would know it to look at this wizened husk of a body, but I was. Skin like cream and hair the colour of summer corn, I had. My waist was slim and my limbs were strong and supple.' She sighed and glanced down at her knotted, ancient hands as if she could not believe they belonged to her. 'That was so long ago. So many decades since I was tutored at the citadel of Goodstone, but I still remember as if it was yesterday. The names, the faces, what happened. It was my duty to go to the mill once a week and collect the flour for baking. Whether it was rain or shine, I would never mind the task because I got to see *him*. Dimetri, the miller's son.' Garnet shifted uncomfortably on the stony ground and cleared her throat. With Rosequartz as her companion, she had heard plenty of stories about the risqué dalliances of lonely and frustrated apprentices to the Ley with various youths in the local area. It was one of the things would-be Ley Ryders were sternly warned against: to remember the value of their maidenhood and the vows of chastity that they would take on receiving their Stone Name; the desire of youth was a powerful temptation. Still Garnet did not see how such a tale was appropriate for a time like this. She thought Chiastolite should have known better.

As if reading her wary thoughts, the elderly Ryder focused her attention sharply on Garnet. 'Understand,' she said sharply, 'there was nothing improper between us. I understood my duties and he was a true gentleman. But I cannot deny that he was very sweet towards me and most handsome. He used to help me carry the sacks of flour back to the keep and we would talk and laugh together. He would share with me the gossip of the town and I would tell him stories from the visiting Ryders. It was nice to have a few moments away from my studies and my service to the Ley.'

A strange thing happened as Chiasolite spoke of her childhood sweetheart. All the traces of weariness and old age that masked her pale face seemed to melt into relief and she was filled with the animation of youth, be it mixed with a sorrowfulness of something that never was. Reaching out she brushed Garnet's hand gently and said, 'Sometimes the sweetest things in our life are not what we have or what is given to us by the Ley, but what never was, what never could be. Deep down, we both knew that our friendship could come to nothing. That I was to be bride only to the Ley. That's what makes what happened all the more bitter; such a sadness. He would have made someone a good husband, even if it hadn't been me.'

Cold sorrow suddenly filled Chiastolite's dark eyes, but it was strangely twinned with the Ley light gleaming there, hard and real at the core of her being. Garnet wanted to say that she did not have to say any more but she knew that this story was at the centre of who she was. It was a Ley blessing, tinted with agonising pain and Garnet must understand its teaching. 'What happened to him?' she asked quietly.

Chiastolite turned back to gaze into the crackling glow of the fire, the markers of age all at once returning to her face. 'It was an evening in early October when it happened,' she continued softly. 'The air was sweet with the scent of fruit and the stars were just beginning to show. Dimetri had walked me back to the keep as he often did. We were chatting, enjoying the beauty of the dusk. When we reached the citadel, he asked me something he never had before. He asked if he could kiss me.'

A choked sound caught in her throat and she covered her eyes with her tanned hand as if, despite her need to share this tale with Garnet, she could not bear to let her see the pain it brought her. When she spoke again her voice was small and lonely.

'It is wrong to say I regret what happened, because I do not. I do not regret that our lips met and in that brief moment I saw the colours and rhythms of the Ley flowing over my closed eyes so brilliant and clear that I finally understood the meaning of all my lessons, that I had shared this moment of destiny with someone who I was so very fond of. I opened my eyes to tell Dimetri the wonder of my revelations but instead of him standing smiling before me, he was still and motionless on the ground at my feet. I tried to revive him with the stone skills I had learnt in my training, skills which seemed so much easier now, but nothing worked. I ran crying for aid to my Sister Ryders in the keep and brought them to where he was but there was nothing that could be done. The Ley sets a lifespan for us all, sometimes many years, sometimes a mere few and that night It had deemed Dimetri's life-force would join It once more and in doing so awaken me to Its power.'

Garnet gasped in horror and reached out to place a hand on Chiastolite's arm in comfort. 'Sister,' she exclaimed compassionately, 'my heart weeps for you. I never knew someone could be summoned to the Ley in such a heartbreaking way.'

The old woman lowered her hand from her face. Garnet expected to see tears in her eyes and was surprised to see her expression stoic and accepting. 'Cast not your pity on me, Sister Garnet,' she said with a sad smile. 'I do not tell this story to gain your sympathy, merely to make you understand this simple fact. The day my Dimetri died and I took the name Chiastolite, Handmaiden to Death, I learnt that the Ley brings agony and sorrow as well as joy and comfort. At every deathbed I attend, ever pyre I light, I see how the power we serve can harm people in the grief and loss of their loved ones. The Ley is divine and merciful and each life has a length and purpose set by It, but the human heart, even one of a Ryder, struggles to accept such finality. We have to come to terms with the fact that there will be those who see us as agents for a brutal force.'

Garnet remained silent for a moment, casting her turbulent thoughts broodingly into the dark flow of Ley that billowed through her mind. Until Amethyst's death, she had never experienced the heartbreak and sorrow Chiastolite knew so well. Now she felt the Ley was driving her to change her view of It. She knew that change and movement was the fabric of the Ley's nature, never truly remaining in one place or being one thing. But to accept the Ley having a darkness to It, a brutality that would cause folk to hate It and Its followers, was a hard challenge.

'Amethyst spoke of an alteration in the Ley, one that related to the mute apprentice Petronia. It is difficult for an experienced Ryder such as I to deal with such notions of darkness and hate when they are connected to my duty, accept It as a thing to be feared and loathed by some. I worry how someone such as she would meet with such challenges.'

Chiastolite blinked her watery eyes and shrugged. 'The Ley has chosen to put her on such a path, just as It chose me to be servant to the dying,' she said simply. 'Sometimes it is beyond our present understanding what is expected of us and why certain problems are placed in our way. But the Ley does it for a reason and by tackling such heartaches and trials we learn to become who we are meant to be. To resent such things is foolish.'

Turning her head, Garnet watched Rosequartz as she stirred and muttered in her sleep, her dreams still lined with traces of the darkness that had temporarily invaded her body. 'And who are we three?' she pondered quietly. She answered herself barely a moment later in a voice that sounded more certain and pragmatic, more truly Garnet than she had felt since learning of Amethyst's murder. 'We are the witnesses and aids to Petronia. We shall follow the path that leads to her and see what the Ley has prepared for her fate.'

Chiastolite shuffled over to the slumbering Rosequartz and repositioned the crystal pendants that lay on her chest to ease her troubled slumber. 'Wisely spoken, Sister,' she breathed. 'But not until morning. For now we must rest and prepare ourselves for whatever is to come.'

Then, together uttering a final prayer to the Ley, she and Garnet settled down on the ground to sleep, held safely in an unmoving bubble of present awareness and past pain, wise enough not to look with either hope or dread at what was not yet to be seen.

Chapter 31

WRITTEN IN STONE

In the strange chamber of rock and metal within Kelhalbon, Hayden slept deep and restful, his mind unwound by a combination of sheer physical exhaustion and immense relief that Petronia had returned to him. The realm of the dwarves was in style and distance far removed from Ravensbrook, but his heart and thoughts were at ease in the knowledge that his sister was unharmed and back within his watchful protection. His dreams were shapeless, but in them he was aware of the hopeful notion that perhaps their journey and troubles were drawing to an end and that they could somehow find a state of peace and safety once more. They had previously been situated in Ravensbrook and always had been since they had started their strange journey. Now they hung in an uncertain place, somewhere inhabited by a maiden with silvery, cobwebbed skin and colourless hair.

He awoke and presumed it was morning, although night and day were indistinguishable in the windowless caverns of Kelhalbon. His sleep was disturbed by the sound of the heavy iron door to his chamber creaking open and Petronia tiptoeing in. Wiping the sleep from his eyes, he beamed contentedly reminded that his sister was indeed safely back. Sitting on the end of his bed, she gestured good morning and asked if he had slept well.

'Like the dead, dear Pet; my mind could finally rest knowing you were safe.' Pushing off the metallic woven cover from him, Hayden reached for his shirt and pulled it on.

Petronia's brown eyes shone warmly. Despite her annoyance at his worrying, she too was grateful that they had been reunited. During their time apart, she had grown a greater understanding of what it was like to fret about your sibling's safety and now that they were back together again, made a conscious decision to be more tolerant of his anxiousness towards her.

She waited for him to dress before standing and giving him an affectionate embrace. *'I'm glad you are safe, Brother,'* she signed. *'I feared that I might not see you again. I will thank Bracken a thousand times for keeping you safe on your journey.'*

Hayden found himself unexpectedly blushing at the mention of the Ley apprentice's name and quickly averted his eyes from his sister's keen gaze. 'Indeed,' he said softly, 'and what a journey it was too! I have much to tell about our adventures and can't wait to hear about yours.'

Petronia made no response. Despite her relief at being reunited with Hayden, she still felt a churning within, the growing, dark power of words and energy that the Ley had awoken. She would be happy to think that her arrival at Kelhalbon was the end of her quest but, if anything, being in the crystal-walled chasms made her more aware that there was some unknown challenge calling. She kept thinking about the dark life-force that animated the iron Golem and felt that here she could understand her affinity with it more fully. She wanted to tell her brother about this new ambition but was reluctant, knowing how much he worried and mistrusted the Ley.

As if reading her mind, Hayden looked at her suspiciously. 'Is there something wrong, Pet?' he asked worriedly, studying her pensive face. 'You weren't harmed in your journey?'

Recognising the familiar anxiety for her well-being in her brother's tone, Petronia sighed and crossed her arms defensively, showing that she was not going to let him stop her following the path she was being drawn to. But to her surprise the concern never came.

'Worry not, Sister,' he told her, holding up his hands in submission. 'I can see now that I have no power to dissuade you from your decision to follow the Ley. During our time apart, some force, be it the Ley or your own will, has kept you safe. Whichever it is, I must learn to allow you to live your own life, though I will confess it will be a challenge for me to do so.'

A grateful smile passed over her face on hearing these words and she placed her hand lovingly on Hayden's arm. It heartened her to know that she had his blessing at last to follow the Calling that was opening up before her. The trials lain down by the Ley were going to be more perilous and dark than her brother could realise. There was a darkness within her too, awakening and powerful, that Hayden would be disturbed by if he knew, a darkness that spoke in a language that Petronia was only just beginning to understand. She felt that a voice and purpose to her life, two things that she had lacked for so long, were going to come within her reach. However, their arrival might not manifest in the way she would have hoped for. Would they change her when she possessed them?

A soft knock on the door interrupted the siblings' reunion. Opening the heavy, metal portal, Hayden discovered Aarold waiting patiently in the stone hallway beyond, his strange steed and companion Phebus lurking a few feet behind him. The young prince bowed his head politely when he saw Hayden. 'Good morrow, Master Hayden,' he greeted with a shy smile.

Respectfully, the blacksmith's son bowed. 'Your Majesty,' he said solemnly, 'please come in.'

Aarold shuffled awkwardly; having people grovel before him because of his status always left him feeling uncomfortable. 'Please,' he begged, 'do not stand on ceremony, I am merely looking for my sister Bracken. I am keen to get to know her after so many years apart.'

He peered inside Hayden's chamber and catching sight of Petronia, gave her a warm smile. 'Greetings, Mistress Petronia,' he said, his cheeks colouring slightly when the pretty Ley apprentice beamed back at him. 'I trust you had a peaceful night.' Happy to see her travelling companion, Petronia crossed the floor to greet him with a smile and signed, *'Good morning.'*

Self-consciously, Aarold ventured to grin shyly back before glancing down at his feet to disguise his timidity. 'I don't suppose either of you have met with her this morning,' he continued. 'Phebus and I visited her chamber and found it empty. I was hoping to speak with her privately so we might learn more about each other. I am eager to know everything there is to know about my new sister.'

Hayden and Petronia looked at each other and shook their heads. 'We have not seen her since we retired last night,' Hayden said on both of their behalves. 'But no doubt she will be found with Mistress Bahl or her grandfather, Prince Ion. The sudden revelations of the true nature of her family seemed to have come as quite a shock.'

Aarold's face turned sallow and disappointed at hearing this and he flexed his wasted leg in embarrassment. 'Oh,' he breathed, wetting his narrow lips, 'I understand. Never mind, my, *our* father always encouraged me not to hamper my weaknesses on to others. I will not trouble her.'

Compassion flooded Petronia's heart when she saw the disappointment in the expression of the young man whom she had grown quite fond of. She reached forward and brushed his hand reassuringly to indicate that he had no need to feel inadequate.

Likewise, Hayden shook his head. 'You miss my meaning, good prince,' he explained. 'I had no thought that Mistress Bracken might regret discovering you were her sibling. I was simply noting that to find out after a childhood of complete ignorance that one is descended from such an alien race as that of the dwarves would overawe any person. She is bound to be emotional at this time.'

A cold shiver of unsettled energy once more ran through Petronia as her brother spoke. There was no doubt in her mind that the atmosphere in Kelhalbon, although outwardly organised and hospitable, held within it a hidden bitterness and ill-ease. From what she had seen of the disturbed Prince Consort, he was hardly the welcoming family an orphaned soul would hope to be returned to.

Aarold's expression relaxed at Hayden's kind words and he nodded in agreement. 'Of course,' he breathed, 'although from what I have read of the histories of the dwarf race, she should feel privileged. They are a great and honourable people. I'm sure she will learn to be proud of them.'

Behind him, Phebus grumbled and cast Aarold a withering look.

'One would hope so,' he remarked. 'It would do better for her to contemplate her maternal line than learn of the uncouthness of her father. I trust you will be delicate with your new sibling, dear boy, when she asks about her barbarian of a sire.' The prince gave his friend a cold glance. 'Phebus,' he reprimanded, 'I certainly hope that you aren't going to infect Bracken's mind with your judgemental opinions of our father. It's hardly the best way to welcome a sister into the family.' The Equile bleated to himself and ran his pink tongue over his glossy black beak, but said no more.

Leaning on his cane, Aarold moved over to stand next to Phebus. 'I suppose it would be best that I go and seek her out,' he informed the others; 'no doubt the good lady Bahl will know where she is.'

Hayden and Petronia nodded in agreement to that sentiment and decided that they would join him. Together the four of them walked along the dim, low-ceilinged corridor that led from the sleeping quarters back to the main chamber where the dwarves had already begun the activity of the day. The mighty furnaces glowed with scarlet heat as the skilful artisans of Kelhalbon toiled at their metal craft. They strolled across the bridges and walkways that connected the stone plateaus of the kingdom, watching as the dwarf smiths created and maintained the iron structures that formed their land. After some time, they found Bahl in a small cubicle situated on one of the quieter islets, seated at an ornate black iron desk, sorting through piles of thinly-cut stone tablets and giving instructions to a continual flow of female dwarf ministers and officials who filed in and out of her study. When the humans entered, she glanced up from her work and smiled and held up her hand to silence the bureaucrat who she had been previously talking with.

'Good morning, my friends,' she said, putting down the plaque she was studying. 'I trust you slept well. You will excuse me for not greeting you earlier. My role of overseeing the business of the kingdom on the queen's behalf is quite an arduous one, and after recent events I have got somewhat behind.' She gestured to the stacks of tablets piled high before her.

Aarold, being familiar with the administration of government, nodded in understanding. 'I apologise for the interruption to your duties,' he said, glancing at the unfamiliar script carved on one of the slates. 'We were merely enquiring after my sister as none of our party has seen her this morning.' The young prince was still getting used to the novelty of having a sibling and it gave him an unusual joy to say the words "my sister" rather than use Bracken's name and this confused Bahl for a brief moment.

'Oh, you mean Lady Bracken. Yes, indeed I consulted with her early this morning. She understandably found it difficult to sleep after yesterday's revelations and I did my best to reassure her of my support while she comes to terms with the knowledge of her royal birthright.' She drummed a rough grey finger thoughtfully on her chin. 'She then asked me if she might spend some time in the crystal fount. It does not surprise me that she should ask that, not with her being under the guard of the Ley Ryders for so long. I expect she is still there.' Hayden looked puzzled and glanced at his sister in the hope that the Ryders might have mentioned such a place but Petronia shook her head.

Getting to her feet, Bahl walked from behind her desk. 'The crystal fount is one of the greatest bonds between we dwarves and the Sisterhood of the Ley Ryders,' she explained. 'It is where the crystals they use to channel the Ley develop, and the sisters consider it a sacred and intense arena of Ley energy. Many Ryders have said they have come to a greater realisation of the purpose the Ley has for them by standing within the chamber. I will escort you there, but understand that it is a place of reverence and must be treated with the greatest respect.'

Beckoning to them, the vizier of Kelhalbon led the way out of her office and back into the hurly-burly of the main chamber. The party followed her across the web-like structure of twisting metal pathways and staircases that spanned the chamber, heading toward the rear wall of the immense cavern. They passed many smiths working at their anvils and fires, a number of whom stopped to greet Bahl or ask her questions in guttural Dwarfish. The capable vizier answered them with swift official politeness before carrying on her way. After a while, Hayden and the others noticed that they were entering into a quieter, less populated area of the chamber. There were less forges and general activity as if this section of the cave had been set aside to remain untainted by the everyday noise and business of dwarf life; even the fiery glow from the great chandeliers above them was muted into a cooler, more shadowy gloom reminiscent of the hour after sunset. In this more peaceful atmosphere, Hayden found his attention drawn to a vast, dark wall of stone. As they drew closer, he was struck by the presence of strength and power that emulated from the heavy rock. A mood of powerful protection seemed to be inbuilt within the wall, a proud resistance that ran through it in hair-thin veins of glittering metallic ore, guarding something intensely precious and holy, as if whatever lay beyond watched over Kelhalbon like a living deity.

They crossed over one final bridge to a narrow shelf of stone that jutted out from the mighty mountainside. At this range, the barrier of granite hung before them like an unmoving black curtain, folds and curves of rock bulging outwards as if straining to withhold the secret beyond. Unlike the rest of the dwarf kingdom, this space was sparsely embellished with very little ironwork. There was no sign of a door or passageway cut into the solid stone, nor were there any crystals visible in its faultless surface. A large, semicircular basin had been carved in the rock to one side of the ledge into which a narrow flow of spring water trickled from some unseen point higher up, its thin constant echo filling the hushed air. At the very centre-point in the wall, a large, ornate wheel had been set, its axle driven firmly into the bed of the stone.

Reverently, Bahl strode across to the stone bowl and meticulously bathed her large, grey hands and face in the purifying flow of the spring, like a pilgrim preparing to enter a sacred shrine. She then approached the iron ring and turned to face the others.

'The crystal fount is an extremely important and hallowed place,' she explained soberly. 'It is where all the jewels used by the Ryders in their duties grow and develop. Not only does it emit a tremendous amount of Ley energy but the crystals draw in and feed off the emotions of others. I do not want to risk contaminating the growing gemstones by overwhelming them with the presence of too many unprepared minds so

I ask you all before we venture any further, to be sure that you will bring nothing within your thoughts that will stain their maturing power.'

Her eyes rested on Petronia as she spoke, hoping that she, as an apprentice to the Ley, would understand the importance of her words. Petronia thought hard for a moment, her eyes resting on the solid iron dial fixed to the dark wall. She was curious to see the birthplace of the mighty power that had so altered her life in the past few weeks but was also acutely aware of the surging, murmuring blackness that whispered silently within her. She knew that given time she could master this dark instinct, but dared not risk entering such a holy and rarefied sanctum with such a feral force churning within her thoughts. Solemnly, she looked at Bahl and slowly shook her head, indicating that she neither felt worthy nor prepared to venture any further.

The dwarf nodded understandingly. 'A wise choice,' she said. 'Many Ryders find it helpful to visit the crystal fount as it gives them greater clarity of the Ley's nature, but it is indeed an intense and emotional experience and not suitable for one at the start of her apprenticeship.'

Suddenly feeling nervous, Aarold rested his hand against Phebus's scaly flank. 'Though I detest admitting it,' he said softly, 'I am aware that my constitution is not very strong and the past few days have been an ordeal for me. Perhaps it would be better for me to wait here with Phebus and Mistress Petronia.' Proud that his companion was at last starting to show some signs of sensible caution, the Equile rested his beak affectionately on top of Aarold's head. 'Quite so,' he agreed. 'I think you have had enough stimulation to last you a lifetime.'

'Very well,' said Bahl before extending her hand towards Hayden. 'If you are ready, we shall proceed.'

Hayden could not think of any good reason for him not to enter the crystal fount, and even if he could have he felt it was only right for Bracken to know that she had at least one familiar face on hand at this confusing and emotional time. She had, after all, stood by him and tried to offer comfort and support when he had been separated from his sister. It would be rude of him not to do the same. Stepping forward, he crossed over to the stone vessel into which the stream of water trickled and solemnly washed his hands and face in its purifying flow. The water was extremely clean and lukewarm, heated by the same hot springs that created the dwarves' bath house. When he felt he was suitably clean, he moved over to stand beside Bahl, ready for her to uncover the hidden entrance to the blessed cavern.

The dwarf vizier carefully rested her large, pale grey hands on the rim of the iron wheel and took firm hold. With strong but steady motions, she began to twist it on its axle, first a few degrees clockwise then a few in the opposite direction, as if entering the combination to some mighty safe. A low, clunking, grating sound emulated as the wheel was turned; the movement seemed to awaken something within the solid fibre of the stone wall. As she slowly spun the dial this way and that Bahl began to hum a deep, resounding, monotone chord, a note that was twinned with the vibrating key of the rock itself. Hayden watched in amazement as numerous cracks and fissures began appearing, stretching out across the dark granite surrounding the wheel. They were not like normal breaks in stone, zigzagging haphazard paths, but straight, precise and angular, as if cut by some invisible blade. They etched purposefully into the wall and the stone surrounding them seemed to shiver and become malleable, like a thick but pliable veil covering a precious treasure. Rays of sharp, bluish-silvery light pierced brightly through the cracks, flawless and brilliant, joining together to mark out a clear portal on the stone.

Bahl ceased her chanting and removed her hands from the iron wheel with a reverent sigh. Resting one hand gently on Hayden's shoulder, she pressed the other firmly against the altered texture of the stone and guided him through. Hayden did not know what to expect or feel as he passed through the enchanted doorway and had only a brief moment to register the sensation. It was as if the wall had become little more than an immense shadow passing over his body before he was greeted by an intense, glaring white light that was in stark contrast to the gloom of the great chamber. It completely blinded him to his surroundings, causing him to squeeze his eyelids shut and bring his hand to his brow to shield his vision. At first, he assumed he must have stepped back out on to the snowy mountainside for the glare that engulfed him did indeed have the same brilliance and purity as sunlight off snow. The air was cooler away from the toil and heat of the dwarf forges, but in no way cold enough to resemble the violent blizzard he and Bracken had fought their way through the day before. Instead, the atmosphere was fresh, still and indescribably silent, as if all noise, all life beyond this hallowed place, ceased to exist.

Slowly, Hayden's sight returned to him and after blinking a few times he was able to see where he was. He found himself not outside after all but within another giant grotto, the beauty and tranquillity of which took his breath away. It was around the same size as the chamber that he had just left, but instead of being dominated by shadow, fire and ironwork, this place sparkled and gleamed with the iridescence of countless crystals of every shade and variety, growing in angular clusters over nearly every inch of the wall, ceiling and floor, like abstract flowers in some bewitched meadow. They blanketed everything, their sharp, rigid faces and peaks stretching forth at every angle, each one proudly glowing with colour and pureness, from bloody ruby and garnet to the aquatic majesty of sapphire and lapis lazuli. They burst from every surface in great, glittering formations. Diamonds, so large their worth would mock the richest monarch's coffers, glinted as clear as chunks of cut glass. Stranger, lesser known stones clung alongside their sisters, their multicoloured shades running with delicate, marbled veins. Even the floor was a vast sheet of intertwined rivers of polished colour, shimmering with specks of vibrancy. The twinkling stones stretched and crept over themselves to form magnificent natural structures, bowing columns and archways, dissecting the chamber into countless alcoves and grottos. But for all their wealth and rarity, these precious crystals were no common treasure trove. Each stone, each gem seemed to glow with a unique radiance that merged together to flood the chamber with a spiritual brilliance, as if there was within each of their solid still cores a seed of powerful virtue, changing each stone into a chrysalis of energy and goodness.

Cautiously, Bahl moved through the chamber, her dark eyes wandering over the glittering walls, respectfully regarding their countless shades of brilliance. She made a small, reverent bow as if to show servitude to some unseen master before turning to address Hayden. 'This is the crystal fount,' she explained, in a hushed whisper, 'birthplace of every gem that reflects the Ley's power. Every stone you see is alive, though not in the way a creature or plant is. Remember what I told you, the crystals are aware of your thoughts; try, if you can, not to bring too much negativity into this place. I fear that Mistress Bracken was troubled with many perturbing thoughts when she asked me to bring her here.'

She beckoned to Hayden to follow her deeper into the cave and he obeyed. He soon discovered that the cavern was in fact a complex honeycomb network of interlocking alcoves and grottos, segmented by vast columns and walls of glittering gems. Rainbow beams of colour and brilliance sliced through the still, hallowed atmosphere, forming transparent imitations and reflections of the vast banks of jewels. The whole space was an immense, glittering hall of irregular mirrors, the naturally polished faces of the crystals forming a myriad of pathways and dead ends. Very soon Hayden found that he had somehow become separated from Bahl and was wandering alone through this beautiful, ethereal arena. He moved as silently as he could, barely daring to breath, less he disturb and shatter the cool, bright, almost brittle air of the chamber. He felt as if he was captured within a huge, crystal orb and that somewhere beyond its translucent walls, a vast benign entity was observing him through a million tiny, bright eyes.

After wandering for some time, Hayden turned a corner and found Bracken, seated on the polished floor within a small alcove beneath an arch of jagged green emeralds. She was once more wearing the patchwork robe of a Ley apprentice, the skirt spread out across the ground like a less impressive imitation of the glittering rainbow walls of the chamber. She had taken down the ornate hairstyle of coils and plaits that had crowned her the previous evening and her long, wild locks now hung about her shoulders, each hair gleaming with a reflected shade of the countless gems that filled the cavern. Her face was pensive, almost emotionless, but as Hayden drew closer he saw redness in her eyes that betrayed recently dried tears. Hearing him approach, she turned her head and gave a small smile of greeting. 'Good morrow, Master Hayden,' she said softly, her voice filled with disguised emotion. Hayden walked over to her and took a seat on the cold, hard ground.

'Good morning,' he replied. 'Mistress Bahl said we would find you here.'

Bracken sighed and shook her head. 'I did not sleep well and rose early,' she explained. 'I read about this place in the library back at the citadel and asked Bahl if I might spend some time here. Did you know it is said that when a Ryder comes to the fount, the intense power of the Ley within the crystals allows her to see what the Ley has destined for her?'

Hayden glanced at the millions of chinks of brightly coloured light reflecting in the angular surfaces of the jewels all around them. 'She mentioned something about it. I was surprised that my sister wasn't more keen to see the fount, being as she seems so determined to join the Sisterhood.'

Bracken barely seemed to register what he had said. Resting her forearms on her knees, she leant forward, her dark, green eyes fixed intently on an expanse of bloody rubies and flawless diamonds that formed part of the wall opposite them. 'Do you know what I feel sitting here?' she murmured, almost to herself. 'Nothing. Oh, I can see the splendour of the crystals, understand better than most the immense power of the Ley held within them. But as for it altering my soul and revealing to me some great personal insight, my mind and spirit remain unchanged. And now it's clear to me why.'

She took a deep breath and bowed her head as if battling to control the urge to weep in despair. 'Bahl explained to me why dwarves cannot feel the Ley. There is something different in our hearts, a hardness that humans do not possess. We guard this great repository of the Ley's power, but we can never experience it. I know that I am not fully dwarf, that my father was a king of men, but there is enough of my mother's nature in me to deny me of the role I long believed would be my destiny. How else could I sit here and not be moved? I cannot help feeling that all the teachings of Sister Amethyst and the other Ryders were a waste. I don't know who I'm truly meant to be.'

The despair in Bracken's voice moved Hayden's heart to pity and he struggled to make sense of how discovering her lost family could bring the maiden such woe. He knew that Bracken never saw herself as an orphan. Her family, her identity, were moulded and shaped by the Ryders' upbringing. To find out that something you were born with denies you the one ambition and destiny that you strived all your life to achieve must be disheartening. *How do you learn to take on a whole new role in the world?*

'But surely you must think the Ley has brought you back to your kin, the place you belong?' he asked, placing a comforting hand on her shoulder. 'You must feel a small amount of gratitude and peace of mind to meet your grandparents and brother?'

Bracken looked up and forced a small, sad smile. 'It should do, shouldn't it?' she said softly. 'Hayden, I know how important you feel blood family to be and perhaps in time I shall grow to see myself as part of the dwarf race. But right now I am finding it very difficult to feel any sort of affection for my mother's parents.' A great sadness and concern filled Bracken's dark green eyes. 'My grandfather has clearly been damaged by the loss of his daughter and as for Queen Penn,' she gave a little shudder, 'I have never seen such hatred and bitterness in a person. It is terrifying. You cannot imagine what she's like. She has such a loathing for me, for the world, I do not see a way of making a connection. Perhaps I could accept her unhappy, chosen fate if it didn't concern me that part of the brutal, unforgiving character may belong to me through our bloodline. How could I be descended from such an uncaring and venomous individual?'

Hayden shook his head. 'You are your own person and mistress of your own fate,' he said plainly. 'Throughout our journey, you've always maintained that it was the lessons and upbringing of the Ryders that formed your view of the world. Sixteen years of that guidance can't be undone by one meeting with a damaged relative. Just because you can't feel the Ley doesn't make Its teachings of mercy and kindness any less profound. The nature of your Dwarfish kin cannot change what your adoptive family has made you.'

Nodding thoughtfully, Bracken got to her feet and wandered over to gaze at a section of cavern wall, its surface encrusted with millions of sharp, crystallised plains that reflected her ponderous features back at her, tinted in shades of deep sapphire and vibrant, green jade. 'It is true,' she uttered solemnly, 'the Ley has given me a guide by which to live but it is the life of a contented servant, not a leader of people. After seeing the venomous state of my grandmother, Queen Penn, it is clear that the dwarves see me returning to them as a chance to have a reasonable and sane sovereign again, but it is a role that I have no aptitude to fill. I fear they look to me as a saviour and ruler when I am not.'

Hayden wished very much he could offer Bracken some words of comfort or advice regarding her predicament but did not quite know what to say. A simple blacksmith's son such as he had no guidance to give regarding the appropriate way she might fulfil her birthright as queen of the dwarves. He only wished that Bracken could feel the same joy and connection with her new-found family that he did at being reunited with Petronia. He thought back over his reluctance to accept his sister's apprenticeship to the Ley and how that now, seeing that she was safe and capable of journeying this far without his guidance and protection, made him realise that perhaps the strange, blind hermit Emouchet was right. It was down to each individual to survive life and seize whatever fate threw in their way. Bracken was a good, just woman and now she knew the truth of her heritage, it was down to her alone to somehow take the responsibility laid at her feet.

He was just wondering how to express this sentiment in the kindest, most subtle way when Bahl stepped from behind the barrier of shimmering jewels that stood to the right of them. The dwarf vizier greeted Bracken with a smile and bowed her head respectfully. 'Your Highness,' she addressed, in her low, throaty tone, 'I'm glad I've found you; your companions were concerned as to where you were. I explained to them you felt the need to immerse yourself in the celestial aura of the crystal fount. I trust your meditation here was soothing to your mind.'

Bracken sighed downheartedly at Bahl's words, loathing the respect and reverence in them. 'Alas, no. As always, the influence of the Ley is lost on my mind. And I do wish you wouldn't refer to me as Your Highness. I know that is how I am seen in this kingdom but the title sits uneasily with me. I mean no offence but there is so much here in Kelhalbon that I am struggling to accept. Perhaps I have too much human blood in my veins to truly be your princess.'

A strange look shimmered in Bahl's wide, black eyes. It might be compared to the human emotions of compassion or sympathy although the nature and facial features of dwarves made those concepts hard to express.

'My mistress,' she said levelly, folding her large grey hands before her, 'I can tell you are concerned by discovering the nature of your birth and by what is expected of you by your people.' She paused for a brief second and took a deep breath before speaking again in the gentlest tone her harsh, gravelly voice could muster. 'May I speak frankly, my lady, not as your vizier but as someone who knew your mother?'

Bracken shrugged and nodded for Bahl to continue.

The wise dwarf frowned slightly and she chose her words slowly and carefully as if speaking in a language unfamiliar to her. 'It is in my opinion,' she stated carefully, 'that your mother did not *love* your father or even fall enamoured of him. It is not in our nature. The brittleness of our hearts means that the idea of romantic love and paternal love is challenging for us. Most dwarves are fond of their partners and offspring, respect and enjoy their company, but the concept of love is difficult for us to conceive. For millennia it has been thus and our past queens have always maintained that to rule without compassion or heated desire was the correct way to govern. But I believe your mother Duun saw a flaw in this mindset. She studied the ways of humans, the Ryders, and noted that it seemed to be their ability to bond with others that gave them strength. Your grandmother always had an unforgiving character, even before she succumbed to the bitter darkness of Ac-Nu. Perhaps your mother deliberately chose to bear a child that mixed human blood with that of her own brutal dwarf kin in the hope that her offspring would grow into a more merciful and just leader for our people.'

Bracken hung her head wearily and sighed. 'Mercy and justice are

471

truly virtues taught to me by my adoptive family and I have always tried to live by them, but the will and ability to govern and lead are not part of the way of life for followers of the Ley.'

Taking a step backwards, Bahl pressed her palms together and bowed her head. 'I can offer you no more words of comfort other than those I have spoken, my mistress. But know that I am the steward of Kelhalbon and have been a loyal servant and advisor to your family. I have aided your mother and grandmother to the best of my abilities and will do the same for you.'

'I hope your faith in me is not misplaced,' breathed Bracken. 'I can only use the guidance instilled in me by the Sisterhood.'

The dwarf's striking features formed an expression of stoic assurance. 'I do not doubt your abilities for a moment, mistress,' she stated surely; before adding, 'you have greatness in you, you merely need to trust yourself and realise it.'

Her words made Bracken recall the woman who had raised her. Sister Amethyst had always said the day would come when Bracken would uncover her destiny. For a long time Bracken thought that meant the day when her spirit finally felt the force and guiding flow of the Ley and her eyes would at last be opened to Its mysteries. Only now she was beginning to come to terms with the notion that the skills and lessons bestowed on her would have to be used for a much different but equally as noble a cause and that she would have to start looking within her own heart and not to the Ley for wisdom.

Turning on her heel, Bahl began to stride back towards the jewel-covered wall of the chamber. She paused momentarily and beckoned to Bracken and Hayden to follow.

'Come,' she called, in her familiar, throaty emotionless tone, 'we have troubled the crystal fount enough with our earthly concerns. Lingering here will not lessen my mistress's worries any more than it has done already. I have many duties to attend to and if Lady Bracken truly wishes to understand the nature of her people it would be best if she accompanies me. We dwarves are an industrious race and are better known through deeds than words.'

Swiftly, she led the pair back through the glittering majesty of the cavern to the spot where she and Hayden had entered. The exit to the hallowed realm was barely visible against the glistening patterns of crystals, simply a dark outline etched against the countless colours of the jewels. With a gentle touch, Bahl pushed the portal ajar and ushered both Hayden and Bracken back into the semi-darkness of the chamber beyond where Aarold, Petronia and Phebus were awaiting them.

The young prince regarded his sister worriedly as she emerged from the sacred grotto. 'Are you well, my Sister?' he asked her tentatively, somewhat surprised by his feelings of brotherly concern.

Stiffly, Bracken nodded, unwilling to linger any further on the doubts and insecurities that troubled her mind. 'I am fine,' she reassured him. 'I guess I am still a little in shock after learning of my royal heritage. I suspect such responsibilities and duties are familiar to you, having borne them all your life, but for me it is quite overwhelming.'

Aarold smiled sympathetically and placed his hand on her arm. 'I understand such insecurities more than you could realise,' he said knowingly. 'The mantle of a sovereign is a weighty one and causes a person to question how their flaws might bring misfortune. I can only advise that you do as I have attempted to in my role as prince of Geoll and use knowledge and guidance to do what you think is right.'

'A fine sentiment!' remarked Phebus tartly. 'It would be good if you took it now and again, dear boy, instead of being driven by whims and fancies.' His scarlet eyes glanced in Bahl's direction and he respectfully bowed his head. 'No offence to you or your kingdom, Mistress Bahl. I simply refer to the foolhardy exploits that brought us here. My master and companion, the prince, is highly educated and well-meaning but he doesn't always think through his actions and is easily led.' He flared his nostrils and looked knowingly at Petronia.

Hayden noticed the Equile's haughty expression and turned to his sister for clarification. 'What does he mean by that?' he queried suspiciously, eyeing Aarold with protective mistrust. Prince or not, he still did not feel he knew enough about what happened between him and his sister whilst they had been parted.

Petronia's cheeks flushed crimson for a moment, but she gestured dismissively and signalled that there was no cause for her brother to be concerned.

Together, the party followed Bahl back across the bridges and overpasses to the main hub of forges and workshops, leaving the sacred tranquillity of the crystal fount behind them as they re-entered the clanking din and bustle of dwarves engaged in toil and craftwork. Hayden, Petronia and Phebus walked a short distance behind the others, idly watching the powerful and skilled workers going about their business of creating and maintaining their ornate home, while Bracken walked slowly ahead of them, Bahl to her left and Aarold to her right, half listening to the dwarf vizier as she tried to explain the duties and chores carried out by each craftsman they passed.

Petronia was wondering whether she should try and give some gesture of comfort to Bracken when a sudden surge of powerful awareness flooded into her brain, turning her thoughts away from her companion's plight. Dark whispers and sensations stirred within her head like the coiled muscles of a wild animal suddenly becoming aware of nearby danger. All at once, she felt the need to prepare herself, summon her strength in readiness for a great challenge. Glancing around, she scrutinised the workshops and smithies for an indication as to where this threat would appear but could see no clue, only the disquiet in her own thoughts. She was aware of a great secret restless to be revealed.

As Bahl and Bracken were about to pass the doorway of one of the workshops, the large figure of a dwarf stepped out from its shadowy depths bowing in greeting to the vizier and Bracken. The group watched and waited as he then proceeded to garble in urgent Dwarfish, gesturing for Bahl and the others to join him inside his smithy. A feeling in the pit of Petronia's gut led her to guess what the dwarf was saying, that it related to the surge of energy and power she once again felt flowing through her thoughts, but she waited for Bahl to confirm her suspicions.

The steward of Kelhalbon listened patiently to her fellow dwarf before turning to explain what he had said. 'You remember Tunk,' she said, her gaze lingering in particular on Bracken, eager for her to begin her lessons in the culture and arts of their race. 'He is one of our finest engineers and has been examining the iron Golem that Prince Aarold and Mistress Petronia say attacked them on the borders of our realm.'

Aarold's pale face grew tense at the mention of the strange, metal automaton that had ambushed them so violently. 'Has he discovered where it came from?' he asked nervously, resting his hand on Phebus's neck for reassurance. Sensing his nervousness, Petronia reached over to the young prince and gave his hand a comforting squeeze.

Solemnly, Bahl shook her head. 'He has studied it thoroughly and has made a number of discoveries but on the whole is still unsure as to its true nature,' she explained as Tunk grunted another phrase in Dwarfish and pointed towards Bracken. 'He wishes that I and Princess Bracken, as well as our human guests, see the Golem for ourselves in the hope that our fresh eyes might bring clarity to the mystery.'

Anxiously, Aarold shrank back against Phebus and swallowed. He hated himself for his cowardice, but the memory of the mechanical beast and its jagged razor-like fangs made him unwilling to confront it again. He had wanted this quest to enlighten his mind but so far it had done more to make him realise his limitations. 'I feel it would be prudent if I remain outside,' he said, 'at least until we know for sure what manner of creature we are dealing with.'

Petronia, however, had no apprehensions. In fact, as the others had stood talking, she had become more and more aware of the dull tone of energy churning within the hidden workings of the unseen Golem. It sang out to her above the clattering sounds of the everyday world of dwarf toil like a low, buzzing drone, a discord that put her nerves on edge. It felt somehow incomplete, stirring within her mind a similar but greater tone that was master to it. Petronia's heart beat faster at that notion, as strange and arcane words began to push themselves once more from her subconscious; alien yet at the same time familiar, she felt them urge her onwards.

Leaving Aarold outside in Phebus's protection, they followed Tunk inside the workshop. The smithy was meticulously tidy, with lines of well-oiled tools hung neatly along three of the four walls, organised in size from a mallet as tall as a grown man to a pair of pliers so delicate it was impossible to think a dwarf could use them without crushing them between his fingertips. A scarlet-hot forge blazed along the fourth wall, fed and maintained by an ingenious clockwork device that shovelled coals and pumped bellows without the need of outside attention. On the workbench that occupied the centre of the room, illuminated by the brilliant orange glow of the flames, was the motionless Golem. Something churned and murmured within Petronia's brain as she gazed upon the metallic automaton. She recalled its violent assault on her and Aarold and although it now showed not the tiniest hint of life or movement, knew that the thoughtless power that drove it still slumbered beneath the strange curved markings on its domed shell. The dull, inaudible note that emulated from its cold, iron form to her brain was constant, like a thin, metal wire that trembled with forceful vibrations at the slightest touch of her thoughts.

Striding over to the workbench, Tunk meticulously checked the thick, heavy shackles that bolted the Golem's spindly legs securely to the table. When he was sure all precautions had been taken, he beckoned for Bracken, Bahl and the others to draw closer.

His huge hands gesturing confidently around the Golem, the dwarf craftsman spoke in harsh, guttural phrases, his dark eyes darting between the machine and Bahl as he waited for her to translate. 'He says that there is no doubt that this creature is dwarf-made,' Bahl stated at last, as Tunk indicated to the lower rim of its shell as if the way the metal was cut and formed was evident proof for even the most untrained eyes. 'He is even convinced he knows which of his fellow smiths made it. It bears some of the signature style of a dwarf by the name of Krogg. He disappeared some months ago while out on a hunt.' Bracken knitted her fingers together and glanced awkwardly at Petronia. Even though she had only known she was heir to the throne of Kelhalbon for a few hours, it made her feel slightly embarrassed to think one of her race was responsible for creating the machine that had put the life of her half-brother at peril.

Stepping away from the workbench, Tunk faced the group, anxiety

476

and doubt etching his craggy, grey features. When he spoke his voice was low and earnest. 'He says that although he is convinced the Golem was fashioned by Krogg's hand, there is more to its workings than normal Dwarfish clockwork. A power, an enchantment of some kind, imbues it with will and energy.'

Bracken studied the motionless metal beast before them for a few seconds, feeling like her dwarf blood should make her possess some insight as to what caused the Golem to operate. 'Like the Ley you mean?' she asked Bahl.

In unison, the vizier and the craftsman shook their heads before engaging in a short, serious conversation in Dwarfish. After a few moments, Bahl addressed the others. 'Tunk says, there are undeniable similarities between the sacred force of the Ley and the might that dwells within the workings of this machine, they both emit immense energy, but they are undoubtedly not the same. The sorcery within the Golem is full of dark hunger, a thoughtless and wicked need to devour and possess.' She indicated to the weighty chains that Tunk had attached to it. 'Tunk says he knows little of sorcery and witchcraft and cannot identify the spell or curse placed in the metalwork but dwarf shackles are practically impenetrable if fashioned well and these should safely bind the Golem so it can do no more harm.'

Petronia tried to listen to the dwarf vizier as she spoke to gain some clue towards the connection she felt binding her to the dormant Golem, but the voices of Bahl and her other companions seemed strangely muted and muffled by the ever-growing muttering of her own thoughts. A constant stream of shadowy syllables and sounds surged through her brain, their meanings growing ever clearer and more concrete by the moment. The mystical language no longer seemed so alien to her now, as if each time it rose from her subconscious, her understanding and familiarity with it grew, reaffirming the bizarre but true knowledge that it was indeed part of her. She gazed upon the unmoving metal beast secured to the bench before them and at once felt notes of unswerving clarity surface from the deafening hum of utterances in her mind. She did not fear the Golem now, but instead was intriguingly drawn to it, seeming to sense a force within its hidden iron workings that was twinned with the new power growing in her own mind. The automaton showed no signs of life or movement yet Petronia was aware of a dark, mindless energy coiled within, gazing out at her from beneath the solid shell, subservient and awaiting her command.

Before she had time to doubt herself, Petronia had stepped towards the bench, her hands outstretched to make physical contact with the iron creature. Her throat felt peculiar, like the cool, hard steel shaft of a bugle awaiting a breath of air to fill it with sound. The constant babble of noise within her thoughts was becoming more ordered now, the powerful whispering roar consolidating into two or three definite, clear profound words that seemed to hover at the very centre of her awareness, so well defined that she could almost taste them. Hayden saw his sister move towards the Golem and placed a hand on her arm to restrain her. 'Pet, no,' he begged, 'take care!' Turning her head toward his anxious face, Petronia's awareness of the language shared by her and the Golem was lost for a moment and she was overwhelmed by the desire to speak directly to her brother and reassure him she knew what she was doing. Unreleased sound burned like lightning across the edge of her tongue but something told her to keep silent as the words that would come were not for Hayden's understanding.

Bahl's dark eyes quickly scrutinised the young Ley apprentice and instantly she could tell by the trance-like expression on her face that the Ley was speaking to her. Reassuringly she touched Hayden's shoulder with her large, grey hand. 'The Golem is securely anchored,' she told him; 'it will not break free.' Despite the vizier's calming words, Hayden still watched uneasily as his sister crouched down before the Golem, her eyes trained on it intently.

The atmosphere around the iron beast seemed to ripple slightly as Petronia grew closer to it, causing a static charge to run across her skin, making her flesh prickle with energy. Her breathing was steady and deep, each exhalation a small, sure tug at the phrases held within, drawing them closer and closer to release. Lightly she rested the fingertips of both her hands on the solid dome. The metal was dully cold against her skin as she slowly traced the forms of the strange symbols carved into its armour. There was sharply woven sorcery etched into the markings, piercing the rigid iron and twisting its nature, a force that was beyond Petronia's understanding. She focused her thoughts, driving the forceful language down from her mind to fill her empty throat in readiness. The heat of her hands warmed the cool metal to the temperature of flesh as she dug deeper past its iron casing, her consciousness summoning up images of frozen cogs, springs and wheels. Beyond the casement of the machine, she envisioned its complex and well-crafted workings, wound and expertly balanced, an intricate display of dwarf skill and design. Petronia's mind delicately touched the carved teeth of the gears and ran along spiral paths of screws and wire coils, searching, grasping for something other than lifeless metal: that dark, hungry unnaturalness that whispered submissively to her. She could feel her mind sinking down into the innards of the automaton, a restraining weight of Ley energy pressing firmly down on the thoughtless shadowy entity that dully coated every inch of the hidden clockwork, holding the violent intent of the machine at bay and at the same time awakening it with the clarity of her thoughts.

Clearly, Petronia considered the command for the iron scarab to obey her, yet the word that formed definitely in her mind bore no resemblance to the mortal phrase for obedience, but was moulded from that darker, more ancient dialect that she was slowly beginning to decipher, a forgotten language of stone and magic. As the statement crossed into her thoughts, she felt the blackness within the Golem stir, reaching out towards her will, covering the wheels and cogs with its obedient power as it did so, trying to shape itself to her command.

She pushed harder, feeling her intent transform into a solid entity of its own, a thin, hard needle of determination that skewered the core of the blackness. Everything within, her mind, her thoughts, her gullet and tongue, seemed to have taken on the aspects of metal. Her focus was iron-strong and unyielding, her throat and mouth a polished passageway for the language and sound that was boiling into existence. Her tongue and palate flexed like molten steel, shaping themselves unnaturally to utter the unutterable. Pulling back her lips, Petronia allowed the powerful whisper to hiss like dark steam from her body, an almost silent breath filling the workshop with its might, painfully ringing in the ears of all who heard it as it seized command of the motors of the Golem. The clockwork trembled with the power of the phrase, once more filled with mindless animation. Petronia felt the link between her and the metal beast restored as it had been in the mountain cave and threads of glistening Ley power and shadowy sorcery bound her mind to every part, like the spidery strings of a puppet.

As easily as sending the idea of forming a fist to her hand, Petronia tugged on the unseen bounds within her thoughts, clicking the metal joints of the creature into action. Teeth slowly meshed together as gears tightened, drawing the metal insect slowing up on to its feet, straining against its heavy chained shackles. Its empty instinct strived towards Petronia's command, entwining its manufactured dark spirit with the brilliance of the Ley. Its jagged iron maul snapped open with a vicious creak as it hissed and moaned for her to feed it with blood, hate or misery. The dull, grating note of imprisonment issued loud and low from Petronia's mouth, holding the Golem's desire for carnage firm. Dark notions of its purpose tugged, making her thoughts burn and her heart beat faster, ideas of dominance, murder and destruction. The foul urge almost overwhelmed her in a sudden flash; the timbre of her echoing voice changed from a note of energy and power to one of termination. A sharp chord like a mighty trap snapping shut pierced the air, instantly sapping all life and energy from the room. The Golem juddered for a moment, its legs trembling and tottering rigidly as its clockwork innards jarred and jammed with a grating crunch, before the weight of its shell forced its limbs to give way as it collapsed into a heap with a lifeless metallic clang.

Petronia staggered back from the automaton, feeling suddenly drained of all strength, her breathing heavy as she tried to steady her nerve. The muscles of her chest and throat throbbed as she inhaled and her mind felt clouded with silvery remnants of Ley energy as her thoughts slowly realigned themselves with the world. As she battled to reconnect with her surroundings, Hayden rushed over and threw his arms around her in joy and disbelief.

'Pet,' he breathed, overwhelmed by the unexpected revelation of hearing a voice issue from his sister's throat. 'You, you spoke! The language I did not understand; truly there must indeed be some sort of sorcery in you. But to hear any words from your tongue is a wondrous miracle. If your muteness is cured, I beg you, say something else that I might understand, say my name or your own or that of our parents. Prove that this arduous journey has yielded a worthy reward.'

He gripped her hand pleadingly, tears of happiness in his eyes. Awkwardly, Petronia opened her mouth, longing to utter some intelligible phrase, more for her brother's sake than her own, but as ever the only sound she could force from her larynx was a small, dry gargle. The mighty commands of metal and Ley power that had brought the Golem to life still hung as ringing, weighty reverberations in the air, disturbing the thoughts of all who heard them, but Petronia knew that mortal ears would never make sense of the language which blossomed from her tongue. Sorrowfully shaking her head, she planted a comforting kiss on Hayden's cheek before tugging her hand from his grasp and haltingly formed the sign, '*Alas, dearest Brother, I cannot.*'

Meanwhile, across the workshop, Bahl and Tunk stood beside the inanimate Golem conversing in heated, anxious Dwarfish. The skilled smith was once again examining the metal scarab, checking the security of its shackles before taking down a selection of implements from the wall to cautiously pry open its shell. Bahl was muttering uneasily, partly to Tunk and partly to herself, seeming to be at a loss as to what to do next. Resting her hand absent-mindedly against her smooth scalp, she intently studied the Golem as if it reminded her of something she could not quite recall.

A long, black-scaled face appeared around the doorway of the smithy and Phebus glared at Petronia with disapproving scarlet eyes. 'Do you mind showing some care?' he hissed icily. 'I warned you, Miss Petit-Fours or whatever you're calling yourself, I'm not going to stand for you shrieking heathen hexes and all manner of coarse Ryder magic around the prince. His condition is very delicate and besides it is thoroughly unladylike!'

'You mean, you spoke in this language before?' asked Bahl, turning her attention on Petronia in a way that made her feel very uneasy.

Phebus flared his narrow nostrils. 'Indeed she did!' he remarked. 'It was while we were sheltering in the mountains not far from here. First that metal monstrosity attacks us and then that little harlot starts gabbling all kinds of indecent hoodoo and nearly causes the young master to have one of his episodes.'

'Phebus!' exclaimed the unseen Prince Aarold from outside the workshop. 'That is not how it happened and you know it! Mistress Petronia was using that language to restrain the Golem and save our lives.'

Bahl barely listened to the Equile's lamenting complaints, her attention focusing suspiciously on Petronia. 'So you have uttered such words before?' she repeated earnestly. Petronia swallowed nervously under the dwarf's interrogating stare. She had the dark fear that the power that welled up within her was something wicked beyond her control and now it seemed that her suspicions had foundation. She felt as if it was an alien entity residing within her and the only way to deal with it was to understand its language and become its mistress. Timidly, she nodded her head, her eyes lowered in shame.

Just as she suspected he would, Hayden was instantly at her side, chiding her for her carelessness. 'I told you, Petronia,' he said in a tone that was both loving and scolding, 'I warned you about the dangers and dark powers of this world. Stay at home, I said, and do not go seeking with the Ryders for more than you have.'

Petronia pouted tensely and looked as if she was about to cry yet her eyes remained dry. She stared at the unmoving automaton broodingly before unclenching her frustrated fists to sign. *'I'm sorry, Hayden, but I had to. It was something I couldn't fight. I meant no harm.'*

'Has my sister committed a sin towards your people?' Hayden asked, turning towards Bahl. 'If she has, it was surely not her intent.'

The dwarf vizier looked perturbed and muttered something to Tunk that made him cease examining the Golem. 'I cannot truly say,' she said finally. 'There are legends about power languages in the Dwarfish lore of old. A mystical skill spoke of by the Ryders. But I, myself, have little knowledge of such stories.' She fell silent for a moment before starting decisively towards the door of the smithy. 'I must consult with the keepers of the histories,' she stated firmly, beckoning for the others to follow. 'Everything that has been, regarding our kingdom, is known to them. I must seek out the appropriate texts before coming to any decision.'

Petronia turned to her brother, a horrified and panicked look in her eyes. She really had not intended any crime with her strange words; her intent had been to control the Golem and stop it doing further harm. Yet when the dark language rose within her, it took all her might to command it.

'Decision?' pressed Hayden, desperately. 'What decision? She meant no harm. What is this language of which you speak? Does it relate to her muteness?'

Hurrying after Bahl, Bracken rested a hand on her arm to slow her stride. 'Mistress Bahl,' she said, trying and somewhat failing to sound authoritative. 'I swear on whatever loyalty you had for my mother that my guardian Sister Amethyst declared to me that Petronia had the potential to be a great Ryder. She would not say such a thing if she felt she had wickedness in her.'

They had left Tunk's forge by now and Aarold and Phebus had joined them, the Equile listening intently to the suggestion that the Ley apprentice who had bewitched his friend was in trouble. 'I knew it, I knew it,' he muttered to the prince triumphantly. 'I said she was trouble from the start!'

Pausing mid-pace, Bahl took a deep breath and turned to face them all. 'Please,' she begged, summoning all the tact her brutal dwarf nature could allow, 'I am not accusing Mistress Petronia of any misdeed. However, it is clear to me that she has a power within her that is uncommon, even among followers of the Ley. Our scholars have collected much knowledge through the millennia and may be able to reveal to us more about this language that Mistress Petronia speaks.'

With that she took firm hold of Petronia's hand and led her across the bridges and staircases of Kelhalbon, towards the east of the chamber. Eagerly, Hayden and the others followed, keen to know what fate might lie in store. They arrived at the wall of the great chamber and found themselves standing before an ornate, dwarf-sized iron door, decorated with countless lines of tiny script, barely visible to the human eye. The portal was slightly ajar and the flickering orange glow of candlelight glimmered through the gap. Without knocking, Bahl pulled the door open and stepped to one side so the others might enter before her. They found themselves in yet another immense cavern not dissimilar from the chamber they had just left. It too was lit by large metal cauldrons of fire suspended from chains in the ceiling. Despite its size, the cave was extremely crowded. Huge piles of countless stone slabs were stacked in neat rows in every direction, forming massive precariously balanced columns that stretched all the way up to the vaulted roof and lining the walls like shelves of weighty books. Interspersed between the stony towers stood several long, granite benches, two or three studious-looking female dwarves seated at each, hunched over in intent concentration as they worked with delicate brass chisels to etch detailed lines of script on more tablets. Their huge hands moved at unbelievable speed as they worked, dancing lightly over the rock lozenges leaving behind elegant lines of angular Dwarfish text. They wrote as if it was a thoughtless instinct, their fingers moving automatically as they chatted to each other in low, serious whispers. The chamber had a hushed atmosphere, the studious silence only broken by the whizzing of a number of metal carriages that ran along a network of narrow rails in between the mountains of stones, carrying various tablets in and out of the archive.

The group gazed about them in wonder at the impressive store of information and the scholarly Aarold could not help but let out a little squeal of excitement. 'Phebus!' he gasped, trying to steal a glance at the writing on one of the tablets. 'Look at it! Look at where we are!' The Equile bristled gleefully, flaring his nostrils as if to breathe in the knowledge hanging in the stale air. 'I know, dear boy,' he exclaimed, 'the legendary records of Kelhalbon, largest and most detailed history every collated. Just imagine the learning on a single shelf of this place! The old dodderer Grahmbere would sell his grandmother's bones just to stand where we are now. Oh, if I could be left alone in here for a single hour with a half-decent guide to the Dwarfish dialect, I could die happy.'

Like an eager puppy, he trotted over to Bahl and gently tugged on the sleeve of her tunic with his beak. 'Mistress Bahl,' he said politely, fluttering his leathery eyelids in what he hoped was an appealing manner, 'might I enquire on the chance of two appreciative scholars such as myself and your princess's royal brother having the opportunity to admire some of your kinsfolk's remarkable literature?' The dwarf vizier smiled knowingly and affectionately patted Phebus's horned crest. 'You may,' she said, 'that is if you can persuade the keepers of the archive to allow you, which I doubt very much. The historians guard their tomes more fiercely than a she-wolf guards her cubs. They are utterly devoted. Even I have been disciplined many times for not showing their records fitting regard.'

She hurried ahead of them, leaving Phebus looking highly disappointed and peering longingly at the towers of information that he would never be allowed to devour. Hayden and Petronia regarded them also, but with fear and apprehension, wondering whether they held within them the key to the strange and dark language that had commanded Petronia's tongue.

Bahl moved swiftly over to one of the large stone tables behind which was seated a dour-faced and serious-looking dwarf. Heavy lids like crescents of granite half covered her glossy black pupils as she peered engrossed down at her work and her straight, full lips murmured slightly as she muttered to herself in Dwarfish what sounded like a long list of facts and figures. Her figure was like that of many female dwarves: broad shouldered with ample bust and full but strangely unfeminine curves; her lower arms and hands seemed uncommonly dainty for her size and build, as if decades of constant scripture had honed the muscles and tendons. Between the elegant fingers of each hand she gripped a long, sharp, golden scalpel with which she feverishly scribbled two entirely different scripts on to the pair of tablets before her. The blades danced like an expert skater upon a frozen lake, leaving line upon exquisite line of Dwarfish text. She glanced up as Bahl and the others approached, her skilful hands not slowing for the briefest of moments as if they laboured with a will of their own.

Bahl nodded politely in greeting. 'Good morrow, Ind,' she said, resting her hand lightly on the table. The dwarf scholar gazed at her coolly and delicately flicked some debris from her left-hand tablet with her little finger. 'Bahl,' she stated matter-of-factly, 'have you checked the reports on the maintenance of the greater north-east staircases? I have been waiting for two days.' The vizier's posture stiffened slightly like a schoolgirl who had not returned her homework to a particularly strict teacher. 'I will make sure you receive them as soon as possible,' she reassured as Ind sniffed doubtfully and added a flourish to the piece of text on the right of her. 'But of course, you understand I have been very busy attending...'

'To the returning Princess Bracken, daughter of the late Princess Duun and King Elkric of Geoll, yes of course.' Ind completed her sentence for her while glancing over to where Bracken stood. Her tone was rasping even for a dwarf, as if she was usually too concerned with her writing to bother with conversation.

Bahl extended her arm towards her companions. 'May I introduce Kelhalbon's chief historian and high mistress of records and writing, Ind. Ind, these are our guests.'

Ceasing her writing with her right hand, the scholar gestured at her visitors with her delicate quill. 'Prince Aarold of Geoll, son of King Elkric and Princess Neopi, his steed and companion Phebus of the Equiles, Mistress Petronia, apprentice to the Ley and her brother Hayden of the hamlet of Ravensbrook,' she listed knowingly. 'And of course, our own long-absent princess. All of whose arrival have been noted, recorded and, unlike the reports on the north-east staircase, logged within the archive.' She gave Bahl a smug smile as her hand went back to its frantic writing.

Bahl pursed her thick lips irritably but ignored the scribe's biting comment. 'I wish to consult something in the archive,' she requested politely, leaning on Ind's desk. 'The ancient writings by those who laid down its first volumes. It's regarding the myths and teaching retained from the first Ley Ryders, anything relating to the name Stone-Tongue.'

Sighing wearily, Ind made a great show of putting down both her quills, annoyed at having her work interrupted. 'Arcane human folklore,' she muttered in a dull tone, as she eased herself from her bench and strolled down to the far end of the table. 'I would think that our vizier was too old and busy for bedtime stories. But I will not question. I am merely caretaker of the records and will retrieve what is requested.'

She moved over to a large, brass tray balanced on the pair of rails that ran up to the edge of the table, stretching out in between the rows of shelves shrouded in the half-light of the archive. Around the edge of the tray, there was a console of numerous dials marked with digits and Dwarfish writing, with which Ind fiddled meticulously for several moments. Symbols shifted into place against arrows with satisfying clicks before the trolley suddenly sprung to life and whizzed at breakneck speed away from them down the track, disappearing from sight.

Hayden and the others stared after it in wonder at the rate it travelled and Aarold and Phebus once more marvelled at the genius and vastness of the dwarf library. 'I must say,' breathed the Equile in admiration, 'the whole place is outstanding, simply outstanding. As a creature of no small education, I admire it greatly.' A pleased smile graced Ind's sour features for a moment as she proudly swept the powdered granite from her desk. 'You have libraries in the kingdoms of man,' she stated confidently. 'But nothing to match this. Everything's on paper, useless, flimsy stuff. It rips and burns, gets marred by damp and age. Stone is a far superior material. The words in these records will last to the end of time.'

After just a few moments of patience, the sound of rapid wheels against brass rails whistled through the air and like a metal hound returning dutifully to its master, the trolley slid back into sight from the shadows of the archive, stopping with a light bump against the edge of the table. Ind reached inside and as carefully as a mother lifting her infant from its cot, retrieved the ancient tablet. The corners of the stone were worn round and smooth and the surface was mottled, but the definite lines of Dwarfish script were as clear as the day they had been engraved. Ind peered at the ancient tome and let out a contented sigh. 'This *is* an old one!' she remarked proudly, carrying it across to Bahl. She placed it carefully in her hands, adding sharply, 'Mind how you treat it and don't even think about sticking it back on the shelf just anyplace when you're done; vizier or not, I will not have you disorganise a millennial-old system.'

Taking the stone, Bahl forced a congenial smile and nodded her head. 'As always, your assistance has been indispensable,' she told the record-keeper in a sardonic tone. 'Good-day to you, Mistress Ind.' Ind grunted a terse farewell and waved her hand to dismiss the bothersome visitors, before returning to her seat and retrieving a blank slab of granite on which to record the details of their encounter.

Hayden and the others followed Bahl as she walked across to a stone reading desk at a suitable distance from where Ind laboured. She placed the arcane ledger down and adjusted the flickering candle held by a hinged iron arm so that it illuminated the text. She remained in silent study for some time, her hands resting either side of the tablet as her gleaming black eyes scanned the text. Anxiously the others watched, waiting for some kind of explanation. Hayden could not stop himself from gripping tightly hold of his sister's hand. She had just been returned to him and the thought that she had unwittingly committed some misdeed that would part them again was unbearable. Motionlessly, Petronia stared at the strange symbols etched on the rock. She knew nothing of their meanings, but the electric buzz of Ley energy seemed to hang in their lines and shapes, informing her the truth of her destiny was hidden within this stone. Bracken, Aarold and Phebus scrutinised the writing, trying to spot familiar phrases or words but the Dwarfish alphabet was so different to the one they knew, it was impossible.

Finally, Bahl stopped reading and turned to face them. 'It is an old prophecy,' she said in her usual emotionless tone, 'written at the birth of the Sisterhood of Ley Ryders. It explains how they will be dutiful servants to It, following Its will for good. But it also tells that a time will come when one will join the order who doesn't merely hear the language of the Ley but can utter it as well. The tablet says that it will be the only voice she will possess and with it she will do many miraculous deeds.'

Hayden glanced uncertainly at his sister who was still staring awestruck at the stone. 'And you think that this foretold Ryder could be Petronia?' he asked softly.

'It is not for me to make such accusations,' said Bahl, shaking her head. 'But she did display tremendous power just now, the like of which I haven't seen a Ryder wield before. They do say that fated children know within their hearts they are so. I ask you then, Mistress Petronia, does what is written ring true with your own spirit?'

Petronia did not reply, did not nod or shake her head or show any expression of reply, but within every corner of her mind the Ley danced with colour and light, declaring in her thoughts, '*Yes, I am she.*' Her soul and knowledge seemed to have shifted as Bahl spoke and she knew without a doubt that this was why she had been born. She did not feel the need to declare it to the others, however, the truth was within her and this alone was enough.

Sombrely Bahl turned back to the stone. 'There is more written,' she said severely. 'The prophecy states that this fabled Ryder will appear at a time when the colour and nature of the Ley is altered. That she also has the ability to command within It fouler shades, reveal within It notions of hate and violence. If evil seizes her heart she could become a beast of unstoppable destruction.'

Defensively, Hayden wrapped his arms around Petronia. 'That would never happen,' he told Bahl fiercely. 'My sister has a pure, strong spirit.'

Behind Bahl, Phebus snorted self-satisfied, and pawed the stone floor with his front claw. 'I knew it!' he hissed smugly to Aarold. 'Right from the beginning. You never listen to what I say but I warned you that little strumpet was nothing but trouble. We Equiles have a very sensitive instinct for this sort of thing. Did you hear what this wise and knowledgeable dwarf said? A beast of unstoppable destruction. Not suitable company for a royal prince to say the least!' He turned his scarlet eyes approvingly toward the dwarf vizier. 'I take it an appropriate punishment will be undertaken. May I suggest burning at the stake? I believe that's a very affective method of dealing with practitioners of evil magic!'

Aarold was horrified by his companion's harsh words and gazing at the pretty young maiden before him found it near impossible to believe that she was capable of even the slightest vicious act. In fact, she had done nothing but protect him from harm during their time together. 'Punishment without proof is a heinous suggestion, Phebus!' he said sharply. 'You've studied the laws of my kingdom well enough to know that!' The Equile ground his shiny, black beak. 'Exceptions can always be made, if circumstances require it!' he muttered darkly under his breath.

Bahl rested her hand lightly on the stone tablet. 'You seem to have misunderstood the interpretation of the prophecy, my good Equile,' she told him. 'The powers imbued on what the writings call The Stone-Tongue are not evil, nor are they virtuous. She has the ability to uncover evil and destruction within the Ley, she also has the ability to nurture it or control it so its wickedness does not harm others. Whether she becomes an agent for devastation or an angel of salvation is entirely down to the fabric of her spirit and the strength of her will. It is not the place of I or any other dwarf to say what she will become. That is down to Mistress Petronia alone.'

She turned her eyes towards Petronia, seeming to make a silent request that she reveal to them the true nature of her spirit, but Petronia was unable to even if her life depended on it. She wanted very much to announce in word or deed that her soul was wholly pious, that the power that coursed through her mind and had given sound to her tongue gleamed with nothing but holy, golden Ley energy, but this would be a lie. Her ability to speak this mystical language only occurred when blackness and violence summoned it: during the attack on the Ryders' keep; studying the corpse of the fallen Ryder within the lodge; controlling the iron Golem. On all these occasions, Petronia had felt the shadowy rush of power surge from her enemy, calling longingly to her in a way that felt so organic that their wickedness had to live within her also. Every word forged in metal, stone and magic from her tongue was as heavy with darkness as it was Ley power, as if the utterances she made came directly from the two crushing against one another.

Picking up the stone tablet from the desk, Bahl sighed grimly. 'Whatever Mistress Petronia's nature is, one thing is for certain,' she stated soberly, 'and that is I cannot allow her to remain in Kelhalbon a moment more than is necessary.'

'What?' declared Hayden, shocked by the sudden accusations that seem to be heaped upon his sister. At a loss at what to do, he looked to Aarold and Bracken in the hope that their royal positions might have some influence over the matter and bring some mercy on his sister's fate. Kelhalbon was not Ravensbrook but it had proved the safest refuge in their journey so far.

The dwarf vizier turned to him, her glossy black eyes displaying helpless sympathy. 'Believe me,' she said, trying with all her might to bring compassion to her gravelly tone, 'I bear no personal grudge or spite to your sister or any of you. You have brought back our lost princess and for that we dwarves will always consider you valued friends. But I am steward of Kelhalbon and I cannot harbour her here when her powers might bring disaster to our kingdom.' Cautiously, Bahl reached out and took Petronia's hand. 'I speak these words for your benefit also, Mistress Petronia,' she told her gently. 'If you are to master your mystical abilities, you must return to your fellow Ryders and study their example. Their skills and virtue will give you the best chance to fight the darkness within the language you speak.'

Petronia nodded in understanding but secretly felt that there was very little the Ryders could do to explain the power that surged within her. She had come this far unaided and felt that if the darkness she felt within her was to overwhelm her completely there would be very little anyone else could do to stop it.

'I'm coming with you!' stated Bracken suddenly, stepping forward.

Shocked by this statement, Bahl got to her feet, cradling the ancient stone prophecy carefully in her arms. 'Your Majesty,' she ventured as tactfully as she could, 'forgive my bluntness but it was naturally assumed by myself and your grandfather, by all of your people, that you would remain here and take your rightful place as queen. We have been without a proper ruler for so long and were overjoyed by the miracle of your return.'

Bracken looked embarrassed by Bahl's words and anxiously fingered her crystal pendants for comfort. 'It isn't that I'm ungrateful at knowing who I am or unwilling to take on the role that is expected of me,' she explained gently. 'I was raised by Ley Ryders and taught never to abandon a fellow Ryder in need. I feel that I must see Mistress Petronia returned to the Sisterhood before I leave my duties to it completely. Besides, the Ley would not wish my guardians to be left ignorant of my own fate. You have my word I will return as soon as the Ley allows me.'

Bahl sighed discontentedly and pressed the stone tablet to her chest. 'You speak with noble intent, my lady, and as your humble servant it is my duty to follow your wishes. I have served in your mother's and grandmother's stead for these past sixteen years, what is a few weeks more?'

Walking across to where Ind sat, Bahl carefully laid the tablet back into the metal tray, ready to be returned to its correct place, before returning to the others. 'Come,' she told them, 'you must prepare to leave. The journey south is long and arduous.'

Phebus let out a weary whine as Aarold raised his hand to gain Bahl's attention.

'If I might make a suggestion,' he said. 'If my memory of the maps I studied of this part of the world serves me well, we are a great deal closer to my grandfather's castle in Etheria than we are to Goodstone. I'm sure we would be welcomed there and could send word to the Ryders about Mistress Petronia.' Phebus sniffed and cast a hateful glance in Petronia's direction. 'Oh wonderful!' he groaned. 'I finally get to return to the land of my birth and it's as an escort to the angel of death!' He rested his head on Aarold's shoulder and whispered crossly in his ear. 'If I live to get to the colonies of my own species in your grandfather's meadows, I am staying there, permanently! Taking up a position of early retirement due to emotional stress and mental trauma.' Aarold hushed him and told him not to be so over-dramatic as Bahl led them all out of the library and began instructing various dwarves to make preparations for their departure.

Petronia dawdled unwillingly at the back of the group, suddenly feeling very tired and small. The great rushing weight of her inner darkness lingered at the back of her consciousness, silent but seemingly made more solid by the revelation of its true nature. Unseen and heavy, it bore down on her, driving all of them forward into the unfamiliar kingdom of Etheria where the ultimate strength of its nature would very soon be realised.

Chapter 32

REUNION AT
THE FALLEN INN

The news of their princess's departure worked the dwarves of Kelhalbon up into an understandable frenzy of woe, and as Bahl attempted to make preparations for the party's journey into the neighbouring country of Etheria many individuals approached Bracken, reminding her of the unhappy state of her grandparents and begging her to stay. Guilt filled Bracken's heart when she saw the disappointment in their eyes and time and time again she reiterated to them what she had said to Bahl, that she did indeed intend to return to them once she had completed one final duty to her adopted family. Prince Ion was, of course, overwhelmingly distraught to hear she was leaving so soon. Wailing and crying in a most disturbing fit of despair, he threw himself around his chamber, smashing furniture and beating at the stone walls with his mighty fists like some terrifying oversized child in a fit of temper. It took at least a dozen burly dwarves to overpower him and wrestle him to the safety of his bed, holding him there until the strength of his woe subsided to exhaustion and he fell into a whimpering fitful slumber, mewling the names of his wife and daughter. Bracken was horrified when Bahl sombrely told her of the sorry episode, realising again exactly why the vizier was so unwilling for her to leave, but she could not go back on her duty to Hayden to ensure his sister's safety. Though she now knew that it would never be her destiny to feel the Ley, she was sure that It would soon enough bring her back into contact with the Ryders, so that she may pass on the news to Sister Amethyst that she had indeed found the truth about who she was. She would then entrust them once more with the care and education of Petronia whose own fate seemed now vital to the future of so many.

After gathering together their few belongings, the five companions met with Bahl in the centre of Kelhalbon's great hall, all nervous and apprehensive about the uncertain and perilous journey that lay ahead of them. Many of the dwarves had gathered there also to say a disheartened farewell to Bracken. The vizier was speaking to Tunk and Rett beside a metal barrow when the group arrived. Pulling a dark, woollen cape around her broad shoulders, Bahl turned to face the nervous travellers. 'I trust you all have warm garments,' she told them in her usual brisk tone. 'The climate of Etheria is damp and chilly for human blood.'

Hayden, Aarold and the others all nodded mutely although the truth was that apart from the Equile Phebus none of them knew what to expect of the country to the north.

Reaching out to seize her arm, Rett leant across and whispered something in Dwarfish to Bahl who nodded in complete agreement. 'Rett says, and it is a sentiment shared by us all, that whatever the prophecy says about Mistress Petronia's power, you are all considered friends of the dwarf race. You have returned to us the royal heir we thought was lost and for that we are grateful beyond measure.'

At her signal, Tunk pushed the barrow towards the group.

'As tokens of such thanks,' Bahl continued, 'it is tradition to present you with gifts that might aid you on your journey.' Tunk lifted from the barrow a bulging, rather pungent leather satchel which he placed over Phebus's head. 'For you, our Equile friend,' said Bahl, 'a selection of our finest fungi and lichens, deadly to humans, of course, but I think your discerning palate will appreciate their unique flavour.' Eagerly, Phebus nosed his beak into the satchel, greedily sniffing the odour of the rare delicacies. 'Cave Berries, Bronze Gilled Mushrooms and what a rarity, Black Devil's Bugle! I never thought I would have the pleasure of sampling some of these again.'

Affectionately, Aarold scratched Phebus's scaly neck. 'See, old friend,

I said this adventure would be rewarding.' Phebus withdrew his head from the satchel. 'Well, I might as well get *some* compensation for what I've had to endure,' he said icily.

Returning to the barrow, Tunk lifted out the next gift and approached Aarold. It was a peculiar-looking object, a contraption of long, delicate bars and hinged metal belts; an invention that appeared to be equally light and strong. Tunk knelt down before the prince and carefully began to unfasten the buckles that held the item together.

'Prince Aarold,' Bahl said tactfully, 'you are the sibling of our dear Princess Bracken and we would never mean to cause you offence. But when Rett aided you in the baths, he noticed the affliction that ails your leg. He has designed this in the hope that it might aid your stride and lessen the pain in your wasted muscles.'

Aarold said nothing at first but stared thoughtfully down at the brace. Sympathetically, Phebus brushed his beak against Aarold's arm as Bahl shifted uncomfortably. 'We dwarves know little of the delicacy of human emotions,' she said when the prince did not respond. 'If such a gift is offensive or inappropriate then we deeply apologise.'

'No,' declared Aarold sharply, raising his head, before adding in a softer tone, 'I am grateful of Rett's thoughtful concern for my welfare.' Getting awkwardly to his knees, the young prince carefully took the support from the dwarf, examining the joins and bars with his keen student's eyes. Like all dwarf metalwork, it was both well-made and beautiful.

'The metal has been fired so that it's not only strong but incredibly light, similar to that we weave with,' explained Bahl, as Aarold moved his fingers across it. 'The fittings at the foot, knee and thigh are cast to fit your body alone. Rett believes if his work is correct that you shall not feel it when it's on.' Aarold looked at her earnestly, his pallid face tense and somewhat unsure. 'Will I be able to walk without my cane?' Bahl nodded stiffly. 'That is the intent,' she told him. 'Sadly, it will not cure your affliction but it should allow you to move with less support.'

An expression of mixed feelings passed across Aarold's face, showing a combination of both hopeful excitement and self-conscious apprehension. Awkwardly he shifted so that his wasted limb was as straight as it could be. 'If you wouldn't mind assisting me,' he asked Rett, quietly. With the utmost care, the dwarf aided Aarold in moving his lame leg into the brace. The prince winced slightly with uncertainty as the stiff, metallic boot enclosed his twisted foot, but relaxed when he discovered that it was lined in soft fur and held his sole securely but without discomfort. Carefully, Rett showed him how to fasten the supports at his ankle, knee and upper leg. The bands of iron were snug, having just enough give to allow him to move and flex without his muscles drawing his leg into its normal inward arch. Curious, Aarold moved his leg, bending his knee and ankle to feel the motion and weight of the device. He found that he could lift it with very little effort while the unbending struts added strength to his weary tendons. 'Marvellous,' he breathed in wonder, gently touching the screws that held it together. 'I can barely feel it.' He motioned for Rett to give him his hand. 'Help me to stand, good sir. I am eager to try and walk.'

Forgetting about his own gift, Phebus stepped forward as the dwarf helped Aarold to his feet, resting his beak protectively against his back. 'Careful, dear boy,' he said wearily as Aarold steadied himself against Rett's muscular forearm. 'Don't you go charging off and doing yourself a mischief.'

The prince was duly cautious, using Rett to make sure of his balance as he experimented with how much of his weight the brace would support. Tentatively, he loosened his grip on Rett and daringly took a step forward. The brace added strength to his stride and allowed him to stand taller than with his cane. Excitedly, he began to stroll up and down before the crowd, his gait still somewhat slow and faltering, but straighter and more upright than before. A proud smile spread across his face. 'Do you see?' he asked, almost in disbelief, 'I am walking with no cane! This is wonderful.'

Bahl clapped her hands approvingly and Hayden called out, 'Well done, Your Majesty!'

Beaming, Aarold turned towards Petronia, eager for her approval. 'Look, Mistress Petronia,' he exclaimed, 'I have never walked like this before. Aren't the dwarves ingenious? Don't you approve?'

Petronia nodded enthusiastically and gave a small smile. The brace seemed to imbue Aarold with a new confidence and the polished and engraved plates of the brace had a look of heroic armour to them that was truly quite dashing.

Hobbling back across to Phebus, Aarold took a moment's rest, leaning against the Equile for support as Rett muttered something to Bahl in Dwarfish. 'He wishes to know whether it is comfortable and says adjustments can be made if it is not,' she explained. The young prince gazed down at the plates that encased his foot and flexed his ankle. 'Not at all,' he grinned, 'it is most well-fitted. I am overjoyed with it. Thank you, a thousand times, thank you.'

Bahl related his message of gratitude to Rett who smiled proudly at the appreciation of his handiwork before shuffling merrily over to the barrow to retrieve the next gift: a thick leather girdle laden with heavy looking pouches which he passed to Bahl.

The dwarf vizier approached Petronia. 'For you, Stone-Tongue,' she said solemnly, as she fastened the belt around the girl's waist. 'A collection of freshly harvested jewels from the most sacred part of the crystal fount. No human hand has touched them and the power commanded by the Ryders resides strongly in their cores. May they aid you to fulfil your destiny and master the abilities you have been given. There is another gift also: a warning. The power within you has two faces, the more you become mistress of It, the greater Its might and ability to destroy. Only by maintaining a virtuous heart can you work for good. Others may guide you but only you can determine the nature of your soul.'

Delicately, Petronia ran her fingers across the leather pouches fastened about her waist and felt the sparkling buzz of the many-shaded aspects of the Ley filter through the stones inside. The crystals showed the countless, virtuous facets of the Ley, but beneath these blessings she was also aware of the surging undercurrent of darkness that lingered in her mind, a feral destructive beast that she had to tame. Eager to show she fully understood the burden of her task, Petronia brought her palms together and bowed soberly before Bahl.

The dwarf vizier nodded approvingly. 'I wish you strength, Mistress Petronia, for all our sakes.'

Moving across to the barrow, Bahl retrieved the item that was to be presented to Hayden. He gasped with surprise as she passed it to him. 'My sword!' he exclaimed as he took the familiar weapon. 'The one my father gave me when we set out on this journey.'

'A fine blade,' agreed Bahl, as he fastened the baldric around him, 'skilled craftsmanship for a human smith. But we did take the liberty of adding a certain unique strength to it that may come in useful. Draw it and you will understand.'

Carefully, Hayden slipped the sword from its scabbard. The steel blade had been buffed to a mirror-like shine that gleamed in the fiery light of the chamber like liquid mercury. An image caught Hayden's eye, reflected in the surface of the metal, and he stared in awe and wonder as he saw the vista of his own home in Ravensbrook, just as peaceful and tranquil as he remembered. There was his father toiling at the forge and his mother sweeping the doorstep of their simple dwelling. Everything so bright and real, so safe that it soothed the apprehension in his heart and he was able to feel as he once did before this arduous journey. As he gazed at the blade, Bahl's voice came to him. 'Our Princess Bracken explained that you are a man troubled by many fears and concerns,' she said. 'Such feelings can freeze the heart and stop you taking action. It is the core of this that turns our kind Ac-Nu. This enchantment of metal will not save a dwarf heart but it will hopefully make a human spirit recall what is important. It will give inspiration to take courage when things seem hopeless.'

Hayden reached out and gently touched the smooth surface of the blade with his fingertips. He could almost smell the smoke that rose from the chimney of his home and feel the bright sunlight as it filtered through the trees at the edge of the wood. Strangely enough, it did not make him feel melancholy or homesick, but filled him with new-found strength.

'Do you think my sister and I will ever make it back to Ravensbrook?' he asked Bahl, curiously. The dwarf shrugged her shoulders. 'It is impossible for me to say,' she said tactfully, 'but as long as you have that weapon, forged by your father, imbued with our magic and your memories, your heart will always find peace.' Hayden smiled contentedly to himself and taking one last glance at the homely scene, sheathed the blade securely in its scabbard.

Removing the final object from the barrow, Bahl gestured for Tunk and Rett to wheel it away before carrying it across to Bracken. Kneeling down before her, she presented it reverently, her head bowed. Resting across her broad palms was a heavy mace of thick, black iron, yet another example of skilled dwarf craft. The weighty head was sculpted into the form of a clenched fist, the middle finger sporting a replica of the dwarf queen's ring of office and the thick handle was engraved with line upon line of Dwarfish script. It was an impressive instrument, brutal and unyielding, and as Bracken stared at it she could not help but recall the rage and hatefulness of Queen Penn.

'Your Majesty,' breathed Bahl, solemnly, 'may I present the weapon wielded by your mother in battle, the sacred war-hammer of the dwarf queens, the Might of Kelhalbon.'

Beneath the burning glow of the chamber's torchlight, the mace's black surface gleamed with dull reflections of blood and fire. Bracken was once again reminded of how at odds she felt with her birthright, how the human blood in her veins and the teachings of the Ryders seemed ill-fitting with how the dwarves viewed her as their leader.

'I was well schooled in the art of fencing by the Ryders,' she said clearly, touching the rapier at her side. 'This sword will protect me well enough but I do not know how to wield such a weapon.'

An anxious murmur ran through the collective dwarves when they saw Bracken make no move to take the mace. Raising her head, Bahl stared at Bracken with piercing black irises. 'This is no mere instrument of war, Your Majesty,' she told her seriously. 'This is your inheritance of sovereignty. A covenant in metal between a ruler and her people. It is by this that Kelhalbon has been led since the birth of our race. A gift from the Ley Itself to mark out our sovereign. Strike the earth three times with this mace anywhere in the known lands and Kelhalbon's finest warriors will be at your side.'

Gazing at the staff, Bracken felt a strange sense of acceptance and responsibility fill her heart. Queen of Kelhabon was not a title she felt prepared for or worthy of but the Ley drew a path for each life, no matter what hopes and expectations one held for the future. Some things could not be altered by want or will and she had been brought by fate back to her mother's people at a time when their leader was crippled by spite and hatred. She thought for a moment about what Sister Amethyst would advise and knew at once that her guardian would remind her that the Ley compelled them to put the needs of others above their own. As much as she desired to, Bracken could not continue to flee from her inheritance. Carefully, she reached out and lifted the weapon from Bahl's hands. The Might of Kelhalbon felt cold and heavy in her grasp, as weighty as the loyalty and responsibility it symbolised. Throughout the cavern, dwarves cried out throatily and dropped to their knees as an indication of willing devotion to their uncrowned sovereign. Fastening the war-hammer on to her baldric, Bracken leant forward and whispered to Bahl. 'I can only promise that I will return and take up my mother's mantle once my duty to the Ryders is complete,' she told her uneasily. 'I do not claim for a moment to know what this realm expects of their queen. As steward, I will look to you for guidance.'

Bahl fixed her jet-black eyes on Bracken's face but her features as usual displayed little emotion. 'I am your servant,' she said in a dull, simple tone. 'What you request of me shall be done.'

Getting to her feet, the vizier adjusted her cape around her broad shoulders. 'Now we must away,' she told Bracken and the others. 'I shall escort you from Kelhalbon via the north-west face of the mountain and down the pass to the foothills that mark the border between our kingdom and Etheria. From there the path is easily followed.'

*

Gathering up their gifts and belongings, Bracken and the others were led across the bridges and staircases of the great chamber towards the torch-lit tunnel that would bring them back to the outside world. A phalanx of dwarves accompanied them as they departed, playing a strange, tuneless tribute to their newly-found princess on hooting bugles and clanking percussion instruments as they went. The mobile orchestra dwindled as they continued down the narrowing passageway, returning to their various crafts and duties until only the five travellers remained trekking after Bahl through the shadowy torchlight. The further they went, the less of the ornate metalwork decorated the stone walls until little remained to indicate that the caves were home to civilised creatures.

Finally they arrived at a vast, heavy iron door barring their way, fixed securely into place across the tunnel by a complex system of bolts, locks and latches. Taking a large bundle of keys from her belt, Bahl set to work opening the portal. Wheels and cogs ground and with much scraping, bars were drawn aside before Bahl heaved the mighty door back on its hinges and the icy, clear gleam of winter sunlight flooded the cave. After so long in the dimly-lit dwarf kingdom, Hayden and his companions were nearly blinded by the brilliance of unfiltered, natural sunlight and spent quite a few moments blinking like hibernating animals awakening to spring before they could see well enough to continue.

A steep, narrow stairway of ancient steps had been unevenly carved into the mountain-face, leading from the tunnel-mouth and winding precariously through the rocks and snow. Bahl set out ahead, clearing the path of any boulders or heavy snowfall to make way for the others. Bracken and Hayden followed her closely, somewhat fearfully as they recalled the avalanche they had encountered on the southern slopes. Despite his new brace, the stairs were too steep and icy for Aarold to dare descend on foot so he rode, chilly but in high-spirits, astride Phebus who seemed uncharacteristically cheerful about the trek. Equiles, with their sturdy build and agile talons, were naturally at home in an alpine environment and the journey appeared to put Phebus in a nostalgic mood. He sniffed at the cool air and declared, 'You know, I do think I remember coming this way with your mother when we travelled to your father's court, all those years ago.'

'Really?' asked Aarold curiously.

The Equile paused for a moment to take in the snow-dusted,

rocky landscape through which they journeyed. 'Oh yes,' he declared confidently, 'this is all becoming very familiar now. We'll soon be in the land of my race, dear Etheria. What a joy it is to be returning to its fragrant mists and rolling pastures once more. Even if it does have to be with a certified herald of the apocalypse.' He cast Petronia a hateful glance and sped up his pace slightly so they moved ahead of the girl who had been, up till then, walking at their side. Aarold twisted round to look back at her apologetically. 'He doesn't mean that,' he mouthed with a compassionate smile.

Petronia nodded. She had learnt to accept and ignore Phebus's clear dislike of her: there were much more troubling matters filling her mind than the creature's disapproval. She repeatedly turned over in her mind the prophecy regarding her fate, her inner instincts reaffirming that everything Bahl had said was true. The words written on the stone seemed to add form and substance to the churning power that moved constantly through her thoughts, making it both easier for her to grasp and more unfathomably dangerous. Its whispers and movements barely left her thoughts now, even when she managed to focus her mind on something else. It remained as a constant background to everything she did, even when she slept, forming new words and commands to the Ley; a mystical language that Petronia carefully stored and filed away in her mind for the moment that they would need to be released from her tongue. What that moment would be, Petronia did not know but she felt as if she had been brought across the mountains into this strange new land to bring it about.

Onward they followed the dwarf's path, down from the steep, unforgiving stone slopes on the high mountain peaks to the easier foothills that skirted the northern face. Here the climate was less icy and windswept and the thick blankets of snow dissolved away into the black earth, leaving the terrain wet and boggy underfoot. Despite the moistness of the ground, very little vegetation grew on the mountainside and the only visible plant-life were numerous sparse clumps of knotted, sharp-leaved trees that only grew as tall as Hayden's shoulder. Large flocks of cawing, black birds with brown-striped, hooked beaks roosted among their knotted branches. Hayden watched as they swooped in spiralling rings in the colourless sky above and recalled the strange blind seer Emouchet and what he had read in Bracken's palm. His mind had been open to so many miraculous wonders and terrors through his journey that it made him wonder no longer if he would ever return home, but whether he could. Everything about him was changing, perhaps Hayden was changing too.

The atmosphere of the lower slopes was moist and chilly, a thin, damp fog filling the air, giving the daylight the oddest quality. It sapped all colour from the landscape, turning everything to shades of black, white and grey. The moisture in the air clung to Aarold's face and hands and made him shiver with a chill that went right to his bones. He remembered his aunt saying more than once that the dry, warm air of Geoll was not good for him and therefore assumed that if he returned to his mother's native lands it would somehow improve his health. Looking about him he saw little evidence that this would be the case. Although he dared not confess it to Phebus, the climate and countryside of this place made him feel uneasy.

When they finally reached an expanse of land where the last of the snow and ice had melted away, Bahl stopped and allowed the others to catch up. 'This is where I leave you,' she told them as they rested in the shelter of a lofty standing stone.

'This marker denotes the border between Kelhalbon and Etheria and we dwarves have little business in the lands of men. Carry on this eastward path for a few more miles and you will come to a tavern bearing the name The Fallen Inn. You will find food and accommodation there for the night.'

She turned towards Bracken and bowed reverently. 'I shall return to my duties as steward of Kelhalbon and prepare for your return,' she told her in her usual sombre tone. 'I pray your business with the Ryders will be carried out swiftly and easily and you return to your rightful place as leader of our people soon.'

Bracken nodded her head acceptingly, although she did not feel fully worthy or capable of taking up her birthright. Uncomfortable with

Bahl's veneration towards her, she rested her hand lightly on the dwarf's forearm, indicating that she should stand. 'You are a wise and faithful servant to your people,' she told her as Bahl raised her head. 'I do not have the words to express the gratitude I feel for the loyalty you have shown to my mother and grandparents during these past unhappy years and the guidance and patience you have given me as I learnt the truth about my origins.'

The dwarf regarded her with her inscrutable dark pupils. 'It is my role in life to do so,' she replied in a tone devoid of emotion or pride. She then turned her attention to the other travellers. 'I wish you all luck and strength in the challenges ahead. Trying times grow close and the darkness they bring will test us all, but none more so than you, Mistress Petronia. Many lives depend on your gift and I pray that you have the strength of spirit to follow the virtue of the Ley when using it.'

Soberly, Petronia nodded, the icy wind of the mountainside gusting restlessly about her while within her consciousness other hidden tides of surging blackness and brilliance ebbed and churned, bolstering against her thoughts.

Without another word of farewell, Bahl turned away and began the trek back into the snowy, unforgiving cliffs of the mountains of Kelhalbon. Bracken and the others stood a while watching her depart, the lofty, powerful figure as stoic and sturdy as the brutal landscape growing smaller and smaller as she slowly vanished into the fog.

*

The air was bitter and it chilled them to stay still for very long so they soon put thoughts of the warm shelter of the dwarf kingdom behind them and continued on the path Bahl had showed them into Etheria. As they travelled, the moist terrain evened out, becoming less sloping and hilly yet retaining its grim, boggy climate. They saw little increase in plant-life as the path they travelled became broader, transforming into a more defined muddy road. Memories of the snow-capped peaks they had left behind remained in the dampness of the gloomy scenery in the form of countless streams and trickling rivulets. Draining down from the upper slopes, they merged to form numerous shallow, murky pools where strange, camouflaged amphibians bubbled, croaked and belched as they feasted upon the swarming yellowish clouds of gnats that buzzed over the water. Phebus knowledgeably informed them that many of the creatures that dwelt within these ponds were considered delicacies and perfectly palatable to both humans and Equiles, but no-one seemed keen on taking up the offer.

It was hard to determine when dusk actually settled for the pale sun never seemed to win its battle with the thick clouds and clinging mist in this environment, but they soon began to tell by the lengthening of their shadows that nightfall was growing near. As the hour of twilight grew close, they came to the hostelry Bahl had informed them of, standing ramshackled and crooked at a turn in the road.

The Fallen Inn needed no sign to identify it for its name was well matched to its odd and seemingly neglected appearance. The ancient building of bowing, dark timber and crude mountain granite looked so unstable and precariously built that it seemed the slightest gust of breeze might cause it to collapse. The whole structure leant sideways on its sloping foundations, as if it had once belonged further up the mountainside, however time and gravity were working arduously together to drag it to a gradual crumble. The great blocks of stone that formed the walls were stacked haphazardly up one on top of the other with no regimented order to give them strength or security. They leant away, pulled by the camber of the ground and thick, wooden struts had been erected to brace the far side from toppling completely. Small, unevenly spaced windows were crammed into gaping holes in the visage of the building, their twisted and creaking frames forming odd shapes around mottled and bubbling glass and the gutters and lintels sagged like the numerous frowning brows of a deformed and woeful face. The roof arched to a sharp point like the wimple of an ancient widow, its surface littered with misshapen and broken tiles, and a narrow chimney zigzagged towards the drizzling sky, emitting a thin plume of pale smoke. The front door slumped on its hinges, cracked and broken on all sides so that large gaps were visible above and below it. To the right of the crumbling dwelling and slightly behind it, there was a smaller, less rundown building that resembled a small stable with a chalkboard sign that read "Equile Accommodation Only. Please house all other mounts in barn at rear of Inn". Oddly, despite its rickety appearance, The Fallen Inn had a strange sturdiness to it, as if it had experienced so much ill-weather and decades of neglect nothing could destroy it. It may creak and crumble but it would never be demolished. Hayden found that comforting somehow.

Aarold dismounted and led Phebus to the shelter. Inside they found a piece of furniture somewhere between a table and a trough laden with hunks of cheese and a few mushrooms, and several cosy stalls equipped with woollen blankets and pillows. The stalls were empty all but one in which resided an elderly Equile who was half asleep after his dinner. Overjoyed to come into contact with a companion of his own species, Phebus politely roused him to introduce himself in the hope of kindling a friendship, but the creature was a short-tempered military type who seemed to be suffering from some kind of Equile senility and repeatedly kept yelling at Phebus to 'drive the dirty blighters back', until Phebus decided it was better to leave him to fall back into slumber.

Once his friend had settled in, Aarold rejoined the rest of his companions and they entered the welcome of The Fallen Inn. The interior of the tavern was shadowy, sparse but hospitable, a suitable rest point for any traveller. A fire crackled warmly in the hearth and several tables and nooks were occupied by groups of merchants, soldiers and other folk partaking of the food and shelter offered by the tavern. Feeling a little out of his depth among the other patrons, Aarold kept the cowl of his cloak drawn up and tried to hide behind the others. A tall, sallow youth with the native Etherian appearance of very pale skin and thick black hair polished tankards behind the bar. Hayden was about to approach him and ask if he and the others might obtain food and lodging for the night when a familiar voice called out from near the fireside.

'Ley be praised, can I believe my eyes?'

Surprised and almost incredulous, Hayden turned towards the three figures sitting close to the fireplace. It was Garnet, looking tired and pinched but overjoyed to see them, her fellow Ryder Rosequartz sat close at her left-hand side. The red-haired maid wore the same warm smile as she always did although her emerald eyes seemed strangely dim and sad. Across from them, Aarold and Petronia recognised the elderly Handmaiden to the Dead, Chiastolite.

With a cry of joy at seeing her adoptive family, Bracken hurried towards them. Rosequartz and Garnet embraced her tightly and uttered prayers of thanks to the Ley before eagerly welcoming the others to sit down.

'We feared you were dead,' Garnet told Bracken and Petronia after they had called for the innkeeper to bring them more food. 'There are dangerous enemies following our Sisterhood, you in particular Mistress Petronia, and we were anxious that we would not find you before them. Praise the Ley for giving you safe passage to this place.'

Bracken nodded sombrely, lightly brushing Hayden's arm as she did so. 'Much has happened since the siege of Goodstone,' she said. 'I am grateful for the companionship of Master Hayden for getting me through it.'

Together, they informed the Ryders of all that had happened since they last met. Bracken and Hayden told of their journey through the Great Forest and Garnet and Rosequartz listened with wonder and pride as Bracken revealed to them the mystery of her blood parentage. She introduced Aarold as her half-brother and he in turn relayed the story of what had happened to him and Petronia since their sudden disappearance from the Ryders' lodge. Finally they divulged what they had discovered in the records of Kelhalbon and how it appeared to apply to Petronia. Garnet and Rosequartz listened without comment to the whole tale, their faces patient and understanding.

'So, you are aware of the truth of your gift?' said Garnet seriously when the story was finished.

Sombrely, Petronia nodded, feeling her dark shadows of language and power stir at the corners of her mind when the topic arose. She looked expectantly at Garnet, hoping the Ryder might have returned to her with some kind of training that would aid her in becoming mistress of the darkness within. However, something warned her that the Ryders had little practical knowledge of what it was to exist with such an ability.

'You knew?' Hayden asked Garnet. The Ryder took a sip of water from her tankard. 'We had our suspicions from the beginning,' she confessed. 'Your sister did display remarkable abilities, even for an individual summoned by the Ley. Couple that with her muteness, my sisters and I, Amethyst in particular, couldn't help but remember the writings and legends of the Ryders of old. It is foolhardy to jump to such conclusions but other forces have removed any doubt.'

Rosequartz laid her hands on the table in front of her and gazed intently at Hayden. 'And what are your feelings towards all of this, Master Hayden?' she asked curiously. 'After all, in the past you have made your concern clear about your sister joining our order.' Hayden looked thoughtfully at Petronia and rested his hand lightly on hers before answering. 'It has always been my greatest concern to keep Petronia safe and protect her from harm,' he said honestly. 'For the longest time I believed that involvement with your Sisterhood would put her in peril but Petronia has shown more resilience and courage than I ever dreamed she could possess.' He thought about all that had happened to his sister and him since they had left Ravensbrook. 'There are many things in this world that I have witnessed that are beyond the realm of belief of a simple blacksmith's son,' he confessed with a shake of his head. 'I thought that a man was master of his own fate, but I can no longer stubbornly ignore the powers and magic that shape our lives. I never desired to take up any quest or travel this far from home; I am no knight or hero. All I am is a son who swore to his father that he would protect and aid his sister and that is an oath that I will not break, no matter what destiny says.'

Tenderly, Petronia leant across and lovingly planted a kiss on her brother's cheek, grateful that he no longer seemed to mistrust the ways of the Ryders. Garnet seemed grateful of his new-found acceptance too. 'Spoken nobly and with love,' she told him. 'Mistress Petronia will need much support in the days to come. Agents of evil are already aware of her gifts and are set to claim her as their own. Be on your guard, Mistress Petronia, for already they hunt for you with the mind to claim your talents for wicked ends.'

Aarold listened fearfully to the Ryder's words, concerned for the safety of the maiden of whom he had become fond. 'Who are these agents?' he asked earnestly. 'Tell me their identities and I will send word to the royal troops to hunt them down. My whole army is at the Ryders' command if it means keeping Mistress Petronia safe!' He would have very much liked to have said that he himself would ride out and track them down, as his father might have, but such acts of chivalry were beyond his physical abilities.

Her face pale, Garnet woefully shook her head. 'Although these villains have already tried to stop us finding you and bringing you aid, we are still unaware of their identities,' she told them grimly. 'The dark sorcery they wield hides their names, even from the Ley Itself, it taints their spirits and aids them with their subterfuge.'

Feeling helpless and troubled by the Ryders' distress, Bracken turned towards Garnet. 'You must return Mistress Petronia to Goodstone as soon as possible,' she implored. 'Take refuge in the citadel and ask Sister Amethyst for guidance. She will aid you to use your powers to serve the Ley.'

A heavy silence fell over the group as the three Ryders bowed their heads woefully. Bracken saw the sorrow etched upon their faces and an unnerving dread ran through her, cold and fearful. Beside her, Petronia felt the Ley stir towards Amethyst's adoptive child, brushing unseen and unfelt against her form. Chiastolite felt it too, the emptiness of love and grief rushing in ready to fill the gap left by the tearing apart of Bracken and Amethyst's spirits. Tenderly, she reached her wrinkled, arthritic hands to take Bracken's in a gesture of compassion. The girl gazed into the kind, black eyes of the Handmaiden of Death and felt her heart shatter with the agonising, unuttered truth.

'No,' she whispered, in a horrified hoarse tone, 'no. Sisters, it cannot be.'

She drew back from Chiastolite's compassionate touch as if the mere caress of the old woman's fingers would make real what she dare not conceive. She looked to Garnet and Rosequartz for them to deny it, but could only see the tears of heartbroken grief in their eyes. The truth and horrors Bracken had learnt of her blood family seemed so trifling now, mere fables when compared to what she must now hear from the Ryders' lips.

Rosequartz swallowed and sadly shook her head. 'You do not know how it breaks my heart to bring you this news,' she told the stunned Bracken.

Bowing her head, Bracken felt her insides begin to tremble with loss and grief. It no longer seemed to matter that her true identity was known to her now that the woman she viewed as her true parent, the loving Ryder who had raised her with so much wisdom and kindness, was dead. It was not within her character to cry easily. It had taken all the doom and bitterness of Ac-Nu and witnessing the hateful character of Queen Penn to bring tears to her eyes. However that gulf of sorrow seemed like nothing compared with hearing about Amethyst's demise and her eyes suddenly were burning with tears. 'How?' she asked in a throaty, dull tone, her hands clasped before her on the table to stop them from shaking. She silently prayed to the Ley that Amethyst's life had come to a peaceful end, a freed spirit merging with the Ley brought on by old age, a reward after decades of dutiful toil. However, the threats the Ryders spoke of against their way of life seemed so relentless and wicked that her dreading heart informed her that this was not the case.

Once more Chiastolite compassionately took Bracken's hand and this time the girl knew it would do no good for her to pull away. Her beloved Amethyst's life on this plane had come to an end, and denying the understanding touch of the Servant to the Dead would not change this. Beneath the table, Chiastolite caressed a well-worn fragment of apache tear, an obsidian crystal. Drawing the power of the Ley through its polished black solidity up into her elderly heart, she prepared to pass its comfort on to the woeful girl as Garnet tentatively told her of her guardian's demise.

'I will not mar your heart any more than needs be by revealing what we three witnessed,' she said sadly, 'only to inform you that Amethyst was dutiful to the end and fell defending Mistress Petronia's safety. She realised the importance of her gift and gave her life defending her from her enemies.'

An ache of guilt gripped Petronia's heart when she heard this. She saw the heartbreak in Bracken's eyes and it made her acutely aware of the weighty burden her strange abilities brought with them. As she thought on this very matter, she felt the fibre of the Ley language stir within her a soft, almost aching loving pulse, summoning up spiritual recollections of the wise Ryder Amethyst and the great affection she felt for her cherished ward. She wished her mystical language would allow her, at that moment, to express to Bracken the shadow memory of her adoptive mother's love, but no words of power came to her lips. All she could do was reach across and rest her hand in silent sympathy on Bracken's arm.

'She was murdered.' Bracken's voice, usually husky and low, seemed even more manly as she uttered the statement bearing in it an almost icy note of hatefulness.

Slowly Rosequartz nodded in affirmation. 'Alas it is so,' she uttered softly, a hint of her own sorrow and unjust fury colouring her voice. 'But believe me, dear child, we will hunt down the villains that took her life and exact on them the justice of the Ley. We have sworn this as her Sister Ryders; it is our duty.'

Bracken's dark green eyes flashed brightly with pained emotion. 'And what is my duty to her?' she asked bitterly. 'My fate isn't to feel the Ley's touch!'

Before anyone could reply or comfort her, Bracken got to her feet and swept from the tavern. Twisting awkwardly in his seat, Aarold turned towards the door to call after her. 'Sister!' he pleaded. 'Don't walk away! We will find the fiends who have committed this deed.' However, Bracken had vanished out into the bitter early evening of the brutal Etherian landscape.

Swallowing hard, Rosequartz watched her walk away, a distressed expression of concern in her normally jovial eyes. 'Dear child,' she murmured, 'I knew this sorrowful news would break her heart. I must go and bring her comfort if I can.' She stood up as Sister Chiastolite did the same, hauling her ancient body stiffly from her seat. 'I will accompany you on that task,' she said decidedly. 'The Ley has awarded me the role of comforter to those who have lost loved ones. I have dried a million tears shed in grief.' Rosequartz offered the elderly Ryder her arm to steady her, but Chiastolite did not take it. 'Does it get any easier?' she asked the old woman curiously. 'Dealing with those whose hearts have been crushed by the agony of Death's separation?' Chiastolite paused thoughtfully for a moment. 'The Ley blesses me with strength to bear for others what they cannot,' she said at last. 'I see It flow around them like a balm when they are gripped by loneliness and despair. All I can do is act as an agent for that solace,' she sighed. 'Of course, it is always more tragic when you witness someone who you know personally in such anguish.'

Hayden watched as the two Ryders headed towards the door of the tavern and felt his heart become heavy with sorrow for his companion. He wondered how the Ryders could continue to see the Ley as a just and fair force, when It allowed Bracken's beloved guardian to be taken from her before the girl had the opportunity to let her know that she had discovered her true birthright? Amethyst's death had been brutal and sudden; he struggled to see how anyone, even if they had faith and devotion to the Ley, could meet their end peacefully when the fate of the child they had devoted their life to was so doubting and unclear. The faith and abilities of the Ryders gave them strength to deal with the loss of their fallen sister. Bracken's half-dwarf nature meant that her heart could not feel the soothing rhythms of the Ley and recall from it loving memories of her cherished adopted mother. Bracken's devotion to protecting Hayden had known no limits during their perilous journey and only in hindsight did he realise the gratitude he owed her. The least he could do was to offer compassion. He glanced at Petronia sitting across from him and for the first time felt strangely grateful of his sibling's rare gifts; perhaps she would have the power to bring to an end the heinous darkness that stalked the Ryders and had ended Amethyst's life.

Keen to bring Bracken what solace he could, Hayden left the others and followed Rosequartz and Chiastolite outside.

Night had begun to draw its veil over the rocky hill-country of the Etherian borderlands, covering the boggy wetlands that surrounded The Fallen Inn, robbing the bleak landscape of any noticeable character. The damp, clinging mist hung heavy in the air, masking the sky of moon or starlight so that the only illumination available came from a small lantern that hung from the crooked gable of the tavern. Beyond the lantern's dim glow Hayden and the Ryders could see the tall, strong silhouette of Bracken, motionless as stone, standing in the murky half-light, her gaze trained east towards the mighty mountains whose snowy majesty was lost in the blackness. She did not move as they approached, seeming totally numb to any stimulus, held lifeless and frozen by grief. Only when they were right next to her did she turn her face towards them and Hayden witnessed the drained and harrowed expression on her face, a mask of agony that seemed to stretch beyond human sorrow. No tears marked her pallid face; perhaps if there had been signs of weeping she would have looked less troubled. Her eyes were dry but the emerald irises seemed darker, narrow and chillingly dull in her round, pale-skinned visage, as if the gentle light of her soul had been snuffed out and been replaced with something damaged and bitter. Her expression was tense, severe, holding within it an unnerving lack of feeling as if the hurt was so deep it would destroy her physical being if she released it from her shattered heart. All hope and tenderness seemed to have fled and in this cold and wounded state Hayden could see in her, unnervingly clear, the savage and unfeeling nature of her dwarf blood: the brutality that could turn into Ac-Nu.

She held their concerned gaze harshly for a second before turning back towards the hidden mountains that marked the border to her path. Stepping forward, Rosequartz touched her arm tenderly, sending out an imploring tendril of loving Ley energy. 'Dear Bracken,' she murmured, 'let us ease your pain and loss by joining it with our own. Amethyst's death wounded all our hearts and although the Ley holds her life-force, the grief we feel for what is no more is as raw as yours. Weep if you must,

I too have cried many tears as I journeyed here. Bellow with rage and injustice if that is what is in your breast, but do not lock us out.'

Bracken did not respond to Rosequartz. The news of her guardian's demise seemed to have filled her with an iciness, a numbing anaesthetic that wrapped tightly around her hurt and grief like a coffin of stone, replacing her despair with quiet, remote fury. Her eyes still searched the mountains of her kinsfolk; lost in the black night, she subconsciously reached down to caress the hilt of the war-hammer that was the symbol of her birthright. 'I made an oath this morning,' she said quietly, not making eye contact with Rosequartz, 'to return to Kelhalbon and take up the throne. I believed that Sister Amethyst's love and teachings had moulded me enough to leave her care behind. I thought I could grow to be content with having a duty that was not connected to the Ley, but the agony of losing her reminds me that the Sisterhood is still my true family.'

Silently, Chiastolite reached into a pouch on her girdle and took out a piece of fire opal. She felt the power of the Ley twist within, ready to unlock and release Bracken's sorrow. Gently she placed it in the girl's hands, uttering. 'She would be proud to know you had discovered the truth. All Amethyst ever wanted for you was to find happiness and fulfilment. She always said you had great potential.' The sorrowful girl turned the orange gem over in her thick pale fingers, but could only feel the icy smoothness of its shape and none of the healing relief of the Ley. She realised now that the stoicism of her dwarf blood denied her the aid of Ley comfort and felt very alone and trapped within her grief. Not even the words of comfort offered by the Ryders brought succour.

'There is a duty of royal lineage to take the throne and lead a people,' she said, gazing down at the stone. 'There is a duty when a Ryder takes her Stone Name to follow the Ley and do as It bids. But isn't there a greater duty than these, a duty of love and family? Do the feelings and hurt of a wronged daughter, albeit an adopted one, not carry the responsibility for her parent? I cannot move forward knowing Sister Amethyst's killers roam free. My heart will not rest until I know they are brought to account.'

Coolly, she handed the fire opal to Rosequartz. The Ryder studied it, seeming to question why its power had brought no comfort to Bracken. 'You know the Sisterhood's loyalty to our own, the natural justice of the Ley,' uttered Rosequartz. 'We will not rest until these murderers are found; the Ley will surely lead us to them.'

'It is not enough!' Bracken's voice was unnervingly cold, brutal and filled with fury. 'I cannot allow you to seek them out without me by your side. They thought it necessary to take from me the kindest, wisest guardian I could've wished for and I demand to confront them.' Rosequartz looked uneasy upon hearing the bitterness in Bracken's tone, but Chiastolite nodded sympathetically. 'This is a common desire,' she reassured her fellow Ryder. 'When death takes someone, the Ley often guides their loved ones to follow the last steps of their path. It will heal Bracken's grief to see us bring Amethyst's killers to justice.'

She smiled compassionately at Bracken, but the young maiden shook her head. 'You misunderstand, dear Sisters,' she uttered darkly as Hayden drew closer to join them and add what sympathy he could to Bracken's plight. 'I do not intend to stand back and watch as the Ryders subdue these heartless villains. I take up my own quest.' With a swift movement, she reached to her belt and drew the weighty and menacing war-hammer Bahl had presented her with earlier that day. A cold feeling of unease ran down Hayden's spine as the dim light glinted on the black, iron fist. 'I swear, as heir to the throne of Kelhalbon and Amethyst's adoptive child, I will find her killers and put a bloody end to their existence. They do not deserve the mercy of the Ley.' The loathing in Bracken's words chilled Hayden's blood. He had never seen her like this, so unforgiving and filled with rage. He could not help but recall the story Bahl had told them of the violent madness that twisted Queen Penn after her daughter's betrayal. Was it possible that Amethyst's death could bring such a hateful curse on her granddaughter as well?

Coming close to her side, he rested his hand on her raised arm and spoke firmly but gently. 'Hear yourself, Mistress Bracken. Think of what you are saying. You speak of murder, of blood for blood. Can you truly say that your beloved guardian would want such a thing? You are not a Ryder; it is not your place to bring justice.' There was an alteration in Bracken's brooding expression, her emerald eyes softened and she looked as if she might cry but did not. 'Perhaps,' she admitted, 'but tell me, Master Hayden, if your parents or sister were murdered would not your soul cry out for revenge. Wouldn't you want to strike down those who took your family away from you?'

Hayden looked at the tall, wild-haired girl and was struck by the strange contradiction in her appearance. Her dwarf heritage gave her the loftiness and strong bearing of a warrior but her eyes still betrayed the fear and doubt of a young woman uncertain of how to carry on. Despite knowing her birth family, Bracken seemed still very unsure of her place in the world and Hayden could not blame her if the death of her guardian had cast a painful shadow over her heart. 'No doubt I would,' he confessed. 'No doubt the agony of loss would injure my soul. But I beg of you, think before you make any decision.'

He felt the elderly Ryder move close to his side, gesturing for him to step back. She gently took Bracken's round face in her wizened hands. 'The Ley always brings punishment to those who have wronged It and taken a life in hate,' she told her softly. 'Whether it be by the word of man's law or by their own violent death, I have never, in my many years, seen a murderer who has gone unmarked, if not in this life then the next.'

Rage filled Bracken's heart. There was no punishment or guilt that she could imagine great enough to pay for the death of a woman so noble and kind as Amethyst. A wrathful voice was inside her head and it shrieked for their blood. 'And might that punishment come at my hand?' she asked darkly, her fingers tightening on the hilt of the Might of Kelhalbon.

Chiastolite looked scared, disturbed by Bracken's angry words. Wringing her hands, she studied the girl's grief-stricken face intently, as if to weigh up the hidden nature of her wounded soul. 'It might,' she confessed at last, her voice thin and quiet. 'I have known of too many incidents where a life has been taken for another. But to choose to do such a thing always damages the person who commits the act. The Ley cannot remove hate after such a deed. It guides us to celebrate life, not to revel in death. But you know the teachings as well as I. The Ley can only guide our actions; the choice of what we do is always our own.' The old woman looked warily up at Bracken, silently praying for the Ley to bless her aching heart with comfort and mercy. She knew well the rage that the death of a loved one could ignite in a soul and had seen first-hand the destruction it could bring on an individual. She would not wish such painful bitterness to besmirch the young woman's heart.

Bracken remained stoic and silent for a moment, staring up at the tightly clenched iron fist of the Might of Kelhalbon as if it clasped within its metal fingers the last tenuous bounds between her and Sister Amethyst. Her face remained inscrutable but after a few moments she seemed to come to a decision and lowered the war-hammer. 'I must come with you to track down these monsters,' she said, reattaching the weapon to her baldric. 'But I cannot promise what I will do when we come face-to-face. You speak wisely, Sister Chiastolite, and my teachings inform me that what you say has great merit, but I am not the person I once was: I am no longer an apprentice to the Ley. Only time will tell what manner of justice the heir to the throne of Kelhalbon will exact.'

Turning on her heel, Bracken retreated back towards The Fallen Inn, striding as purposefully as a soldier towards an impending battle. Filled with concern for the anguish that she bore, the others watched her go, Chiastolite and Rosequartz fretfully clasping their pendants and praying to the Ley.

'Poor child,' said Rosequartz as they headed back inside. 'I'm glad we are with her to watch over her as she grieves.' The elderly Ryder nodded solemnly. 'We can only do what the Ley allows us to, Sister,' she said grimly, 'and I fear that the powers that took our dear Sister Amethyst from us and attacked us in the forest grow to threaten the Ley Itself. We need to guide Stone-Tongue so that she may use her unique power to defeat it. I fear she might be our only hope.'

Neither of them addressed Hayden or even seemed aware that he was at their side, but he knew that the Ryders would be acutely alert to the concern within his own heart as the challenge his sister had to face grew ever greater.

Chapter 33

A VINDICTIVE ALLIANCE

Impatiently, Tristram Kreen watched the insipid winter dawn as it broke across the rocky southern foothills of the Kelhalbon Mountains, his heart restless with a mixture of longing for his beloved White Duchess and his desire to continue the hunt for her lost nephew. Following their run-in with the Ley Ryders, he had reluctantly followed Coal-Fox's trail towards the north, riding through the night, keeping near to the gory scarlet path that led them ever onward. They had reached the foot of the brutal mountain range in the gloomy last hours of the night, and made a makeshift camp where they patiently waited for the arrival of the Duchess Maudabelle. Neither of them slept, but instead they spent the chilly pre-dawn watching each other in silent mistrust in the dim glow of the firelight.

The captain of the Royal Guard stretched his legs on the hard ground where he sat and stared over the rustling grasslands of the Greyg Steppes for any sign of life. 'Where is she?' he murmured. 'It is not proper for a lady of the duchess's standing to take such a perilous journey alone.'

Beside the camp fire, the enigmatic Coal-Fox sat cross-legged, idly whittling away at a twig with her dagger. She glanced at Tristram with sly amusement through the narrow slits in her leather mask. 'You mewl like an infant whining for his nursemaid,' she told him dryly. 'Has anyone ever told you that?' The captain of the guard bit his lip in anger as he glared at the masked huntress. The presence of his beloved duchess's sinister servant needled him and he felt that if Maudabelle had placed him solely in charge of rescuing her nephew, Prince Aarold would be back in the safety of the palace by now. Darkness and corruption seemed to cloak Coal-Fox as fittingly as the leather mask that shielded her face and Tristram felt her very company hampered his mission. 'Mind your tongue, woman,' he uttered broodingly, poking at the glowing scarlet embers of the fire. 'I grow impatient to meet with Her Grace the Duchess again so I may tell her that her trusty Coal-Fox seems more intent on murdering Ley Ryders than hunting for the prince. This rendezvous wastes precious time in my quest for the prince's safety, but if it means the duchess sees you truly for the cut-throat you are and allows me to continue alone it will be time well spent. If she's wise, she will see fit to put you in your proper place, in gaol with the rest of the bandits and footpads.'

Coal-Fox seemed completely unaffected by this terse threat and slipping her dirk back into its scabbard, lazily got to her feet. 'If that is the case, then my judgement is now at hand,' she said dryly, gesturing to the misty grassland before them. 'Our lady approaches.'

His heartbeat quickened to see his beloved duchess. Tristram turned and peered through the bleary dawn haze, seeing the striking silhouette of Maudabelle mounted on her thoroughbred piebald mare, cantering toward them. She was as beautiful and stunning as ever, clothed for her journey not in her usual finery but in polished armour that glinted dully in the early morning light. Her steel breastplate was engraved with an intricate version of the serpent emblem of her birth-land and a weighty skirt of chain mail hung elegantly to her mid-calves. A barbute helmet with a flowing indigo plume covered her long, ebony tresses, the T-shaped opening in the front making her refined but serious features look even more exquisite. She spurred her steed onwards with the heels of her boots, looking every inch like a regal Valkyrie, ready for battle.

Tristram was on his feet and hurrying down the slopes the moment he caught sight of her, eager to reach her before Coal-Fox. Seeing the pair approach, Maudabelle brought her horse to a halt and waited coolly in the saddle, surveying the mountains before her. Reaching her side, the loyal captain chivalrously fell to his knees and kissed the duchess's gauntleted hand in greeting, while Coal-Fox remained at a distance, suddenly unsure of what the meeting might bring.

'Your Grace,' breathed Tristram as Maudabelle dismounted, 'you honour us with your presence. I am sorrowful that you have been forced to come all this way, when we have yet to find the prince.'

The White Duchess regarded him coldly with vivid green eyes. 'Save your apologies,' she told him curtly as she removed her helm, allowing her long dark braid to tumble down her back. 'I do not have time for them. I entrusted you with a specific task and you were unable to carry it out. There is little else to say.' She glanced across at Coal-Fox with an expression that said she was equally disappointed in both of them. The captain winced, pained by his dear duchess's harsh words. Irate he stole a look in Coal-Fox's direction to see if the mysterious huntress bore any guilt for the failure of their mission. Her masked face, of course, gave no clue of her feelings but her posture seemed tense.

'Your Grace,' he said as smoothly as he could muster, making sure his tone was loud enough for Coal-Fox to hear, 'forgive my rudeness but I do feel that if I had been allowed to carry out the search single-handed, it may well have been more successful. This individual who you have appointed to the task has some very unsavoury and dare I say violent characteristics that aren't suitable for a servant of the court.' Turning towards her mysterious servant, the White Duchess assessed her with vivid green eyes. 'Yes,' she breathed coolly, 'I had hoped that she would have dealt with the situation better than she has, but nevertheless she does possess skills that I do find invaluable.'

From her position a little way off, Coal-Fox tilted her head in a mock bow. 'I am but a humble retainer,' she breathed, her voice dripping with sarcasm. 'The whole purpose of my life is to serve. Forgive me if I do not meet the lofty standards of the Royal Guard.'

Irritation flamed within Tristram at Coal-Fox's impertinence and he failed to understand why the duchess tolerated being spoken to in such a disrespectful manner.

A small, ironic, knowing smile played upon Maudabelle's lips as if she and Coal-Fox shared a secret joke; it only lasted a moment, however, before her expression became serious again.

'However,' she continued abruptly, her eyes straying to the foggy mountains to the north, 'it is clear that my initial plan to leave the matter of my nephew in the hands of you both has not been successful and I feel the need now to glean help from another ally.'

Captain Kreen followed her gaze towards the horizon. 'The dwarves?' he queried doubtfully. 'You believe that they might be able to help locate the prince?' The duchess looked thoughtful. 'Perhaps,' she murmured. 'The trail that leads to my nephew seems to be heading northwards. There is a good chance they might have seen something.' Dismounting, she strode decisively towards Coal-Fox. 'I have a contact within the dwarf court,' she announced briskly. 'You will accompany me to meet with them and discover if they have any information about the prince.'

Tristram prepared to follow but as he did, the White Duchess held out her hand to stop him. 'Coal-Fox shall accompany me on this journey,' she informed him. 'The dwarves are an extremely private race and will not welcome a large entourage.'

Biting his lip in frustration, Tristram glared at Coal-Fox but did not argue. 'As you wish, Your Grace,' he muttered with a respectful bow.

*

Without another word, the White Duchess and her mysterious servant left Captain Kreen to wait with the horses as they began the trek through the coarse grass into the foothills of Kelhalbon. They did not speak for a very long time as they made their way up the steep mountain path that rose into the unforgiving jagged cliffs of the range. It was only when they were a good distance from the royal captain and sheltered from unwanted attention that the masked woman dared voice her feelings.

'It would be a great deal easier if you would allow me to dispose of our companion and seek out the brat myself,' she muttered darkly as Maudabelle carefully picked her way through the icy boulders. The White Duchess considered Coal-Fox's sentiments for a second; as brutal as they were there was a pleasing simplicity to them, and she could not help but wish things could be that straightforward. 'Be grateful that I was able to negotiate a rescue party of one soldier who is in my sway, rather than having the whole Royal Guard on the prince's trail,' she said as they climbed higher. 'We are nearly in the kingdom of my uncle, we can deal with both Captain Kreen and the boy there. I doubt a cripple, even a royal one, will have much protection alone in a strange land. I've made sure that he is far from resourceful.'

Coal-Fox looked doubtful. 'I hope you are not underestimating the ability of the Ley Ryders to interfere with our intentions,' she reminded the duchess pointedly. 'They have been a thorn in our side for too long and now that Stone-Tongue walks among them their power is even greater.'

Maudabelle stopped dead and spun to face Coal-Fox accusingly. 'It was your job to deal with them,' she accused sharply. 'A task in which you've failed miserably. Still, no matter, I am convinced that you will be able to carry out your role in my new plan with aplomb once I retrieve the necessary item from Kelhalbon,' she smirked knowingly. 'As for Stone-Tongue, I have made special considerations for her.'

They carried on their way higher into the rocky terrain as a light shower of snowflakes began to tumble icily. The White Duchess led the way carefully, staying a good distance from any noticeable entrances to the dwarves' kingdom. They veered from the path, clambering over slippery boulders until they reached the precise point that Maudabelle had been searching for: an isolated outcrop, sheltered from the biting wind by the mountainside. Thoughtfully, the White Duchess wandered about the deserted ledge, gathering its position in relation to the hidden realm below.

'This will do,' she decided finally, slipping the leather knapsack from her back. 'I should be able to contact her from here.'

Idly, Coal-Fox leant against the solid cliff face and watched as Maudabelle prepared for the meeting. 'Are you sure the dwarves will aid us in our quest?' she queried dubiously. 'It is not in their nature to be involved with the affairs of men.'

A cruel, knowing smile curled Maudabelle's scarlet lips. 'It is in her nature to help me,' she said slyly. 'She will give me what I seek whether she wishes to or not. It pours from her very being.'

With that, the White Duchess set about completing the ritual. Drawing the sword from her hip, she scored a small, tight circle on the pale ground in which she sat down cross-legged. Reaching into her satchel, she retrieved a small drum which she sat between her legs, and an empty leather flask etched with runes and marked with sorcery which she handed to Coal-Fox. 'Keep this open and ready for the moment I return,' she told her faithful servant as she placed it in her hands.

Taking a deep, steadying breath, Maudabelle closed her eyes and focused her mind, clearing it of all thoughts as she began to put herself into a trance. Her fingertips rested lightly on the taut skin of the drum, beating out a light, regular rhythm that matched her own pulse. Her trained and powerful mind was soon able to cast away all notions of where she was, concentrating only on the core and life-force at the centre of her being, the essence of her wily spirit. It was a technique she had mastered over many years of study, a state of being alert to her own conscious will and being able to disconnect it from her physical body. After a few moments, the drum fell silent as her hands became still and the only movement within her body was her deep breathing and the slowed pulse of her heart keeping her mortal form alive as Maudabelle commanded her awareness to rise out of her body and mind. She existed for a moment, still and totally alert outside her resting body, conscious of everything around her on the mountainside, from the icy fragments of snow tossed by the wild wind to the stoic figure of Coal-Fox standing watch over her entranced form. It gave her no alarm or unease to see her body from outside; she had practised this ritual so many times that to leave her physical self behind felt perfectly natural.

Summoning her will, the White Duchess drove her consciousness downwards, allowing her spirit to slip easily into the solid fibre of the alpine rock. The darkness of the earth engulfed her as she urged her awareness towards her destination, melting through the impenetrable granite as fluidly as a fish diving through the black ocean. At last, out of the silent weight of the mountain, a void of brightness and activity opened up before her and in her unearthly state Maudabelle could witness the entire panorama of Kelhalbon laid out before her. A slight buzz of exhilaration caught her as she drifted unnoticed past the toiling smiths and astute record-keepers, dwarves engrossed in the day-to-day work with no awareness of her malicious plot. The sights and sounds of the subterranean realm were as clear as they would have been if she had stood among them in her physical body, but they held little interest for her as she sought out a darker, more hate-filled power. Like an unseen spectre from the land of the dead, Maudabelle's consciousness drifted stealthily across the plateaus and gleaming bridges of Kelhalbon until her mind was brought to the rim of a great, dark ravine that ran through the centre of the cavern. A terrible sense of hopelessness and bitter despair cried out silently to the White Duchess's thoughts from this shadowy pit, and Maudabelle's senses felt rigid with the gloom and loathing that ran through it. She paused for a moment, calling into her soul numerous enchantments of nourishment and resilience to strengthen her in her quest, before pressing her mind onward merging into the sorrow and vile hatred of Ac-Nu. The rocks and solidity of the caves seemed to dissolve as she plummeted lower, her trained awareness becoming attune to the relentless misery and resentment that echoed forever in the blackness. Despite all her powers and mental control, she could feel the cold wretchedness of the forgotten dwarves within their self-built prison shriek into the rueful depths of her own memory, bringing forth the wrathful purpose of her own vicious endeavours. But this was not enough for what she required; her enemies deserved something far more potent.

A thousand wails, mutterings, and screams of grief and fury filled Maudabelle's mind as expertly she analysed each one as she sought out the twisted and brooding soul she needed. At last, a singular dark mass of simmering loathing and nursed hatred encountered her thoughts, heavy with bonds of rage, growling and spitting with long-recalled injuries. The White Duchess knew she had found her quarry. With all her cerebral might, the wily duchess formed, in her disembodied thoughts, a respectful salutation, sending it into the brooding blackness from her entranced mind. 'Hail and reverent greetings to you, Queen Penn, rightful and wronged monarch of Kelhalbon.' The groaning, sagging mass of rage did not respond at first, cloaked so deeply was she in her own thoughts of betrayal and revenge. Insistently, the White Duchess enforced the greeting again, thrusting it sharply into the void, until she felt the soulless raging consciousness of the trapped dwarf queen grip cruelly on to it and heard the half-alert, contemptuous reply hiss out, 'Who are you?' In her focused awareness, Maudabelle saw a singular, slit pupil scowling with disinterest out of the shadows. Keenly, she clung on to this image, this connection with the hateful queen, ready to draw from her the toxicity that would be her foe's undoing. 'My name is Nothing and I am nobody,' she uttered humbly as Queen Penn groaned and moaned grimly in her tomb. 'I am merely here to offer comfort to your heinous plight. Tell me of those who slighted you, of those blood-traitors who besmirch your royal name.'

The White Duchess's concentration shook violently as a terrible roar of fury and soulless agony emitted from Queen Penn's fanged maul. 'Harlot!' she shrieked. 'Vile discharge squeezed from my glorious loins. How dare she cross her royal mother and rut with that stinking human scum? How dare she live to drop that foulness into the world? I thrive on the image of her rotting carcass but death is an unfit punishment. I AM QUEEN PENN AND I AM WRONGED! Pay to me what is due. Bring me my vengeance!'

Each utterance of poisonous anger quaked the gloom of the cavern and summoning all her dark sorcery, the clever White Duchess caught them carefully in her agile mind. The destructive force of Ac-Nu scorched her spirit as swiftly she formed her consciousness into a psychic vessel to capture the precious spite.

'Traitor!' raged the manic queen. 'Slut and filth. A curse upon her soul and bones. A thousand curses upon her damned usurping bastard who had the gall to walk before me and claim she is of my line. May justice strike down the followers of the Ley for not throttling her in the cradle!'

The hot fury of Queen Penn's malformed spirit dripped and oozed into Maudabelle's mind like oily poison. Carefully, the White Duchess took command of each murderous sentiment, binding it with her own intricate magic until it merged into a bubbling cloud of thundering darkness. The hatred was like a potent venom and it took all of her concentration to gather up every droplet of its corrosive power. When she had collected as much as she dared, Maudabelle dragged her attention away from the vile rantings of Queen Penn, lifting it upwards out of the wailing despair of Ac-Nu, dragging with her the churning malcontent of the dwarf's rage. She felt it burn and claw within her soul, eager to destroy and corrupt everything it came into contact with. It forced her to recall her own private bitterness towards Elkric and the land of Geoll and it took most of her skill not to allow it to overwhelm her. Once more, she returned unnoticed to the upper tiers of the dwarf kingdom and was just about to continue her path back to her physical body when a vengeful muttering from Queen Penn's stolen resentment caught her attention and awoke within her a mild curiosity. Altering her intent, Maudabelle drew her attention from her upwards trajectory to a point across the far side of the immense chamber. In that instant, she found herself before the imposing doors of the dwarves' detailed archive and with little effort slipped her thoughts easily into the massive safe-house of records and information. The vast store of complex history lay before her keen mind and for the briefest of moments, Maudabelle felt overawed by the amount of content that spread out before her cunning mind. The details of thousands of scribes over millennia jostled together with the sound of sharp chisels against granite, vying for her attention. Within her spirit form, Maudabelle sensed the rueful complaints of the embittered Penn, cursing one half-recalled name and swiftly she pierced the countless carved lines of text to seek it out. Coded dwarf text unravelled itself before her inquisitive mind until one passage came glowing brilliantly into her knowledge, revealing to her all she sought.

With this confirmed fact clenched firmly in her thoughts and the destructive venom of the dwarf queen's loathing trapped within her spiritual grasp, Maudabelle allowed her awareness to turn once more to her mortal body and as she did so the caves of Kelhalbon melted into darkness. The slowed, rhythmic tattoo of her own pulse filled her mind and an icy chill shook her awareness back into the mountain clearing. A jagged gasp of cold air filled her lungs as her eyes snapped open, blinking with pained tears in the brilliant morning light.

An agonising, sapping sensation gripped her hands and urgently she let out a cry. 'The flask!' she shrieked as Coal-Fox realised her mistress had come out of her trance. 'Quickly!'

Dropping to her knees, Coal-Fox thrust it towards Maudabelle. Within the White Duchess's cupped hands, there had formed a small pool of deadly churning black fluid, that hissed and bubbled with the sounds of despairing wails. It clung greedily to the lily-white flesh of her hands as if trying to suck the very life and soul from her.

Urgently, the White Duchess raised her trembling hands to the open neck of the flask and her fingers flexed as she attempted to expel the strange and toxic entity from her skin. The hateful mass writhed and squirmed violently, clawing with greedy desire to consume and destroy another spirit, but summoning her magical knowledge, Maudabelle whispered compelling enchantments of dominance to drive the noxious power from her fingers. With a resentful rip, the blackness oozed from her, moaning and wailing as it was sucked into the awaiting vessel. As the final strand of despair vanished within the flask, the duchess quickly crammed the cork securely into the neck and seized the bottle from Coal-Fox. She could still sense the restless grief of Ac-Nu battling and raging within, alive with the poisonous memories of Queen Penn. Gripping the flask, Maudabelle ran her skilful white fingertips across the runes and symbols of sorcery etched upon its tanned surface, causing them to glow dimly as she forced the dwarf misery to submit to her will. Too lethargic and self-pitying to offer any kind of resistance, the imprisoned darkness soon fell into a groaning half-consciousness, mewling and hissing to itself. Turning the flask over in her hands, Maudabelle studied it inquisitively. 'Bitterness can be a powerful weapon,' she mused as she passed the vessel back to her loyal servant, 'even against a virtuous Ryder. But I needn't remind you of that, need I?'

The assassin's black-gloved fingers tightened broodingly around the flask betraying her hidden emotions but she did not respond to the duchess's comment. 'What do you wish me to do, Your Grace?' she asked darkly.

Getting to her feet, Maudabelle brushed away the snowflakes that had clung to her cloak. 'No doubt you are familiar with the Weald of Megrim to the far north of my uncle's kingdom. It is said that the trees and plants there thrive on misery and sorrow. I am sure that with the aid of Ac-Nu's power you will be able to nourish them. Don't worry about Prince Aarold or our friend Captain Kreen. Once within the borders of Etheria I will have the facilities to deal with them both.'

Coal-Fox's eyes glinted cautiously through the slits in her mask. 'I do hope you haven't undervalued the talents of Stone-Tongue,' she uttered warily.

A sly smile creased the White Duchess's shapely lips. 'Oh no,' she told her servant smoothly, 'I haven't underestimated her at all. In fact, I am acutely aware of the power she possesses and it is of greater interest to me than perhaps you can imagine.'

She turned her glistening green eyes towards the pass through which they had travelled. 'Come now,' she said briskly, as they started to make their way back to where Tristram awaited. 'We waste time and our prey has already a day's ride on us. I am sure you are eager to be reunited with the followers of the Ley.' Hanging back for a moment, Maudabelle watched her deadly and determined assassin pick her way carefully down the icy path. 'By the way,' she called to her idly, a note of amusement catching in her smooth Etherian accent, 'while I was in the halls of Kelhalbon I discovered a small nugget of information that might entertain you, my friend. The apprentice to the Ley, Bracken, who escorts Stone-Tongue – I know the identity of her birth parents. She is the daughter of my cousin-in-law King Elkric and heir to the dwarf throne. The mating is what caused Queen Penn to become Ac-Nu.'

Coal-Fox stopped where she was for a moment as she mulled over this information.

'A half-breed,' she chuckled to herself, toying with the flask at her side. 'A royal half-breed, true, but still a sorry mistake of nature. The Ryders are weak if they are willing to take on such mongrels.' A cool, merciless confidence swelled within her as she followed her mistress down the mountain path, confident that the legacy of the Ryders would perish at her hand.

Chapter 34

THE BAIT AND THE SNARE

Sleep did not come easy to the travellers housed at The Fallen Inn. The news of Amethyst's death weighed heavily on the hearts of even those who knew her fleetingly, making them even more aware of the power and threat Petronia could face. For the Ryders and Bracken in particular, dealing with such a painful loss filled their hearts with sorrow that the Ley did little to heal. Hearing that her beloved guardian had been slain so viciously seemed to release in Bracken a new and detached nature that mirrored the brutality of her maternal race, giving her companions cause for concern. It troubled Rosequartz and Garnet to see the girl they loved so full of heartache and bitterness. They feared for the condition of her soul if she was to continue the journey with them, as they guided Petronia onwards towards her destiny. They longed to send her away, back perhaps to the relative safety of her birth race in Kelhalbon, where the hurtful temptation to avenge Amethyst's death would not be so close. However, the true nature of her bloodline could not wash out the love and grief that struck her soul. Bracken was officially free of all duty and responsibility to the Ley, but her heart and mind were still trained on the damage the faceless enemy had caused to the Sisterhood who had saved her. She had set herself to see this battle through to the end, no matter how Chiastolite warned her about the scarring effect of revenge.

Petronia rested that night with an uneasy heart. The legend revealed to her by Bahl about her nature had made the instincts she had felt seem certain; her strange gift of dark and powerful language was to be used to stop a great evil, a wickedness that she seemed to sense growing more and more tangible each moment they were within the borders of this eerie and misty country. Lying silently in her bed beneath the twisted beams of The Fallen Inn, she tried to bring her mind to clarity and command the churning, muttering blackness that tugged at her thoughts to reveal its intent and identity. Although the disquietening shadows of power taunted and teased her constantly, when she tried to bring them into a clear notion, something maliciously pushed her away and all knowledge was lost. In this state of frustrated ignorance, Petronia found her concentration repeatedly drifting to thoughts of the young prince who had accompanied her for much of her challenging journey. Each time it did she felt her heart ache with feelings of affection and concern. She had the unnerving impression that she could fall in love with the sensitive and thoughtful youth; the idea of this made the battle she faced even more daunting. With her destiny so perilous and unknown, it did no good to contemplate notions of love. Caring for Aarold made him a liability and he had faced enough dangers of his own, dauntlessly, without being involved with her and her arduous destiny. She tried to console herself with the thought that they were heading towards the palace of his maternal grandfather and he would find sanctuary, but still the taunting utterances of her inner language bubbled violently within her soul as they burned with cruel menace around the edges of Petronia's concern for Aarold.

It was still dark when the party rose from their beds and breakfasted in readiness for the journey towards the fortified castle known as Murkcroft where King Hepton held court. Hayden suspected that the hour was later than it appeared and sunlight shunned this country until late in the day, if indeed it ever blessed the earth at all. Aarold had money enough to rent horses for Hayden, Bracken and Petronia from the innkeeper and with the three Ryders mounted on their steeds and Aarold secure on Phebus's back the group set off westward, following the directions of the prince's memory of the charts he had studied of his mother's birth-land.

The atmosphere was chilly and damp as they travelled across the marshy countryside and a light drizzle fell constantly, keeping sunlight at bay. The dour weather matched the mood of Garnet, Rosequartz and Bracken as they rode in silence, their thoughts consumed with mourning for Amethyst and sombre concern for what lay ahead. The elderly Chiastolite trotted apace beside them, fragments of brilliant purple sugilite clasped in her arthritic fingers as she softly chanted prayers to the Ley to heal her companions' grief. Hayden and his sister brought up the rear of the group, riding side-by-side in silent companionship, Petronia's senses anxiously alert with the awareness of the shadowy power alive within her.

Garnet surveyed the dull landscape for features that would tell her where they were heading. 'I trust you know the location of your grandfather's palace,' she murmured. 'It has been many a year since I rode to war in this land.'

Aarold tried to look confident. 'Well, I was tutored in the geography of Etheria,' he said, trying to sound sure of himself, 'but I haven't personally been here before. I'm sure though I have a good knowledge of where we're heading.' Phebus snorted doubtfully. 'Oh yes,' he sarcastically muttered, 'and your bearings on this expedition have never been wrong before, have they? Fortunately, I have made the journey personally as a foal and we Equiles have a natural compass towards our homeland.' Feeling slightly guilty that there was more than a gleam of truth in what Phebus had said, Aarold did not bother to chastise him for his sharpness. The truth was that he had indeed been relying on his Equile friend to lead the way.

Momentarily distracted from her thoughts of grief, Bracken looked across to her brother. 'But you did know our father, didn't you?' she said quietly. 'What was he like?'

All the party were startled by hearing Bracken speak. She had remained broodingly silent since the previous evening, her concentration seeming to be completely consumed by her anguish at losing her guardian and determination in seeking out the murderers. All of the group were very aware of her tender, emotional state and wondered why she would ask such a thing.

Aarold twisted awkwardly to look at his sister. 'I beg your pardon?' he asked politely. Bracken took a deep sigh. 'I feel I have little connection left with who I truly am, perhaps even less than when I didn't know the identity of my birth parents. My dwarf grandparents are not properly mentally equipped to give me an honest picture of who my mother was and now that Amethyst is...' She halted mid-sentence, unable to even speak of the sorrowful loss of her guardian without feeling the rawness of her grief. 'I would like to know of the blood we share. I hear the king, our father, was well admired.' Phebus made a doubtful sound. 'By some he was, certainly,' he remarked tartly. 'Though if I'm completely truthful, I can't say I was among them. He did have such a boorish nature, no appreciation for more intellectual matters. Thank goodness dear Aarold took after his mother.'

The prince shook his head at his friend's criticism of his father. 'Phebus didn't take to father very greatly, but there is some truth in what he says. Our father was a leader of courageous action rather than introspective thought, characteristics that my delicate nature would make it difficult for me to share. I do believe, though, he would have liked you a great deal. He would have been proud that one of his children inherited his fearless spirit and was capable of resolute action.'

Bracken nodded stoically but did not carry the conversation further. Her mind had been brought back to the resolution she had made the night before, to hunt down those who had murdered Amethyst and make them pay for the grief they had caused her. She felt the Might of Kelhalbon weigh heavy at her hip and knew such a quest could only end in blood, but such logic and reason did not lessen the anger in her damaged heart. Hearing about her father's character made the burning desire for vengeance on Amethyst's killers seem all the more just.

Petronia heard Aarold's words and felt a pang of sympathy for his self-doubt. Gesturing to her brother, she spelt out a message with her fingertips for him to translate to the prince. 'My sister says, you do yourself a disservice, Your Majesty,' repeated Hayden. 'She says, to have come so far from the security of your royal home shows great determination and character.' Aarold glanced over his shoulder and smiled a modest thanks at Petronia but even as she looked at him, she felt the churning language that troubled her thoughts growl loud in her consciousness, that the prince's difficulties were far from over. In fact as she looked about her at the drab and windy landscape through which they travelled, a certainty filled her heart telling her Aarold was in grave danger.

They rode on for most of the morning, guided by Phebus's infant memory of the murky countryside, following the barely visible light of the sun ever north-eastward. The landscape was monotonous: a seemingly never-ending wasteland of colourless long grass and coarse reeds, interspersed by dwarf, twisted trees with knotted black trunks and tangled, thorny branches that dripped with mossy foliage. Once they passed near to a hamlet, not even as big in size as Ravensbrook, merely a collection of two or three ramshackled wooden shelters. Phebus informed them these were probably the dwellings of marsh-farmers: common, hardy folk who lived off the fish and other aquatic creatures in the numerous pools and bogs that scattered the wetland.

The company seemed to journey on forever with no sign of human life till Hayden's mind started to question if the prince's Equile actually knew his homeland as well as he claimed to. Then, in the mid-afternoon, just as the insipid sun was beginning to dip into the misty gloom ahead of them, two mounted figures in armour appeared out of the dank fog to the south, calling out for the party to stop. Bringing their horses to a halt, the Ryders and their companions rested as the duo grew closer.

'At last,' breathed Garnet, as Chiastolite rubbed her ancient hands together to warm them, 'life in this cold land.'

Shifting in her saddle, Petronia felt her stomach tighten. The damp air around them seemed to be alive with dark utterances of peril and foreboding calling out to her; she was baffled that none of the other Ryders seemed to detect it. The pair grew closer, a regal-looking lady in polished armour and a ruddy, auburn-haired soldier, bringing their mounts to an even trot as they approached across the damp ground. Aarold let out a cry of recognition. 'Aunt Belle!'

The White Duchess and her escort halted before the group and

Captain Kreen bowed respectfully when he saw the young prince.

'Your Majesty, thank the heavens you are safe. Your noble aunt and I have been searching for days.' He eyed the Ryders with icy suspicion.

Guilt and disappointment filled Aarold's heart as he realised that with the return of his aunt, his adventure away from the restraints of court life would very likely be coming to an end. 'Greetings, Captain Kreen, Aunt Belle,' he said jovially, as he tried to disguise his sadness at the reunion. 'How wonderful to see you again.' The White Duchess scrutinised her charge closely with her vivid emerald eyes. 'The court has been in utter turmoil with worry, Aarold, not to mention my own concern for your welfare,' she said, her elegant voice displaying not the slightest trace of anxiety. 'We believed you had been kidnapped. I myself, with the trusty aid of Captain Kreen, headed up the hunt for your safe return.'

Aarold lowered his eyes in shame for the trouble his escapade had caused. In his heart, he knew that this moment would arrive sooner or later and he would have to return to cosseted normality.

From her mount at the back of the group, Petronia found herself watching the exchange with a curious intensity. In her mind, her supernatural awareness drew itself to a razor-sharp point, focusing on every word and gesture of the beautiful duchess as if drawn to her like a magnet. Her chest felt tight with unease and her throat and tongue seemed to become dry and heavy with the urge to release the power that churned within her mind.

'I heartily apologise for any trouble I might have caused you or my loyal servants,' Aarold uttered dully, pulling his cape across his lap to hide the leg brace he had received from the dwarves. 'There is no-one to blame but myself and my own foolishness. I grew bored within the confines of the palace and curious to see more of the world. It was only when things got away from me that I realised what a perilous mistake I had made.'

'Indeed,' sniffed Phebus knowingly. 'I can testify, dear Maudabelle, this whole expedition has been one crisis after another. Oh the stories I could tell you! I did warn him, I did try and dissuade him from the whole foolish notion, but he refused to take sound advice. I am only grateful that I was there the whole time to see that no mortal harm befell the boy, though what mental scars have been left on my delicate psyche only time will tell.' He blinked his scarlet eyes hopefully at the White Duchess anticipating some reward for his loyalty and level-headedness. Maudabelle gave a curt nod of thanks to the Equile and beckoned him carry the chastised prince over to her and Captain Kreen.

As they moved away from the group, Petronia felt a sickening tug of urgency fill her heart. It was totally appropriate for Aarold to be returning to the safety of his regal aunt instead of setting out with her and the rest of the Ryders to face an unknown and dangerous threat. But as she witnessed the White Duchess cast her cool emerald gaze over the young prince, something pulled desperately at Petronia's thoughts, warning her to fear for Aarold. Glancing uneasily at the Ryders at her side, she felt baffled that none of them seemed able to detect the troubled atmosphere that she felt so acutely.

Maudabelle rested the cold metal of her gauntleted hand lightly beneath the prince's chin as she examined his face for any sign of illness or injury. 'Still,' she said thoughtfully, once she was content that Aarold's well-being was intact, 'no harm seems to have befallen you. I guess I should be grateful that you crossed paths with the noble and valiant Ley Ryders on your adventures. They have clearly kept you out of danger.'

Turning towards Garnet and the others, she gave a gracious smile. Gallantly, Garnet bowed her head. 'Our duty is to serve all those in need,' she informed the White Duchess politely. 'It was an honour to escort Prince Aarold back to you.'

Bile and anxiety rose in Petronia's throat as she heard Garnet speak so cordially to the duchess. She felt she wanted to cry out a warning to the Ley Ryder. 'Look! Can't you see what is happening?' But even if she had possessed the ability to voice her unease, she did not fully know the nature of the threat that she felt hanging over Aarold. Without realising it, a nervous bleat escaped her lips, capturing her brother's attention.

'What is it?' Hayden asked, looking at her in concern.

Closing her eyes, Petronia tried to form in her mind the clear reason she felt so strongly that the young prince should not leave the protection of the Ryders. The dark energy that fuelled her thoughts was thick and palpable in her mind, an enigmatic whisper that simultaneously called her to it and drove her away from the truth of its identity. She pressed herself closer to it, attempting to glean some sort of mastery over its strength, but it remained tauntingly distant. Opening her eyes, she found herself caught in the White Duchess's piercing and strangely knowing gaze.

At Maudabelle's side, Captain Kreen still studied the Ryders and their companions with reserved mistrust, unable to forget the concerns the duchess had confided in him and what he had witnessed personally in front of the lodge in Veridium. 'So we are leaving the Ryders to go about their business?' he asked uncertainly. A dismissive laugh caught in Maudabelle's throat. 'Why of course, Captain. I see no reason to detain them from their noble duties,' she smiled sympathetically. 'I hope you understand the loyal captain's coolness towards you; it is my fault entirely. Distraught as I was at the notion of the prince being abducted, my foolish maternal mind concocted the paranoid suspicion that the Sisterhood had taken him. I hope you will forgive such an idiotic mistrust. It was born out of frantic desperation.'

For the first time since their meeting, a small expression of discomfort ghosted across Garnet's face but she quickly disguised it with an understanding smile. 'Such things are bound to cross our thoughts at times of crisis, Your Grace. We take no slight.'

Maudabelle glanced knowingly at her young nephew, a contented smirk playing across her ruby mouth. 'Well it is now obvious that the young prince could not wish to have had better guardians during our time apart,' she said, taking up the reins of her horse. 'I thank you for his safe return and we shall trouble you no further. Your Majesty, thank the Ryders for their aid and bid them farewell. If we set off now we will reach your grandfather's castle by nightfall.'

Longingly, Aarold gazed at the Ryders and his newly discovered half-sibling, filled with the gloomy suspicion that he would never see them again, not at least without his aunt's watchful supervision. His eyes locked with Petronia's and he felt a desperate lurch of yearning fill his chest, urging him to express just how fond he had grown of her. It seemed cruelly ironic that after all the countless books and odes he had read in the royal library, at this crucial moment, when he felt he should speak, words failed him and he felt as mute as her.

'Farewell, good Ryders,' he stammered at last, softly. 'Farewell, Mistress Petronia. I am grateful to you, for everything.'

With a kick of his spurs, Captain Kreen urged his horse towards the foggy east, leading the way ahead of Phebus as the Equile carried his mournful friend away. With a final bow of respect, the White Duchess departed to follow her royal ward. The group of six travellers watched them go until the trio disappeared once more into the icy fog.

Garnet let out a thoughtful sigh as Aarold and his two new escorts vanished from view. 'The Ley go with him,' she breathed quietly. 'It is a dangerous time that we live in. It is better for the prince to be in the safety of his grandfather's palace than with us, especially with such unknown dark powers abroad. I don't feel this land is safe for the vulnerable.'

At her side, Petronia swallowed and nodded her head. She tried very hard to find comfort and truth in the wise Ryder's words, telling herself that it had always been their intention to bring Aarold back to his royal family, but she was unable to shake the effect the imposing presence of the White Duchess held over her. The striking memory of her beautiful but imposing visage still burned with powerful resonance in her mind's eye like a potent beacon that slipped into her consciousness, drawing to it the full force of the troubled, shadowy murmurings of her thoughts. Something within her cried out desperately from the core of her heart that it would be a deadly mistake to allow Aarold to return to that woman, that within the White Duchess was a nature of malice.

The group once again began their trek west across the mist-covered bog, Petronia reluctantly taking up the rear of the party; her thoughts were unable to leave the mental image of the defenceless Aarold trapped within the sinister sway of his cool but powerful aunt. Around her, she was aware of the Ryders making idle conversation as they rode, planning their path ahead, but their voices seemed somehow muffled and distant beneath the feeling of urgent concern that filled her mind. With every yard they moved away from Aarold and the White Duchess, Petronia became more and more aware of the desperate cry of the expanding, dark energy in her mind, swirling like an eddy around the recollection of Aarold's face, like a powerful bind compelling her to be back with him; an instruction and urge just as definite as the one that had drawn her up to the parapets of the Goodstone citadel. Low, hissing tones whispered in her mind, telling her that her powers were needed not with the Ryders but back at Aarold's side, defending him from the hidden danger within the White Duchess's emerald eyes.

Unable to deny her fearful instincts any longer, Petronia tugged on the reins of her horse, bringing the beast to a halt and turning to looking anxiously over her shoulder, desperately searching the misty landscape for a signal that Aarold and his escort had not been lost to her. She could not see their figures amid the colourless fog, but the acute focus of her stony, sharp awareness trained her eyes on a point on the near horizon and she instinctively knew that was the direction she must head in.

Noticing his sister's distraction, Hayden stopped his own steed at her side. 'What is it?' he asked in concern as Petronia stared intently into the distance. Aware of the commotion, Bracken and the Ryders ceased their journey and followed the troubled girl's anxious stare.

Petronia could barely hear her brother's worried question above the urgent cries of darkness from within her own thoughts, screaming out for her to pursue Aarold before it was too late. Her mouth and gullet felt rigid as stone and seared with a fire of mystical language that was burning to be released. Trembling, she disentangled the reins from her hands and signed the phrase, '*Something's wrong. I must go after him!*'

Hayden glanced at the Ryders. 'She says we should follow the prince,' he said grimly, but Petronia shook her head and pressed her hand firmly against her bosom, indicating that it was she alone who could help him. Before anyone could say anything to dissuade her, she dug her heels into the flanks of her horse and set off at a gallop across the misty marsh.

Streaks of shadowy power and gleaming Ley energy knotted like darting ribbons along her path as Petronia rode urgently through the damp mist. A thousand powerful words and phrases gabbled and hissed in her consciousness, not quite distinct enough for her to understand, taunting her and driving her onwards in her chase. Filled with dread for Aarold's safety, she leant close to her horse's neck and urged the beast to run faster, a knot of growing energy and nerve tightening in her abdomen.

Her heart lurched as suddenly, out of the paleness of the distance, a solitary figure mounted on horseback, calm and motionless, appeared out of the mists, a solid focal point for the growing darkness that drove her on. Petronia felt her breath growing short as the mystical words within her prepared themselves to be uttered, but before she was even conscious of the sensations of stone and magic transforming the muscles of her throat and tongue, the moist cold air of the heath darkened with the forceful power that until that moment Petronia had believed dwelt only within her. *'You naïve fool! Did you think that you were the only person to command such might, simply because an accident of fate twisted your tongue?'* Each phrase rained painful and clear down on Petronia like a barrage of stone daggers, chiming with the icy tones of the White Duchess. Waves of malicious power echoed out from her dark silhouette, reverberating into Petronia's consciousness, ripping jaggedly at the ancient language within, awakening it and snatching it away from her tenuous control. Words twisted like cawing carrion crows all around her, demonstrating the White Duchess's mastery of this wild force.

'I wasn't born with this ability like you, ignorant of what you are. I had to study alone and in secret for decades, use sorcery and cunning to unravel the mysteries that lurked in the forgotten dark edges of the Ley. But what I lack in natural aptitude I make up for in knowledge and practice.'

As the duchess's voice rang through her, Petronia felt an icy grip of control seize her body, crushing around her shoulders and waist and lifting her like a doll caught in a gale from the saddle of her horse. Ley light and billowing shadows twisted both around her and in her own thoughts as she battled to keep charge of the feral energy that tore at her spirit. Her lungs felt heavy with each inhalation she took as words of command and self-protection began to form within her mind. With all her strength, she forced them to flow, lava-hot into her flexing larynx, a great torrent of sound and power surging upwards to fill her mouth. Lips parted, the granite-hard cry of might ripped out from her: a long, thick strand of trembling language that swirled like a steel serpent from her heart, flowing out towards Maudabelle. The stream of energy coiled and twisted like smoke in the cruel wind, finding its path through the cold air towards its target, but the White Duchess remained untroubled. With minimal effort, an off-hand gesture of her arm and a breathy uttered command, Petronia felt her exalt her will over the attack, holding the shadow of her violently spoken words still in the air for a moment, like a hound called to heel, probing and twisting the released energy with her own trained ability until she possessed it completely. Maudabelle's voice and thoughts skimmed lightly through the fibre of the dark sound until they whispered in her head. *'Yes, dear girl, that's right. Release it, let it out, don't fight the blackness within.'*

Maudabelle's intent shifted the movement in Petronia's shrieked power, forcing it back in on itself, reversing the flow so that it billowed and retracted, withdrawing back into Petronia's body and mind with a sudden jolt of pain and shock like a wave crashing over her, sapping her of all strength and control. The strange and wild spirit that was the darker counterpoint to the Ley, the language that flowed fleetingly in and out of Petronia's mind seemed to be everywhere now, swallowing up the world at the duchess's command, engulfing all her senses. What had once been part of her, dwelling half-sleeping, half-waking in her subconscious, now filled her entirely, a dreadful, wonderful fountain-head of unbridled blackness that charged every inch of her with words and shadows and deadly energy. Through the swirls of feral power, the disembodied voice of the White Duchess echoed as clear as her own inner monologue, sounding almost maternally proud.

'Dear girl, you have no idea what you truly are, the awesome potential you possess. You are unique, a vessel for such magic that could command the Ley Itself. Those foolish Ryders would have you chain it down, limit what's

naturally in you. But I would set your true self free. In my control, you will become the Angel of War and Death.'

Petronia desperately wanted to fight, wanted to resist the sway of the White Duchess's persuasion, but the very will that she wrestled to use in regaining restraint was the same entity that bubbled from within, forcing her to give herself over to it completely. Colours of Ley light danced before her eyes, brilliant and vivid but each one tinted with darker, more powerful hues of destruction and evil. Her mind, her throat, her whole body brimmed to bursting point with cold, hard language, the sound of which Petronia knew would bring only havoc and murder. There was such vileness within her heart and it repelled her to realise that the only thing that stopped it from being released was Maudabelle's control over her. All her life, Petronia had felt there was something buried deep within her, kept hidden by her ignorance and muteness, and now it was being set free, transforming her into her true nature, something beyond human, something savage and unrestrained. A creature of pure energy and wickedness and, Petronia recoiled inwardly at the notion she could not deny, she welcomed it.

A sudden, dull weakness numbed her wild thoughts, forcing her to submit into sleep, cradled in the bonds of Maudabelle's sorcery. The last strands of her awareness sagged as the White Duchess soothed her. *'Hush, Stone-Tongue. Save your strength. Soon, all of Geoll will hear the terror of your voice.'*

A final brief slither of consciousness illuminated her mind just as the unnatural slumber overwhelmed her: a memory, hardly seeming more than a fantasy or waking dream, of having a family and a desire to follow the Ley; of a young prince with brilliant blue eyes and of a girl who Stone-Tongue thought she once was.

Chapter 35

THE WEALD OF MEGRIM

His heart burning with growing concern, Hayden urged his steed onward across the mist-covered heath in pursuit of his sister, Bracken and the other Ryders close at his heel. The fog seemed to suddenly grow thicker, like a vast tide of icy, grey smoke washing over the land until anything more than a few feet away became invisible. He strained his ears for voices or hoof-beats, any audible sign of where Petronia had headed after Prince Aarold and his entourage. He believed for a moment he heard on the moaning wind harsh words shrieked out in some wild language of rock and magic that drove him onward with more determination, but then all was silent once more.

Petronia, the prince and the rest of the party seemed to have vanished like phantoms into the cold landscape of Etheria, leaving Hayden and his companions lost and disorientated.

Bringing his steed to a halt amid the rough grassland, Hayden surveyed the empty landscape and called out his sister's name. His voice rang out in the empty, cold air; a pointless call to which there was no response. Dread gripped him as he feared that his sibling had once more been unexpectedly snatched away. 'Where did they go?' he uttered anxiously, as Bracken and the others halted at his side, searching the distance for any sign of life. 'They couldn't have out-ridden us so quickly. It's like they vanished into thin air. Something isn't right.'

Pensively, Garnet nodded and began to search the leather pouches suspended from her belt. 'I agree, Master Hayden. I fear there is more here than meets the eye. Your sister may have detected something we missed.'

Looking uneasily around at the grim countryside, Rosequartz's senses grew acute and aware as the Ley swirled agitatedly around, whispering to her in brief fragments of what had occurred there moments before. 'The Ley has been disturbed here,' she agreed. 'Something has upset It.'

Climbing down from her saddle, Garnet paced through the rippling grass and coarse heather. In her outstretched palm, she held a large fragment of highly polished black obsidian which she swept through the air in broad, slow circles as she partitioned the Ley to reveal to her what had happened. 'Show us,' she breathed. 'You are the truth, so show the truth to us.' Focusing her will on the shining, dark crystal, Garnet felt a sudden surge of Ley energy being sucked into it as the echoes of what had taken place were attracted like iron filings to a magnet to its glossy surface. Her eyelids fluttered closed and her breath grew shallow for a moment as the Ley filled her mind with traces and impressions of the battle Petronia had faced.

'Sorcery,' she whispered at last, painfully blinking open her eyes, 'the same dark evil that attacked the citadel and murdered Sister Amethyst. It has taken Mistress Petronia and the prince.'

Hayden gasped with dread at the notion of his sibling being in deadly peril. 'Say it isn't so,' he begged; 'tell me she lives.'

Garnet shook her head in ignorance and looked apprehensively towards Chiastolite, the Handmaiden of Death, for confirmation. The elderly Ryder surveyed the misty air thoughtfully with her watery eyes, searching the strands of Ley she witnessed hanging there for the familiar signs of mortality. 'They survive, for now,' she told them grimly. 'But destruction draws close to them both, Stone-Tongue especially. Perhaps not her own demise, I don't sense that, but a power of devastation that threatens to overwhelm her.'

Bracken gasped with horror as Chiastolite's words made her recall the prophecy told to them by Bahl in the Kelhalbon archive. 'Just as the legend said,' she breathed. 'We have to stop them before it's too late.'

A cold sickness filled Hayden's throat as he thought about the darkness, spoken of by the dwarves, that dwelt within his sister's mysterious gift. 'No,' he muttered through gritted teeth. 'I will not have it. Petronia wouldn't willingly harm a soul.'

Placing the black obsidian back into its pouch, Garnet mounted her steed once more. 'Pray to the Ley you are correct, Master Hayden,' she said soberly, 'but I fear these agents of evil will stop at nothing to break her resolve. We must find them before it's too late.'

Hayden was about to fearfully ask in which direction they should begin their search when a cry from behind made them turn in surprise and anxiously reach for their weapons. From the direction they had come, the sound of galloping hooves rose from the fog and a figure clad in gem-studded leather armour materialised out of the gloom. Sister Jet tore towards them, the moisture of the air clinging to her flowing ebony tresses and cape, her fine features even more pale and severe than usual. She called out in greeting to the group as she grew closer, waving her arm for them to wait.

'Hail, Sisters!' she cried, bringing her steed to a trot as she approached. 'I have grave news.'

Garnet and Rosequartz stared at each other in amazement at seeing their old companion and rode out to welcome her. 'By the Ley,' gasped Garnet when she saw Jet's weary and stern face. 'Sister Jet, we thought you were lost. Such strange and violent powers stalk these lands since we last met, I feared we had lost all of our Sisterhood.'

Rosequartz studied her fellow Ryder's drawn face. 'Rest, Sister Jet, while you can and speak of where you have been. There is little time for recovery though, for the Ley calls us on a vital mission.'

'I know,' uttered Jet sombrely, glancing at Hayden and Bracken for a moment. 'The girl we brought to Goodstone, she is the one of legend, the Stone-Tongue. I had my own suspicions from the start.'

Chiastolite regarded the younger Ryder and felt an unnerving sense of dread tremble at her instincts as it always did when death was near at hand. 'Where did you learn of this news?' she queried.

Jet looked shocked by this question. 'I need no mortal messenger to inform me of such,' she remarked sharply. 'These are grim times and the Ley has called me to pursue those who seek to damage it. Since leaving Goodstone, I have been on a relentless hunt for those who seek to destroy Its flow. I hoped that Stone-Tongue would have sanctuary within the citadel until I sought out the identities of our foes. Was that not the case?'

Sadly, Garnet and Rosequartz hung their heads in grief at the memory of what they had witnessed within the keep. Grimly, Bracken stared at Jet. 'Sister Amethyst is dead,' she said, her tone heavy with the woe she felt for her lost guardian. 'The citadel was breached and she was murdered defending it.'

The raven-haired Ryder grimaced slightly as Bracken spoke of Amethyst's demise, but her expression remained stoic and unemotional. 'A tragic loss to our Sisterhood,' she stated in a cool, level tone. 'Sister Amethyst was wise but in the winter of life, no match to defend Goodstone unaided. But what of Petronia?'

Hayden sighed worriedly. 'My sister did manage to escape from the citadel on the night of the attack, but I fear she is free no longer. Just moments before your arrival, she set out after Prince Aarold and his aunt only to vanish into thin air before we could catch up with them. She seemed to suspect that the prince was in danger and it seems she was right.'

Jet lowered her emerald eyes broodingly. 'It is as I thought,' she muttered. 'Sisters, during our time apart, the Ley tasked me with hunting out the identity of the persons who brought this shadowy evil to our land. I have discovered the perpetrator is none other than the White Duchess Maudabelle. She plans to murder the prince and use dark magic to overwhelm the country of Geoll.'

The other Ryders gasped in horror at this revelation. 'Then we must ride out at once,' cried Rosequartz in alarm. 'Go after them before it's too late.'

Gritting her teeth, Jet turned her narrow gaze northward. 'We will not catch her that way,' she uttered grimly. 'This is the duchess's homeland and no doubt she will have agents to assist her in her flight. Fortunately, she is not the only one who is familiar with the country of

Etheria. This was the land of my birth, I dwelt in these climes before joining the Sisterhood and the memory of the terrain is still clear to me. We are best heading north and circling round to approach Murkcroft from that angle. It will take us through the Weald of Megrim which is a less known path, unfamiliar to those who aren't natives. They won't expect us to come that way.'

Garnet and the others turned to follow Jet's gaze towards the northern horizon. Already the dank gloom of the later hours of the day were growing dense, thickening the colourless fog of the marshes until it made any vague landmark in the nondescript terrain indistinguishable. It was the sort of featureless landscape in which an inexperienced traveller could get hopelessly lost. Rosequartz sniffed the chilly, dusk air distrustfully. 'Are you sure you'll be able to find the correct path in this foul mist?' she asked.

A strange, confident smile crept over Sister Jet's striking face as she looked over her shoulder at her fellow Ryders. 'Of course, Sister,' she reassured her, urging her steed to begin the journey onwards. 'I know exactly which way to lead you. Hurry now, there are lives at stake.'

With a kick of her spurs, Jet quickened her horse's pace, leading the way ahead of her five companions through the long grass that carpeted the wet soil. The three Ryders trailed after her in single file while Hayden and Bracken brought up the rear, both painfully anxious for the welfare of their siblings. The spongy texture of the moist earth squelched and slipped with wet unpleasantness beneath their horses' hooves as they rode, the tangled undergrowth so lushly wild and high in places that the damp, greenish-brown blades of grass clung to their boots as their animals seemed to sink lower into the sodden ground with each step. At one point, Sister Garnet took out a fragment of brilliant yellow jasper from her belt and gripped it between her fingers as she held on to her reins. The stone seemed uncommonly colourful in the grim, grey atmosphere, but although Garnet willed it to speed their path back to Aarold and Petronia not even the Ley seemed capable of showing them a firmer route. The disorientating mist continued to swirl around them every step of the way growing ever heavier as the weak daylight drew to an ominous end.

Like a blind man, Hayden's knowledge of the world came mainly from the sounds of nature that groaned and chattered and croaked all around him. The mist heavy with the noises of the alien, hidden wild things of Etheria made him anxious. Doggedly, he kept his gaze on Bracken's silhouette, terrified of losing sight of the rest of the party for even a second. Yet despite the arduous landscape, Jet never slowed nor stopped to rest, only briefly looking behind her every so often to check her followers were still keeping up.

Gradually, slight changes began occurring in the drab scenery through which they travelled. The ground beneath them grew dryer, more firm, transforming from sloppy mud to slippery, uneven shards of brittle shale, like plates of fractured ice that shattered sharply when their steeds trod on them. Her suspicion roused, Garnet halted for a moment and dismounted to examine the ground. Running her fingers across the strewn debris, she found the soil deadened beneath her touch, devoid of any trace of Ley. Picking up an icy fragment, she examined it more closely. 'There are pieces of shattered metal amid this earth, crushed bone also,' she exclaimed.

A chill seized Hayden as he pictured what kind of ogres might lurk in the cover of the gloom, but Jet simply laughed. 'These are dangerous parts,' she explained as Garnet climbed back into the saddle; 'thieves and bandits use these paths. But nothing we can't handle between us. Surely you aren't losing your courage, Sister?'

Garnet swallowed deeply as a sudden, unnerving feeling of gloomy trepidation washed over her. Fear awoken, stirring low in the pit of her stomach, but she could not fully identify what troubled her. 'Come,' she said sharply, 'let us continue without further delay.'

Peering down at the debris-covered earth, Chiastolite felt her pulse quicken as the intense memories of all the deaths she had witnessed in her lifetime flowed suddenly and painfully into her mind. 'This is a place of troubled spirits, of woeful killings,' she uttered quietly as they set off again. No-one replied and it was as if they had not heard her.

Onwards they went, silently following Jet's lead. Soon the empty landscape of the barren grasslands began to disappear as out of the moist mist there came into view strange, drooping trees rising like still mournful widows in billowing veils of purplish grey. They grew sparsely at first, odd, lonely shapes with bowed trunks and long, trailing, willowy branches that sagged wearily down to the ground, trembling and rocking to and fro in slow, hypnotic patterns. Hayden found himself helplessly unable to look away from the thin, seemingly lifeless foliage and noticed that the branches were strangely lacking in buds or leaves, possessing instead a covering of narrow, fleshy tubes, translucent, dark and oily with dripping moisture. Each of these appendages flared outwards slightly at the tip to form a tiny mouth that quivered and puckered as if searching out nutrients. The fog that had hung so relentlessly around them slowly began to ebb away as they drew deeper into the shadows of the wood and Hayden pondered idly for a moment and wondered if the trees gained their sustenance from the moisture in the air. The atmosphere certainly seemed to shift as the plant-life increased, growing clearer but somehow more heavy with each step they took; it was as if it was pressing in on them, making it hard to breathe, the still air leaden with darkness. It was not long before the thought crossed his mind that Sister Jet might have forgotten the terrain of her birth-land and they were wandering hopelessly, becoming even more lost. His mind kept being drawn back to the thought of Petronia, in danger and helpless, captured by the White Duchess, and as the trees became denser he could not help but feel further away from Petronia, away from anything that was familiar and safe. The murky atmosphere seemed to adhere to his worries and feelings of isolation until he swore that he could hear his own internal train of thought echoing audibly in the lifeless air. As he found himself focusing more and more on his grave concerns for his sister, his eyes became increasingly drawn to the bizarre foliage that swung from the branches overhead; the lazy, hypnotic swaying seemed to both block out his awareness of his companions and cause him to become acutely aware of the loneliness and weary despair that weighed down upon him.

Amid his melancholy introspection, he was momentarily alerted to a sound outside his own thoughts. Ahead of him, lost to his sight by a heavy, colourless curtain of succulent tendrils, Bracken let out a distraught sob, a plaintive sound of grief that pierced the deafening silence like a cry from a wounded bird.

'Sisters,' she wept, her voice somehow seeming like that of a spectre, distant and lost, 'I do not know what to do. All I can think of is how I miss Sister Amethyst. Oh why did she have to die?'

As Bracken lamented, a singular, sinewy wet strand of insipid growth brushed, icy and clinging, against Hayden's face like a tear shed by the forest itself. It remained there, lifeless and chilling on his skin, a strangely comforting gesture of awareness to his downhearted mood that he could not find the strength to wipe away.

Up ahead, he heard Garnet heave a weary sigh. 'Her loss was a tragedy,' she uttered mournfully, her voice stirring the delicate patterns of drooping branches. 'She was too old and frail to defend the citadel alone. Why didn't I realise that and stay behind to aid her? She might still be alive if it wasn't for me.'

Forcing his eyes momentarily away from the mesmerising bowers above him, Hayden half-heartedly tried to glimpse his fellow travellers amid the gloom of shadows and creepers. He saw them briefly, slump-shouldered, bow-headed forms on horseback, trekking just beyond the field of his awareness. The grief they felt for the loss of their sister seemed to have descended heavily upon them once more, as if the dreary climate of the wood had brought to the fore the reality of their sorrow. A feeling of hopelessness filled the cold, still air, its weight tangible as it pressed in on Hayden, clouding his thoughts and turning them once again to Petronia's plight. He was vaguely aware that they were meant to be riding to her rescue, but now within the seemingly never-ending cocoon formed by the bowing trunks and branches the task appeared futile. A notion hung somewhere in his subconscious, woven between the drifting creepers that drooped all about him in every direction: was his sister still alive? He tried valiantly not to dwell on that despondent idea but the more he attempted to reassure himself it was untrue, the more obvious the notion became. A sigh of despair caught in his chest as a curtain of transparent foliage brushed against him, the moist, clammy tendrils clinging to his form, adhering lazily to his garments and skin as their wetness sank into him. In his despair, Hayden was once more briefly aware of the voice of one of his companions.

Wearily, Rosequartz reached into one of the pouches on her belt to retrieve a fragment of the crystal that bore her name. 'Take heart, Sisters,' she murmured hoarsely, seeming as if it took all her effort to find the words to speak. 'Please, take heart. There must be comfort in this black world somewhere, there has to be. The Ley named me as the Bringer of Joy. Say there is happiness somewhere or what has been the purpose of my Calling?'

Hayden could tell that Rosequartz was desperately trying to summon some form of comfort and reassurance from the Ley, but in his heart he knew this was futile. The atmosphere around them was so devoid of life and hope, he was sure that not even the most skilled Ryder could find the smallest glimmer of power in the wet and oppressive air. All around seemed a blank, never-ending ocean of grimness and thick, drifting vegetation that hemmed them in on every side until the very air was transformed into a muted pupa of his own heavy, bleak ruminations. There was no wind to stir the strange, lush trees, and yet Hayden thought he heard the constant sound of breath in the air, whispering with an echo of his heart's deepest fears and sorrow. Their limp, damp tendrils brushed against his body with every melancholy thought, the moist fibre of the supple stems tangling around his world-weary form, cradling him with lulling subtlety until, without realising, Hayden ceased riding and remained suspended in the coils of the trees, inert and overcome with loss.

The dampness of the foliage pressed thickly against him as painful notions of his inability to keep Petronia safe tormented his mind. The creepers pulsed and twisted their translucent flesh as the woeful, tired sound of Chiastolite's ancient voice drifted through his dulled senses. 'Joy is only an illusion, Sisters,' she sighed faintly as Hayden's lethargic mind struggled to grasp her words, 'death is the only certainty; I know, it has been my companion for so many years. Sister Amethyst is no more now; it is a state that will come to all of us in the end.'

Death. The word, the complete and perfect notion broke over Hayden like a blissful wave of darkness, filling his body and mind with pure, unblemished despair. That was the answer, of course it was, the solace from all desperation and feeling, to surrender everything and escape. The idea consumed him, both brilliant and terrible, until all else faded into shadow. This macabre longing possessed him, drawing closer with it the knotting, hungry coils of the trees, curling greedily around his limbs and torso, lifting him from the saddle into their crushing embrace. The moist tips of the creepers nuzzled against his flesh, drawn closer to him by the crushing misery that crippled his body. Through his semi-catatonic awareness and the translucent pupa of icy fibre that encased him, Hayden sensed the silhouetted figure of Jet before him and watched with helpless apathy as she reached into the folds of her cloak to retrieve a leather flask.

'You wish to know how she died, Sisters?' Jet's voice cut cruelly through the bulk of the foliage, heartless and icy, all pretence dropped now that she saw her companions trapped helpless in despair. 'It was me. I slew her with my own hands, watched her perish as you will in this forest of broken souls.'

With a swift movement, Jet pulled the stopper from the vessel, allowing the blackened, dense anguish of Ac-Nu to billow out into the chilled, lifeless air. Then a terrible sound filled the glade, a cry brought from the deepest core of the trapped Ryders' souls as the power of the dwarf queen's wretchedness fuelled the hunger of the leech-like trees. Hayden felt his gut constrict with an animalistic scream of inner agony of the grimness of life. Unable to contain it, he allowed it to spill forth from his throat to form succour for the vegetation that suffocated his spirit. The vines contorted vice-like around his body just as tightly as weakness and grief did around his mind. All about him were the sounds of melancholy, the weeping and moans of Bracken, Garnet, Rosequartz and Chiastolite as brutal truth, and the forest, bound their souls.

'Say it is not true.' Garnet's plea tortured Hayden's aching heart. 'For the sake of the Ley, Sister, tell me you would not do such a thing.'

A bitter laugh echoed from Jet's throat. 'The Ley,' she sneered, dismissively, 'what has the Ley ever done for you? You were blind to the traitor in your own Sisterhood. What has It ever done for me? I delivered myself to It when my country, this land was ravaged by the Geollease army, hoping I would find comfort in It from the grief of the kinsfolk I had lost. But all I became was a servant to bring mawkish false sympathy to others. My heart still remains shattered, my soul hungry for revenge.'

Insipid tendrils twisted eagerly towards Jet, ravenous to drink of her fury and loss but she swiftly cowered away before they could entrap her. 'No longer,' she snarled. 'Farewell, Sisters. Farewell to you and the pitiful Ley. I know of a greater might, dwelling in the breast of Stone-Tongue, and even as the last strands of existence seep from your husks, the White Duchess is working to extract it. She will be the weapon with which we shall strike back for all that has been taken!'

Seizing her reins, Jet dug her heels into her steed's flanks and galloped away with the swiftness of the wind, leaving her victims bound and enchained by crippling sorrow as the trees of Megrim set about consuming them, flesh and soul.

Breath and pain poured out of Hayden's form as the woeful notion of his sibling's fate caused the branches of the trees to grasp him even more tightly. One particularly thick, powerful bower forced itself mercilessly against the centre of his chest, directly over his aching heart as if to crush every last ounce of hurt, life and feeling from his body until there was nothing left. His form convulsed, a violent, tortured spasm of agony that trembled through his bones as the creepers held him fast, shaking his sword loose from its scabbard. The dwarf-polished blade gleamed iridescent amid the desolation and murk of the forest, a brilliant beam of mirrored silver that glittered unrelentingly through the gloom. In his leaden thoughts of grief at his inability to save his sister, Hayden's weary awareness suddenly stirred, captured from his train of self-hatred by the spark of something reflected back to his mind in the blade's shining surface. Through darkness and grief, he saw an image, narrow but filled with colour, of Ravensbrook, his home. A searing warmth of recollection and love blazed like sunlight into his weeping mind, battling against his desire to submit. Hayden was suddenly filled with a knowledge, a realisation that there still remained a world beyond this foul glade that was worth fighting for. His parents, his sister, they were not dead yet. As long as he drew breath there was still a chance things could be altered. As long as he lived he could fight.

The blade twisted through the cold, dark air before him as if wielding itself ready for battle. The joy of Hayden's homely memories danced along the honed steel as it fell against the heavy sinews of the tree that bound him and the wet fibre hissed with repulsion at the notion of happiness. Cutting metal and the concept of hope sliced through the creepers, granting Hayden thankful leeway to move. With an almighty effort, he willed his arm to reach out for the sword's hilt, focusing every ounce of consciousness on the idea of his family and home. Agony seized at him again as the ravenous tendrils frantically clung to their prize, taunting him with seductive offers of surrender and death. Hayden felt his chest heave with effort as he battled the blackness for each breath; each sensation informed him that he must keep living. Each inhalation brought a wave of agony and mental nausea, each breath a dragging drain of vital energy, but he dared not rest. Suddenly, a new, alien sensation broke over him, an awareness of his outstretched fingers coiling round the solid, sure hilt of the sword, confirming the reality of life within. His muscles still ached, his heart still wept but he knew he could survive.

With a bellow of agonising effort, he swung the blade manically towards his suspended body, not daring to think whether it would rend his own flesh. His only concern was to bring the brilliance of his family's memory closer until it burned away the icy, black strands of grief that imprisoned him. The creepers wailed and clung frantically as he hacked at them, ripping at his flesh and spirit as they fell away. Fear and terror blazed like coals in his gut as he flung his body desperately around, kicking, struggling and carving as life flooded back into his body. The damaged fibres of the vines lashed out, caressing his tender, weakened flesh with haunting promises of numbing relief; fearfully Hayden repelled them with the shimmering recollections imprinted into the metal of his weapon. He dared not stop, dared not pause to think even for the briefest of seconds, in case the creeping, dark clouds of sapping melancholy drifted back into his thoughts and trapped him once more. His awareness remained held safe in the memory of his home and family.

With one last great struggle of physical and mental effort, Hayden felt his body at last tear away from the chilling clutches of the ravenous tree with an agonising rip of pain that made one final frantic attempt to claim his strength. With a furious cry of suffering, he tumbled from the branches' possessive hold and fell to land in a heavy pile on the stony ground. The landing sent shock-waves of bruising pain through his shoulder and ribs, but it was welcome relief compared with the mental torment he had endured moments before. Air gushed easily, cold and stagnant, in and out of his lungs as his mind tentatively realigned itself with the reality of the world. Gloom still hung like an unseen assassin over his thoughts and he carefully focused on the guidance of the inspiring blade clasped in his hand to keep it at bay.

His legs trembling with adrenaline and anxiety, Hayden scrambled to his feet and frantically looked about him for the rest of his party. The forest was still eerily lifeless and sombre, black strands of foul Ac-Nu hung in knotted curls in the icy air, whispering with sighs and moans of hopelessness. The greedy tendrils of the foliage curled menacingly all around, beckoning him to return to their embrace of misery. Keeping the shimmering sword raised and ready, he stalked forward, searching for any sign of the Ryders. Muffled weeping and gasps filled the air, issuing from between the tangles of colourless shoots. Peering eagerly into snarled masses of moist, grey plant-life Hayden could clearly make out the forms of listless limbs. Hurrying closer to the immense clump of twisting creepers, he felt the great misery of this hateful place threaten to overwhelm him once again as from within the trees' grasp a lost voice let out a moan of woe. Swiftly, Hayden brought the glimmering blade up before him and drove the tip firmly into the throbbing cocoon. The vines hissed in bitter protest as the sharp metal pried them apart and Hayden watched as a new vision of peaceful countryside glimmered within the polished steel. As he cut away at the pulsating knot, the sight of villagers grateful of the aid the Ley had brought them danced lively within the metal. The insipid foliage writhed furiously as Hayden ripped it asunder, frayed tips lashing hungrily in the stagnant air as from within the knot a human body began to stir to life once more. With an agonised cry of pain and effort, Garnet flexed her heavy limbs, awkwardly casting away the thick, meaty cords that had imprisoned her. Her normally tawny skin was deathly pale and moist with sweat and tears, and her breathing was ragged and uneven. She blinked hard, trying to wake herself from the catatonic mental torment of the trees and re-engage her mind. A harrowing scream issued from her throat as she stumbled free of the creepers' grasp, almost collapsing beneath her own weight as she did so.

Taking a step back, Hayden gave her room to breathe. 'Are you all right, Sister Garnet?' he asked anxiously, his eyes already surveying the gloomy woodland for signs of the rest of their party. Gripping her head in her hand, the Ryder let out a weary moan. 'I am for now, thanks to you, Master Hayden,' she said, trying to shake off the ill effects of the trees' draining hold. 'The Weald of Megrim, that's where we are. Of course, how could I have been so foolish not to recognise it straight away. I thought the potency of this place on fears and woes was just a myth.'

Hayden glanced around him, his eyes ever watchful of the strange, greedy tendrils that even now threatened to recapture them, if their minds drifted into thoughts of unhappiness for the briefest moment. 'It would appear not,' he said grimly as Garnet unsteadily got to her feet. 'But somehow my sword seems to have the ability to repel the trees. I believe it has something to do with the magic the dwarves imbued in it.'

Garnet took in the familiar and reassuring images that danced across the gleaming surface of the blade. 'Bahl mentioned to me that this weapon would help remind me of what is of value in life,' he murmured thoughtfully, 'and it seems like it has a similar effect on others. We must search for our companions before it is too late.'

With Garnet keeping close by his side, her golden eyes ever dancing between the inspiring images caught in the blade and the swirling foliage that billowed all around, Hayden stalked carefully through the gloom and chill of the wood. Both youth and Ley Ryder kept wary watch for any sign of their companions trapped within the seductive coils of misery that twisted down from the boughs above, straining their ears for any sigh or despairing sob that might betray their location.

After just a few moments searching, Garnet seized hold of Hayden's shoulder to raise his attention and pointed in the direction of a thick, oily vine that coiled down from the canopy, the inert, trembling form of Rosequartz wrapped in its taut spiral. Cold grief filled Hayden's heart when he saw the once-jolly face of the Ryder, a pale, drawn mask of despair, her bloodless lips moving in soft, breathless utterances of inward thought. The grey flesh of the broad creeper pressed closely against Rosequartz's sallow cheek, absorbing from her very flesh the deepest, hidden darkness of her mind.

Stepping closer to her imprisoned sister, Garnet reached out to gently touch Rosequartz's icy hand, calling her name in a soft but firm voice. The woman's emerald eyes flickered feverishly open, her green pupils blurry and awash with a thick haze of tears. Her lips parted and a weary, woeful cry emitted from her throat. 'Rosequartz,' she gasped, her voice thin and weak with despair, 'who is Rosequartz? The Bringer of Joy. Not I. Not any more. I have no joy in my heart left to bring to the world. The world is empty of happiness.'

Concern throbbed in Garnet's chest when she witnessed the wretchedness that was consuming her fellow Ryder, and this anxiety made the creepers that draped down from the shadows above inch subtly closer to attempt to ensnare her once more. 'That isn't true, Sister,' she enthused, although a hint of fear and doubt crept into her voice. 'It's this foul place; it turns your thoughts dark and tries to devour your spirit.' Swiftly, she turned to Hayden, urgency shining in her golden eyes. Hayden did not wait for her to speak a word. With one swift strike, he brought the shimmering tip of his blade down upon the throbbing vine that knotted around Rosequartz. The steel seemed to sing joyously as it sliced easily through the thick foliage; bright images from the Ryder's past gleamed in brilliant jewelled hues within the silvery metal. Life flickered once more in Rosequartz's emerald pupils as the sword filled her mind with powerful memories of the happiness that her blessed Calling and her exuberant character had brought to people. Her consciousness was suddenly enlivened by recollections of the laughter of children playing around her as she sang and told them stories, of words of hope and comfort she had uttered to those whose spirits she had lifted, of lewd jokes and stolen flirtations made with handsome fellows on her travels: the fragments of joy that knitted together to form Rosequartz's robust personality. The cool air seemed to sing with peels of laughter as Hayden carved through the sinewy bonds that gripped her body, and with a ragged gasp the awoken Ryder slipped free from her mental and physical prison. She tumbled to her knees before Hayden and Garnet, her body trembling with a sudden burst of energy as she battled to steady her uneven breath.

With shaking hands, Rosequartz reached into the pockets that hung from her girdle and retrieved a large fragment of the soft, pink stone that bore her name, clutching it desperately in her trembling fingers. Bringing it reverently to her lips, she held it there, eyes shut tight in a grateful rejuvenating prayer to the Ley until after a few moments her breathing became more even and the colour returned to her cheeks. 'I am Rosequartz,' she uttered assuredly to herself as the darkness lifted finally from her thoughts. 'The Bringer of Joy, Mistress of Happiness.'

A peaceful smile graced her lips as she kissed the crystal one final time before putting it away and getting to her feet. Gratefully she gazed at Garnet and Hayden, her eyes sparkling with spirit once more. 'My thanks a hundredfold, Master Hayden, for bringing back to me the memory of who I am,' she said earnestly. 'A few moments more and my spirit would have been lost completely.'

Hayden shook his head. 'No time for words of gratitude, Sister Rosequartz, ' he said, 'Sister Chiastolite and Mistress Bracken are still lost. We must seek them out and flee from this poisonous place before it claims us all.' A strange and sudden anxiety gripped Hayden's heart when he uttered Bracken's name. All at once he was aware what a tragedy it would be if brave and virtuous Bracken was lost to the world, moreover lost to him. The urgency he felt to find her burned within him as fiercely as the one to find his own sister.

Anxiety gripping his heart, Hayden resumed his search through the depressing gloom of the woodland shadows, both Garnet and Rosequartz remaining close to him, wary to stray from the protective power of the enchanted blade. Eagerly, all three scrutinised the tangled masses of swaying branches and gnarled trunks for any sign of their companions, ever fearful that the sapping influence of the numbing arboretum had already absorbed the lives of Bracken and Chiastolite completely. The forest did seem unnervingly devoid of any human existence apart from their own, the air cold and filled with the merest maundering whispers of swaying foliage that attempted to call out to them in tones of weighty doom, tempting them to surrender back into the possessive embrace of their twisting tendrils. Hayden kept his sword drawn, brandished firmly before him so that he and the others could always keep one wary eye on the heartening images reflected in its surface and thus strengthen themselves against the temptation to give up hope. The insipid, pallid creepers knotted complexly together, interweaving tightly with each other to form thick, sinewy ropes of growth and abstract coils and tangled clusters that seemed to resemble the half-formed imagery and twisted faces of fevered nightmares. Hayden studied these strange, chilling shapes closely, searching for a glimpse of the two lost travellers between the matted vines, his hand gripping furiously on to the hilt of his weapon so that he was ready to cut them free. The drooping foliage stirred lazily before his eyes, the translucent flesh flexing and pulsing like the bloodless intestines of some mighty beast as it digested a meal and within that slight movement Hayden caught sight of a lost, colourless face, weeping silently from within the imprisoning grasp of the tendrils.

The weak and grief-stricken form of Bracken was barely visible amid the dense growth that cocooned around her body. Thick lengths of plant-life pressed in tightly, coiling like ravenous serpents along her arms and legs as their sensitive tips stretched determinedly towards her heart. A vast bower, twice as thick as a man's arm, encircled her torso possessively, squeezing and crushing her around the waist with such force that it looked as if it might break her in two. Her face was terrifyingly lifeless, her normally pallid complexion turned practically transparent from lack of energy and tiresome sorrow. Her lips trembled slightly as shallow breath eked in and out, twitching now and again as if she wished to release the torturous sorrow that consumed her soul. Heavy, dark grey lids weighed down over her moist pupils until only a narrow band of shadowy muddied green was visible, dull and soulless as she gazed blankly out at the world. This visage, sickly and aged with inner agony way beyond its years, hung like a ghostly spectre amid the gloom of the branches, a watery replica of the person Bracken once was, haloed by a mantle of countless, smaller vines that wrapped themselves tightly around her head. These worm-like growths curled and traced tightly across her moist brow and temples, clinging so fiercely to her pasty skin that puckered lines and indentations formed around the paths they took, as if these new shoots were merging with Bracken's scalp, drawing out the sorrow and mourning that filled her mind.

A sickening horror gripped Hayden as he looked upon the agonised, trapped girl, and sorrow for her state made his hand tremble on the hilt of his sword. Reaching out to her with his free hand, his fingertips compassionately brushed her sallow cheek, finding that her flesh was unnervingly cold and clammy. 'Have strength, Mistress Bracken,' he uttered, 'I will free you.'

The tormented girl's woeful face flexed and twisted spasmodically and her hooded eyelids lifted to show the deadened, empty despair that dwelt within her soul. Tears gushing down her broad cheeks, her dry lips quaked as she opened her mouth and let out a heart-wrenching, bleating cry. 'I am alone,' she wailed as the tendrils of the heinous tree pulsed and squeezed her tightly. 'Sister Amethyst is dead, my parents are dead, my grandparents despise me. My life serves no purpose.'

As she cried and bitterly shrieked with lonely sorrow, Hayden took firm hold of his blade and raising the glimmering sword mightily aloft, brought the shining metal down upon the undulating vines with all the power he could muster. The cutting edge of the enchanted steel collided with the slippery fibre of the vegetation with a dull thud, the brawny bowers juddering as he struck them before contorting even more possessively around Bracken's form. The girl trembled and sobbed, lost in misery as Hayden sliced and chopped at her life-choking captor, but the vile plant remained unharmed. Sweat of desperation and effort formed icily on Hayden's skin as he fought against Bracken's woe. Flashes of colour and half-formed images darted across the metal of his blade just as they had done before only now they seemed strangely fragmented, the half-formed features of Sister Amethyst floating in and out of view as if the tree's fierce hold over Bracken's spirit was too firm to allow even the magic of her kinsfolk to reach her. Hayden felt his breath catch in his chest as he hacked and chopped at the ever-knotting bonds that laced around the maiden. His hearty efforts seemed useless against the rubbery stems: the honed edge of his sword falling dully again and again against vine and branch leaving only the thinnest white scars upon the pliable bark. Bracken's grief was dense: a tangible veil surrounding her, embroidered with ravenous tendrils, weighty and black as iron. Hayden's eyes grew blurry, his vision clouded with tears of effort and desperation as the sorrowful effects of Megrim threatened to overwhelm him once more, and he realised Bracken was all but lost.

'What's happening?' Garnet's voice rang out to him through the heavy atmosphere, her tone shrill with concern. 'Why can't you sever the vines?'

Too intent on his hopeless task, Hayden did not look round. 'I'm trying!' he implored fiercely, dealing a volley of powerful blows upon the broad tendril that reached down like a massive serpent to encircle Bracken's brow, 'but they're too strong.' Once more, he struck the creeper but the hateful plant still bore no damage. Instead, it flexed its sinews more powerfully, driving its narrow, creeping offshoots deeper into the pale skin of Bracken's temples. Trembling in tortured agony, she let out a high, pleading whimper and bleated her dead guardian's name.

Another desperate voice mingled with Bracken's cries in the maundering air of the forest: a rasping, throaty whisper, quavering with the rattle of near-death but clear as it uttered the words. 'It isn't enough.'

Drawn by the strangely familiar tone, Garnet and Rosequartz

searched the brooding woodland for its owner. At first, the voice seemed to come from nowhere, an ancient, dry note born from the icy air itself. The trees empty, the last member of their party no more than a phantom or memory. But her breath, a gravelly, heavy gasping, guided them towards where Chiastolite was, her elderly body pressed taut against the pale trunk of a willowy tree. A network of transparent tendrils wove around her brittle, aged form, encasing all but her head like a strange, living bridal gown of shimmering lace. Small, almost delicate coils of growth spiralled around her arthritic fingers and caressed her wrinkled throat like the soft hands of a lover. She gazed at them, her round, dark eyes shimmering with moisture and grief, but at the same time brilliantly lucid as if the exhausting depression of the forest had yet to fully claim her consciousness. The plant-life that cocooned itself around her ancient form bound her tightly to the smooth, pale trunk of one of the trees, the rigid support of the slim prop forcing her twisted spine to straighten so that she once again could stand to her full height. It was odd but, far from being trapped or drained by the pale growth taking possession of her, Chiastolite seemed to almost welcome it as if the sorrowful trees and vines were a long missed part of her persona as Handmaiden of Death. Her moist pupils filled with grief and knowing; she regarded her fellow Ryders and with agonisingly slow and deliberate movement, she raised her gnarled hand to beckon them to her.

Wary that the dense and mournful foliage might once more ensnare them with grief, Rosequartz and Garnet stepped carefully towards their elderly comrade. Chiastolite strained to keep her gaze on them, battling against the oppressive influence: the dark atmosphere that fogged her mind. Her creased lips puckered and twisted as she struggled to croak coherent words. 'The boy,' she gasped dryly, her head jerking tautly in Hayden's direction. 'I, must, speak with, the boy.'

A graceful coil unfolded itself from the shady boughs above, caressing her dry, puckered cheek as it did so. Her horrified eyes still trained on the trapped elderly Ryder, Sister Garnet swiftly stepped back, hurrying in the direction of where Hayden continued to battle with the fibrous bonds that held Bracken prisoner.

'Master Hayden,' she cried urgently, as the boy once again pressed his shimmering blade unsuccessfully against the thick, resilient boughs that wound themselves firmly around Bracken's trembling body. The sword and its bright colours of hope and memory left a pale, thin scrape on the smooth, bluish-grey texture of the knotted tendrils: a minute trace of the hopeless effort he had spent to free the girl from her cocoon of despair. The vine rippled, like a warrior flexing his muscles, and formed another choking loop around Bracken's forearm, the futile mark left by Hayden's blade dissolving into flawless, pallid stem. A gagging sob contorted Bracken's throat as if her sorrow and agony were so immense that they squeezed the very air from her lungs. A growl of frustration rumbled in Hayden's throat. 'Why isn't this working?' he roared, before adding in a softer tone. 'Try and hold on to life, Mistress Bracken, don't allow these vines to strangle your hope.'

Garnet reached out and gently touched the boy's arm to gain his attention. 'Master Hayden,' she said in a soft, firm voice. 'Come quickly. We need you to free Sister Chiastolite. She is old and I fear doesn't have the strength to last much longer.'

Hayden did not move at first but stood frozen mid-action, sword raised over his shoulder, ready to submit another strike upon the tangle of branches that gripped the woeful girl. He looked into her pale, wet face, trying desperately to lock his gaze with her sea-green eyes and see within them one faint glimmer of life or spirit.

'I can't leave her,' he uttered softly, a pained ache of fearful loss filling his chest as he looked upon Bracken, her head drooped forward, shivering with exhausted tears and wails. Garnet gazed at her too, bitterly woeful at the sight of the maiden she knew so well reduced to a shell of grief. 'I know, Master Hayden, ' she stammered, reaching up to place her hand over his own where it closed around the sword's hilt, the Dwarfish magic giving her strength to deal with the thought she dared not consider, that Bracken was beyond help. 'But you must. Come now.'

Hayden resisted for a second as Garnet tried to lead him away. With his free hand, he reached out to caress the girl's colourless cheek, unnerved by the icy coolness and damp of it. Bracken inhaled a ragged sigh and Hayden thought he saw the glimmer of something other than despair in the depths of her eyes before her lids fluttered shut with exhaustion.

A rasping, urgent cry rang out once more through the dark woodland, the voice of Sister Chiastolite calling to them, battling to keep hold of her own consciousness and deliver her message before the darkness claimed her. Swiftly, Hayden and Garnet hurried back to the place where Rosequartz stood watching over the ancient Ley Ryder. Greedy tendrils reached out to ensnare them as they ran, hungry for the grief and concern for Bracken's plight but Hayden batted them away with his sword: the memory of a life beyond this hopeless forest.

When they reached Chiastolite, her feeble, elderly frame was barely visible amid the complex lattice-work of pale plant-life that worked its way around her fragile body like a protective casing of living lace, drawing her further and further away from the horrors and realities of the outside world, not draining her of who she was but transforming her into itself, the Handmaiden of Death eluding normal mortality in favour of some other existence. Only her face and hands remained wholly in their human state, her crooked fingers beckoning them towards her, dark, moist eyes brimming with the knowledge she had to impart. Hurriedly, Hayden raised his glittering blade and prepared to skilfully swipe away the intricate covering of vines that embraced her, but the ancient Ryder met his eyes with a bright, lucid gaze and held up her tanned, wrinkled palm to bar him from action.

'No,' she declared firmly, although her tone was little more than a dry, hoarse whisper. 'I have no need for your salvation.' As she spoke, spiralling, pale growths of plant-life wound and caressed her leathery throat.

Garnet cried out as Hayden paused from his rescue. 'Sister Chiastolite, do not say such things. It is the hateful influence of this dark realm warping your mind. Allow Master Hayden to set you free of your bonds and you will see the folly of what you are saying.'

A strange, sad, but knowing smile creased Chiastolite's mouth and she turned her eyes towards the mass of foliage that cradled her. 'My mind is clear, good Sister,' she croaked peacefully, 'I know exactly the power of this forest and what it craves. It thrives on grief and sorrow, emotions that I have allowed to fill my heart to brimming with through my work as Handmaiden of Death. I am old and this existence of woe is too familiar to me. I know every shadow and shade of misery that allows this forest to grow and they hold no horror for me. I welcome them as old friends.' As if to prove her point, the Ryder's ancient body moved, flexing and twisting awkwardly within her fleshy, silver cocoon. The vines that hung about her rustled and shifted, stirred by her movement and more thin tendrils wormed and coiled around her, merging with her ever-thickening veil. Chiastolite's wrinkled features contorted as the tree embraced her as preciously as a lover and an expression crossed her face that was difficult to read, a mixture of grief, agony, bliss and acceptance. Her eyelids fluttered closed for a moment as the forest drew the feelings of over eight decades into itself, and Hayden and her fellow Ryders feared that death may have claimed her. Then with a heartfelt sigh of effort, Chiastolite's eyelids opened once more and she gazed earnestly around, her dark eyes finally coming to rest on the glittering dwarf-made blade in Hayden's grip.

'It isn't enough,' she uttered firmly once more, her voice still barely a whisper but still retaining the emotional wisdom of her countless years of service to the Ley. 'You will not save Bracken with a weapon that merely mirrors past joys. Her grief, the loss of Sister Amethyst, discovering the true, hurtful nature of her birth family. These things are too raw, too real in her mind to be driven back by happy recollections. She will not be saved unless she is given something worth living for.'

The distant sound of Bracken weeping bitterly for her lost guardian tore through the chilling, shadowy atmosphere, ripping desperately at Hayden's heart. The notion of her torturous suffering filled him with a dread tangible to the greedy trees and vines, making them writhe eagerly towards him. Swiftly, Hayden raised his sword and sliced them away with a thought of returning home before they could infect his body and mind once more. Before him, Chiastolite let out a heavy, ragged gasp, her entangled form twisting and writhing almost gracefully as the repelled creepers sought refuge around her limbs and waist.

Cautiously, Hayden leant closer to the elderly Ryder as she squirmed and trembled beneath the caress of the intertwined foliage. 'Tell me then, Sister!' he begged as Chiastolite made a strange, high-pitched whimper that spoke of both intense joy and burning loss. 'Tell me what I must do to free her!'

The old woman awkwardly twisted her face towards him. Long rivers of grey-blue branch and supple, fresh growth flowed so lushly all around her that it was impossible to make out any shape or outline of her body. The brittle, white hair, withered muscles and aching bones of Chiastolite were no more, dissolved, transformed and reborn as healthy wood and vine. Only her face remained as it had been, wrinkled and seemingly without pallor, tears overflowing from liquid, ink-black pupils filled with a profound knowledge about the true nature and wonder of life. Her creased lips, virginal, but for a singular stolen kiss received all those years ago, parted and breathed a soft whisper. 'You know.'

Awe-struck, Hayden found himself lost in the realisation he saw reflected in Chiastolite's eyes. For a brief second, he thought he witnessed the wondrous shades of the Ley glittering within the shadows of the old woman's eyes, an understanding of fierce tenderness and longing that was at once universal and unique to his heart. Love. Love that had existed between Chiastolite and her long lost beau; love that dwelt within his heart for Bracken. The misery that made the Weald of Megrim flourish could not exist without the loss of love to furl it and in turn it was love that would release Bracken from its grasp.

*

The cherished memory of her beloved Dimetri flickered brilliantly for a moment within Chiastolite's eyes, intense with both sweet passion and crippling loss. A tsunami of grief, not only for her own girlhood sweetheart, but for the countless souls she had witnessed join the Ley in their final moments, grew within what was left of her heart before crashing over her. Tears, like the whitish sap from the ravenous trees, washed over her cracked mouth as her lips fell open and a sound, more than a human cry or wail of sorrow, a gut-wrenching, bare note of grief was released, filling the cold, forest air with a noise that seemed to echo with the tears of every lost person who had fallen prey to the wood. Vines swayed and boughs creaked and stirred as Chiastolite's cry called out to them with the misery they craved and swiftly they surged on her like hungry vipers, flowing thoughtlessly over each other, cracking themselves free from their trunks as they tried to swallow up the grief and agony.

*

Overwhelmed by what he had just experienced, Hayden stumbled back from what remained of the Ryder Chiastolite, tumbling into Garnet and Rosequartz as he did so. The startled Ryders caught him before he could fall, swiftly moving to avoid the great insurgence of vines that swum in from every direction. Numb with wonder and astonishment, the trio stood frozen for a moment watching as plant growth raced in from every direction to join and become one with Chiastolite's shrivelling body. Vine upon supple, fresh vine wound over each other, desperate to coil as close as possible to the core of the wretched cry, as if the old woman's feeble remains had now been transformed into the very heart and mother root of the forest. Awkwardly, Hayden and his companions backed away as the vast knot of entangled plant-life knotted more densely round Chiastolite until nothing of the Ryder's form was visible, leaving the pained, raw wail of grief as the only trace of her spirit. The cry pierced the icy air, almost blocking out the sound of shifting branches and rustling creepers, a loud defiant note that was a deafening imitation of the low, breathy, pathetic sobbing that called out to Hayden, barely audible in the lonely chaos of the wood.

Looking frantically about him, Hayden searched the gloomy shadows and shifting boughs, seeking out the owner of the dying voice, his heart now doubtless about what he had to do. In moments, he had spotted the insidious tangle of bonds where Bracken was still held prisoner of her own grief. Her weary and motionless body hung suspended like shrivelling fruit within a complex nest of matted vines, the singular thick coil that embraced her exhausted form squeezing and throbbing as it wrung the final dry gulps of despair from her body. Hair-like tendrils etched across her temples and cheeks, smothering her face with a transparent veil of death and sorrow as tiny sobs of weak misery escaped from her puckered lips.

Hayden dashed towards her across the stony, cold ground, weaving between the serpentine branches as they stretched out towards the gnarl of sorrow that once had been Chiastolite's body. The ancient Ryder's shrieks of angst still trembled the cold air as did the cries of urgency from Garnet and Rosequartz for him to hurry before it was too late, but Hayden was barely aware of these sounds. All he could hear was Bracken's jagged respiration, the arduous intake of air and the sobbing outward gasp that told him that he might still be able to save her.

He reached her living prison, thoughtlessly wading into the dense mass of deadly foliage that gripped her. He felt hungry, eager shoots reach out to pull him into their sapping embrace, dark notions of hopelessness once more fogging his thoughts as they wound about his waist and wrists. Bracken's pallid face was now inches away from his own, her features distorted beyond recognition by bleak loneliness. The mesh of delicate plant-life wove across her moist, half-blind eyes and small sounds of misery moaned plaintively from her lips. Her body was still alive but it seemed as if her soul was lost, somewhere unknown in the blackness of the branches overhead.

Tears clouded Hayden's eyes as he recalled all that Bracken was: brave, loyal, filled with unprejudiced love and compassion. A woman whom he had not realised he had grown to care for and who now might be destroyed by the belief that there was no-one left in the world who loved her.

Tenderly, he took her round face in his hands. The slippery texture of the vines scalded his fingertips with bitter sadness, beneath them her cheek felt deathly cold. Bracken stirred slightly at his touch, fresh tears flowing to water the foliage that masked her eyes, a heartbreaking whisper of isolation sighing from her for the guardian she had lost. Her grief squeezed painfully at Hayden's heart and unable to bare it a moment more, he pressed his mouth gently again her almost lifeless lips. The kiss filled his with burning, icy pain as the despair within Bracken cried out silently to him and the relentless vines battled to tighten their hold. She breathed into him, the air from her lungs a cruel winter wind, lost and desolate, filled with fresh hurt and sorrow. Selflessly, Hayden inhaled it into his body, taking the grief and desperation it carried, reassuring her splintered soul that she was still loved. Heat and life bloomed upon Bracken's lips as the visage of numbing misery shrivelled on her skin and she returned Hayden's kiss gratefully. About them, a sickening creaking hiss filled the air as the branches that embraced her turned brittle, retreating into the inky gloom like scalded beasts. Bracken stumbled forward with a mixture of loving gratitude and exhausted weariness into Hayden's arms. Breaking away from the kiss, she blinked her tear-filled eyes as reality dawned upon her once more.

'What's happening?' she slurred weakly as Hayden wrapped his arm protectively around her waist while at the same time drawing his dwarf-forged blade. 'Where are we?'

Nearby, Garnet backed carefully away from what remained of Bracken's shattered prison as it swarmed eagerly towards the echoes of Chiastolite's wails. 'Somewhere we would rather not be,' she uttered anxiously, her eyes watchful of the twisting creepers that slithered around them. 'We have to get out of this hateful forest but which way?'

Her final words were drowned out as another wrecked cry of inhuman agony rang out from the twisted shadows where Chiastolite had once been. The dark forest of misery responded with creaks and groans from every direction as the pale trees and grasping branches shifted and bowed like the sinewy limbs of rag-clothed mourners, stretching out to become one with the ever growing knot that wailed with a thousand griefs. Even the unbroken canopy that hung broodingly above them arched and lifted, like a bank of ebony cloud torn by the wind, and through the bent and crippled shapes of the trunks a thin and anaemic corridor of daylight broke through.

'There!' cried Hayden, gesturing in the direction of the hopeful passage with his sword. 'Follow me.'

Fearful and awe-struck, Bracken stared about her at the writhing creepers that surrounded them, unable to will herself to move. 'But what of Sister Chiastolite?' she queried urgently. 'She is not with us.'

The morbid notion of the Ryder's painful sacrifice clouded Hayden's mind with gloom for a moment as he felt a slithery, chilling tendril divert from its path to coil like smoke over his shoulder. Swiftly, he brandished the shimmering blade and sliced it away with the hopeful idea that their escape was close at hand.

'Don't think about her,' he ordered urgently, seizing hold of Bracken's hand as he steered her towards the narrow pathway of light and escape. 'All of you, we must keep our minds clear.'

He set off at a pace towards the small glimmer of daylight that eked between the dim shadows, Bracken trotting close at his side. Rosequartz and Garnet followed swiftly, swerving and ducking to avoid contact with the numerous vines and branches that flowed in around towards Chiastolite's hypnotic cry, like sleek, pale salmon teeming up a river. As he ran, his eyes ever trained on the colourless glow of distant salvation, Hayden battled to keep his mind free of any solid thought or clear feeling, knowing that if he paused mentally, even for the briefest moment, the forest's dark power would seize him again, knotting him in its depressive grasp. Even as he concentrated on his aim of escape from this hellish domain, he could sense the presence of the seductive gloom of the shadowy vines reaching out to him from every angle, barbs of hopeless thought stinging the outer edges of his consciousness with taunting notions that he dare not examine. The resounding, plaintive notes of the transformed Ryder's wails of grief rose and fell in desperate cords in the dull atmosphere, mingling with the low, unnerving whispers of the mystic foliage until the sound of the old woman's cries became hushed and lost and all trace of humanity vanished in the cold air. Misery made Hayden want to glance back out of respect for Chiastolite's heroic sacrifice but he dare not, and instead urged his sore muscles, aching and tired with emotion and exhaustion, onwards through the tunnel of vines and darkness. His senses told him of what was around him, the feeling of Bracken's chilled hand gripping tightly his own, too fearful to let go, the sounds of the heavy, running footfall and frantic, sobbing breathlessness of the two Ryders dashing after them, but even these definite truths of reality were not secure enough to build any safe awareness upon. All he could do was keep running onward, his eyes unfalteringly trained on the encouraging glimmer of his sword.

They ran for what seemed like hours, cloaked all around by the desperate chorus of the forest, haunting them, calling them back to its empty, soulless heart. At last the lonely whispers drifted into the mundane sound of the winter wind, and sunlight began to defuse the oppressive shadowy atmosphere of the Weald as the hungry trees became less dense, losing their dominance over the land and their thoughts. Hayden felt a change in his demeanour, the brooding black cloud lifted from his mind and the tightness in his chest diminished as the forest relinquished its grip over his thoughts. His awareness became clearer, more focused and able to deal with the realities of his emotions and he found himself crying as he ran, not the hopeless tears of misery wrung from him by the forest, but tears of an exhausted relief that his feelings were once more his own. Finally, he felt confident enough to glance behind into Bracken's emotional, pale face and felt a blossoming courage as he witnessed the strange beauty in her troubled, green eyes.

Drained and strangely euphoric, they broke free of the last traces of gloom cast by the forest and tumbled, trembling and crying on to the barren, colourless grassland of the Etherian plains. The misty, damp air clung to their skin making them feel at once both hot and cold in the same moment and they revelled like maniacs at being able to experience this sensation. Falling to his knees, Hayden sunk into the long, wet grass and pulled Bracken into a grateful embrace. For a blissful moment, everything else in the world seemed to melt away and they simply held each other, laughing, kissing, touching and weeping as life returned to their bodies and minds. Moments after their salvation, Garnet and Rosequartz emerged from the darkness of the wood, gasping for breath, crying prayers of thanks to the Ley. The Ryders collapsed, unable to run any further and for a long interval the four of them lay silent, gazing up at the clouded sky, thankful to be alive.

*

Soon, however, the exhilaration of their escape subdued and harsh reality returned. Sitting up, Rosequartz reached into the pouches on her belt and retrieved four smooth fragments of the blushing crystal whose name she shared and handed one each to her companions. The pink stone felt warm, almost fleshy in their hands and they basked gratefully in its loving, life-affirming power. Getting to her feet, Rosequartz turned sombrely and looked back at the hateful trees that had claimed the life of their fellow Ryder. Digging a small hole in the soft, moist earth, she dropped a smooth piece of brown chiastolite and an angular fragment of deep blue-green dioptase as a profound, symbolic tribute to her fallen sister's noble sacrifice. 'Farewell, Sister Chiastolite,' she breathed sadly, burying the crystals in the soil and uttering a mournful prayer of remembrance. 'By giving yourself to those heinous plants, you surely spared us our lives and gave us access to freedom once more. You shall be honoured by our Sisterhood.'

Standing up, Garnet nodded in sober agreement. 'Ley take her soul,' she murmured softly, as Hayden held Bracken in a comforting embrace. 'She was a loyal servant not just of death but of love. If the Ley is merciful, It will reunite her with the sweetheart she lost long ago.' Stealing a glance at Hayden and Bracken, she smiled quietly to herself.

With a heavy sigh, Rosequartz rubbed the inner corners of her eyes and shook her head as if she had awoken from a heavy slumber. 'Was it just a dark fantasy, then?' she asked, studying the shadows of the forest. 'What we saw, what we felt among those vines? Was it all merely a nightmare?'

She turned hopefully towards her Sister Ryder but Garnet grimly shook her head. 'Those trees could not have fed on our feelings so verdantly if they weren't true. The forest simply drew from us the darkness that was already there.'

With a shudder of betrayal, Bracken broke away from Hayden's embrace as the cold truth of her guardian's murder washed over her. 'Then that means Sister Jet killed Sister Amethyst,' she uttered in a bitter, low tone. 'Betrayed the Ley, betrayed us all.'

Garnet regarded her and noted a hard coldness in her dark emerald eyes that had nothing to do with the horrific enchantment of the forest. 'It would appear so,' she said quietly. 'Never did I believe that a Ryder would be turned against the Ley out of sheer personal vengeance, but it seems Sister Jet has laid her allegiance with the rulers of this land to turn Mistress Petronia into a weapon of evil.'

Dread and desperation sickened Hayden as he was struck by his sister's plight. He recalled the prophecy read to them in the library of Kelhalbon, a prophecy that warned that the Stone-Tongue could be transformed into an angel of destruction if her spirit was not strong or pure enough. Such a wicked fate seemed wholly at odds with the sibling he loved so dearly. Was her heart truly brave enough to resist the dark powers which now held her captive? 'Then we must do something!' he declared urgently, looking towards Garnet. 'Stop them, save my sister before it is too late, not just for her but for everyone!'

Garnet met his eye. Her posture was tense, full of nerve and ready for action but the expression on her features was filled with uncertainty. 'Agreed,' she said in a grim hesitant tone, glancing in Rosequartz's direction. 'Agreed. We must do something while it is still in our power. The prophecy was clear as to what will happen.'

Garnet's words seemed to shake Rosequartz from her thoughts of their loss and Jet's treachery. Approaching her Sister Ryder she placed a pleading hand on her arm. 'I fear that I know your mind, Sister,' she said anxiously, 'but surely you realise such a plan has only the faintest glimmer of succeeding. And besides, for the mercy of the Ley, think of the boy, think how this will destroy him.'

A reluctant sigh escaped Garnet's lungs and she hung her head. It was as if the entire weight of the world bore down upon her. 'You know, Sister Rosequartz, this isn't my decision. From the moment we found Stone-Tongue, I held in my heart grand hopes for her potential, what her existence would mean to the Ley and our Sisterhood.' Shaking her head, she looked west across the grassy, colourless marshlands towards the war-palace of Murkcroft where Petronia was surely being held. 'But the Sisterhood isn't about our hopes and dreams, it's about devoting ourselves to the greater good and protecting those most vulnerable. It pains me to say it but our duty is clear. If wickedness has claimed Stone-Tongue for its ends we must destroy her before her power is fully unleashed.'

Chapter 36

PHEBUS TO THE RESCUE

After their rendezvous with the Ryders, Maudabelle sent the rest of her party on ahead, informing Tristram that she would contact her servant Coal-Fox and tell her of Aarold's safe return before taking a more northerly road to her uncle's castle to make ready for their arrival. The journey from the low, misty grasslands to the rocky high-country to the far west of Etheria, where King Hepton held his court and the majority of the Equile population had established their permanent home, was a relatively short one for Captain Kreen, Prince Aarold and his loyal companion Phebus who the White Duchess had charged with guiding them to the home of his infanthood.

Shortly after leaving the company of the Ley Ryders and heading west, they found the vast grassy plains transformed into a more jagged and sloping climate as the dark, bouldered land rose almost abruptly into the uneven foothills that served as markers to the imposing fortress of Murkcroft. The mountains here were quite different to the snowy peaks that sheltered the realm of the dwarves to the east. The slopes were vast, narrow jagged shards of black stone, reaching up through the chilled, grey fog of the lowlands, surveying all before them like a ring of gaunt giants, their uneven faces naked of any ice or foliage. Smoke and smog hung in trails around their irregular apexes, the dim orange glow of distant fires and beacons reflecting on the natural walls of ebony slate from the narrow windows and watchful lanterns of the monstrous castle that sat in the core, central valley of the range. Murkcroft had been built centuries before, a fortress at one with the brutal terrain that surrounded it. An impressive curtain wall snaked in between the sudden ravines that parted the mountains, dotted with lofty merlons from which blazing lanterns and watchful guards surveyed the dark landscape. A myriad of mismatched turrets and towers peered above the protection of the outer ramparts, sturdy structures of threatening black stone from which flowing banners fluttered in the colours of midnight blue and gleaming silver of the royal house of Etheria.

Feeling apprehensive and agonisingly cold, Aarold peered nervously up at his maternal grandfather's castle. The immense structure seemed like a huge beast with countless glowing eyes, at rest within the safety of the mountains, and he felt a strange sense of dread as they travelled closer. The icy air made the weak muscles of his chest grow painful and tight and he longed very much to be back in the safe, warm company of his beloved Mistress Petronia and the Ley Ryders.

Seeing the worry and paleness in the young prince's face, Captain Kreen flashed him a reassuring smile. 'Take heart, Your Majesty,' he said as Aarold pulled his cloak more tightly around his weakened frame. 'We are nearly there. Soon you shall be in front of a blazing hearth with your aunt and grandfather and all your troubles will be behind you.' He regarded his young master's pinched and slender face and wondered hopefully whether once the prince had recovered his strength whether it would be the fitting moment to ask him for Maudabelle's hand in marriage. Aarold looked at Captain Kreen, his blue eyes watering in the harsh wind and, his teeth chattering too severely to answer, gave a curt nod.

They continued for what seemed to Aarold like a lifetime along the narrow, twisting pass. It wound its way between slopes and cliffs until they came to a fork in the road where a smaller path broke away from the upward route, to coil down into a natural depression sheltered between two cliffs. Captain Kreen paused and gestured that Aarold should dismount from Phebus's back.

'The College of the Equiles is down that path,' Tristram told Phebus as he assisted Aarold to climb in front of him on his horse. 'There you will find food, lodgings and the company of your own species.'

Eagerly, Phebus peered down the neatly paved road that wound its way between the rocky barriers and felt at last a sense of relief fill his tired body. He had found the entire expedition with his curious master on the whole a harrowing ordeal with one perilous event after another. The thought of finally recuperating among his fellow Equiles seemed a more than deserved reward for his loyalty. 'At last,' he sighed with gratitude. 'Believe me, Captain Kreen, the trials I have faced in the last few days due to the prince's foolish desire for adventure would chill even your hardy warrior's spirit. I am long overdue for a sabbatical!'

He trotted over to Aarold who was wearily trying to keep himself seated upright in Captain Kreen's saddle and pushed his beak chidingly against his knee. 'I hope this little jaunt of ours has cured your wanderlust, dear boy,' he berated the shivering prince. 'I shall be very interested to know what your aunt has to say about you sneaking off to cavort with dwarves and dally with wayward Ley apprentices. Goodness knows what direr scrapes you would have gotten into if it hadn't have been for me.'

His breathing ragged with exhaustion and cold, Aarold reached out an icy hand to gently pet Phebus's muzzle. 'Good, good boy, Phebus,' he whispered wheezily, his eyelids drooping with fatigue. 'You are such a devoted friend.'

Phebus's heart softened as he gazed upon Aarold's sickly pallor and pinched features. 'Aren't I just,' he muttered as his friend withdrew his bone-white hand back into the warm folds of his cloak. Turning his scarlet eyes towards Tristram, the Equile asked gently, 'You will stay with him until his aunt returns? Make sure they give him a good, hot bath and some plain, wholesome porridge.'

Tristram placed his hand on his chest and bowed his head loyally. 'On my word to the White Duchess,' he said before taking up the reins of his horse and continuing on his route along the steep, narrow path that led to Murkcroft.

*

Phebus stood and watched until they disappeared around a sharp bend in the mountain pass before turning to make his own way along the winding track that led to where his fellow Equiles made their home. He felt tired beyond words, but also happy in the knowledge that Aarold was finally returning to the safe watch of his royal family and he could set aside his worries and return to the comforts he well and truly deserved. As he walked along the sheltered pathway, the Equile mulled over all that he had endured during his travels with the prince. From footpad attacks and seductively dangerous Ley Ryders to mechanical golems and the hospitality of dwarves: the whole thing made for quite a thrilling tale and Phebus considered the idea of putting the next few months aside to organise it into a proper memoir. People would bound to be interested in the well-composed life story of a brave and intelligent beast such as himself.

Phebus found that the passageway through the cliffs opened out into a fair-sized valley, sheltered from the howling winds by the protective walls of the mountains. The peaceful arena housed a quadrangle of stylish buildings constructed from near-black granite and dark ebony beams, adorned with plain but elegant pillars, delicately curved gutters and fine frescoes of Equiles engaged in various gentile pursuits such as reading, writing and political debate along the outer walls. An archway opened out into a well-sized courtyard with mosaic floor and a large, round stone table set in the centre, laden with various bowls of cured meats, pungent cheeses and assorted fungi and mushroom dishes to tempt the cultured Equile palate. Metal braziers of crackling fire blazed in each corner of the square, keeping the enclosed space at a comfortable temperature despite the bitter wind. Phebus assessed the lodgings approvingly. *This is most acceptable*, he thought; *so nice to be in quarters designed and well suited to my breed.*

There were no other Equiles to be seen at present, but Phebus was too tired to make idle conversation anyway and decided there would be plenty of opportunity to ingratiate himself to the resident community once he had been properly fed and rested. Taking a place at the large table, he set about partaking on the succulent array of fare on offer. Everything was deliciously prepared and Phebus enjoyed a leisurely meal, content in the pleasant surroundings, and reassured that Aarold was being appropriately looked after. As he feasted, he wondered how long it would be before he had an audience with the White Duchess. He had quite a few matters to discuss regarding the security surrounding his master, and was sure that the subject of rewards and honours would be raised once Maudabelle learnt of his courageous loyalty to her nephew.

Once his appetite had been sated (rather overly so, if Phebus was honest as he was in the habit of letting his gluttonous nature get away with him), he set out to explore the various chambers that led off the central courtyard. During his idle investigations, Phebus was pleased to discover a number of inspiring rooms: well-stacked libraries, artistic studios equipped for painting and sculpture, and a tidy laboratory for those Equiles whose interests laid more within the sciences than the arts. There was also a large gymnasium with a running track, racks of weighted harnesses for strength training and a plunge pool. This was clearly where the Equiles of Murkcroft kept themselves fit and ready for their duty guarding King Hepton, although this "torture chamber" bore little interest for a beast as inclined to inaction such as Phebus. Despite this, he found himself liking this abode of his fellow creatures more and more, and the luxuries he was uncovering made him even more certain that his decision to enter retirement was the correct one.

At the end of his investigation, Phebus came across a collection of luxurious sleeping apartments, furnished with comfortable Equile-sized beds of feathered mattresses, satin cushions and velvet comforters. Such temptingly plump and lush furnishings made Phebus remember how exhausted he was and picking out a chamber that appeared to have no signs of an owner, he made himself comfortable among the soft pillows and soon fell into a deep slumber.

Weary and with a full belly, Phebus would have rested there for many hours, but a short time later his sleep was disturbed by the voices of other Equiles chattering near his sanctuary. The tone that awoke him was female, brisk and official.

'Come along, come along, you two. No shim-shalling now. We're wanted on guard duty at the castle, first watch, don't you know. Very important what with the duchess and the prince returning.'

There was a heavy sigh before another female spoke, sounding older and more weary than the first. 'There's no rest for the wicked, is there, Reeva? I must be positively satanic. I don't suppose you have heard anything about my annual leave. I did put a request in over a month ago.'

The first voice huskily cleared its throat. 'It's *Captain* Reeva to you, when we're on duty. And as you know I'm not involved with personnel.'

From his cosy nest, Phebus opened a single, lazy red eye. He wondered whether it would be polite to rouse himself and make his presence known, but his tired limbs seemed to have become stuck to the mattress. Instead, he remained where he was and continued to listen as a third voice entered into the conversation.

'Maudabelle has returned?' it quizzed interestedly. 'I *knew* something was going on, Esway. This is curious. I bet the rumours about what she's been up to are true.'

Phebus heard the jaded Equile, whose name was clearly Esway, sigh. 'Not this nonsense again,' she moaned. 'Haven't we got enough to do without you obsessing over some obscure piece of folklore?'

Through the translucent green curtain which hung across the partly open door of Phebus's hideaway, he saw the crest of the barely formed horns of a young female Equile bob into view as she arrogantly reared her head. Fearful of being spotted and causing a major faux pas, he buried his beak under a large silk pillow and tried to remain still.

'And when was the last time you took any interest in studying the finer aspects of arcane sorcery or listened to what was happening in court?' the third voice retorted boldly. 'Stone-Tongue is far from a myth! The king is very keen on having the duchess seek her out!'

A shocked snort caught in Phebus's nostrils and he trapped the silk pillow over his beak tightly with his claws to stop it escaping. Stone-Tongue? That troublesome coquette who had caused him and the prince no end of grief since Aarold had fallen under her spell? Had she followed them all the way to Murkcroft? Phebus's heart fell at the thought of seeing that little madam again. Silently, he cursed the Ley Ryders. *They should properly discipline their students instead of letting them wander anywhere seducing young, vulnerable princes and fulfilling apocalyptic prophecies.* He considered the notion of the White Duchess finding out about Mistress Petticoat leading her nephew astray. No doubt Maudabelle would find an appropriate punishment.

Reeva's voice chimed outside his door, coolly controlled and well-informed. 'Predma is quite correct actually. The White Duchess has returned in the company of a young woman who I have been informed is the fabled Stone-Tongue, though how Predma found out such a top-secret nugget of information when I have only just found out I would very much...'

The young Equile seemed totally unperturbed by Reeva's dissatisfaction of her nosiness. 'Ah-ha,' she said triumphantly. 'See, Esway. I told you. Show an interest in what's happening around you, keep an eye open and who knows what you might learn.'

'Keep an eye open and someone will poke it out for you, that's what I've learnt!' came Esway's grumbling reply. 'Stone-Tongue is here, so what?'

The youngest Equile gave a short snort of scorn at her curmudgeonly companion's disinterest but made no further comment. 'This is fascinating,' she continued to Reeva.

'Might I enquire what Stone-Tongue actually looks like? There is only so much of an impression you can gain from speculative scripture.'

Beneath his pillows, Phebus felt his own tongue stick to the roof of his mouth with the urge to give his own very clear opinion on Petronia. What was Stone-Tongue like? That was a very pertinent question indeed and he could think of a number of choice adjectives to describe her, many of which he considered himself too cultured to utter.

'To be totally honest, chaps, I only caught a glimpse of her as she was led through the courtyard.' Reeva's tone seemed to have relaxed into a more informal manner of speech. 'But from what I saw you would be disappointed. She just looked to me like a normal, human peasant rather than a sorcerer.'

'Ha!' The sound of scoffing disbelief had escaped Phebus's throat before he had the chance to stop it. At once, he froze in silent fear of his outburst giving away his location; he lay as rigid as a statue as the trio outside became aware of the sound.

Did you just hear someone speak?' Predma asked the others after a few seconds silence. There was another long pause as they all listened carefully and buried beneath his bedding Phebus peered out to watch the Equile-shaped shadows move about beyond the semi-open door. He held his breath, convinced that even this would betray him.

After what seemed like a lifetime, Esway gave a dismissive sniff. 'Probably just Marnious doing his routine in the gymnasium,' she sneered; 'he's been reading all about this new deep breathing technique for improving muscle strength or some such. Frankly, I tune out half the time.'

This explanation seemed to satisfy for she grunted approvingly before continuing in her more officious tone. 'Anyway, no matter what Stone-Tongue looks like, the White Duchess must know what she's doing. She is, after all, an informed expert on all things magical. We will be getting our orders through the usual channels soon enough.'

Phebus heard Esway mutter something morosely that he could not make out. He carefully shifted his head from among the pillows just in time to hear Predma utter, 'So there's no official say on when the execution will be? I wonder if we will be given permission to witness it.'

Despite his eagerness to remain hidden, Phebus could not help his ears twitching with interest when he heard mention of capital punishment. He knew that he could rely on Maudabelle to deal with that troublesome girl in an appropriately severe manner! A grim smile passed across his beak. Little Miss Petit-Fours would not be causing Aarold any more mischief once her head was on the end of a pike! Laying as still and silently as he could, he listened carefully for further details, but Captain Reeva remained vague.

'That is all going to happen in good time,' she breezed officiously. 'Her Grace will have to familiarise herself with what powers Stone-

Tongue possesses. We wouldn't want anything to go awry after so much has been put into this endeavour.'

'Macabre,' snorted Esway scornfully. 'That's what you are, Predma. A sick ghoul. Let me tell you, my girl, when you have fought as many campaigns as I have you'll be less inclined to revel in death and gore.'

Phebus saw the silhouette of the youngest Equile turn sharply towards her gloomy companion. 'Well, excuse me if I want to witness a piece of history. It's not every day that a prince gets executed by a legendary force of sorcery. I can't wait to see the duchess harness Stone-Tongue's abilities!'

Phebus felt like someone had burst into his cosy chamber and tipped a bucket of ice water over him. Forgetting his attempt to stay out of sight, he sat up suddenly, tossing his camouflage of cushions and covers aside as his brain scrambled to try and put Predma's words together in a way that made logical sense. *Execute the prince? The prince as in Aarold? No, no, that couldn't be right. That didn't make sense. Why on earth would Maudabelle murder her own nephew?* The very notion was beyond ludicrous. He had to think. This Predma must have gotten confused or perhaps he had misheard what she had said. He was, after all, extremely tired. This could just be a stress-dream brought on by exhaustion and worry. His brain still attempting to find a rational explanation, Phebus gave himself a small nip on his leg. The sharp pain told him that he was unfortunately wide awake.

'Well, I don't see why they've had to make such a circus out of the situation.' Esway's bold opinion jostled into his frantic thoughts. 'If it had been me and King Hepton had sent me undercover to the Geoll court...'

'Esway,' came her superior's warning tone, 'it isn't up to us to question His Majesty's plans for the invasion.'

'If I was the White Duchess,' the world-weary Equile continued undeterred, 'I would have put a pillow over that royal brat's face the moment my weakling cousin had given birth!'

'Yes, Esway,' Predma replied sarcastically. 'A brilliant plan. Murder your enemy's son in his castle, right under his nose, right after he desolated your country's army. I really don't know why Maudabelle went to all that trouble of seeking out Stone-Tongue when all that was needed was a bit of infanticide!'

The eavesdropped conversation spun through Phebus's head as he desperately tried to make sense of this new, terrible information. His basic instinct was to deny it all, search for some other explanation, no matter how unbelievable. This was not meant to happen. He had gone through all these ordeals and now everything was meant to be safe and right. Maudabelle was taking charge of Aarold's care, not planning his assassination and taking over Geoll. Phebus prided himself on his wits and dazzling intellect; if this plot had been going on surely he would have sensed it.

Esway muttered something Phebus could not make out, but Reeva cut her off before she could continue her bellyaching. 'Whatever your opinion, now is not the time to get into a debate about it. The White Duchess is working to harness Stone-Tongue's power as we speak so the outcome will be known soon enough. As for the pair of you, orders have been given and you are wanted on guard duty up at the castle, so chop-chop!'

There was the sound of Esway's grumbling and the sharp clip of Equile claws trotting away as the trio departed, leaving Phebus still lying in a state of frozen shock within the comfort of the sleeping chamber. He remained perfectly motionless, rooted against the soft bedding, his heart drumming nineteen to the dozen as he tried to organise his thoughts and convince himself that everything he had just heard was a terrible mistake. His brain worked overtime to come up with a satisfactory reason why he should dismiss all he had heard and remain where he was. However, a highly annoying sense that was completely at odds with Phebus's sedentary nature needled him to take action, although what action, he was not completely sure.

'Aarold is fine,' he muttered quietly to himself, as he climbed out from amid the pillows and sheets. 'I mean, just fancy, Maudabelle planning to kill him and using that silly Ryder girl to do so. What utter rot! The gossip people pick up on.' His words sounded strangely unconvincing though and as hard as he tried he could not shift the dread the other Equiles had raised in him.

Unable to settle his worried mind, Phebus checked that the coast was clear before leaving the cover of his sleeping chamber and making his way swiftly back along the corridors and across the courtyard where he had dined a little earlier. It did no harm, he thought, just to make his way up to the castle to meet with the White Duchess and check that Aarold was settled in and inform her of the trouble Petronia had caused her nephew. Phebus was sure she would be grateful and it would, after all, be what his old friend, Aarold's mother, Neopi would want. He thought for a moment about Maudabelle and the ridiculous stories he had overheard about her. Surely he knew the White Duchess better than some Equiles who had probably never met her. He paused for a moment as he suddenly realised that he could not actually recall a singular occasion when he had talked with the duchess about Aarold's well-being. Now that was an odd thought and one that did not sit well with Phebus, as he found himself entering the ravine that led back to the main pass. *Suppose, just suppose, I believe what I've overheard. Is it that infeasible? Etheria and Geoll had been fierce enemies until Neopi had married Elkric. It was highly possible that Hepton had sent his niece to report back on his daughter's marriage to his enemy and once Aarold had been born and with him being so sickly and his mother dying so soon after...!*

Suddenly, Phebus felt very ill and very foolish for not having seen what had been going on right under his beak. No wonder the Royal Guard had not come looking for them after they escaped the palace! Maudabelle must have been hoping Aarold would have some terrible *"accident"* and he would have done, if it had not been for Petronia. Now Maudabelle held her captive and Aarold too. That had to mean, *good Lord!* Phebus was sure he was going to vomit. Trembling with shock, he leant against the sheer wall of the rocky ravine for support as he felt a swoon threaten to overcome him. *No!* He could not do this. Now was not the time to faint like some simpering fop or foolish girl. Aarold was in perilous danger and Phebus was his only ally. Oh why did the boy's warmongering father have to be dead when he was needed so badly?

Elkric would have been bound to know what to do in a situation like this. Phebus tried to recall all he had ever read about battle and siege warfare. He was going to have to storm the castle, overcome the guards, break through the main drawbridge and confront Maudabelle single-handed. Taking a deep breath, he glanced up at the innumerable turrets visible over the crest of the cliff. The battlements would be groaning with trained archers and beyond them lay league after league of the king's skilled warriors. Phebus was a single, slightly overweight Equile whose greatest weapon was his barbed tongue. He was going to die and so was Aarold.

The sound of footsteps beyond the opening to the passageway made Phebus jump in terror and quickly he scuttled behind an outcrop in the cliff out of sight. Trembling with fear, he listened as the harsh voice of one of the castle guards called out, 'Halt! Who goes there?'

Barely daring to breathe, Phebus shifted his head an inch to the left and peered through the narrow space between his cover and the ravine entrance with one scarlet eye. He watched as a woman, a Ley Ryder it appeared, dismounted. Phebus's heart leapt with hope for a second. Perhaps the Ryders had come to the prince's rescue.

The sallow-faced Ryder raised her hand in greeting. 'At ease, soldier, I am expected by your lord and the White Duchess.'

The guard lowered his halberd and stepped towards the newcomer. 'Ah,' he said, a note of admiration in his voice. 'Coal-Fox, I presume. The duchess indeed awaits your company. She insisted the ceremony not go ahead until you were present.'

Phebus studied the Ryder as closely as he could from his vantage point, trying to match her features to the trio of women he had encountered at The Fallen Inn. He always struggled to tell the difference between human faces, to him they all appeared alike, but he noted that this newcomer had long black hair and sharp, angular features that he did not recall seeing before. She smiled cruelly as she removed her gauntlets.

'The White Duchess is most hospitable,' she said in an icy, ironic tone. 'I wouldn't miss Stone-Tongue's formal welcome for the world.

I'm sure she will forgive my tardiness though, I had pressing matters to attend to with my sisters.'

There was something in Coal-Fox's voice that made Phebus feel utterly nauseous and he glared at the Ryder intently. There was nothing in this woman's manner that spoke of the virtue and nobility of the Ryders he had met and her words filled him with dread for the maidens that might have been Aarold's saviours.

He heard the guard gasp, clearly impressed by what Coal-Fox had implied. 'They have been dealt with, as the king requested of you?' he queried, seeming unsure whether to trust her. 'His Majesty was very adamant that there was to be no chance they would interfere.'

The woman laughed, a cold, short, sharp sound that lacked any warmth or humour, and lazily massaged her palm with her thumb. 'Trust me,' she said darkly. 'No-one escapes the Weald of Megrim, not once the trees feast on their misery.' Her gaze wandered away from the guard to the shadows of the valley and Phebus drew back against the wall just in time to avoid being seen.

'But we waste time with idle gossip,' she said sharply, turning her eyes back toward the guard as Phebus breathed a sigh of relief at not being spotted. 'Escort me to the duchess so that our work may begin; we have dallied from action long enough.'

Phebus remained frozen with hopeless fear hidden behind the cliff, listening as Coal-Fox departed with the guard. Once the sound of their footsteps had disappeared into the moaning howl of the mountain wind, he pressed his forehead despondently against the hard rock of the cliff and let out a cry of despair.

The Ley Ryders were defeated; how was he ever going to find troops to save Aarold now? Phebus had no delusions about the severity of his situation. Without help, his friend would surely perish at the hands of his aunt and it was all because he had not seen her murderous intent when it had been right under his beak. Tears of frustration and grief filled his scarlet eyes. It would take an army to seize the castle and stop Maudabelle's plans, skilled warriors with an armoury of weapons to even stand a chance. Warriors like Aarold's father or his sister or – dwarves!

The idea hit Phebus's mind like a bolt from the blue, causing his sobbing to suddenly cease. *There is something I can do! Hadn't the dwarf vizier Bahl sworn her people would assist them any way they could? Aarold was their princess's half-brother; they had to help*! Gulping back his tears, Phebus raised his gaze once more to the turrets and battlements that perched atop the jagged peaks of the mountain. His agile mind raced as he tried to work out how long it would take him to reach Kelhalbon. Grimly, he realised that dwarf soldiers would probably not get there in time to spare Aarold from his fate, but they just might be able to hamper Maudabelle in whatever she had planned for Geoll. His heart aching with sorrow, the Equile gave the alpine keep one final mournful glance. He had failed to protect Aarold but he would not fail to protect Geoll. Stepping out from his hiding place, he set out eastward down the narrow pathway as fast as his spindly legs would carry him.

Chapter 37

THE DESTROYING ANGEL

She was trapped. Not just physically but in every sense. Trapped within the unending darkness and noise of her own mind, unable to release or escape the burning torrid power that churned within her; an energy of words that she foolishly believed she was learning to master now seemed twisted and full of menace. There was nothing but pitch blackness and hateful noise stretching out from her awareness in every direction, filling every thought and notion that fluttered into her whirling mind. A never-sated hunger for death and chaos that longed to consume the world and every scrap of life in it into a vortex of emptiness. Worst of all, the thought of this carnage thrilled her beyond words. She felt as if she knew, as if she had always known, that this was her true nature. She was the darkness, the noise and the fury, the rushing, surging power of energy that laid to waste all before it and left only cinders and wreckage in its wake. Flashes of fearful memory flickered fleetingly amid the ever-growing might and destruction, glimpsed moments of her past filled her with terror as they reminded her that she was once something other than this force. Voices, places and people she battled fiercely to recall. The name Petronia entered consciousness and she shuddered with fear that that woman, the woman whose life she had once inhabited, was lost forever.

Now only the other tone commanded her, gave her purpose and guidance. Her faceless mistress that kept her wild desires in check, set the darkness within her free while at the same time restraining it, moulding and nurturing her demonic might, telling her that now was not her moment but praising her for awakening who she truly was. Again and again the name Petronia and the notion of the Ley intruded into the wondrous darkness, forcing her mistress to beat it away, lowering her consciousness until at last she fell into an awaiting state of dreamless slumber.

'Awaken.'

As if controlled by a mechanical switch, Stone-Tongue's eyes snapped open and she became aware of the stark environment she was in. The chamber was cylindrical, a dimly lit tower of dull grey stone, sparsely furnished and illuminated by the yellow light of unseen, flickering tapers. A narrow window pierced the dark wall directly in front of her, but only a featureless patch of dark sky could be seen through its thin casement. A wooden table intruded into the right periphery of her field of vision, littered with bottles and other strange implements that she could not quite make out. She attempted to turn her head to see what they were but found this movement impossible. Cold, clasping agony gripped her throat in a choke-hold like a metal hand squeezing the life from her. Her neck seemed to tighten, transforming into a ratcheted iron brace that was being drawn in notch by notch until only the smallest gasp of air could eke into her lungs. Frantically, she panted for air, feeling the violent, hot power of her restrained wild nature rail high in her chest, unable to break through the solid barrier that seized her throat. Gagging and choking, she clasped at her neck, her fingertips encountering the icy curved form of the heavy collar that imprisoned her. Desperate for breath, she returned her head to its original position, feeling the collar loosen slightly as she did so. Breathing in sharp, fearful inhalations, she tentatively explored the contraption that encircled her throat, her hands trembling unbearably in fear that she might touch some trigger that would snap her neck. The rigid brace of icy metal trapped her whole throat, beginning at her collar bone and stretching up to just below her jaw. The iron was smooth and chilled against her skin, resting so snugly against her flesh that it was impossible for her to press even her fingernails between the two. A thick, flat strut extended up from the front of the collar, tracing across her chin and lower lip before forcing itself brutally into her mouth. It pressed down agonisingly on her tongue, trapping it against her lower teeth. The metal filled her mouth with a vile taste and coarse texture that made her want to vomit or spit to expel the foreign article. Automatically, she flexed her tongue against the painful splint, the rough surface rasping on the tender muscle as it attempted to free itself. A violent, burning energy swelled within her throat, formed of crushing words and mighty intent, but the unmoving control of the device remained firm.

Her hands felt heavy, weighed down with weariness, and holding them up before her face, she saw that her wrists were encircled by thick iron shackles attached to a slack chain that snaked through a sturdy ring secured firmly into the flagstone floor a few feet away. Similar restraints bound her ankles. Crushing gloom overwhelmed her as the hopelessness of her situation dawned and she sank to her knees in despair, bitter tears coursing silently down her cheeks, the powerful choker not even allowing her to release the softest wail or sob of misery.

'There, there, dear Stone-Tongue. Now isn't the time for tears.' The female voice was chillingly familiar to her, the almost maternal tone laced with a cool, removed command that she found impossible to ignore. Her rueful tears seemed to freeze like droplets of clear glass within her eyes and apprehensively she lowered her hands from her face to gaze upon the graceful and imposing figure that stood before her.

In the golden glow of candlelight, the White Duchess was a striking presence, beautiful and powerful, the air of triumph emulating from her like an aura. She was clothed in a close-fitting gown of lush black-work that clung to her elegant frame like a robe of shadow. A black velvet wimple framed her striking features and a simple but exquisite coronet rested on her brow. Her pale face seemed to glow with cruel but exultant victory, her emerald pupils glistening excitedly as her scarlet lips formed into a wide grin.

The shackled girl saw the face of the White Duchess and in doing so, a million fragments of memory were triggered like sparking flints in her mind. This woman was going to harm the prince! Emotions churned in her belly as thoughts of vulnerable, kind Aarold flooded her mind, each one tumbling like a domino as it forced her to recall more and more. Aarold, the Ley Ryders, the dwarves of Kelhalbon, her brother Hayden and their parents! It was all coming back to her now! She had an identity, a name: Petronia! As the realisation of who she was became clear to her once more, a furnace of wild emotions erupted inside: fear, anger and hate. *Hate.* There was so much hate, not just for this woman, but for everything. She could feel it, hot and black like a choking phantom filling her body. She felt like she wanted to tear the world asunder.

Teeth bared fiercely against her metal gag, Petronia lurched angrily at the White Duchess, her dark eyes wild with fury. The smiling duchess remained coolly unaffected by this sudden attack, simply taking a graceful step back, her hand raised as if baying a disobedient lapdog to stop barking. As Petronia lunged towards her, the brutal iron of the enchanted collar contracted once more, crushing viciously against her throat, squeezing from her both breath and rage. Gagging for air, she tumbled forward, her hands clawing desperately for support, before crashing face down on the hard flagstones at the duchess's feet. The front bar of her bridle jammed painfully against her lower lip as she landed, ripping the soft flesh and producing a steady stream of scarlet blood. Trembling with agony, Petronia raised her right hand to nurse her injured lip while her left ruefully rubbed the cold metal of the collar as it slowly relaxed against her windpipe.

As she tried to comfort herself, Maudabelle strolled across the room to the table and took from it a small swatch of white linen. Returning to where Petronia crouched, the White Duchess knelt by her side and softly dabbed her stinging wound. Petronia flinched, both through the pain of her injury and mistrust of her captor. Warily, she regarded Maudabelle's beautiful face, feeling her loathing for her grow inside. She was still filled with the urge to lash out, but was not foolish enough to risk it again. The discipline of the magical collar had done its work.

Once Petronia's mouth had stopped bleeding, the White Duchess folded away the stained bandage, tucking it into her cuff.

'I know,' she uttered with unnerving compassion as Petronia

cautiously fingered the metal encircling her neck. 'It is a heinous device. Necessary, I hope you appreciate, but brutal nevertheless. Still, do not be concerned, you'll be released from it soon enough.'

With shadowy grace, the White Duchess stood up and began pacing up and down before her. Taut with loathing and trepidation, Petronia remained on her knees, her eyes suspiciously tracking the older woman's movements back and forth. 'I wouldn't want you to have the assumption that I would do anything to deliberately harm you,' she said coolly as her footsteps dully sounded against the stone. 'You are a much too unique creature for me to even consider such a thing. No doubt by now you have some notion of the power you hold but I wonder if you truly realise your full potential.'

She stopped right in front of Petronia and turned to face her, her green eyes bright with admiration, even jealousy. In response, Petronia stared defiantly up at her, her dark eyes blazing with hate. In her mind, she recalled what the dwarf Bahl had said to her about the legend of Stone-Tongue, how she could be a mighty crucible for good or wickedness. Her mind was fixed that she would not let this woman's evil intent tarnish her spirit even though shades of destructive language warped beneath her bridle.

'No doubt, the Ley Ryders have spoken to you about your ability to understand and utter the dialect of life and death.' Maudabelle's tone sounded flat and ominous. 'But their teachings and rules have their limits and you, my dear Stone-Tongue, deserve a more informed tutor.'

She swept suddenly towards the far right of the chamber, out of the line of Petronia's restricted vision. Petronia could hear her touch the bottles, flasks and other items on the workbench hidden from her view and desperately wanted to turn her head to see what she was doing, but dared not defy the collar's control. She could only listen as the White Duchess's voice rose once more above the sounds of moving stones and glass.

'I pride myself, dear Stone-Tongue, on being a diligent student on numerous forms of sorcery,' she said sounding highly pleased with herself. 'It has been my lifelong duty, a personal passion as well as a patriotic calling. My uncle, King Hepton, you see, sent me to Geoll not just as handmaiden to his daughter when she was married to that brute Elkric, but as an agent to oversee his interests within the enemy court. He knew, of course, that the marriage would only bring about a temporary peace and soon Etheria would rise to avenge the wrongs done against her. Elkric had made sure that our forces were damaged enough that an immediate retaliation was impossible, but never underestimate the ability of feminine guile and cunning against male intellect and strength.' She paused for a moment and allowed herself a small chuckle of pride at her own abilities.

'It was I who nursed my cousin through her pregnancy, using my skills in potions to ensure the baby was born sickly and malformed. Poor naïve Neopi never suspected a thing; she was always slightly dim-witted, my late cousin. I honestly believe she was even growing to love her idiotic husband. Still, I won't take undue credit. I never intended for her to die so soon after childbirth. However it did help my cause not having her cooing and clucking around the baby but I doubt she would have held much weight in court even if she'd lived. And as for Elkric's loathing of his son's infirmities, well, you can blame his own ignorant character for that. It was also, I confess, of much convenience that he chose to have himself killed so foolishly in that riding accident, but I do not claim commendation for that either. Not that I wouldn't have been more than willing to drive a dagger through his chest, but I prefer to think myself more tactful in my endeavours. I was merely well placed to remind the Geollease court of the fragility of Aarold's nature and advise that it was best he didn't take the throne until his health improved. This bought me plenty of time.'

Once more, the White Duchess stepped into Petronia's field of vision, this time carrying a small, clear glass vial containing a watery liquid of pale green. Petronia squirmed rebelliously as Maudabelle approached her again but the magical force of the collar prevented her turning her head away. Delicately, Maudabelle brought the bottle close to Petronia's face and tilting it, allowed a few droplets to trickle on to her swollen lip. She winced as the medical potion stung against the fresh gash, purifying and aiding it to heal. The White Duchess regarded her work thoughtfully. 'Such a pretty mouth,' she mused absent-mindedly. 'Quite a fitting vessel for the power that flows from it.'

Her words made Petronia's skin crawl with their tenderness. Listening helplessly to all that the White Duchess had said, the heartless way she had manipulated Aarold's fate, crippling his body and robbing him of his livelihood, made her sick to her stomach. She wanted to block it out, forget the duchess's cruel plans, but even as Maudabelle spoke, Petronia could feel the wicked intent of her ambitions rouse the swirling shadows that bubbled within her chest.

The White Duchess sat back on her heels, her pale hands resting neatly on the rich, dark fabric of her skirt as she regarded the captured girl with curious interest, her head tilted slightly to one side. 'Do you think me conceited?' she asked, sounding genuinely concerned. 'I honestly do not want you to think I overestimate my talents. I am skilled in sorcery, but I have had my failures. For all my efforts I could not master the means to form a reliable weapon to channel the darker potential of the Ley. The experiment with a human receptacle was a complete disaster and while I was fairly pleased with the dwarf-made automaton it paled in comparison to what you can achieve.' Her green eyes sparkled with eagerness as she contemplated the powerful entity that knelt before her in the form of Petronia. 'Oh no, like I say, you are truly more miraculous than you know.'

With a sigh of contentment, the White Duchess got to her feet and paced slowly round to stand behind Petronia. 'I suppose you could call it fate, if you wished, the divine providence of the Ley; no doubt your Ryder friends might say that our lives were destined to combine to make something glorious.'

Firmly but gently, Maudabelle placed her cool hands on Petronia's thick ebony tresses, smoothing and caressing them as she spoke. 'You will be a terror like the world has never known,' she breathed proudly. 'A magnificent creature of beauty and deathly destruction. An angel of this country's vengeance who will twist the very fabric of the Ley and whose existence will be spoken of with fearful awe down through the ages. And you shall call me mistress.'

Petronia trembled as the White Duchess stroked her hair, the brutal description of what she could become chilling her to the core. With every touch of Maudabelle's hands on her scalp, with every terrible word she spoke, Petronia could feel the shadowy force and language within her body swell and become more dominant. Dark, heinous words of destructive power began to take shape within her mind, formed of the same mystical dialect with which the Ley once called out to her, but now they were devoid of hope, wonder and love. Now just the rotten fester of awaiting death remained and its consuming might was only barred by the forceful bridle that gripped her tongue and throat. She battled against the hate and hunger for devastation that churned feral within her, desperately trying to concentrate her will on something pure and hopeful, something that she could not bear to destroy. The faces of her loved ones flickered through her mind, each one resting within her consciousness for a brief instant before being swallowed up by the wicked glee and eagerness to watch the world burn to ash at a single utterance from her lips. As she felt the duchess's delicate, skilful fingers slip down to draw light patterns on the sensitive skin at the back of her neck, summoning the wild spirit within her to rise up, she dug her own fingernails into her palms to grip on to the desire to fight for who she was.

'I know what you're thinking.' Maudabelle's voice was soft and intimate in her ear. 'You're thinking "It's my mind, my thoughts and words. She can't force me to become a monster." You're quite right too, of course. Your natural power outweighs mine beyond measure. But ask yourself this. Why would you want to fight something that's deep at the core of your being? The Ley wouldn't have awoken such words within you if It didn't want you to utter them. Look inside your heart, Stone-Tongue, and confess what is there. Haven't you always known that there was more to you than a simple, mute country girl? Haven't you always desired something else, wanted to awaken your destiny?'

Within her mind, an icy darkness was cast across Petronia's thoughts, a wondrous yearning for awakening and knowledge, to see how far her power would carry her, to become a creature of unimaginable greatness.

A voice cried out within, filled with ominous warning, telling her that if she succumbed to this desire, there would be no way back. She would fill the lands before her with blood and fire, crush the very mountains to dust. Fear gripped her chest as she became aware of such notions of destruction filling her mind. The sentiment of such anarchy spoke to her in profound tones, making her blood sing thrillingly in her veins, and her spirit became inflamed with excitement. It disgusted and shocked her that such wild and evil longings could be alive within her and she battled with every ounce of will to suppress them. She tried with every fibre of her consciousness to fight the blackness, all the time painfully aware of the feather-light touch of the White Duchess's fingers against her nape, caressing and stimulating the force of shadows and powerful words that churned within.

Suddenly, the heavy, potent atmosphere of the dim chamber was broken by a sharp rap on the door as a man's voice rang out, brisk and official. 'His Royal Highness King Hepton wishes to enter.'

Maudabelle let out an almost reluctant sigh and stroked Petronia's throat one last time before taking her hand away. The moment she did, Petronia felt the wild, hot, destructive desire that burned within her abate slightly, leaving her mind clearer and more filled with terror at the heinous notions that had been summoned.

The White Duchess lightly brushed a stray strand of dark hair from Petronia's forehead, tucking it neatly behind her ear. 'It would seem your moment of glory is close at hand, my dear Stone-Tongue,' she breathed smoothly as she swept across the room before Petronia's limited field of vision. 'My uncle will be most eager to meet you. I have spoken highly of your potential and trust you won't disappoint him.'

Terror and helplessness engulfed Petronia's body, leaving her cold and trembling. She wanted to curl herself into a ball and hide away from the ominous threat that loomed darkly over her, but knew that even if she could hide from the White Duchess it would do her no good. The true horror, the dormant monster that was about to be awakened, lay within her own being.

Frozen with trepidation, she listened as Maudabelle opened the heavy wooden door and greeted the King of Etheria, her voice rich with relish and triumph. 'King Hepton, beloved uncle. It is an honour to be in your company once more. I am joyous to have returned to Murkcroft with such success for your campaign. It has been too many years.'

Petronia heard heavy footsteps on the cold, stone floor and the sound of the door swinging shut behind the king as he entered. Fearful curiosity made her want to turn her head and see him, but the unyielding restraint of the collar made this impossible. Instead she kept her eyes lowered in dread, her hands nervously gripping the material of her skirt as she heard King Hepton address Maudabelle.

'Indeed it has, my faithful niece, too long by half. There were some in my court, foolish folk with loose tongues, who said you were failing in your duties, had forgotten why I sent you as my daughter's handmaiden when she married. But I would not suffer such malicious gossip. You are, after all, my sister's child and a fitting heir of her loyalty, intellect and cunning. I knew you wouldn't fail me. Idle tongues do not flap so when they are cut out.'

The voice seemed to fill the gloomy chamber: authoritative, low and silken; the deep, chilling baritone of a man who was used to not being questioned. The White Duchess chuckled appreciatively. 'Your belief in my endeavours flatters me, Your Majesty. I only seek to serve our motherland and avenge the crimes exacted upon her. Though, I must confess, that in bringing Stone-Tongue into your service I have achieved more than I believe even my late mother would have dreamed.'

An unpleasant surge of energy lurched within Petronia's stomach as Maudabelle uttered the name Stone-Tongue, as if the White Duchess was already mistress of the dark language which dwelt within her. Unspoken words of death and magic leapt like dancing embers in her mind, barricaded from action by the firm iron plate that held her tongue, making her pulse race with feral euphoria. Once more she was overcome by the heady desire to allow this destroying might to claim her, transform her into an untamed spirit of mayhem. Swallowing hard, she tried to force this heinous power to quieten itself as King Hepton turned his attention towards her.

'Is this she?' he queried briskly, stepping towards Petronia to examine her like a prized trophy of war. Summoning all her courage, Petronia lifted her head to stare defiantly up at the imposing presence of the famed warrior king. He towered over her, back straight, figure lean, but strong despite countless battles and any ill effects of his seven decades. His countenance was severe, ruthless and without a flicker of emotion, strangely similar to the stone-like features of the dwarves. But the hardness rendered within Hepton's flesh was a long-developed mirroring of the brutal coldness within. His leathery, pallid skin was a map of lines, deep creases of maturity mingling with uneven scars like lines of cruel writing on colourless parchment that told a story of a ruler who was as cunning and patient as he was merciless. Narrow, dark eyes sparkled like black diamonds, surveying the world and everything in it with shrewd intelligence, evaluating, judging, planning. His cheekbones were high and sunken, his nose prominent with flared nostrils that gave the king the watchful resemblance of a bird of prey, the sharp look of a practised hunter. Thick lips turned downward in a permanent sneer of scowling displeasure. A crown of weighty, hammered gold rested with proud arrogance on his pale, hairless brow. It was not an ugly face, perhaps in his youth the king could have been judged as having a striking handsomeness, but time and the nature of its owner had twisted the features so they now resembled the brutal soul and calculating mind who owned them. Petronia looked into King Hepton's cold, bright eyes and saw that their gleam came not from humanity, but heartless guile and determination.

Hepton astutely considered the girl kneeling before him. 'A rather ordinary looking little thing, is she not, my dear niece?' he mused, reaching out to stroke Petronia's cheek with his leather-clad forefinger. Petronia flinched and drew back from him in disgust. 'Hardly a monster at all. More like one of the serving wenches from the kitchens.'

An amused laugh rumbled in his throat as his thick, sneering lips spread into a cruel grin. It made Petronia feel nauseous to look at that humourless smile. The king's face was imposing, unforgiving when he scowled, but it took on a much more disturbing air in mirth, almost demonic.

The White Duchess echoed her uncle's laughter with a soft chuckle and moved to stand behind Petronia once more. 'Do not be deceived by her everyday appearance, Your Majesty,' she uttered smoothly, resting her hands lightly on the girl's shoulders. 'I can vouch that the abilities of Stone-Tongue here are truly remarkable.'

Petronia felt the pressure of Maudabelle's hands, warm and persuasive, pressing against her collar, the gentle weight of her palms causing the black energy within to fill her brain with a flood of mystical words. Her tongue grated painfully against the metal plate that held it, eager to release the wild might that her utterances could exact.

Crossing his arms, King Hepton took a half-step back from Petronia and grinned with conceited appreciation at his niece. 'I do not doubt it for a moment,' he said slyly. 'You always did have an acute sense for judging such matters. Tell me, have you witnessed her capabilities yourself?'

The White Duchess allowed one hand to slip from Petronia's shoulder, while the other remained, idly caressing the edge of the metal brace with her thumb. 'Only briefly, my lord, but I have enough information from reliable sources to not be in any doubt. With the proper guidance I'm convinced she will fulfil her great potential.'

With a dark chuckle, Maudabelle leant over Petronia's shoulder, allowing her breath to blow warm against her cheek. Petronia stiffened with contained hatred for her captor, as once more molten rage coursed through her, tinged with the ancient dialect of her gift.

Straightening up, the White Duchess released the girl at last from her potent touch. 'But all in good time,' she told her uncle. 'There are formalities that have to be addressed regarding our honoured guest here. I do hope you have extended adequate hospitality to your grandson.'

Dreading concern filled Petronia for Aarold as she saw a malicious gleam ignite in the king's cruel eyes as he let out a short humourless laugh. 'The boy is well watched over by my personal guards, for now. The journey has taken its toll on his delicate constitution. I fear the climate of my draughty castle makes his health look considerably uncertain.'

His gaze once more drifted to the girl knelt before him and Petronia was at once aware of the ominous unspoken meaning in his words. Terror and anger filled her for what this wicked pair had planned for the sweet, gentle-natured prince she had grown to love. *No, it would not be!* There was no power they could exact over her to force her to harm a hair on his head. She would rather die than speak the words that would rob him of his life.

Enraged with contempt and fury for their heartless plot, Petronia staggered unthinkingly to her feet and flung herself, arms outstretched, fingers clawing towards King Hepton. The king let out a cry of shock as she lunged for him, which transformed into a gleeful laugh as the enchanted iron encasing her throat tightened, causing her to gasp desperately, collapsing to the floor in a helpless, choking heap.

'A feisty one!' he crowed merrily clapping his hands, as Maudabelle stepped forward to drag the trembling girl to her knees. 'I was wrong to dismiss you as just a common wench! My niece was correct, you do have fire in your belly. Worry not, my little hell-cat, you'll soon have ample opportunity to display your might!'

The White Duchess settled the gagging Petronia on the floor, neatening her gown and dishevelled hair with her skilled, light touch. Petronia bristled with rage and loathing as Maudabelle's cool hands lingered on her jaw. She longed to lash out again, but the pressure of the collar was an effective deterrent.

Once she was happy that her prisoner was adequately subdued, Maudabelle gracefully crossed the chamber to stand at her uncle's side. With a self-satisfied smile towards Petronia, she continued their conversation as if nothing had happened. 'What of our loyal agent Coal-Fox?' she asked with a hint of contempt. 'Has she returned yet?'

The king nodded. 'Indeed. She arrived not an hour ago. I was listening to the report of her duties when you sent for me. She is waiting outside the chamber. Shall I bid her join us?'

The White Duchess's posture stiffened slightly and a displeased expression crossed her face as if she had tasted something sour. 'If Your Majesty wishes,' she uttered coldly. 'I do suppose she does deserve some credit for her part.'

Ignoring his niece's clear hostility, King Hepton stepped across to the door and opened it. 'Enter, Coal-Fox,' he summoned.

Petronia once more heard the sound of boots on the flagstones as the newcomer silently entered the room. Horror and bitter betrayal filled her heart as she recognised the cunning servant of King Hepton as none other than Sister Jet. Free of any disguise or charade, Jet stood before Petronia, her icy blue pupils glittering with triumph. Petronia's mind spun with the sick revelation of the treacherous Ryder's presence. Furious energy boiled and formed hateful words within her bosom as the extent of the foul plot became clear to her. This had been what Jet had wanted all along, right from the moment Petronia had revealed her abilities to her. The Ley glistened like a wispy golden thread in her mind, a precious, sacred blessing that Jet had besmirched with her cruel trickery. What kind of heartless villain would do such a thing?

A smug grin twisted Jet's mouth as she gazed down at Petronia. 'We meet again, Stone-Tongue,' she murmured, in an amused tone.

Petronia did not respond, did not move a muscle or attempt to make a sound. Her flesh felt cold and hard as if the growing sense of hatred within her had swelled to such an extent that it had turned her to stone. Not just her muted tongue but every atom of her form felt as numb and dead as granite. And yet the burning contempt still raged within for the trio that stood staring at her like a prized trophy. Somehow she had a recollection of Bahl's words of warning, a sense that she had to hold on to some fragment of virtue or love to stop herself becoming a creature of utter destruction but that seemed an impossible task. The world was a bleak and heartless place and she was part of it.

King Hepton bowed respectfully towards Jet. 'My apologies for interrupting our earlier discussion, my loyal Coal-Fox. But I was eager to see that my niece was giving suitable instruction to our most honoured guest.'

The mutinous Ryder's eyes flashed to King Hepton and the White Duchess for a moment before coming back to rest on Petronia. A shudder raced along Stone-Tongue's spine when she boldly met Jet's intense eyes. There was something twisted and broken within the woman that unnerved her more than the cold brutality that existed in King Hepton and his cunning niece. An incalculable savagery had long remained hidden behind a mask of respectability, growing angrier and more bitter by the day and had now been given an opportunity to reveal itself. An unhinged spirit of murderous disregard lurked beneath her composed, warrior's exterior. Her very presence within the room seemed to heighten the wildness pulsing within Petronia's own spirit. She had the air of a wild beast, a ravenous tigress that even the king she served wouldn't have the power to call away once she had her target in mind.

'Please, Your Majesty. Too many years have I hidden behind masks and lived within identities that did not fit as my own. Now I only wish to be called by my birth name. It is in the memory of my slaughtered family I serve, the father, brothers and betrothed who were slaughtered by your wretched enemy. I am Aerona.'

A curious smile twitched King Hepton's thick lips. 'As you wish it, Mistress Aerona. Though it shall be *Lady* Aerona and more besides if you have brought about all you have promised. I am much pleased with the gift of Stone-Tongue. Perhaps there is more good news to follow. Who knows, if Stone-Tongue possesses the power you have promised, I might feel inclined to make a wife of the maid who uncovered her for me.' Folding his hands together, he regarded the former Ryder with admiration.

An avaricious gleam twinkled in Aerona's eyes as she pondered the prospect of being queen and ruling over not just Etheria and Geoll, but the White Duchess herself. She and Maudabelle had been dual agents for Hepton's cause but that did not mean they had each other's respect. She bowed her head modestly. 'You give me too much praise, Your Highness,' she said smoothly as Maudabelle glared at her in disdain.

The cruel humour drained from the monarch's face and his features once more looked ruthless. 'Indeed,' he told her dryly, 'well you remember it. Now tell me, what of the Ley Ryders? I trust they will cause no further issues.'

Pushing her ambitious thoughts to the back of her mind, the former Ryder smiled respectfully. 'I have dealt with them in a most adequate fashion, Your Majesty,' she informed him, knitting together

her leather-clad fingers. 'I took them and Stone-Tongue's brother on a little trip through the Weald of Megrim and made sure they had enough melancholy notions to arouse the appetites of the hungry vegetation. When I left, they were quite literally drowning in their own sorrows.'

A satisfied smile broke across the king's thick lips and once more he laughed a soft, humourless laugh. 'Foolish folk,' he uttered. 'You would think Ryders would know better than to linger amid such notorious woods. It is, I hear, a most slow and torturous death. They say the heart and mind of one ensnared by the boughs there can continue to exist for over a decade while the trees sap their life-force. I commend your actions, Mistress Aerona.'

Glaring at her uncle, the vivid scarlet drained from Maudabelle's lips. This was meant to be her moment of glory and now it seemed like Sister Jet, or *Aerona* as she was now choosing to call herself, was moving to steal her thunder. 'Actually, Uncle,' she interjected sharply, 'leading them into the Weald was my plan. It was I who obtained the misery of Ac-Nu from the queen of the dwarves to leaden their spirits. Coal-Fox was acting on my orders. She doesn't possess the wit or skill to undertake such deals unaided.'

Beside her, crouched on the floor, devastated on hearing Jet's wicked tale, Petronia felt numb to the women's petty bickering and power play. The extent of the fallen Ryder's betrayal stabbed her bruised heart, making the shadows that swirled within her grow even more dense and blackened. Her dear brother Hayden, whose only wish had been to lead a safe and mundane existence, was no more, slaughtered by darkness and grief trying to save her. All he had ever wanted was for her to return home and forget about the power that now threatened to consume her completely. Petronia rued bitterly every time she had dismissed his warnings, turned her overambitious sight away from his loving concern. Now all hope was gone and she struggled to even recall the sound of his tender voice amid the maelstrom of greedy, evil language that screeched within her mind.

King Hepton batted his hand impatiently, displeased by the rivalry between his niece and servant. 'I will not tolerate such trivial vying for my favours,' he announced sharply, his cold eyes gleaming. 'The Ryders are no more and we have Stone-Tongue at our disposal; all else is trivial. I am eager to see the full extent of her capabilities. I trust you have trialled your power over her, White Duchess?'

Maudabelle regained her composure and the flush of ire seeped from her pale cheeks as her uncle moved to take a seat at the far corner of the chamber in unemotional expectation. Exactingly she paced slowly in a circle around the knelt, shivering girl, her cunning emerald eyes running over every detail of her form from her nervously clasped hands to the mystical lettering inscribed on the iron collar at her throat and the rigid strut that protruded from her mouth. Petronia was so consumed with sorrow and terror that she was barely aware of the White Duchess as she moved to stand close behind her, hands gripping her shoulders forcing her back to straighten, the cool metal of her collar shifting slightly against her skin. She hardly felt Maudabelle stoop down to rest her lips next to her ear or heard her whisper, 'See, dear Stone-Tongue. The last remnants of your old life are no more. Your moment is at hand.' Her mind was filled with nothing but the sorrow of all she had lost.

Her pale hand still resting on the iron collar, Maudabelle rose again to address her uncle. 'I believe that we are both fully prepared to serve you, Your Majesty. Although I would advise a test to prepare our dear guest for her new role. I feel she is suffering from a mild case of stage fright.'

Understanding gleamed cruelly in the king's eyes. 'Do you have a suitable candidate in mind, my niece?'

Petronia felt the White Duchess's hands shift slightly on her throat and heard her chuckle. 'As a matter of fact I do. The captain who has escorted your grandson here has been most loyal in his wooing of me. I do believe it is time his persistence is rewarded.'

Amusement danced gleefully over King Hepton's callous features and he shifted impatiently in his chair. 'Mistress Aerona, would you be so kind as to fetch Captain Tristram Kreen here at once.'

With a solemn bow, Aerona left the room to fulfil his request, leaving the king, Maudabelle and Petronia alone in expectant silence. In the weighty quiet of the chamber, Petronia could feel the White Duchess's skilful hands move in light, complex patterns over her collar, drifting now and again to caress the skin of her jaw and cheeks. Her fingertips were laced with finely-honed sorcery and as they darted across the metal and her skin, Petronia could feel the great, unforgiving darkness stir hungrily within her, flooding her brain with wicked power and phrases. Frantically, she searched her mind, trying to grab on to the raw, grieving memory of her brother, a notion that would move her to compassion before the thoughtless might that was rising within her consumed her will completely.

After what seemed like an age, the sound of the door to the chamber broke the suffocating silence and a new figure entered, striding across to stand before King Hepton. The man dressed in Geollease armour had long, fine red hair and mismatched but determined eyes. His watchful gaze cautiously surveyed the room, studying Petronia's prone form with curiosity and lingering with loving admiration on the woman who stood behind her. His eyes returned to the king and respectfully he fell to his knee in a gallant bow.

'You summoned me, Your Majesty?'

Lazily, Hepton gestured for him to rise. 'Indeed I did,' he said as the man got to his feet once more. 'You are Captain Tristram Kreen of the Geoll Royal Guard, are you not? It was you who was responsible for escorting my grandson here?'

Seeming slightly doubtful, the man ventured a small nod in reply. 'This is true, my Lord. I was servant to your late son-in-law and now am in the service of Prince Aarold and, of course, his guardian, your lovely niece Maudabelle.' He paused for a moment, his attention drifting once more to gaze wistfully at the White Duchess. Petronia felt the hands resting on her collar stop moving briefly and sensed that the duchess was smiling knowingly at him.

Ceasing his romantic daydream, Tristram continued with his speech. 'I was charged by your niece to seek out the prince after he was kidnapped. It was a duty I endeavoured to carry out to the fullest of my abilities. Though I must confess that I was indeed aided on my quest by the duchess herself and her loyal servant Coal-Fox.'

A broad smile crept across King Hepton's face. 'You are much too modest, my good captain. My niece has already told me of your devotion to her and the prince as well as your ability as a soldier. I'm sure that without your bravery my grandson would not be in the safety of my castle and the one responsible for his kidnapping not be so securely captured.' He gestured towards where Petronia knelt at Maudabelle's feet. Tristram regarded her once more, pondering how such a simple-looking girl could be responsible for such a crime. Staring back with desperate, large eyes, Petronia silently pleaded with the captain to see the foul truth behind the charade before it was too late. Already Maudabelle's touch was sculpting the surging language in her mind, bringing violent words to the forefront of her awareness, compelling her to rend and kill.

'But,' Hepton went on, sounding almost light-hearted, 'such ill concerns are behind us now and we should not trouble ourselves with past worries. No, Captain Kreen, you have behaved both chivalrously and wisely in your duties and my niece and I were discussing how to appropriately reward your actions.'

Tristram's heart leapt hopefully on hearing this and he stole another glance at his beloved duchess's beautiful visage. Falling respectfully to his knee once more, he tactfully ventured. 'King Hepton, if you would permit me to be so bold. I have been enamoured of the duchess's beauty and wisdom for many a year now. If it pleases both you and she, I would ask for no more reward than her hand in marriage.'

Hepton thoughtfully ran his hands along the wooden arms of his chair. 'An interesting proposal, my good captain, and not unwarranted. I will need time to consider your suit, but meanwhile I had in mind a more immediate honour.'

He once more directed Tristram's attention towards where Petronia knelt. 'As I explained, this individual is the one responsible for the prince's abduction. She is a crude magic-worker, a witch of sorts, her mind addled with madness. My niece is well studied in such areas and has managed to neutralise her power. I believe that as you have aided so much in her capture, it should be your hand that ends her life.'

The captain turned to face the pitiful prisoner and studied her sorry appearance suspiciously. He recalled seeing a girl looking very much like her fleeing from the Ryders' lodge in Veridium pursued by a great cloud of dark sorcery but as he gazed upon her now, it was hard to believe that she was capable of any malevolence. Still, Tristram was wise enough to remain cautious.

With a smooth movement, Maudabelle caressed the curved metal that sat beneath Petronia's chin. Petronia shivered slightly as the magic of the collar silently called out to the darkness within her. 'The neckband is of my own crafting,' the White Duchess told her suitor sweetly. 'It has drawn into it all power or spells she might possess. She is totally harmless. Once it is removed, simply sever her head from her body and she will cause no further woe or mischief to the innocent.'

Her hands clasped in terror, Petronia was barely able to comprehend the layers of lies and trickery spread by the king and duchess. Within her, she could sense the blackest hues of her powers take solid form, like a coiled viper of fatal words kept in check by the enchanted band at her throat; she knew at once what would happen once the restraint was removed. It both terrified and thrilled her and her heart raced in her chest as words of death and control readied themselves within. In desperation, she gazed deep into the soldier's mismatched eyes and begged him silently to see the truth, see what was truly within her, the monster that would be released at Maudabelle's command. '*I will destroy you,*' she thought in a sudden passion of excitement and revulsion. There was no warning she could give through sound or gesture. A thousand words throbbed in her mind, ready to fill the air, but never before had she felt more helpless or silent.

Tristram faltered doubtfully as he looked into the girl's dark eyes. There was something deep within them, wild and immeasurable, that unnerved him. Glancing back at King Hepton, he asked, 'Are you sure all her wickedness has been subdued?'

A quizzical expression passed over the king's face and he leant forward slightly in his seat. "You doubt the abilities of my niece in judging such things?' he accused darkly.

Tristram felt his mouth become dry with nervousness. Gazing at his beloved White Duchess, he drank in the beauty and guile in her vivid green eyes and his nerve became firm once more. He would do anything she asked to win her hand.

'Draw your blade, Captain Kreen.' The king's instruction was emotionless and measured.

As if in a trance of absolute devotion, Tristram took a firm grip of the hilt of his sword and pulled it smoothly from its scabbard. The sound of sharpened iron against leather sang in Petronia's ears, a high-pitched note resonating with the memory and intent of violence that made her nerves come alive with yet to be spoken utterances of destruction. Her insides were burning, her belly, throat and tongue licked with dark hell-fire confined from the outside world by the simple metal strut within her mouth. Maudabelle's hands rested lightly but firmly on the back of her collar and with a flinching sensation of dread Petronia felt a clicking of shifting metal locks being slowly unfastened. The restraint moved slightly, the iron rubbing up against her jawline and the plate twisting within her mouth, small motions that warned her that the darkness the collar choked into obedience would soon be set loose. Vicious exhilaration rose within her like the heady scent of warm blood, filling her chest with a razor-like stream of deadly words and sound. Through swirling confusion, she gazed up at the man standing before her, trying desperately to convey a sense of warning to him, let him know that he should flee before it was too late. He seemed frozen in the moment of action, as if time had been called to a halt, his sword raised over his shoulder, muscles coiled ready to strike, loyalty and doubt wrestling for control within his eyes. She felt the White Duchess's fingertips push firmly against the base of her skull, the pressure heightening the ready energy that surged from her breast into her larynx, driving out all notions of mercy and turning her thoughts murderous. The person before her was no longer a man now, but a pitiful vessel of life to be drained, consumed and controlled.

The White Duchess whispered something, an utterance that Stone-Tongue could not hear above the shrieking maelstrom of language in her own mind, and with one swift gesture the collar was undone.

The sturdy iron bit fell from her mouth and free from its restriction, her tongue lashed wildly against her palate and gums like a cracking whip. Overwhelmed by the force that had built up within her, she fell forward on to her hands, spine arched like a hissing cat, muscles contorted beyond her control as a torrent of heinous, hateful sound poured out of her. Long-dormant words carved from the magic of the Ley formed themselves clearly within her mind, crafted and sculpted by the unrelenting grip of the duchess on her neck and jaw. Her body jerked and trembled as her abdomen tightened into a hard knot, driving the long, low, hellish note of power from her. It shredded her inners, turning her nerves to wire and her breath to molten lead, flowing unforgiving out into the world like an ascending demon on a river of blood. Desperate to gain some mastery over her will once more, Petronia searched the howling dark of her awareness for a glimmer of golden Ley light, but Maudabelle's will over her was too strong. Every note of power carried by her gasping breath was seized, snatched from her control and transformed into something hateful and deadly.

The curdling echo of the devilish scream filled the icy chamber like a swelling tidal wave, turning the chilled air white-hot with passion. Petronia's stomach retched helplessly, unseen flames gusted from her lungs, licking the inside of her throat and turning to venomous bloody sound as her tongue shaped them. She struggled to control the power, turn the destructive din into stony silence, but Maudabelle's command of the darkness within her was absolute. She straddled the tormented girl's form, her right hand clasped around her neck, draining the hateful power from her. Frozen with terror and deafened by the unnatural blast, Tristram Kreen remained bolted to the spot, unable to comprehend what was happening. Petronia's helpless stare locked with his terrified pupils and her mind struggled to register him as anything more than a soon-to-be extinguished light. Another baying spasm of sound and rage ripped through her body with exquisite rapture and her singed, bloodied tongue spat out a growling note of command. Her breath turned black, a shadowy, curling plume snaking ominously from her jaws with one sole intent: enslavement.

Still subduing Stone-Tongue's flexing body beneath her weight, Maudabelle cast out her left hand, allowing the curls of blackness to caress her colourless palm and fingers, letting it become aware of her desire. With a violent thrust, she stretched her clawed hand out towards the horrified Tristram. The billowing mist surged from Stone-Tongue's lips with a possessive shriek, engulfing his body in silken, churning wings of shadow. He opened his mouth to scream, but the only sound that could be heard was the mystical words of ownership that tore from Stone-Tongue's lungs. The darkness consumed his form with greedy speed, pouring like dark liquid into his gaping mouth and wide eyes, clinging to every inch of him like a swarm of shrieking insects. Within her heart, Petronia felt a quiver of deadly terror as she witnessed the bleak force from her seize hold of the helpless man's form, swallowing up every fragment of life and matter within him. The note that poured from her seemed to rip a soulless gash in the universe, an empty space once inhabited by Tristram Kreen and now filled with thoughtless, un-dead shadow. A final ripple of resistance shook the shadow-figure, running from the heels of the boots to the tip of the sword, a last memory that this vaporous entity had once been a thing of flesh and life, then nothing and the dark phantom stood motionless, its smoky fibre vibrating with power and sound.

Force clasped suddenly at Petronia's throat and the feral cord of her mystical voice faltered to choked silence as the enchanted brace was once more pulled tightly round her neck, the icy burn of the mouth-plate forcing her lashing tongue to silence. She felt the hateful, leaden note within her draw back, turning to molten metal in the pit of her belly and the exhaustion of the power that had been ripped from her crushed her body so that she collapsed, face down on the cold floor, limbs shaking.

Pleased with her impressive achievement, Maudabelle allowed her hand to run through Petronia's dishevelled dark hair a final time before delicately stepping over her prone form to approach the shadow-figure. The man-shaped patch of swirling darkness stood erect before her, its face featureless, its form crafted from undulating blackness. The hushed echo of remnants of Petronia's mystical language rustled within the fibre of its being, a replacement for living breath. Its dark sword still drawn, it turned its head towards the White Duchess, mindlessly awaiting her command.

A victorious grin broke across Maudabelle's face as she inspected the creature. From his seat at the side of the room, King Hepton gazed proudly at his niece and brought his hands together in a slow round of applause. 'Impressive, my dear Duchess,' he commended as Maudabelle gracefully raised her arm and uttered words of enchantment softly to the shadow warrior. At her command, the dark figure sprung into movement, flourishing its sabre in skilful, deadly circles through the air.

The White Duchess watched the demonstration for a few moments, guiding the phantom now and again with subtle whispers and gestures before uttering one final phrase that caused the figure to fall inactive once more.

'A warrior of sorcery and Ley magic, totally within my psychic control,' she explained proudly. 'Without thought, without fear, without weakness. His will is my will, his sight, my sight, his words, my words. His greatest wish was to be held within my heart and now he is slave to my mind, a shadow of my very thoughts. Through him, I will strike down our enemies and lead your warriors while I remain in the safety of the palace.' To demonstrate her point, Maudabelle motioned to her uncle to pass her the sword he wore. Taking the weapon, she plunged it with all her might into the being's dark abdomen. The gleaming steel blade vanished smoothly into the swirls of blackness as easily as if it had been cutting through thin air. The creature did not move, did not call out in pain, but simply remained still and unaffected by the attack. The White Duchess removed the blade and handed it back to the king. 'Totally impervious to mortal weapons, it cannot be killed and will obey my every order.'

Examining his unbloodied sword, King Hepton nodded approvingly. 'With an army of such soldiers, Geoll will fall to its knees before me,' he said triumphantly before glancing across to where Petronia lay, curled woefully on one side, her eyes barely open as she tried to comprehend the horror she had created. Maudabelle followed her uncle's gaze to where Stone-Tongue lay and a cold smile creased her lips. 'She will regain her strength soon, I will make sure of it,' she crowed as if reading her uncle's thoughts. 'The more power that is released from her the more accustomed her body and mind will become. I can foresee her even growing to relish her new role. After all, it is her true nature.'

A sickening shudder of anticipation ran through Petronia's exhausted body at the White Duchess's suggestion. It revolted her how her instincts seemed to rejoice at the prospect of such heinous action when her conscious mind only feared and loathed it. Already, the churning, muttering darkness within her was beginning to rise once more against the chastisement of the weighty collar, its appetite sharpened by turning the unfortunate man to shadow. Stubbornly, she kept her mind turned towards the narrow, glimmering thread she could barely sense running through her spirit: the undying flow of the Ley that not even death could extinguish.

King Hepton sheathed his sword and turned back to his niece. 'I am eager to witness more of Stone-Tongue's abilities. I trust she is as adept at destroying life as she is transforming it.' His eyes glittered with a brutal malice that was mirrored in Maudabelle's expression. The White Duchess grinned morbidly as she sensed her uncle's thinking. The moment she had waited fourteen years for was imminent. 'A brief rest should be all she needs, Your Majesty. Send for your guards to bring Prince Aarold here.'

A malicious, cold laugh caught in Hepton's throat and with a final bow he departed to set in motion the next stage of their plan. Along with her unnatural creations, the White Duchess allowed herself a moment of quiet jubilation. Proudly, she circled the dark spectre that stood like a tower of inky storm-cloud, unthinkingly awaiting its mistress's will. Gazing into its blank visage, Maudabelle idly recalled the foolish, misguided man whose life-force it now possessed. Tristram Kreen's romantic desires for her had always made him follow her every whim. It seemed doubly appropriate then that he was the first to be transformed into this ingenious avatar for her might. She drummed her fingers thoughtfully against her palm as she excitedly considered battalion upon battalion of such creatures tearing the city of Veridium asunder. Stone-Tongue would need vessels to do her work, but there were plenty of prisoners in the castle dungeons. The White Duchess chuckled darkly to herself. Perhaps she could persuade her uncle to get Coal-Fox to "volunteer".

Leaving her treacherous plans for the former Ley Ryder to one side, Maudabelle turned her attention to more pressing matters. Turning her back on the shadowy warrior, she strode purposefully across the chamber to where Petronia lay, exhausted and abused, gripping herself tightly as she battled to maintain control over her own mind.

The bubbling language of her thoughts quietened in obedient awe as Maudabelle drew closer and Petronia's fingernails gripped the stone floor as she felt her consciousness ready itself to do the duchess's bidding. Standing at the wooden table, Maudabelle hummed softly to herself as she mixed together various unknown ingredients in a ceramic pestle. Taking the dish in her hand, she once more knelt down beside Petronia and embraced her around the chest with her free arm. Petronia wanted nothing more than to fight back, to push her away and escape her controlling touch, but she did not have the physical or mental strength.

Maudabelle brought the pestle up before Petronia's face, tilting it slightly towards her as if to encourage her to drink. Petronia gazed at the contents, a deep scarlet, almost black liquid, and felt its powerful aroma wash over her. It smelt delicious, dark and decadent: the heady scent of warm blood, magic and power. The rich odour seeped into her as she breathed deeply, nourishing her weary, aching body and intoxicating her mind until she could barely recall anything but the wonder and the might of the words that spun within her brain and how she hungered to speak them again. In this fit of rapture, she drifted for what seemed like centuries, nursed within the White Duchess's possessive embrace as she whispered to her of the violent deeds they would commit together.

Chapter 38

THE SUBTERRANEAN ARMY

Hayden knelt motionless, the long whispering grass rippling around him like dark, green waves, unable to move as he tried to take in what Garnet had just said. He felt as if the sickening bleakness of the Weald of Megrim from which they had just fled had escaped the shadowy gloom of the carnivorous trees and taken root amid his thoughts once more. The words that the dwarf Bahl had translated from the ancient tablet were brutally undeniable in his mind, ominous sentiments about dark angels and prophecies of doom. Carnage and death brought about by one woman: his beloved sister. The grimness in Garnet's voice told him all he needed to know. The hope the Ryders held for Petronia's resistance was failing and they were now searching for ways to avert the calamity foretold by their disloyal comrade. They had to stop the White Duchess's plans at all costs.

'You can't kill Stone-Tongue. It's unthinkable! There has to be another way.' The cry of desperate dissent did not, surprisingly, come from Hayden. Bracken had dragged herself to her feet, leaving her new-found love's side, and marched over to where Garnet knelt dejectedly at the edge of the dark forest. Weary with emotion, Garnet looked up into the girl's angst-ridden face. 'Please, Bracken,' she uttered, her voice hoarse as she battled to control her sorrow. 'We cannot allow our emotions to affect us at this time. The task will be hard enough, both physically and emotionally. We must try and do what the Ley asks of us.'

Cautiously, Rosequartz stepped toward the irate Bracken, a fragment

616

of calming, creamy moonstone in the palm of her outstretched hand. 'No-one wants this, child,' she told her gently. 'But we cannot allow this evil to go ahead unchallenged.' She was interrupted mid-sentence by Bracken violently knocking the crystal from her hand. 'Don't try and *heal* me, Sister Rosequartz,' she hissed, the memory of Jet's betrayal aflame in her breast. 'Neither crystals nor the Ley Itself could dampen my emotions enough to consent to this plan. Look into your hearts, both of you, and tell me dutifully do either of you have the courage to see this action through? To rob a gifted innocent of her life because she has been usurped by heretics and devils? To take from a virtuous man his loyal sister and cut silent the very voice of the Ley with your blade? Does the Ley truly give you strength to do such a deed?'

Both Garnet and Rosequartz fell into silence as they contemplated the weight of Bracken's question. It was an unsettling prospect that they were, indeed, attempting to take on and the irate girl had simply voiced the uncertainty they each felt as they considered what had to be done. It frightened them deeply to consider the act that must take place to ensure the future, a deed that seemed to go against every instinct they had as loyal followers of the Ley.

Awkwardly shrugging off the connotations of what lay before them, Rosequartz gazed at Bracken with sympathetic eyes. 'Your fury isn't wholly with us, Bracken,' she said softly, reaching out to touch the girl's shoulder. 'It is with Sister Jet. It is for the deep betrayal and heinous misdeeds she has inflicted on our order, on our family. I understand and share your loathing.'

Bracken's brooding expression twisted with rage and treachery as something within her seemed to break. 'Do not speak that name to me!' she hissed, her dark green eyes turning almost black. 'No Ryder, no person should give her credence by speaking the title she has no right to wear. She has denounced the Ley. She murdered Sister Amethyst!' Her voice trembled with passion as she spoke the final sentence and her hand clasped the hilt of the Might of Kelhalbon that hung from her belt. Her wrathful countenance made all those in her presence recall the bitter oath she had sworn the night she had learned of Amethyst's death: to see her killers brought to justice. A dark atmosphere hung in the chilled air, still and ominous with the foreboding of imminent bloodshed. The Ley seemed to recede into Itself, becoming removed and distant, as if tensely watching to see what action Its servants would take. Reaching out, Rosequartz gently touched Bracken's cold cheek. 'I know she did,' she told her softly, sorrow heavy in her tender voice. 'I know she did. Which is why we must act swiftly before they can harm anyone else.'

Her words were ambiguous as if already the prospect of defeating Stone-Tongue was too immense to even speak of. She turned to look at Garnet for mutual support, but her fellow Ryder's golden eyes bore the same level of doubt that she felt. Not a word was spoken, but the uncertainty they felt was profound. Whether it was the residual effect of the Weald's gloom or the hurt exacted on them by Jet's treachery, they could not say, but inwardly neither Garnet nor Rosequartz were sure they had it in them to go ahead with the mission. Then, in that moment of doubt, a voice spoke, low and emotionless.

'I'll do it.'

Unobserved by Bracken or the Ryders, Hayden had got to his feet and was staring bleakly towards the west where the very tips of the upper turrets of Murkcroft were just visible against the cloudy horizon. Her heart swelling with love, pity and horror, Bracken rushed back to him, flinging her arms around his neck, barely able to comprehend the gravity of his suggestion. Hayden held her tightly, drawing strength from her embrace, his mind awash with woeful memories of his sister.

Colour drained from Garnet's cheeks as she stared overawed at the grim-faced youth. 'No,' she said finally, when she had regained her speech. 'Master Hayden, I, we cannot allow you to take on such an arduous burden. Think of what you are saying. Stone-Tongue is your sister! It would be unthinkable for you to even attempt it.'

Her words rained against Hayden's beaten soul, making the grief within him burn even more fiercely. He would have given anything to find another way out, lay his fate at the Ryders' feet and allow them to decide Petronia's destiny. But Hayden was a man who would not leave his life or that of those he cared for to chance. Memories of his sister were vivid in his mind, recollections of their simple carefree childhood, of watching her make brightly coloured pebbles dance and spin across the floor before his innocent infant eyes. Each instance from their past stung like a wound as he recalled Petronia, his strong, clever, free-spirited sibling who had come so far to disprove his doubts in her abilities. Abilities that now appeared to stretch further than he dared consider. Hungry for certainty and support, he gripped the hilt of his sword and asked, 'Tell me once more what the dwarf prophecy said would happen if Stone-Tongue succumbed to darkness.'

Garnet felt a tug of Ley energy course through her body, urging her to speak. Dully she uttered the ancient words that It called into her thoughts. 'If evil lays claim to Stone-Tongue's soul, she will become an instrument of relentless destruction,' she told him, feeling tears spring to her eyes. 'She will have the power to end life with a single word, twist the fabric of nature with the very sound of her voice and corrupt the Ley Itself to darkness. She would no longer be the soul she once was but become consumed by an unquenchable hunger for destruction. She would become the Angel of Death, Herald of the Apocalypse.' Overcome by what she had just said, Garnet fell silent once more and took a fragment of snowflake obsidian from her belt, pressing it to her lips to purify them of the dreadfulness they had been forced to utter.

Hayden took in every word Garnet spoke with silent acceptance, his breathing heavy. Lightly, he rested his hand on the hilt of his sword but made no motion to draw it as he recalled the promise he had made to his father, to watch over and protect Pet. Familiar feelings of uncertainty and mistrust in the true nature of the world came back to him and once more he found himself wishing that he had never left Ravensbrook. 'My sister has a strong spirit,' he said quietly as Bracken rested her hand compassionately on his arm. 'I've always known that. But during her travels she has proven it to be even stronger than I imagined. She will fight any wickedness that tries to claim her with every ounce of strength in her soul. If it overwhelms her, crushes the goodness that dwells within her heart, then what remains, the monster of which you speak, will no longer be my sister. I will slay it in her memory, to preserve the mercy of the Ley and the woman she once was.'

Approaching him, Rosequartz reached out to take his hand in her own, placing an unpolished fragment of speckled grey and green rhyolite in his palm to help him summon his strength and courage. Hayden ran his fingertips across the rough stone, feeling an intense warmth within its uneven surface. 'For inner strength,' she explained gently. 'Ley bless you, Master Hayden, for being willing to take on such a burden.'

Hayden closed his eyes and summoned to mind Petronia's beautiful face. Silently, he sent a prayer to his sibling, telling her that he believed in the resilience of her soul and begging her to fight the darkness within. He truly did not want to accept that his sister had become an entity of evil that must be destroyed.

His sombre thoughts were interrupted by Bracken letting out a cry of warning which told them that someone was approaching from the west. Fearful of the imposing threat they faced, Hayden became alert once more, drawing his sword as he and the Ryders turned readily to meet the newcomer. In the mid-distance, making its way at haphazard speed, a stocky dark creature picked its way with anxious swiftness through the shifting grass of the rocky plain. At first it appeared to be a small, sable pony that had thrown its rider and was now running loose in the brutal wilderness. But as it drew closer, Hayden and his companions could clearly make out the slick, leathery scales and bony crest of horns that unmistakably belonged to an Equile. The frantic beast soon caught sight of them and began trotting towards them as quickly as his spindly legs could carry him. Phebus's familiar husky, dramatic tone could be heard carried on the cold wind.

'Help!' he cried plaintively, between weary gasps. 'Treachery! Foulest of foul murder!'

Scarlet eyes streaming with frightened tears, he cantered up the hillock towards them, his limbs trembling with exhaustion and emotion. Eagerly, Hayden and the others rushed to greet him and the traumatised Equile gently touched each of them with his beak, seeming to struggle to believe they were really there.

'Oh, you're alive!" he exclaimed in relief. 'The Ryders, Aarold's sister too, thank the stars, you're all alive!'

Hayden rested a compassionate hand on Phebus's smooth neck, trying to calm the creature down. 'Yes, we are still alive, but barely. The Weald of Megrim nearly saw otherwise and it was due to Sister Chiastolite's noble sacrifice that we stand before you.'

Barely paying attention to what Hayden was saying, Phebus wearily lowered his head and let out a whine of fatigue. 'Yes, dear boy, but be quiet. You must hear me, all of you. I have terrible, frightful news. Prince Aarold, my dear companion, has been taken hostage and you'll never guess by whom. His own aunt, the White Duchess Maudabelle! She's been a spy for Etheria all this time, under the orders of King Hepton, Aarold's grandfather! They plan to use your comrade Stone-Tongue to kill him and invade Geoll. Oh the horror of it all!' He began sobbing distraughtly as Garnet stroked him tenderly on the snout. 'Try and calm yourself,' she told him. 'We know exactly the White Duchess's plan for the prince and Stone-Tongue. Our disloyal Sister Ryder Jet works with them in this evil plot. We have all tasted betrayal this day.'

Phebus's red eyes grew wide with amazement and he stopped crying. 'You knew?' he declared, the familiar irate tone slipping back into his voice. 'I risk my life galloping here to find you and you already knew? Well then, don't just stand there, woman, do something! We've got to do something!' He began pacing up and down in front of them, eager for some kind of action to be taken.

Turning her gaze westward, Garnet considered the distant spires of Murkcroft spiking like narrow pins on the horizon. 'Fear not, my good Equile,' she told him. 'We already have a plan. The Ley won't let us fail.'

Phebus stopped his pacing and snorted indignantly. 'You will need more than just a plan,' he remarked. 'Murkcroft is a stronghold guarded by scores of professional warriors and marksmen. What we need is an army!'

Sighing gravely, Garnet continued to study the far-off towers of the enemy fortification. 'That,' she said grimly, 'is something we don't possess. We will have to give our trust to the Ley to empower our small band with the strength and courage of many.'

The Equile looked at her impatiently and clicked his tongue. 'What kind of talk is that?' he muttered, trotting over to Bracken. 'I credited followers of the Ley with more intelligence. Do I have to think of everything? No army, indeed. Why, this young maiden here is the heir to the throne of Kelhalbon. I saw steward Bahl present her with the war-hammer of the dwarf queens myself! And what were her words to you? Strike it against the ground thrice and the finest warriors of your mother's people will be summoned to your side.'

He blinked expectantly at Bracken while her companions looked towards her, each of them wondering how they could not have thought of the idea themselves. Bracken wavered for a moment and looked doubtful. The truth of her royal identity still sat uneasily with her, but this was not the time for uncertainty. Rosequartz placed an encouraging hand on her shoulder. 'It would add great strength to our plan if the dwarves were to fight by our side,' she prompted.

Swallowing her nervousness, Bracken briefly smiled at the Ryder before stepping away from the group to find enough room to draw the mighty mace. The icy wind tugged at her hair and garments like the invisible flow of the Ley as she drew the Might of Kelhalbon from her belt. The dim light of dusk gleamed dully over the strong, black iron fist at the tip of the weapon and as she lifted it high above her head, Bracken thought she felt a pulse of ancient energy, a power twinned with her ancestry and the will of the Ley, flow from the metal into her palms. In that brief moment, she at last experienced a connection with her Dwarfish heritage.

'I, Bracken, daughter of Princess Duun, summon your aid.' The command was unnecessary and her voice shrill with trepidation, but Bracken felt the need to recognise herself as the Might of Kelhalbon's true mistress. With all her strength, she brought down the weapon upon the firm ground, the metal knuckles sending up small clouds of dry soil where they met the earth. A low, reverberating tremor echoed out through the ground beneath their feet like the pre-shock of a coming earthquake.

Shaken a little off balance, Hayden shifted his footing and moved closer to Phebus. The muted boom spread out from the hilltop, a wave of energy travelling at powerful speed outwards in every direction, carrying the command of the queen of the dwarves that the subjects of the mountain realm were being summoned by their leader. Bracken waited a few, brief seconds for the deep echo of the blow to spread far out into the earth like an ancient long-dormant voice, before raising the mace again and bringing it down a second time, her confidence in her actions growing surer. This time the impact upon the dry ground was louder, more brittle, like a rigid crack of thunder as a lightning strike hit the earth. Jagged clefts split out from where the iron hand had struck, spilling across the crust of the stone on which they stood in angular paths, marking out large rectangular sections amid the sparse plant-life. The hill, the whole land beneath their feet, seemed at that moment strangely fragile, a splintering and hollow shell under the unquestionable strength of the weapon in Bracken's hands. Large, newly formed plates of rock shifted up at uneven angles to reveal shadowy caverns of the cold underworld. From these narrow portals the creak and trundling of weighty machinery echoed low and unseen, along with the distant guttural voices and tramping steps of dwarves drawing closer as the flickering glow of flaming torchlight began to brighten the gloom. A strange thrill of hope and exhilaration filled Bracken's heart as for the third and final time she struck the shattering ground, the trembling shards of stone falling with unnatural neatness and ease to form staircases and ramps leading down into the darkness below.

Bracken and her companions moved back from these newly opened entrances and gaped in awe as out of the gloom, team upon team of dwarves emerged into the daylight. Armoured in heavy breastplates and pauldrons to guard their broad shoulders, many brandished brutal, spiked clubs or large pikes while others worked in squads of three or four to haul mighty war engines, catapults, trebuchets and battering rams from the tunnels. At the head of this army, Bahl, the steward of Kelhalbon strode forth, overseeing everything, shouting orders in unemotional, blunt Dwarfish. She made a powerful sight, her tall, lean form clad in a suit of heavy chain mail adorned with glinting medallions of crystal and an ornately engraved barbute helmet, the T-shaped opening of which accentuated her strong, symmetrical features even more acutely. On her back were strapped a pair of curved twin blades, razor-sharp and each nearly as tall as Hayden. She moved deliberately, almost gracefully as she walked among the warriors of her race, dealing out instructions. It was easy to see from her muscular physique why King Elkric had been so keen to make an allegiance with the dwarves when he had fought the Etherian army.

Bahl sank to her knee before Bracken in a gesture of respect. 'You summoned the army of your people, Your Majesty?' she asked in her usual, throaty, aloof tone.

Taking a deep breath, Bracken tried not to feel fearful of the drastic situation before them. For a brief moment, her mother and father crossed her mind and she wondered whether the legendary King of Geoll or the dwarf warrior princess had felt terror before a battle. 'We need your aid, Bahl,' she said, willing her voice to sound masterful. 'We need the strength and courage of my people to help stop a cataclysm that threatens us all. Petronia, Stone-Tongue, has been captured by the Duchess Maudabelle. We believe she is going to use her sorcery to release the dark power within her mystical language against Prince Aarold and ultimately Geoll itself.'

Bahl listened intently. Her face, as always, was an inscrutable, blank mask, but her glossy black pupils shone bright with trepidation. 'How did this happen?' she asked dully.

Sore fury burnt within Bracken's belly and her fingers gripped tight around the hilt of the dwarf-made mace. 'We were betrayed,' she uttered hoarsely as she recalled Jet's sneering face. 'A traitor, the vilest murderess who wore the guise of a loyal Ryder while all the time remaining a servant to the wicked duchess and her foul aims. She guided us to the dismal forest of Megrim and left us for dead. If it hadn't have been for the sword that my people gifted Master Hayden and the noble sacrifice made by Sister Chiastolite we would have all drowned in our sorrows.'

A look of disgust crossed Bahl's striking features. Pursing her thick lips, she uttered something coarsely in the language of her people before getting to her feet and turning to greet Garnet and Rosequartz. 'My greatest sorrows to you, Sister Ryders, that one who claims to be of your Calling could betray the Ley in such an unholy manner.' Grimly they accepted her condolences. 'Her Stone Name was but a mask,' Rosequartz said bitterly. 'She never served the Ley within her heart. I pray It will forgive her.'

Bahl tilted her head slightly and scrutinised both of them with an intense stare. 'I take it you know what must be done,' she said flatly. 'Stone-Tongue cannot be allowed to exist as an oracle of destruction. She must perish. I know human hearts struggle more to accept such a deed. I willingly offer my blade or that of any of these dwarf warriors to spare you the pain of the task.'

Sombrely, Garnet shook her head as Hayden stepped forward. 'A most courageous heart has already volunteered for the sad deed,' she said reverently as Bracken laid a tender hand on his shoulder.

The steward of Kelhalbon studied Hayden's angst-ridden but resolute expression and her unsentimental dwarf heart struggled to understand the complex emotions that motivated his actions. 'Her brother,' she said, with surprised incomprehension. She paused thoughtfully for a moment before shaking her head. 'The more I try and understand human ways the less sense they seem to make. You are truly a most perplexing, remarkable species.' She extended her broad, iron-gauntleted hand to him. 'I respect you greatly for seeing the necessity of what must happen, Master Hayden. May you have the strength of heart to carry it out.'

Hayden took her hand briefly but did not reply. In his heart, he still prayed for the resilience of his sister's soul to resist the evil that sought to command it and hoped that Petronia still existed.

Once more, Bahl stared critically at Garnet and Rosequartz. 'Just the pair of you from your Sisterhood, I see,' she uttered with grim acceptance. 'I would have hoped the Ley would have summoned more of Its followers to confront this enemy. Still, I doubt your skill and courage no more than I doubt that of my fellow dwarves. I trust the Ley will act strongly through you when the moment arrives.'

She turned back towards the massing companies of armed dwarves and let out a powerful exclamation in brisk Dwarfish to call them to attention. At once, the dull rumble of guttural voices fell silent and the engineers attending the mighty siege machines ceased their work. Surveying the army of sturdy, granite-grey-skinned creatures, Bahl uttered a few short, firm phrases, her low voice strong and inspiring even to those who did not understand her language. The dwarves listened and grunted now and again in understanding and compliance. Then one of them raised his muscular arm and pointed directly at Bracken before saying something in a tone that sounded like a distant avalanche. Bahl nodded and beckoned for Bracken to step forward. 'They ask that our true leader, the owner of the Might of Kelhalbon, commands them,' she explained. 'Tell them what has happened and I will translate.'

Bracken faltered briefly. As an apprentice to the Ley, her role in life had always been a submissive one. Now she was being asked to lead, to command. It went against her nature, all that she had been taught, but Bracken realised that the Ley had never intended her to be a Ryder. This was the destiny It had created for her.

With Bahl's assistance, Bracken climbed on to the cart upon which one of the trebuchets was mounted. She was by no means a petite or delicate figure, but she was still a great deal shorter than the rest of her people and this platform gave her a better vantage point from which to address them.

'Dwarves of Kelhalbon,' she called, her husky tone sounding strangely high compared to that of Bahl's. 'I humbly request your aid in stopping a great evil that threatens us all.' She paused for a moment to allow Bahl to repeat her words in monosyllabic Dwarfish. 'My friend, the one they call Stone-Tongue, has been taken by the White Duchess Maudabelle and King Hepton. They intend to force her to use her command of Ley language to wreak terrible destruction and chaos. Once unleashed, this power will spare no soul, no dwarf, Ryder or human. They must be stopped at all costs. I know you have been leaderless for a long time. I know my grandmother has been incapable of being the queen she once was. I understand how it feels to be uncertain of who you are. All my life I have been intent on a goal, a fate that could never be my own. But now, I realise who I truly am and I am proud to take my place among you. Many years ago, my father King Elkric turned to your strength and bravery in his hour of need. Today I do the same. My mother, your Princess Duun, fought bravely at his side to defeat Hepton and his army. Today I stand shoulder to shoulder with you and we will not rest until this darkness has been vanquished for good. Fear not, for the might of the Ley is with us all and that cannot be destroyed!'

The power of Bracken's words echoed as Bahl uttered them forcefully in the tongue of her people. Dwarfish and common language mingled stirringly in the icy air of the hilltop, reaching to all that heard it like resilient strands of Ley-spun music. A low mumble rippled through the assembled dwarves, an utterance of proud and heartened consent for their new sovereign. Rhythmically, their heavy feet began stomping on the stony ground as the murmurs and grunted words became a repetitive chant. Slightly unnerved by this strong reaction, Bracken climbed down from her perch on the cart as the regimented hordes turned westward and began to march slowly towards the distant mountains. 'What are they saying?' she asked Bahl, as a squad of dwarves once more took command of the trebuchet that had acted as her platform and began to trundle it downhill.

Bahl watchfully assessed the troops as they fell into line. 'It is a war song,' she explained above the roar of booming voices. 'Basic meaning being "we will not falter, we obey our queen". A pledge of obedience to you.' Bracken baulked slightly at hearing this but this was no time for modesty.

Bahl then turned her attention to Garnet and Rosequartz. 'Your sister's treachery has gifted us with an advantage,' she told them in her usual bluff manner. 'No doubt by now the enemy believe you to be dead, they will not suspect an ambush, but I will wager Murkcroft will be well guarded nonetheless. It would be wise to conceal our presence until the last moment. Is it possible for the Ley to aid us?'

Garnet evaluated the brooding, shadowy slopes of the distant mountains. 'I believe there is an old trick that may suit the purpose, considering the nature of the terrain, though it will not be easy to move such a large number of us undetected.'

Phebus trotted across to stand next to Hayden and gave his arm a gentle nudge. 'Master Hayden,' he said, 'it would do me a great honour if you were to allow me to act as your steed during this assault. I am no great beast of war but I will do my utmost to carry you as far as I can towards your goal. It is the least I can do for my poor, dear Aarold.'

The Equile sniffed away a tear and Hayden patted him gratefully on his beak before climbing astride his broad, smooth back. He soon discovered that riding an Equile was quite different from riding a horse. Phebus's scales were leathery, almost slippery beneath him and it took several moments for Hayden to find secure purchase. There were, of course, no reins or stirrups to secure himself so he had to make do with maintaining a firm hold of the lowest bony protuberance of Phebus's neck crest.

Before Hayden was fully aware, the company was off, heading with grim purpose towards the dark slopes that preciously guarded Hepton's stronghold and Petronia's prison. The army moved steadily across the barren grasslands as they climbed higher towards the west, filling the still, cold air with the weighty trudge of dwarf footsteps and the creak of the wheels of the mighty siege engines. The warriors of Kelhalbon snaked forward, a long trail of immense, powerful, grey bodies, marching two or three abreast, huge, double-headed battle-axes and spiked maces slung over their shoulders. At the heart of the procession, just behind Bahl and guarded on all sides by dwarves, Bracken marched, flanked on either side by Garnet and Rosequartz. She walked at a steady pace, keeping in step with the Ryders, her eyes fixed unwavering on the line of powerful dwarves ahead of her. Every so often, her hand would drift to the hilt of the Might of Kelhalbon that swung with weighty rhythm at her side as if the heaviness of the iron war-hammer helped her maintain her courage. Mounted on Phebus just behind her, Hayden gazed at her tangle of deep grey tresses and wondered what she was thinking. He was trying very hard to keep his mind in the here and now, focus on this exact moment, fearful to contemplate too much on the aim of the expedition, of the violence and enormity of the task that lay ahead. The silent trek gave him too much time to think about what he had agreed to and a sensation of self-doubt and sorrow stirred within. His mind kept conjuring images and memories of his sister and it tortured him to know that all that was of virtue and goodness within her might already be destroyed, leaving only darkness and hate. Even if that was the case, a part of him still doubted that he could summon the ability to end her life. It would kill him to take such heinous action, but the notion of placing Petronia's fate in another's hands was even worse. If Stone-Tongue had to be vanquished it should be done by someone who loved her.

Dusk drew in swiftly as they trekked through the bleak countryside and all too soon they found themselves departing the misty marshlands and beginning the ominous climb into the rocky slopes of the mountains where Murkcroft lay. Night drew across the jagged and uneven peaks like an immense, featureless blanket of ebony cloud, the mixed vapours of wintry fog and swirling smoke from the castle blocking out any natural illumination of moon or stars. Only the fierce flicker of flaming torchlight from the imposing turrets and battlements resting high above dispelled the forgiving blackness that covered them as they approached. Once the legions of dwarves were fully in the cover of the twisting pass, Bahl drew one of the sabres from her back and raising it aloft over her head, let out a short, sharp order in Dwarfish for her battalions to halt. At once, the sound of marching feet stopped and the mass of dwarves waited silently for their next instruction.

Glancing at the black peaks that towered over them, Bahl turned back towards the two Ryders. 'We best go no further without the protection of the Ley to shield us from our enemies,' she told them in a whisper. 'If you would be kind enough to do the honours.'

Garnet did not reply, but instead looked thoughtfully around the gloomy valley they found themselves in, while Rosequartz searched the pouches on her belt for the correct crystal. Eventually, she retrieved a large fragment of unpolished black jet. Removing her gauntlets, she moved to stand beside her Sister Ryder, the dark stone cupped in her outstretched hand. Garnet too took off her glove and with a delicate, careful touch lay her fingertips upon the matt surface of the shadowy crystal. A ripple of tension ran through the Ryders' bodies as they focused all their attention on the stone, silently sending out a respectful plea to the Ley to grant their request. An aura of taut energy enveloped them, emulating from some unseen alteration deep within the heart of the jet, making the pale contrast of their hands against the stone grow less apparent. Together they inhaled sharply as the Ley power coursed through them, reverberating into the darkness of the mountain night surrounding the army. Hayden started with sudden apprehension as a silken movement shifted noiselessly in the gloom of the jagged peaks and gorges of the pass. At some unuttered command, the blackness of the wintry night seemed to converge, draw together like trickling droplets of blood or ink, to become a singular flowing mass of blackness. Responding to the Ryders' prayer, the Ley twisted the very fabric of the night, transforming it into a pool of shade, like the immense shadow of some mighty dragon soaring high above. In a motion of graceful silence, it spilt out to cover the awaiting ranks of the dwarf army, turning every hue of skin, cloth and metal to match with the gloom of the cliffs and sky. Gazing down at his own hand, Hayden attempted to make out the shape of his fingers. They were not invisible or transparent, but remained just solid outlines of black against black, as if he and the others around him had become a living part of the landscape.

The supernatural cowl cast over them brought with it a muffling hush, deadening the sound of their movements as well as hiding them from mortal eyes. The dark rested upon them with the texture of black velvet, as weightless and silent as a shadow, ghosting over their progress as the intrepid warriors once more commenced the climb towards Murkcroft. The nature of their camouflage gave the terrain a strange, unreal quality before them. Hayden felt oddly removed from the world as they journeyed towards their grim destiny. The peaks and cliffs, the narrow, twisting track, the featureless sky, even the ominous towers and imposing walls of the looming castle appeared more like a darkly painted mural. Despite this, the brutal truth of what awaited and his sister's terrible fate seemed undiminished and Hayden found himself praying that the Ley would alter her destiny.

Soon the dwarf troops stood within the very shadow of Murkcroft itself. High above them, blazing torches flickered along the parapet, outlining the movement of soldiers and guards. Bahl uttered a singular word of command in Dwarfish and with fluid speed the engineers and crews took to their machines of war. At the same time, legions of dwarf warriors brandished their axes and maces ready to attack. Garnet and Rosequartz drew their swords. A note of terror gripped Hayden's stomach and swallowing hard, he gripped the hilt of his own blade, his free hand clasped tightly around one of Phebus's horns. Behind, he could hear the Ryders utter a supplication to the Ley to imbue them with strength for the battle ahead.

Bahl's dark eyes expertly surveyed the towering bastion. Suddenly, she stopped, her attention caught by a strange, dark shape moving swiftly like a column of living smoke back and forth along the ramparts.

'Hold!' she ordered, in a gruff, anxious whisper. 'What is that?' Reaching into a pocket of her tunic, the dwarf vizier drew out a small, brass spyglass which she brought to her eye. After a moment's inspection, she handed the telescope wordlessly to Garnet who studied closely the fire-lit top section of the wall.

'No idea,' replied the Ryder in a hushed tone, lowering the spyglass, 'but it's not a good omen.'

Urgent panic heightened in Hayden's heart as he thought of his sister. 'Let me see,' he pleaded taking the instrument from the Ryder and fearfully peering through it. At first, he could make out nothing clearly, just partially glimpsed fragments of stone illuminated in the torchlight. Then as his sight grew more focused, he saw a tall, lean, featureless figure move with eerie grace and swiftness between the narrow embrasures of the battlements like a phantom of colourless mist. It ghosted in and out of the firelight, the golden glow of the flames flitting across its smoky skin like sheet lightning caught amidst stormclouds. It possessed the silhouette of a warrior armed with a broadsword, but in the brief moments when it was fully visible, no armour, hair or face could be seen, only the dark grey surface of its form which bore no signs of human nature. Moving with unnatural ease, it clambered atop the wall, leaping from parapet to parapet like some macabre acrobat, poised and balanced, without the slightest hint of fear for its own life. Suddenly it stopped, as motionless as a gargoyle carved of sable slate, right on the cusp of the outer edge of the wall, its form crouched like a panther, one leg hanging over the parapet as if it was about to jump. The head of the creature bowed to survey the landscape of stony gloom beneath it, its absent face turned directly towards the hidden warriors below. Even at this distance, Hayden could feel its gaze upon him, eyeless but with a supernatural perception that pierced the protective shadows drawn to them by the Ley, exposing their presence. In a singular, lithe gesture, the spectre that once was Tristram Kreen raised its dark blade and let out a brutal cry ringing with sorcery: a woman's voice, the voice of the White Duchess Maudabelle.

'Intruders!' it shrieked like a banshee to the guards and archers stationed beside it. 'Do not let them enter!'

Chapter 39

THE TAKING OF
MURKCROFT

In an instant, the bleak night sky was ablaze with flame as a barrage of burning arrows flew from the bows of the Etherian archers, painting the turrets and mountaintops wrathful scarlet and gold. The missiles fell like satanic shooting stars from the empty heaven upon the dwarf army, dispersing the inky blackness which cloaked them into a million fractured shadows. The dwarves roared with rage as fire and flint peppered their number. Clasping crystals of iron pyrite and fire agate, Rosequartz and Garnet raised their hands towards the sky, compelling the Ley to protect them. A vibration of pure energy shook the atmosphere, rising from the crystals the Ryders held aloft in rolling waves towards the sky to form a mighty arc overhead, shielding them from the rain of flame. The substance of the Ley was invisible, but the hem of Its reach was marked as the blazing arrows collided with it, veering off in every direction to paint the night with their sparks. With a terrifying, guttural snarl, Bahl cried for the dwarves to assault the walls of the castle and at once the teams of skilled engineers leapt to their catapults while other dwarves scurried in earth-shaking bounds to the rocky slopes of the valley to haul from the ground boulders to use as ammunition. They dug swiftly as if the unforgiving terrain was as pliable as clay, dragging out large chunks which they passed dwarf to dwarf until they reached the catapult. Once there, these missiles were hurriedly loaded and with an inhuman cry the engineers released the tightly wound cords, sending flurry after deadly flurry of stones toward the battlements. The rocks peppered the parapets, crumbling them to dust. Still the archers released their bows, changing their target to a lower angle, aiming at the base of the wall so that their fiery bolts swooped beneath the arcing shield of Ley energy. This strategy was more successful and Hayden watched in fearful horror as darts of fire rained down, setting the catapults smouldering. The dwarves seemed barely troubled by the attack, brushing the blazing projectiles from their thick skin as if they were no more than irritating insects.

A fiery shot struck the ground inches from where Phebus stood and the Equile fearfully reared up with a cry of alarm, nearly shying Hayden from his back. The boy gripped the creature's bony neck for dear life, and uttered calming words barely audible above the roar of battle as the blaze was trampled underfoot by the dwarves surging once more towards the keep.

Amid the blaze of flame that lit the battlements, the strange shadow-figure danced hither and thither, apparently uttering unheard orders to the Etherian warriors. The soldiers atop the wall responded, some setting down their bows to rush to the gate-tower. The dark phantom accompanied them, dashing fearlessly along the edge of the curtain wall in athletic leaps and bounds. Hayden watched with dread as the defenders of Murkcroft amassed around an immense, wooden hoist mounted on the tower top. He let out a cry of warning to Bahl as the Etherians swung the huge crow into action, its arm reaching out in a wide semicircle over the heads of the dwarves. The brave dwarf vizier barked an order to the troops around her, stepping forward to put herself between Bracken and the incoming attack. The massive chain attached to the end of the crow's arm swung through the air with a weighty crash, the deadly hooked anchor suspended from it ploughing into the ranks of dwarves. Phebus darted skilfully back against the lower slopes, along with Bracken and the Ryders, as the crow's vicious hook sliced through the throng of dwarves. The air was filled with the sickening din of crumbling stone and mangled limbs as the great weapon sent at least a dozen dwarves to their demise. Its curved blade rammed into the heavy flesh of one poor individual, skewering him through his breast and hoisting him carelessly into the air like some giant fish on a line, before casting his lifeless body on to the black cliffs.

Soundless amid the clamour of war, the unnatural phantom jumped with a singular vaulting step to land on the very tip of the moving arm of the engine, crouching there, its hands caressing the manacle from which the chain was suspended. Dark tendrils of its smoky being ran in gleaming serpents of power through the links, ensuring that the weapon followed the most destructive path. The crow reversed its arc, swinging back into the flanks of dwarves once more as they scattered towards the mountains.

Rosequartz's heart lodged in her throat as she watched the carnage. Her focus trained on the nightmare astride the hoist, she drew out a black wand of quartz and tourmaline crystal and aimed the jagged point at the creature. The Ley rushed through the fibre of her body, burning liquid golden as she compelled it to destroy the beast. Brilliant yellow light flamed from her fingertips, refracted into a singular intense beam that spilt from the stone's tip, arching like a shimmering fountain across the valley towards the dark being. The phantom raised its head, the glow of the Ley power turning its featureless visage ice white for a second as it brazenly stretched out, from its dangerous perch, tapered fingers spread wide like the struts of a bat's wing. Coils of smoky flesh knotted tightly around the ray of Ley power, sinewy tendrils that squeezed and crushed, shredding the concentration of Rosequartz's energy into scattering fragments. She gasped and let out a shrill cry of shock and pain as the crystal wand exploded into razor-like shards in her hands, slicing her flesh to bloody ribbons.

In an instant, Garnet was at her side to give aid. 'Sister,' she cried gazing at Rosequartz's scarlet hands.

Rosequartz gritted her teeth against the stinging agony and wiped the blood on her cape. 'Tis but a scrape,' she laughed bitterly. 'No more than a darning needle's prick. Worry not for me but for the harm that abomination does to the Ley. It refuses to submit to Its will. At least from this distance.'

Garnet turned her honey-coloured eyes towards the shadow that danced along the cross-beam of the crow. Flashes of flame illuminated the castle wall and surrounding peaks with flickering orange and scarlet as the archers on the battlements continued to release volley after volley of burning darts.

'There has to be another way,' she muttered thoughtfully as the fire painted the blackness. 'The Ley wouldn't desert us.'

Reaching into the pouches of her girdle, she drew out a chunk of brilliant orange fire agate and another of vivid blue lapis lazuli. Gripping one crystal in each hand, Garnet spread her arms wide, her lips moving in reverent plea to the Ley. An unnatural warm wind at once began to curl about her, tugging at the Ryder's cape and chestnut hair. With a cry of sheer effort, Garnet suddenly brought her hands together above her head, the stones colliding between her palms. Golden sparks burst into existence as if the crystals had been flint, and overhead the archers' bolts were ripped from their trajectories, caught within the magnetic pull of the Ley. The unseen force drew them in, merging their heat and flame into one pulsating spot of fire, a miniature sun that flared with angry heat directly above Garnet. The Ryder held it there for a moment, her back poker-straight, her posture rigid as she allowed the Ley to flow through her up into the fireball. Then with one swift movement, she brought her arms suddenly down and forward, her fingertips stretching towards the castle wall and the crow, sending the fiery orb blazing back towards the battlements. The sphere of roaring flames zoomed over the heads of the dwarf army and collided with the wooden struts of the crow, engulfing them in flame. Fire licked hungrily at the swinging beams, reaching scolding fingers towards the parapets as the lithe figure of the shadowy phantom bounded skilfully back to the safety of the wall, its shape barely distinguishable amid the chaos of darkness and fire.

The searing heat of the blaze quickly engulfed the mighty wooden device and with a crack like thunder, the burning mass of oak and metal broke from its hinges, crashing down into the midst of the dwarves. With bellowing cries they scattered from its path as it tumbled to the ground in a rain of fierce sparks before they once more took to the siege engines to attack the vulnerable castle.

Out of the surging mass of dwarves, a lone figure broke free, making her way swiftly through the warriors and engineers, shouting orders as she went. Through the fire, rocks and chaos the powerful figure of Bahl strode towards Hayden and the Ryders, a terrifying visage of war. The smoke from the fallen crow had blackened her grey skin and gleaming armour so completely that her appearance seemed to mirror that of the ghastly spectre that taunted them from the battlements. The blades of her twin sabres gleamed scarlet as they reflected the countless fires that lit the valley. A large gash scarred her right cheek, just beneath her eye, exposing a triangular wound of purplish, weeping flesh.

'Well aimed,' she cried as she watched the engineers set fly another round of boulders at the castle walls. 'They won't hold out much longer.'

Hayden felt Phebus tremble fearfully as they watched yet more massive stones being hurled against the sturdy walls, seemingly with little effect. 'You're sure about that?' the nervous Equile screamed. 'They seem to be doing pretty well at keeping us at bay to me. I don't know exactly what Maudabelle has in mind but I can assure you she doesn't waste time.'

Rosequartz nodded in agreement. 'We need to get through the gatehouse as soon as we can.'

A triumphant, almost demonic expression crossed Bahl's face. She looked proud, almost exhilarated as if she had been waiting too long to display her people's prowess in battle. 'You Ryders just concentrate on how you are going to bring down that foul creature of darkness. Leave bringing down the fortification to us. Kelhalbon's best miners are already at work.'

Bracken looked at the vizier in puzzlement. 'Miners?' she asked baffled as Bahl cast her eyes agitatedly across the length of the curtain wall. 'You mean we're going to tunnel under?'

An amused chuckle like a falling avalanche rumbled in Bahl's throat and her eyes glinted like black diamonds. 'Under, Mistress Bracken? My word, no. We are going through! There isn't a wall built by humans that we dwarves can't topple. As we speak, the miners are digging away at the very mountain beneath our enemies' feet to find and destroy the foundations of the castle at any moment!'

Stopping mid-sentence, Bahl rested the tip of one of her blades against the ground. She stood still for a moment, her sword's hilt resting lightly in her palm as if dowsing the earth for some hidden sign. A second later the ground beneath them vibrated with a tattoo of short tremors. Shouting triumphantly, Bahl cried out in Dwarfish to the throng behind them before pointing to a spot not far to the right of the gatehouse.

'Quickly,' she urged Bracken and the others. 'Draw your weapons and ready yourselves. They have broken through!'

Hayden watched in amazement as the ground at the base of the wall bulged and buckled and large cracks began to spread across the pale stones. With a great avalanche of crumbling masonry and dust, a wide section of the castle's outer wall tumbled as the dwarf miners burst through. Snarls of war filled the air as the army of Kelhalbon turned their attention from the gate-tower to the newly formed opening, surging forward, their axes and clubs drawn ready to assault their enemy. Urging Phebus into a gallop, Hayden set off after them, Bahl and Bracken close behind, while the Ryders drew their stone-tipped blades and called to the Ley for strength.

The first of the dwarf warriors reached the gap in a matter of moments, ambling easily over the strewn debris in weighty bounds. The walls and inside of the courtyard seemed to teem with life as Etherian soldiers left their stations and rushed to fend off the attacking masses. The ranks were swelled with many men-at-arms, experienced warriors, many of whom had faced dwarves before during the Great War against Geoll and were not shaken by their size or strength. Fearlessly, they launched themselves at the front guard of dwarves, skilfully armed with narrow spears and javelins which they aimed with crude accuracy at the few vulnerable spots in their attackers' physiques: the eyes and throats. The dwarves overpowered the men with brute strength, sweeping the humans aside with mighty blows from their clubs, but still many of the Etherian missiles landed true, striking into eye-sockets and severing arteries in spurting fountains of dark brown blood.

Hayden felt his heart in his throat as he willed the frightened Equile onward through the breach in the wall, the carnage all about them. He crouched low over the creature's leathery neck as arrows and missiles whizzed by from every direction. Bahl's coarse voice rang out from somewhere nearby, ordering him to stay amid the protection of his dwarf guard. He turned towards the sound of her words and was met with the sight of an Etherian solider hurtling towards him, his sword raised. Adrenalin flooded Hayden's body as Phebus struggled to shy away from the attack, throwing Hayden from his back. A whirl of blades sliced the air between him and his assailant as Bahl materialised out of the chaos like some terrible guardian angel. Her curved, twin scimitars danced in a deadly flurry of metal and blood, so swift Hayden was barely able to register, decapitating and gutting the man with a precise dual action. Hayden and Phebus regarded her, stunned for a moment, as the emotionless dwarf turned back towards them, her blank, stoic face dotted with flecks of scarlet. 'Go,' she commanded. 'Find Stone-Tongue.'

At that moment, a terrible note of violent sound rose above the clash of battle, an echoing, metallic shriek of pain, energy and impending death that howled like an unseen iron wolf through the courtyard, filling Hayden's heart with dread. From its seat atop the battlements, the shadow-figure of Captain Kreen surveyed the carnage with its eyeless gaze before leaping dauntlessly from its perch to join the fray. Scurrying down the inner wall like a dark-skinned lizard, it landed amidst the warring armies with powerful, velvety grace, its blade of pure blackness drawn and ready. Like a deadly panther it moved swiftly across the courtyard, its spectral sword leaving murky trails of grim mist as it sliced and carved its path towards Hayden, murdering human and dwarf with the same thoughtless efficiency. Its dark sabre seemed sharper than steel: a narrow, unforgiving band of death that took life with the merest flick of movement. It carved through solid dwarf flesh and sinew with sickening ease, casting limbs asunder in a cascade of rust-coloured blood and anguished cries.

Terror swallowed Hayden as he realised the warrior of darkness and destruction was focused on pursuing him. Bravely, he dismounted Phebus and placed his palm firmly on the hilt of his sword, ready to draw, feeling the joyous throb of the dwarves' mystical blessing warm the steel.

The dark creature continued on its deadly, purposeful path, its heinous blade etching the air with savage bands of murderous sorcery. The atmosphere surrounding it crackled with an electric aura of power and menace and beneath the clamour of battle, its presence stirred with an ominous whisper. Thin tendrils of smoky magic spilled out of its form, reaching hungrily towards Hayden.

A sudden flash of brilliance sparked across the courtyard, flowing with gleaming streams of green and flame-orange fire. Hayden felt an intense rush of energy wash around him as Rosequartz and Garnet dashed towards the entity, brandishing emeralds and fire opals. The trails of Ley energy emulating brightly from these stones knotted in broad ribbons of light around the being's form, knitting a cage around it. Viciously, the shadowy creature slashed at the bands encircling it, severing one after another with blows of its mighty blade. Hayden heard the Ryders gasp with pain and effort as sorcery bit into the coils but still their resolve stayed firm and they summoned yet more bands, barring the being's way. Looking round, he saw the resolute expression on Garnet's face, urging him to continue his mission.

'This way!' A hand grabbed his arm, dragging him from the scene of the Ryders battling to contain the supernatural warrior. Hayden turned and found Bracken at his side, urging him to follow. Her pale face was smeared with sweat and blood and her wild hair gleamed almost crimson in the fierce glow of battle. Hayden did not respond at first, his body motionless with the shock of the chaos. The glare of the Ryders' cobweb of gleaming power fizzled violently behind them as the dark warrior battled to break free of its restraints. Fear flashed in Bracken's eyes as she witnessed Rosequartz and Garnet struggle with all their effort and will to hold back the soulless apparition.

'Come on!' she urged, dragging her eyes from the terrible scene. 'Follow me. I've found a way into the keep.'

The shock that had paralysed Hayden shattered as quickly as it had seized him and without really thinking, he found himself racing after Bracken towards a wooden door. They reached it in a matter of moments and with a few powerful kicks broke the portal from its hinges. Tumbling inside, Bracken and Hayden found themselves in a vast hall of cool dark stone. Striking statues of the past monarchs of Etheria lined either side of a broad staircase and the gloomy walls were hung with standards of dark navy and silver.

As soon as they were inside, a horrendous sound tore the cold air around them, echoing in sickening discord within the space. A nerve-jaggling shriek sounding neither human nor beast rose in a vicious note, like a blade of pure noise, ready to rip asunder the very fabric of life. Falling to their knees, Hayden and Bracken pressed their hands to their ears to try and block out the petrifying cry, but the sound still echoed within their skulls, flooding their minds with images of carnage and death. The heinous note rose to a pitch like a thin, piercing needle of steel, before tapering into silence once more, leaving Hayden filled with a grim terror at confronting its owner. Hauling herself to her feet once more, Bracken looked towards the flight of stone stairs before them.

'Stone-Tongue,' she uttered, her voice a dull whisper after the hellish cacophony that had preceded it. 'She's up there somewhere. Hurry.'

Before he could realise it, Hayden was running, taking the stairs two at a time, his muscles trembling with fear and exhaustion. The memory of the soulless scream filled his mind and he struggled to connect it with the loving, quiet notion of his sister. The creature that made that sound was a ghastly monster, an unimaginable being of terror and death, just as the dwarves had foretold. Petronia filled his thoughts, all that was good, loving and brave about her seeming like notions from another place and time, far removed from his quest. In the horror he had found himself in, Hayden's mind had split the idea of the individual others called Stone-Tongue in two: the dark angel he must slay and the sibling he had sworn to protect. He dare not tell himself they were one and the same.

The staircase rose forever, carrying them higher into the upper apartments of the keep. They raced through room after room, barely taking a moment to be aware of their surroundings, hoping and at the same time dreading that in the next chamber they would find Stone-Tongue and the White Duchess. Intermittently, the wicked call sliced the atmosphere to shreds, a baying siren that goaded them onwards with every murderous note even as it tortured them. Each time it died away, the silence that filled their thoughts bore blood trails of the carnage it would cause if Hayden failed in his aim.

The cry seemed to be calling directly at them, drawing them towards where Stone-Tongue was, as surely and swiftly as if the Ley Itself guided their feet. The path led them to a narrow corridor winding away from the main chambers of the castle, a deserted passageway ending in a spiralling staircase. The stone walls were scarred with fresh cracks and the floor covered with dust and masonry from where the vicious shouts of destruction had worked their evil sorcery. Another shriek ripped through the dusty air, making reality quake with the threat of oblivion. Debris crumbled from the roof as the sheer power and might of the sound shook Hayden's awareness and for the briefest of moments his vision failed him. The demonic voice fell silent, its tone dying in an almost piteous sob. Turning to face the staircase once more, Hayden and Bracken found a figure now barred their way.

*

Shock and rage froze Bracken to the spot as the fallen Ley Ryder Jet stepped into the half-light. She was as striking and lithe as ever, but the crystal-encrusted leather armour of her former guise had been replaced by chainmail and a breastplate as black as her silken hair. A sword of cold steel edged with jagged stone rested lightly in her right hand, the same blade she had used to slay Bracken's beloved guardian. A manic look of grim anticipation danced within her gleaming emerald eyes as she regarded the duo maliciously. She flexed her free hand almost lazily at her side and from the debris-strewn floor of the passage, a smoky coil of darkness rose like a mesmerised serpent to caress and wind around her fingers.

Hayden glanced sideways at Bracken. The girl's piebald complexion had turned pale with fury, her eyes fixed in an unblinking glare. Her broad shoulders rose and fell with heated breath and her lips sneered with utter contempt. In a rumbling tone low with hate, she uttered a singular word. 'Murderer.'

An icy heartless smile broke across Jet's face. 'Well, well, well,' she purred, her eyes flitting between the pair. 'Who have the mighty Ryders sent to save them from Stone-Tongue? An uneducated blacksmith and a half-breed bastard. How utterly pathetic.'

Bracken's whole body trembled with rage. It was as if she had forgotten all about Hayden and their purpose for being there. Her face took on the same cold, brutal expression Hayden had seen at The Fallen Inn when they had learnt of Amethyst's death. All that mattered to her now was the treacherous Ryder and her betrayal.

'You killed her.' Bracken's voice dripped with utter loathing. 'You murdered my mother.'

Tilting her head to one side, Jet studied the enraged girl, an unhinged pride gleaming in her emerald eyes. 'No,' she said in a soft, strangely patronising tone as if she was trying to teach a somewhat dim child. 'You killed your mother. She was foolish enough to throw her life away bringing you into this world. I killed Sister Amethyst, a senile old woman who raised you out of soft-hearted sentiment and was too stupid to realise the true potential of Stone-Tongue. Not that you should worry yourself with such trivial semantics. The age of the Ryders ends this night; the White Duchess will see to that.'

Cold fear and dread chilled Hayden's veins as he anxiously wondered if there was any scrap of his sister's soul that remained. 'We're here to stop you,' he stated firmly. 'You will not corrupt her for your own wicked ends.'

The former Ryder's grin grew broader, revealing her even, pearly teeth. She moved her left hand in small, swift circles at her side, whipping the dark trail of sorcery into a pliable, silken band that knotted around her fingers. 'I was so hoping you would say that,' she purred. 'Now I get the pleasure of slaughtering you both.'

Gripping his blade, Hayden stepped forward to confront her but was instantly halted by Bracken barring his way with her arm. 'No,' she growled to him through gritted teeth. 'I made a vow in Sister Amethyst's name. This fight is mine.'

Hayden met her eyes and saw the bitter wound within her soul. Jet chuckled darkly and swished her rapier through the dusty air in a series of practice parries. 'Come, come, Master Hayden,' she mocked, 'surely you're not so ungentlemanly as to barge in before a lady? A *princess* no less. Mistress Bracken here demands satisfaction by facing me in a duel and I'm more than happy to oblige.'

Hayden could do little more than watch as Bracken drew her sword and stepped forward to confront her personal nemesis. The two women circled each other slowly, both waiting for the other to make the first strike, their movements and forms at polar opposites. Jet, lithe and graceful, stepping almost like a dancer, her narrow blade at the ready as the drifting trail of vaporous, dark magic floated serpentine from her free hand. In comparison, Bracken stalked with all the contained might of her tall, muscular physique, a brooding mantle of simmering rage enveloping her powerful movements, her hand tightly clasped around the hilt of her sword.

Jet grinned glibly as Bracken glared at her. 'Now, young Bracken,' she taunted, 'let's see how well you remember your fencing lessons. Concentrate on your gait, keep your guard up, very good.'

The girl did not respond. Her face remained stoic, a brooding mask of mottled marble, her eyes blazing with green flames of hate. Hayden could hear her deep, heavy breathing and wondered if she was attempting somehow to summon the Ley. But still she made no motion to attack.

Spreading her arms wide, Jet gave the thick strand of magic in her hand a little flick. 'Don't be so shy, dear girl. I know you want to kill me. Look, I'll even let you take first blood, an allowance I didn't even extend to Amethyst and she was practically waiting for death when I faced her. You must have better abilities than that old hag, even without the Ley to aid you.'

This insult to her guardian was all it took to erupt Bracken's rage. With a fierce roar, she lunged at Jet, her blade raised to slice at her throat. Skilfully, Jet side-stepped as her adversary came hurtling towards her. Bracken's blow was true but Jet was faster and the edge of Bracken's blade simply grazed Jet's cheek as she swiftly leapt out of harm's way. As she did so, she raised her left arm, allowing the sheet of translucent magic to ensnare Bracken. The girl stumbled, her actions careless from anger as she fell against the shapeless shadow that hung like a net from Jet's hand. The fibrous darkness bulged and stretched as it swallowed up Bracken's form, the outline of her shoulder and face visible through its surface. With a flick of her wrist, Jet sent a wave of energy through the black entity, making its consistency alter from silky to that of a thin sheet of flexible metal that bowed for a moment before snapping back to hurl Bracken viciously against the opposite wall. The girl let out a pained groan as her body collided with the brickwork. Hayden was about to rush to her side when another deafening note of terror shook the atmosphere, shattering his grasp on reality and making blood sing in his head.

A knowing laugh emanated cruelly from Jet's lips as she wiped away the blood that Bracken had drawn from her cheek. 'A crude strike, child,' she sneered as Bracken determinedly staggered to her feet to face her again. 'But brute strength can't overshadow finesse. Now, it's my turn.'

Before Bracken could properly regain her balance, Jet lunged at her, the stone and metal of her rapier slicing through the air like a scorpion's sting. Just in time, Bracken blocked the blade with her own, before it sliced into her stomach, pushing it to one side and clambering to her feet. The once-beautiful Jet looked like a green-eyed demon as she lunged again and again at Bracken, her face the cruel emotionless mask of a deadly killer. Her attacks were swift, honed from years of experience, and even though Bracken bettered her in sheer muscle the two were well-matched. Bracken deflected blow after deadly blow but her lack of participation in proper battle meant that she was unable to lay her blade anywhere near the older woman. As she attempted to strike her enemy,

Jet wielded the dark cloud of noxious magic about her like a smoky cape that hampered Bracken's view. Tendrils of mist clung to her limbs and body like an unnatural armour, deflecting Bracken's sword with slippery ease.

Once more, the sound of Stone-Tongue's shrieks shredded the air like the claws of death. Jet's own manic laughter echoed them as the piercing notes caught Bracken's limbs in a shocked spasm.

'Listen!' she screamed insanely. 'Listen! The Angel of Death sings! She sings for you all!' With a powerful blow, she drove the sword from the girl's momentarily weakened grasp, sending it clattering across the stone floor, leaving Bracken exposed for her fatal blow. Triumph dancing manically in her eyes, Jet raised her sabre to cleave into Bracken.

Gazing into the mad woman's face, a strange strength and instinct filled Bracken quite unlike anything she had experienced before. Without even thinking, she reached for the Might of Kelhalbon that hung at her hip. The cold, black metal seemed to merge instantly with the flesh of her hand, becoming a natural extension of her body as if it had been waiting for her to summon its power. Her pulse reverberated through the heavy iron, right to the tips of the fist's curled fingers, causing them to uncoil. Powerfully she raised the mace before her to deflect Jet's lethal strike. Victory turned to shock in the woman's eyes as the metallic hand took firm grasp of the blade of her sword, snapping it in two like a brittle twig before snatching the hilt from her hand.

Clarity washed across Bracken's mind as the Might of Kelhalbon responded to her will just as it had the dwarf queens' who went before. With a vicious swipe, she landed a blow across Jet's jaw. The fallen Ryder reeled back stunned, spitting blood and shattered teeth as she tried to recover as the Might of Kelhalbon struck once more. This time, the sacred mace collided with her ribs, filling the air with a sickening crack as they broke. Crumbling to the ground, Jet cursed, her lips dripping with scarlet blood, her alabaster skin purple from Bracken's attack. Amethyst's ward loomed over her, her eyes burning with hatred as another deathly cry shook the passageway. At Bracken's internal command, the fingers of the iron hand brutally reached out and grasped with unforgiving might around her throat. Summoning all her physical strength, Bracken pinned Jet spitting and gasping for air against the wall.

'Master Hayden,' she barked, not turning away from the woman trapped within her grasp, 'fetch me my sword.'

Hayden felt his blood run cold as he heard the furious tone of Bracken's voice and recalled her vow of vengeance for Amethyst's murder. Swiftly, he found Bracken's blade amidst the rubble and placed it in her outstretched hand.

Struggling within the Might of Kelhalbon's unrelenting grip, Jet let out a half-choked wicked giggle. 'Too late,' she croaked with macabre glee. 'The dye is cast. Kill me if you wish, stupid girl, it won't stop Stone-Tongue. Geoll will quake before her. There is nothing *you* can do!'

Violently, Bracken shook the Might of Kehalbon, slamming the back of Jet's skull against the wall. 'Silence your tongue,' she spat. 'You traitorous bitch! I want you to listen, I want you to understand. Understand how much you disgust me, how deeply I detest you. Not because your black heart cost me the only parent I ever knew and that you slaughtered her in cold blood. Not that you deliberately left me and your fellow Ryders to waste away in the misery of Megrim. It's not even that you allowed Stone-Tongue's gift to be perverted by twisted sorcery. I loathe you for all those vile sins but what makes me want to end your life is that you were a Ryder, blessed to see the glory of the Ley, and you turned against It, betrayed Its love for unholy carnage.'

In the darkness of the passage, Jet sneered. 'The Ley,' she spat through bloodied lips. 'What did It do to avenge the death of my fellow Etherians when they were slaughtered? Nothing. I gave them justice by my own hand. Life for life, spilt blood for spilt blood. The Ley will pay for Its indifference when Stone-Tongue brings forth justice! Do what you will with me, it will alter nothing.'

An expression as hard as granite came across Bracken's features. Taking a firm grip of the Might of Kelhalbon, she dragged Jet away from the wall, twisting the mace in her hand before driving its hilt firmly into a high lenient in the crumbling brickwork. Choking for breath,

Jet struggled to free herself, her toes barely able to touch the ground. Bracken stepped back as a look of peace came to her eyes.

'No,' she stated. 'I loathe you. But if I were to kill you, because I detest you and all that you have done, it would be an act of spite and malice. An act not worthy of someone guided by the Ley. An act that would make me like you and nothing would disgust me more. Your life isn't worth taking.'

With a final look of revulsion, she turned back towards Hayden. 'Go,' she urged him, glancing in the direction of the stairs from which Jet had descended. 'I will see she doesn't break free. Do what must be done.'

Stepping towards Bracken, Hayden wrapped his arm around her waist and leant close to place a kiss tenderly on her mouth. Her lips tasted of blood and tears but he knew that her soul was satisfied, the memory of her guardian avenged. Bracken had met the challenge of her fate and he loved her for that. Now everything relied on him.

Breaking away, he gazed into her dark green eyes. 'I love you. I will end this and return.' His words sounded like a vow but his mind was still filled with doubt that he could see the heartbreaking task through.

As if to prey on his fearful uncertainties, another terrible cry echoed from high above. Maliciously, Jet let out a choked, gasping laugh. 'Run, boy,' she sneered despite the iron hand crushing her throat, as Hayden dashed toward the steps. 'Heed the call of Stone-Tongue. Face her and witness the wonder of death she has become!'

Chapter 40

THE VOICE OF THE LEY

An unnatural rhythm of sound and silence bombarded Hayden as he raced up the staircase that led to the top chamber of the tower. A disturbing pattern of beastly, inhuman cries like the snarls of a demonic dragon awoken from the bowels of the earth rose in sharp discord with a weighty, deafening quiet akin to the false peace at the heart of a storm. One moment, Hayden found himself frozen in shock by the sheer violence of the noise, convinced that the very notes themselves could cleave the life from him. The next, the shadows of the spiralling stairs fell into such a grave and ominous quiet, it seemed all life in the world had been halted, but for the pounding of his own frightened heart. It was in these terrible respites that Hayden found his thoughts reaching desperately for Petronia, searching for any clue that the tiniest scrap of his sister might remain. Even as he climbed step by step nearer to end her life and halt the awesome power of Stone-Tongue, Hayden prayed that Petronia was still alive. In those dark, soundless moments, he knew that he would give anything to know she could still survive, to see her face or feel her hand in his. Then with the cruellest irony his wish was granted as the roar of twisted sound and destruction rose like a wailing banshee once more to prove that Stone-Tongue existed in all her terrible, unstoppable glory.

A flickering gleam illuminated the darkness of the tower as the hungry cry of destruction died abruptly, emulating from beneath the door ahead of him. Suddenly, he became aware of the resonance of his every movement in the chilly dry air and froze, ears straining as he heard voices filtering through the darkness.

A retching cough rang brutally out, almost robbing the words from its owner. 'You traitors! How could you! My own aunt! My own grandfather!' The voice was Aarold's, weak with fatigue but fierce with fury.

A man laughed cruelly, a deep, throaty humourless chuckle, followed by the voice of a woman, her words soothing but her tone like ice. 'Hush now, young prince. It will all be over with soon, I promise.'

Hayden heard feminine footsteps move lightly across the floor and another sound that he struggled to identify, like a drugged animal straining against heavy chains.

Stealthily, he crept closer to see if he could find a keyhole through which to peer but finding none nor any other gap that would allow him to see inside.

'You can't make her do it, you know,' Aarold's tone was brazenly defiant. 'Not with all your magic or all your swords. You can't force her to kill me. I know her. Mistress Petronia is a kind, noble Ley Ryder; her heart is pure. If you want me dead, have the courage to kill me yourselves! I'm not afraid!'

The male voice laughed, amused by the bravado of his sickly grandson. 'Listen to him! A pathetic echo of his blow-hard father. The same idiotic self-belief but with none of the strength. It's pitiful really.'

A terrible, muffled sound shook the air as Stone-Tongue struggled to suppress another fearful note of destruction. Mingled with the sound of Petronia's unnatural tones, Hayden could hear the White Duchess uttering complex incantations to twist and control the power in her voice. Once again the strange intonations died away to silence.

The voice of Maudabelle rose once more, filled with a cool arrogance. 'Ah, and you are such a good judge of character, aren't you, Your Majesty? Placing your utter trust in me, your faithful aunt to watch over your kingdom until the day you came of age, never thinking for a moment that I might have my own motives. Silly boy. Well, now your beloved Ryder is under my command and we will see the true nature of her power.'

Hayden's heart pounded wildly in his chest as he realised he could not spare another moment. The White Duchess's heinous plot was about to be unleashed and he had to stop it at all costs. Eyes closed, he allowed himself one last memory of Petronia, his sister, the brave, determined girl who he had grown up with before this awful darkness had taken hold of her soul. He told himself that she would not want to become a beast of death, that the act he must commit was as merciful for her as it would be for the rest of the world. Drawing the joy-blessed blade gifted to him by the dwarves, Hayden summoned his strength and charged shoulder first into the barred door.

With the sound of splintering wood, he crashed into the chamber, unsure what horrors awaited inside. Anxiously he surveyed the scene, his brain racing to make sense of what lay before him. To the far right of the room, crouched helplessly upon the stone floor, lay Prince Aarold. Though no person gazing upon him would suspect he was anything other than a wretched, crippled beggar too stubborn to submit to the weakness that claimed his form. Gone was the leg brace fashioned for him by the dwarves; he sat vulnerable, his wasted limb curled awkwardly beneath him, the agony of the contorted muscles etched on his pale but defiant face. His sapphire eyes were fixed with a mixture of hate and fear upon the man who towered over him. King Hepton gazed down at his grandson, arms crossed, his face a mask of brutal indifference to the boy's plight. His eyes were black and dead, the eyes of a man who had killed and killed again so that now ending a life had no effect on his heart, even when it was his own flesh and blood. He looked like he could, at any moment, draw the sword that hung at his hip and slit Aarold's throat, but curiosity made him wait to watch the actions of the two other figures.

Hepton's soulless eyes flickered to where the White Duchess stood, an elegant, dark figure of confidence and power. Her poise was relaxed and ready, one hand on her hip, the other resting with quiet impatience on the metal collar of the being who knelt motionless at her side. Hayden barely recognised his sister at first, for the girl seated next to the White Duchess did not look like his strong-willed, lively Petronia.

In fact, her appearance was so eerily beautiful and lifeless, she more resembled a sculpture of ebony and ivory than a living creature. Her skin was bone white against the black of her hair and gown, her face blank and filled with hate. The pupils that had always been dark were now pitch black, staring straight ahead as if she was in a deep trance, her mind locked by the duchess's sorcery. She knelt like a dog, frozen with the scent of blood in its nostrils, her back arched, fingers gripping the floor. Her colourless lips twitched and curled with trembling fury and her teeth grated against the iron bar within her mouth as muted sounds of violence boiled. Traces of ominous black etched her gums and the creases of her lips with the impending malice of twisted power that swelled within. Staring at her, Hayden's heart ached and he understood how the dwarves feared her as the Angel of Death.

His unannounced entrance made the king and White Duchess turn towards him but Maudabelle seemed strangely unperturbed. A small smile twisted her scarlet mouth and she laughed softly to herself. 'It would seem that our faithful Coal-Fox has allowed an intruder to interrupt us, dear Uncle,' she said smugly as Hayden pointed his sword towards her. 'I always suspected she was lax in her diligence.'

Chuckling sinisterly, Hepton skilfully drew his blade ready to tackle the interloper. 'No matter,' he uttered darkly, 'I'll dispatch of this whelp myself.'

But his niece held up her pale hand to halt his actions. 'Do not bother to bloody your sword, my lord,' she informed him smoothly. 'He is but a common blacksmith and not worthy of the effort. The Ryders do not even possess the nerve to send one of their own to face Stone-Tongue; instead they use this fool. Perhaps they believe that by capturing my shadow warrior, our power has somehow weakened. But no matter, Stone-Tongue can always make me more.'

At the mention of her name, the being in the iron collar snarled a low, choked growl, eager to be allowed to speak. Triumphantly, Maudabelle reached down and proudly stroked her silken hair.

Disgust and fear knotted in Hayden's stomach as he saw the White Duchess stroke Petronia his sibling like a tamed beast. 'What have you done to her?' he spat as Stone-Tongue's breathing rasped in jagged snorts. 'What have you done to my sister?'

The White Duchess glared, her emerald eyes flashing with victory. 'Your sister is dead,' she declared confidently. 'That pathetic charade of a life is no more. She does not need it. She is Stone-Tongue, the mouthpiece of death. I have set her free, elevated her to her true destiny. Did you honestly think that you had the ability to confine her soul, to stop her obtaining the power that was rightfully hers? I saw what she truly was and unleashed what those foolish Ryders would have curtailed. She serves me now.'

As the White Duchess spoke, the girl at her feet lifted her head, staring thoughtlessly at the world with inhuman, dark eyes, black tendrils of hair framing her ghoulish visage. Under her metallic neckband, tendons of stretched muscle contorted beneath her pallid skin. Hayden stood transfixed, searching the monstrous countenance for a glimmer of his sister's soul.

'It isn't true,' he uttered in a low voice. 'She won't obey you. I know Petronia, she's strong, she will be mistress of her own fate.'

The cunning Maudabelle smiled once more and moved to stand directly behind the crouched girl. 'We will see,' she said in a silken tone. 'You are indeed correct, Stone-Tongue will choose her own destiny. So let us see what it will be. Will she listen to the one who restrained her, held her back all her life out of fear and ignorance or the person who looks to celebrate the greatness she can embody?'

The White Duchess extended her pale elegant hand and beckoned for Hayden to approach where she stood. Lowering his sword, Hayden slowly walked forward towards where his sister knelt, her body tense with contained power, the echoes of evil growling deep in her chest. Across the chamber, Aarold bravely shuffled an inch closer, reaching towards the girl whom he had fallen in love with. 'Be strong, Mistress Petronia,' he whispered. 'I believe in you.'

Abruptly, his grandfather seized the back of his collar and hauled him back toward him, dumping the crippled prince roughly on the stone floor. 'Hold your tongue, you mewing invalid!' he barked as

Aarold cried out in agony, his injured leg twisted beneath him. 'You will die soon enough.'

The prince's yelp awoke Stone-Tongue's attention and like a hound suddenly aware of the scent of prey, she fell forward on to all fours, muscles taught as if ready to attack, her fathomless, dark pupils fixed blindly on Aarold.

Before she could move any further, Hayden stepped between Stone-Tongue and the petrified boy. Sharply, the girl raised her face to gaze mindlessly upon him. All human expression in her face was void as if her soul had fled from her body, leaving only a monstrous, trapped power. Hayden studied the face glaring up at him, the features that he had known all his life now twisted with rage and unforgiving brutality. His mind screamed woefully that the worst had come to pass, that all that had been his sister had been destroyed and that what lay before him now was an unthinkable terror wearing her flesh, a vile evil that he must destroy. His eyes told him this was the truth, but his heart refused to believe it.

With careful, slow movement he lowered himself to his knees before the brooding Stone-Tongue, the dwarf blade still clasped in his hand. Violently, the girl jerked forward, her throat straining against the restraint of her collar, breathing in shallow, angry snorts. Her teeth grated viciously against the iron bit as mystical language struggled to be released from her mouth and her eyes swirled with the inky black depth of her power.

Bringing his face inches away from his sibling's, Hayden rested his sword carefully on the ground beside him and gazed deep into her eyes. He stared deep into her, beyond the mask of heartless flesh that she wore and the bottomless black that clouded her eyes. He looked for his sister, looked not with his eyes but with his soul for that glimmer of unbreakable spirit that was Petronia, looked and looked again for the thing that had become so lost. When he spoke, his voice was low and gentle, a loving whisper that he prayed the White Duchess could not hear.

'Pet, I know you can hear me. Dearest Sister, I know you're still

654

in there. I know it's hard and I know there is so much noise in you but please try and listen to me. I need you to hear this, I need you to remember the truth.'

The dull, inhuman pupils in the pallid mask stared blankly back at him in threatening spite as Stone-Tongue tautly pressed her lips against the metal of her gag. With a soft, low laugh, Maudabelle moved to stand behind her prize, resting her fingertips lightly on the catch that would release the collar.

Tenderly, Hayden reached up to caress Stone-Tongue's bloodless cheek. Her skin was warm and soft, but she made no response to his touch. Hot tears of grief and frustration blurred the visage of what his sister had become and Hayden knew that he did not have the strength to stop her.

'I was wrong, Pet,' he wept. 'I always believed that I could stop you, protect you, but I was wrong. The Ley was always with you. It would have called you no matter what I tried to do. Nothing could change that. I always loved you but only now do I understand you. Only you can decide your fate, dearest Sister, only you can choose how the words that are in your heart are spoken. Be what you must be.'

Stone-Tongue remained motionless, locked within an inner world of language and power, silently awaiting the moment of her release. Defeated, Hayden bowed his head, knowing he could do nothing to save her. Grief shredded his heart as he recalled memories of the person his sister used to be. A sinister laugh issued from Maudabelle's scarlet lips as she loosened the catch on Stone-Tongue's collar. The rhythm of the girl's breathing altered, her shallow gasps lengthening into deep, even inhalations as she awaited her release.

Terror seized Hayden and instinctively his grip closed around the hilt of his sword as he heard the heavy shifting of the metallic clasp. In a moment of self-preservation, he found himself lifting his weapon, the enchanted, dwarf-made blade glimmering like a silvery-white beacon of love and memory, filling his heart with a surreal happiness and joy as the images reflected in it passed before his eyes. The polished metal seemed to glow even more brilliantly than it had in the Weald of Megrim, casting radiant strands of golden light, like the shimmering tails of fallen comets.

Stone-Tongue's body bucked violently as the chain fell from her neck, her jet black eyes turning to liquid gold as they reflected the Ley light from the sword. Possessed with a sudden surge of life and power, she flung her head back and released an earth-trembling tone of might and sound as if every atom in the universe was crying out at the same moment, every living thing uniting in one voice that issued through the avatar of this silent maiden. A column of blinding luminescence burst from her open mouth as if her body contained within it the sun and stars themselves.

Dazzled by the noise and brilliance, Hayden tumbled backwards, petrified but unable to look away from the godhead of power that poured from his sister's body. Wonder-struck, the White Duchess staggered backwards, shielding her eyes from the blazing glow. The full power of the Ley was now visible to them all, born in flesh in Stone-Tongue's transformed body. From across the room, Aarold wept with fear as he beheld such a sight.

The shimmering avatar drew itself to its feet, its movements graceful and slow. From out of Petronia's face, inhuman pupils glowed, glittering with every conceivable hue and her lips, teeth and tongue gleamed molten silver and gold. It gazed around, regarding with divine wisdom the awe-struck faces of those before it and spoke in a voice that seemed to bypass audible tone and enter straight into their minds.

'*Step forth she who has summoned me to her command!*'

Maudabelle let out a stunned chuckle as she cautiously edged forward to address the embodiment of the Ley. 'It was I, glorious Stone-Tongue,' she uttered, her voice seeming like a whisper compared with the beauty and resonance that issued from Stone-Tongue's mouth. 'I brought you here to release you so you might honour me with your wondrous power. You are at last transformed into your true state, free from the pitiful guise of life that imprisoned you.'

Stone-Tongue turned to face the White Duchess. She moved as if she was underwater, every gesture deliberate and considered, knowing that her smallest motion held within it the potential to cause shockwaves of effect throughout the fibre of the universe. The swirling radiance within her pupils bore into Maudabelle's soul, allowing her nowhere to hide. Sparks of blistering, golden fire leapt like shooting stars from her lips and the still atmosphere of the chamber trembled with the fury and strength of her words as if they were altering the very fabric of existence.

'And who are you to weigh the value of a life? I am the Ley, that has always existed and always will be. This flesh vessel is only a transient incarnation, an instrument for My voice. I have deemed it so, to allow My will to come to pass. Her fate is no less or greater than any other. By My will are the paths of life laid, the thread spun, measured and cut. You seek to command the fates of others by corrupting this avatar for your own means, to bring about death in place of life. But this shall not be!'

Flashes of blazing white light shot from Stone-Tongue's throat as her shrieking words filled the air, dancing brutally across Maudabelle's stunned face like bolts of silver lightning. Fear filled her eyes as Stone-Tongue glided towards her, her soundless footsteps causing the flagstones beneath her to crack and crumble. The full might of the Ley burned wild and untameable within the maiden's eyes like rivers of mercury washing into consume her. 'I sought only justice for my king and my people,' she cried out as the aura surrounding Stone-Tongue began to shimmer with a misty, pale energy that licked the air with restless tendrils.

The possessed girl bared her metallic teeth causing a wrathful serrated din to rip through the air, contorting the bodies of those present with agony. Her words sliced like knives at the duchess's skin.

'What you sought was vengeance, to pay death with death. I am the Ley; I alone can deal justice, give back what was taken. Were you not blessed despite your suffering, gifted with wisdom, power, wealth and beauty? Were not the countries of Geoll and Etheria united when Elkric wedded your cousin? The thread was spun for you but this foul tapestry is woven by your own hand. Your destiny is of your own choosing.'

The awesome words transformed into an echoing howl that whipped deafeningly around the circular room filling the space with suffocating sound that crippled all those who heard it. Hayden found himself crushed, paralysed against the floor like an insect in amber, helplessly watching as Stone-Tongue reached out towards Maudabelle, bands of gleaming iridescence spreading from her fingertips. The White Duchess was screaming, eyes round with terror, mouth gaping yet her voice was lost beneath the call of the Ley. Her skilful hands drew intricate patterns before her, summoning trailing black vapours of sorcery like silken scarves around her body to protect her. Stone-Tongue closed in on her, arms stretched wide to embrace the blackness, crushing the shadows back in on Maudabelle's form. Waves of Ley power rippled over the duchess's body as Stone-Tongue's hands clasped powerfully on her shoulders. The avatar's glowing face became distorted and elongated as its mouth stretched, opening wider and wider with the force of the sound and brilliance that poured out of it. The hellish shriek rose to a chillingly shrill pitch as Stone-Tongue brought her face close to Maudabelle's, the unrelenting stream of light engulfing the duchess's pale features until they were no longer visible. A cascade of liquid gold poured from the screaming metallic jaws of the avatar, enveloping the duchess utterly, until nothing of her could be seen. The flowing tides of the hereafter swelled into the room through the floodgate of the Ley's avatar, merging Maudabelle's body and spirit with the divine power of the Ley until her mortal shape melted into a pool of ebbing radiance at Stone-Tongue's feet.

Frozen with shock, Hayden, Aarold and Hepton stared as Stone-Tongue stepped towards them, her multicoloured eyes locked on the king. Hepton's cruel features were as fearless as ever as the incarnation of Ley energy closed in on him, her lips gleaming silver with mystical language. '*She acted at your command. You too must be made to answer.*'

Brazenly, King Hepton bared his teeth. With one sudden movement, he hoisted his grandson from the floor and drew his sword. Aarold screamed with helpless terror as the steel blade was pressed against his throat, frantically lashing out to try and escape.

Hepton's dark, soulless eyes bore fearlessly into Stone-Tongue's gleaming face. 'You will not take me,' he barked as the young prince squirmed to get free. 'Utter another word and I will cut his throat.'

Hayden gazed between the king and the being that once was his sister. Stone-Tongue's expression was knowing and unperturbed by these threats. Innumerable flecks of colour glittered within her eyes as if they reflected the very core of the crystal fount. Gracefully, she raised her right hand, strips of Ley power caressing her fingers as once more the commanding tone of her words filled the air. *'It is not his time to die. Strength of spirit is greater than steel and might.'*

Hepton's eyes gleamed manically as his gaze flickered to the shimmering pool that remained of his niece. 'We shall see,' he spat. 'I have not come this far to surrender. Let his blood be on your hands!'

With a flick of his wrist, he drove his blade viciously into Aarold's breast. A bloom of scarlet erupted from the centre of his white shirt and his body sagged lifelessly to the ground. A chilling note of power and vengeance erupted from Stone-Tongue's mouth and her lips turned the shade of blackened steel.

'It shall not be,' she shrieked, the terrible sound of her voice turning the air of the chamber dark. The texture of her utterance seized the fresh gore that flooded from the boy's wound, moulding it in the air like a billowing wave that curled with golden Ley to wrap itself around Hepton. The old man let out a shout of fury as the silken sheath of blood enveloped his body, squeezing tightly around him. Stone-Tongue's lips continued to move with mystical, dark magic, recalling not only Aarold's life but the countless slain at King Hepton's command. The never-ending flow of the life-force closed in death around him, crushing his bones with a singular reverberation that seemed to shake the castle to its foundations.

Hayden crouched terrified amidst the intertwining rivers of blood and sparkling Ley power. The air stank of death and destruction, yet from the gleaming liquid around him there was a rhythmic pulse of unnatural energy as if Aarold's blood teemed with a thousand souls. Unsure what to do, he dragged himself through the strange eddying swill to the younger man's lifeless form. Aarold's face stared soullessly at him, his pale skin painted with smears and speckles of scarlet, his vivid blue eyes dim. A terrible, gagging spasm gripped his form as his lungs drowned in his own fluids. Horrified, Hayden touched his pale wet skin, unable to offer any sort of aid in his final moments. He found himself speaking but his words of comfort and Aarold's sickening gasps were silent beneath the all-encompassing cry of Stone-Tongue as she shrieked her mystical chants.

Turning his head away from the horror of Aarold's corpse, Hayden saw the being that once was his sister spring like a banshee of light and sound to the high window-ledge, her gleaming eyes searching the brutal carnage below like twin lighthouse beams piercing the darkness. Once more, her jaw split open to form an unnaturally gaping maul, a lone, silvery note of order unfurling in a trembling but resolute cord across the battleground. Stars leapt from her palate, illuminating the night, causing the warring armies to stop in their tracks. Far below, the misty form of the shadow warrior turned noiselessly, its featureless visage upturned towards the shimmering avatar. The utterance fell silent in Stone-Tongue's throat, casting a deathly quiet across the courtyard. Her glittering lips puckered and like a mighty stream withdrawing with the tide, she inhaled. A tangible ripple of Ley movement dragged across the minds and souls of all those present and even Hayden felt a sensation, like dexterous fingers being drawn through his thoughts, picking out all traces of terror and sorrow. The shadow-figure emitted a strange, noiseless gasp, like a relieved, dying breath, before being carried through the air towards Stone-Tongue. As it floated, the fibres of its vaporous shape began to uncoil as the White Duchess's corruptive influence over the Ley ebbed away and the energy of Tristram Kreen's form was released. Stone-Tongue breathed, her respiration steady and profound, the final trails of darkness being adsorbed into her blessed form. Stretching her arms wide, the incarnation of Ley power tilted her head back as it felt each fibre and atom of life pass through the flesh of Petronia. In one sublime instant, all that had been and all that was yet to come was held within her, eternal and fleeting.

Footsteps echoed off the stone staircase outside and Hayden's stunned wonder was broken by Garnet, Rosequartz and Bracken bursting through the doorway. At once, Bracken's horrified gaze fell upon the bloodied, lifeless form of her half-brother and with a sobbing cry she fell to her knees beside Hayden to cradle his body.

'We heard the call,' she wept softly, gently trying to wipe the hideous stains from Aarold's pale skin. 'Stone-Tongue. Her voice forced back our enemies. It crushed the life from Sister Jet before my eyes. We thought her salvation meant my brother had been spared.'

Tenderly Hayden wrapped his beloved in his arms and held her close. He knew her pain too well for even though his sister's form remained alive, breathing lyrical sighs of Ley power as it hovered phantom-like beside the window, he felt that this being no longer held within it the mortal essence of Petronia. Stone-Tongue existed, a goddess incarnate, untouched by Maudabelle's enchantment, but to Hayden it was a cruel and unwanted replacement.

'I'm sorry,' he whispered as Bracken buried her head against his chest. 'He was a brave and intelligent man. I would have given my life to have saved him if I could.'

'*Each strand of life is unique and has its own measurement and purpose. One cannot be exchanged for another.*' Stone-Tongue's tone was achingly gentle, seeming to echo within each of their hearts. Lighter than gossamer, she stepped down from her perch beside the casement, her toes causing tiny ripples as they rested amid the streams of scarlet.

Dumbstruck to witness the Ley birthed in human form, Garnet and Rosequartz fell to their knees before her, heads bowed in reverence of her gleaming pupils. Stone-Tongue smiled upon them, the radiance and warmth of the Ley issuing from her silvery lips. '*My most loyal and cherished Ryders,*' she said, stooping to rest her hands lovingly on their brows. '*Your service to me and this humble body has been greater than any Ryders throughout the aeons. You have moulded this vessel with love, courage and wisdom and your ordeal is nearly through. But no state is eternal apart from that of love and I have one final task to complete before my flow continues.*'

The Ryders looked at Stone-Tongue in trepidation and to their wonder saw the memory of the features of their lost sisters, Ammonite, Amethyst and Chiastolite, ghosting across Petronia's visage.

Easily, Stone-Tongue strolled across the bloodied floor towards where Aarold's body lay. With each step she took, the crimson liquid at her feet shimmered in the glowing radiance of her aura giving it the appearance of flawless ruby. When she reached Bracken and Hayden's side, she gracefully knelt down beside them, the warmth and love radiating from her, falling across their grieving forms. Conscious of this gentle glow, Hayden turned from comforting the weeping girl to look at the life-form that now possessed his sibling's body. The face and shape of her were so achingly familiar that he wanted to embrace her, but the immortal power that glowed within her pupils made his spirit tremble.

'*The flow of life is eternal.*' Stone-Tongue's voice issued through her gleaming lips like a river of warm honey, a balm to quieten their sobs. '*Each soul has a destiny, whether I choose to reveal it to them or not. The flow may be diverted but it will always reach its goal. No life ends meaninglessly.*'

She gestured gracefully to Hayden to lift Aarold's sorry remains on to her lap. Her movements were so obvious, so like the clear hand signals through which Petronia had once communicated, that it brought tears to Hayden's eyes and with painful care, he took the young prince's body in his arms and lifted him gently on to Stone-Tongue's dark skirt. Aarold's body was so thin and wasted that he seemed to weigh no more than an infant. His pallid complexion was stained with blood and looking upon his wasted, misshapen remains it was hard to believe that he had once been a prince, or anything more than an unfortunate invalid whose brave soul had finally been overwhelmed by the cruelty of existence.

Strands of silvery and golden light twinkled into existence within Stone-Tongue's aura as Aarold was tenderly placed on her lap, weaving in dancing patterns over his lifeless face like darting fish in a clear stream. Bracken let out a bleating cry of woe as Hayden took her brother from her and as soon as the prince's form had been placed in Stone-Tongue's care he returned to comfort her. The divine avatar seem oblivious to Bracken's cries; her brilliant, molten gold pupils gazed down into the face of the dead boy as if he was the only thing in the universe. The fibres of her mystical power flitted swiftly across the brutal gash at his breast, illuminating the deadly wound in searing clarity as her slender fingers traced his features with almost curious gentleness. Once more, her voice rose in words both new and ancient. *'What is death but a shadow of life, what is life but a shadow of death. They are one and the same. They are I and I they.'*

She lifted her head, her serene face gazing expectantly at Garnet and Rosequartz. *'I possess a thousand shades,'* she declared softly, her hands outstretched towards them. *'Crystals are eternal, but life is ever-altering.'*

The Ryders looked at each other, as a sense of realisation passed between them. Hurriedly, Rosequartz opened a pouch on her belt and took out a large nugget of golden yellow chrysoberyl and an angular black and white pyramid of merlinite. The gems seemed to glow brilliantly with a fresh inner light in the presence of Stone-Tongue.

Gently, Garnet opened the front of the dead boy's shirt and with breathless care Rosequartz arranged the crystals on his sallow, still chest, the merlinite resting directly over his heart, with the radiant, green-tinted chrysoberyl just beneath it. Hayden watched intently as she worked, his arm still around Bracken's shoulder. 'Can you really raise the dead?' he asked, as Rosequartz carefully positioned the stones.

Uncertainty filled Rosequartz's face as she studied Aarold's open wound. 'It is not normally within our powers to take back from the Ley what It has retrieved,' she uttered softly.

Rosequartz finished arranging the stones but before she could remove her hand, Stone-Tongue gently took hold of it and guided it to remain on the pyramid of merlinite, her gleaming eyes imploring Garnet to do the same. *'I am the Ley,'* she reiterated profoundly. *'Each soul will return to Me in its time.'*

Apprehensively, the Ryders positioned their fingers on the sharp surface of the monochrome prism. As they touched it, the merlinite burned intensely against their skin, the heat flooding into their bodies, spreading powerful tendrils out into their souls, making them recall the moment they first heard the Ley utter their Stone Names.

Inhaling deeply, Stone-Tongue moved her graceful fingertips in deliberate patterns across Aarold's lifeless face and body, her touch leaving flowing trails of glittering scarlet flecked with fragments of gold.

Her silvery lips and tongue moved as a note of angelic beauty and power rose from within, filling the chamber with its majesty. The volume of the tone was soft at first but swelled louder and larger until its resonance filled the room, making the stones of the tower and atoms of the atmosphere sing along with it. As if she was conducting a grand symphony, Stone-Tongue flung out her left arm and with the centre finger touched the pool of Aarold's blood glistening next to her. A ripple of metallic sound and light ran like a wave of stardust through the scarlet pool as the brightness of Stone-Tongue's aura grew and spread to engulf both her and Aarold. The blood swirled with crimson spirals like distant galaxies of ruby and silver, flowing up into the heart of the light that now blazed like a white-hot sun around both prince and avatar. Hayden, Bracken and the Ryders felt their hearts grow full with the love and splendour of the Ley that filled the space. They longed to gaze into its beauty but the intensity was so blinding it was impossible to do so. Instead, the lovers clung to each other as the Ryders gripped the fragment of crystal, all cloaked within the wondrous music of the Ley.

The sound and light rose like a blazing phoenix to a shattering crescendo before splitting into a star-burst of released energy, flinging a million shards through the universe. The room seemed to spin with silence that rushed in to replace the lost sound. Dizzy and shaken, Hayden fearfully raised his head from Bracken's shoulder.

The pool of blood was no more, the flagstone floor clean and dry. Nearby, Garnet and Rosequartz clung to each other, shaking with joyful shock at the miracle they had just witnessed. In the centre of the stone floor, two other individuals rested, barely moving. The boy, pale and slim, one leg withered slightly, lay on his back, his breathing shallow but steady. He lay peacefully slumbering, his head resting in the lap of a dark-haired girl who was stooped over him, her long tresses falling like a dark curtain across their faces. No golden power or goddess-like energy hung about her form as she sat there. She appeared no more remarkable than an ordinary maiden, head bowed to awaken her sleeping lover with a kiss.

With silent apprehension, Hayden crawled across the floor towards where the girl sat. He remained quietly knelt at her side for a moment, fearful, uncertain, making it difficult for him to hope that his sister had truly returned. His hand trembling slightly, he reached out and gently touched her arm. The girl flinched as if awoken from a trance and lifted her head, causing the slumbering youth resting in her lap to also stir and waken. She turned towards Hayden, her face peaceful if slightly baffled.

Studying her features uncertainly, Hayden looked deep into her dark, chestnut eyes. 'Pet?' he murmured apprehensively, 'is that really you?'

A broad smile spread across Petronia's face and overwhelmed with joy, she flung her arms around her brother's neck and embraced him tightly. Relief flooded Hayden's heart and tears sprung to his eyes as he held his sister close. All that she had been, dark angel, avatar of the Ley, melted into insignificance. She was his own beloved Petronia, his sister and she was alive.

'Oh Pet, I thought I'd lost you,' he whispered, his tears falling on her long, dark hair. 'When Stone-Tongue took your form, I feared it was too late.'

Drawing away from her sibling's embrace, Petronia wiped tears of happiness from her eyes, her hands shaking. She did not try to speak but her fingers moved frantically as they spelt what was in her heart. *So did I, dear Brother. I was lost, so lost in the power of the Ley, I thought I'd never find my way back to who I was. But it's different now and I am so glad.*

Hayden cried with joy as his sibling signed to him. He had thought for the briefest instant that the Ley would have granted his sister the gift of speech as recognition of her great service, but the truth was such a token mattered little to either of them now. Petronia had a voice, she had always had one, not one that was audible to the ear, but through deed and courage. With a brave heart and loving actions she had always expressed herself.

Stirring from his rest, Aarold coughed and struggled to sit up. Concerned for her brother's well-being, Bracken hurried to his side to help. Composed from his frightful ordeal, the young prince steadied his breathing and looked around, searching for Petronia. When his eyes did fall upon her, a relieved smile broke across his face and he reached out to take her hands in his.

'I knew it,' he whispered tenderly, sapphire eyes shimmering, 'I knew they couldn't overpower my brave, true Ryder. You saved me, Mistress Petronia, you healed me.'

Leaving her brother's embrace, Petronia gazed into the prince's kind face and felt an overwhelming surge of love for the shy, kind young man whom she had grown to care for. Her mind and heart felt cleansed, silent without the eternal utterances of the Ley and in their place the peaceful certainty of her own true emotions.

Firmly, she shook her head. '*No, it was Stone-Tongue that brought you back, saved us all. She is gone now. I don't think I need to be her anymore.*'

Happiness filled Aarold with a courage he had never felt before. His life had been gifted back and he did not want to waste a moment. 'I don't care what you choose to call yourself, all I know is that I owe you my life and that,' he paused for a second as his natural shyness threatened to overcome him, 'I love you.'

Petronia's cheeks flushed scarlet as she realised she felt the same. A glint of bright colour in the centre of Aarold's bare chest caught her attention. Where his grandfather had driven his blade into his breast there now was a narrow pale scar, the edges of which were trimmed with tiny, multicoloured crystals that shimmered beneath the surface of his skin. Aarold studied this new wound as Petronia gently traced it with her fingertips, trying to sense any sign of Ley power within, but felt nothing more than Aarold's warm skin.

From her spot beside Rosequartz, Garnet moved forward to inspect the strange mark. The microscopic gems twinkled as she touched them, pulsing with a soft Ley energy. 'It would seem that the Ley has laid Its highest blessing upon you, Your Majesty,' she smiled. 'You are very fortunate.'

Petronia frowned and studied the scar intently once more, desperately trying to sense any message from the mark. Confused, she signed something to her brother. 'She says that she can't feel anything there; in fact she says she can't feel the Ley at all.'

A gentle pulse stirred Rosequartz's aura with a sense of Ley energy that was very familiar. 'Perhaps that's because It doesn't want you to,' she suggested with a knowing grin. 'You have done the Ley a great service, Mistress Petronia, it would seem fitting for you to be rewarded. The Ley does not take hearts if they belong elsewhere.'

Eagerly, Aarold motioned to Bracken to help him to his feet. Steadying himself, he took Petronia's hands gently in his own. 'Dear Mistress Petronia,' he said tenderly, 'I know it is not the destiny that you believed you would have, I know I am not perhaps as handsome or brave as other men but I do love you with all my heart. Would you do me the honour of marrying me and becoming Queen of Geoll?'

A broad smile broke across Petronia's face. Now the influence of the Ley had left her, the true intensity of her feelings for the sweet young prince became clear and she was certain that she wanted nothing more from life but to spend it as his wife. Despite his insecurities, Petronia could not imagine there being a kinder or sweeter man than Aarold. Leaning forward, she kissed him tenderly in reply as her brother looked on happily.

The joyous moment was interrupted by the sound of heavy footsteps running up the tower stairs. The door swung open and Bahl burst into the chamber. Her grey skin and heavy armour was smeared with blood but her face wore a triumphant expression.

'Murkcroft has fallen; our enemies have surrendered,' she announced. Her tone was as emotionless as always but victory shone bright in her dark eyes. 'Praise the Ley for Stone-Tongue's strength in helping us succeed.'

Chuckling, Rosequartz slapped her hand on Bahl's shoulder. 'She is Stone-Tongue no longer, my friend,' she said gesturing to the happy pair. 'The Ley has sent her a new title.'

'We are to be married,' Aarold explained as Petronia wrapped her arm affectionately round his waist.

The dwarf took this information in her usual impassive manner. 'A good match,' she nodded, cleaning her twin swords on her cape. 'If she is as loyal to you as she has been to the Ley, you have made a wise choice.'

'You and your people must come with us to Veridium for the wedding. I feel I owe the dwarves so much, not least the blessing of a sister.'

Bahl looked awkwardly in Bracken's direction. 'There is still much to be done,' said the steward of Kelhalbon as her thick, dark lips twitched and deep creases appeared around her glossy eyes. It took a few moments for the others to realise, but Bahl was smiling. 'Why not,' she declared at last, 'it is a time of celebration. Princess Duun's daughter has returned and the Ley is triumphant. We shall camp tonight and ride out in the morning.'

*

This they did, returning to the city of Aarold's throne in great splendour and joy after many days of travel. Once re-established in the palace, preparations began for Aarold and Petronia's wedding and coronation. Word was sent to Ravensbrook to bring Godfrey and Beatrice to court. Petronia and Hayden were overjoyed to be reunited with their parents after so long and the blacksmith and his wife cried many tears of relief and happiness to see their children safe once more. For many months they had believed the promise made to them by the Ryders had been nothing more than a cruel lie and that they would never see their son and daughter again. To hear that they were not only alive, but that Petronia was to marry a prince seemed nothing short of a miracle.

The people of Geoll adored their new monarch and his bride despite their impairments. What Aarold lacked in physical ability he made up for in kindness and wisdom, lowering the taxes his aunt had put in place and freeing those jailed for non-payment. The dwarf Krogg who Maudabelle had kidnapped was also released so he might return to his people. The wedding celebrations lasted over two weeks, with Aarold and Petronia being married by Rosequartz. Hayden could not have been prouder or happier for his sister. At last Petronia had found her true destiny: guiding her husband in governing the kingdom with all she had learnt from the Ryders.

Between attending the many balls and galas and making up for lost time with his mother and father, Hayden's thoughts turned to what his future might hold. Clearly Petronia no longer needed his protection and he felt it was time to consider what he would do without her. Always during these moments of contemplation, Hayden's thoughts turned back to Bracken. Whatever the future held for him, he secretly hoped that she would be part of it. He loved her dearly and was sure that she felt the same though he was painfully aware that she still had a duty to her people. Aarold, as king, had the liberty of marrying Petronia even though she was a commoner, but did Hayden have the right to ask a dwarf princess to become the wife of a common blacksmith? However, the festivities of the royal wedding prevented him raising the issue with her. It would seem that whenever they met it was in the company of others, until one evening, several days after his sister's wedding, Hayden found himself searching the palace corridors for Bracken only to be told by one of the guards that she and the other dwarves had departed early that morning to return to Kelhalbon.

The news hit Hayden brutally although he dare not show it. Bracken had been raised to put her duty to others ahead of her own desires and wishes. Hayden realised that if Bahl had told her that her responsibility was to take over from her sickened and embittered grandmother in the role of queen, nothing could make her stay. It pained his heart, but her loyalty was one of the reasons that he loved her. The Ley had drawn a path for each of them: rewarding Petronia with a loving husband and fulfilling life; Bracken with the truth of her identity; and Hayden with the existence he had always wanted: the contentment of his old life at his father's forge, safe in the knowledge that his sibling would be cared for, for the rest of her days. With a quiet heavy heart, he said farewell to his sister and the friends they had made and returned to Ravensbrook.

THE SMITH OF THE HEART

All was as it had been in the quiet hamlet of Ravensbrook, peaceful and untroubled by events in the outside world. People worked, talked with their neighbours and cared for their families as they had done for generations. Of course, now and again a rumour or story would give the villagers fresh gossip to trade with one another, tales of a war in the north, a great battle involving the Ley Ryders and dwarves. There was even word that the mute daughter of the blacksmith had married the new king, but for as many who believed such was true there were equal numbers who said she had gone mad and run away, never to be heard from again. Either way, folks gained little truth from her brother when he returned from his travels for he did not socialise much, mostly being content in his work. There was a sorrow in his dark eyes that people suspected had something to do with his lost sibling, but he spoke nothing of it not even to his parents. In fact, days would pass where he would not say a word to anyone. He told them there was great value in being silent.

Weeks turned to months; winter gripped the earth with its icy hand only to retreat once more as the fresh shoots of pale green pushed their way from the soil. It was on an evening at this time that Hayden took a walk in the woodlands near his home only to find his melancholy thoughts interrupted by familiar voices.

'Well, if you refuse asking for directions what do you expect?' came a haughty tone as the sound of weighty footsteps disturbed the peaceful spring air. 'We are going to be wandering round the countryside, forever.'

'I have plotted a logical route and can say with all certainty we are not lost,' came the flat reply. 'Besides, may I remind you what happened when we last approached someone? They took one look at me, one look at you and ran away screaming!'

'Country folk can be so ignorant,' the first voice snorted disdainfully.

Hayden looked round in surprise to see two unusual figures walking side by side towards him along the riverbank some distance off. The pair were a strange sight in the spring woodland, a horse-like creature with a coat of shiny black scales and a bony crest of horn along the back of his neck, trotting at the side of a looming, muscular individual whose hairless scalp was covered by a cowl of heavy, metallic fabric that looked too hot for the pleasant climate. Pausing for a moment, Hayden studied the pair, hardly believing what he saw. When he was sure his wishful imagination was not playing tricks, he let out a cry of delight and hurried towards them.

'Phebus! Mistress Bahl! Greetings! What in the world are you doing this far south?'

Hearing his name, the Equile trotted eagerly towards the young man while Bahl carried on at her same steady pace, leaning leisurely on the ornate iron staff she carried. Happily, Hayden patted Phebus's leathery neck and went to greet the dwarf with a friendly embrace before recalling her reserved nature and stopped himself.

'My old friends,' he declared as Bahl greeted him with a formal bow. 'I cannot believe it's you! What brings you here? Are you well?'

Phebus gave his head a little shake, clearly weary from their journey. 'I am in rude health, my boy, I am happy to say. The mountain climate of Kelhalbon has done wonders for my physical welfare.'

Hayden looked puzzled. 'I thought you were in the royal palace of Veridium with Aarold and my sister?'

The Equile blinked his scarlet eyes. 'I am gratefully retired,' he sighed joyously. 'Besides, newly-weds don't want an interloper like me intruding. No, I decided to use the rest of my days broadening my understanding of dwarf culture, which is a great deal more sophisticated than I formerly imagined.'

Bahl gave Hayden a knowing look. 'He spends his time eating his way through our fungus and lichens stores and bothering Ind and the other record-keepers,' she said candidly.

Phebus snorted, wounded by Bahl's frankness, but the dwarf ignored him.

'And you, Mistress Bahl, you are well I trust?'

Bahl nodded stoically. 'I am in good health, Master Hayden, thank you. My work as Steward of Kelhalbon has given me cause to seek you out and Phebus agreed to keep me company.'

'Seek me out?' asked Hayden, feeling confused and concerned. 'Is there something the matter? Does Petronia need me?'

The dwarf waved her large, grey hand dismissively. 'There is no need to worry,' she told him, turning back the way she came. 'It is a minor, administrative issue that needs attending to. Would you come with me?'

Bewildered, Hayden followed Bahl and Phebus along the path of the stream and through the newly budding trees to a small clearing dotted with primroses and other wild flowers. In the centre stood a light, two-wheeled gig crafted in distinctive dwarf iron-work. On the fur-lined seat, a regal figure sat looking like an angel cast in silver. She wore a loose gown of woven metallic threads, shimmering with a delicate pattern of fish scales in bronze and platinum. The cut flattered her tall stature and was cut away at the shoulders to expose her pale, marbled skin. She was adorned with bejewelled chains and pendants and the Might of Kelhalbon hung loosely from her girdle. Her long tresses were wound in a singular plait around her head and they shone in the sunlight with a pale, jade glow. She looked what she was, a noble and worthy queen, but her round, colourless face and dark emerald eyes were those of the loyal apprentice to the Ley who Hayden loved so dearly.

He stood stunned for a moment, gazing at her, not knowing what to say. For many months, he had kept the vision of her alive and vivid in his mind, silently rehearsing the words he wanted to say, but now she was before him his plans and thoughts seemed to vanish and he found himself not knowing where to begin.

Bracken gave him a shy smile that seemed at odds with her royal countenance. 'Hello,' she said softly, as Bahl opened the door of the carriage and folded down a small flight of steps so she could climb out.

The Dwarf Queen walked towards him across the fresh, new grass, clearly trying to keep her pace regally elegant despite her slightly ungainly nature and gently rested her hand on his arm. 'You look well.'

Emotions crashed painfully in Hayden's heart, elation at seeing her again, hurt and anger for the way she left without even saying goodbye. Now she was back, appearing as unexpectedly as a dream, and he did not understand why. There was so much he wanted to ask but the only words that would come out were, 'You too.'

Oblivious to the awkwardness between the pair, Bahl reached beneath the carriage's seat and took out a small slab of stone and a metal chisel. 'Your Majesty,' she called to Bracken, 'if we can get on with things. I will act as scribe. Ind will, of course, be keen to have all details recorded for the archive.'

An awkward, unwilling expression passed over Bracken's face and she sighed.

Rolling his scarlet eyes, Phebus muttered something to himself and trotted over to stand beside the dwarf. 'I think,' he announced deliberately, 'we are running low on supplies for our onward journey. Perhaps it would be wise if you and I seek out provisions before attending to the matter in hand.'

Bahl looked at him blankly, ignorant of his hint. 'I hardly think that's a priority in the circumstances,' she replied flatly.

Bracken chuckled wearily and turned to address her vizier. 'It would be of great help if you and Phebus asked in the village for food,' she encouraged.

The dwarf's smooth brow creased with puzzlement. 'As you wish, m'lady. But I did stock up when we stopped at Goodstone.' She paused, looking between the laden packs fastened on the back of the gig. 'This is one of those human "emotional" matters we talked about,' she stated finally.

Relieved, Bracken nodded. Bahl placed the slate back under the seat.

'Very well, Phebus and I will set forth to source provisions. How long do you think this "emotional" matter will last?'

Groaning, Phebus took the arm of Bahl's tunic in his beak and tugged her towards the edge of the clearing. 'Remind me to lecture you in the finer details of human mating and courtship,' he told her, as they left the couple.

The Steward of Kelhalbon gave her mistress one last cautionary glance as they departed. 'I would find that most enlightening,' she told the Equile. 'Their emotions appear to make things so impractical!'

*

Alone in the gentle glow of the warming spring sunlight, the awkward silence once more fell upon Hayden and Bracken. They looked at each other, each one longing to say so much but unwilling to break the blessing of each other's company with base words.

Together they walked a little way to an ancient beech tree that grew at the far corner of the clearing, its twisting branches freshly dressed with newly green buds. Its roots ran close beneath the earth, pushing out of the ground to form a ridge upon which mosses and grass grew and it was on this soft mound that Bracken sat, motioning for Hayden to join her. The fine fabric of her metallic gown looked out of place against the grass and wildflowers and Hayden wondered if it was seemly for a queen to sit on the ground, but then Bracken had always been slightly out of place wherever she was.

'It's beautiful here,' she breathed as he settled beside her, 'so peaceful. I can understand why you were so eager to return. You must be very happy now.'

'Must I?' Hayden asked doubtfully, before he realised it. The truth was that he had not been happy for some time and struggled to recall when he had last been.

Bracken plucked a flower from the grass and rolled its stem between her fingertips.

'You have everything you told me you wanted. You have returned safely home to your village and family, your sister is happily wedded to a man who loves and understands her. I would say the Ley blessed you.'

Hayden nodded thoughtfully but did not answer. He wondered whether any person knew truly what they wanted in life. Maybe that was why the Ley existed, to guide people towards what they needed even when they told themselves otherwise.

'And you? Does being a queen compensate for not being a Ryder?'

She contemplated this for a second, smiling to herself. 'In a way. There is much I still have to learn of my people. Bahl is an immeasurable help to me. I now believe it is where I belong, where I am needed. I try to lead with wisdom and kindness.'

Her voice drifted to silence as she touched the large, purple crystal that rested against her chest. Her eyes were sorrowful, filled with shades of the Weald of Megrim.

Tenderly, Hayden took her hand in his. 'She would have been proud,' he told her softly. 'Sister Amethyst never doubted you would find your path. That's why she sent you with me; she knew how brave and loving you were.'

Her hand felt warm in his; dwarf skin was cool and hard to the touch but Bracken's was not, neither was her heart. Suddenly, Hayden felt unable to remain silent. 'You left,' he whispered bitterly. 'After the wedding, you left and didn't say goodbye. Didn't it matter to you?'

Pained tears filled Bracken's eyes and she tried to turn away, but Hayden refused to let go of her hand. 'I didn't want to leave you like that but it was the only way. My place was in Kelhalbon. I couldn't follow my heart. A Ryder's duty to others always comes first. If I had tried to tell you I was leaving I wouldn't have been able to.'

Hayden hung his head, unable to look at her, unable to gaze upon her strange, inhuman beauty and strength and know she could never be his. 'Then why are you here now?'

Bracken swallowed hard, filling her voice with strength as she recalled the words Bahl had told her. 'When a dwarf queen takes to the throne, our laws state that she must take a consort. A smith whose skills she holds above those of any other. There is no smith, no man, who I think of more greatly, whom I love and wish to call husband more than you.'

Hayden raised his head and looked at her, seeing not the Queen of Kelhalbon, but the courageous and kind girl who had learnt compassion and justice from a benevolent force that she had never been able to witness. A young woman whom he had grown to love.

Bracken gazed at him, her face filled with doubt. 'I realise what I'm asking is a lot,' she said. 'You have the peaceful life you always wanted and I don't expect you to give it up purely for my sake. I just have to know for sure. What is it that you want?"

Hayden considered the question, realising that for the longest time he had been unsure of the answer. There had been times when he thought he knew what it was that he wanted, times when the uncertainty of what lay ahead made it impossible to bring form to his dreams. But in this moment, for perhaps the first time in his life, Hayden was in no doubt. Something in his heart told him what must be.

Tenderly, he took her hands in his and leant forward to place a soft kiss on her mouth.

'The Ley has brought me exactly what my heart most desires,' he told her gently, 'and for that I will be eternally grateful.'

The sweethearts embraced, their hearts filled with happiness and love, as above them rays of spring sunlight danced through the tree branches, glittering with a divine brilliance.